Georg Long

The Decline of the Roman Republic by George Long

Georg Long

The Decline of the Roman Republic by George Long

ISBN/EAN: 9783742830739

Manufactured in Europe, USA, Canada, Australia, Japa

Cover: Foto ©Andreas Hilbeck / pixelio.de

Manufactured and distributed by brebook publishing software
(www.brebook.com)

Georg Long

The Decline of the Roman Republic by George Long

THE DECLINE

OF

THE ROMAN REPUBLIC.

BY

GEORGE LONG.

VOL. II.

LONDON:
BELL AND DALDY, FLEET STREET.
CAMBRIDGE: DEIGHTON, BELL, AND CO.
1866.

PREFACE.

I HAVE a remark to make on the way in which I have used some of my authorities in these volumes. In a few short passages I have kept so close to the originals that my text is almost a translation. I have done this purposely. It makes no difference sometimes whether a man professes to translate a portion of an ancient writer or gives it as near as he can without making a translation. The object in both cases is to present the evidence or statement just as it is without adding to it or taking from it. There are cases in which it is useful for the reader to have the exact words of a witness, that he may be able to estimate their value, and be certain that the modern writer has not altered the meaning of the ancient writer by dressing it in his own words. There is more reason for doing this sometimes than many persons can see, unless they have tried the experiment of making an historical narrative out of insufficient materials. The taste for adding ornament to the simplest facts is now become a fashion, which some writers indulge in to a great extent, and some readers appear to admire. The practice is supposed to relieve the almost unavoidable dullness of a narrative, when the events themselves are not such as to fix the attention and move the feelings. If a man could thus amuse a few idle persons without deceiving them, it would be a harmless pastime; but there are readers who prefer truth to fiction, who think that the romance writer and the writer of history ought to have different purposes, and find the bedizening of plain facts with fine words a very tedious and not a clear way of writing. The love of ornament certainly leads both to the imperfect representation and the misrepresentation of facts. It would be easy to show by examples how truth, or such evidence as we must accept for want of better, is often slightly altered by some writer who has taken the trouble to look at the original authorities, and is then perverted by others who only copy him and copy one another.

I have sometimes given Plutarch's words from my own translation of thirteen of the Roman Lives. In the notes to these Lives I have also translated passages of Greek and Roman writers, and I have used in this volume (pp. 217, 367) at least two of those translations of short passages, one of them with a few slight alterations. I am careful to mention this, that I may not be supposed to have copied them from another book, in which one of the versions appears with a few alterations, and the other with the change of a single word, which is not an improvement.

G. L.

ROMAN CONSULS

FROM B.C. 105 TO B.C. 72.

(CLINTON'S FASTI.)

B.C.		B.C.	
105.	P. Rutilius Rufus.	93.	C. Valerius Flaccus.
	Cn. Mallius Maximus.		M. Herennius.
104.	C. Marius II.	92.	C. Claudius Pulcher.
	C. Flavius Fimbria.		M. Perperna.
103.	C. Marius III.	91.	L. Marcius Philippus.
	L. Aurelius Orestes.		Sex. Julius Caesar.
102.	C. Marius IV.	90.	L. Julius Caesar.
	Q. Lutatius Catulus.		P. Rutilius Lupus.
101.	C. Marius V.		The Social or Marsic War.
	M'Aquillius.	89.	Cn. Pompeius Strabo.
100.	C. Marius VI.		L. Porcius Cato.
	L. Valerius Flaccus.	88.	L. Cornelius Sulla.
	Birth of C. Julius Caesar [1].		Q. Pompeius Rufus.
99.	M. Antonius.	87.	Cn. Octavius.
	A. Postumius Albinus.		L. Cornelius Cinna.
98.	Q. Caecilius Metellus Nepos.	86.	L. Cornelius Cinna II.
	T. Didius.		C. Marius VII.
97.	Cn. Cornelius Lentulus.		Death of C. Marius.
	P. Licinius Crassus.	85.	L. Cornelius Cinna III.
	Human sacrifices at Rome for-		Cn. Papirius Carbo.
	bidden by a Senatusconsul-	84.	Cn. Papirius Carbo II.
	tum.		L. Cornelius Cinna IV.
96.	Cn. Domitius Ahenobarbus.	83.	L. Cornelius Scipio Asiaticus.
	C. Cassius Longinus.		C. Norbanus.
95.	L. Licinius Crassus.	82.	C. Marius.
	Q. Mucius Scaevola.		Cn. Papirius Carbo III.
94.	C. Caelius Caldus.	81.	M. Tullius Decula.
	L. Domitius Ahenobarbus.		Cn. Cornelius Dolabella.
		80.	L. Cornelius Sulla II.
			Q. Caecilius Metellus Pius.

[1] See Note p. 877.

CONTENTS.

CHAPTER I.

GALLIA.

B.C. 107—103.

CHAPTER II.

THE ROMAN ARMY IN THE TIME OF C. MARIUS.

CHAPTER III.

THE WORKS OF MARIUS ON THE RHONE,

B.C. 104—103.

CHAPTER IV.

THE CIMBRI AND TEUTONES.

B.C. 102.

CHAPTER V.

C. MARIUS AND THE CIMBRI AND TEUTONES.

B.C. 102.

CHAPTER VI.

Q. LUTATIUS CATULUS AND THE CIMBRI.

B.C. 102, 101.

*Livy, Epit. 68; Plutarch, Marius; Frontinus, i. 5. 3; iv. 1. 18; Vale-
rius Maximus, v. 8. 4; Orosius, v. 16; Florus, iii. 9; Tellstus, ii. 12.*

CHAPTER VII.

THE SECOND SLAVE WAR IN SICILY.

B.C. 105—99.

Livy, Epit. 69; Diodorus, 631; Dion Cassius, Frag. 101, &c.

CHAPTER VIII.

L. LICINIUS CRASSUS AND M. ANTONIUS.

*Cicero, Brutus, 26, 36—40; De Oratore, i. 16, 39; ii. 1, 14, 73;
iii. 1, 20; De Officiis, iii. 16; Diodorus, Excerpta, p. 600.*

CHAPTER XII.

SPAIN, AND BRITAIN.

B.C. 97—92.

Livy, Epit. 70; Appian, Hispan. c. 99; Frontinus, l. 8, 5; ll. 10, 1; Strabo, III. p. 175; Diodorus, v. 21; Plutarch, Sulla; Justinus, lib. 38; Appian, Mithridat. cc. 10, 12, 14, &c.; c. 57, &c.; Velleius, II. 13; Cicero, Brutus, c. 29, 30; De Oratore, III. 24; Suetonius, De Claris Rhetoribus liber; Gellius, xv. 11.

CHAPTER XIII.

THE TRIBUNATE OF M. LIVIUS DRUSUS.

B.C. 91.

Livy, Epit. 70, 71; Dion Cassius, Fr. 100, 110; Florus, III. 17; Velleius, II. 13, &c.; Pliny, H.N. 33. c. 18; Appian, Civil Wars, I. c. 35; Aurelius Victor, De Vir. Illustr. c. 66; Cicero, De Oratore, III. 1, 2; Diodorus, Excerpt. Val.; Obsequens, calv.; Orosius, v. 18.

M. Livius Drusus a tribune of the people—The quarrel between Drusus and Q. Servilius Caepio—The consul L. Marcius Philippus—The designs of Drusus—His Lex Frumentaria—Drusus promises to give the Italian allies of Rome the Roman citizenship—The various measures of Drusus towards accomplishing his projects—The invective of the consul Philippus before the people against the leading men in the Senate—Drusus com-

CHAPTER XIV.

POLITICAL CONDITION OF ITALY.

B.C. 90.

*Livy, Epit. 71; Appian, Civil Wars, i. 37; Valerius Maximus, viii. 6. 4;
Diodorus, Excerpta, 538, &c.; Savigny, Vermischte Schriften, vol. i.
Jus Italicum, Nachträge, p. 61, &c.*

The law of the tribune Q. Varius directed against those who had encouraged the Italians to take up arms—The trials under this law—The
preparations of the Italians for war and the massacre of the Romans at
Asculum—The condition of Rome and her dependencies at the beginning
of the Social War—The condition of the Roman provinces—The political
condition of Italy—Alien laws at Rome   164

CHAPTER XV.

THE SOCIAL WAR OR MARSIC WAR.

B.C. 90.

*Livy, Epit. 72, 73; Appian, Civil Wars, i. 38—55; Diodorus, Excerpta,
538, 539; Strabo, p. 211; Velleius, ii. 15, &c.; Orosius, v. 18;
Plutarch, Marius and Sulla; Gellius, iv. 4; C. A. F. Briland,
De Bello Marsico, 1834; C. G. Keferstein, De Bello Marsico, 1812.*

The confederate Italians make Corfinium their capital—The force of the
confederates—The preparations of the Romans for war—The authorities
for the history of this war—The defeat of the Roman consul L. Julius
Caesar, of Perperna, and of P. Licinius Crassus—Nola is betrayed to the
confederate consul Mutilus, who undertakes the siege of Acerrae—The
story of Oxyntas, a son of Jugurtha—The victory of L. Caesar before
Acerrae—The defeat and death of the consul P. Rutilius Lupus—The
folly and defeat of the Roman commander Q. Caepio—The consul Caesar
is defeated by the confederate general Marius Egnatius—Sulla and Marius
are acting together against the enemy—The interview of Marius and the
confederate general Pompaedius—The military operations on the east side

CHAPTER XVI.

THE SOCIAL WAR.

B.C. 89.

Livy, Epit. 74, 75, 76; *Cicero, Philipp.* xii. 11; *Pliny, H. N.* iii. 6 and
iii. 8. 9; *Orosius,* v. 18; *Frontinus,* i. 6. 17; *Dion Cassius,* 43 c. 51;
Gellius, xv. 4; *Cicero, Pro Cornelio, Frag.* 27, p. 451; *Asconius,
In Cornel.* p. 70, ed. *Orelli.*

The social war continues, and L. Julius Caesar has a command as pro-
consul—The interview between the consul Cn. Pompeius Strabo and the
confederate commander P. Vettius Cato or Scato, at which M. Tullius
Cicero was present—The services of L. Cornelius Sulla in this year—
Albinus, commander of the Roman fleet, is murdered by his own men—
Sulla's campaign in Samnium: he takes Bovianum—The defeat and death
of the consul L. Porcius Cato—The campaign in the south-east of Italy—
The confederates after several defeats remove the seat of government from
Corfinium—Q. Pompaedius Silo has the chief command of the confederates,
who make a last desperate resistance—The great battle before Asculum
between the Romans and the confederates—The capture of Asculum by the
consul Pompeius Strabo—The romantic history of P. Ventidius Bassus—
The Jus Latii or Latinitas is given to the Latin colonies north of the Po—
Struggle between debtors and creditors at Rome, and the murder of the
Praetor Asellio—The Lex Plautia de Vi—The Lex Plautia Papiria and
the object of it—The sumptuary law named Lex Licinia—The Lex Plautia

CHAPTER XVII.

THE TRIBUNATE OF P. SULPICIUS RUFUS.

B.C. 88.

Livy, Epit. 76, 77; *Appian, Civil Wars,* i. c. 55 &c.; *Diodorus,* lib. 37. ed.
1; *Appian, Mithridat.* c. 112; *Cicero, De Divin.* i. 33, ii. 30; *Brutus,*
c. 55; *Auctor ad Herenn.* ii. 28; *Plutarch, Sulla, and Marius.*

L. Cornelius Sulla consul—The defeat and death of the confederate
general Q. Pompaedius Silo—The negotiations of the confederates with

CHAPTER XVIII.

C. MARIUS.

B.C. 88—86.

Livy, Epit. 77, 79, 80; Plutarch, Marius and Sulla; Appian, Civil Wars, i. 61, &c.; Velleius, ii. 19, &c.; Plutarch, Pompeius; Dion Cassius, Frag. 168. 172; Granius Licinianus; Orosius, v. 19; Diodorus, Excerpta, 614.

CHAPTER XIX.

DOMESTIC EVENTS.

B.C. 86.

CHAPTER XX.

MITHRIDATES VI. EUPATOR, KING OF PONTUS.

CHAPTER XXI.

SULLA IN GREECE.

B.C. 87.

CHAPTER XXII.

SULLA AND MITHRIDATES.

B.C. 86—84.

CHAPTER XXIII.

SULLA IN ITALY.

B.C. 84—83.

Livy, Epit. 84, 85; Strabo, p. 609; Appian, Civil Wars, i. 76, &c.; Plutarch, Sulla, Crassus and Pompeius; Velleius, ii. 24, &c.

CHAPTER XXIV.

THE CIVIL WAR.

B.C. 83—82.

Livy, Epit. 85, 86, 87, 88; Appian, Civil Wars, i. 81, &c.; Plutarch, Sulla, and Pompeius; Cicero, In Verrem, Act ii. 1, c. 18, &c., and c. 27; Orosius, v. 20, 21.

a

CHAPTER XXV.

SULLA, DICTATOR.

B.C. 82—81.

Livy, Epit. 89; Appian, Civil Wars, i. 95, &c.; Plutarch, Sulla and Pompeius; Lucan, Pharsalia, ii. 175; Q. Cicero, De Petitione Consulatus; Cicero, Pro A. Cluentio Habito, c. 7; Appian, Mithridat. 64—68.

Sulla's character—He determines to punish his enemies—Sulla's proscription lists—The proscribed are murdered, and their property is sold—The cruel death of M. Marius Gratidianus—The charge against L. Catilina—Sulla's men receive lands, houses and money—The story of M. Aurius, who was made prisoner at Asculum—The final reduction of Nola, and the death of Papius Mutilus—The submission of Volaterrae to Sulla—The for-

CHAPTER XXVI.

C. JULIUS CAESAR AND M. TULLIUS CICERO.

B.C. 80—79.

Plutarch, Caesar, Lucullus; Suetonius, C. Julius Caesar; Appian, Civil Wars, 1, 102; Cicero, Pro Sexto Roscio Amerino; Cicero, Brutus, c. 89, &c.

CHAPTER XXVII.

SULLA'S DEATH.

B.C. 80—78.

Livy, Epit. 90; Appian, Civil Wars, 1. 105, &c.; Plutarch, Sulla; Granius Licinianus.

a 2

CHAPTER XXVIII

SULLA'S REFORMS.

Zachariä, L. Cornelius Sulla als Ordner des römischen Freystaates; Cicero, Pro A. Cluentio Habito, c. 40; Appius, Civil Wars, l. 59; Becker, Handbuch der Römischen Alterthümer; Polybius, lib. vi.; Savigny, Vermischte Schriften, vol. 1., Verbindung der Centurien mit den Tribus; and vol. III., Tafel von Heraclea.

CHAPTER XXIX.

SULLA'S REFORMS.

CHAPTER XXX.

M. AEMILIUS LEPIDUS.

B.C. 78—74.

*Livy, Epit. 90, 93; Appian, Civil Wars, i. 107; Sallust, Historiae;
Plutarch, Caesar, Pompeius; Orosius, v. 22; Strabo, 668, 671; Florus,
III. 6; Cicero, In Verrem, II. 1. 21; Velleius, II. 43; Thucydides, i. 4;
Beaufort, Karamania, 1818; Suetonius, Caesar, c. 3, &c.*

CHAPTER XXXI.

SERTORIUS IN SPAIN.

B.C. 82—76.

*Livy, Epit. 91, 92; Appian, Civil Wars, i. 108, &c.; Plutarch, Sertorius;
Orosius, v. 23; Sallust, Historiae; Cicero, Brutus, c. 48; Caesar,
Gallic War, III. 20; Drumann, Geschichte Roms, 4 Th., Cn. Pompeius
Magnus.*

CHAPTER XXXII.

CN. POMPEIUS IN SPAIN.

B.C. 76—75.

Livy, Fragment of the 91st Book; Frontinus, Strat. II. 5. 31; Sallust, Historiae.

Cn. Pompeius makes a road across the Alps—He passes through the
Pyrenees into Spain, and advances against Sertorius southwards to Lauron,
near the Sucro—Sertorius lays an ambuscade for the foragers of Pompeius,
and destroys them together with a legion—Sertorius takes Lauron and
burns it—Pompeius retreats—The severe discipline of Sertorius—He be-
sieges and takes Contrebia—He goes into winter quarter, holds a meeting
of the friendly Spanish States, and establishes a workshop for the fabrication of arms—Sertorius sends Perperna to the coast—The policy of Sertorius as to the conduct of the war—His operations along the river Ebro—
Hirtuleius is defeated by Metellus and killed—The battle on the Turia,
and the victory of Pompeius—The battle on the Sucro between Pompeius and Sertorius—Pompeius and Metellus join their forces—The flown
of Sertorius—The battle at Saguntum—Sertorius retires to Clunia, whither
he is followed by Pompeius—Pompeius from his winter quarters addresses
a letter of complaint to the Roman Senate 460

CHAPTER XXXIII.

THE DEATH OF SERTORIUS.

B.C. 74—72.

*Livy, Epit. 91, 92, 93, 94, 96; Appian, Mithridat. c. 68; Civil Wars,
l. c. 111, &c.; Cicero, In Verrem, ii. 1, 34; Pliny, H. N. 3, 4, 3; 7, 27,
20; 37, 6, 2; Strabo, iii. p. 160; Sallust Historiae.*

THE DECLINE

OF

THE ROMAN REPUBLIC.

CHAPTER I.

GALLIA.

B.C. 107—103.

WHILE C. Marius was conducting the campaign against Jugurtha, his colleague the consul, L. Cassius Longinus, was in Transalpine Gallia. The Tigurini, one of the four cantons of the Helvetii, occupied that part of Switzerland which lies between the Jura mountains, the Rhone, and the Lacus Lemanus, now the lake of Geneva. At this time the Cimbri were ravaging Gallia, and it is not unlikely that the Tigurini were joined by some of these marauders. The Tigurini, under a leader named Divico, crossed the Rhone, and entered the territory of the Allobroges, who were now the subjects of Rome. The consul Cassius advanced to meet the Tigurini, and we may conjecture from the narrative of Orosius that he gained some advantage over them, for he is said to have pursued them "to the Ocean," an expression which is manifestly absurd. Thierry suggests that the ocean may mean the lake of Geneva; but Orosius, who is our authority, if he really wrote the "Ocean," could never have supposed that he was writing about the lake of Geneva. Nor is the difficulty removed by supposing that Longinus followed the Tigurini to the Atlantic in some emigration like that of the whole Helvetic nation, which Caesar checked in B.C. 59; for the campaign was in the country of the Allobroges east of the Rhone, where the consul fell into an ambuscade and lost his life. His legatus, L. Calpurnius Piso, who had been consul

VOL. II. B

in B.C. 112, also perished. This Piso was the grandfather of
L. Piso Caesoninus, the father-in-law of C. Julius Caesar.

Part of the Roman army escaped to their camp under the
command of C. Popillius Laenas, another of the legati of
Cassius. Being blockaded by the enemy, Popillius had no
way of avoiding total destruction except by an ignominious
surrender. He accordingly agreed to give the Tigurini
hostages, and one half of every thing that the army had, as
Orosius says; but it is more likely that he gave up every
thing. We have the evidence of Caesar himself in his Commentaries that the army of Cassius was sent under the yoke;
and it would be a fair conclusion that the Romans laid down
their arms.

Popillius thought that he had done the state some service
by saving an army, which had been lost through the im-
prudence of the consul; but on his return to Rome, he received notice of a public trial. He was prosecuted on a
charge of Perduellio, or treason, before the Comitia Centuriata.
The prosecutor was the tribune, C. Caelius Caldus. The
popular assembly still voted openly in such cases, for the
Leges Tabellariae had not been extended to trials for Perduellio. But before the matter was put to the vote, Caldus
proposed and carried a Lex Caelia Tabellaria, which empowered the popular assembly to vote by ballot in prosecutions for Perduellio. His object was to ensure the ruin of
Popillius, by enabling the voters to satisfy their passion by
the conviction of an unsuccessful commander, who might
have found protection under the influence of his own friends,
if the voting had been open. Popillius left Rome, and perhaps before the day of trial. His punishment was purely a
party question, and effected by the lying and misrepresentation of political enemies. Caldus afterwards attained the
consulship; and Cicero says that he repented of having
carried a law which was injurious to the state. Like other
demagogues, when he rose to power, he changed his opinions
to suit his new circumstances.

The consuls of the next year (B.C. 106) were Q. Servilius
Caepio and C. Atilius Serranus. Atilius had Italy for his
province, and Caepio had Transalpine Gallia. The Servilia

Lex, which was proposed and carried by the consul Q. Servilius Caepio, was probably enacted early in the year B.C. 100, and before Caepio left Rome for his province. This law, which is generally named the Lex Servilia Caepionis, in order to distinguish it from a subsequent Lex Servilia of Glaucia, restored the Judicia, as the Romans termed it, to the Senate, and consequently repealed one of the laws of C. Gracchus (vol. i., p. 264). This revolution shows that the party of the Optimates had a temporary superiority in Rome. The great orator, L. Licinius Crassus, supported the proposal of Servilius in a speech in which he maintained the authority of the Senate, and inveighed against the party spirit of the equestrian order and of those who had acted as prosecutors under the law of C. Gracchus. When Crassus was a very young man, he had supported the proposal for the establishment of the colony of Narbo against the Senate, who opposed it. This apparent change in his opinions brought on Crassus the charge of political inconsistency; but it is possible that Crassus thought that the Senate did wrong in opposing the settlement of Narbo, and also that he believed that the law of C. Gracchus, which gave the office of judex, or juryman, to the Equites, had been proved by sixteen or seventeen years' trial to be a bad measure. The records of this period are so very defective that it has been doubted whether this Servilia Lex of Caepio was carried; but the only fair conclusion that we can derive from the ancient authorities is, that the Lex was enacted, though it was very soon repealed. The statement that the Servilia Lex of Caepio made the judices eligible from the senators and the equites rests only on the authority of Obsequens. Crassus, says Cicero, was thirty-four years of age when he delivered this speech for the Lex Servilia; and, he adds, "it was the year in which I was born." This speech served as a kind of oratorical lesson to Cicero, when he was a boy; but it had not been fully reported, for some of the chapters contained only the substance of what was said, and not the words.

By establishing the colony of Narbo the Romans secured a road from their Gallic province into Spain, and fixed themselves near the rich valley of the Garumna (Garonne). The

Volcae Tectosages occupied the upper basin of the Garonne, between the western prolongation of the Cévennes and the eastern Pyrenees. Their chief town was Tolosa (Toulouse), on the river Garonne, in the French department of the Haute Garonne. The Romans had formed some kind of alliance with the Tectosages, and had contrived to place a Roman garrison in Tolosa; but the people, encouraged by the presence of the northern barbarians, who had broken into this part of France, perhaps also being under the pressure of fear, and with some hope of ridding themselves of the Romans, rose on the garrison, and put the soldiers in chains. When Caepio came to Gallia, he advanced upon Tolosa, and some traitors let him into the city by night. The consul found a great quantity of the precious metals in Tolosa. There was a story, reported by Justinus, that the Tectosages were in the army of Brennus, and that they brought home the gold and silver which they had gained by plunder and sacrilege; but on their return these robbers were attacked by a pestilent disease, which was not stayed until they followed the advice of the priests, and sunk all the treasure in the tanks of Tolosa. It was also said, as Strabo reports, that this treasure was part of the plunder of Delphi; but Posidonius, who had travelled in Gallia, refutes this story. The temple of Delphi, he says, had been well stripped by the Phocians in the Sacred War; and whatever was left would be very little when it was distributed among the men of Brennus. But the fact is that these plunderers did not take the temple of Delphi: they were bravely repulsed. Many were killed or died of disease; and we know that the remnant of the Tectosages of Brennus made their way into Asia, and finally settled in that part which, after their nation, had the name of Galatia. Besides this, there is no certain evidence that the Gallic followers of Brennus emigrated directly from Gallia. Long before the attack on Delphi, in B.C. 279, the Galli had crossed the Alps into Italy, and had extended their incursions east of the Hadriatic into the basin of the Danube; and it is more probable that these were the barbarians who fell upon Macedonia in the reign of Ptolemaeus Ceraunus, and under Brennus made an unsuccessful assault on Delphi. The treasure at Tolosa was the produce of the auriferous regions of the Pyrenees and of the offerings of the superstitious Celts. The amount that was found by the Romans, says Posidonius, was about fifteen thousand talents, part of which was in the temples, and part consisting of masses of gold and silver was sunk in the sacred tanks. When the Romans became masters of the country of the Tectosages they let those tanks to the publicani, or farmers general, who fished up out of them masses of hammered silver.

Caepio laid his hands on all that could be found in the town; he did not spare even the temples, an act of sacrilege which, as the Romans believed, finally brought ruin on himself and his family. The booty was sent to Massilia under an escort, but the men were waylaid and killed, and the treasure was carried off. Nobody knew how this happened, but the consul himself was accused of being the robber. The memory of Caepio was always connected with the plunder of Tolosa, and the expression "Aurum Tolosanum," the gold of Tolosa, became a proverb, which was applied to all who got money by dishonest means, and came to a bad end. Indeed, Strabo, when he is speaking of the plunder of Tolosa, expressly asserts that Caepio was driven out of Rome for plundering the temples, and ended his life miserably; but this statement does not mean that the punishment of Caepio followed immediately upon his offence.

At the elections of this year (B.C. 106) P. Rutilius Rufus and Cn. Mallius Maximus were elected consuls for the next year. Q. Lutatius Catulus was also a candidate, but the people gave their votes to Maximus, a man of no family, without merit, without talent, and mean and contemptible in all respects. Such are the terms in which Cicero, in one of his orations, speaks of this unfortunate consul, and the harsh judgment is accepted on the authority of a man who might have given Maximus a different character if it had suited the purpose for which he was then talking. The proconsular authority of Marius in Numidia was continued. Rufus stayed in Italy, and Maximus was sent into Transalpine Gallia to oppose the northern barbarians. Caepio also still remained there at the head of an army, which seems to show that he had not yet been censured for his conduct in the affair of Tolosa.

The incompleteness of Livy's Epitome is shown by the fact that it contains no mention of the plunder of Tolosa, though this event must have been spoken of in Livy's sixty-sixth book. This book also probably recorded the election of the consuls, P. Rutilius Rufus and Cn. Mallius Maximus, and we may therefore conclude that M. Aurelius Scaurus, who is named by the Epitomator (Epit. 67) the "consul's legatus," was the legatus of the consul Maximus in Gallia. Scaurus had been consul in B.C. 108, and having now the command of an army (B.C. 105) somewhere in Transalpine Gallia, he was defeated and taken prisoner by the Cimbri. Orosius states that Scaurus was made a prisoner in the great battle in which Mallius and Caepio were defeated; but this is a mistake, or at least the assertion is contradicted by Livy's Epitome, Dion Cassius, and the fragments of Licinianus, who briefly states that Scaurus fell from his horse, and being taken prisoner, was brought before an assembly of the Cimbri, but he neither did nor said any thing unworthy of his rank, and "so he was killed, when he might have escaped." This imperfect narrative implies that he might have escaped death if he had done or said something dishonourable. The Epitome explains this by the statement that when Scaurus advised the barbarians not to attempt to cross the Alps with the view of conquering Italy, for the Romans were invincible, one of the chiefs, named Boiorix, in a fit of passion stabbed him on the spot.

Maximus being consul had the command in Transalpine Gallia, and Caepio, as already observed, was still in this country at the head of an army. The consul was on one side of the Rhone, and on the other side of the river was the proconsul Caepio, as he is called by our authorities, though it is a manifest inconsistency to speak of a consul and a man with proconsular authority being in the same province at the same time. As the two armies were on opposite sides of the river, we must suppose that the enemy was also on both sides; or one army may have been intended to protect from invasion one side of the river, which was at that time not occupied by the barbarians. However this may be, after the defeat of Scaurus, Maximus ordered, and even entreated Caepio to join him, but Caepio at first refused, wishing, it is suggested, to gain a victory, and to have all the credit of it. When Caepio did cross the Rhone, he boasted to his soldiers that he was going to help the timid consul, but he would neither form any plan of joint operations with him, nor would he listen to the commissioners who had been sent by the Senate to exhort the two commanders to act unanimously for the interests of the state. Caepio had placed his camp between Maximus and the enemy. The barbarians seeing two armies in front, hesitated to attack them, and they sent an embassy to Maximus to see if any terms could be made. They were probably tired of their vagabond life, and would have been glad to settle in the sunny basin of the Rhone, if they could remain unmolested. The barbarian envoys on their road to the consul passed the camp of Caepio, who, it is said, was vexed because the men did not address themselves to him. He gave the envoys churlish words, and they narrowly escaped with their lives from his hands. But a fragment of Licinianus implies that the Cimbri did address themselves directly to Caepio, for it states that the men who were sent on this business expressed their wish for peace, and asked for land and corn to sow on it; but they were sent back in such an insulting way that, having no hope of peace, they attacked on the following day the camp of Caepio, which was not far from that of Maximus. Even then Caepio would not unite his army to that of Mallius, "and the greatest part of it was destroyed." This is the statement of the annalist Licinianus, and here unfortunately the fragment is imperfect, but we collect from the few words which follow that a remnant of the defeated army or armies made their escape.

Dion states that the clamour of the soldiers at last compelled Caepio and Maximus to join their forces, but greater proximity only increased the ill-will of the two commanders, and the ruin of the Roman army was the necessary consequence of divided authority and want of subordination. It

was in this state of affairs that the enemy, who consisted
of Cimbri, Teutones, Tigurini, and Ambrones, attacked the
Romans, who lost eighty thousand men and forty thousand
camp-followers, as Q. Valerius Antias, quoted by Orosius,
writes. The same numbers are given in the Epitome of
Livy, though Livy, who often quotes Valerius, accuses this
annalist of monstrous exaggeration. Two sons of the consul
fell in this dreadful fight; and only ten men are said to have
escaped, a statement which we cannot accept; and it is indirectly contradicted by the fragment of Licinianus. But the
fact is certain that the Romans sustained a signal defeat.
There is no indication of the site of the battle-field [1]. The
day was the sixth of October, B.C. 105, and it was one more
black day added to the Roman calendar.

Q. Sertorius, a name afterwards well known, was in Caepio's
army. He lost his horse and was wounded, but he saved his
life by swimming in his armour across the rapid current of
the Rhone. The barbarians got possession of two camps
and an immense booty, all of which they wasted for some
religious reason, or in pursuance of a vow, as Orosius conjectures. They tore in pieces the dress of the soldiers, threw all
the gold and silver into the river, hacked the coats of mail,
and destroyed the horses' housing. The horses were pitched
into the Rhone, and the prisoners were hung on trees. Such
wild vengeance and waste seem quite incredible, but so the
story is told.

Caepio deserved punishment for his scandalous misconduct;
and, according to Livy's epitomator, he was condemned by a
vote of the popular assembly, his property was seized to the
use of the state, and he was deprived of his proconsular
authority. Nothing is said by the Epitomator about the
punishment of Maximus, but it would be consistent with

---

[1] In the text of Livy's Epitome (67), where the old reading is "secundum
populi Romani Jusoturm," it has been proposed to read "secundum Arausionem," and to place these words at the end of the preceding sentence, which
refers to the defeat of Mallius and Caepio. It may be doubted if the old text
is right; but it is also certain that the new reading, "secundum Arausionem,"
even if there were more authority for it than there is, cannot be accepted as
Latin. Arausio is Orange, on the left bank of the Rhone, north of Avignon.

Roman practice to find that both Maximus and Caepio were immediately called to account. Indeed, some have concluded from a passage of Cicero that Maximus was tried, and that he was defended by M. Antonius; but this conclusion cannot be derived from the words of Cicero. It would be quite as fair a conclusion that Maximus perished in the great battle, for nothing is ever said of him afterwards, except in a passage of Licinianus, which states that "Cn. Mallius was ejected from Rome by a plebiscitum proposed by L. Saturninus, and for the same reason that Caepio had been ejected." But this passage is interpolated in the text out of the order of time, and cannot be relied on as a part of the genuine text of Licinianus, for we must assume that the proceedings of Saturninus against Caepio took place in the tribuneship of Saturninus, of which we shall speak hereafter. The expression in the text of Licinianus also implies that Mallius Maximus was ejected from Rome after Caepio had been ejected. It is said, on the authority of Asconius, that in B.C. 104, the year after the defeat of Caepio and Maximus, L. Cassius Longinus, a tribune, carried several laws, the object of which was to weaken the power of the nobility. One of these laws was to the effect that if a man had been condemned by the people, or deprived of that authority or commission named by the Romans Imperium, he should lose his place in the Senate. Cassius, in carrying this law, had in view the punishment of his enemy Caepio, who had been deprived of his commission for his misconduct in the war against the Cimbri. This enactment was a usurpation of power by the popular assembly, which had no constitutional authority for determining who should sit in the Senate. In consequence of the original vote of the assembly Caepio would lose all his property and his rank of senator; and it appears probable also that he was obliged to leave Rome. But if he left Rome, he certainly came back, for he was tried again, as we shall see, though there is some difficulty in determining the year of his second trial and final ruin.

This loss of two armies in Transalpine Gallia spread alarm through Italy. All men turned their thoughts to Marius, who was still in Africa; and notwithstanding the law about

re-election, Marius in his absence was chosen consul for the
year B.C. 104, and the Provincia Gallia, or the south of
France, was assigned to him. But if Marius was not elected
till the news of the defeat near the Rhone reached Rome, the
consular elections of B.C. 105 must have been delayed much
beyond the usual season.

While Maximus was in Gallia, his colleague, P. Rutilius
Rufus, was well employed at home in raising troops to resist
the threatened invasion. He required an oath from all the
juniors, or those under a certain age, who were bound to
military service, that they would not leave Italy; and men
were sent to all the coasts of the peninsula and the harbours
to give notice that no man who was under thirty-five years
of age should be taken on board a vessel. There must have
been some apprehension that many men would leave the
country in this moment of peril, and save themselves while
they were depriving Italy of their services. It was also
necessary to improve the discipline of the Roman army and
to prepare the recruits to meet a formidable enemy. The
consul began by setting a good example. He might have
kept his son about him as one of his staff, if he chose; but he
made him serve in a legion. As men are not fit for soldiers
unless they have been trained, Rutilius instituted a new
practice. He took a number of men who had been used to
train gladiators, and employed them in teaching his new
soldiers the art of attack and defence. Valerius Maximus
attributes to Rutilius the introduction of a regular training
of men to the use of arms; and Freinsheim supposes that
this was the origin of the Campidoctores, or masters at arms,
though the name, as far as we know, was not used till a
much later period. The Roman soldier was taught to thrust
with the sword, and not to cut, as Vegetius remarks, and
thus his blow was more efficient and his own body was less
exposed than if he cut with the edge of the sword. In the
Roman way of fighting every thing depended on the courage,
strength, endurance, and bodily activity of the soldier; and
the constant exercise which was necessary to prepare him for
a campaign gave him also healthy occupation during the
seasons of repose. Rutilius prepared the men who, under

C. Marius, dispersed the hosts of the northern invaders and deferred to a distant time the horrors of a barbarian conquest of Italy. In this emergency the Romans did not trust to their superior wealth, nor yet to numbers, for in this matter they were far inferior to the enemy. They proved the falsehood of the saying that money furnishes the nerves of war: they saved themselves by the courage of their men and the skill of their general.

Marius remained in Africa after the capture of Jugurtha (vol. i., p. 490), which event is placed by Clinton early in B.C. 106. It has been inferred from the last chapter of Sallust's Jugurthine war that the Numidian king was captured in B.C. 105, but this is a very uncertain conclusion from the vague words of the historian. It is also inconsistent with the narrative of the campaigns of Marius, for he went to Africa in his consulship in B.C. 107, and Sallust speaks of him going only once into winter-quarters before the capture of Jugurtha. But the historian's chronology is so loose that we can place no confidence in it, and it has been shown (vol. i., p. 470, &c.) that the events which Sallust describes in the campaigns of Marius could not possibly have taken place in the short period which he allows for them. For this reason then it is very probable that the capture of Jugurtha was not accomplished before B.C. 105; and indeed we can conceive no sufficient reason for Marius remaining so long in Africa, if the war was ended early in B.C. 106. There was little for Marius to do in Numidia after he had secured Jugurtha. The Romans did not form Numidia into a province, which was their usual policy after a conquest. They had already in their province, named Africa, as much as they could look after in that part of the world; and if they had settled Numidia as a province, they could only have held it by keeping a large force there, which they could not do at a time when they wanted men, and Italy was threatened by the northern invaders. If the Romans kept their promise to Bocchus, his dominions were enlarged by the addition of a large part of western Numidia. The rest of the kingdom was probably given to Gauda, the brother of Jugurtha, or rather his half-brother, if Gauda was legitimate, as Sallust's

narrative implies, for he tells us that King Micipsa had
named Gauda in his testament as his heir, in case of the
failure of the line of his sons, Hiempsal and Adherbal, and
his bastard nephew Jugurtha (vol. i., p. 412). It is supposed
on the authority of an inscription that Gauda was the father
of King Hiempsal II., whose name will occur afterwards.

At the close of B.C. 105 Marius returned to Rome with
Jugurtha. Marius entered on his second consulship with
C. Flavius Fimbria on the 1st of January B.C. 104, and on
this day also he had his triumph. Jugurtha, loaded with
chains, and his two sons with him, passed in the procession
through the streets of Rome. There was a great display of
the precious metals, both coined and uncoined, the booty of
the Numidian campaign, for Marius had employed his time
well since the capture of Jugurtha in taking for the use of
the Roman state the accumulated wealth of the Numidian
princes. After the triumph Jugurtha was thrown into the
foul hole named Tullianum. This prison, which is said to
have been built by King Servius Tullius, was a subterranean
dungeon: the lower part of it still exists on the Capitoline
hill on the right of the present ascent from the Forum. It
was usual to strangle great captives after the triumph, and
Eutropius says that this was the end of Jugurtha; but,
according to Plutarch, he had a worse fate. When he was
brought to the Tullianum, some of the executioners tore his
clothes from his body, and others, eager to secure his golden
ear-rings, pulled them off and the lobe of the ear with them.
"In this plight, being thrust down naked into a deep hole,
in his frenzy with a grinning laugh he cried out, 'O,
Hercules, how cold your bath is!' After struggling with
famine for six days, and to the last moment clinging to the
wish to preserve his life, he paid the penalty due to his
monstrous crimes" (Plutarch). Probably both the sons of
Jugurtha were spared. One of them at least, named Oxyntas,
was living a prisoner at Venusia when the Social War
broke out.

Marius had summoned the Senate to meet in the Capitol,
and as soon as the pompous pageant was closed, he stepped
from his car and entered the house in his triumphal robe.

Whether this breach of custom arose from his insolent disposition or his want of good manners, he had wit enough to see that the senators did not like it, and accordingly he soon went out, and returned in the usual dress of a magistrate. The state of public affairs would of course be the matter for deliberation, and as the province of Gallia had already been assigned to Marius, it only remained to provide him with an army. He was allowed to make his own choice, and he took the troops which Rutilius had been drilling. His colleague Fimbria had Italy for his province.

It is not known where Marius was or what he was doing during the years B.C. 104 and B.C. 103, in which year he was consul for the third time. He was employed, says Velleius, in making preparation for the war, but we cannot suppose that he was at Rome all this time, nor yet in Italy. If he was in Transalpine Gallia, he had certainly no conflict with the enemy, who seems to have made no movement towards Italy after the defeat of the Romans on the Rhone. A passage in "Livy's Epitome," and another in "Plutarch's Life of Marius," offer the only explanation of the difficulty. The barbarians, instead of crossing the Alps, wasted all the country between the Rhone and the Pyrenees. Probably Massilia and the Massaliot settlements were protected by their walls. On their road to the Pyrenees the invaders would pass the new Roman settlement of Narbo; and we may be certain what was the fate of this colony, if it was not in a state of defence. The men of the north crossed into Spain by the defiles of the eastern Pyrenees, where they would find a road ready made. They wasted every thing as usual, but they were now in a country from which every invader has at last been compelled to retreat; and in Central Spain they found in the Celtiberi an enemy who was more than a match for them. They returned into Gallia, and there joined the Teutones, as the Epitome says. The invaders of Spain were the Cimbri, according to the same authority. This brief notice of the invasion of the Spanish peninsula may be an historical fact. The final contest between the Roman and the barbarian was deferred to B.C. 102; and the invasion of Spain by the northern barbarians during the years B.C. 104

and 103 was a piece of good luck for Marius, as Plutarch says.

Among the legati of Marius was L. Cornelius Sulla, who had the credit of bringing the war with Jugurtha to a close by his daring and his cunning. Marius, himself a vain man, was jealous of the reputation of Sulla, who also was of an arrogant temper, and not disposed to let his services be forgotten. Sulla had a seal-ring cut in commemoration of his successful perfidy, and he wore it constantly. The subject was Bocchus surrendering and Sulla receiving the surrender of Jugurtha. Yet Marius knew that Sulla would be useful; and he had him as a legatus in his second consulship, B.C. 104. In this year Sulla, who had already caught one king, succeeded in laying hold of another, who is named Copillius, king of the Tectosages. This confirms the conjecture that Marius was in the south of France in B.C. 104; or if Sulla only was there, we must still suppose that Marius was not far off, somewhere in North Italy.

Perhaps these two years saved Rome. Marius had time to bring his recruits into good discipline, to strengthen them by exercise, and to gain the confidence of his men. He was inexorable in punishing all breaches of military order, but he was also just, and he gave his army a signal example of his impartiality. Marius had a nephew serving under him, an officer whom Plutarch names C. Lusius. This man conceived a passion for a young soldier under his command, named Trebonius, and had often ineffectually attempted to seduce him. One night he sent a servant with orders to bring Trebonius. The young man came in obedience to his superior, and was introduced into the tent, but when Lusius attempted to use violence, Trebonius drew his sword and killed the villain.

Marius was absent when this happened, but on his return he brought Trebonius to trial. There were many, says Plutarch, who joined in making the charge against Trebonius, and there was not one to speak in his favour. The officers perhaps thought that such a breach of discipline deserved punishment, and if they were no better than Lusius, they would view his crime as a small matter. But Trebonius must have had some friends, for after boldly telling the whole story, he produced witnesses to prove that he had often resisted the importunity of Lusius, and had always rejected the temptation of money. The general commended the conduct of Trebonius, and with his own hands placed on his head a crown such as was conferred for noble deeds according to an old Roman fashion; a fit reward, says the biographer of Marius, for such an act at a time when good examples were much needed.

The report of this just judgment of Marius was carried to Rome, and contributed to his being elected in his absence consul for the year B.C. 103. His colleague was L. Aurelius Orestes. Marius still had the province of Transalpine Gallia, for the barbarians were expected early in the year 103, and there was no other man to whom the defence of Italy could be safely entrusted. But this year also passed quietly, and nothing was done in Gallia. The consul Orestes died during his office, and Marius, leaving Monius Aquillius in command of the army, came to Rome to hold the Comitia. There were now many candidates for the consulship, but Marius wished to be elected again. For this purpose he gained the assistance of the popular leader, the tribune L. Appuleius Saturninus, who addressed the electors, and recommended Marius for a fourth consulship. Marius affected to decline the honour, on which Saturninus called him a traitor to his country for refusing the consulship at so critical a time. The force was plain to all, but as the danger from the north was not past, the electors voted for Marius. Q. Lutatius Catulus, who was esteemed by the nobility and not disliked by the people, was the other consul.

CHAPTER II.

THE ROMAN ARMY IN THE TIME OF
C. MARIUS.

FROM the time of Marius there was a change in the constitution of the Roman legions. The census ceased to be the
foundation of the delectus or conscription. The mass of
citizens was poor, and the property was in the hands of a
small number. The tribune, L. Marcius Philippus, who
unsuccessfully attempted to carry an Agrarian Law (B.C. 104),
declared that there were not two thousand citizens who possessed any property—an assertion which is probably a great
exaggeration, but still some indication of the state of society
at that time. Cicero, who quotes this statement of Philippus,
says nothing about the truth or falsehood of it: he only remarks on the pernicious tendency of such talk, and that it
leads towards schemes for the equalization of property; and
what greater mischief, he asks, can there be than this? The
passage of Cicero has been perverted by some critics in a
strange way. They admit that a Roman agrarian law related to the resumption by the state of public land only; and
yet they suppose that this law of the tribune Philippus proposed that there should be a general equal division of landed
property. Such a monstrous proposal was never made in any
country, nor can we believe that Philippus made it at Rome,
whatever he may have said about the land being held by so
few owners, and so many persons being unable to get any
share of it. If Cicero had really said what these critics suppose him to say, we might reasonably doubt the truth of his
statement; but any man of sound judgment, who looks at
the original, will see that Cicero only says, that such talk

tended to encourage wild revolutionary schemes. In whatever way the question about the concentration of the land in the hands of a few owners may be ultimately settled, no change will ever be effected by any scheme so absurd as some modern writers have falsely attributed to the tribune Philippus.

After the Social War, B.C. 90, when the Roman citizenship was given to a large part of Italy, the means of supplying the Roman legions with soldiers were still more abundant. Muster-rolls of all the Italians able to bear arms were doubtless still kept; but the strict old conscription was no longer necessary. The poor man by enlisting in the army got pay, sometimes booty, and he had a prospect of a grant of land when his term of service was over. The legionary soldiers, instead of being disbanded when they were not wanted, remained in service for a long time. Those persons who had any means of living, and no taste for war, though not legally excused from service, would certainly not be summoned, when willing men could be had, as many as were wanted. A few of the richer class would join the army as officers, with the hope of promotion and rising to the highest honours of the state. Though we have no reason to believe that there was any legal change in the mode of raising soldiers, for the Romans kept the forms of old institutions long after their purpose had ceased, it is certain that from the time of Marius the armies had the character of volunteer paid troops, and the modern system of standing armies was firmly established. Thus an instrument was ready to the hands of successful generals for the overthrow of the constitution, an inevitable result in all systems of government which are founded on popular election, when a large part of the citizens are converted into soldiers.

A Roman army now consisted of the legionary soldiers, the auxiliary infantry, the cavalry, the artillerymen and engineers, and the general's staff, and the troops about his person.

Up to the time of the Social War the Latini and the Italian allies were the auxiliary troops. The employment of foreign mercenaries in the Roman army began before the time of Marius, and it was continued.

As far as we can conclude from the ancient authorities, great changes in the military system were made in the time of Marius; but we cannot assign to him every innovation. We have no history of these changes; and we must collect what they were from scattered passages. It is only in Caesar's writings that we have the campaigns of a Roman army written by a Roman commander, and a living picture of the Roman military system. We now possess from a modern soldier a commentary[1] on the campaigns of Caesar. It is a small book, like the original, but as unassuming and as full of matter as the immortal work of the conqueror of Gallia.

It is sometimes affirmed that in the time of Marius the Roman cavalry was no longer employed, and that the legion consisted only of infantry. A certain number of cavalry, as we learn from Polybius, was a part of the old Roman legion; but it is said by some modern writers that the men in the Roman cavalry (equites Romani) now served only in the praetorian cohort of the commander, or as tribunes of the legions and as praefecti, or were employed on extraordinary commissions. This conclusion is derived from some passages in Sallust's Jugurthine war; but Sallust is not evidence enough for a fact of this kind, nor do those passages prove the conclusion, even if we accept them as evidence. In Caesar's campaigns the cavalry appears to have consisted entirely of auxiliaries; and in the Gallic campaigns his cavalry was raised in the Provincia and in the Gallic states which were friendly to him; and he also had some German cavalry. To mount his men properly Caesar got horses even from Italy and Spain; and he had some Spanish horsemen in his service.

The artillery, as we may call it, or the engines for the discharge of missiles, and those used in sieges, must have been carried with the armies, for we cannot suppose that materials for constructing and repairing engines could always be found on the spot; nor if the materials could be found would there always be time and means for making engines. We shall see in the Gallic campaigns of Caesar how he

---

[1] Heerwesen und Kriegführung C. Julius Cäsars, von W. Rüstow, Zweite, verbesserte Auflage, 1862.

employed his artillery. In the campaigns of Metellus and
Marius in Africa, it is certain that engines must have been
carried with the armies, if Sallust's description of the assaults
on some of the strong places is true. The conveyance, the
repairs, and the management of this cumbrous machinery
would require the services of a set of men trained for the
purpose; but, as Rüstow observes, we do not know how this
part of the service was managed. He conjectures that the
Fabri, or engineers, had this duty assigned to them, and as
we know no other body of men who could manage the
engines, we may assume this conjecture to be true. In
Marius' campaigns in Gallia and North Italy, there would be
no occasion for the employment of the heavy artillery, but he
must have had a large body of Fabri, as will soon appear.
These Fabri were under the direction of a Praefectus
Fabrorum, or officer of engineers, and they formed a distinct
part of the army. They were employed to build bridges,
make roads, construct huts for winter-quarters, and to form
the defensive works of the camps. But a good part of the
hard labour was also done by the legionary soldiers under the
inspection, as we may suppose, of the Fabri. There were
Fabri Ferrarii, or workers in iron, who, as Rüstow conjectures, also repaired the weapons, and particularly the Pilum,
which would be damaged in every fight. The carpenters'
work was done by the Fabri Lignarii.

I find nothing about surgeons in the Roman army, and
yet broken limbs and ugly wounds would require more skill
and attention than a soldier could have from his comrades.
The Fabri, who were able to use their hands, might give
some help; but it is hardly possible that there were no
surgeons or physicians in a Roman army, when they were
employed to look after the health and wounds of gladiators.
Caesar on one occasion speaks of delaying some days on a
battle-field to look after the wounded, but he does not say
how this was done.

The Fabri were attached to the staff of the army, which
consisted of the commander-in-chief and various officers.
First were the Legati, a term which means "men with a
commission." They were generally men of senatorian rank,

perhaps always, who were assigned to the commanders of the
armies, and served as generals of division or in any other
way that the commander-in-chief might employ them. The
Quaestor, an officer who was assigned by lot to the commander-in-chief out of the body of the Quaestors who were
annually elected, had the care of the military chest, paid the
soldiers, looked after the supplies of the army, and with his
subordinates discharged all the duties of a commissariat
department. The Quaestor made the arrangements with
the contractors or great merchants for the delivery of all
that was required for the use of an army; and we even find
instances of a Quaestor commanding a division of the army
when his services were wanted.

It was the practice for young men of rank to accompany a
general on a campaign as volunteers, for the purpose of
learning the art of war. If they showed talent and courage,
they would have opportunities of being employed by the
commander and distinguishing themselves. They were named
Contubernales, and formed a part of the Cohors Praetoria, or
body immediately attached to the general-in-chief. We read
of the younger Scipio Africanus forming a body-guard for
his own protection, when he undertook the Numantine war
with an army which was in a disorderly state (vol. i., p. 87).
This may have been the origin of the Cohors Praetoria.

The body-guard of the general was composed of such
troops as he enlisted for this special purpose, such as the
German cavalry for instance, which Caesar employed in the
Gallic War, and of the class called Evocati. These Evocati
might be any men who joined the general upon his invitation;
but they were properly veterans who had completed their
term of service, and either stayed with an army or joined it
again on the summons of an old commander.

The Roman discipline allowed no women in the camp;
but when large bodies of sutlers followed an army, we must
assume that they were accompanied by women, for women
would follow the army, even if men did not. Lipsius con-
tends that the two thousand whom Scipio drove away when
he was reforming his army before the siege of Numantia
(vol. i., p. 88) were not women, and his interpretation is

possible; but, if it is true, it would show a state of demoralization, which is incredible.   The change in the way of raising soldiers did not corrupt the discipline of a Roman army.   It is probable, as Rüstow suggests, that it contributed to the maintenance of the old discipline, which Polybius tells us was very strict.   The men who now voluntarily took service in the Roman army would be of the lowest class, often coarse and brutal, and such men both submit to, and require, a very severe discipline.   The ancient discipline, it is true, was as severe as it well could be; but in the altered condition of Roman society after the Punic wars, it would hardly have been possible to keep up this discipline in an army where all the soldiers were citizens and electors, and by their votes could help to give or refuse the consulship to an officer according as he was popular or unpopular.   "But discipline was maintained by surer and better means than merely by the fear of punishment.   Of such means the traditional military system of the Romans supplied abundance to a general who knew how to use them.   The daily fortification of the camp during a march left the soldier little time to think of any thing except his duty.   In the longer intervals of rest, the completion of their fortifications, the making the camp comfortable, and the strict watches that were kept, all contributed to the same object.   The Roman method of fighting made the personal dexterity of the soldier a necessary condition of success, and consequently there was constant practice in the use of arms, which occupied the time of the men profitably.   To all this we must add the rewards for faithful discharge of duty and for great courage, which rewards at this time did not consist of crowns of leaves, but sums of money.   Thus we may conceive that a Roman commander was not driven to the necessity of punishing continually " (Rüstow).

The pay of the Roman soldier in the time of Marius is uncertain.   Polybius in his time says that it was two oboli a day for the soldier, four for the centurion, and six oboli, or a drachme, for those who served in the cavalry.   About two-thirds of an Attic medimnus, or four modii of corn, were allowed for each soldier monthly.   The cavalry had

seven modimni of barley a month, and two medimni of wheat,
which is twelve modii. The barley was for the horses. The
auxiliary infantry had the same as the legionary soldiers ;
and the cavalry one medimnus and a third of wheat, and five
medimni of barley. The medimnus is estimated by modern
metrologists at twelve imperial gallons nearly, or one bushel
and a half. But in the case of the Roman soldiers a deduction was made from their pay both in respect of clothing,
arms, and food. The auxiliaries received no pay from Rome,
but the allowance of corn was made to them cost free. Cuius
Gracchus either carried or proposed a law for supplying the
soldier with his clothing by the state without any deduction
being made from his pay (vol. i., p. 263). From a passage
in Tacitus we learn that in the time of Tiberius the soldiers
still complained of deductions being made from their pay for
their clothing, arms, and tents.

Polybius says that the regular strength of a legion was
4200 men and 300 horse; but we read on many occasions
of the number of a legion being much larger. There is no
authority after that of Polybius for determining the regular
force of a legion. We do not learn this even from Caesar's
writings. We only know on certain occasions what the
actual strength of his legions was. In the time of Polybius,
and before his time, the legion consisted of four divisions,
differently armed, Hastati, Principes, Triarii, and Velites,
light-armed soldiers or skirmishers. The three first divisions
were completely armed, and a man's place in one of them
was determined by his age.

In the legions of Marius the distinction of Hastati, Principes, and Triarii did not exist. All the soldiers of the
legion wore complete armour, and all were armed alike. The
Velites are mentioned for the last time in a passage of the
Jugurthine war (c. 46). Probably from the time of Marius,
and certainly in Caesar's armies, all the light-armed troops
were auxiliaries, and formed no part of the legion. The
offensive weapons of the legionary soldiers under Marius were
the pilum or heavy javelin and the sword. The pilum is
particularly described by Polybius, who says that every
soldier had also a light pilum. We do not know when the

light pilum was laid aside, but it is certain that Caesar's men used only the heavy pilum. The wooden shaft of the pilum was about three pechcis (cubits) long, or four feet and a half, and four-sided. The iron part was as long as the wooden shaft, but the lower four-sided part of the iron was fixed to the wood in a groove, which was half as long as the shaft, and consequently only the upper end of the iron, which was also four-sided, and terminated in a point[1], projected beyond the end of the wooden shaft. The whole length of the pilum was four and a half pechais, or about six feet and nine inches. The iron head was fastened to the shaft by several iron rivets or nails, as Polybius says, but by two only, as Plutarch's description implies. Marius is said to have retained one of the nails, but in the place of the other he used a wooden peg, "the design being that the spear, when it had struck the enemy's shield, should not remain straight, for when the wooden peg broke, the iron head would bend, and the spear, owing to the twist in the metal part, would still hold to the shield, and so drag along the ground" (Plutarch). This heavy missile was only used for throwing, and it could not be used with effect except at a very short distance. When it was fixed in an object, such as an enemy's shield, the weight would be sufficient to bend the iron point without the contrivance of Marius. When the soldier had discharged his pilum, he used his sword, which was straight and short, with a double edge and sharp point.

The Roman soldier required for his use various tools besides his arms, such as saws, spades, axes, baskets, which were used in fortifying, scythes or reaping-hooks for foraging, hand-mills for grinding the corn, cooking utensils, and, as Josephus says, chains or gyves to secure captives. He was heavily loaded, as we know, but he could not carry all these things, and some of them must have been included in the

---

[1] Polybius (vi. 23) names the Pilum βέλος ὑγεωστρωτός, which is rendered "telum hamatum," and by Hampton is translated "turned outwards at the point in the form of a double hook;" others translate the words "a barbed iron head." But this cannot be the meaning. Such a weapon would be useless. Rüstow (Table 1. Fig. 1) has a drawing of a pilum. The head is a four-sided pike, terminating in a point.

baggage (impedimenta) of the legion. Rüstow observes that the stakes (valli) for forming the palisade of a camp were not carried by the soldiers in Caesar's time, and were cut on the spot where they were wanted. But it is not credible that the old Roman soldier, in addition to his arms and other things, was burdened with several stakes. Polybius fixes the number of stakes which the soldier carried at three or four; and this may have been the case on particular occasions. The soldier also carried his own food on short expeditions; but nobody will believe that the legionary soldier usually carried several weeks' provisions besides the rest of his load.

It was the design of Marius to diminish as much as possible the baggage of the legion, and to make the soldier's burden easier to carry. For this second purpose he invented the "Marian mules" (muli Mariani) as they were named. The soldier's utensils and food, says Frontinus, were formed into a bundle (sarcina), fastened to a board, and the whole was fixed at the end of a forked pole (furca), which the soldier on his march carried over his shoulder, as a traveller may now carry his bundle or his knapsack on a stick. Lipsius has given two representations from the Trajan column of a Roman soldier carrying his pole nearly upright with the bundle at the top, which seems to make a frightful load, and the arrangement does not appear very convenient. However the weight does not rest entirely on the shoulder. Under this heavy burden the Roman soldier often made long marches, but he was trained for them by previous exercise.

The legion now consisted of ten cohorts or battalions, the number of men in which would of course depend on the strength of the legion. Each cohort consisted of three manipuli or companies, and the manipulus contained two divisions named ordines, and perhaps centuriae also; though Rüstow observes that we cannot determine from Caesar's Commentaries whether the name centuria is given to half of a manipulus. The name cohort was not a new name, for Polybius says that three manipuli (σπεῖραι) form a cohors. The change then that Marius is supposed to have made consisted in drawing up a legion in cohorts for the purpose of fighting; and the legions for all purposes of attack or defence,

and movement before the battle and during it, was considered
as composed of cohorts, and not of smaller divisions. This
was so in Caesar's time at least.

Marius, in his second consulship, says Pliny, made the
eagle (aquila) the chief standard of the legion, and it was
entrusted to the first cohort, and specially to the oldest centurion of that cohort. The eagle was of gold, perhaps gilded,
or of silver, and fixed on the top of a pole. It is conjectured
that the eagle was also used as the standard (signum) of the
first cohort; and that every other cohort had its separate
standard. But some critics suppose that in Caesar's time
every manipulus had its colours or standard, and that the
cohort, which was composed of three manipuli, had no
colours. But there appears to be no proof of this fact, and
there is some evidence, and considerable probability, against
it. Rüstow observes, "It was not the manipulus, but the
cohort which was at this time the tactical unit, and the probability is therefore that the colours belonged to the cohort,
and not to a division of the cohort."

The chief officers of the legion, "tribuni militum," were
six in the time of Polybius, and we suppose that this number
was continued, for there is no evidence of any change in it.
Each manipulus had two centurions, one of whom commanded
the first division of the manipulus, and the other commanded
the second. The cohorts of the legion had rank according
to their number, the first cohort, second, and so forth, to the
tenth; and the rank of the centurions depended on the
number of their cohort. Within each cohort there was also
a gradation of rank among the centurions. This is Rüstow's
view of the matter: "The six centurions of the first cohort
form the first class of centurions (primi ordines), those of the
eighth cohort, the eighth class (octavi ordines), and so on.
The regular course of promotion was this; the youngest centurion in a cohort must pass through all the grades in his
cohort before he can be removed into the next higher cohort,
into which he enters as the youngest or lowest centurion.
Thus he proceeds in regular order of promotion till he
reaches the first cohort, the centurions of which have a
superior rank to all the rest in the legion, and are constantly

members of the military council. The highest rank in the first cohort is the rank of first centurion (primus pilus), and with this, as a rule, the promotion of a centurion ended." Extraordinary promotions were sometimes made for unusual services in battle, and they followed of course after great fights, in which centurions were killed, and when new legions were formed, they would have their centurions from the old legions. Centurions were not often promoted to the rank of tribunus. Rüstow supposes that there was something like the same kind of difference between centurions and tribunes that there is between the non-commissioned officers and the officers in the English army.

Some objections have been made to Rüstow's simple theory of the promotion of the centurions, and those who are curious may turn to his book, where they will see how he answers these objections.

The Centurions were taken from the lower classes of society. The tribuni militum belonged to the higher classes. They were young men of education and property, who, under the system of conscription, which existed in the later Republic, might easily have avoided military service. If such men had an inclination to serve in the army, they obtained recommendations to some general on foreign service, and were attached to him as members of his Praetoria cohors. When they had proved themselves worthy of promotion they were made tribuni militum.

This is Rüstow's statement as to the practice in Caesar's army, but this does not appear to have been the only way in which tribunes were appointed at that time. It is plain indeed from Caesar's Commentaries, that the tribuni were not employed by him to command legions; that he made little use of them, and he seldom mentions them. He gave the command of each of his legions to a legatus, to some man who was devoted to him. His manner of proceeding was so arbitrary during his long campaign in Gallia, that we may infer that, though he could not remove the tribunes from the legions, he reduced them to insignificance, and trusted only to his legati and centurions. At the battle of Philippi, Horace says that he commanded a legion; and so we may conclude that if

Caesar did not employ his tribunes in that way, it was because he did not choose.

In the time of Polybius, "the command of the legion was divided among six tribuni militum, each of whom commanded the whole legion for two months." This is Marquardt's explanation of the passage in Polybius (vi. 34), in whose words there is some obscurity. Such a clumsy arrangement would not have suited Caesar in his Gallic campaigns. However we cannot deny that tribunes were still appointed in Caesar's time, as they had been before. It is said that all the tribuni militum were originally appointed by the consuls. When two consular armies of two legions each were raised in the old fashion, there would be twenty-four tribunes for the four legions. In the course of time, six of these tribunes were annually elected by the people in the Comitia Tributa; and afterwards sixteen in the same way. In B.C. 171, during the Macedonian war, the practice of electing "tribuni militum" was suspended, and the choice was left to the consuls and praetors, who would do the work better than the electors. In B.C. 169, says Livy (43, c. 14), the people elected all the twenty-four tribuni militum of four extraordinary legions, which were then raised. The tribuni militum, who were appointed by the people, were named the tribunes of the first four legions, and classed among the magistratus, as we learn from Cicero; and also from the more trustworthy authority of the Lex Servilia of Glaucia (see chap. ix.). Another passage in Livy (44, c. 21) states, that the Senate passed a resolution, that for eight legions the consuls and the people should appoint an equal number of tribuni militum — that is, the consuls would appoint twenty-four, and the people would elect the other twenty-four. I think we must conclude then that Caesar had in his Gallic army both tribuni who were elected by the people at Rome, and others whom he appointed himself, for it is certain that he did appoint some tribunes. We cannot tell what the practice was in the army of Marius; but he would have the power of appointing some of the tribunes, if the resolution of the Senate mentioned in Livy (44, c. 21) was still in force.

The impedimenta, the heavy baggage of a Roman legion,

was carried on mules and horses. Rüstow supposes that the
sutlers and traders only had waggons, with which they followed the army. But the artillery and heavy engines must
have been also conveyed in waggons, if they were conveyed
at all from one place to another. The want of roads in some
countries would probably prevent the use of any carts or
waggons, either by the legion or the camp-followers, and
every thing that the soldiers could not carry must have been
put upon beasts. The soldiers' tents were a chief part of the
incumbrances of a Roman army. They were made of prepared skins, in fact of leather. The supply of skins and
hides for the Roman army was one of the requisitions laid
on the provincials. Sicily, says Cicero, among other things,
supplied Rome with skins; and we read, at a later time, of
Drusus imposing on the Frisii a fixed contribution of cow-
hides for military use. Besides the tents, there would be tent
poles to carry, with food, utensils, tools, and a variety of things.
By making certain assumptions as to the capacity of horses
and mules for carrying, and also assuming the weight of the
tents and other incumbrances, it is possible to approximate to
the number of beasts required for a legion, including the
camp servants (calones), and the riding-horses and pack-
horses of the tribunes. Rüstow thus arrives at a sum total of
520 beasts for each legion. When an army went on a short
expedition no beasts would be used, and every soldier carried
all that he required.

As the cohort was the unit of the legion, even in the time
of Marius, it is probable that his way of drawing up the
troops for battle did not differ from that used by Caesar,
which we know. The cohort was made by the combination
of three manipuli. The legion was formed for battle by
placing the cohorts in two, and sometimes in three lines
behind one another, with intervals between the cohorts, when
the ground allowed it. When there were three lines (acies
triplex), three cohorts were placed in front; the three in the
second line were placed respectively opposite to the intervals
in the first line; and the three cohorts in the third line, as
we may conjecture, were opposite to the intervals in the second
line, or, in other words, opposite to the cohorts of the first line.

So far as I have described it, this may be a tolerably correct statement of the constitution of a Roman army in the time of Marius. This description is founded on the authorities quoted at the head of this chapter, and a comparison of them with the passages of the ancient writers. As we have no historical writings for the period of which we are now treating, there is nothing to say about the movements of the Roman armies in the field beyond the vague and general expressions of the extant authorities. It is only when we come to Caesar's proconsulship of Gallia, and the wars which followed his invasion of Italy, that we have to deal with the writings of a man who tells us what he did and how he did it.

CHAPTER III.

—

B.C. 104—103.

THOUGH wo do not know where Marius was, or what he was doing in B.C. 104 and B.C. 103, we may conjecture that he was in the Provincia, or south of France, part of this time at least, and well employed. Plutarch supposes that he entered Gallia by one of the passes of the Alps, but this statement cannot be relied on. It is more probable that ho carried his troops by sea to the French coast. The supplies for his army were certainly taken that way, and brought to the Rhone. The mouths of this river at that time were choked with mud and sand, and the entrance was thus made difficult, and too shallow for the Roman vessels. Marius employed his men in cutting a now channel from some point on one of the outlets of the Rhone to a convenient place on the coast which had water enough for large vessels, and was safe against the wind and waves (Plutarch).

The ancient geographers did not agree about the number of the outlets of the Rhone, and Polybius found fault with Timaeus for saying that they were five. Polybius reckoned only two, and Artemidorus three. Strabo agrees with Plutarch in assigning to Marius the credit of improving the navigation of the river; for, observing that the outlets were choked with the alluvium brought down by the stream, and that the entrance was difficult, he made a now cut, into which the greater part of the water was divorted. There was beyond (east of) the outlets of the Rhone a salt lake, called Stomalimne, which contained abundance of shell-fish and other fish. Some geographers, says Strabo, reckoned the outlet of this lake as one of the mouths of the Rhone, and especially those who made seven outlets of the river, or five outlets, as the passage of Strabo stands in the present corrected text. But Strabo does not admit this outlet of the lake to belong to the river, for, he says, there is a hill which separates the lake from the river. The Stomalimne is supposed to be the modern Étang de l'Estouma, which lies between the east outlet of the Rhone and the great Étang de Berre, supposed to be the Mastramela Stagnum. "There does exist, in fact, a chain of hills to the west of the gulf, and on these hills is built the village of Foz; but, by turning this hill, Marius made the waters of the Rhone flow into the gulf of Stomalimne, from which we see that those who made this gulf one of the mouths of the Rhone were not mistaken, as Strabo says that they were" (Statistique du Département des Bouches-du-Rhône) [1]. But I think Strabo's conclusion is right, for such a canal as that made by Marius did not really constitute a new mouth of the river.

This cut of Marius appears to have been made in a straight line from the Étang de l'Estouma westward to a point on the east branch of the Rhone about a mile above the mouth. The canal was named Fossae Marianae, from which word it is assumed that Foz is derived, the name of a village which stands above the place where the canal entered the salt lake Stomalimne. On one side of the line or hollow, which marks the position of the canal, there has been a cutting into the rock at the base of a hill. West of Foz is the Marais de Foz, which was crossed by the canal. The Marais de Foz terminates in an étang of the same name, which joins the Étang de Galéjon, where it is supposed that in the time of Marius was the outlet of the Massaliotic or eastern branch of the Rhone. The hill which Strabo mentions may be the high ground between Foz and Istres or Distres, which is on the west side of the Étang de Berre. The distance from the

---

[1] This work is by the Comte de Villeneuve, Marseille, tomes i., ii., iii., iv., with an Atlas, 1821—1829. It is a complete description of the department named Bouches-du-Rhône. The archaeological part of this work contains much valuable information, but the author's sketch of the military operations of Marius (ii. 219, &c.) is of no value: it is a piece of fiction founded on a few facts.

commencement of the Fossae (Foz) to the point where it reached the east branch of the Rhone is sixteen Roman miles in the Maritime Itinerary. At this point on the east bank of the Rhone was a port named Gradus Massilitanorum, which may have been established by the Massaliots before the time of Marius. But it is asserted by the author of the Statistique, that the canal of Marius did not receive the water from this part of the Rhone. The canal, he says, was continued due north for about twelve miles from Gradus to the étang of the Desuvites, which comprised the marshes of Arles, of Mont Majour and of the Baux, and into this étang flowed also, at least in part, the Louérion, a canal derived from the river Durance near Orgon. It was the Louérion strictly which supplied the Fossae Marianae. There was a road by land from Massilia, which passed through Calcaria and Fossae to Arelate (Arles). Between Fossae and Arles the road would cross the Cumpi Lapidei, or the stony plain, now called Crau, part of which is traversed by the railway between Arles and Marseille.

Marius made this new cut in order that the Roman vessels might be able to enter the Rhone and bring his supplies up the river into the interior of the Provincia. Without this precaution his army would have been in danger of perishing in a country which had been wasted by the barbarians, and he could not have waited for an opportunity to fight a battle. Marius gave this canal to the city of Massilia for their services to him during the campaign in Gallia. The Massaliots derived profit from the canal by exacting tolls from the vessels which passed by it up and down. But the channel, adds Strabo, is still difficult owing to the violence of the stream, the formation of alluvial matter, and the lowness of the country, which cannot be seen from the sea in misty weather even when you are near it. The Massaliots built towers along the coast to serve as beacons, and a temple of the Ephesian Artemis in that part where the outlets of the Rhone form an island.

Though the evidence of the ancient writers as to the great canal of Marius is so small, it is confirmed by an examination of the ground. The authority for what follows is the author of the Statistique. I assume that we may trust his description of the localities, though we must reject his account of the campaign of Marius. The writer supposes that Marius placed himself with the greater part of his forces on the border of the sea in an impregnable position, in a camp on the tongue of land which projects between the Étangs of Estouma and Engrenier, on an eminence which has retained the name of Marisct or Mariet. At that time the étangs communicated with the sea by a canal. The Foasme carried the waters of the Rhone into the gulf, so that the camp was surrounded by water on the south and the east and could not be turned. On the west were extensive marshes, and consequently the camp could only be approached from the north; but this side also was protected by a great ditch, which Marius is supposed to have made. It may be admitted that Marius would make a fortified place near the outlet of his new cut; but it would have been absurd to fix the main body of his army in a place to which the invaders would not and could not come. This is an arid country too, but the author of the Statistique informs us how Marius got a supply of water, though he does not tell us how the army subsisted before the great works were made. Marius, he says, made his soldiers construct great reservoirs in the tongue of land between the Étangs of Estouma and Engrenier for receiving all the waters from the hills to the east of the Étangs. These waters were received into several aqueducts, which first flowed into a single reservoir near Merindol. From this reservoir there was another aqueduct on arcades, which crossed the marshes and gulf of Stomalimne in the part which was narrowest and most shallow. The transport vessels could pass under these arcades. The aqueduct terminated in the cisterns on the point of land already mentioned. The enclosures of two of these cisterns exist: they are now filled with earth and planted with vines. The arm of the sea which was crossed by the aqueduct is now a tongue of sand. There were standing not long ago seventy-seven arcades extending from this tongue of sand to Merindol. These arcades are more or less ruined. They are in general six mètres, or above eighteen feet wide; but one of the

arcades which crossed the channel into the gulf was fifteen
mètres wide, as appears from the foundations which were
buried under the sand.   The aqueduct, which was supported by these arcades, was two mètres wide, so as to contain
a body of water more than six feet in width.   The author of
the Statistique admits that this aqueduct is partly a modern
work, but he says that the lords of Foz merely repaired an
ancient ruined work in order that it might serve the original
purpose; for the bases of the pillars and some arcades are
entirely Roman.   In the demolitions also recently made
several Roman medals have been found, two of which were
consular medals.   The author's conclusion is that this aqueduct of Marius was at first roughly executed, and that it was
strengthened and improved under the empire, on account of
its use to the town of Fossae Marianae, which was a place of
some traffic when Arelate (Arles) became one of the most
important cities of Gaul.   We may certainly conclude that
under the empire at least the maritime town of Fossae was
supplied with water by a magnificent aqueduct, and that
Marius made the canal which always bore his name.   It is
probable too that his camp near Foz was the origin of the
town of Fossae Marianae, and that he began at least those
useful works which were necessary for supplying Fossae with
fresh water.   But we cannot admit more.

The Romans wanted men to oppose the northern nations,
and they had accordingly empowered Marius to take soldiers,
if he could get them, from parts out of Italy.   Marius is said
to have sent for men even to the king of Bithynia, Nicomedes II., who had assisted the Romans in the war against
Aristonicus.   But if this statement is true, Rome must have
been reduced to a miserable condition to send for soldiers into
Bithynia.   The answer of Nicomedes was as strange as the
application: he said that the greater part of the Bithynians
had been kidnapped by the Roman Publicani, or farmers of
the taxes, and were now slaves in the Roman provinces.
now Bithynia was still an independent kingdom, and the
Roman Publicani had nothing to do there; but it is possible
that the Publicani in the adjoining province of Asia were
purchasers of slaves, and bought them from those who kid-

napped the subjects of the Dithynian king or any other men whom they could catch. The answer of Nicomedes led the Roman senate to make an order that no free man belonging to a state in alliance with Rome should be kept as a slave in a Roman province, and the governors of the provinces were to take care that this order was executed. The application of Marius to Nicomedes was probably made either in B.C. 104 or B.C. 103.

In B.C. 104 or in B.C. 103 Italy was disturbed by domestic troubles. There was danger both from abroad and at home. In the neighbourhood of Nuceria, in Campania, thirty slaves planned an insurrection, but they were soon punished. Two hundred slaves near Capua made a like attempt, and had the same bad luck. The third rising was more serious, and it is a bit of romantic history. T. Minucius, a Roman eques, and the son of a rich father, conceived a desperate passion for a slave girl. The master could not easily be induced to part with her, but Minucius was so importunate that the owner at last consented to sell his slave for seven Attic talents on credit, for Minucius was trusted on account of his father's wealth. When the time for payment came, Minucius had not the money ready, and though the time was again extended, he again failed in payment. Dunned by his creditor and maddened by passion, for the story implies that the girl had not yet been delivered to him, he seems to have gone downright crazy. He bought on credit five hundred suits of armour, and taking them secretly to an estate in the country he armed his own slaves, four hundred in number. So far he resembled an insolvent, who attempts to get rid of his difficulties by a revolution, or by turning brigand; but if, as Diodorus says, he assumed a regal diadem, royal purple, and other insignia of power, appointed lictors, and called himself a king, we must conclude that he was mad. He began his reign by flogging and beheading the men who were sent to demand the price of the girl. Going with his armed slaves to the neighbouring farms, he gave arms to those who joined him and killed those who refused. His men soon increased to more than seven hundred, and were formed into military companies. He made a fortified camp,

and received all the slaves who came. Thus this fellow
became the centre of a general servile insurrection. The
senate acted promptly. They sent the praetor, L. Lucullus,
probably a son of the consul of B.C. 151, who left Rome with
six hundred picked men, a force which on his reaching
Capua had increased to four thousand, and four hundred
horsemen. Vettius, as he is now named in the text of Diodorus, and perhaps this was the man's real name, hearing
of the approach of Lucullus, occupied a strong hill with
his force, which had grown to more than three thousand
five hundred men. In the fight the slaves had the better
position and gained some advantage. Lucullus however
bribed Apollonius, a Greek, as the name proves, and the
general of the new king. This fellow sold his master on
receiving from Lucullus the assurance of a full pardon from
the Roman state. Apollonius now did his best to help
Lucullus, and attempted to make his master a prisoner, but
Vettius, who knew what he had to expect if he was taken,
made a decent end of a mad freak by killing himself. All
his band was destroyed except the traitor Apollonius. If
the praetorship of Lucullus is rightly assigned to B.C. 103,
we are enabled to give the time of this affair of Vettius.

The Romans had always war abroad, and they were never
quiet at home. Instead of the old contests between Patricians and Plebeians, there were the contests between the men
of opposite parties. In B.C. 103, T. Albucius was brought to
trial on a charge of Repetundae. He was a man learned in
the literature of the Greeks, which was now fashionable at
Rome; and, indeed, says Cicero, he was almost a Greek.
When he was a young man, he studied at Athens, which was
already visited by the Romans as a place of education, and
he became a follower of Epicurus. Cicero has preserved some
biting verses of Lucilius, which are addressed to Albucius in
the name of the illustrious jurist, the augur Q. Mucius
Scaevola, the son-in-law of C. Laelius, the friend of the
younger Scipio Africanus. Scaevola had administered the
province of Asia as propraetor B.C. 121, the year in which
C. Gracchus lost his life. On his return from Asia, Scaevola
passed through Athens, where the young puppy Albucius

came to pay his respects to the learned lawyer. Scaevola,
who loved a joke, and knew that Albucius affected Greek
fashions, is represented by Lucilius as addressing Albucius in
Greek instead of Latin, using the word χαῖρε, " welcome."
All the lictors of Scaevola, and all who were about him, took
up the word, and Albucius was received with a round of
salutations in Greek. The young pedant did not forget this,
for it is said that there was no other ground for his prosecuting Scaevola in B.C. 120 on a charge of Repetundae. It
was usual for young men, who aspired to political eminence,
to begin their career by attacking some man of note; but
Albucius assailed a person whose character was unassailable,
and he had not been made an orator by his Epicurean studies.
Scaevola was acquitted. In B.C. 105, while Albucius was
governor of Sardinia, he put down some trifling insurrection,
for which he was silly enough to ask the Senate for a suppli-
catio, or public thanksgiving. His request was refused,
partly because he had already had a kind of triumph in
Sardinia, which was an irregular proceeding. In B.C. 103
he was prosecuted for Repetundae; and there were two men,
C. Julius Caesar Strabo and Cn. Pompeius Strabo, both of
whom claimed the office of prosecutor. But as Pompeius had
been the quaestor of Albucius, it was not thought right that
he should be the prosecutor; for the quaestor was considered
to have a kind of filial relation to his superior, the governor
of a province. Accordingly Albucius was prosecuted by
Caesar, a young man who had been requested by the Sardinians to undertake their case, and he made his first essay in
this line on Albucius, as Albucius had done on Scaevola, but
with a different result. The Epicurean, who ought to have
been content with little, if he had imitated the founder of his
school, was convicted of having robbed the Sardinians; and
he left Rome to reside at his favourite Athens. The young
orator Caesar gained great reputation by his speech against
Albucius; and the future Dictator Caesar made use of some
parts of this speech in one which he delivered himself when
he was a young man.

Velleius places the tribunate of Cn. Domitius Ahenobarbus
in the third consulship of Marius, which was the year B.C. 103;

but Asconius fixes this tribunate in the consulship of Marius
and C. Flavius Fimbria, which was the second consulship of
Marius, and in B.C. 104.

M. Junius Silanus, consul B.C. 109, had been unsuccessful
against the Cimbri (vol. i., p. 436), and he was now prosecuted by Domitius, perhaps not really because he had attacked
the Cimbri without authority, or because he had failed, but
for some private pique, so far as we can make it out. The
charge was Perduellio, and his judges or jury were the people
voting in their tribes. However, Silanus was acquitted by
all the tribes except two.

Domitius, who was an active man, soon found another
person against whom he could employ his talents, M. Aemilius Scaurus, who, as Cicero says, was a defender of the state
and an enemy of all the men who excited disturbance from
the time of C. Gracchus to Q. Varius. Scaurus, one of the
firmest of the Optimates, never had much rest. He was often
prosecuted, and he was often a prosecutor. He had been
consul a second time in B.C. 107 after the death of Longinus
(p. 1); and his competitor, P. Rutilius Rufus, who had lost
his election, prosecuted Scaurus for Ambitus, or bribery, after
his election and before he entered on his office. Scaurus was
acquitted, and then he prosecuted Rutilius also for bribery at
the same election, and Rutilius was acquitted too. Scaurus
was a member of the college of augurs, and on the occurrence of a vacancy in the college Domitius wished to have
the place; but Scaurus had influence enough to prevent his
colleagues from electing a man who belonged to the popular
party, and probably was no friend to him. It was the fashion
among the old Romans, as Cicero informs us, for the members
of these colleges to live on terms of intimacy with one
another, and not to elect any man who was unfriendly to a
single member of the college. They formed a close club, in
which a single black ball would exclude a candidate.

Domitius revenged himself by summoning Scaurus before
the popular assembly, and proposing to fine him on the
ground that many religious ceremonies of the Roman people
had been neglected by him. The particular charge, or one
of the charges, was, that through the fault of Scaurus the

religious services of the Dei Penates, which were celebrated
at Lavinium, had been performed irregularly, and without
proper respect. Macrobius says, that there was at Lavinium
a temple of the Dei Penates, and it was an ancient custom
that consuls, praetors, or dictators, when they had entered on
their office, should celebrate a religious service at Lavinium
to the Penates and Vesta. Rubino assumes, for I know no
proof of the fact, that Scaurus was Pontifex Maximus; and
that he was brought to trial before the people in their tribes
for neglect in discharging the duties of his office. But
neither the College of Pontifices nor the Pontifex Maximus
was responsible, as we know, to any other authority in
matters pertaining to religion. The college was the supreme
ecclesiastical court; and, according to the Roman constitution, not even the popular assembly could rescind what the
college did, or in any way call the college to account. Nor,
if Scaurus had neglected the ceremonial of religion in any
way, whether as consul, or when holding any other office,
could he be answerable to the people. The whole business
must have been irregular; and one of those acts which
marked the decline of the old constitution and the usurpations of the popular party. If Domitius merely attacked
Scaurus out of spite, we can hardly understand why he should
have acted with so much apparent generosity, when a slave
of Scaurus came to him and offered to make some charges
against his master. Cicero, our authority for the anecdote,
says that Domitius seized the miserable wretch and handed
him over to Scaurus. We may safely assume that this slave
could not appear as a witness against Scaurus; and indeed
the form of proceeding instituted by Domitius precluded all
the formalities of a trial. The slave could have done no
more than denounce his master; and a Roman, a slave-owner
himself, would not make such a mistake as to establish a pre-
cedent like this. The attack of Domitius on Scaurus is
intelligible enough, if we suppose Domitius to have been a
knave. He used the name of religion for the purpose of
damaging a political enemy; and the trick has been repeated,
and is repeated up to the present day. The Romans must
have kept records of many of these trials. They were the

great events of the times, matter for talk among the people,
and traditional stories; and so we learn that three tribes
voted against Scaurus, and thirty-two voted for him; but in
each of these thirty-two tribes there was only a small
majority of votes (pauca puncta) in favour of Scaurus.

The tribune C. Licinius Crassus had made in B.C. 145
(vol. i., p. 49) an unsuccessful attempt to alter the way of
filling up the vacancies in the colleges of priests. New
members of the colleges were still appointed by the priests
themselves. Domitius, it is said by Suetonius, had failed in
being elected a member of the college of Pontifices in place
of his father, consul B.C. 122, who was dead, and as he was
very ambitious of ecclesiastical dignity, he determined to
take from the colleges the power of appointing their own
members. When we read of political struggles in ancient
states, it is often very difficult for us, at this distance of time
and under circumstances so different, to comprehend fully
their meaning. But a little reflection will enable us to see
that sometimes a great political change was made, of which
we have no record except a few words; and if we would fully
comprehend those few words, we must now express the facts
contained in them in a way that cannot be misunderstood. The
two great priestly colleges were those of the Pontifices and
the Augurs. Between them they directed the religion of the
state, which was a powerful instrument for keeping the
people in subjection. It was an old principle, as old as the
religion of Rome, and a wise one too, that the people could
not appoint the members of these colleges, and this is true in
whatever sense we take the word "people." Only priests
themselves could name other priests to those high places.
How it happened that the Pontifex Maximus, the head of
the college of Pontifices, was elected by the popular vote, if
this was now the regular practice (vol. i., p. 49), I can neither
explain nor understand; and I leave to others the solution of
this difficulty, which is increased by Cicero's remark on the
occasion of speaking of the Lex Domitia. He says that the
Pontifex Maximus could not be appointed by the people, for
the Roman rules of religion did not allow them to participate
in the religious ceremonial of such an appointment, and yet

on account of the dignity of the office of Pontifex Maximus
it was settled at some uncertain time that the candidates, as
Cicero expresses it, should humbly sue to the people for the
office. It seems that the mode of electing the Pontifex
Maximus was the same which by the law of Domitius was
fixed for the election of other members of the priestly colleges. If the people did now elect the Pontifex Maximus,
that was merely a designation of the person who should fill
this high office, for the Pontifex Maximus must be inaugurated, that is ordained, by the Augurs. Domitius proposed
that, when a vacancy occurred in any of the priestly colleges,
seventeen out of the thirty-five tribes should be chosen by
lot, and that a majority of these seventeen tribes by their
votes should fill up the vacancy; but still the form of co-
optation was retained, that is, the popular vote determined
the new priest, and the colleges went through the old form
of choosing, as their new member, the man whom they could
not refuse. So far the practice resembles the way in which
we now appoint English bishops, with this difference, that
the king or reigning queen names the new bishop and re-
commends him for election to the dean and chapter of his
cathedral, who are too prudent to refuse to do what they are
told, for they know the penalty of refusal. But though the
crown can name a man who shall be made a bishop, the
making of the bishop can only be the work of ecclesiastical
hands; and so it was among the Romans. The electors
named the person, and the sacred colleges made him a priest.
Thus we see at Rome that the agitators continued to battle
away at the old fabric of the constitution, as if they could
not see that they were bringing down the whole building on
their heads. The direction in which the popular party was
moving was to extend the principle of popular election, when
the only safe course at Rome would have been to regulate
and limit it.

No reason is given by the ancient authorities for the election of the priests under the law of Domitius being made by
seventeen tribes instead of being made by all the thirty-five.
It was probably a way of evading the religious difficulty, for
it was an old principle that the people could not appoint men

to priestly offices. Now, if seventeen tribes made the appointment, it could not be said that it was made by the people, that is, by the electors in their tribes, for seventeen is less than half of the whole number, and a majority of nine would really appoint. This seems to be Cicero's meaning, and if it be replied that this was a childish evasion of an old principle, that is no argument at all against the truth of the fact. Such an arrangement would not be disagreeable to candidates, for if the priestly offices were to be filled by the people, it was better for the candidates to have only seventeen tribes to canvass, and to bribe if necessary, than to have thirty-five to deal with. The choosing of the seventeen by lot also gave a religious colour to the business, for when a thing was determined by lot, it was the same thing in Roman theology as if it was determined by the will of the gods. Goettling has observed that seventeen is equal to the number of the eight Pontifices, not including the Pontifex Maximus, who made the ninth, added to the number of the Augures, who were nine; and that it is possible that for religious reasons this number seventeen determined the number of the seventeen tribes.

CHAPTER IV.

THE CIMBRI AND TEUTONES.

B.C. 102.

THE northern nations had for some years been knocking at the doors of Italy. In B.C. 113 (vol. i., p. 346) the consul Cn. Papirius Carbo was defeated by them. The facts of this defeat are very imperfectly known, but the Romans then became acquainted with the name of the Cimbri. Obsequens, who is no authority, found somewhere that these new enemies were both Cimbri and Teutones, or Teutoni. In B.C. 109 the consul M. Junius Silanus was defeated by the Cimbri in Gallia, as the better authorities affirm, though Eutropius says that Silanus defeated the Cimbri. Again, in B.C. 107, the consul L. Cassius Longinus, as we have seen, was defeated and killed in Gallia by the Tigurini. Then came the defeat in Gallia of M. Aurelius Scaurus by the Cimbri; and in B.C. 105 the total overthrow of Cn. Mallius Maximus and Q. Servilius Caepio again by the Cimbri in Gallia. Sallust, when he is speaking of the same event, gives the name of Galli to the people who defeated Mallius and Caepio. Then followed the invasion of the Spanish peninsula by the Cimbri, their defeat by the Celtiberi, and their retreat into Gallia or the south of France, where they joined the warlike Teutoni[1].

---

[1] Livy. Epit. 67, "reversique in Galliam bellicosis as Teutonis conjunxerunt." The "bellicosis" is objected to by some critics. It is said that the MSS. and most of the old editions have "imbellicosis," which is certainly not genuine. Mommsen says that we should read "reversi in Galliam in Vellocassis as Teutonis conjunxerunt." With the aid of this arbitrary correction he describes the Cimbri, after being driven out of Spain, as passing northward along the Atlantic coast of France as far as the Seine. While they were in the

In B.C. 102 C. Marius, now consul for the fourth time, was
in Gallia and ready to meet the northern invaders. But we
are informed by Plutarch, our only authority for this fact,
that the barbarians had divided themselves into two bodies,
and had agreed that the Cimbri should march through the
country of the Norici over the Alps against Q. Lutatius
Catulus, the colleague of Marius, and force the eastern
passage into Italy. The Cimbri then would enter Switzerland from the country of the Allobroges who were in the
Roman Provincia, and advance by a road north of the great
mountain masses. They might cross the Rhine somewhere
between the Lake of Constance and Chur, and so find their
way over the Inn to the head of the valley of the Athesis
(Adige), by which they could enter Italy. It was a long
and difficult road from the country of the Allobroges; and
we might conjecture that the Cimbri were already in Noricum
and did not march there from the banks of the Rhone. But
we can only take the facts as they are told. It was settled
that the Teutones, with a people named the Ambrones,
should march through the Ligurian country to meet Marius.
Thus it appears that it was the plan of the barbarians to
invade Italy by two roads, and if the two armies could have
met in the plains of the Po, it is possible that they would
have desolated a large part of the peninsula. But the plan
of the campaign, which would appear not bad even for
regular armies, was a combination which might be frustrated
by events which no man could foresee.

The ancient writers did not know who these Teutoni and
Cimbri were, nor whence they came. Modern writers have
not been more successful in their inquiries. Plutarch, who
did not affect to write history, and had no great turn for
historical investigations, has written a sensible chapter on
this matter in his life of Marius. He has reported what was

territory of the Voloraacs (the Vexin of France, before the great revolution of
1789), on the north bank of the Seine, they were joined by the three cantons of
the Helvetii, "apparently about this period," and by the Teutones who had been
driven from their homes on the Baltic, and now appeared on the banks of the
Seine. This is a wonderful amount of history extracted from a single word, and
this single word itself a fiction.

said about these people, and he has come to the conclusion that all that was said was rather founded on conjecture than on sure historical evidence. It was soon after the news of the capture of Jugurtha that the Romans heard of the advance of the Cimbri and Teutones, "three hundred thousand armed fighting men, bringing with them a much larger number of women and children, in quest of land to support so mighty a multitude and of cities to dwell in, after the example of the Celtae before them, who took the best part of Italy from the Tyrrheni and kept it." The report of the number and strength of the invaders was not believed at first, but it turned out that the report fell short of the truth. It was not an army that threatened Italy: it was a nation or two nations seeking a new home. These invaders had no intercourse with other nations; they had traversed a great extent of country, and nobody knew "who they were, or where they issued from to descend upon Gaul and Italy like a cloud." The most probable conjecture, Plutarch says, was that they were Germani, a name which the Romans learned from the Galli or Celtae of Gaul; that they belonged to the nations which extended as far as the northern ocean; and "this opinion was founded on their great stature, their blue eyes, and on the fact that the Germans designate robbers by the name of Cimbri." Others thought that Celtica or the country of the Celtae extended from the external sea (the Atlantic Ocean) and the subarctic regions to the rising sun and the Lake Maeotis (the sea of Azoff); "and it was from this region, as they supposed, where the tribes are mingled, that these invaders came, and that they did not advance in one expedition nor yet uninterruptedly, but that every spring they moved forwards fighting their way, till in the course of time they traversed the whole continent." In these last words we have no doubt an historical fact, the continual movement of the nations in the great plain of northern Europe. Others again connected the name of Cimbri with that of the Cimmerii, a name known even to the author of the Odyssey. These Cimmerii, whose home was between the Dnieper and the Don, broke into Asia Minor during the time of the Lydian kings and took their capital Sardes, except the acropolis. The Ionian Greeks saw these horrible barbarians wasting the fertile lands of Asia. A single line of the poet Callinus of Ephesus is the only direct contemporary evidence that can be alleged of this Cimmerian invasion of Western Asia, though there is no reason to doubt that Herodotus and Strabo had some authority for what they say on this barbaric invasion. The Roman word Cimbri is a correct verbal equivalent for the Greek word Cimmerii, but a name is not enough to establish the fact of the descent of the Roman Cimbri from the Greek Cimmerii.

The two names, Cimbri and Teutones, still exist; and first as to the Teutones. The Germanic nation has never called itself German; nor was there ever, so far as we know, any tribe which called itself German. The German name for themselves is Deutsch, or Teutsch, with other varieties in the older forms; but if we admit that the Teutones of Marius were Germans, we cannot conclude, either from any evidence or with any probability, that this was a name for the whole Germanic nation. It is much more likely that the Teutones were only one of many Germanic tribes; and that there was yet no name for the whole Germanic nation. The Teutones mentioned by Mela, the geographer Ptolomaeus, and by Pliny, occupy a part of Germany, north of the lower Elbe; and if we trust Pliny's testimony (xxxvii., c. 7), Pytheas of Massilia placed them in these parts, and near the Baltic. Caesar was informed, when he was in the country of the Belgae, that most of the Belgae were Germans, who, in remote times, had crossed the Rhine, and settled in the fertile parts on the west side of the lower course of the river after expelling the Galli. It was also a tradition that, when the Teutoni and Cimbri entered Gallia, the Belgae were the only people who repelled them. The invaders must, however, have passed through the Belgian territory on their road to the Roman province and to Italy, for Caesar found in these parts a people named Aduatici, who were the descendants, as he was told and believed, of these Cimbri and Teutoni. The barbarians left behind them the beasts and baggage which they could not conveniently take with them, and six thousand fighters to look after their property. We must suppose that

these men who were left had wives and children. They
maintained themselves in the country west of the Rhine,
after their friends perished by the Roman sword, often
attacked and sometimes attacking their neighbours, until, by
general consent, the Belgae made terms with them, and they
quietly occupied the country where Caesar found them.

The Cimbri and Teutoni, after leaving the country of the
Belgae, entered the territory of that compact mass of the
Celtic population of Gallia, who lived between the Seine and
the Garonne, and between the upper Rhine and the ocean.
The Celtae fled into their towns to escape from the invaders;
and many of them at last were reduced by a long blockade
to the greatest extremities. Those who, by reason of their
age, were unable to be of any service in the war, were eaten
by the rest. This resolute resistance saved the towns of
Celtica. The barbarians ravaged the country, and leaving a
waste behind them, entered the Gallic territory of the
Romans, which suffered in the same way.

The two nations, Cimbri and Teutoni, according to this
story, joined in this emigration towards the south; and this
fact is some presumption in favour of their being people of
like race, and language, and habits. According to such evidence as we have, we must conclude that these Teutones
issued from the north-west part of Germany. Strabo has said
nothing about the geographical position of the Teutones;
indeed, he only speaks of them once, when he says, that "the
Belgae alone resisted the attack of the Germani, the Cimbri
and Teutones." It appears from this passage that he supposed the Cimbri and Teutones to be Germani; and in
another passage he speaks of the Galli and Germani as being
in their nature (their physical character, probably) and
political institutions like one another and akin. But this is
not stated by him as a positive fact; it is an inference which
he makes from very insufficient premises.

The man who knew most of what was said about the
Cimbri was Posidonius. He was probably about thirty years
of age, or somewhat more, in B.C. 102. He travelled largely
in Gallia, and he was acquainted with Marius in the latter
years of the life of Marius. Posidonius may have known no

more of the Cimbri than he heard from Marius and other
Romans; but he is the only contemporary who has left us
any information about these people. He rejected the idle
story of the Cimbri being driven from their homes in a
peninsula by a great invasion of the sea. He conjectured
that they were a nation of robbers and wanderers; that their
incursions extended to the Maeotis, or sea of Azoff; and that
the Cimmerian Bosporus took its name from them, the
Greeks having given the name Cimmerii to the Cimbri.
Posidonius also said that the Boii once occupied the great
Hercynian forest; and that the Cimbri having come to these
parts, and been repulsed by the Boii, moved off to the Ister
(Danube) and the Scordisci Galataee (Galli); the Cimbri
then came to the Tauristae, or Taurisci, who were also Galli;
finally they went to the Helvetii, who were rich in gold, but
a peaceable people. Now, when the Helvetii saw that the
wealth which the Cimbri had acquired by robbery was much
more than they possessed, they were so much moved, particularly those divisions of the Helvetii named Tigurini and
Tougeni, that they joined the Cimbri in their wanderings.
All of them, however, were overpowered by the Romans,
both the Cimbri themselves and those who joined them; the
Cimbri as they were crossing the Alps, and the others beyond
the Alps.

Posidonius in this passage does not conjecture what was
the original abode of the Cimbri, and herein he shows his
good sense. Nor does he say whether they were Celts or
some other nation; but he supposes that a people named
Cimbri advanced as far eastward as the sea of Azoff, and
that they were the people to whom the Greeks gave the
name Cimmerii. Instead then of conjecturing that the Cimmerii came from the east, he supposes that the Cimbri
moved from the west to the east. The hypothesis of Posidonius is as good as any other; and it is consistent with the
Cimbri being a Celtic people, as some suppose. It is certain
that the Celtae once occupied a large part of Europe, and
that they entered many countries long before our historical
records begin. The first Celtic invasion of the Italian peninsula which was known to the Romans was assigned by them

to the time of their king Tarquinius Priscus, but the names of many of the rivers and mountains in north and central Italy prove that a Celtic nation was there long before Rome existed. If these Cimbri were Celtae, their rambling habits were conformable to the character of the people and the remote period to which these migratory races belong. The ancient speculators had an advantage over the modern in not being fettered by certain preconceived notions which check free inquiry. They had neither the notion that the move-ment of the earliest populations was always from east to west, nor were they confined within the narrow boundaries of time to which modern writers have limited the history of man and of the earth. Herodotus in his speculations on the formation of Egypt supposes a period of twenty thousand years, during which the Nile may have been depositing alluvium, nor does he in any way leave us to conclude that he thought that man did not exist during this time.

As the Galli invaded Asia in the third century before the Christian aera, and finally settled in Galatia, to which they gave their name, so men of the same race may have invaded the western parts of Asia many centuries earlier, under the name of Cimbri, or in the Greek language Cimmerii. For in those remote times we may assume among great numbers of the human race a long continuance of those physical characteristics, language, and ways of living which lead us to classify people as nations. It seems that many nations whom we are now acquainted with, such for instance as the negroes of Africa, have preserved the same character and habits for countless generations; and it is doubtful if we know a single barbarous people who have abandoned their national habits and advanced to what we call a civilized state by their own efforts and without the influence of other nations superior to them in knowledge and the arts.

The women of the Cimbri always accompanied the expe-ditions of the men, which must be the case with all nations until they have renounced a nomadic life and fixed themselves firmly on the soil. The Cimbri had priestesses, grey-haired women, clothed in white linen, with a belt of copper, and they went barefoot. These holy women, armed with knives, used to meet the captives who were brought into the camp, put crowns on their heads, and lead them to a huge copper vessel. There was a step or stool near the vessel, and the officiating priestess, standing on this stool and leaning over it, cut the throat of every prisoner as he was held up to her. As the blood streamed into the vessel the women made their divinations, and others cut open the bodies of the victims, and examining the viscera announced victory to their people. While the men were engaged in fighting, the women used to beat the leather coverings of their wicker carts and make a monstrous noise.

Strabo believed that the Cimbri in the time of Augustus occupied their original country, which he describes as being between the outlets of the Rhine and the Elbe. He places the Sugambri as well as the Cimbri in these parts. These Cimbri sent to Augustus the holiest of their vessels or caldrons, that we may suppose which these beastly barbarians had most frequently drenched with human blood, and they asked for the great man's friendship, and prayed that the past might be forgotten. Their prayer was granted, and they returned home. If this story is true, it proves that these Cimbri believed that they were of the same stock with those who had once made an attempt to storm the bulwarks of Italy; and that, if the Cimbri issued directly from the north-west angle of Germany to the conquest of the south, some of their people remained behind, for we have no reason for supposing that any of the emigrants made their way back from the bloody fields of Gaul and Italy to the neighbourhood of the Baltic, though some may have escaped the Roman sword and Roman slavery.

Strabo's statement is sometimes used as evidence that the Cimbric Chersonese, or Jutland and Schleswig, was the original country of the Cimbri, as if they had any original country. Strabo, indeed, places these Cimbri south of the Elbe, for which he may have had as good authority as those who placed them north of the Elbe. The fact of this northern peninsula, which is included between the Baltic and the North Sea, having been named Cimbric by the later geographers, proves nothing beyond the fact of an opinion that there was then in these parts a people whom they supposed to be Cimbri, or at the most a people who were named Cimbri. Pliny gives the name of Promontorium Cimbrorum, a point which the Roman fleet reached in the time of Augustus, to the termination of the peninsula of Jutland, which peninsula, he says, is named Cartris. He also mentions in the Baltic a bay named Lagnus, which borders on the Cimbri. So we may conclude that he supposed the Cimbri to be in his time in Holstein and the parts north of it. He reckons the Cimbri and Teutoni to belong to the great nation of the Ingaevones, to which the Chauci also belonged. Bordering on the Rhine were the Istaevones, part of whom were also Cimbri. Tacitus also speaks of the Cimbri in his Germania as placed on the Ocean in the north part of Germania; a small people in his time, but of great renown. He says that there are in many parts traces of their ancient fame " on both banks, encampments, and spaces, by the extent of which you may estimate the magnitude and numbers of the nation, and what credit is due to the story of such a great migration" (Germ. 37). This is obscurely said, but Tacitus perhaps means that there were still traces of this great Cimbric migration on both sides of the Rhine.

If the men who were sent to Augustus really called themselves Cimbri, we have evidence of their true name, for the fact of the Galli in the time of Marius and the Romans giving the name of Cimbri to the invaders from the north is not a proof that these people named themselves so. If the Cimbri who entered Gaul, Italy, and other parts of Europe emigrated from the Cimbric Chersonese and the adjoining parts in such enormous numbers, they must have been a people who cultivated the ground, but there is no reason for supposing the invaders of the south to have been an agricultural people, who were bound to the soil; for this kind of life implies private property in land and permanent dwellings; and we know from Caesar that even in his time some at least of the Germanic nations had not yet reached this state of social existence which we consider to be the first element in civilization. The result of all our inquiries is that we cannot fix on any country as the permanent abode of those people

who are named Cimbri by the Romans, but wo may affirm
that this great emigration proceeded from the country between the Rhine, the Danube, and the Baltic, and we have
therefore a reasonable probability that all the invaders belonged to the great Teutonic nation. As to their name, no
safe conclusion can be derived from the word Cimbri; and
certainly not the conclusion that they belonged to the Celtic
nation.

The name Kymri, or Cymry, still exists. It is the name
that the Welsh give themselves, but I am not aware that any
other people have called them by that name. These Kymri
are a branch of the great Celtic people, and this resemblance
of the words Kymri and Cimbri has led many modern
writers to assume that the Cimbri were also a Celtic people,
as many of the ancient writers name them. But those ancient
writers are principally the later Greeks, who are no authority
at all on such a matter, for they often confound Celts and
Germans where the distinction is quite clear. Sallust indeed
says that the Galli defeated Caepio and Mallius, but he has
made a great mistake; and to quote him as authority for the
Cimbri and Teutones being Celts is a strange perversion of
evidence. It is plain that Strabo, Pliny, and Tacitus believed
the Cimbri to be Germans, and Mela agrees in placing both
the Cimbri and Teutones of hisday in the Codanus Sinus, or the
western part of the Baltic. Nobody doubts that the Teutones
were a Germanic people, and Cimbri and Teutones are named
together as having joined in this great southern emigration.
The name Cimbri has perished in Germany, while that of the
Teutones, by some strange accident, is now the name of the
whole Germanic population.

Plutarch has given a hint which may assist us in dispelling
false conclusions founded on accidental resemblances of name.
He says "that the Germans designate robbers by the name
of Cimbri." Cimbri then is not the name of a people,
but a name characteristic of these fierce northern invaders,
who were called, and doubtless called themselves by some
native name, which the Romans represented by Cimbri.
Whether the name Cimbri, says a learned modern writer [1],

---

[1] J. Molleri, Flemb. Imgoge ad Historiam Chrwonard Cimbricae.

is derived from Gomer, the son of Japhet, or from the Cimmerii, or rather from a native word Kaemper, "fighters," he leaves to the inquiry of those who take a pleasure in investigating the mysterious origin of proper names, and love to dwell on trifles. The first two etymologies, he adds, seem absurd to all sensible men; the third is more probable, but not certain. We may perhaps then take Plutarch's statement, that Cimbri was a general name for fighting men, and the nearest thing to the genuine word which the Romans could devise. We may admit also the evidence of the Cimbrian mission to Augustus as a proof that in his time the nations about the lower Elbe and north of it were of the same stock as the bravest of the northmen, who had been known for about twelve years to the Romans before their final and decisive defeat in the South of France and in North Italy. During this terrible period these invaders had been in Illyricum, the basin of the Danube, France, and Spain. They met with a stout resistance in all these countries, some of which were protected by their natural strength as much as by the bravery of the people. France suffered most, for a large part of France is a plain country, and easily overrun by an invader, if he is not met by superior force. The scanty notices that are preserved of the Cimbric invasion of France show that this country never had a more formidable enemy preying on her fertile fields. If the elder Pliny's work on the Germanic wars had been preserved, we should know something more of the violent disturbance of Europe by the warlike migratory nations east of the Rhine and north of the Danube.

Mignet, in his essay on the introduction of ancient Germany into civilized society, has some instructive remarks on the unsettled state of northern Europe for a long time before the wandering nations were firmly fixed to the soil. He says, "The introduction of the German race into the regular societies, and the union of their territory to that part of the European continent which was already subjected to a like organization and the same moral law, is an event of the highest importance. This great event, without altering the proportion of the geographical masses between the civilized

world and the barbaric world, has changed the proportion of
their strength. It has closed the principal road by which
the nomadic tribes of northern Europe and of the plateaus of
Asia advanced from time immemorial to the borders of the
Ocean and the Mediterranean, driving every thing before
them. This event prepared and hastened the happy trans-
formation of the peoples and the countries in the north of
Europe; and they, in their turn, have extended the circle of
the civilized world. Accordingly, the addition of a whole
race, numerous, strong, and intelligent, to that civilization
which it was capable of accepting, but not of producing; the
formation of a central barrier, strong enough to stop this
flood of barbarians, which from time to time inundated the
regions of the west and the south; and finally the formation
of a European unity:"—these are the important results which
led the author to the consideration of a subject, which he has
handled with great ability.

The conversion of the Germans to Christianity in the
eighth and ninth century was the beginning of German
civilization. The arms of Rome first carried civilization
beyond the Alps, and attempted to stop the progress of bar-
barism from north to south. When the western empire had
fallen under the repeated blows of the Northmen, Rome
resumed her work of conquest under the banners of the
Christian faith. The monastic institutions established in
Germany were religious colonies, the centres of civilization,
and the origin of many towns. The formation of a Germanic empire opposed an obstacle to the incursions of the
eastern peoples; but many generations passed before Europe
was secure behind the barrier of Germany. Even in the
thirteenth century the Mongols extended their incursions
from China to the Vistula, and threatened to overrun Europe
with their nomadic hordes, and bring back the ancient bar-
barism. The Mongols were defeated on the Danube by the
Germans; and the threatened danger did not pass west of
the Germanic frontier. In the sixteenth and seventeenth
centuries the Germans checked the Turks on the Danube, and
stopped for ever the progress of one of those Asiatic peoples
who have been the greatest enemies of European civilization.

"Thus, on one side, the German race became for the north of Europe the instrument of civilization; and, on the other, their territory was for the south a barrier against the invasion of barbarous peoples" (Mignet).

But how many centuries had elapsed before this result was obtained? Nobody can tell. Southern Europe consists of three large peninsulas, each of which is protected on the north by mountain barriers. The rest of Europe, with the exception of the central mountains of France and the upper basins of the great rivers of Europe, is an immense plain. This plain extends along the Atlantic from the western Pyrenees to the entrance of the Baltic, and along the southern shores of the Baltic eastward to the Volga, and to the steppes and deserts of central Asia. Within these wide limits, during ages far beyond the narrow bounds of historic time, nations were jostling against one another, sometimes moving in one direction, sometimes in another, but never at rest. The Celtic nation played a great part here before the history of the Germanic races, so far as we know it, had begun. The Celts in their migrations penetrated into Spain and Italy, and into Germany and the basin of the Danube. When the Celtic nations in the west had made the Rhine a frontier between themselves and the Germans, they enjoyed some repose; the different tribes became a stationary people; they built towns, and began to participate in that civilization which prevailed in the Hellenic and Italian peninsulas. Perhaps for several centuries before the Romans entered Gallia this fine country was in the state in which Caesar describes it. But the Gauls were still pressed hard by their German neighbours, themselves probably suffering from a pressure still further east; and now at the close of the second century before the Christian aera we find the barbarians of the great European Plain attempting to pass the barrier of the Alps. It may not have been the first time that Italy was threatened by the people of northern Europe; but we know nothing of any former Germanic invasion, and we know no more about this invasion of the Cimbri and Teutones than the few facts which the scanty records of those times have preserved.

The Roman writers, in their ignorance of the geography and the nations of northern Europe, could only form a very imperfect judgment of the character of this barbaric irruption; but the Italians felt that their existence was in danger, and their hope rested on a single man.

CHAPTER V.

C. MARIUS AND THE CIMBRI AND TEUTONES.

B.C. 102.

WE know little of the campaign of Marius against the barbarians except the result. He established a fortified camp on the east side of the Rhone, and brought up his supplies by the river. Orosius reports that the camp was near the junction of the Rhone and the Isère, which would be not far north of Valence; and there he waited for the enemy, who soon made their appearance "in numbers countless, hideous in aspect." They covered a large part of the plain. There was in the army of Marius an Italian named Sertorius, who put on a Celtic dress and acted as a spy among the enemy. Marius kept his men within their intrenchments, with the view of making them familiar with the sight of the barbarians.

If Marius did advance as far north as the Isère, we must conclude that a large body of the barbarians was still in the northern part of the Roman province; but it is impossible to make any consistent narrative of the movements of the invaders. Nor do we see why Marius advanced so far north to meet them, unless we conjecture that by fixing himself in a safe place on the upper Rhone, he would have a full view of his enemies, and when they had passed his camp might follow in their rear and choose a fit opportunity of fighting them.

The barbarians, according to Orosius, consisted of Teutones, Cimbri, Tigurini, and Ambrones. The Cimbri, according to other authorities, were already on their way for the purpose of entering Italy on the eastern side of the Alps. The

Tigurini were one of the Swiss cantons, near the lake of
Geneva, who had joined the barbarians. Plutarch speaks
only of Teutones and Ambrones being in the Roman province.
The Ambrones are a nation entirely unknown. The only
name like theirs is that of the Ombrones, whom Ptolemaeus
places in Eastern Sarmatia. But Strabo mentions both
Tigurini and Tougeni, or Tugeni, as being combined with
the Teutones. Now it is almost certain that the Tugeni were
one of the Helvetic cantons. Caesar, who fixes the number
of these cantons at four, names only the Tigurini and Vor-
bigeni or Urbigeni. The name of the fourth is still wanting,
and as those Ambrones did not belong to the northern
nations, so far as we know, and as the name occurs in no
part of Gallia west of the Jura, it is possible that they were
the fourth of the Helvetic cantons. If these conclusions as
to the Tugeni and Ambrones are true, a large part of the
Helvetii joined the Teutones in their migration; and even if
the Tigurini were the only Helvetic people who joined the
Teutones, still we find part of this nation attempting to do
what the whole nation attempted, when the proconsul Caesar
(B.C. 58) stopped their bold enterprise.

The Roman soldiers were impatient to leave the camp and
fight the enemy, who were plundering the country and
challenging the men of Marius to come out to meet them.
But Marius told his men that he was only waiting for the
time and the place of victory promised by the gods. He had
in his camp a Syrian, or perhaps a Jewish woman, named
Martha, whom he carried about in a litter and treated with
great respect. This woman had formerly applied to the
Roman senate and offered to foretell future events; but this
illustrious body had their own way of managing such matters
and would not listen to the stranger. However, Martha got
access to the Roman women, whom she convinced of her
skill, for women, as Strabo says, are the prime movers in all
superstition. On one occasion, when Martha sat at the foot
of Julia, the wife of Marius, she told what gladiators would
win, and this led to her being presented to Marius. The
story may not be true, for it is difficult to believe that the
Roman women of that time were present at the fights of

gladiators; but we may maintain the credit of the anecdote by supposing that Julia saw the gladiators before they entered the lists. However this may be, we know that in the time of Cicero the Jews and Syrians flocked to Rome in great numbers. They came to traffic, and to make profit out of Roman superstition. Martha accompanied the army of Marius "and assisted at the sacrifices in a double purple robe fastened with a clasp, and carrying a spear wreathed with ribands and chaplets." Some doubted whether Marius really believed in the woman, or only used her for his purposes.

There were great signs in those days. Two vultures were hovering about the army. Those birds were well known, for the soldiers had once caught them, and after putting brass rings round their necks let them go. Whenever the birds appeared while the army was moving, the soldiers rejoiced, for they considered it an omen of victory. It was reported from the Italian towns, Ameria and Tuder, that at night there was the appearance in the heavens of fiery spears and shields, "which at first moved about in various directions, and then closed together, exhibiting the attitudes and movements of men in battle; at last part gave way, and the rest pressed on in pursuit, and all moved away to the west." About the same time there appeared at Rome Bataccs, the priest of the Great Mother from Pessinus in Phrygia, and he reported that the goddess had declared that victory would be on the side of the Romans. The Senate accepted the announcement and voted a temple to the goddess in commemoration of the expected victory. This is Plutarch's narrative. The fragment of Diodorus does not mention the promised victory nor the temple, but it contains some other curious matter. This impostor told the magistrates and senate that the religious ceremonial of the goddess had been polluted, and it was necessary that there should be a public purification at Rome. The priest wore a strange dress. He had on his head a large golden crown, and his flowered robe embroidered with gold gave him the appearance of a royal personage. He was allowed to address the people from the rostra, and he is said to have greatly excited their superstitious fears; but whether he spoke in bad Latin or through some interpreter, we may attribute the effect to the man's appearance more than to his words. He was entertained as a public guest, but Aulus Pompeius, one of the tribunes, would not allow him to wear his golden crown. Another tribune, however, again produced him before the people on the rostra, and questioned him about the matter of the sacred rites of the Great Mother. The priest's answers only increased the people's alarm; but Aulus Pompeius persisted in his irreverent treatment of the holy man, who went off to his lodgings in very bad humour, and would not come forth any more. He said that the treatment he had received was an act of impiety to himself and the goddess too. Thereupon Pompeius was seized with a violent fever: he lost his speech, and an attack of quinsey killed him in three days. His death, as most people considered it, was a judgment for his wicked behaviour to the priest and the goddess; for, as Diodorus observes, the Romans are very superstitious. Butaces was now permitted to wear his priestly dress, and was entertained in splendid style. On his departure from Rome he was escorted some distance by a crowd of men. The women of course were there.

The barbarians, after an unsuccessful attempt to storm the Roman camp, began to move southward. The number was so great that during six days without interruption the long line of waggons was passing the intrenchments of Marius. The barbarians, as they marched by, jeered the Romans, and asked if they had any message to send to their wives, for they would soon be with them. When the enemy had advanced some distance, Marius followed, always halting near them; and according to the fashion of the Romans, carefully fortifying his camp against attack by night. The barbarians still went on, and Marius followed till both the armies were near the new Roman settlement of Aquae Sextiae, now Aix (vol. i., p. 311). The enemy were now on the road to Italy; but there was no way except along the Ligurian coast, and it is certain that they could never have taken their waggons by that route. Their destruction was inevitable, if they went on, and it was not easy to retreat, nor have we any reason for supposing that they thought of retreating. The new settlement of

Aquae may have been protected by walls against any sudden
assault, for nothing is said of the town having suffered from
the barbarians.   Aquae was only about twelve Roman miles
from Massilia, for the old Roman road was more direct than
the present road.   A place named Septèmes, seven miles
from Aix, and five from Marseille, still represents the Roman
milestone Ad Septimum.   Marius now prepared for battle
with his formidable enemy in the plain of the Arc.   East of
Aix the little stream of the Arc flows in a valley between two
ranges of hills, one of which is named Sainte-Victoire, or
Notre-Dame des Victoires.   Marius placed himself on one of
those ranges, where his position was secure, but there was no
water.   When the men were complaining of the site chosen
for the camp, Marius pointed to the stream in the valley,
where they would find water, as he said, but the price was
blood.   The men asked to be led against the enemy while
they were still fresh.   The general's answer was, that the
camp must be secured first.   In the mean time the slaves
having no water for themselves or their beasts went down
to the river armed to fetch water, even if they must fight ·
for it.   They met with little resistance at first, for most of
the barbarians were eating after having bathed, and some of
them were still in the water.   "For a spring of warm water
bursts from the ground here; and the Romans surprised some
of the barbarians who were enjoying themselves, and making
merry in this pleasant place" (Plutarch).   There are warm
springs not only within the limits of the ancient colony of
Aix, but in the territory of the town on the east side.   As
the barbarians were not in the town of Aix, but outside of it
to the east, we may suppose that their host extended from a
place named Jouques, about four French leagues north-east
of Aix, where it is said there is a source of water, to Meirar-
gues, which is within two leagues of Aix.   Thus the field of
battle seems determined to be in the country which extends
east of Aix to the mountain which bounds the horizon in that
direction.

The shouts brought the barbarians to the spot where the
bathers were attacked; and Marius could hardly check his
men any longer.   They were afraid of their slaves being

destroyed by the enemy, for the Ambrones, the bravest among them, had sprung up, and were running to arms. They had just eaten and drunk wine, but still they advanced in good order, calling out the name Ambrones, either to encourage one another or to frighten the Romans; for Plutarch observes, and we may suppose that he found some authority for the remark, that it was the Ambrones who defeated the armies of Mallius and Caepio. The Ligurians were the first of the Italic people to go down to battle with the Ambrones. We have Plutarch's authority for Ligurians being in the army of Marius, and it is confirmed to some extent by a passage of Frontinus; but when Plutarch adds, that the Ligurians responded to the enemy by calling out their own national name, which was also Ambrones, we are perplexed by this identity of name between Ligurians, of whom we know something, and Ambrones, of whom we know nothing. The Ambrones could not all cross the stream before the Ligurians, who were running down the hill, fell on the first ranks of the enemy; and the Romans, hurrying to the support of the Ligurians, and rushing on the barbarians from the higher ground, broke them, and put them to flight. Most of the Ambrones were cut down in the stream, where they were crowding on one another, and the river was filled with dead. The Ambrones retreated to their waggons, where the women with furious yells, and axes, and swords attempted to drive back both the pursuers and the pursued. They mingled with the combatants, and fought and struggled till they fell beneath the blows of the enemy.

The Romans had destroyed many of the Ambrones, but they passed a night of alarm. Their camp was imperfectly protected, and there still remained a mighty host of barbarians. All night long were heard the lamentations of the Ambrones, who had joined their brethren, and the cries and shouts from such numbers filled the plain and kept the Romans in expectation of an attack in the dark. But the enemy remained quiet both that night and on the following day, being busy with preparations for the final battle. Marius, observing that the position of the enemy was backed by hills and deep ravines shaded with trees, employed a

stratagem which Frontinus has recorded. He sent M. Claudius Marcellus the night before the battle with a small force
of infantry and cavalry to a place in the rear of the enemy;
and he also sent with them grooms and camp-followers, and
a large part of the beasts used to carry the baggage. The
beasts had their horse-cloths on, and the men being mounted
on them would present the appearance of cavalry. The army
in the camp supped in good time, and had a night's rest.
On the morrow the Romans were drawn up in front of
the camp, and the cavalry advanced into the plain. The
barbarians would not wait till the Romans came down to
fight with them on fair ground. They moved up the hill to
meet them. Marius directed his officers to keep the men
steady till the enemy were within reach of the pila, and after
discharging these weapons they were ordered to draw their
swords and close with the barbarians, who would have the
disadvantage of the lower ground. The pila of the Roman
soldiers discharged against the front rank of the barbarians
would be like a volley of musketry at short distance. It
checked the advance of the enemy, who were compelled to
retreat to the plain. They moved back slowly, and while
they were re-forming in the plain a loud shout burst from
the hills behind them. It came from the ambuscade of Marcellus, which fell on the rear of the barbarians. Attacked
both in front and behind, the barbarians gave way, followed
by the Romans, who slaughtered them without mercy. How
many perished, nobody can tell. It was two hundred thousand
according to one story; but it is not an easy matter to kill
two hundred thousand men, even if they offer themselves to
be butchered. A king Teutoboduus, or Teutobocchus was
killed, says one authority. He appeared in the triumph of
Marius, says another. The tents, waggons, and property fell
into the hands of the conquerors, and, we may certainly conclude, many of the women and children. There was a story
that the barbarian women sent to Marius to pray that they
might be spared and given to the Vestal virgins. This
absurd fiction, reported by three writers of little authority,
is past all explanation; but the fate of the women, as
Orosius, one of these authorities, reports it, is very probable.

Their request, whatever it may have been, was refused, upon which they dashed their children's heads against the ground and destroyed themselves by hanging or by the sword. This was the only way of escape for these unfortunate women from the brutality of a victorious army.

Marius collected the arms and spoils of the barbarians, which were suited to make a show in a triumphal procession. The rest was piled in a great heap. The soldiers were standing by in their armour, and Marius in his purple robe was going to set fire to the pile when some men appeared riding quick towards the general. The horsemen leaped down and greeted Marius with the news that he was elected consul for the fifth time, and they delivered him letters to this effect. The army sent forth one universal shout, the officers crowned Marius with another wreath of bay, and he completed the solemn ceremony by setting fire to the heap of spoil (vol. i., p. 8).

It was said that the people of Massilia afterwards made fences round their vineyards with the bones picked up on the field of battle, or it may be that they used the bones for manure. This bloody plain, where thousands died and rotted, was so fertilized that it produced an unusual crop the next year.

We might reasonably expect to find even still some local evidence of this great fight. The French archaeologists have carefully collected all that they could. The place now named Meyrargues was named Mairanicum in certain old documents; but in still more ancient titles it was named Marii Ager. A small valley near Aix, where there were at least fifty years ago remains of an aqueduct, was named Vallis Mariana in ancient writings. A piece of evidence, reported by M. Fauris de Saint-Vincens, is more precise. There is or was an old charter signed at Marseille in the second year of the reign of Conrad, probably one of the German emperors, but that is not said. This charter contains a donation of Count William to the abbey of Saint Victor of Marseille of a certain domain "quod est in Campo de Putridis prope montem qui dicitur Victoriae vel Santo Venturi." The Campus de Putridis is now the village of

Pourrières, which is bounded on the east by the hill of Victory, which has a considerable elevation. There was once a convent of Carmelites on the top of this hill, where a hermit afterwards fixed his residence. The chief comfort of the good man must have been the prospect, for he would find little else there. The defects of evidence as to this mountain of Victory are supplied by the statement that Marius built a temple on this mountain. He may have done so, but we have only the word of a modern writer for it. If this mountain was named Mons Victoriae after the victory of Marius, it is quite consistent with modern practice that the name Sainte should have been added. A curious annual procession used to be made to Sainte Victoire by the inhabitants of some of the neighbouring villages, and particularly those of Pertuis, which is north of the river Durance. One authority says that the festival was on the twenty-fourth of April : another says that it was in May. They made a pile of wood on the mountain, and crowning themselves with flowers set fire to it. They then moved round the fire crying out Victoire, Victoire. On their return to Pertuis they cried out Sancta Victoria, and went to the church to thank "the god of armies who had not allowed their ancient country to be subjugated by the northern barbarians" (Millin). This festival lasted till the great French Revolution.

If we admit that the names Marii Ager, Putridi Campi, and Mons Victoriae were intended to commemorate this victory, we shall not admit that a part of the territory of Aix, named Malousse, is a corruption of "mala ossa," and that these "wicked bones" are the bones of the northmen. The name of Mont Sainte Victoire has perhaps the best title to be considered a genuine record of the victory. The Latinized names of Marii Ager and even Putridi Campi may certainly indicate that those who used them had heard the story of the victory ; but our inquiry is about names which should be as old as the victory itself, and the evidence for the antiquity of these names is very defective. We may also admit, as seems to be proved, that there was once a pyramidal building near Aix, which commemorated the battle. But this edifice was two leagues and a half from Aix on the Toulon road, and whatever it was, we cannot assume that it was contemporary with Marius, much less that it was erected by him. We must use the French archaeologists with great caution, and we must not forget that we are in the country of falsities. At Marseille they used to show the house of T. Annius Milo, who retired to that city after his trial at Rome; and at Arles among the numerous monumental inscriptions is one to "Calpurnia the most dutiful daughter of C. Marius and conqueror (victrici) of the Cimbri." The impudence and ignorance of forgery can go no further.

In this year there was a triumph at Rome. M. Antonius praetor in B.C. 104 had been sent in B.C. 103 with the title of proconsul to Cilicia. There was no province Cilicia at that time, if we understand Provincia in the ordinary and later sense of a territorial government. Antonius was said to have had Cilicia for his province, because he was commissioned to act against the pirates, whose haunts were in the harbours of the south coast of Asia Minor. These sea robbers had increased during the decay and the troubles of the Syrian kingdom. But piracy alone would never have made these Cilicians so powerful. Their great profit was derived from taking men prisoners and selling them in the market of Delos, the great dépôt from which the Romans supplied themselves with slaves in the second century before our aera. As the trade was profitable, the Cilicians seized men wherever they could both by sea and land, and sold them as slaves. They sold any body that they could lay hold of, even their own people, and finally they made the Mediterranean unsafe for the voyager. We do not know the particulars of the campaign of Antonius, but he must have had some success, or he would not have had a triumph, though it is probable that at this time a triumph was easily granted by the senate. The pirates however were as bold as ever, for in a few years they were off the west coast of Italy, where they landed and seized the daughter of Antonius, who was making a journey somewhere near the coast. The father, who had triumphed over the Cilician pirates, had to pay a heavy sum for the ransom of his daughter.

CHAPTER VI.

Q. LUTATIUS CATULUS AND THE CIMBRI.

Q. LUTATIUS CATULUS the colleague of Marius in B.C. 102 was sent to stop the passage of the eastern Alps against the Cimbri. The barbarians were expected to descend upon Italy by the Saltus Tridentinus or the long valley of the Adige, in which their road would lead them past Tridentum (Trento) to Verona, where the great plain of North Italy begins. This conclusion is made probable by the narrative of Plutarch, and it is confirmed by a passage of Frontinus. Catulus however gave up the defence of this pass, and probably he was compelled to retire. M. Aemilius Scaurus had a son in the army of Catulus, and he disgraced himself by flying from the enemy at the defile of Trento. The father, who had the spirit of a Roman of the better times, forbade the young man to come into his presence. The son was so overpowered by his disgrace that he died by his own hand.

It appears that the retreat from the valley of the Adige took place in B.C. 102, for according to Plutarch's narrative Marius received intelligence of the entrance of the Cimbri into Italy a few days after the defeat of the Teutones and Ambrones near Aix.

The Athesis (Adige) rises in the Rhaetian Alps and after running some distance receives another stream, the Eisach, which comes from the Brenner. Catulus intended to place in his front the Adige, which at the place where it comes out of the valley at Verona is a deep and rapid river. Accordingly we must suppose that the barbarians came down the valley on the east side, which would be the more practicable route, and

Catulus probably posted himself just below Verona on the west bank. At any rate he chose a position where he expected that the barbarians would attempt the passage of the river. He had a camp on each side of the stream, and he made a bridge to establish a communication between his two camps. Plutarch names this river the Atison, and some writers have supposed that he meant by it the Natison, which flowed near Aquileia at the head of the gulf of Venice; but this cannot be the river which Catulus defended. When the enemy reached that part of the river where Catulus was posted, they attempted to dam up the stream with trees and rocks and earth. Probably they thought that they could thus make a passage for their people and waggons over a river which they could not ford. They also threw heavy pieces of wood into the stream which floated down against the wooden piles of the bridge of Catulus and shook it violently. The Romans were terrified and fled from their camp on the west side of the Adige in such confusion, that Catulus could do nothing more than place himself at the head of the fugitives with the view of giving the flight the appearance of a retreat. The men on the east side of the river defended their camp so obstinately and bravely that the barbarians when they got possession of it, in admiration of their courage let the men go on certain conditions, which were sworn upon a brazen bull. This bull was taken after the great battle in which the Cimbri were defeated and became the property of Catulus. The barbarians now crossed the Adige and wasted all the country. The army of Catulus fled before the Cimbri, who pursued and stopped all further retreat by occupying the bank of a river, which Catulus must cross in order to escape from his enemies. He accordingly made use of a stratagem to effect the passage of the river. He drew his men to a neighbouring height where the Cimbri could see what he was doing, and he made preparations as if he were going to encamp there by setting up a few tents, lighting fires, and doing other things calculated to deceive the enemy. The Cimbri, expecting that Catulus was going to make some stay, set about making a camp themselves and were dispersed over the country in search of supplies. Catulus now availed himself of the opportunity to cross the river and even to attack the camp of the Cimbri. Freinsheim supposes that Catulus made good his retreat across the Po; but if this is so, he must have crossed it again when he joined the army of Marius before the decisive battle near Vercellae. It is more probable that Catulus moved westward, and that it was at the Ticinus (Ticino) that he practised this successful stratagem.

Marius visited Rome after his victory in Gallia. The senate had voted him a triumph, and it was expected that he would celebrate it now; but the army was not there, and a triumph without the men who won the victory would have been ridiculous. He left Rome to join Catulus, and sent for the soldiers from Gallia. In whatever way these men came, some time would pass before they could assemble in the plain of the Po and reinforce the army of Catulus. On the arrival of the men from Gaul Marius crossed the Po, for the barbarians were still on the north side of the river, and they were in no hurry to fight, because they were expecting the arrival of their allies the Teutones. They also sent to Marius to demand land and cities for themselves and their brethren in arms. The interview between Marius and the ambassadors of the Cimbri is probably ornamented in Plutarch's usual style; but if there was any embassy, we can believe that Marius convinced the Cimbri of the fate of the Teutones by producing some of them in chains.

The king of the Cimbri is named Boiorix, which is a Gallic name. He was a gallant chieftain and ready to decide the question of the possession of North Italy by a pitched battle. He invited Marius to fix a day and a place for the fight. Marius replied, as any other sensible commander would do on such an occasion, that the Romans never took the advice of their enemies about fighting; however he agreed that the battle should be on the third day from that day, and the place should be the Raudian plain near Vercellae (Vercelli), which is on the river Sesia about half-way between Turin and Milan. The whole country between the Adige and the Sesia in length above one hundred and twenty miles had been overrun by the Cimbri, and as this country had not been visited by any enemy for a century, we may imagine

what the cultivators had suffered from this barbarian visita-
tion, when we read of the plunder and waste committed even
now in an invaded country. The Cimbri, as already remarked, were in Italy in B.C. 102, and their final defeat did
not take place until the summer of B.C. 101. If Marius consented to fight in the plain of Vercellae, we must either suppose that he thought the position as good as any other in
this flat country, or what is quite as probable, he was
compelled to fight in order to stop the progress of the
invaders.

Marius had employed Sulla in Gallia, but Sulla seeing or
supposing that Marius was jealous and unwilling to give him
opportunities of distinguishing himself, joined Catulus, who
entrusted him with matters of the greatest importance.
Plutarch speaks of Sulla reducing a large part of the Alpine
barbarians, a statement that might be intelligible if we had a
history of the campaign. On one occasion when the army
was much in want of provisions, Sulla brought into the camp
enough for the men of Catulus and also for the soldiers of
Marius, who were suffering from scarcity.

The centre of the Roman army was occupied by Catulus
with twenty-two thousand three hundred men. Marius had
thirty-two thousand who were distributed on each of the
flanks. This small force was all that the two generals had to
oppose to the Cimbri. Plutarch used Sulla's memoirs for his
description of this battle, and as Sulla did not like Marius, we
must receive the following statement with some caution:
" Marius expected that the line would be engaged chiefly at
the extremities and on the wings, and with the view of appropriating the victory to his own soldiers, and that Catulus
might have no part in the contest and not come to close
quarters with the enemy, he took advantage of the hollow
front of the centre, which usually results when the line is
extended, and accordingly divided and placed his forces as
already stated." Catulus also wrote a book on his consulship
and his campaigns, and though he wrote in a good Latin
style, his work, says Cicero, was no better known than the
three books of the Memoirs of M. Aemilius Scaurus. Plutarch had not seen this work of Catulus, but he derived from

other writers, who had used it, the fact that Catulus accused Marius of want of good faith.

The infantry of the Cimbri advanced in a square, each side of which was thirty stadia, or more than three miles. This is all that we are told, and it is neither intelligible nor probable. The barbarian cavalry was fifteen thousand. The horsemen had helmets "which resembled in form the open mouths of frightful beasts and strange-shaped heads, surmounted by lofty crests of feathers, which made them appear taller; they had also breastplates of iron and white glittering shields." The horsemen's practice was to discharge two darts and then to use their swords.

The barbarian cavalry did not move straight upon their enemy, but deviated a little to the right with the view of drawing the Romans gradually in that direction and attacking them when the Romans had placed themselves between the cavalry and the Cimbric infantry which was on the left. The Roman generals saw the manœuvre, but they could not stop their men, for there was a cry that the enemy was flying and the whole army rushed to the pursuit. If we had Sulla's memoirs we might learn what this large body of the enemy's cavalry did. Orosius has preserved the fact that it was driven back upon the Cimbrian infantry and thus contributed to their defeat. Plutarch takes no further notice of the cavalry, but as he has spoken of a pursuit before the Cimbrian infantry had come up to the Romans, he must mean a pursuit of the cavalry. In the mean time the barbarian infantry came on like a huge moving wave, and the battle began. Here something happened to Marius which Sulla has recorded, and he considered it as a divine retribution. The opposing armies were wrapped in a cloud of dust so thick that Marius hurrying in pursuit of the enemy missed them altogether and was for some time in the plain without knowing where he was. Thus it happened that the barbarians closed with Catulus, and the chief struggle was between the Cimbri and the men of Catulus, among whom Sulla says that he fought. He also reported that the enemy had the sun in their faces, which was not an accident, but the result of Marius' choice of a position. Marius had given his men a good meal before the battle and placed them in front of the camp, leaving to the enemy the fatigue of crossing the space which separated the two armies. He had also so chosen his ground that the enemy should have sun, wind, and dust in their faces. This prudent precaution of the Roman general has been recorded by a military writer who could appreciate the value of the stratagem (Frontinus, Strat. ii. 2.8). The barbarians, who were well inured to cold, could not stand the dust and heat of this dreadful day, for the battle was fought in the hot season, "three days before the new moon of the month which the Romans at that time named Sextilis or the Sixth, but afterwards Augustus." This day would be the thirtieth of July. The dust which enveloped the armies was also favourable to the Romans, for it obscured the mighty host of the enemy, and the Roman soldiers engaged man to man with the barbarians without feeling the terror which the mere sight of overpowering numbers might have created. The men of Catulus were so well trained that " not one of them was seen to sweat or pant, though the heat was excessive and they came to the shock of battle running at full speed, as Catulus is said to have reported to the honour of his soldiers." The men from the north, who had been accustomed to live in the open air and live poorly, had been corrupted by the luxuries of Italy, and enervated by the climate and excessive indulgence in wine. They were no match for the Romans on Italian soil, and their numbers and want of discipline only made the battle a savage butchery.

The Cimbri had fastened together the men in the first rank by long chains which were passed through their belts, in order to prevent the line from being broken. Such an absurd contrivance would only make their defeat more certain. When the Cimbri gave way, they were driven back to their waggons, where their own women turned upon them, massacring both the fugitives and the Romans who pursued. When the women could no longer resist, some strangled their children, and then maddened by desperation destroyed themselves by every horrible form of death that was in their power. Two chieftains died in mutual combat. Two other kings named Lugius and Boiorix fell like men on the battle-field.

Claodicus, which looks like a Teutonic name, and Cesorix were captured. The number killed was estimated at 120,000 or 140,000, and above sixty thousand prisoners were taken and made slaves in Italy. The valuable property was the booty of the men of Marius; but the military spoils and standards were carried to the tent of Catulus, who relied chiefly on this evidence in claiming the victory for his own men. The soldiers of the two generals also had disputes, which it is said were referred to some commissioners from Parma who happened to be present. The soldiers of Catulus, leading them among the dead bodies of the enemy, pointed out that the barbarians were pierced by their spears, which were recognized by the marks on them, for Catulus had taken care to have his name cut on the shafts. Yet Marius got the chief credit of the victory, both because he was consul and on account of his success in Gaul the year before.

This great battle decided for a long time the superiority of the Italian over the northern people, but the Transalpine nations have never ceased to covet the great plain of Italy, and the Teuton is still lord of one of the fairest parts of it. Plutarch is the only writer who has fixed the locality of this fight near Vercellae. Velleius and Florus place it at the Campus Raudius or Campi Raudii without any indication of the position of this plain. The news of the victory was immediately carried to Rome, not by runners or relays of horsemen or birds, all of which were ordinary means, but by the gods. On the very day of the battle, in front of the temple of Castor and Pollux some young men crowned with bay handed a despatch to the Praetor Urbanus. This would not surprise the Romans, for the defeat of the Macedonian king Perseus was announced at Rome in a like manner on the day of the battle, and, as it was supposed, by Castor and Pollux. Great was the joy at Rome for this deliverance. Marius was named the third founder of Rome, for he had averted a danger as great as the Gallic invasion, and in their thanksgivings the name of Marius was coupled with the gods. He alone was considered to deserve a triumph, but Catulus had a triumph also, either because Marius wished to show

that he was not too much elated with his victories, or for the
better reason that he feared the soldiers, who were ready
to obstruct the triumph, if Catulus did not share it with
him.   Marius was contented with a single triumph for
both his victories, for the defeat of the Teutones in Gallia
and of the Cimbri at Vercellae.   Catulus triumphed over
the Cimbri only.   Florus reports that king Teutobodus or
Teutobocchus walked in the procession, though other authorities state that he fell in the battle near Aix.   But it
would not be difficult to find some huge barbarian among
the captives to act the part of king.   This fellow was so
big that he 'towered,' as Florus says, 'above his own
trophies,' whence we may estimate his height at ten or
twelve feet if we follow the strange opinions of Peiresc and
Froinsheim.

It had long been a practice for successful generals to raise
some memorial of their victories, and the present was a
worthy occasion.   Marius erected a temple to Honos and
Virtus.   On the dedication of his temple Marius exhibited
some Greek plays or spectacles in Greek fashion, whatever
they might be; but he had no taste for such things, and
though he came to the theatre he only sat down a short
time and then went away.   This temple of Honos and Virtus
is often mentioned by Cicero, who sometimes names it the
'memorial of Marius' (monumentum Marii).   An extant
inscription also records that Marius erected a temple to
Honos and Virtus from the spoils of the Cimbri and Teutones.
The situation of this temple is unknown.   Catulus built on
the site, where the house of M. Fulvius Flaccus once stood
on the Palatine, a colonnade which was named Porticus
Catuli.   He also erected a temple to the 'Fortune of this
day,' the day being the day of battle with the Cimbri, on
which he had made a vow to dedicate this temple, but the
title would be good for all time.

The epitome of Livy records a horrible crime in this year.
Orosius, who has also preserved a notice of it, places it after
the triumph of Marius.   One Publicius Malleolus, a man of
noble family, with the assistance of his slaves, murdered his
own mother.   Being convicted of this crime, which the

Romans named Parricidium, he was sewn up in a sack and
pitched into the sea. Both the authorities say that this was
the first instance of such a crime at Rome; but Plutarch
mentions a man named L. Hostius, who murdered his father
after the second Punic war.

CHAPTER VII.

THE SECOND SLAVE WAR IN SICILY.

B.C. 105—09.

THE chief authority for the second slave war in Sicily is Diodorus, whose narrative is very sober and circumstantial. He connects the origin of this insurrection with the execution by the governor P. Licinius Nerva of the senate's order (chap. iii.) made on the occasion of the answer of king Nicomedes II. to the demand for soldiers to assist the Romans. Diodorus was a native of Sicily, and he may have had good opportunities of getting information about both the slave wars. It is certain that he took some pains with this part of his general history.

Dion Cassius says nothing about the order of the senate, but he makes another and a very improbable statement in his own peculiar style. P. Licinius Nerva hearing that the slaves were not fairly treated in some matters, or being moved by a desire of gain, for he was not above taking a bribe, sent round notice to all the slaves who had any cause of complaint against their masters, and promised that he would relieve them. The slaves came in great numbers, some to complain of their wrongs, and others to make charges against their masters, for they all thought that the time was arrived for safely accomplishing what they wished. The masters combined to resist the slaves and did not yield. Nerva being afraid of both parties, and seeing that he might be in danger from those who were defeated in the appeal to him, refused to listen to any of the slaves. He sent them away with some assurance or comfort that they should suffer no wrong for the future, or with the hope that when they were dispersed,

they could make no further disturbance. But the slaves
now feared their masters against whom they had made
charges, and forming themselves into bands they turned to
robbery. Whatever truth may be hid under this statement
of the origin of the insurrection we cannot determine. The
following is the more simple and probable story of Diodorus.

When the senate had passed the decree that no ally of the
Romans should be kept in slavery and that the governors
of the provinces should look after this matter, the governor of Sicily P. Licinius Nerva released many men from
servitude after inquiring into their case. In a few days
more than eight hundred men were declared free. This gave
all the slaves in Sicily hopes of recovering their freedom, though
the grounds on which a few were released could not apply to
all. Those slave-owners who had influence urged the
governor to stop his proceedings; and either because he was
bribed, or for other better reasons, Nerva put a stop to all
further investigation into the cases of those who claimed their
freedom, and told the men to go back to their masters.
Upon this the slaves left Syracuse, where we must suppose
that the governor was then residing, and flying to the
asylum of the Palici began to think of revolt. The lake of
the Palici is a small pond, once probably a volcanic crater, in
the interior of Sicily and west of Leontini, sacred to the
Sicilian deities named Palici. The lake is now the Lago di
Naftia. There was here a consecrated piece of ground with
a temple, to which slaves used to fly when they were badly
used, and the masters could not forcibly take them away.
Accordingly runaway slaves stayed there, and were of course
maintained by the guardians of the temple, until the masters
came to reasonable terms with the slaves and confirmed the
agreement by a solemn oath, which no master was ever known
to have violated. The fear of the deities of the place secured
the performance of the oath; for divine vengeance soon followed an act of perjury. Some perjurers had been deprived
of their sight on the spot. Thus superstition had its uses.

The rising began with thirty slaves belonging to two
brothers who were rich. The insurgents were headed by a
slave named Oarius. The men murdered their masters by

night in their sleep, and then went to the neighbouring plan-
tations to stir up the other slaves. In this first night the
number of the insurgents was increased to one hundred and
twenty. They seized a strong place, which they made still
more secure, and they gained an accession of eighty armed
men. Nerva was soon on the spot, but as he was not strong
enough to take the place, he employed C. Titinius Gadaeus to
deceive the slaves. This fellow had been condemned to death
two years before, but he escaped and became a robber. He
had killed many free men, but harmed none of the slaves.
Nerva promised Titinius a pardon, if he would help him in
his designs. The robber, with some slaves whom he could
trust, came up to the place professing his wish to join the
rebels. He was let in, chosen the leader of the slaves, and
he betrayed them. Some of the insurgents fought till they
were killed, and others threw themselves down the precipices.
This was the end of the first rising.

As soon as the soldiers of Nerva had returned to their
homes, news came that the slaves of a Roman Eques P.
Clonius had murdered their master and were forming a large
body of insurgents. The governor misled by advice and
having his men dispersed gave the slaves time to strengthen
themselves. However with such force as he could collect he
set out, crossed a river which Diodorus names Alba, and
passing by the rebels who were posted on a hill named
Caprianus he came to Heraclea, a town on the south coast
near the mouth of the river Halycus (Platani). The river
Alba is not mentioned, I believe, by any other writer, but it
is very probably the river Allava in the Antonine Itinerary.
If the governor crossed this river before reaching Heraclea,
it must be a stream east of Heraclea, but some geographers
have identified the Allava with a river west of Heraclea. As
the governor did not attack the slaves, they thought that he
was afraid, and they stirred up others to join them, and soon
mustered two thousand. The governor, who still shut himself up in Heraclea, hearing of this increase of the insurgents
appointed M. Titinius to command six hundred men taken
from the garrison of Henna. Titinius attacked the slaves,
but they had the advantage of numbers and position. Many

of the men of Titinius were killed, and the rest threw away
their arms, which the rebels picked up. This success brought
on a general rising, and in a few days there were above six
thousand slaves in arms.

The rebels elected for their king a slave named Salvius,
who was supposed to be skilled in divination. He had also
been accustomed to accompany the women in their Bacchic
ceremonials. The king kept his men away from the towns
for fear of their being corrupted by idleness and luxury. He
made three divisions of his troops with a commander for
each, and he ordered them to scour the country and meet at
a certain place and time. Salvius was thus supplied with
beasts and horses, and he was able to muster above two
thousand mounted men, and twenty thousand foot soldiers
trained to military exercise. With this force Salvius suddenly fell on the strong town of Morgantine or Morgantia.
The situation of this place is not certainly known, but it was
probably somewhere in the valley of the Symaethus (Simeto).
The governor advanced by night to the relief of the place
with about ten thousand men, Italian Greeks and Sicilians.
Finding the rebels engaged about Morgantia he attacked
their camp, which was guarded by a few rebels, and filled
with captured women and booty. He easily got possession
of the camp and then moved on to Morgantia. But the
rebels, who were in a strong position, attacked the governor
with great fury, and his army was routed. Salvius made
proclamation that no enemy should be killed, if he threw down
his arms. This stratagem was successful. The governor's
men threw away their weapons, and Salvius not only recovered
his camp, but got a great supply of arms. The governor lost
about six hundred men, and four thousand were made prisoners.
This success brought Salvius many fresh recruits, and he was
now master of all the open country. He again began the
siege of Morgantia, and made proclamation that he would
give liberty to all the slaves in it. But the masters in Morgantia made the same promise to their slaves, if they would
fight in defence of the town, and the slaves accepted the offer
of their masters, and bravely repelled the rebels. The Roman
governor however revoked the promise of freedom which had

been made to the slaves of Morgantia, and many of them
went over to the insurgents.

There was also a rising of the slaves in the west part of
the island, about Segeste and Lilybaeum (Marsala), and
other neighbouring parts. The leader was Athenion, a
Cilician born, and the bailiff of two rich brothers. He was a
man of courage and could read the stars. He first persuaded
the slaves who were under him, about two hundred, to rise,
and then the slaves on adjoining farms. In five days he had
above a thousand men. Athenion was chosen king and he
assumed the diadem. His conduct was different from that
of all the other rebels. He made soldiers only of the best of
his men. He compelled the rest to remain at their work
and supply the wants of the fighters. He pretended to learn
from the stars that he should be king of all Sicily, and he
told his men that they must spare the land with the animals
and the produce on it, for every thing was theirs. When he
had got together above ten thousand men, he began the siege
of Lilybaeum, but as he made no progress in the siege he
determined to withdraw, and he told his men that he was
obeying the command of the gods, who said that if they
persisted in the siege, they would have bad luck. While
Athenion was preparing to retire, some vessels arrived at
Lilybaeum bringing a picked body of Mauri, who had been
sent to relieve the town under a commander named Gomon.
As Athenion's soldiers were making their retreat by night,
Gomon and his Mauri suddenly fell upon them, and killed
and wounded many of the rebels, who were amazed at the
accuracy of Athenion's predictions.

Sicily was in a most wretched condition. It was overrun
by revolted slaves, and plundered by the poor freemen, who
had no means of subsistence, for the insurrection had deranged all regular industry. These people formed bands and
spread all over the country: they drove off the cattle, robbed
the granaries, and murdered all who came in their way, both
free and slave, that there might be none to give evidence
against them. There was anarchy literally, for the Romans
did not maintain the authority of the law, and every man
did just what he liked. Those, who were once the rich and

tho chief persons in the towns, lost all that they had in the country, and they were compelled to submit to the insolence of the free poor. The slaves were in possession of all the lands of their former masters, whose bad treatment they did not forget, and though they had got more than ever they expected, they were not satisfied. The slaves in the towns were all disposed to revolt, and though they could be kept in check by the combination of the masters, they were a cause of continual uneasiness and alarm to them.

Salvius after his failure on Morgantia overran the country as far as the rich corn plains of Leontini (Lentini), which are north of Syracuse. He had now thirty thousand good soldiers. As a thanksgiving for his success he sacrificed to the Palici and dedicated to them a purple robe. He assumed the name of Tryphon, the same name as that of the man who had usurped the throne of Syria in B.C. 142; and in this he followed the example of the slave king Eunous, who took the name of Antiochus (vol., i. p. 120). No reason is given by Diodorus for Tryphon leaving the east side of the island and establishing himself in the west, but we may conjecture that as he had failed before Morgantia, and there were on the east side of Sicily the large cities Messana, Catana, Syracuse, and others, the new king did not feel quite safe there. Tryphon having moved westward summoned Athenion to come to him, as a king would summon one of his generals. It was expected that this order would make a division between the rebel chiefs, and so the insurrection would be easily broken. But Fortune, a goddess who played a great part in Roman history, made the two leaders agree, as if she were purposely increasing the slave power. Tryphon came to Triocala with all his force, and Athenion joined him with three thousand men, having sent the rest to overrun the country and stir up the slaves to revolt. But Tryphon, suspecting that Athenion would take some opportunity to attack him, put his general in prison.

Triocala, which Tryphon chose for his royal residence, was naturally a strong place. It was so called, as people said, but perhaps they did not say true, because it possessed three good things, abundance of excellent water, a territory rich

in wine, oil, and grain, and perfect security, for it was a large
impregnable rock. Tryphon surrounded the place with a
wall eight stadia in circuit, and a deep ditch. He filled the
town with abundant supplies, and built for himself a palace,
and a large Agora or public place for the use of the citizens.
If he formed a council of the wisest men, as Diodorus reports,
he acted like a wise man himself; but if he also assumed the
purple robe of royalty, as we are told, and went abroad preceded by lictors with axes, and in every thing aped a king,
we must suppose that he was a vain silly fellow: for though
the outward signs of power dazzle and delude mankind, and
so far are useful to kings, they are not worth much unless
power has a sure foundation, and Tryphon could hardly yet
believe that he had established a royal dynasty.

In the interior about twelve miles from Sciacca, the site
of the hot springs of Selinus, there is a place named Calatabellotta, a town of Saracen origin, as the name shows. The
position of Triocala is supposed to be near Calatabellotta, and
if it be true that there was an old church here which had the
name Triocala, that is some confirmation of the conjecture;
but there is no direct evidence which enables us to determine
the position of Tryphon's royal residence.

The Roman Senate sent L. Licinius Lucullus into Sicily
with an army of fourteen thousand Romans and Italians,
besides eight hundred Bithynians, Thessalians, and Acar-
nanians, and six hundred men from Lucania commanded by
Cleptius, a skilful and brave man.   There were also six hundred other soldiers, and so the whole force was sixteen
thousand, or seventeen thousand as Diodorus has it, by some
error in some of the numbers.   This force was sufficient to
crush a servile insurrection if the men had been good for
any thing, but Rome now felt her weakness in a matter
where all nations suffer who are always at war. She wanted
men. When the news came to Rome, says Diodorus, of
many thousand slaves having risen in Sicily, the Romans
were in great trouble, for they had lost near sixty thousand
of their best soldiers in the fight with the Cimbri in Gallia,
and they had no reserves of well-tried soldiers. Diodorus is
here evidently alluding to the defeat of Mallius Maximus

and Carpio in B.C. 105, and he means that the Sicilian insurrection began soon after. This is consistent with his narrative about Tryphon's movements and the fortification of Triocala by the slave king. As Lucullus was succeeded by C. Servilius, and Servilius was succeeded in B.C. 101 by Aquillius, the year in which Lucullus was sent to Sicily was B.C. 103, if Lucullus and Servilius each had his year of command, as we must assume. But the allusion to the defeat of Mallius Maximus and Caepio shows that the island was in a state of insurrection two years before, and the Romans had done nothing effectual to put it down.

Tryphon took Athenion out of prison to advise with him about the war. The king thought of standing a siege in Triocala, but Athenion persuaded him not to shut himself up to be blockaded, but to fight in the open field, and the advice was good. The rebel king posted himself near a place named Scirthaea with forty thousand men, about twelve stadia from the Roman camp. The battle was well contested, and there was great loss on both sides. Athenion with two hundred picked horsemen about him covered the ground with the dead bodies of the enemy, till at last he was disabled by wounds, and then the rebels turned their backs, and Tryphon fled with them. Athenion lay as if he were dead, and made his escape from the field when night came. The Romans had a decisive victory and killed twenty thousand of the rebels, exactly half their force. The rest escaped during the night to Triocala, and it would have been easy, says Diodorus, for Lucullus to have pursued and killed all the rebels. But the loss of the Romans also may have been very large, and Diodorus, or the authority that he followed, could have only a feeble conception of the difficulty after a hard day's fight of slaughtering twenty thousand men who were retreating in the dark through a country which they knew better than the Romans. The rebels were so dispirited by this defeat that many of them thought of returning to their masters and submitting, but the opinion of the braver part prevailed, who resolved to fight to the last rather than surrender. Lucullus did not appear before Triocala until the ninth day after the battle. He began the siege, but retired after suffering some

low, and the rebels recovered their courage. Lucullus was
blamed for not doing all that he ought to have done, either
through want of activity or because he was bribed. · It is
not easy to suggest how he was bribed, but it is very easy to
believe that his sixteen thousand men reduced in numbers
by a hard-fought battle were not a match for the rebels.
However he was prosecuted on his return to Rome. The
charge against him was Peculatus or the unlawful appropria-
tion of public property, as some authorities say. But a more
serious offence is implied in a fragment of Diodorus, where it
is said that when C. Servilius had crossed the straits to supersede him, Lucullus disbanded his men, and burnt his military
material, with the intention of depriving his successor of the
means of carrying on the war. Such treason, which would
be impossible in any well-regulated state, is almost incredible
even in the Roman Commonwealth at that time; but if it is
possible, it could only happen in a government where place
depends on a popular vote. However we must conclude that
Lucullus merited some punishment for his conduct in Sicily,
or that party spirit and popular clamour were strong against
him.   Lucullus was married to a sister of Q. Metellus
Numidicus, consul B.C. 109, but Metellus refused to say any
thing in favour of his brother-in-law. The prosecutor was
an augur named Servilius. Lucullus retired from Rome into
exile. Metellus himself left Rome in B.C. 100, and therefore
Lucullus was either prosecuted in that year before Metellus
went away, or the prosecution took place after the return of
Metellus to Rome, which was in B.C. 99.

Caius Servilius, as Diodorus names him, succeeded Lucullus
in Sicily. Tryphon died, and Athenion taking his place
prosecuted the war. He besieged cities and overran the
country with impunity, for Servilius did nothing. Florus
states that Athenion took the camp of Servilius, an expression which has no exact meaning. He also speaks of
Lucullus' camp having been taken, but he mentions it after
the capture of Servilius' camp. The name of Tryphon is not
mentioned by Florus. His brief narrative of the second
Sicilian slave war is contained in a few sentences, such as
historical epitomators write who have a rhetorical turn. We

may probably refer to the year of Servilius the attack of
Athenion on Messana. The inhabitants of this town, which
is naturally strong, brought into it all their moveables from
the surrounding country, and thought that they were quite
safe. But Athenion surprised the Messenians as they were
celebrating a festival in the suburbs, killed many of them,
and very nearly took the town. He then occupied a strong
place named Macella, and ravaged the territory of Messana.
Servilius, so far as we know, did nothing, and when he returned to Rome he had the same fate as Lucullus.

In the next year Marius was consul for the fifth time with
M'Aquillius for his colleague, who is incorrectly named
Caius in Diodorus' text. We thus determine accurately this
year of the slave insurrection to be B.C. 101, for Aquillius
was sent to Sicily, and he stayed there till he finished the war.
Aquillius defeated the slaves in a great battle, in which he
engaged in single combat with Athenion and killed him.
Aquillius himself was wounded in the head. After this
defeat there were still ten thousand slaves in arms, but they
fled to the strongholds in the island, which Aquillius took by
blockade. There remained now only one thousand rebels
headed by a man named Satyrus, and Aquillius was preparing to attack them, when they surrendered. Aquillius took
the men to Rome, where they were employed in fighting with
wild beasts to amuse the people, probably on the occasion of
the triumph of Aquillius, who had an ovation for his Sicilian
victories. But some say that the prisoners made a glorious
end, for instead of fighting with the beasts, they turned on
one another with their arms till only one was left, whom
Satyrus despatched and then heroically killed himself.
"This," says Diodorus, "was the tragical end of the Sicilian
slave war, after it had lasted near four years." When
Diodorus says that the war lasted near four years, perhaps
he reckoned the commencement from the government of
Lucullus in B.C. 103; for if Lucullus and Servilius had each
a year in Sicily, and Manius Aquillius finished the war in his
proconsulship, we have four years of war without including
Nerva's administration of Sicily, which would be in the year
B.C. 104. Accordingly the slave war ended in B.C. 100, unless

it was in the second year of Aquillius' proconsulship that
Satyrus surrendered. In Livy's Epitome (69) the termination of the slave war is placed after the return of Metellus
from exile in B.C. 99, and accordingly the slave war could
not be ended earlier than this year, if we may trust this
evidence.

There is a passage of Posidonius, quoted by Athenæus, in
which it is said that there was a rising of the slaves in Attica
during the second slave war in Sicily. Orosius (vol. i., p. 122)
has recorded a slave revolt in Attica during the first Sicilian
servile war. It is possible that Orosius has made a mistake
about the time, or there may have been two risings in Attica.
These slaves worked in the silver-mines in fetters and had a
hard lot. Having killed their overseers they seized the
citadel at Sunium and ravaged Attica for some time. Cæc-
cilius of Calacte in Sicily, a rhetorician of the time of
Augustus, wrote a work on the slave wars in Sicily, and
Athenæus appears to quote him as the authority for the
assertion that above a million slaves perished in these insur-
rections. Such extravagant numbers cannot be accepted as
any thing else than the expression of the fact that in these
wars Sicily lost a great part of the men whose labour
enriched the island. Cæcilius, who was a contemporary of
Diodorus, could not know more of these rebellions than
Diodorus did.

We shall hear little more about Sicily till we come to speak
of the famous prosecution of Verres the governor of Sicily by
Cicero. The island recovered in some degree from the effects
of this second servile war before Verres plundered it. An
honourable governor was fortunately sent to Sicily after the
suppression of the revolt by Aquillius. Diodorus names
him Lucius Asyllius, which does not appear to be a genuine
Roman name. Freinsheim assumes the true name to be L.
Sempronius Asellio, but I know no proof of this; and so we
must be content with a short record of an honest governor,
whose name cannot be ascertained. This man found Sicily
in a state of ruin, and restored prosperity by his prudent
administration, in which Diodorus seems to think that he
imitated the jurist Q. Mucius Scaevola, who had administered

wisely and equitably the province of Asia. This Scaevola
was governor of Asia in B.C. 94, and therefore Asellio, or
whatever was his real name, was governor after this date,
according to the opinion of Diodorus. The governor of Sicily
took with him as legatus and adviser Caius Longus, his best
friend, and an honest man. He also was assisted by a Roman
Eques, named only Publius by Diodorus, who was the chief
of all the Roman Equites who resided in Syracuse, rich,
generous, and of excellent character. The governor resided
close to his two friends, whose assistance he had in restoring
the administration of justice and in the general improvement
of the province. He attempted to stop malicious informers
and pettifoggers who make law an instrument of oppression;
and he took care to protect those who particularly require
the protection of the law, women and orphans. It had been
the custom of former governors, in accordance with Roman
practice, to appoint trustees and guardians for orphan children and for women who had no kinsmen to protect their
interests. The governor declared himself the guardian of all
such women and children, and by his own inquiry and care
he settled all disputed matters in which they were interested,
and gave them relief against the oppression of unjust men.
This declaration contained a principle which, if it was new
in Sicily, was a great improvement. The governor, who held
in his hands the civil and military authority as the representative of the Roman people, constituted his court the general
guardian of those who by reason of their age or sex required
a guardian. We can hardly suppose that the court affected
to look directly after the administration of the estates of so
many persons who might live far from Syracuse, but it
assumed the power of calling to account all persons who in
any way managed or meddled in the affairs of orphans, and
of women who had no male kinsmen to protect them.

CHAPTER VIII.

L. LICINIUS CRASSUS AND M. ANTONIUS.

THE great men of Rome were soldiers, lawyers, and orators, men actively engaged in public affairs, not retired students or philosophers. The orators were not those who were only distinguished as speakers in the Senate. A Roman orator's great fame was acquired by popular harangues, by speeches made either in the prosecution or defence of men charged criminally, and on occasions when important questions of property were in litigation. The two most distinguished orators of this time were L. Licinius Crassus and M. Antonius, both of whom have often been mentioned.

Crassus, who came forward as a speaker when he was a very young man (vol. i., p. 320), was Quaestor probably in B.C. 109, and in Asia, where he devoted himself still further to oratorical studies under Metrodorus of Scepsis, a rhetorician of the Academy, of whom Crassus had a high opinion. Among the Romans a man did not attain to oratorical eminence without long and laborious study. It was not considered sufficient to speak much and often, for though a man may thus acquire confidence and facility, his confidence may have no sure foundation of knowledge, and his facility may be a mere readiness in pouring out words, a quality in which any sharp-tongued woman will excel him. It was the opinion of Crassus that men were deceived by the saying that we learn to speak by speaking: for most men in this way practise only their voice, and not even that according to any principle; they practise their strength also and acquire volubility of tongue, and they are pleased with their abundant flow of words. But the true saying is, that by speaking badly men very easily learn to speak badly. Speaking without preparation is useful, but it is better to think well on the matter first and then to speak with due preparation, and more exactness. But the chief thing is to write much, and that is a kind of labour which most people shun. Oratory accordingly has its rules and principles, and it requires the discipline of training, that a man may avoid faults and acquire the power of instructing, pleasing, and finally of convincing, which is the purpose of the orator's art.

The first teacher of Crassus was L. Caelius Antipater the historian, who was a good writer, considering the time when he lived, and a very excellent lawyer. He had many pupils. Crassus himself entered so early on his oratorical career that, as he said himself, he had not often been a hearer of the learned men of his time, for he was always employed in the Forum, except during his absence from Rome as quaestor. But he availed himself of this opportunity, as we have seen, and he learned to speak Greek so well, that you might have supposed that he knew no other language. But though Crassus could speak Greek, he did not affect to write Greek. He read the best Greek orators and translated them into Latin when he was a young man, and thus he learned to find appropriate words to express the meaning of the original, and sometimes he made new words in imitation of the Greek, but he took care that they were such words as were fit for his purpose. Bishop Burnet observes in the preface to his translation of More's Utopia that "the French took no ill method, when they intended to reform and beautify their language, in setting their best writers on work to translate the Greek and Latin authors into it." These old French translators, of whom Amyot the translator of Plutarch is one of the best, both improved their own language by these translations, and opened to their countrymen a new source of pleasure and improvement by enabling them to read the works of antiquity. North's translation of Amyot's version of Plutarch's Lives is one of the best specimens of English style in the early part of the seventeenth century.

On his return from Asia Crassus went through Macedonia

to Athens, where he carefully read with Charmadas the
Gorgias of Plato, in which dialogue he most admired that
Plato while ridiculing orators showed himself to be the
greatest of orators.   He heard other philosophers and
rhetoricians at Athens, and he would have stayed longer,
if he had not been vexed because the Athenians would
not repeat for his pleasure the mysteries, which had
been celebrated two days before the arrival of Crassus at
Athens.

M. Antonius used to read Greek authors as well as Latin
in his retirement at Misenum, for he had little time at Rome.
He did not read for the direct purpose of improving himself
in oratory, but for amusement.   He said that when he
walked about in the sun, though he walked for another purpose, still the natural consequence was that his complexion
got some colour, and so he felt that his language was coloured
by what he read. He also said that he could only understand
those Greek writings, which the writers intended to be
understood by every body.   When he met with the philosophers, who treated of virtue, justice, honesty (in the Roman
sense), pleasure, and the like, he found that he was only
misled by the titles : he could not understand a single word,
so crabbed and concise were these discussions.   He never
attempted to read the Greek poets, for they wrote almost in
a different language.   His pleasure was in reading the historians or orators, or those who wrote as if they wished to
be understood by men like himself, who were not among the
very learned.

It was a common opinion, says Cicero, when he was a boy
that L. Crassus knew no more than what he acquired in his
early education, and that M. Antonius was altogether without
learning.   But Cicero even in his youth refuted these asser-
tions on the authority of his father, of C. Aculeo the husband
of his mother's sister, and of his uncle L. Cicero, who accompanied Antonius to Cilicia, and often spoke to his nephew
about the pursuits and acquirements of this great orator.
Cicero, his brother Quintus, and his cousins, the sons of
Aculeo, followed a course of instruction which was recommended by Crassus, and under the same teachers that Crassus

had; and so Cicero had the opportunity of knowing, and
even as a boy could judge how well Crassus spoke Greek;
and he used to observe that he would put such questions to
Cicero's teachers, and in his conversation make such remarks
as showed that nothing was new or strange to him. Antonius also had opportunities of improving himself during his
quaestorship in Asia (B.C. 113), and again when he had the
province of Cilicia (B.C. 103). He visited Athens on his way
to Cilicia, and had daily conversation with the most learned
men there. He had also the same opportunities at Rhodes.
Cicero, when he was a very young man, knew Antonius, and
often used to put questions to him, so far as proper respect to
so distinguished a man would allow.

Cicero in his treatise on the Orator, the best of all his
writings, attempted to expound the opinions of Crassus and
Antonius about the principles of their art, and to preserve as
far as he could the memory of these two illustrious Romans.
This would hardly have been necessary, he says, if these
orators could have been estimated by their writings; but
Crassus wrote little, or at least very little of his writings had
been preserved, and that little was written when Crassus was
a young man. Antonius wrote nothing except a short treatise
on oratory of no value, and he was sorry that ever he wrote
it. Cicero retained a lively remembrance of these great
orators, and he thought it his duty to make their fame imperishable, as far as he could. If he had been writing about
the orators Servius Galba (vol. i., p. 22) or C. Carbo, he says
that he might have invented, if he chose, for there was
nobody living who could contradict him; but when he wrote
of Crassus and Antonius, he was writing of orators whom
many of his readers had often heard.

The style of these two men was very different. Crassus
was dignified, and yet he could be humorous and witty.
His language was studiously elegant, but there was no appearance of effort. His sentences were short. He stated a
case clearly, and when he was arguing a legal question or
treating of principles of equity, he was fertile in argument
and in discovering points of similarity. He had little action,
little variety in his tone; he never moved about as some

orators did, and seldom stamped his foot. But sometimes
his language was vehement, and expressed passion and indignation.   Cicero informs us that he was a very ornate
speaker, and yet he spoke with great brevity; and this is a
rare combination.   In sharp answers and repartee he had no
equal, and he knew how to deal with a witness and to draw
him on to make admissions.   A man named Silus had given
evidence against Piso the client of Crassus: it was hearsay
evidence, which the Romans allowed, but they did not over-
value it.   Crassus in his cross-examination of Silus said to
him: It is possible, Silus, that the man from whom you say
that you heard this said it in a passion.   Silus assented.   It
is possible too, continued Crassus, that you may have misunderstood him.   Silus admitted this by such a ready nod of his
head as to put himself altogether in the hands of Crassus.
It is possible too, said Crassus, that you never heard at all
what you say that you did hear.   This unexpected conclusion
brought on a burst of laughter which put an end to the
evidence of Silus.   Crassus was engaged in all kinds of
cases, and, as we have seen, very soon attained the highest
rank among the orators of Rome.   Most of the short fragments of his speeches are from orations delivered in the senate
and in public assemblies; and this was the kind of oratory in
which he excelled.

Antonius was a forensic orator, and perhaps there has
never been his equal.   When he spoke, he had all his matter
at command, and he put every thing in the right place,
where it would be most effective.   He had a very great
memory, and no appearance of preparation.   His style was
not exactly what could be called the most elegant, but in the
selection of his words, their position and combination in a
period, he had always in view a principle and some reference
to art, which indeed was much more apparent in the embellishment and the turn of the thought than in the expression.   Besides these great qualities, his action was
peculiarly his own; and if we distribute action into gesture
and voice, we may say that his gesture was not that which
merely expressed what words might say, but it was in
perfect harmony with the thought—the hands, the motion

of the shoulders and sides, the stamping of the foot, the
stationary attitude, the gait, and every movement. His
voice was steady and uniform, but naturally rather harsh.
This accomplished advocate was powerful, vehement, passionate; always well prepared and fortified in every part of his
case. Vigorous, acute, and perfectly clear, he would dwell
on the strong points of his case: when he was hard pressed
by his opponent, he would retire with a good grace, but he
followed up every advantage with energy; he could inspire
terror, move compassion, and employ all the endless variety
of speech without ever wearying his hearers. Antonius tells
us himself, or Cicero tells us for him, how he used to manage
a case. He concludes with a remark which may be useful:
an advocate should ever be on his guard, and Antonius was
particularly anxious on this head, not so much to attempt to
strengthen his case, as to take care that he did not injure it.
A man must of course try to do both, but it is much more
disgraceful to an advocate to damage his case than not to
improve it. (De Orat. ii. 72.)

Crassus and Antonius were sometimes opposed, as in the
case of C. Sergius Orata. M. Marius Gratidianus had sold
to Orata a house which he had bought from Orata a few
years before. This house was subject to a Servitus, as the
Romans named it, which means that the enjoyment of the
ownership of the property was limited by a right which the
owner of some adjacent property had with respect to the
house of Marius, such, for instance, as a right to the passage
of the rain-water through the premises of Marius, or any
other right which comes under the head of Servitus. Marius
had not mentioned this Servitus in the conditions of sale, and
Orata brought an action against him for damages, probably.
Crassus was the advocate of Orata, and Antonius was for
Marius. It was purely a legal question. Crassus maintained
the strict legal right of Orata; that as the vendor had not
mentioned this Servitus, which impaired the value of the
property sold, he was bound to make compensation. Antonius
in reply urged what the Romans called 'aequitas' or fair
dealing: this Servitus was not unknown to Orata, for he had
first sold the house to Marius, and there was therefore no

occasion for Marius to mention it, and Orata was not
deceived, for he knew that the property was subject to a
Servitus. The question was whether the letter of the law
should prevail or the meaning of the rule of law. Antonius
had the right side to defend. It was the rule of law that no
defect should be concealed from the buyer of a thing, and
here there was no concealment, for the purchaser Orata knew
that the property was subject to a Servitus. Still there
was something to say on the side of the literal interpretation
of the rule, that all defects in a thing known to the seller
should be declared to the purchaser. But when we look to
the purpose of the suit, whether it was to rescind the contract or to claim damages, we are at a loss to know
what kind of an argument Crassus would make, for his
client had suffered no damage by the informality in the terms
of sale.

This is an instance of the kind of questions that arose
sometimes even among so practical a people as the Romans.
Roman usage separated the office of ' jurisconsultus ' or lawyer
from that of ' orator ' or advocate. The lawyer was often no
speaker, and the speaker often knew little of law, though he
knew enough to argue a legal question, or at least he was
able to master so much of the law as each case required. It
was the orator's business to deal with direct evidence and to
establish facts, or where the evidence was defective, to draw
probable conclusions. The application of the law when the
facts were ascertained would not generally be difficult, for
most questions, however complicated they seem, may be
reduced to a simple form; and as the wise know, it is not so
much the uncertainty of law that we have to complain of,
as the difficulty of establishing the facts to which the law
may be applied.

Orata was a man fond of good living and a friend of
Crassus, who had also a taste for luxury, and possessed a
splendid house on the Palatine hill. In order to be less
dependent on the winds and waves, Orata had made salt
ponds for various kinds of fish, and whatever the weather
was, his table was always well supplied. He had also erected
spacious and lofty buildings on the shores of the salt lagoon

named the Lucrine Lake, for the purpose of breeding oysters.
But the lagoon was public property and let to a Publicanus
or public contractor, named Considius, who complained of
Orata's encroachments on the lagoon, and brought an action
against him. Crassus was on this occasion the advocate of
his friend Orata.

There is a fragment of Diodorus on the increase of luxury
at Rome, which may be fitly introduced here, though we are
not quite certain what chronological place it occupied in his
history. He begins with speaking of those old times, such
as people now-a-days talk of, when the Romans had good
principles and good habits, by which they slowly increased
in power till they attained the most glorious and extensive
dominion that any nation ever had. But in more recent
times, after subduing most nations and enjoying long peace,
they changed their old frugal habits for a pestilent rivalry.
As the wars ceased, the young men fell into habits of luxury
and intemperance, and wealth supplied them with the means
of gratifying their desires. Men began to prefer the costly
to the simple, and an indolent life to the study of the military
art. A man was considered fortunate by the vulgar not for
possessing merit, but for enjoying through life the pleasures
that he liked best. Accordingly expensive dinners became
the fashion, and rare scents, and rich coverings for couches
with patterns of flowers, and furniture ornamented with silver
and ivory and all other costly materials, on which the artist's
most elaborate skill was displayed. Wines which gave a
moderate degree of satisfaction to the taste were rejected, and
only Falernian and Chian, and other wines of equal quality
were used. Of fish too and other things for the table those
which had the highest repute for pleasing the palate were
freely consumed. The young men used to go about the
Forum wearing clothes remarkable for their softness, so thin
that the form could be seen through them, and in fineness
like women's dresses. Now as there was a demand for every
thing that contributed to enjoyment and pestilent display,
the prices of all such things rose to an incredible height.
A jar of wine was sold for a hundred denarii, and a jar of
salt fish from the Euxine at four hundred. Such cooks as

excelled in the art of preparing dishes sold for four talents;
and slaves remarkable for their beauty were purchased at the
price of many talents.

The picture is naturally drawn, and true for all time.
When a nation is in the enjoyment of peace and is growing
rich, the corruption of manners inevitably follows. But the
prosperity of Rome had a less stable foundation than that of
modern states, in which wealth is founded on industry, and
on the inventive powers by which the labour of man is made
more productive. Yet even in modern states, where the
opportunities of growing rich by successful enterprise and
industry far exceed all the means which the Romans had at
their command, society does not escape the evil which is ever
mixed with that which we call good. The luxurious habits
of the rich are seen and known : wealth is coveted by coarse
and sensual men because it supplies the means of pleasure ;
and those who cannot grow rich honestly attempt to
accomplish their end by extravagant speculations and by
fraud. The few who by ability, self-denial, and hard labour
win their way to wealth, often foolishly aspire to establish a
family which shall not exist by the same virtues which the
founder practised, but shall be supported in idleness by the
produce of the ancestor's labour. The young are proud of the
place to which a father's ability has raised them. They have
done nothing to serve mankind, or even to serve themselves,
and they spend in riot and intemperance that which another
has earned. The mischief does not end here. Their companions, whose fathers have been less successful in gaining
wealth or have had nobler objects in view, imitate the bad
example. They wish to do as the rich do : they would enjoy
before they have laboured ; and so kicking against the law
by which society exists, they bring ruin on themselves and
often on others. Thus even the wealthiest and most fortunate of our modern societies consist of one set of men, who
have laboured for their own good and that of their country,
and of another set, who will not labour, but are mean enough
to live on those who have done the work. Thus society
is cursed with a number of pestilent fellows, devourers of
substance, lazy, mean, and ever on the watch to get by

borrowing, by begging, or by fraud, that which others have got by labour. The evil increases till it breaks out in crime, and even threatens revolution. The evil is manifest. The remedy is a return to plainer ways of living, to a simpler life; and an inexorable resolution on the part of those, whom knaves disturb, to crush them by any severity that is necessary to clear the world of those who prey upon it.

CHAPTER IX.

THE LEX SERVILIA OF C. SERVILIUS GLAUCIA.

THE date of this Lex cannot be accurately ascertained, because we cannot determine in what year C. Servilius Glaucia was tribune. Glaucia was praetor in the sixth consulship of Marius B.C. 100, in which year he lost his life in a riot. As the Lex Servilia of Caepio was enacted in B.C. 106 (p. 3), and the Lex Servilia of Glaucia was later, we must place it between B.C. 106 and B.C. 100. It has sometimes been assigned to B.C. 100, but in that year Glaucia was praetor, and, as Klenze remarks, it was usual up to the time of Sulla for popular measures to be enacted by the Comitia Tributa and to be proposed only by tribunes.

Glaucia is enumerated by Cicero among the "seditiosi" or disturbers of the public peace. He was the greatest knave ever known, if we accept Cicero's opinion, who compares him to the Athenian Hyperbolus, a man who has a bad character in the contemporary Attic writers. Glaucia was very sharp and cunning, and witty enough to make his hearers laugh. With these qualifications he rose from the lowest condition to the praetorship, and he would have been elected consul for the next year, if there had not been two obstacles or perhaps only one. There was a law, the Lex Villia, which prevented a man from being a candidate while he held an office, but this law had been violated repeatedly in the case of C. Marius, and it might have been violated again, if the career of Glaucia had not been cut short in his praetorship. He had gained the favour of the common sort by qualities which they could appreciate, and he had secured the support of the equestrian order by carrying a law which restored to them the judicial office and the consequent political influence of which the Equites had been deprived by the Lex Servilia of Caepio. Such a man was qualified to rise in a corrupted state, where office is conferred by the popular vote. His cunning and his jokes, his low origin and his coarseness would have floated him into power by the suffrage of his admiring fellow-citizens.

The fragments of the Lex Servilia have been put together, restored and explained by C. A. C. Klenze, Berlin, 1825. The tablet, of which the present fragments are part, contained on one side the Lex Servilia, and on the other the Lex Thoria (vol. i., p. 355). Bluhme examined the existing fragments of this bronze tablet at Naples, and Klenze those at Vienna. Both agree that the whole tablet was originally made and adapted to receive the Servilia Lex only, and that the Thoria was afterwards written on the back of the bronze. The face, on which the Servilia is cut, is smoothed and polished: the back is rough like those bronzes which are written only on one side. The letters of the Servilia are well formed and regular: those of the Thoria are very irregular, some large and others small, and the lines are generally oblique and unequal. This is not the only example of a bronze tablet written on both sides.

With the aid of Klenze's valuable restoration of the text of the Servilia and his notes we now know something of the Servilia Lex of Glaucia, and of the constitution of the courts for the trial of the offence named Repetundae (vol. i., p. 25). The first Lex on Pecuniae Repetundae was that of L. Calpurnius Piso, the next was that of M. Junius, and the third was that of C. Servilius Glaucia. In the fragments of the Servilia Lex no laws are mentioned except the Calpurnia and the Junia, and we know nothing at all about the Junia. The Servilia was followed by the law of M'Acilius Glabrio, then by the Cornelia of the Dictator L. Cornelius Sulla, and last of all by the Julia enacted in the first consulship of C. Julius Caesar B.C. 59. All these Leges dealt with a matter which was a fruitful cause of discord in the declining Roman state.

The fragments of the Servilia show that it was both a Lex on the subject of Pecuniae Repetundae and on the constitution of the court for trying those who were charged with this offence.

The first chapter of the Servilia Lex of Glaucia names all those Magistratus, greater and less, as the Romans called them, against whom legal proceedings might be commenced for taking or receiving from any Roman citizen or Socius or any Latin, or from any person belonging to a foreign nation under the protection of the Roman people or in alliance with them, any money in any one year above a certain amount, which amount cannot be determined in consequence of the imperfect state of the fragments. The Latin terms in which the offence is defined (ablatum captum coactum conciliatum aversumve) are wide enough to comprehend any kind of taking or receiving even under the name of a gift, for a thing might in form be a gift, though it was extorted by force, threats, or fraud. Gifts under a certain amount might perhaps be received under the Servilia, as we know that such gifts were allowed at a later time. This first chapter also provided that, when the amount for which proceedings had been instituted was ascertained, and such amount was not in the defendant's possession, there might be fresh proceedings for the recovery of this deficiency from any person into whose hands it was proved that any part of the amount claimed had come.

No man who held any "magistratus" or "imperium" could be proceeded against during his term of office. That there might be no mistake about the terms "magistratus" or "imperium," the persons comprehended in these words were specially enumerated, from Dictator, Consul, Praetor, and so on to the military tribunes of the first four legions (chap. iii.).

The law provided for a patronus or prosecutor being appointed by the Praetor, before whom the charge had been made; but we must assume that this appointment of a prosecutor only applied to those who could neither prosecute themselves nor appoint others as their advocates; and the

persons under these disabilities were socii and other aliens
(perogrini).   The practor was prevented from naming certain
persons as prosecutors, such for instance as kinsmen of the
defendant, and others.   The plaintiff might reject the
patronus, whom the practor appointed, if the patronus was
a man of suspected character, and the practor must appoint
another (chap. iv. v.).

The sixth and seventh chapters are important. They treat
of the Judices or jurymen who are to be appointed by the
Practor and placed in the Album for the year.   Klenze has
a valuable note here.   The determination of the class who
should act as jurymen on trials for Repetundae, and in other
cases also, was a great matter in dispute between the two
parties at Rome from the time of the Gracchi to the time of
Octavianus Caesar, but for want of sufficient evidence it is
very obscure.   These two chapters, though both of them are
imperfect, can be restored with certainty from one another;
and Klenze has done it. Before proceeding to explain chapters six and seven, Klenze makes some remarks on the agreement between these chapters and what we know in other
ways about the appointment of Judices.   The common statement is that the law of C. Gracchus took away from the
Senators the privilege of acting as Judices and transferred it
to the Equestrian order, who kept it till Sulla's time.   As to
the Servilia Lex of Glaucia also, Cicero states that Glaucia
gained the favour of the Equites by what he did for their
order.   But there is no mention of the Equites in the sixth
and seventh chapters, though those chapters can be restored
so completely that it is hardly possible that any thing can be
lost, nor is there mention of the Equites in any other part of
the fragments of the Servilia. Klenze concludes that the
office of Judex was never given in direct terms to the Equites,
but that these popular laws gave the Equites the opportunity
of having the greatest influence in the trials, and that this
was already effected by the law of C. Gracchus, which deprived the senate of the power of being Judices, as the Servilia certainly did, for they are excluded by chapters six and
seven.   The whole question then is reduced to this.   The

Servilia Lex expressly excluded senators and others, as we shall see, from the office of Judex; and the law of C. Gracchus probably did the same. All those who were not expressly excluded from the office of Judex must have been admissible to it.

The following is the substance of the sixth chapter as restored by Klenze. It provides for the appointment of 450 Judices by the Praetor Peregrinus for the first year following the enactment of the Lex Servilia, and within ten days after the enactment. The law does not state from what class or classes the praetor must choose (legat) the Judices: it only declares that he must not choose persons from certain classes. The Praetor must not appoint any Tribunus Plebis, Quaestor, Triumvir Capitalis, military tribune of the first four legions, any man who is or shall be a Triumvir for the assignment of lands, or any man who is or shall be in the senate, or any man who has been hired for pay or wages, or any man who has been condemned in a Quaestio, or in a Publicum Judicium, in consequence of which he was not eligible to the senate, or any man under thirty years of age or above sixty, or any man who does not dwell in Rome or does not dwell nearer to Rome than five miles, or any man who is the father, brother, or son of a man who is or shall be in the senate, or any man who is beyond seas. Every man who is selected by the Praetor must declare his father's name, the name of his tribe, and his cognomen. The names of the 450 Judices must be written on a white tablet with black characters with the name of each man's father and tribe. After the Praetor has selected the Judices, he must take care that the names be read before the people, and he must swear that he has appointed the Judices pursuant to the law. The names of the 450 so selected must be retained in the public tables "in perpetuo," which means "all through the year."

The seventh chapter provides for the appointment of 450 Judices annually for every year following the first year after the enactment of the law. This chapter is the same as the sixth except in the beginning which determines who is to appoint the 450 annually. The person who must appoint

appears to be one of the Praetors, chosen by lot, as Klenze
conjectures. Accordingly by the sixth chapter the Praetor
Peregrinus would name the Judices for that part of the year
which would remain after the enactment of the law, and at
the beginning of the next year one of the Praetors for that
year chosen by lot would appoint the 450 Judices and preside
at all the trials for Repetundae for that year.

The enumeration of persons who are excluded from the
office of Judex contains only the Minores magistratus, but
the words (queivo in Senatu siet fueritve), "who ever is in
the senate or shall be," comprehend the Majores magistratus,
such as Dictator, Consul, and so on. The terms of this Lex
however show that the persons enumerated before the Senators are not considered as Senators by virtue of their office,
though they may have been Senators in some other way.
The Senators as such are distinctly excluded by this chapter
from the office of Judex.

The words "or any man who has been hired for pay or
wages" are partly restored by Klenze's conjecture (queivo
mercede aliqua conductus sit). Sigonius made a different
restoration, but it cannot be accepted. Klenze's conjecture
is certainly probable, but his explanation of the restored
words is not satisfactory (p. 30, note 7). The terms of this
exception would require the Praetor in choosing the Judices
to exclude any man who had ever given his services for hire
in any way. It would therefore exclude a great number of
the poorer people, and any body, whether rich or poor, whom
the terms of the law would comprehend. The law excluded
also persons below and above a certain age, and all who did
not live in Rome or within a certain distance from Rome.
These exclusions would limit very much the number of persons from whom the Judices could be selected, and some of
them would apply to the Equites. Unfortunately the text of
the law is deficient in that part which should state whether
the Praetor could name any person who was not included in
the exceptions above mentioned, and Klenze's restoration of
this part cannot be considered certain. But the whole tenour
of the chapter leads to the plain conclusion that any Roman

citizen not included in the exceptions might be selected as a
Judex by the Praetor. It is however almost certain that he
would choose the Judices from those who had some property,
and the money class were the Equites. Thus by the complete exclusion of the senators the law of Glaucia in theory
at least made the office of Judex open to every Roman
citizen, with certain exceptions. This was a great change.
It deprived all members of the senate of an important office
which they had once exercised, and gave it to the people.
But it did not go so far as to make the choice of the Judices
depend on popular election. The choice was wisely given to
a Praetor, who was himself appointed by the electors.

The eighth chapter treats of the mode of commencing an
action by him who shall claim a sum of money under the law,
and of the choice of the Judices out of the four hundred and
fifty (De nomine deferundo judicibusque legundeis). This
chapter is very difficult, and we can derive no help from the
history of the Judices for filling up the gaps in this part of
the Lex. It seems however that we may safely conclude
from what Sigonius and Klenze have done for the restoration of
the text, that the way of proceeding was this. The plaintiff
or prosecutor named one hundred persons from the Album
Judicum or jury list for the year, and the defendant selected
fifty out of them, or in other words he rejected fifty. In the
same way the defendant named one hundred Judices, and
the plaintiff or prosecutor rejected fifty. Thus there would
remain one hundred Judices for the trial. As this is an
even number there must have been some provision in the Lex
for the case of the jury being equally divided in their verdict,
if the whole number of one hundred sat on the trial. So far
the meaning of this chapter appears tolerably certain.

The thirteenth chapter treats of the mode in which the
Judices should give their votes at the trial. The voting-
tablet (sorticula) was made of box-wood and of certain speci-
fied dimensions, and covered with wax on which the Juror
must write A or C or N L, which letters respectively denoted
acquittal, condemnation, or indefinite adjournment. The
Praetor must have a voting-box prepared, named Sitella in

this chapter, and he must instruct the Judices to place their
voting-tablets in this box; and the Judices must place the
tablets in the box in such way that it may be certain that
each Judex casts only one vote, and he must cover with his
fingers the letter which is written on the tablet. The Praetor
(chap. 15, 16) after counting the tablets pronounced the condemnation or acquittal according to the majority of the votes.
If a man were condemned or acquitted, the judgment was
final, unless it should be proved that there had been 'prae-
varicatio' on the part of the prosecutor, which means col-
lusion between the prosecutor and defendant, by means of
which the defendant had been acquitted; or unless there
might arise some question in respect of the Litis aestimatio
or amount of the damages; or some question respecting the
'legis sanctio.' The meaning of this last exception is doubtful. Klenze says that it provides for the case of an acquittal
being obtained by the defendant through bribing the Judices.
If the defendant were convicted, the Quaestor, he who had
charge of the Aerarium, as Klenze conjectures, with the consent of the majority of the Consilium, was required to call on
the defendant to give securities (praedes) for the amount at
which the damages might be assessed in the Litis aestimatio;
and if securities were not given, the quaestor must take possession of the defendant's property in the name of the state.
This Consilium, or body of jurymen, may be, as Klenze conjectures, those who, as we shall presently see, were appointed
to assess the damages; and a majority of this Consilium
determined what should be the amount of the security.
(Chap. 17.)

The eighteenth chapter is 'de leitibus aestumandis.' The
plural form was necessary to express the fact, because there
might be many claims against the defendant, and the whole
amount of damages could only be ascertained by adding
together the assessed damages of each complainant. The
amount of damages for money wrongfully taken before the
enactment of this Servilia Lex was 'simplum,' as the Romans
termed it, or the amount of the damage, and no more.
Nothing is said about the costs of the plaintiffs, which might

be large, though the Patroni received no fees. But the
Servilia Lex declares that in respect of money wrongfully
taken after the enactment of the Lex, the assessment must
be double the amount of the actual damage, and thus the
plaintiffs would get some compensation for their expenses.

If a defendant should leave Rome before his trial and
conviction, or have gone 'into exile,' as the Romans expressed it, the practice was, as it seems, for this exile to be
declared a part of his sentence. The eleventh chapter has
something on this matter, but the chapter is so imperfect that
we can hardly accept as certain all the restorations. Klenze
in a note has expressed an opinion that banishment from
Rome was no part of the penalties of the Servilia Lex, or
of any subsequent Lex de Repetundis ; and that banishment
only became a part of the offender's punishment, if he left
Rome before judgment was pronounced against him. But
other writers are of a different opinion, and they refer to the
case of P. Rutilius Rufus, and to the expression of Cicero
(De Or. ii. 47) in the case of M'Aquillius, which words seem
to imply that if Aquillius had been convicted, he must have
left Rome.

The nineteenth chapter provides for the payment of the
sums due to the several claimants in a suit under this Lex.
The first part of the chapter appears to provide for the payment to a Roman citizen of such money as he had claimed
either on his own account or acting as a Patronus for another.
The money recovered from the defendant was first paid into
the Aerarium, and then paid out to the persons who were
entitled to it. The second part of this chapter provides for
the payment of sums recovered on behalf of any king or
foreign people. The money which was paid into the Aerarium
in order to be paid out again, when the time came, was kept
in sealed Fisci. A Fiscus was a wicker basket or pannier in
which the Romans kept large sums of money and carried it
about when necessary.

The twenty-third chapter is entitled "de coivitate danda,"
"on giving the Roman citizenship." If any man, who was
not a Roman citizen, should complain to the Praetor, who

had jurisdiction under this law, of a Roman who had brought himself within the penalty of the law, and such Roman should be convicted under the law, then the man who had laid the information, and his wife, children, and son's children became Roman citizens by virtue of this chapter of the Servilia. Cicero in his oration for L. Cornelius Balbus says that the "Latini, that is the Foederati," could obtain the Roman citizenship under the Servilia Lex by prosecuting a senator to conviction. Accordingly the learned have inferred from this passage of Cicero, that only Latini enjoyed this privilege, but here we have the evidence of the Servilia Lex itself that this privilege was given to any man who was not a Roman citizen (qui civis Romanus non erit); and hence we must conclude with Klenze that Cicero only mentioned Latini and Foederati, because his client Balbus belonged to a foederate state. But we must also conclude that this is another of the many examples of Cicero misleading us by his remarks. Again, Cicero speaks of prosecuting a senator to conviction; but it was not necessary that the person prosecuted should be a senator, though it would generally happen that he was a senator. But there is no authority for the assertion sometimes made that a prosecutor by prosecuting to conviction obtained the same rank in the Roman state which the convicted man had held. Such a rule would be very absurd. The foundation for the opinion, I suppose, is a passage of Cicero's oration for Balbus (c. 25); but the passage does not contain this meaning.

CHAPTER X.

L. APPULEIUS SATURNINUS.

B.C. 102—100.

WHEN L. Appuleius Saturninus was quaestor, he had the Provincia Ostiensis, or the business of looking after the corn supply of Rome which came in at Ostia, a town at the mouth of the Tiber. He mismanaged the business, or people were dissatisfied with him. The Senate removed him from his office, which was a very unusual proceeding, and appointed in his place M. Aemilius Scaurus, Princeps Senatus. This insult, as Saturninus considered it, may have driven him to the party of the Populares. He reformed his life, which was rather irregular, and becoming a sober steady man, or seeming to be such, he was elected tribunus plebis, and held that office in B.C. 103, as we may conclude from the fact that in this year as tribune he recommended C. Marius to the Roman electors for a fourth consulship (p. 15). Aurelius Victor attributes to him a law for giving to each of the veteran soldiers of Marius a hundred jugera of land in Africa. Baebius, the colleague of Saturninus, who resisted the law, was driven away by the people with a shower of stones. If Victor has rightly assigned this law to the first tribunate of Saturninus, it could only apply to the men who had served under Marius in Africa, and even many of these men were probably with Marius this year (B.C. 103) in the south of France.

The censors of B.C. 102 were Q. Caecilius Metellus Numidicus and another, whose name is unknown; but the Lustrum

was held in B.C. 101. Appian states that Metellus attempted
to remove from the senate for their bad lives both Servilius
Glaucia, who was a senator, and Saturninus, who had been
tribune, but Metellus was prevented from doing what he
wished, because his colleague would not assent. Metellus
also refused to admit on the censorian lists a man named
L. Equitius, and consequently he would not allow that
Equitius was a citizen. This fellow pretended to be a son of
Tiberius Gracchus, and Aurelius Victor has preserved a story
of Sempronia, the sister of the Gracchi and the widow of the
younger Africanus, being produced as a witness to the claims
of Equitius, but neither threats nor entreaties could induce
her to acknowledge "the disgrace of the family," whatever
that may mean. Saturninus is also said to have been the
prime mover in this matter. The people, who had not forgotten the Gracchi, pelted the censor, because he would not
admit the claims of Equitius.

In the interval between the first and second tribunate of
Saturninus, and consequently either in B.C. 102 or B.C. 101,
but the year is not determined, there came to Rome an embassy from King Mithridates. The only authority is a
fragment of Diodorus. The ambassadors came, as he says,
with a large sum of money for the purpose of bribing the
senators. Saturninus seized the opportunity of showing his
spite against the senate, and insulted the ambassadors in a
violent way. The ambassadors complained, and the senate
supported them. Saturninus was brought to trial for a
breach of the law or usage of nations, which gave ambassadors protection in the country to which they were sent. The
charge against Saturninus involved the penalty of death, says
Diodorus, and as the senate would compose the Judices or
jury, he was in the greatest danger. But we must accept
with distrust both the statement as to the penalty, which may
have been capital (capitalis) in the Roman sense, without
being capital in our sense, and also the statement as to the
constitution of the court by which Saturninus was tried.
Diodorus did not know enough of Roman affairs to tell such
a story correctly. However, Saturninus in his danger had

recourse to the poor for protection. He laid aside his usual
costly dress, and according to the fashion of those times put
on foul clothes, which he might easily find by exchange with
some of his friends of the common sort, or at the shop of an
old clothesman. With his hair neglected and beard un-
trimmed he went about among the rabble, falling on his
knees before some, pressing the hands of others and entreating
them to help him in his trouble. He said that the senate
were factiously combining to ruin him because he was a
friend of the people, and that his enemies were both his
accusors and judges. The people, who were moved by his
prayers, assembled by tens of thousands at his trial, and he
was unexpectedly acquitted. He was now elected tribune
again. We may believe that Saturninus was tried in some
way for some matter connected with this embassy, but the
form and manner of the trial are not truly described by
Diodorus.

There were great disturbances this year when Saturninus
was a candidate for his second tribunate. A man whom
Appian names Nonius, and the Epitomator of Livy calls
A. Nonius, spoke freely against Saturninus and Glaucia, and
Nonius himself was elected one of the ten tribunes. But
Appian is mistaken in saying that Glaucia was then praetor
and presided at the election of the tribunes, for Glaucia was
praetor in the next year B.C. 100. It is true that Glaucia
might have been elected praetor for the next year before the
election of the tribunes, but a praetor designatus would not
preside at an election. Glaucia and Saturninus, who were
afraid that Nonius would use his authority against them, instigated a body of men to set upon him as he was returning
from the Comitia. Nonius fled into a shop, and he was
murdered there. On the next day at dawn Glaucia's party
elected Saturninus tribune before all the people could come
together, and so nothing was said about the murder of Nonius,
for men were afraid to charge Saturninus with the crime, as
he was now tribune. Livy truly says that Saturninus was
elected by violent means.

The Epitome states that Marius gave his support to Satur-

ninus in his election. Marius was himself elected consul this
year for the sixth time, and of course before the election of
the tribunes. To secure his election Marius courted the
electors, and he went farther than was consistent with his
rank, and farther even than suited his own temper, for
though he wished to appear to be one of the people, his real
character was altogether different. This man who was so
brave before the enemy lost his courage amidst the noise of
the popular assemblies, and was easily disconcerted. However it seems that he found a ready answer once. He had
given the Roman citizenship to a thousand men of Cameri-
num, or two entire cohorts, as Cicero has it, who had
distinguished themselves under him in the late war, and
when he was publicly charged with this illegal act, he replied
that he could not hear the law for the din of arms. Marius
was the enemy of the party of the Optimates, and he had an
especial grudge against his old commander Metellus Numidicus. Accordingly he allied himself with Glaucia and
Saturninus, who had at their bidding a number of needy and
noisy fellows, and he also was supported by the men who
had served under him. P. Rutilius Rufus, who was a personal
enemy of Marius, but an honest man, wrote in his history
that by extensive bribery Marius excluded Metellus, who was
a candidate for the consulship, and secured his own election
for the sixth time. This honour had never been so often
conferred on any man except Valerius Corvinus, though
Plutarch remarks that it was said that there was an interval
of five-and-forty years between the first and the last consulship of Corvinus, but Marius after his first consulship held
the office five years in succession: The colleague of Marius
was L. Valerius Flaccus, but he was rather a servant than a
colleague.

The first measure of Saturninus was an Agrarian law.
The Teutones and Cimbri had been in occupation of parts of
the south of France before they were destroyed by Marius, and
we may assume that many of the Gallic people had perished
and their lands were wasted and deserted. The conquest of
Marius gave this land to the Roman state according to

Roman principles, and indeed the Romans might fairly claim
what they had won by the sword, unless any of the former
occupants had escaped and were willing to return to their
farms.   Victor has preserved a notice of a more extensive
Agrarian law, or it may have been part of the Agrarian law
about the lands in Gallia.   This was a proposal to give lands
to settlers in Sicily, Achaea, and Macedonia, and also to
employ in the purchase of land the gold got at Tolosa by
Caepio, from which it appears that some of it must have
reached Rome.   The Lex Agraria of Saturninus contained a
clause by which within five days after the enactment the
senate should swear to observe it, and if any senator should
refuse to take the oath, he should be expelled from the senate
and fined twenty talents.   The object of this part of the law
was to punish those who did not like the measure and to get
rid of Metellus, who was a proud man and would not take
such an oath.   Saturninus named a day for proposing the
law for the popular vote, and he sent round notice to the
country electors, the men on whom he most relied, for many
of them had served under Marius.   There was now a large
number of men who had seen hard service in Africa, Gallia,
and North Italy.   They had saved the Roman State and
might fairly ask for their reward, if the State had any lands
to give.   The Italians, it is said, would derive most advantage
from the law, for many of them had fought in the late
campaigns and were attached to Marius, but the people in
Rome disliked the law, because it would be for the advantage
of the Italians who helped Rome to fight her battles.   On
the voting-day there was great tumult.   Those who spoke
against the law were insulted by Saturninus.   The city voters
called out that it had thundered, and when it thundered on
such occasions, it was not lawful to proceed with the business.
The partisans of Saturninus persisted, upon which the city
men, tucking up their clothes and seizing such pieces of wood
as were at hand, dispersed the country folks, but they were
rallied by Saturninus, and arming themselves with sticks they
fell on the city men, drove them away, and the voting went
on till the law was carried.   It was a violent and irregular

proceeding. The invincible army of Marius, after conquering the men of the north, compelled the voters of Rome
to submit to the will of those who would reward them for
their toils and dangers. The law of Saturninus allowed
Marius to make three Roman citizens for each colony that
should be established, which shows that the colonies were
intended to be Roman, and Marius was to be rewarded for
his great services by receiving the power to oblige some of
his Italian friends. All this disturbance which resulted in
the enactment of a law by violence ended in little or nothing.
The colonies at least were not settled.

But the law served to effect the object of the conspirators,
which was to drive Metellus out of Rome. Marius now
consul (B.C. 100) laid before the Senate the matter of the
oath. He declared that he would never voluntarily take the
oath, Metellus said the same, and the Senate approved their
resolution. But on the fifth day after, at the tenth hour of
the day, Marius hastily summoned the Senate. This, says
Appian, was the last day fixed by the law for the taking of
the oath, and we learn from the fragments of Roman laws
that it was usual to name a short time for the execution of
some things required by a law. Marius told the Senate
that he was afraid of the people, for they were very
earnest about the law, but he had a device which would
meet the difficulty: he said that he would swear to obey
the law as far as it was a law, and this would induce the
country folks to disperse, who were now in a threatening
attitude towards the Senate, and then he would soon show
that the law was not a law, for it had been carried by force
and after thunder was heard, which was contrary to Roman
institutions.

The senators were amazed when they heard this: they saw
that they had been deceived. But Marius gave them no time
to consider. He went straight to the temple of Saturn, where
the Quaestors used to take the oaths. Marius took the oath
first, and then his friends. The rest took the oath through
fear, all except Metellus, who refused. On the next day
Saturninus sent an officer to drag Metellus out of the Senate-

house. As the other tribunes protected Metellus, Glaucia
and Saturninus ran out to the rustics, who seem to have been
always on the spot when they were wanted: they told these
men that they would not have the land nor would the law be
in force unless Metellus was driven out of Rome. They also
proposed a bill of pains and penalties, for such in fact was
the way of getting rid of Metellus by the exclusion of him
from the use of fire, water, and house. The city voters were
very indignant, and they armed themselves with daggers and
formed a guard for Metellus, who commended them for their
good intentions towards him, but said that he would not
allow any danger to befall the country on his account; and he
left Rome. Saturninus urged on the business, and the bill
was carried. Such is Appian's narrative of the disgraceful
intrigues which drove Metellus into exile. Plutarch also
has told the same story shorter and with some variations.
Metellus retired to Rhodes or Smyrna, as Victor says, where
he spent his time in philosophical studies. He received in
his exile testimonies of affection and respect. Plutarch in
his life of Marius has said no more about the exile of Metellus,
but he intended to speak of this matter more particularly in
his life of Metellus, which however he never wrote, or it has
been lost. L. Aelius Stilo, a Roman eques, a Grammaticus
and a partisan of the Optimates, accompanied Metellus in his
exile. This man, who was one of Cicero's teachers, used to
write speeches for others to deliver, after the manner of some
Athenian orators.

Saturninus proposed a Lex Frumentaria "de semissibus et
trientibus," as it is named by the Auctor ad Herennium. It
seems to have been to the same effect as the Lex Frumentaria
of C. Gracchus (vol. i., c. 19), but then we must read "senis
assibus et trientibus" in place of "semissibus et trientibus."
If the proposal was to sell the public corn at the rate of
five-sixths of an as for the modius, that would be almost the
same as giving it. Though we do not know the exact terms
of the Lex of Saturninus, his object was certainly to relieve
the poor by supplying them with corn at a low rate, and thus
to gain the support of the rabble. It is possible that the law

of C. Gracchus had been repealed, or more probably in those
disorderly times it had ceased to be executed after the death
of C. Gracchus, and it might be considered necessary to
revive it. Q. Servilius Caepio, of the same family as the
famous plunderer of Tolosa, and, as some critics have conjectured, his son, was Quaestor Urbanus, and in that capacity he
had the care of the treasury. He informed the Senate that
it was not possible for the state to support so profuse an
expenditure, and the Senate made a resolution that if Saturninus should propose such a law to the people, "he must be
judged to be acting against the common weal." This was a
usual formula at Rome, the object of which was to check
measures of a revolutionary tendency, and to give a show of
reason for the Senate to use force, if necessary. Saturninus
went on with his law, and his colleagues interposed in the
usual way, and so made it illegal for Saturninus to proceed
with his measure. He got the ballot-boxes ready, but Caepio
seeing that Saturninus was acting against the resolution of
the Senate and in opposition to his own colleagues, made an
attack on him with the conservative party, the good, as they
named themselves. The Pontes or passages which led to the
voting-booths were broken down, the ballot-boxes were scattered, and the voting was stopped.

The last law proposed by Saturninus was a law de Majestate, and it was, so far as we know, the first law which had
this title. It is mentioned several times by the Roman
writers, but the exact provisions of the law are unknown.
It may however be reasonably conjectured that one object of
this law was to strengthen the power of the tribunes and of
the popular party. It is said that Caepio who disturbed the
voting on the Lex Frumentaria was tried for Majestas, from
which it might be inferred that the Lex de Majestate was
enacted before the Frumentaria was proposed; but the Lex
de Majestate may have been enacted to meet the case of
Caepio, for such an irregularity would be a trifle in those
times.

The Lex contained no definition of Majestas, for if it did,
M. Antonius in his defence of C. Norbanus, who was tried

(B.C. 04) under this Lex, could not have attempted to define Majestas. The expression of the Lex was general, " Majestatem minucro," and the question would always be, what acts were comprehended in this general expression. We are helped to the Roman notion of Majestas minuta by the terms of the Formula in which the Senate in times of need empowered the consuls to use force, " Ne quid Res publica detrimenti caperet," which means, that the integrity of the state must in no way be impaired. A " Majestatis minutio " was in fact any act which impaired the integrity of the commonwealth. Accordingly a man is said "majestatem minuere " who takes away any of those things which make up the whole of the State; or in other words it is to impair the honour, the fulness, or the power of the Roman people, or of those to whom the people have delegated power; as for instance by opposing a magistrate in the execution of his office. The offence of "Majestas minuta" therefore, or "Majestas," as it was sometimes called, was more comprehensive than the modern term Treason, but under the Imperial system the notion of Majestas came near to that which our law names High Treason.

Caepio was prosecuted under the Lex Appuleia by a man named T. Betucius Barrus of Asculum, whom Cicero names the most eloquent man in Italy with the exception of the Roman orators. It is uncertain to which Asculum Barrus belonged. He must in some way, we suppose, have become a Roman citizen. His speech against Caepio was preserved, for Cicero calls it a famous oration. Caepio's defence was written by L. Aelius Stilo, as Cicero says. We must therefore conclude that Stilo wrote it before he left Rome to join Metellus in his exile. The defence of Caepio was founded on his interpretation of "Majestas minuta." He admitted the facts with which he was charged, but he said that a man impairs the integrity of the state by taking something from it, whereas so far from taking away something, he had saved the state from loss (detrimentum) by preventing the exhaustion of the treasury.

Saturninus was a candidate this year for a third tribunate,

and he was elected. The fellow Equitius turned up again,
and was also a candidate for the tribunate, though he was not
acknowledged as a Roman citizen. Marius put the man in
prison, but the people broke open the doors and carried him
out on their shoulders. Equitius thus secured his election. A
name raised him to place and power, for many persons
believed him to be a son of Ti. Gracchus, though others said
that he was a runaway slave.

At the consular elections of this year (B.C. 100) for the
next year, the distinguished orator M. Antonius was elected
without opposition. The other candidates were C. Memmius
who had been tribune in B.C. 111 (vol. i., p. 401) and Praetor
in B.C. 104, and C. Servilius Glaucia who was now praetor and
consequently not eligible. As Memmius had the better
chance of being elected, Glaucia and Saturninus hired men
with bludgeons to fall on Memmius while the voting was
going on. The candidate for the consulship was murdered in
the presence of all the people, and the election was stopped.
All law, order, and decency were at an end. On the next
day the people mustered in great force intending to get rid
of Saturninus, though he was on the so-called popular side.
But Saturninus was prepared. He summoned his partisans
from the country, and together with Glaucia and a quaestor
named Saufeius he seized the Capitol. It was now a civil
war or a rebellion, and the Senate resolved to put down the
turbulent tribune who had defied the law. The consuls
Marius and Flaccus were empowered to act by a resolution in
the form usual on such occasions with the assistance of such
of the praetors and tribunes as they should think proper.
All the tribunes except Saturninus, says Appian, and all the
praetors except Glaucia joined the consuls: but we must
except Equitius from the number of the tribunes who were
on the side of order. Marius was not well pleased with this
commission to attack his old friends, and he was slow in
making preparation. He supplied his men with arms out of
the temples and the public arsenals, in which arms were
stored, for it appears from what happened on this and other
occasions of arming the people that they did not possess arms

at home, and very probably were not allowed to keep them.
In the mean time the pipes were cut which supplied with
water the Capitol or the temple of Jupiter, as Cicero has it.

Orosius has some facts which are not in Appian. After the
murder of Memmius, he says, Saturninus held a meeting in
his house, where he was named King by some and Imperator
by others; which is a most improbable story. But it is
quite certain that the insurrection was not put down without
bloodshed. Marius drew up his men in regular companies,
planted his colleague with part of his forces on an eminence,
and himself held the gates of the city. M. Antonius, consul designatus, was posted outside the city with an armed
force, probably to prevent the country folks from coming to
help their friend the tribune. All the illustrious nobles of
Rome took up arms in defence of order. The aged M.
Aemilius Scaurus, the chief of the senate, appeared in the
Comitium in arms: he could hardly walk, but his feebleness, as he said, or is supposed to have said, would at least
prevent him from running away. The augur Q. Mucius
Scaevola, a decrepit old man, was there too, leaning on a
spear, an evidence of his feebleness and his spirit at the same
time. All the men who had filled the consulship, all the
praetors, all the nobility old and young were in arms to support the consuls, as Cicero says on an occasion when it suited
his purpose to show that every man of any note in Rome was
opposed to the insurgents. Cicero was too young to have
been present, but he was afterwards intimate with many of
the men who took an active part in suppressing the insurrection. There was a fight in the Forum, in which the party
of Saturninus was defeated, and he fled to the Capitol, the
approach to which through some neglect or want of men had
not been secured by Marius. All the rebels did not make their
escape. Many were destroyed in their flight to the Capitol;
and as the water supply was cut off, the insurgents who
were shut up on the hill suffered from thirst. Saufeius recommended the burning of the Capitol, which would certainly
have given some lustre to this ignoble quarrel; but Saturninus and Glaucia, who trusted in their old friend Marius,

surrendered, and Saufeius followed their example. The termination of the affair is told somewhat differently by the authorities. Marius was urged to put the men to death, but he shut them up in the Curia Hostilia, intending to proceed against them in legal form. Their enemies thinking that this was only a trick to save the men, took off the tiles of the roof and pelted them with stones till they were all killed, a quaestor, and a tribune, and a praetor with the insignia of their office on them. They got what they well deserved, and their old friend and fellow-conspirator, now a consul for the sixth time, let them perish. The authorities of Orosius reported that the doors of the Curia were broken open, and the men were pulled out by Roman Equites and murdered. Glaucia, according to this story, had escaped into a house, but he was dragged out and killed. Many others perished in this quarrel, and the tribune Equitius too. He was tribune for the first time on the day in which he lost his life. As the tribunes entered on office on the tenth of December, the day on which the turbulent Saturninus ended his career was the tenth of December B.C. 100.

Appian, who shows good sense in his judgments, thus concludes: "There was now nothing to look to for protection, neither liberty nor democracy nor the law nor rank nor office, when even the tribunes, whose office was instituted for the prevention of crimes and the protection of the people, and whose authority was sacred and inviolate, committed such crimes and suffered such a penalty."

The year B.C. 100 was memorable for the birth of C. Julius Caesar. In this year also was settled the colony of Eporedia (Ivrea) in Cisalpine Gallia, on the river Duria (Dora Baltea), at the point where the Val d'Aosta commences. It is uncertain whether it was a Roman or a Latin colony. The object of this settlement, as Strabo says, was to protect the country against the Salassi who occupied the Val d'Aosta (vol. i., p. 55); but the colonists of Eporedia had no security against these people till the nation was annihilated.

CHAPTER XI.

FOREIGN AND DOMESTIC EVENTS.

B.C. 99—93.

AFTER the murder of Saturninus the Senate and their partisans called out for the return of Metellus. P. Furius, one of the tribunes, and the son of a freedman, opposed the measure, nor would he yield to the tears and entreaties of the son of Metellus, who by his earnestness in his father's cause gained the name of Pius or the dutiful. In the next year, when Furius was out of office, another tribune C. Canuleius brought him to account for his conduct in the affair of Metellus. Furius had not acted illegally, if he merely opposed a bill for the restoration of Metellus. He was however brought before the popular assembly or obtained permission to address them, but the people would not listen to him, and he was 'torn in pieces' by a mad rabble. This is Appian's expression, but tearing to pieces is a figure of speech, and may mean no more than a brutal and savage murder, which had now become a common thing in Rome. A bill was proposed for the restoration of Metellus by a tribune A. Calidius. The bill was carried, and Metellus returned from exile. He was met at the gates of Rome by thousands, and the day was not long enough for him to receive the congratulations of all his friends. It was the year B.C. 99. We may wonder what Marius was doing all this time. Plutarch is the only writer who has said any thing on the matter. Marius did all that he could to prevent the return of Metellus, but finding that his influence was gone, he left Rome for Cappadocia and Galatia. He pretended that he went to pay a vow to the Great Mother, but he had another object. He

had saved Italy from the barbarian: there was tranquillity at
home, and little doing abroad. In quiet times he would be
forgotten. Accordingly he went to Asia, as his biographer
says, to see if he could not stir up war there, and so find
employment and gain fresh honours. We cannot place much
confidence in Plutarch's report of Marius having visited
Mithridates, and still less in the account of what passed
between them.

The consul of B.C. 99 M. Antonius was no doubt in favour
of the restoration of Metellus, for Antonius belonged to the
party of the Optimates. After the death of Saturninus,
another tribune Sextus Titius attempted to enact again the
part of Saturninus, but he was opposed by M. Antonius, who
gave evidence against this turbulent citizen, from which
fact we conclude that Titius was tried in some way. Antonius
explained in his evidence all that he had done to oppose this
tribune, and what the tribune in the judgment of Antonius
had done against the interests of the State. Cicero in his
oration for Rabirius tells us that Titius was tried by the
Roman Equites and convicted for having in his house a bust
of Saturninus, a statement which in itself carries the evidence
of falsity, though it may be true that Titius had a bust of
Saturninus and that this fact was used against him. We get
something more like truth out of the statement of Obsequens
(100). Titius persisted in an Agrarian law, though his
colleagues opposed it. During the assembly two crows were
fighting over the heads of the people with such obstinacy
that they tore one another with their beaks and claws, and the
Haruspices declared that the proceedings about the Lex must
be deferred. Titius left Rome, or he was driven out by some
proceeding regular or irregular. If he was driven out by
popular clamour or by the popular vote, he had no reason to
complain, for his own conduct about his Agrarian law was
irregular.

The conqueror of the slaves did not fare better than his
predecessors in the war. He was prosecuted in B.C. 98 by
L. Fufius Calenus in the name of the Sicilians for the offence
of Repetundae. Cicero in one passage affirms that many

charges of grasping cupidity were proved against him, but
he was acquitted because he had been successful against the
rebels. M. Antonius defended Aquillius. Cicero in his
treatise on the Orator introduces Antonius as speaking of his
own conduct of the case. Antonius was deeply affected at
the miserable condition of his client. He had seen Aquillius
consul, honoured by the senate for his successful termination
of a dangerous insurrection, and ascending the Capitol in
triumph. The contrast between his past honours and his
present wretched condition moved the feelings of his advocate, and the advocate moved the jury. In the heat of his
passion Antonius rent open the vest of Aquillius and showed
to the court the honourable scars of his client. C. Marius
who was present was melted into tears by the vehement language, the passionate appeals, and the genuine grief of the
orator. This was no trick, as Antonius affirmed : it was not
his fashion to act a part. His gesture, his words, and his
lamentations were the real expression of his feelings, for he
said, and said truly, that if he had not been deeply moved
himself, his speech so far from exciting compassion would
have been only ridiculous. The Epitomator of Livy (Ep. 70)
has preserved this anecdote of the trial of Aquillius, and he
says that Cicero is the only authority for it. Cicero has told
the story twice.

In this year (B.C. 98) in the consulship of Q. Caecilius
Metellus Nepos and T. Didius was enacted the Lex Caecilia
Didia, which Cicero reckons among the laws which were
useful to the state. This law contained at least two chapters,
one of which required every law to be promulgated, that is,
set up in public, for three Nundinae before it was proposed
to the voters. The Nundinae was the last day of the Roman
eight-day week, and the term Trinundinum expressed two
weeks, the first Nundinae being included after the Roman
fashion of reckoning with ordinal numbers. On the Nundinae the country folks used to come to Rome: it was a day of
business and a market-day. The object of the Caecilia Didia
was to let the people know what the law was on which they
would be summoned to vote. The only authority for the

other part of the Lex is the oration De Domo, sometimes
attributed to Cicero, in which it is said that two different
things must not be comprised in one Lex; for such is the
inference from the words "that the people should not be
compelled, if several things were put in one bill, either to
accept what they did not like or to reject what they did like."
But the law itself was an example of the practice which it
professed to stop.

The Spanish peninsula had been quiet for a long time, but
still there were occasional outbreaks, and a very small success
against the natives would be enough at this time to secure a
general a triumph. At the close of B.C. 98 or the beginning
of B.C. 97, L. Cornelius Dolabella had a triumph for some
advantage over the turbulent Lusitani. One of the consuls
of B.C. 98 T. Didius had triumphed over the Scordisci for a
victory gained when he was governor of Macedonia, probably
a few years before his consulship. In B.C. 97 he went to
Spain as proconsul. His Spanish campaign will require a
short notice.

In the year of the city 657, which was B.C. 97, and in the
consulship of Cn. Cornelius Lentulus and P. Licinius Crassus,
Pliny records that a Senatusconsultum was made to this
effect, "that there should be no human sacrifice" (ne homo
immolaretur). This is the only notice that we have of an
act of legislation for stopping the practice of sacrificing a
human victim, when the fears of the people required it (vol.
i., p. 345). Pliny in the introduction to the thirtieth book of
his Natural History has a discourse on the falsity of the
magic art, which, he says, merits a particular notice, as it is
the most knavish of all arts and had prevailed over the world
for many ages. The power of the magic art, he says, cannot
surprise us, when we consider that it combines in itself three
things which exercise the most imperious dominion over the
human mind : Medicine, or the healing art ; Religion, by
which the human race is still kept in a state of darkness; and
Astrology, which professes to read the future in the heavenly
bodies. Magic, he says, still prevails among a great part of
mankind and rules the most powerful of the eastern kings.

Pliny's magic evidently comprehends every superstitious practice by which men hoped to pacify the deities, to deprecate their anger and to secure their favour. His historical sketch of the growth of this pernicious practice is certainly of no value. He mentions Moses and a man named Lotopeas as the authorities for magic arts which still existed among the Jews or some Jewish sect. These men, it is conjectured, were such itinerant exorcists as are mentioned in the nineteenth chapter of the Acts of the Apostles. Harduin observes that Pliny attributes the powers of exorcism to the magic art, and for this reason the learned commentator gives his author the title of atheist. Pliny, who was a wise and humane man, took every opportunity of exposing these gross superstitions, which all experience has proved to be more opposed to human improvement and happiness than atheism or any other form of unbelief. The Gulli sacrificed human victims to appease their deities, until Tiberius Caesar exterminated the Druids; Pliny declares that such human sacrifices still existed in Britain in his time. The Romans too were chargeable with this monstrous crime, which even this resolution of the Senate did not stop, if it is true, as Dion reports, that two men were put to death "as a kind of sacrifice" by the order of the Dictator Caesar in the Campus Martius by the Pontifices and the Flamen Martialis. But this is capable of an explanation: these men were punished for mutiny, and a punishment and a sacrifice are different things. We might as well say that Servetus was sacrificed at Geneva, instead of saying that he was burnt for heresy. Pliny himself however speaks of men and women being buried alive in the cow market, and in such terms that we must conclude that he refers to what happened in his own lifetime. Lactantius also affirms that even to his day Jupiter Latiaris, whose temple was on the summit of the Alban mountains, received human offerings, an assertion which is certainly false. It is however an undoubted fact that human blood has been shed at some time by man's superstitious fears in all countries from the borders of the Atlantic to the Indian peninsula. Only a few years ago a mountain people in Orissa were accustomed to appease the deity of the earth with the blood of human victims; and it required all the prudence and perseverance of a wise administrator to stop the practice.

The censors of B.C. 97 were L. Valerius Flaccus and M. Antonius the orator. Marius, who had been six times consul, but had now lost much of his popularity, did not offer himself as a candidate for the high office of the censorship. He alleged as a reason that he did not wish to make himself enemies by a rigid scrutiny into men's lives and morals, but his real reason is supposed to have been the fear of not being elected. If Marius did not make any figure in political life for want of sufficient capacity, he was not deficient in common sense and cunning. The censors, Flaccus and Antonius, removed from the Senate a man named M. Duronius, because in his tribunate he had repealed a law, but it is not said what law, which checked expense at entertainments. Valerius Maximus reports a few of the words which Duronius used when he was urging the people to repeal this sumptuary law, or, what is more likely, he invented them. It is said that Duronius attempted to avenge himself by prosecuting Antonius for ambitus or bribery in his canvass for the censorship, and this prosecution has been assigned to B.C. 97, the year when Antonius was censor; but those who hold this opinion have been misled by an expression of Cicero, for Antonius could not be prosecuted while he was exercising the consorian office. A false fact being established by a misinterpretation is alleged as evidence that a magistrate could be prosecuted during his office, though it is well known that such an assertion is contrary to Roman constitutional principles. Antonius is said to have decorated the Rostra during his censorship with the spoils of the enemy. We must suppose therefore that he had something to show as evidence of his defeat of the pirates in his praetorship. M. Aemilius Scaurus, who had twice before been named Princeps Senatus, was named Princeps again by Flaccus and Antonius.

A Greek Asiatic king, the third Attalus, had set the example of bequeathing his kingdom to the Roman State (vol. i, p. 203), and a Greek African king followed his example. Ptolemaeus, surnamed Apion, of the royal Greek family which reigned in Egypt, had left by testament his kingdom of Cyrene to the Romans. He died in B.C. 96, and the Roman Senate declared the cities of the kingdom to be free. This is the statement in Livy's Epitome (Epit. 70). Obsequens fixes the death of Apion in the consulship of Cn. Domitius Ahenobarbus and C. Cassius Longinus, but he names him Ptolemaeus king of Egypt. The date of Obsequens agrees with the Epitome, which places the death of Apion between the consulship of T. Didius and Sulla's mission to Cappadocia. Appian has incorrectly placed the death of Apion in B.C. 74. This Apion was a bastard son of Ptolemaeus VII. king of Egypt, named Physcon, who died in B.C. 117 and left Cyrene to Apion. It is clearly to be inferred from Justinus that Apion died in the lifetime of his half-brother Ptolemaeus VIII. Soter king of Egypt, who himself died in B.C. 81. The error of Appian is therefore manifest. The kingdom of Cyrene was immediately made a Roman province, as we might infer from the words of Justinus, but all such conclusions from writers of his class are uncertain. The words of Livy's Epitome, "the Senate declared the cities of the kingdom to be free," merely mean that the chief cities of the Pentapolis, as it was called, should retain their own local administration, and the fact of the Senate declaring the cities to be free implies that the Romans guaranteed this freedom. These cities were Apollonia, Cyrene, Ptolemais, Arsinoe originally Tauchoira, and Berenice originally Hesperides. We cannot conclude from the words of the Epitome that the Senate refused the legacy. Such a refusal would be inconsistent with the policy of the Romans and their design of extending their foreign dominions in the East. The correct conclusion then is that the Romans did occupy the country and gave it some kind of general administration, which would be absolutely necessary to maintain the unity of their new possession. It was afterwards formed into a Province with Crete.

Nothing is known of Apion's reign or his motives for leaving his kingdom to the Romans instead of allowing it to

be reunited to Egypt. Kings never willingly give up any
territory to which they have a claim, and as the eighth
Ptolemaeus of Egypt and his successors did not recover
Cyrene, we may certainly assume that the Romans got it by
some intrigue, and that they kept it because they were able
to hold it. If they had not accepted the legacy, the king
of Egypt would soon have laid his hands on the country.
Apion, like Attalus of Pergamum, probably secured his
kingdom from annexation in his lifetime by promising it to
the Romans after his death.

The kingdom of Cyrene, or the Cyrenaica, extended west
of Egypt along the north coast of Africa from the Cata-
bathmus Major to the Great Syrtis or Gulf of Sidra. It is
only a strip along the coast of the Mediterranean, a table-
land which descends in terraces to the sea, and is backed by
the Libyan desert. The oldest Greek settlement was the
town of Cyrene, whence the whole country subsequently had
the name Cyrenaica. The term Pentapolis was a collective
name for the five chief cities of the Cyrenaica.

The year B.C. 95 had two illustrious consuls, the great
orator L. Licinius Crassus and the jurist Q. Mucius Scaevola,
afterwards Pontifex Maximus, by which title he is distinguished
from Q. Mucius Scaevola called the Augur, who was also a
great jurist. The Augur's daughter Mucia was the wife of
the orator L. Licinius Crassus. In this year Q. Hortensius
made his first speech in the forum at the age of eighteen; and
the poet Lucretius was born.

Crassus had Citerior Gallia or North Italy for his province
in his consulship. Scaevola appears to have stayed in Rome.
Crassus was ambitious of a triumph, which is a proof that
his great talents did not elevate him altogether above the
vulgar notions of his age. But he found no enemy, and had
therefore no military success beyond the destroying of a few
mountaineers, who were either robbers or said to be. He
was weak enough to claim a triumph, but the opposition
of his colleague prevented the Senate from allowing it, and
saved Crassus from a public exhibition which to him would
have been a disgrace. But the conduct of Crassus in North

Italy was free from blame. In his youth he had prosecuted to conviction C. Papirius Carbo (vol. i., p. 320), and the son of Carbo now followed Crassus into his province to look after his behaviour, as Valerius tells us. Crassus did not send him away. He even allowed Carbo to sit by him on the bench when he was holding his courts, and he made no decision without asking Carbo's opinion. Certainly, if this anecdote is true, Crassus used the wisest means for disarming an enemy. Valerius places the Alpine exploits of Crassus in B.C. 94 after his consulship, and Drumann prefers his evidence to that of Cicero, who, he argues, either means "proconsul," when he says "consul," or is mistaken about the year.

Crassus and his colleague proposed and carried a law, the Lex Licinia Mucia, the title of which is not certain. It is sometimes quoted as a "Lex de civibus regundis," and sometimes as a "Lex de civibus redigundis." The Italian allies of Rome wished to be raised from the condition of subjects to the rank of citizens, and it is said that many of them acted as Roman citizens, from which we must conclude that they sometimes voted at Rome, and probably they joined in the noise and tumult of the public assemblies. We have already seen that the Romans attempted by enactments to clear their city of the Latins and Italians, and it is possible that this law only enforced more strictly the existing law, for it is said by one authority that the purpose of it was to compel the Latini and Italian Socii to leave Rome. Further it appears that a very strict inquiry was made under this law into the case of these resident aliens at Rome, but whether it extended to all of them or was limited to those who pretended to be Roman citizens, we cannot tell. However, this Lex caused the greatest discontent among the Italians, and is supposed to have been one of the immediate causes of the war, which broke out in a few years. Q. Servilius Caepio, he who had plundered Tolosa and lost an army on the banks of the Rhone (B.C. 105), was brought to justice. This affair of Caepio is very confused. It was now ten years since his defeat in Gallia, for which he had already been punished with the loss of his property and his senatorian rank (p. 8). Such a

penalty would seem sufficient to satisfy all his enemies. The
passage in Licinianus already cited (p. 9) does not state that
the plebiscitum by which Caepio was ultimately ejected from
Rome was proposed by L. Appuleius Saturninus, though the
passage may possibly bear that meaning. It states that
"Cn. Manlius" was ejected by a measure proposed by
Saturninus, and for the same reason that Caepio was. Now
Maximus could only be punished for the loss of his army,
and therefore according to this authority Caepio had been
punished for the same reason. But, as it has been already
stated (p. 8), Caepio was promptly punished for his misconduct in Gallia, and he would not be punished again for the
same offence. It is possible then that he was now called to
account about the old affair of the gold of Tolosa. But whatever may have been the ground of this second charge, there
is no reason for imputing it to Saturninus either in his first
or his second tribunate, except the passage of Licinianus, and
that is not decisive, even if we accept it as evidence. The
only authority for assigning this second proceeding against
Caepio to the year B.C. 95 is a passage of Cicero (Brutus,
c. 44), who speaks of a speech made by L. Crassus in his consulship in defence of Caepio, an expression which we cannot
understand, if Caepio had been driven out of Rome some
years before in the lifetime of Saturninus. On this second
occasion the tribune C. Norbanus proposed to the popular
assembly the bill, which was intended to complete the ruin of
Caepio. It is affirmed by some modern writers that Caepio
was prosecuted under the Lex Appuleia Majestatis, which
was enacted after the disgrace of Caepio; but he might be
prosecuted for Majestas, as Galba was (vol. i., p. 21), without
being irregularly prosecuted under a law which was enacted
after his offence. Others suppose that he was tried by a court
with a jury of Equites, which is certainly false. When the
bill of Norbanus was proposed to the people, there was a great
tumult, with fighting and throwing of stones. The Optimates
mustered on the occasion to protect a man of their own party.
M. Aemilius Scaurus was struck by a stone; and the tribunes
L. Cotta and T. Didius, who attempted to put their veto

VOL. II. K

on the Rogatio, were driven away. The bill was carried
by violence, and Caepio went to Smyrna an exile. Valerius
Maximus says in one passage that Caepio was thrown into
prison, though he does not say whether it was before the bill
passed or after, and that one of the tribunes L. Rheginus,
an old friend of Caepio, released him, and even accompanied
him in his "flight." In another place Valerius says that
Caepio died in prison, and that his body lacerated by the
executioner was seen lying on the steps called Gemoniae
to the great horror of all the Forum. Strabo states, on the
authority of the historian Timagenes, that Caepio having
appropriated some of the sacred treasures of Tolosa ended his
life unhappily, being ejected from Rome as guilty of sacrilege,
and that his daughters became prostitutes and died miserably.
It is hardly credible that there should not have been a man
in Rome willing to help the daughters of Caepio, if poverty
drove them to prostitution. Such a total ruin of a family is
not however unknown even in modern times. Freinsheim
argues that there is nothing strange in Caepio having been
punished twice; first, for losing his army, upon which he
was expelled from the Senate and his property was confiscated, and secondly by this bill of Norbanus which was
carried by violence, and probably was the penalty for Caepio's
alleged misappropriation of the gold of Tolosa. This may
be possible; but if Caepio lost all his property in B.C. 105, we
cannot understand how he could live at Rome for ten years
longer, or how he could live at all.

A young Roman, who afterwards acquired great reputation
as an orator, P. Sulpicius Rufus, brought Norbanus to trial
under the Lex Appuleia of Saturninus (B.C. 94). The prosecution of Norbanus was perhaps quite as much a party matter
as the prosecution of Caepio by Norbanus. M. Antonius
defended Norbanus, who had once been his Quaestor, and by
his great talents and exertions he secured his client's acquittal. We learn that the jury who tried Norbanus were
Equites, and we may conclude that the Lex Appuleia among
other things provided for the constitution of the court which
should try those who were charged with the offence of

Majestas. There was, as it has been said, no definition of Majestas in the Lex (p. 115). The notion of "Majestas minuta" existed in men's minds as an act that was prejudicial to the State, and on each occasion the jury must decide whether any particular act was an impairing of the Majesty, that is, the magnitude or integrity of the Roman State. So Antonius could argue that a man impaired the integrity of the State when he gave up to the enemy a Roman army, as Caepio had done, not a man, who like Norbanus, gave up Caepio to the people. But the case was not decided on the interpretation of a word. Cicero in his dialogue on the Orator (ii. 48) has put in the mouth of Antonius a statement of the nature of his defence of Norbanus. Cicero was too young at the time of the trial to understand such a question, and as Antonius left no written orations, Cicero must either have been informed by others about this great oratorical effort of Antonius, or he has told us in the name of Antonius how such a case might be successfully defended. In either way the defence is equally instructive.

Antonius said that in his forensic oratory he kept in view three things: first, he laboured to gain the good-will of the jury; second, to inform them; and third, to move their feelings. To accomplish the first a certain mildness and moderation of speech are necessary; the second requires clearness, and the third, energy. For it is necessary, he said, that those who are going to give a verdict in our favour, must either be made well disposed towards us by the inclination of the will, or they must be brought over by arguments, or the orator must master them by exciting their feelings. In prosecuting Norbanus, P. Sulpicius Rufus, who came forward in defence of the State, of the law, and of order, had an honourable office to discharge. Antonius, who had been consul and censor, could hardly in consistency with his high character undertake the defence of a man who was a turbulent citizen and an inexorable enemy to Caepio in his distress. But the fact that Norbanus had once been the quaestor of Antonius could safely be relied on as a sufficient excuse for Antonius defending Norbanus. The art of the orator did the rest.

Antonius in his defence went back to the early periods of
Roman history. He collected instances of the various disturbances in Rome under every kind of circumstance, and he
came to this conclusion, that though all these civil broils had
caused great trouble, yet some of them were justifiable and
almost necessary[1]. Neither could the kings have been expelled, nor tribunes of the Plebs instituted, nor the power of
the consuls limited by so many Plebiscita, nor could the right
of appeal, that guardian of the State and security for freedom,
have been given to the Roman people without these civil con-
tentions. If those great disturbances had been beneficial to
the State, it was not reasonable that any popular excitement
in the case of Caepio should be charged against Norbanus.
Now if there ever was a sufficient reason for popular excitement, there was on this occasion. Antonius then directed his
speech to the disgraceful flight of Caepio and the deplorable
ruin of his army. Thus he revived the sorrow of those whose
friends and kinsmen had perished through Caepio's inca-
pacity, and he stirred up again in the minds of the jury, who
were of the equestrian order, their hatred of Caepio, who had by
his law (B.C. 106) for a short time excluded the Equites from
the jury lists. When Antonius saw that he had secured the
favour of the people who were present, by maintaining their
right even to make disturbance, and the good-will of the jury
either by reminding them of the great calamity that Caepio
had brought on the State, or of the loss of their kinsmen, or
by reviving their angry feelings against Caepio, and now had
brought them to the mood that he wished, he changed his
manner. He assumed a mild and quiet tone. He said that
he was speaking for a friend, for a man who had been his
quaestor, and whom according to the custom of old times,
he must consider as a son; he was in fact engaged in a
struggle for his own reputation and all his best interests, for
nothing would be more disgraceful to him, and nothing could
be more painful than to be unable to help a friend after he
had successfully defended so many citizens who were perfect

---

[1] Compare Machiavelli, Discorsi, I. cap. 4.

strangers to him. He entreated the jury, if they thought that his sorrow and affection for his client were justified, to grant him what he asked in consideration of his age, the offices that he had held and what he had done, especially if they should bear in mind that in all other cases he had only appealed to them to be lenient to his clients, and had never asked any favour for himself.

Thus, observes Antonius himself, he said little about the Lex Appuleia: he only slightly touched upon the definition of Majestas. In fact, as he admits, he had a bad case, and so he said little, where he could not say any thing in favour of his client. He diverted the minds of the jury altogether from his client by rousing their hostility to Caepio, and by recommending himself to the jury as a stedfast friend. "Thus," he adds, addressing Sulpicius in Cicero's excellent treatise on the Orator, "it was rather by moving the minds of the jury than by instructing them that I gained a victory over you in the case of Norbanus."

The great case of Manius Curius was heard in B.C. 93, a little before the time "when I came into the Forum," says Cicero, who was then in his fourteenth year. "Entering the Forum" is a Roman expression equivalent to assuming the dress of a man—the "toga virilis." Perhaps we may conclude that Cicero was not present when this case was argued. The case was this. A testator named Coponius, who, as we must infer, had no children, declared by his will that if a son should be born within ten months after his death, that son should be his heres, or in other words should be his universal successor, should take all his property. Ten months was named because it was according to Roman notions the limit of a woman's pregnancy. The testator further declared that if this child should die before he reached the age when he could legally administer his property, then Manius Curius should be his second heres, or take the property in place of him who was named first. No child was born, and the question arose whether the deceased's property should go to his next of kin one M. Coponius, or to the second heres named in the will, Manius Curius. The cause was heard before the

court of the Centumviri or the Hundred, a court which was
established in early times for the purpose of deciding questions of ownership, and, as we see by this instance, questions
of a disputed succession. L. Licinius Crassus argued the
case for Curius, and his colleague in the consulship Q. Scaevola, the great lawyer, was for the other claimant. Scaevola
contended that the substituted heres, as the Romans named
Curius in such a case, was only conditionally named heres,
and as the condition had not been fulfilled, Curius could not
claim the succession. According to the testament, a son
must be born within ten months after the testator's death,
and he must die before he attained the age of full legal
capacity. Now these conditions were not fulfilled, and Scaevola maintained that M'Curius could not take as heres under
the testator's will. It was his opinion that in interpreting a
testament we should keep to the plain meaning of the words.
Crassus argued against adhering to the plain words of the
testament and in favour of an equitable and fair interpretation, "pro aequo et bono," as the Romans termed it. He
treated the matter in an amusing and humorous way, and
he collected many instances from the popular enactments
(leges), the resolutions of the senate (senatus consulta), and
from ordinary life and common conversation, in which we
could come to no conclusion, if we looked to the words only
and not to the matter. He said to Scaevola, if no will can be
properly drawn up, unless you do it, all of us must come to
you, and you must be the only will-maker. It was clear, he
said, what the testator's intention was: in whatever way it
should happen that he should have no son of sufficient age to
administer his property, either because no son should be born
or being born should die before the time named, it was his
will that Curius should have the property; this was the way,
he said, in which persons drew up their wills, and it had
always been held to be sufficient. Cicero, who has often
spoken of this case, uses the argument of Crassus in the oration
Pro Caecina (c. 18) for his own purpose. He admits that
the words of the testament were not sufficiently precise to
give the succession to Curius. "What then," he says,

" determined the question ? Why the intention (voluntas),
for if our intention could be known without words, we should
not use words at all; but because this is not possible,
words have been invented, not for the purpose of obscuring
but for declaring the intention."   This accomplished orator
could easily have shown the fallacy of his own argument, if
he had been on the other side in the matter of Caecina.   It
is true that the purpose of a will is to declare the intention
of a testator, and words are used because there is no other
way of declaring the intention, and when the words of the
testator are free from all ambiguity, we learn the intention
from the words only, as Scaevola argued. If the testator's
testament is perfectly clear, but cannot be applied to the circumstances in the way which the testator contemplated, he
has made an imperfect will; and then, as Scaevola said, if we
do not follow the words, we must form a conjecture about the
testator's meaning and pervert plain expressions by subtle
interpretations.   The consequence of Scaevola's opinion
would be that men must make their wills more carefully, or
employ some competent person to make them.   The consequence of Crassus' argument would be that we must interpret
a testator's will by some opinion of our own founded on a
conjecture of what the testator would have said, if he had
been wise enough to foresee what he did not foresee, or did
not think about.   Whatever decision may be made or has
been made in modern times in a similar case of conditional
testamentary substitution, the objection that Scaevola urged
against any except the literal interpretation retains all the
force that it had then.

Crassus prevailed, and the court of Centumviri gave judgment for M'Curius.   Quintilian (Inst. Or. vii. 6. 9) mentions
this case in the chapter on the legal questions which arise on
the opposition between intention and the written words.   ·

CHAPTER XII.

SPAIN, AND BRITAIN.

B.C. 97—92.

In B.C. 97 the proconsul T. Didius was in Spain, and he had some success against the Celtiberi, who for some reason, which we do not know, had provoked the Roman arms. Q. Sertorius, the man who had escaped from the slaughter on the Rhone (p. 8), served under Didius as a tribune. Didius had a triumph for his Spanish victories in B.C. 93, and we must conclude that for the greater part of the time between B.C. 97 and B.C. 93 he was in Spain.

. Sertorius during this campaign was wintering in Castulo, which Plutarch names a city of the Celtiberi, but it belonged to the Oretani. Castulo is supposed to be represented by Cazlona on the river Guadalimar, which a little below Cazlona joins the Guadalquivir. If Sertorius had the command in Castulo, he must be blamed for what followed, though any commander might have found it difficult to maintain discipline when his men were scattered about the town. The soldiers were living in great abundance in their quarters, and were generally drunk. The citizens, or the barbarians as they are called, did not get drunk like those who looked on them with contempt, and seeing an opportunity of being rid of the Romans they sent to some of their neighbours for help, and all together falling on the soldiers in their lodgings began to massacre them. Sertorius, who was always ready for any emergency, stole out of the town with a few others and got together all the Romans who had

escaped. The barbarians had left the gates open through
which they had secretly entered the town. Sertorius did not
make the same mistake. He set a watch at the gates, and
hemming the people in the town he massacred all who were
of age to bear arms. After the massacre Sertorius ordered
his men to put on the dress of the barbarians and follow
him to the town from which Castulo had received help.
The barbarians decoyed by the appearance of the men kept
the town gates open, supposing that their friends were
returning from a successful expedition. But most of them
were killed by the Romans near the gates, and the rest surrendered and were sold as slaves. Didius had some hard
fighting in Spain, and he found it necessary to use stratagem
as well as force. One day's obstinate battle was only ended
by nightfall. The loss was great on both sides, but Didius
contrived to bury most of his killed before the day dawned.
There must have been a truce to allow the Romans to bury
their dead, though Frontinus has left us to infer it from the
circumstance of the Spaniards coming out to the battle-
ground when it was daylight. The Spaniards finding that
their dead much exceeded the number of the Roman killed
whom they could see, concluded that they were beaten and
submitted to the terms of Didius. Another stratagem has
some merit. Didius was expecting the arrival of some
legions, and in the mean time, as his numbers were insufficient, he avoided any conflict with the enemy. But he found
out that the Spaniards intended to intercept the legions
which were coming to join him, and accordingly he made
ready for battle, and at the same time ordered his prisoners
to be less strictly watched. Some of the prisoners escaped to
their countrymen and reported that the Romans were going
to attack them. The Spaniards not thinking it wise to
divide their force when a battle was imminent, did not send
the division that was intended to intercept the fresh troops
of Didius, and thus the legions made their way to the Roman
commander without any danger.

Appian reports in these campaigns a slaughter of twenty
thousand Vaccaei, one of the Spanish peoples. It has been

suggested that the name Vaccaei in Appian should be
Arevaci, for the town Termesus "the great city" which
Didius took belonged to the Arevaci. The Roman general
compelled the people to leave this stronghold, which had
always given the Romans trouble, and to live in an unwalled
town on the plains. The proconsul after a nine months'
siege forced also the town of Colenda to surrender, and he
sold all the people, men, women, and children. Probably
the dealers who followed the Roman army would find a
market for their slaves in Sicily, where so many had lately
perished.

Some Celtiberi had been planted by Marius, as Appian
names him, in a town near Colenda (vol. i., p. 398). These
men were poor, and the Romans said that they robbed.
Didius' way of dealing with them was very simple, and it
was approved by the ten Roman commissioners who were
with him for the purpose, according to Roman usage, of
regulating the affairs of the Spanish province. The general
told the chief men of the town that he intended to give them
the lands of Colenda. The people were pleased with this
liberal offer, and were invited by Didius to come with their
wives and children to receive the allotments. On their
arrival at the Roman camp the soldiers left it, and the
Spaniards were ordered to go within the intrenchments, that
the numbers might be taken of the men, women, and children
respectively, with the view of ascertaining how much land
they would require. When the people were within the
camp, Didius placed his men round them and massacred all.
For these exploits, says Appian, Didius had a triumph; and
yet he was as guilty as the butcher Galba (vol. i., p. 20).

P. Licinius Crassus, consul of the year B.C. 97, had also a
triumph in B.C. 93 for victories over the Lusitani. Freinsheim
observes "that the exploits of Crassus are so obscured by
time that we should hardly know that he had been in Spain,
if his triumph had not been recorded, and if Strabo had not
told us that P. Crassus sailed to the Cassiterides from Spain."
Freinsheim correctly refers the passage in Strabo to this
P. Crassus. The passage is this: "The Cassiterides are ten

in number, and they are near to one another, to the north of
the harbour of the Artabri, out in the open sea. One of
them is uninhabited. The rest are inhabited by men who
wear·black cloaks and tunics which come down to the feet
and are fastened about the breast. They walk about with
sticks, and resemble the Furies as represented in tragedies.
They live in nomadic fashion chiefly from their herds. They
have mines of tin (cassiteros) and lead, which metals they
give in exchange, together with skins, to the merchants for
earthenware, salt, and copper vessels. Now, in former times
the Phoenicians only carried on this trade from Gadeira
(Cadiz), and they kept the navigation a secret. The Romans
once followed a certain captain for the purpose of becoming
acquainted with these trading-places, but the captain being
jealous about the secret drove his vessel on a shoal, and drew
those who followed him to the same destruction. The captain
himself escaped on the wreck and received from the State the
value of the cargo which he lost. The Romans however after
many attempts found out .the way at last. After Publius
Crassus had crossed over to these islands and discovered that
the metals were dug out at a small depth, that the people were
peaceable, and now growing rich attended to maritime affairs,
he pointed out the passage to those who chose to make it,
though it was longer than that which separates Britannia
from the mainland " (Strabo, iii. p. 175).

There is no difficulty in this passage, unless it may be in a few
words which do not affect the general meaning (ἐκ περιουσίας
ἤδη τὴν θάλατταν ἐργάζεσθαι). These words are certainly
mistranslated in Groskurd's German version of Strabo. The
Artabri occupied the north-west part of the Spanish peninsula,
the modern Galicia. The bay of the Artabri probably means
one of the various bays in Galicia, which are now the bays of
Coruña, Betanzos, and Ferrol. Strabo has described with
sufficient accuracy the position of the Cassiterides or ten
islands, which are the Scilly islands and probably also the
western extremity of the Cornish peninsula. The name
Cassiterides first occurs in Herodotus, but he says that he
knew nothing of islands named Cassiterides from which tin

comes to the Greeks. The Phœnician trade with the Cassiterides was not from Tyre, but from Cadiz, and Herodotus
who had visited Tyre probably could not have learned any
thing about the western tin trade, even if the Tyrians had
been willing to tell him all that they knew. The exploration
of the shores of the Atlantic was the work of those Phœni-
cians who had been settled outside of the straits of Gibraltar
on the isle of Leon from a date long anterior to any existing
European records. The commerce of Tyre was in a different
direction, and the tin of the early Greeks probably came
from Asia through Tyre. This tin would be the produce
of the Malay peninsula, but it must have passed through
several hands before it reached the eastern shore of the
Mediterranean. Both the metal tin and the name by which
it was known to the Greeks were Asiatic. The Phœnician
commerce with the south-west angle of Britain would be
of later date, and the oriental name Cassiter would be
of course given to the same metal when it was found in the
remote island of the west by the Phœnician settlers in the
isle of Leon. We may thus explain why the tin country
and the adjacent islands received the name Cassiterides,
which accordingly must be a Phœnician and not a British
name. Strabo's story instead of being vague and inexact
has all the appearance of containing substantial truth. The
Scilly islands indeed are now above ten times more numerous
than Strabo describes them; no tin is got there, and it may
be that it never was. But the existence of a tin trade with
the south-west part of Britain is a fact as well established as
any other fact of antiquity. Diodorus, who wrote in the
time of Augustus, has described (v. 21) the working of the
tin in the extremity of the Cornish peninsula, and the
carrying of the metal to an island named Ictis, for at ebb
time, he says, the space between the mainland and the island
was dry and carts could cross over. The island which he
describes is Mount St. Michael, where the metal was bought
by the merchants and taken to the French coast, and then
to the south of France. We learn from the passage of
Strabo that there was at least in B.C. 100 a trade by sea

between Spain and the Cornish peninsula. The tin people were growing rich by the business: they gave their metals and hides for articles which they wanted. If the traders from Cadiz knew that the tin country was part of Britannia, it seems that Strabo's authorities did not know it. The proconsul P. Crassus, though he may not have been the first Roman who visited Britannia, is the first Roman voyager to this island whose name has been recorded.

L. Cornelius Sulla, who had taken Jugurtha prisoner in B.C. 100, and had fought against the Cimbri at Vercellae in B.C. 101, does not appear in public life again until B.C. 93. He did not become a candidate for the praetorship immediately after his return to Rome, as Plutarch incorrectly says. In his first candidateship for the praetorship he failed. He attributed his failure to the common sort, for he said in his Memoirs that it was well known that he was a friend of king Bocchus, and they expected from him a fine show of Libyan wild beasts, which it was usual for a Curule Aedile to give, and they elected others to the praetorship with the view of forcing Sulla to serve as Aedile. He was again candidate for the praetorship in the next year, and by the help of solicitation and bribery he succeeded. In his praetorship (B.C. 93) he exhibited a hundred lions. This was the first time that lions were let loose in the circus. King Bocchus, who supplied the beasts, sent men also to shoot them with arrows.

The affairs of the East were now attracting the attention of the Romans, who were in possession of the province Asia and looking out for opportunities to extend their dominion. Ariarathes V. Philopator, king of Cappadocia, who had assisted the Romans in their war against Aristonicus and lost his life in it, was succeeded by a son Ariarathes VI. Mithridates VI. named Eupator, king of Pontus, commonly called Mithridates the Great, is said to have assassinated (B.C. 96) Ariarathes VI., whose wife was Laodice, the sister of Mithridates. On the death of Ariarathes, Nicomedes II., king of Bithynia, occupied Cappadocia, and Mithridates on pretence of helping his sister sent a force to expel Nicomedes.

Laodice in the mean time married Nicomedes, who was a very old man, but still Mithridates expelled Nicomedes from Cappadocia, and set on the throne one of the sons of Ariarathes the Sixth. Soon after Mithridates proposed that Gordius, a Cappadocian, who had been his agent in the murder of Ariarathes VI., should return to his native country, to which the young king would not consent. Upon this Mithridates prepared a great force to attack his nephew, who also raised an army to oppose his uncle. Mithridates fearing the issue of the war invited his nephew to a conference and murdered him. He then set on the throne a son of his own, eight years of age, and gave him the name of Ariarathes, and made Gordius his guardian. The Cappadocians were soon weary of the tyranny of the agents of Mithridates, and they summoned from the province Asia, where he was then living probably under Roman protection, another Ariarathes, also a son of Ariarathes VI., and made him their king. Mithridates immediately drove out of Cappadocia the new king, who died soon after. Then commenced a series of frauds. Nicomedes found a youth, whom he affirmed to be a third son of Ariarathes, and presented him as a claimant for the crown of Cappadocia before the Roman Senate, and he sent his wife Laodice to Rome to give evidence that she had borne Ariarathes three sons. Mithridates was not behind the king of Bithynia in impudence. He sent Gordius to Rome to maintain before the Senate that the youth to whom he had given the crown of Cappadocia was the son of the Ariarathes who had fallen on the side of the Romans in the war with Aristonicus; but it was not possible that a child of eight was the son of a man who died in B.C. 130. The Senate did not believe either Nicomedes or Mithridates. They took Cappadocia from Mithridates, and Paphlagonia from Nicomedes; and they declared that both these countries should be free, which may mean that they should have no kings. The Cappadocians refused the offer. They said that they could not live without a king, and as the royal blood was spent, the Senate appointed a king named Ariobarzanes I., probably in B.C. 93; or according to Strabo, the Senate allowed the Cappadocians to choose a king by a vote of the people, which seems to be the meaning of Strabo's words.

Mithridates, who was not ready for a final rupture with the Romans, persuaded Tigranes king of Armenia to drive Ariobarzanes out of his kingdom, and to secure his new ally he gave him his daughter Cleopatra to wife. As soon as the army of Tigranes approached, Ariobarzanes packed up and went to Rome. He must have been a very short time on his new throne, for in B.C. 92 L. Cornelius Sulla was sent to the East to settle affairs there. He went out with the title of Propraetor of Cilicia, though Cilicia was not yet a Roman province (p. 66). It does not appear from what quarter Sulla entered Cappadocia, but he probably made his approach from the province Asia. He had only a small force, but it was increased by the Asiatic allies. Gordius met Sulla with a Cappadocian army, but Gordius was defeated, and a still larger force of Armenians who came to support him was also routed by Sulla, who set Ariobarzanes again on his unsteady throne.

While Sulla was near the Euphrates, Orobazus the general of Arsaces IX., king of the Parthians, was sent to visit the Roman commander. This was the first time that a Roman and a Parthian came face to face. The object of the Parthian mission was an alliance and friendship with Rome. At the interview three seats were placed, one for Ariobarzanes, another for Orobazus, and a third for Sulla, who took the middle place, which was the seat of honour. Such behaviour was consistent with Sulla's arrogant temper, and though it pleased some persons to see the barbarians treated in this haughty manner, others thought it was an ill-timed display of pride. The Parthian king resented the insult by putting Orobazus to death on his return. Among the attendants of Orobazus was a Chaldaean, who was or professed to be a judge of men's character. After carefully observing Sulla's countenance and behaviour according to the rules of his art, he declared that Sulla must of necessity become the first of men, and he wondered that he was not so already. It is possible that Sulla may have told the story in his own

Memoirs. He had all through life a firm belief in his good
fortune and great destiny. On Sulla's return to Rome in
B.C. 91, a man named Censorinus, probably C. Censorinus,
whom Cicero enumerates among the Roman orators, instituted
proceedings against Sulla, whom he charged with having
received large sums of money from a king who was a friend
and ally of the Romans. It is likely enough that Sulla made
Ariobarzanes pay for his kingdom. However for some
reason, which is not known, Censorinus gave up the prosecution.

It was probably in B.C. 92 that the trial of P. Rutilius
Rufus took place. It was a party question, and almost produced a revolution. In B.C. 94[1] the learned lawyer, Q.
Mucius Scaevola, who is distinguished by the title of Pontifex from Q. Mucius Scaevola the Augur, was governor of the
province Asia. By his wise and just administration he
gained the affection and esteem of the Asiatic Greeks, who
instituted an annual festival, named Mucia, to commemorate
the services of their governor. Rutilius, who had been consul in B.C. 105, was the legatus of Scaevola, and he contributed
to the happy administration of his superior by protecting the
provincials from the exactions of the Publicani or farmers of
the Asiatic taxes. His integrity made him odious to the
Equestrian Order, to which the Publicani belonged, and he,
who had prevented others from committing acts of rapine
and injustice, was charged with the offence of Repetundae.
Among the men who laboured to ruin Rutilius was a fellow
named Apicius, who was noted for his luxurious habits.
Apicius may indeed have been the prosecutor, but this conclusion cannot be certainly derived from the words of

---

[1] There may be some doubt whether Scaevola governed this province as
praetor or proconsul. If he was praetor, still he might have had the title of
proconsul, as he is named by Livy's Epitomator (Ep. 70). The Pseudo-
Asconius speaks of Scaevola governing Asia as Praetor, but he also says that
Rutilius was Scaevola's quaestor, which is very improbable. If Scaevola
was governor of Asia in his praetorship, his administration of Asia must have
preceded by two or three years his consulship, which was in B.C. 95, and we
cannot admit it to be likely that the enemies of Rutilius deferred their attack so
long. The passage of Valerius Maximus (viii. 16) does not decide this question.

Athenaeus, the only authority that mentions the man's name.
Rutilius was tried under the Lex Servilia of Glaucia. He
defended himself like an honest man conscious of his
integrity. He did not condescend to move the jury by any
of those mean tricks, which were often practised by other
defendants, nor did he attempt to avail himself of any
rhetorical art: he relied on his innocence and the simple
statement of the truth. He would not employ either L.
Crassus or M. Antonius, the two great advocates of the day.
He entrusted some part of his defence to C. Cotta his sister's
son, at that time a young man; and the pontifex Scaevola
said something for him. Scaevola was a clear and elegant
speaker, but he was not an orator: he did not possess the
energy and the eloquence which such a case required.
Rutilius was convicted, and, as we must believe, by a dishonest jury; for all the extant evidence affirms his innocence.
This was one of the most disgraceful transactions in the
annals of the Republic. Rutilius retired to Asia, where he
was well received by the people. He first went to Mitylene
and then to Smyrna, where he received the greatest marks
of respect, and there he spent the rest of his days, though
Sulla afterwards invited him to return to Rome. Rutilius
bore his exile with the resignation of a practical Stoic. His
oratorical powers were not great, but he was well acquainted
with law, well versed in Greek literature, and he had been a
hearer of the philosopher Panaetius, a friend and companion
of the younger Scipio Africanus. One Aurelius Opilius, a
freed man, who had successively taught philosophy, rhetoric,
and grammar at Rome, broke up his school and followed
Rutilius to Smyrna, where the two friends grew old together
and amused themselves with literary pursuits. We may
assume that it was during the leisure of retirement that
Rutilius wrote his autobiography, of which several books are
quoted, and a portion of the history of Rome in Greek, which
contained the war of Numantia. When Cicero was travelling
in Asia (B.C. 78), he saw Rutilius at Smyrna and heard from
him the story about the trial of the Publicani whom C.
Laelius and Scr. Galba defended (vol. i., p. 110).

The censorship of L. Licinius Crassus and Cn. Domitius Ahenobarbus (B.C. 92) was made memorable by a singular exercise of the censorian authority. By an Edictum, or order placed up in public, they closed the schools of the Latin teachers of rhetoric, and the teachers, we must suppose, had to turn to some other occupation, for it was not the fashion in those days to give compensation. The terms of the Edictum are preserved by Suetonius and by Gellius, who may have copied it from Suetonius. They are as follows: "It has been reported to us that there are men who have established a new kind of instruction, and have opened schools to receive youths; that these teachers have assumed the name of Latin rhetoricians, and that young men spend whole days in these schools: our ancestors determined what their children should learn and to what schools they should go: this innovation, which is contrary to the custom and practice of our ancestors, does not meet with our approbation, nor is it judged to be right: wherefore we think that we ought to show both to those who keep these schools and to those who are accustomed to frequent them what our opinion is, which is this, that we do not approve these schools." The Edictum is probably complete, and the concluding words, which express the censors' disapprobation, were a formal condemnation. In B.C. 161 a senatus consultum had been made, which empowered and instructed the praetor M. Pomponius not to allow philosophers and rhetoricians to remain in Rome. It has been conjectured that this order of the senate was probably directed against Greek fugitives and exiles in Italy, many of whom would be men of acquirements, and ready to do something to get their bread. There might be among these teachers also many who were incompetent men and not likely to improve youths either in learning or good manners. We must assume some other reason for this summary expulsion of teachers in B.C. 161 than the mere fact that they taught philosophy and rhetoric; and indeed we are told that they corrupted the Roman youth by their teaching. This is likely enough, for no education could possibly be worse than such philosophy and rhetoric as were then in fashion. The

reasons for the censorian edict of Crassus and his colleague
are not matter of conjecture, if we accept Cicero's statement
of what Crassus said himself (De Or. iii. 24) when he was
discoursing of oratory. He says that it is easy to lay down
principles for the choice of words and their collocation and
their combination in a period, or a man may learn it by
practice only. But as to the matter of discourse, it is very
extensive; and as the Greeks were not masters of this branch
of the subject, and the Roman youth under their Greek
teachers were almost forgetting what they already knew,
Latin teachers sprung up. But I stopped them, says
Crassus, by my edict, not, as some ignorant people said,
because I would not have the wits of our young men sharpened,
but for just the contrary reason, because I would not have
their wits dulled and their impudence confirmed. For as
to the Greeks, whatever they might be in other respects, I
saw that in addition to this readiness of tongue they possessed some learning and cultivation; but these new teachers
could only teach impudence, which even when it is combined
with good qualities, is a thing in itself which should be carefully avoided. As this was all that they taught and their
schools were schools of impudence, I considered that it was a
censor's duty to see that the mischief did not spread farther.

CHAPTER XIII.

THE TRIBUNATE OF M. LIVIUS DRUSUS.

B.C. 91.

THE consuls for the year B.C. 91 were L. Marcius Philippus and Sex. Julius Caesar. In this year also M. Livius Drusus was a tribune of the plebs. He was the son of the tribune M. Livius Drusus, the opponent of Caius Gracchus and consul in B.C. 112 (vol. i., p. 273).

This eventful year preceded and led to the Marsic or Social War, but our authorities are so few and so poor that it is very difficult to state the facts with precision, and perhaps quite impossible to arrange them in their true order. A few chapters in the first book of Appian's Civil War are the only connected narrative of the turbulent tribunate of Drusus. A chapter of Aurelius Victor de Viris Illustribus (c. 66) professes to give a brief biography of Drusus, but the author has apparently confounded the father and the son in some cases, and in others his story is certainly false. All the rest that we can collect about this famous tribune consists of short notices from various writers and of doubtful value. Instead then of describing the position which the second Drusus occupied as a reformer, I shall endeavour to place the facts in such a shape that the probable conclusion from them may be deduced by the reader.

Among the opponents of Drusus in his tribunate was Q. Servilius Caepio. His relationship to the plunderer of Tolosa (p. 5) is unknown; but he belonged to the same

family (p. 115). Drusus and Caepio were once friends, and
even made an interchange of marriages, as Dion reports, but
the meaning of his expression is not certain. It has been
supposed by some critics that Dion means to say that Caepio
married Livia a sister of Drusus, and Drusus married a sister
of Caepio; and this may be the true explanation. The other,
which supposes that they exchanged wives, assumes that this
was sometimes done at Rome; but such critics ought to know
that a Roman could only have one wife at a time, and that if
two married men wished to make such an exchange, each
man must first divorce his own wife, which he could do, if he
liked, but there might be a good deal of trouble about a
settlement of money accounts with the women. If such an
interchange of wives was made, it would be no great evidence
of previous friendship, nor any great reason for the continuance of it. The enmity between Drusus and Caepio was
traced by the anecdote-collectors to the trivial circumstance
of the two men bidding for a ring against one another at an
auction.

After the conviction of P. Rutilius Rufus, Caepio charged
Scaurus under the Lex Servilia of Glaucia. Scaurus had
been sent on some mission into Asia about the affairs of Cappadocia and Bithynia, and there was talk of his having been
bribed and having got money illegally from some of the
allies of Rome. It is not improbable that Scaurus was in
Asia at the same time with Sulla, or it may have been shortly
before. Scaurus, who was always ready, replied to Caepio's
charge by a counter-charge, and managed matters so cleverly
that the charge against Caepio was heard first. The result
of these two trials is unknown. As the Judices were now
taken from the order of the Equites, who had convicted
Rutilius against evidence, and as Scaurus himself had been
exposed to a like danger by Caepio's charge, we can readily
believe the statement of Cicero's commentator that Scaurus
urged Drusus to attempt a change in the constitution of the
body from which the juries were taken.

There is the evidence of Florus, which is followed by some
modern writers, that the consul Philippus was also prosecuted

by Q. Servilius Caepio for obtaining the consulship by bribery,
and they assign this prosecution to the year B.C. 91, during
which Philippus was consul. But if Philippus was prosecuted for bribery at the consular election, he must have been
prosecuted in B.C. 92 after the election and before he entered
on his office. Florus however is a poor authority for this fact,
for he states that Scaurus also was prosecuted by Caepio for
bribery, whereas it is certain that it was for another offence,
as I have stated.

The consul Philippus was well known to Cicero, for
Philippus was living when Cicero was a young man. As an
orator Philippus could not be compared with Crassus and
Antonius, though there was no Roman of his day who approached so near to them. His oratory was characterized by
" the greatest freedom," says Cicero, by which he perhaps
means that his language flowed easily and without any con-
straint; he had much humour, fertility enough in his ideas,
and readiness in expressing them: he was well acquainted
with Greek learning for the times when he lived, and in dis-
putation his humour was not without a certain sting and
abusive tone. Horace has told at some length a practical
joke which Philippus played off on a poor fellow. The story
is not calculated to give us a favourable opinion of a man,
who sought amusement by leading a town-bred dependent to
undertake the management of a farm for which he was
altogether unfit. Philippus was a distinguished forensic
orator. He seems not to have relied on preparation, for,
according to Cicero, when he rose to speak he never knew
what he was to begin with; and he used to say himself, that
when he had warmed his arms, he was then ready for a
fight.

The career of Drusus in his tribunate is represented by
Livy's Epitomator in the following general terms: " In order
more effectually to support the cause of the Senate, which he
had taken up, Drusus moved the Roman allies and the Italian
people by giving them hopes of obtaining the Roman citizenship ; and with their help he carried by force Agrarian Laws
and Leges Frumentariae ; he also carried a Lex Judiciaria by

which the Judicia were equally divided between the Senate and the Equestrian order ;" which means or ought to mean that the jurymen were taken in equal numbers from each order. Thus Drusus appears as a man who adopted revolutionary measures with the view of strengthening the party of the Optimates ; and Velleius gives the same general view of his policy, when he says that Drusus desired to restore to the Senate their former credit and to transfer the Judicia (the office of juryman) from the Equites to that order, and yet he found that the Senate opposed him in those very things which he was designing to accomplish in the interest of the Senate. The testimony of Velleius is not altogether unexceptionable, but it agrees with the Epitomator, and we shall see how far it is consistent with other authorities.

Drusus must have been actively employed during his year of office. Nothing is known of his Lex Frumentaria, for though the Epitome speaks of such laws in the plural number, we cannot suppose that there were more than one. This corn law was, as the name indicates, a law for the distribution of public corn among needy Roman citizens at a price below the market price (vol. i., p. 261). Perhaps Drusus also did a little in the way of settling accounts between debtors and creditors, for Pliny informs us that he debased the silver coinage by mixing with it one-eighth of copper. One-eighth part of copper in place of so much silver was a moderate amount of depreciation, and hardly worth the trouble, as we should suppose, though it would certainly be very agreeable to a debtor to pay seven-eighths of a debt instead of the full amount.

All the policy of Drusus turned upon the great question which had agitated Italy ever since M. Fulvius Flaccus during his consulship gave the Italian allies of Rome the hope and prospect of the Roman citizenship (vol. i., p. 241). Flaccus and his associate Caius Gracchus had perished in their attempt, but the Italians did not despair of attaining their object. They applied to the tribune Drusus, and he promised them his aid. It seems probable that the allies would begin their agitation early in the tribunate of Drusus and sooner

perhaps than he wished.   There was, if we may trust Florus
and Victor, a design on the part of the Latins to begin the
rising by massacring the consuls Philippus and Caesar, while
they were making the annual solemn sacrifice at the Feriae
Latinae to Jupiter Latiaris on the summit of the Alban hills.
Drusus is said to have been acquainted with the plot and to
have warned the consuls.   The Feriae Latinae were not celebrated at a fixed time, but it was the practice for the magistrates or priests, whose business it was to give notice of the
festival, to name the time.   Perhaps we may conclude that
they were generally observed early in the year.

In order to prepare the Roman people to help him with
their votes on the great Italian question, Drusus established
several colonies in Italy and Sicily, which would provide for
a good number of clamorous voters.   Appian observes that
provision had long since been made for these colonies, but
they had not yet been settled.   In the absence of evidence
we can only conjecture what these colonies were.   It seems
most probable that they were the twelve which Drusus the
father of this Drusus had proposed to settle in B.C. 122
(vol. i., p. 274).

If Drusus could gain the popular vote by these grants of
land, he had still a difficulty remaining.   The Senate and
the Equestrian order were at variance about the constitution
of the juries, which at present were so formed as to exclude
the senators; and thus when any senator was brought to trial,
he was at the mercy of men who were his political opponents.
Drusus attempted to reconcile the two orders by a compromise, for it was clearly impossible to restore to the Senate
their former judicial privileges.   But we here encounter a
great difficulty.   Appian, the only writer who has described
the compromise of Drusus, has made a statement which it
is not easy to accept or to explain.   The Senate, he says,
"through the civil commotions," which may mean by the
exile of the members and other causes which we cannot
guess, was now hardly three hundred.   Drusus proposed that
another three hundred should be selected according to merit
from the order of the Equites, and that out of this body of

six hundred the jurymen (judices) should be taken for the future. So far we might understand Appian to mean that the Album Judicum or list of jurymen should be six hundred, half of whom would be Equites and half would be Senators; and this statement would appear to agree with that of Livy's Epitomator. But this explanation cannot be satisfactory, because one object of this measure was to increase the number of senators by the addition of three hundred Equites, and the Senate thus enlarged to about six hundred was to form the body out of which the Judices or jurymen would be taken. Consequently the Equites as an order would be entirely excluded from the functions of jurymen. Drusus also added a clause which gave the newly-constituted court cognizance of cases in which jurymen had been corrupted by bribes, for it was almost forgotten that this was an offence, such bribery being very common. Here we are again reminded of Cicero's impudent assertion that for near fifty years, from the time of Caius Gracchus to Lucius Sulla, during which the jury list was composed of the Equites, there had never been the slightest suspicion of any juryman having been bribed. But we have Cicero's own testimony to the fact that Drusus did propose to examine into the cases of Equites who were charged with receiving bribes in their judicial capacity, and that the Equites opposed this measure. Whether any of them were guilty or not, it is plain that some people thought that they were.

The object of Drusus was the reconciliation of the two orders, but his attempt turned out quite contrary to his expectation. The Senate did not like so great an addition being made to their number all at once by promotions from the equestrian rank to the highest order in the State; and "they also thought it likely that, when these men had become senators, they would combine, and quarrel with the other senators more than before" (Appian). This is a distinct statement that the proposal of Drusus was to put three hundred Equites at once in the Senate; but it is not said how the number of six hundred was to be maintained, and it is evident that we have a very imperfect history of this pro-

posed change. The Equites were not satisfied with the proposal of Drusus: they suspected that this measure, which
seemed so flattering to them, would in the end transfer to
the Senate the judicial privileges, and as the Equites had
enjoyed profit and power, they were much annoyed at the
prospect of losing both. The Equites were also a numerous
body, and there was jealousy among them about the selection
of the three hundred, and the inferior sort looked with envy
on the superior sort, who might be preferred to them. But
most of all the Equites were annoyed at the proposed revival
of trials for judicial corruption, for they thought that such
inquiries had entirely fallen into disuse and would not touch
them.

If the measure of Drusus was what Appian describes it to
be, Drusus was a man of small political sagacity. Such a
law in order to be effectual must have repealed all previous
laws about the constitution of the jury lists, and thus the
Equites would have had their judicial privileges taken from
them, and all that they would have got for the surrender of
this privilege would be the elevation of three hundred of
their number to the rank of senator. Thus Drusus pleased
nobody. The Senate and the Equites, though they could not
agree about other things, agreed in hating Drusus. The
only friends he had gained were those who expected grants
of land by the settlement of the colonies. But the popularity
that he acquired by this measure was counterbalanced by
what he lost in another way. The great object of his tribunate was the settlement of the grave question whether the
Italian dependents should remain in the condition of discontented subjects or be raised to political equality with the
citizens of Rome. It was a subject worth a statesman's
labour, and it would have been an honour to Drusus to solve
this great problem. He could easily reckon all the difficulties
of this undertaking, but he could not, if he was a man of
sense, think of settling so serious a matter by the childish
expedient of bribing all parties by some small advantage
to each to agree about another thing to which they were all
opposed.

The Italians also, to whose interests Drusus was directing all his efforts, were alarmed at the prospect of the execution of the law about the colonies, for many of these people were still in possession of Roman Public Land, which had not yet been assigned under the Agrarian laws; and they were using this land, some having got possession of it by force and others by fraud. They were afraid too that they might have some trouble about their own lands, if these new colonies should be settled; and their fear was not unfounded, for a resumption of public land led in many cases to a general examination of men's titles to their estates (vol. i., p. 183).

Livy's Epitome affirms that Drusus carried all his measures, but not without the help of the Roman allies and the Italian people to whom he gave hopes of obtaining the Roman citizenship. How these people helped him, when they had no votes at Rome, we can only conjecture; but as the Epitome also asserts that the Agrarian laws and the laws about the distribution of grain were carried by force, we must suppose that many Italians flocked into the city at the time of voting. Nor is this statement about the Italians aiding Drusus to carry his Agrarian laws, if there were more than one, necessarily inconsistent with Appian's statement, that the Italians did not like the Agrarian laws of Drusus, because they were afraid of being disturbed in their possessions. The number of men who held Roman Public land would be small; but those who would be ready to resort to Rome at the bidding of a popular tribune, might be a different and a more numerous class. These Italians often mingled in the Roman elections, and sometimes even fraudulently voted. Though the Romans had enactments specially directed to keeping aliens out of the city, the law was not always enforced, nor would it always be easy to distinguish between a Roman voter and an alien who affected to act as a Roman citizen. If Drusus carried his laws by calling in those who had no votes to intimidate those who had, he was not the first Roman who did so. But he was guilty of brutal violence too. The consul Philippus, who had himself in his tribunate attempted to carry an Agrarian law, opposed the Agrarian laws of Drusus, upon which he was

seized by the throat either by Drusus himself or by some
man under his order, and throttled till the blood gushed out
of his nostrils.   This consequence of the outrage only gave
occasion to the tribune to make a coarse joke, which a learned
editor has extracted from a corrupt Latin text.   (Aurelius
Victor, De Viris Illust. c. 66.)

In the month of September there was a scene in the Senate-
house, of which Cicero has preserved a record.   The consul
Philippus in an address to the people had inveighed against
some of the leading men in the State, against the " cause of
the chiefs," as Cicero expresses it; and at this time the influence of the tribune Drusus, which had been used on
behalf of the Senate's authority, was beginning to be impaired.
Philippus was charged with having told the people " that
he would look out for some other advisers; that he could
not administer the State with such a Senate."   The
exact meaning of the consul's declaration cannot be ascertained.   The Senate was the administrative body, and the
consuls could not carry on the government without it.   We
cannot suppose that Philippus thought of any revolutionary
means of getting rid of the Senate.   He was not a bold
adventurer ready to usurp power, and no Roman usurper
ever attempted to govern without a Senate.   His words
probably expressed no more than his disgust at the measures
of Drusus and the majority of the Senate who had sided with
or been led by the tribune.   The words of Philippus however
were of serious import, and the Senate would see that it was
necessary to remove any impression that they had made on
the people.

L. Crassus, who had been staying at his Tusculan villa
during the Ludi Romani, returned to the city on the last day of
the festival.   In the morning of the thirteenth of September
there was a full meeting of the Senate summoned by Drusus,
who complained loudly of the consul, and formally brought
before the Senate the words that Philippus had used in his
speech to the people.   Crassus addressed the Senate, and he
never spoke better.   He deplored the miserable condition of
the Senate, which was like a child deprived of parent or

guardian, for the honour of the Senate had been assailed by
the consul, whose duty it was to protect the body in which he
presided; but it was not surprising, he said, if a man, who
had damaged the State by his own policy, should endeavour
to prevent the Senate from administering it.   Philippus was
not of a temper to bear this imputation in silence: he was
greatly exasperated, and proceeded to check Crassus by an
exercise of authority, which was peculiar to the Romans, but
may be compared to a threat to commit for contempt of court.
Crassus however still went on: he maintained his right to
speak what he liked: if the consul would not acknowledge
his privileges as a senator, he would not acknowledge his
authority as consul: he was not alarmed at threats.   "If
you intend to stop me," he said to Philippus, "you must cut
out this tongue of mine, and even when that is torn out, with
my breath alone my freedom shall resist your tyranny."
After a most vehement speech Crassus finally proposed a
resolution, which was adopted by a full senate, to the effect, as
Cicero's words seem to mean, That the Roman people should
be fully assured that the Senate had always looked after the
public interest faithfully and to the best of their ability.
This was the answer to the declaration of Philippus; but if this
was all, it was a feeble reply to the bold attack of the consul,
and shows that the Senate did not venture to pronounce
a direct censure upon him, or that the party of Drusus was
becoming weaker.   Indeed the very form of the resolution
has the appearance of a compromise between the two parties.
Crassus was one of those who remained to see that this
resolution was formally entered on the journals of the house,
and, according to Roman practice, his name would appear
among the names of those who were present on this occasion.
Cicero appeals to the journals as containing the name of
Crassus prefixed to this resolution.   This was the last speech
of the great orator.   He had been seized with a pain in the
side, while he was speaking, and with profuse perspiration
followed by cold shivering.   He went home with a violent
fever on him, and in seven days he was dead.   Cicero has
recorded the circumstances of the last appearance of Crassus

in the Senate and his sudden death.   In pathetic and
eloquent language he deplores the loss of the great orator;
but if Crassus died too soon for his country, he did not die
too soon for himself.   He did not see the war which soon
blazed through Italy, nor the crimes committed by the
leaders in the State, nor the sorrow of his daughter whose
husband became an exile from Rome, nor the flight of
C. Marius, and the cruel massacres which followed his return.
So, says Cicero, we may consider the death of Crassus a
happy event, when we reflect on the fate of those who are
introduced with him as the speakers in the famous Dialogue
on the Orator.

   We see from this that Drusus and the Senate were still, in
appearance at least, acting together so late as the middle of
September.   Crassus too, if he was not a strong partisan of
Drusus, still defended the policy of the Senate, whatever it
was; and in his late holiday in the country he had been
accompanied by two rising young men, C. Cotta and P. Sulpicius Rufus, who were on terms of great intimacy with
Drusus, and undoubtedly shared his opinions.   Philippus was
called a man of the popular party, but political names are not
always a safe guide to an estimate of public measures and
public men.   All that we know of the conduct of Philippus
in his consulship is that he resisted the Agrarian laws of
Drusus, and complained that he could not administer the
State with such a Senate as he had; but when our evidence
is so small, we must conclude that we are unable to form an
exact opinion of the real nature of the dispute between Philippus and the party of Drusus.   However, what followed
shortly after shows that Philippus was opposed to all the
measures of the tribune.

   It is uncertain if Drusus had carried his judiciary law at
the time of this debate in the Senate, for that was the
measure which brought on him the enmity both of the
Equestrian order and of the Senate.   But it is possible that
this measure may have just been carried, for Cicero remarks
that the power of Drusus was growing feebler.   Thus as the
popularity and influence of Drusus diminished, and his year

of office was drawing to a close, he would have little prospect
of accomplishing his great design, and it is possible that
he contemplated using violent means.   There is a fragment of
Diodorus, which perhaps we may refer to the time of
Drusus' tribunate, and if it does belong to this year, it must
be to the latter part of it.   Pompaedius Silo, an Italian, got
together ten thousand men, who were afraid of being brought
to account, as Diodorus says, and he gives no further information, but I assume that he means for rebellion against
Rome.   Every man had a dagger under his dress, and Pompaedius led them towards the city.   His design was to surround the senate and to demand the citizenship, and if it was
not granted, to destroy every thing with fire and sword.
Such a purpose would be very absurd, unless the Italians
expected to find associates in Rome.   Pompaedius happened
to be met on the way by C. Domitius, as Diodorus names him,
and being asked where he was going with such a train, he
answered to Rome to demand the citizenship, and he added
that he was invited by the tribunes.   Domitius represented
to Pompaedius that he might attain his object with less
danger and more honourably if he did not approach the
senate in a hostile manner, for they were ready to grant this
favour to the allies if they were asked, but they would not
give it on compulsion.   Pompaedius was persuaded by these
reasons, and Domitius had the credit of saving the city from
a present danger.

Another valuable fragment of Diodorus, only recently discovered, tells us something new; and at the same time it
suggests how little we know of the history of this year.   He
has preserved a solemn form of oath, by which those who took
it would bind themselves to consider every man his friend or
enemy, who was the friend or enemy of Drusus; and to
spare neither life nor child nor parent, unless it should be for
the interest of Drusus and those who had taken the same
oath.   The oath continued, "and if I should become a
citizen through the law of Drusus, I will consider Rome my
country and Drusus my greatest benefactor; and I will administer this oath to as many citizens as I can; and if I

keep my oath, may I be rewarded with all good fortune, and
if I break it, may the reverse befall me." We must conclude,
if this oath is genuine, that Drusus was now a conspirator;
and even if the oath is an invention and the conspiracy not a
fact, we have still a probable inference that Drusus was supposed to be combining with the Italian allies to force their
demands upon the Romans. This belief in his traitorous designs is consistent with what followed. Philippus was reconciled to the Senate; and it is said that men from Tyrrhenia
and Umbria flocked to Rome at the invitation of the consuls, and on the pretext of complaining of the law, but in
reality for the purpose of killing Drusus, and they waited for
the comitia. Such is Appian's story; and we must guess,
for he does not tell us, what law he means and what comitia.
All we can safely affirm is that Rome was filled with men
from the country ready for any broil, and Drusus like
Tiberius Gracchus was accompanied by a disorderly crowd
when he went to the Forum and returned home. Of late he
had gone out little, being afraid of his enemies. One evening
as he was transacting business in an ill-lighted part of his
house and was just dismissing the people, he suddenly cried
out that he was wounded and fell down. A knife was found
firmly fixed in his thigh or his side, and in a few hours he
died.

Velleius embellishes the death of Drusus with some
dramatic circumstances. As he was dying, he looked on his
weeping friends who were standing around, and said, " Kinsmen and friends, will the Republic ever have a citizen like
me?" His mother Cornelia was still alive when her son was
assassinated, and she bore her misfortune with a spirit worthy
of her name. Though we have several statements nearly the
same about the manner of his death, there were also reports
that Drusus died by his own hand, and even that he died a
natural death caused by his anxiety about the state of affairs.
It seems most probable that he was assassinated by some
unknown hand. Cicero alone fixes the guilt on Q. Varius.
There was a rumour too that Philippus and Caepio suborned
the assassin.

It is now generally supposed on the authority of a fragment
of Diodorus that all the enactments carried by Drusus were
declared null by the Senate in his lifetime. This conclusion
is not quite certain, though it is certain that before the death
of Drusus the Senate did deliberate on the matter, and there
must have been a great change of policy or opinion in Rome.
It is said that Drusus declared that though he had the power
to prevent any decision being made by the Senate, he would
not do so, for he well knew that those who should do him
this wrong would soon meet with the punishment which
they merited: he added that if his measures were declared
null, the law about the constitution of the judicial body
would be nullified also; whereas, if this law were maintained,
every man who passed his life honourably would escape prosecution, and those who plundered the provinces would be
brought to account for their dishonesty; and so the consequence would be that those who through envy were destroying his fair name, would by their own measures bring trouble
on themselves. However, either shortly before the death of
Drusus or soon after, all the laws passed in his tribunate were
declared null by the Senate on the motion of the consul
Philippus, who had become reconciled to his political opponents on the ground of the public interest, probably the
approaching Social War. The Senate declared that all the
laws of Drusus were carried in violation of the proper
religious solemnities, and that they were not binding on the
people. According to the author of the Oration De Domo,
Drusus in framing his laws had also violated the provisions of
the Lex Caecilia Didia (p. 122). Thus by one single resolution
all the legislation of Drusus was nullified. This power of
the Senate was established by usage, and probably originated
in usurpation. But the assumption of power was ingeniously
founded on a religious principle. Every public act at Rome
was attended with certain solemnities, and if these were not
observed, it was a consistent conclusion that the act was
invalid. The only question then would be, who should be the
judge in such a case. The opinion of the high ministers of
religion must of course decide whether the forms of religion

had been observed or not, but the Senate as the administrative body in the State would naturally seek this opinion and act upon it. Philippus himself the consul was also an augur, a circumstance which may have increased his influence on this occasion. Certainly when party spirit ran high, we may suppose that religion was only the pretext, and whether the proper forms had been observed or not, the Senate would not hesitate to nullify any measure that they did not like. The habit of obedience to the Senate as the administrative body, and the superstitious fears of the Romans, made this exercise of authority possible occasionally. In deciding on the validity or invalidity of an enactment, the Senate occupied a position like that of a supreme court in a Republican system, which is founded on a written Constitution.

This is all that we know of Drusus, his legislation, and his designs. The records of this eventful year and of the troubles which followed are very imperfect. Velleius Paterculus, who is rather severe on the two Gracchi, speaks of Drusus in more favourable terms, and probably out of adulation towards the emperor Tiberius Caesar under whom he wrote, for Livia the mother of Tiberius was the daughter of a Claudius, who by adoption became a Livius. Like the Gracchi, Drusus had great designs; and if we adopt the opinion of Velleius, his abilities and his intentions were superior to his fortune. But to us it seems that it was a foolish thing for any tribune to expect to reform the Roman State in one short year of office, or even in two, if he were re-elected. Drusus is represented by all authorities as a proud, impetuous man, and it is rare to find good sense united with such a temper. He was lavish of the public money and public property, and even boasted, as it is said, that he had left nothing for any one else to give. Tacitus accordingly places him as a profuse and wasteful statesman with the Gracchi and Appuleius Saturninus. If he was really a partisan of the Optimates, and only bribed the people by grants of land and cheap bread in order to get their votes for the accomplishment of his ulterior designs, we cannot assign him either the credit of honesty or the possession of political talent.

The tribunate of Drusus was a year of wonders. At Arretium while people were breaking bread blood flowed out of it. In the country of the Vestini it rained stones and tiles for seven days; on which Scheffer has the instructive remark that you will scarcely find any where else than in Obsequens an instance of such rain; but he remembers one which is recorded by Dion Cassius (40, c. 47). Flames burst from the earth in Aenaria, now Ischia, a volcanic island in the bay of Naples. This is a valuable fact in the history of Ischia, if it is true; but Orosius says that the flame appeared on the mainland in the Samnite territory, where the earth gaped wide and sent up fire to the skies. Rhegium was shattered by an earthquake. At Cumae the famed statue of Apollo sweated. In the year in which the Social War commenced there was a wonder surpassing all wonders. In the territory of Mutina two hills engaged in single combat: they rushed on one another with a terrible crash and then drew back. The collision produced flame and smoke which rose up to the skies: all the houses and the animals which were between the two combatants were crushed. This sight was seen from the Via Aemilia by a great number of Roman Equites, slaves, and travellers. Pliny (H. N. iii. c. 83) says that he found this story in the books of the Tuscan rituals (disciplina), and the event happened in the consulship of L. Marcius Philippus and Sextus Julius Caesar. The prodigy was attested by many witnesses, who in their terror magnified and distorted the phenomenon of a terrible earthquake. Other strange things were reported, things possible and things impossible, invented or perverted by superstitious fears. Italy was agitated by rebellion against the tyranny of Rome, and signs both on the earth and in the heavens portended war and bloodshed, the tramp of hostile armies, and the devastation of the peninsula.

CHAPTER XIV.

POLITICAL CONDITION OF ITALY.

B.C. 90.

THE death of Drusus and the annulling of all his legislation were followed by fresh disturbance. The Equestrian order took advantage of the policy of Drusus for attacking the Optimates, and they persuaded the tribune Q. Varius to propose a law by virtue of which those men should be brought to trial who had aided the Italians openly or secretly against the interests of Rome. The authority of Valerius Maximus is the worst that we can have for establishing an important fact. However he states that the purpose of the law of Varius was to inquire "through whose fraudulent dealing the Italian allies of Rome had been compelled to take up arms." If this is a correct statement of the object of the law, it was a cleverly devised scheme, for it affirmed the fact of the allies being driven to war, and it laid the blame on somebody without stating whether the rebellion was caused by certain Romans encouraging the allies or by the refusal to grant their reasonable demands. Diodorus also derived from his authorities the opinion or the fact that the party of the Optimates in order to strengthen themselves against the popular party had called in the aid of the Italian people, though he does not say how these people could help the Optimates, and that the Italians were encouraged to hope for the freedom of the city; but as these promises were not kept, the Italians took to arms. It seems very probable that some of the Optimates had been tampering with the Italian allies. The words

of Diodorus also imply that the war had already begun
when the law was proposed. The Equites had been the
great opponents of Drusus, and they were opposed to the
claims of the Italians; or they availed themselves of the
opportunity of the rebellion of the subjects of Rome to ruin
an order which had hitherto held the political power. They
hoped to procure the conviction of many of the Optimates
on the odious charge of treasonable dealing, for the Equites
themselves would form the jury, and if their enemies were
removed from Rome, they would possess the political power.
The other tribunes opposed the law of Varius, but the Equites,
and probably others also whom they hired, came armed with
daggers, and the law was carried by intimidation. It does
not appear certain whether the Lex Varia was enacted at the
close of B.C. 91 after the death of Drusus, or early in B.C. 90.
Asconius (in Scaur. p. 22) says that it was enacted after the
Italic war began, but it is difficult to say whether he considered the Italic war to have been begun immediately after
the death of Drusus or early in the following year. The trials
under the Lex Varia certainly took place in B.C. 90, and
Q. Varius was tribune in that year.

L. Calpurnius Bestia, one of the consuls of B.C. 111, who
had made a scandalous treaty with Jugurtha and been
punished for it, was living in Rome in B.C. 90. He was one
of those against whom the law of Varius was directed, but not
choosing to put himself in the power of his enemies, he immediately left Rome. C. Aurelius Cotta was a candidate for
the tribuneship in B.C. 91, a short time after the death of L.
Crassus, but he lost his election. Cotta was a great friend of
the tribune Drusus, and he was prosecuted under the law of
Varius. Though Cotta was a good speaker, he employed L.
Aelius Stilo to write a defence for him, which Cotta delivered.
Probably he was not formally condemned, for it is said that
he left Rome to avoid a conviction, and he must therefore
have gone after he had made his defence and before a verdict
was given. Cotta in his defence maintained his political
integrity and made a fierce invective against the Equestrian
order. Q. Pompeius Rufus, who was praetor urbanus in B.C.

91, was also tried under the law of Varius, but the result of
the trial is not recorded.   Finally, Appian mentions among
those who were prosecuted Mummius, the conqueror of
Corinth.   He was scandalously deceived, says the historian,
by the Equites, who promised to acquit him if he would
stand his trial.   He did stand his trial, was condemned and
retired to Delos, where he died.   But this is a gross blunder.
Freinsheim suggests that the man's name was Memmius, and
we have Cicero's authority for L. Memmius being tried
under this law of Varius.   M. Antonius the great orator
was also brought to trial.   He defended himself with all his
eloquence and powerful gesture.   I saw him, says Cicero
who was present, in the midst of his great efforts bend
the knee and touch the ground with it.   Perhaps he escaped
like old Scaurus.   This veteran statesman, now more than
seventy years of age, was summoned to answer a charge of
having stirred up the Social War.   Though he was only just
recovering from an illness, he came to the Forum supported
by some of the noblest youths of Rome.   His defence was
short; he said, "Q. Varius a Spaniard affirms that M.
Scaurus the head of the Senate has called the allies to arms.
M. Scaurus head of the Senate denies this.   There is no
witness on either side.   Romans, which of the two ought you
to believe?"   Varius was surnamed Hybrida, and said to
have been born at Sucro in Spain of a Spanish mother.   He
had no evidence to support his charge.   Like some plaintiffs
now-a-days he perhaps expected the defendant to prove the
case for him.   But Scaurus was acquitted, or, if the trial did
not come to a verdict, the proceedings stopped for want of
evidence.   It appears however that Q. Caepio again commenced proceedings against Scaurus under the law of Varius;
but we are not told how the matter ended.   There is an
obscure notice of Varius himself being afterwards convicted
under his own law, and he came to a miserable end somewhere, for, as Cicero says, he was tortured to death.   This
could not have happened at Rome.   Freinsheim suggests that
he fell into the hands of the Italian insurgents.   This
turbulent fellow is charged by Cicero with being the assassin

of Drusus and having poisoned Motellus, probably Numidicus, which may be true or false.

While Rome was distracted by these trials and the violence of party spirit, the Italians were preparing for war. They had heard of the death of Drusus and of the persecution of many noble Romans, who had acted, as they supposed, in the interest of the dependent states of Italy. They secretly sent commissioners about to form a league of the Italian states, and in order to secure mutual fidelity they gave hostages to one another. The Romans were so busy with the trials in the city and their own quarrels that they did not know what was going on outside. When they did learn of this great movement, they sent to the Italian cities such Romans as had most intimate relations with the several states, with instructions to inquire secretly into the condition of affairs. An envoy, who was at Asculum in Picenum, had seen a young man sent from that town as a hostage to another town, and he informed Q. Servilius who was in those parts with pro-consular authority. Servilius hurried to Asculum in a passion. It happened that there was some festival going on at the time, and of course there was a great concourse of people. The language and behaviour of Servilius made the Asculani suspect that the design of the Italians was detected, and they murdered both Servilius and his legatus Fonteius. The Roman citizens in the town were also murdered and their property was plundered. This was the first act of hostility on the part of the Italian subjects of Rome, and it took place in the country east of the Apennines on the Hadriatic. This town of Asculum (Ascoli), sometimes named Asculum Picenum, by which term it is distinguished from the Asculum of Apulia, was on the river Truentus (Tronto) in a position naturally strong.

The massacre at Asculum was a signal for the rising of the Italian people. Appian names among the insurgents the Marsi, Peligni, Vestini, Marrucini, and bordering on them the Picentini, Frentani and Hirpini, the Pompeiani or in-habitants of Pompeii, the people of Venusia, the Iapyges, the Lucani and Samnites, nations which in former days

had been dangerous enemies to Rome. The Umbri and
the Etrusci did not at first take any part in the rebellion.
The Picentini were a small people on the west coast of
Italy on the Bay of Paestum and in the south part of Campania, which bordered on the Lucani. The Romans had
some time before transferred to this country a portion of
the inhabitants of Picenum on the Hadriatic, who are named
Picentes in Livy's enumeration of the rebels. Appian also
includes among the insurgents all the people of South Italy
from the Liris (Garigliano) on the west to the Hadriatic Sea,
both the people of the interior and those on the coast. Before
commencing hostilities the rebels sent commissioners to
Rome, to complain that they were deprived of the rights of
Roman citizens, though they had helped the Romans to
acquire dominion. The Senate answered, if they would
repent of what they had done, they might send commissioners
to Rome, and they would be received; but otherwise they
would not. This firm answer showed the Italians that nothing
could be got except by arms, and they prepared for war.

It is necessary to understand the relative position of Rome
and her Italian dependencies at this crisis in the history of
the Republic. When the Social War began, Rome had
brought to a state of dependence all Italy and many countries
beyond the limits of Italy. These foreign dependencies or
provinces were Sicily, Sardinia with Corsica, the two Spanish
provinces Hispania Citerior and Ulterior with the Balearic
Islands, the South of France named the Provincia and afterwards Gallia Narbonensis, part of the eastern coast of the
Hadriatic, Macedonia, with which government the parts of
Greece south of Macedonia were probably connected, the
province Africa, comprehending Carthage, and part of the
old territory of Carthage, the Cyrenaica, and the old kingdom
of Pergamum, now the province Asia. The north of Italy,
or the great plain of the Po, named Gallia Cisalpina was still
a province, and it was not politically incorporated with Italy
until B.C. 43.

The general condition of the Roman provinces and their
relation to Rome may be described in few words. The nature

of a provincial organization will be more particularly considered when we come to speak of the prosecution of C.
Verres for misconduct in the administration of Sicily, the
first possession which the Romans acquired beyond the limits
of Italy. A Roman province in the territorial sense was
a country acquired by conquest, or, as in the case of the
kingdoms of Pergamum and Cyrene in Africa, by the
bequest of the last kings. It was not a burden to the Roman
state, but a possession, a source of revenue; and so Cicero
says that the revenues (vectigalia) and the provinces of Rome
were a kind of farm belonging to the Roman people. In the
provinces the Romans carried on a profitable business: some
enriched themselves as bankers or money-lenders, and
returned home to enjoy their wealth; others who cultivated
the land or pastured cattle and sheep in the provinces, sometimes finally settled there.

In the Republican period, as we see by many examples,
the organization of a province was fixed at the time of the
conquest by the victorious commander with the assistance of
ten senators—in two instances five only are named—who
acted under the instructions of the Roman senate. This
constitution of a Province remained the fundamental law of
administration; but sometimes the laws enacted at Rome
and even the orders of the senate extended to such matters in
the provinces as touched the rights and interests of private
persons. The governors also by their edicts from time to
time made such regulations as were necessary for improving
the administration. The general organization of a province
was founded on a new territorial arrangement, by which a
country was divided into administrative districts, the central
point of which was some large city. The condition of every
province was not exactly the same; it depended, as already
observed, on the original settlement. In the same province
also there were differences in the condition of the towns.
There were in the old provinces a few free cities, whose
condition was secured by treaty. Such was the relation of
Massilia to Rome. There were also other free cities more
numerous, whose condition was not determined by treaty, but

by some special law or decree of the senate, which rewarded
such cities for their attachment to Rome or their ready
submission by making them self-governing communities, and
attaching them by interest to the Roman state. Some of
these provincial towns supplied ships and men for the Roman
navy, as we see in the case of Miletus in Asia, and some of
the Sicilian towns. Thus the Romans who built few ships in
Italy maintained the command of the Mediterranean chiefly
by the means which they derived from the provinces. There
were also colonies established in some of the provinces, as
Narbo in the south of France: some of them were Roman
colonies or settlements of Roman citizens; others were Latin
Colonies, a term which denoted to a Roman their peculiar
civil condition. These provincial colonies, which after B.C.
100 became more numerous in consequence of the establishment of military colonies, served the purpose of providing
for settlers, securing the supremacy of Rome, and ultimately
of Romanizing the foreign possessions of the Republic by the
use of the Latin language and the introduction of Roman
institutions. The towns in the provinces, which did not
enjoy any particular privileges, were under the direct administration of the Roman governor. But the Romans allowed
even these towns to retain their own internal administration and magistrates under the general supervision of the
governor.

The old provinces Sicily, Sardinia, and the two Spains
were originally administered by Praetors elected for the
purpose. It has been said that after B.C. 149, when six
praetors were annually elected, all of them stayed in Rome
during their year of office, and did not take the government
of a province till the following year with the title of Propraetor (vol. i., p. 27). However this may have been, we
learn that when war was going on, the consuls of the year
were sent into the provinces, or the command in the war was
given with the title of Proconsul to some man who had been
consul or praetor. The office of provincial governor was
conferred for one year only, pursuant to the general Roman
principle of limiting the duration of delegated authority and

securing liberty by annual elections. If a governor's authority was to be extended, or prorogued, as the Romans termed it, a vote of the people was necessary, for the term prorogation implies an appeal to the popular vote; and yet it appears that such prorogation was sometimes effected by a resolution of the senate. Such irregularities often occur in Roman history, and we might expect them in a state in which there was always a struggle for power between the supreme administrative council the senate, and the popular power represented in some form. The governor received, after his appointment to a province, the necessary sums of money, soldiers, and a staff or body of officers, of whom the chief were the Legati, and the quaestor. The quaestor for each province was taken by lot from those who had been elected by the Roman citizens. He had the care of the money, which was supplied by the Roman treasury for the expenses of those who were sent out, and he received all the sums which were payable to him out of the receipts in the province. At the end of the year he produced his accounts at Rome. One copy was deposited in the Roman treasury, and two copies of the original in the province. The Legati were appointed by the senate out of their body, and furnished with an outfit like the governor. They were under the orders of the governor, and he could delegate to them such authority as he thought proper, both military and civil; but it is said that the governor reserved to himself the jurisdiction in criminal matters, and this appears to have been the case at least in later times. The governor had also a "praetoria cohors," which consisted of the military officers about his person and young Roman nobles, who went abroad to learn the art of war and civil administration. He had also a numerous train of lictors, clerks (scribae), interpreters, and other functionaries. It is affirmed by some authorities that in the republican time a governor was not allowed to take his wife with him. Whether this was a positive rule or not, I believe no example occurs of the wife of a general accompanying her husband on a foreign expedition or to the government of a province. The Romans thought that women

were an incumbrance in foreign parts, and that a governor
might be sometimes induced by an extravagant wife to prey
on the provincials. But the absence of the wife did not
always save the provincials from the rapacity of a bad
governor, and he sometimes caused great scandal by making
free with the wives of others and the women in the province.

The demands of the governor on the provincials were fixed
by law. He was forbidden to traffic in his province and to
take presents; but all rules were unavailing against the
greediness of a governor, who had impoverished himself at
Rome by buying the votes of the people to secure office, and
who had only a short period of almost absolute rule for
replenishing his empty pockets and making a fortune. It is
true that he might be tried and often was tried on his return
home for malversation in his province, but this was only a
further motive for getting enough for himself, and enough to
bribe the jury who had to decide on his condemnation or
acquittal.

Two other classes of men helped to increase the sufferings
of the provincials, the Publicani or farmers of the taxes, and
the Negotiatores, the money men. The demands of the Publicani were limited by law, but they had many contrivances
for taking more than their due, and though the governor
could check their irregularities, it was not safe for him to
quarrel with men out of whose order the jury was taken
which might try him on his return to Rome, if any man
chose to prosecute him for malversation even without sufficient reason, which was sometimes the case. If he were a
dishonest governor, he would wink at the exactions of the
Publicani or even help them and then share their unjust
gains. The Negotiatores, who carried the precious metals
with them, made enormous gains by lending money both to
towns and individuals, and their profits were the larger as
the money was often borrowed of necessity to meet the
avaricious demands of the governor and the Publicani. Even
Roman senators, who were not allowed to engage directly in
trade, entrusted their capital to the Negotiatores and thus
increased their wealth. The provinces in fact were for the

capitalists merely a place to make fortunes in. Greediness and rapacity were universal, and the extravagant expenditure of the Roman nobles was not supplied merely by the careful management of their large Italian estates, but by the plunder of the provinces. Livy has well described the Publicani, when he says that the Roman state could not do without them, but wherever the Publicani came, there either all law ceased to exist, or all freedom for the provincials was gone.

This oppressive administration was not calculated to secure the fidelity of the provincials during the Social War, and if the contest had lasted longer, Rome might have been unable to hold her foreign possessions to their obedience. But they were separated from one another, and had no means of uniting against the oppressor, so long as the heavy hand of the great Republic could hold them in check and crush insurrection. The Romans probably derived great supplies from the provinces during the Social War. Sicily, we know, sent without any cost to the Romans skins for tents, clothing for the armies, and corn: it was on this and other occasions, as old Cato named it, the storehouse of Rome. Thus though the defection of the Italians placed Rome in great danger, the resources of the provinces helped her to maintain the war, and as long as Rome had the command of the sea and maintained her hold on her foreign possessions, she was more than a match for her Italian subjects.

The political condition of Italy and the provinces immediately before the Social War is explained by Savigny with great clearness. There were included in the Roman State four classes of free persons: 1. Cives Romani or Roman citizens, who were the inhabitants of Rome, also the citizens of the Roman Colonies, and finally the citizens of the Municipia without any respect to the several nationalities. 2. The Latini, who were the citizens of the towns of the old Latin nation, with the exception of such towns as had been raised to the rank of Municipia; and besides these there were the numerous Latin Colonies. 3. The Socii, who were the free inhabitants of Italy; they did not belong to either of the first two classes, and they did belong to different nationalities. 4. The Provincials, who were the free subjects of Rome in the countries beyond the limits of Italy.

We often find the terms Socii and Latini, or Socii and Nomen Latinum, used by Livy and by Cicero, and these names are perfectly consistent with Savigny's enumeration. The name Itali or Italians, if we choose to use it, is not specially applicable to the Socii only, for it would include the Latini as well. It is true that the great war is called indifferently the Social War and the Italian War by the Romans, and it is possible that in using the latter name they referred to the Italian Socii, exclusive of the Latini, who were faithful to Rome during the contest. The word Italian has no reference to the term Jus Italicum as a designation of the political condition of the Socii before the Social War, as some writers have maintained. The Jus Italicum originated at a later time and was a different thing.

Though there were four classes of persons in the Roman State, there were only two political conditions viewed with respect to Rome. These conditions were those of Cives or Roman citizens, and Peregrini or aliens, a political term which comprehended alike the Latini, the Socii, and the Provincials. The Socii and the Latini were Roman subjects or dependents before the Social War, and they became Roman citizens after it, as we shall see.

A few words are necessary to explain more fully the nature of these two political conditions. There were Roman citizens both in Rome and in the Roman colonies. The citizens in the Roman colonies planted in various parts of Italy retained the full rights of Roman citizens: they could vote at Rome and were eligible to the "honores," as the Romans named the high offices of their state. It is certain that all or nearly all these Roman colonies had been formed by sending Roman citizens to occupy towns which already existed in the conquered parts of Italy, and accordingly when any part of the old inhabitants of these towns was allowed to remain in them, they must have formed a community in political subjection to the new settlers. The colonists had their senate; and their town government was an image

of the great city from which they came and to which they
owed obedience. It is nowhere said what was the political
condition of those people who lived in a town which a Roman
colony had occupied, and we can therefore only infer their
condition with probability. Two independent communities
could not exist together; but still it is possible that the
conquered people may have retained their own laws and
usages to some extent under the supervision of their political
superiors, or, as we shall see, they may have had a magistrate
sent from Rome. There is not much foundation for the
supposition that they had the Roman citizenship without the
right of voting; for if that were so, a Roman citizen of the
colony might have married a native woman, and his children
would have been Roman citizens; and also a native man
might have married the daughter of a Roman citizen, and
his children would have had the same political status as
the father, whatever it was. These native inhabitants of the
town might be called citizens in a sense as being in a Roman
city, but in no other sense could they be Roman citizens. It
is possible indeed, as it has been suggested, that before the
Social War these two classes in a Roman colony had become
less clearly distinguished by irregular intermarriage or in
some other way; but we do not know in what way, and there
is no use in guessing.

The term Municipium appears to have been applied
originally to those conquered Italian towns, which Rome
included in her dominion without conferring on the people
the Roman suffrage and the capacity of attaining the honours
of the Roman state. After the overthrow of the Latin
confederacy, B.C. 338, we read in Livy of various towns
to which the Roman citizenship (civitas) was given without
the Roman suffrage. This was "civitas sine suffragio"
or "civitas sine suffragii latione," as Livy has it (ix. 43).
The men of these towns were citizens in a sense, but as
they had no vote at Rome, they were considered to
be, and they were imperfect citizens. If the inhabitants
of such Municipia had every thing Roman except the
right to vote and to be eligible to the Roman magistracies,

they had Commercium and Connubium. By virtue of the
first, such persons could acquire property within the limits
of the Roman state, and could dispose of it by sale, gift, and
testament. By virtue of the second, they could contract a
legal marriage with the daughter of a Roman citizen. Some
of these Municipia were allowed to retain their own town
government, for instance Arpinum and Tusculum; but
others were altogether deprived of it, and must therefore
have had magistrates sent from Rome. It seems that all
these Municipia received the complete Roman citizenship
before the Social War, and many of them are mentioned by
name, such as Tusculum, Cato's birthplace, and Arpinum,
the birthplace of Cicero.

When the inhabitants of these Municipia obtained the full
citizenship, they would of course be included in the Roman
Tribes, which were consequently extended in such way as to
comprise a considerable part of the territory of Italy. It
appears that the towns of one region or country were often
distributed among different Roman tribes, which may
have happened from various causes, difficult for us to conjecture, and we have no evidence to explain this apparent
irregularity. Many of the voters in the distant Municipia
certainly would not and could not come to Rome to vote on
all occasions, and we can hardly conceive that any of them
would come except for the great elections, and sometimes
when important matters were agitated, which affected their
interests; such as Agrarian laws (vol. i., p. 250). When a
Municipium became Roman, we must assume that Roman
law was used there, and it is supposed that all of them were
under the jurisdiction of the Praetor Urbanus, but the office
of judge was exercised by a man sent from Rome annually.
His title was "Praefectus juri dicundo" or Praefect for the
administration of justice. It appears from Festus that these
Praefecti were at one time certainly appointed by the
Praetor Urbanus every year, except four who were elected by
the people out of a body named the Twenty-six men (xxvi
viri). The general definition of a Praefectura by Festus
is this, and it is the only general definition that we have:

Praefecturae was the name of those Italian towns in which justice was administered and markets (nundinae) were held, and they had a kind of community (res publica), but yet no magistrates of their own, and Praefecti were sent to them annually to administer justice. We must accordingly conclude that Praefecti were sent to all the Italian towns included within the Roman political system, that is, to all the Municipia, and consequently a Praefectura would be a Municipium in a sense, and a Municipium would be a Praefectura in a sense. It is not possible to include the Roman colonies in the definition of Festus; but still we may suppose that Praefecti were sent into the Roman colonies also, where a part of the original inhabitants still remained, and for the purpose of administering justice between such inhabitants, and also between them and the Roman citizens in the place. This is a reasonable and consistent hypothesis, and consequently Praefectura would be a generic name comprehending the two species, Coloniae and Municipia. Still we must allow that the Roman Colonies always had their own magistrates, that is, the Roman citizens of such colonies had a complete town community of their own and managed their own internal affairs. Disputes might arise in some cases as to the jurisdiction of the Praefecti in such Roman colonies, but if we admit that they were sent there with direct reference to the native population, we may admit the possibility of a magistrate annually sent from Rome and magistrates of the colony being within the same walls; for some provision must have been made for the administration of justice among the natives; and if they did not appoint their own magistrates, which is exceedingly improbable, they must either have been subject to the magistrates of the citizens, which is possible, or a magistrate must have been annually sent from Rome. Sigonius long ago observed that the Formula, or constitution of a Praefectura was not unlike that of a Province, for as Praetors were annually sent from Rome to the provinces, so Praefecti were annually sent to the Praefecturae to administer them and to do justice. It seems likely that when a town such as Arpinum was first incorpo-

rated in the Roman state, it was made a Praefectura, which
name it would have because a Praefectus was sent there
from Rome, and it was also named a Municipium because it
was incorporated in the Roman state as a member without a
vote at Rome (civitas sine suffragio). Arpinum received the
suffrage in B.C. 188, and we may suppose that from that
time it ceased to be a Praefectura and had its own magistrates. Indeed it appears that most of the Praefecturae
received the full Roman citizenship before the Lex Julia
(B.C. 90), and if any of them had not received the citizenship,
they would have it by virtue of the Lex Julia. But after
the enactment of this Lex we still find Italian towns distinguished as Coloniae, Municipia, and Praefecturae, not only
by Cicero, but in two extant Roman laws. These different
names therefore subsisted though all these towns had then the
full Roman citizenship. Accordingly it is concluded that after
the Lex Julia the Praefecturae differed from Coloniae and
Municipia in this only : the Coloniae and Municipia had their
own magistrates who administered law, " Duumviri juri dicundo," and were chosen by the town senate or Decuriones ; in
the Praefecturae law was administered by a " Praefectus juri
dicundo " sent from Rome. But it is not known why these
towns were not allowed to have their own magistrates.

The destruction of the Latin league was followed by the
complete political subjection to Rome of all the peoples comprised in it ; and it is now generally assumed - that their
political condition is expressed by the term "civitas sine
suffragio :" but they were really subjects, had no vote at
Rome, and as a matter of course they were not eligible to the
offices of the Roman State. The Latin league, while it was
independent, had in antient times established colonies in
Italy ; such colonies may also have been established during
the existence of the league, which was formed between the
Romans on the one side and the Latins and the Hernici
on the other (B.C. 493, 486) ; but though we know the names of
several Latin colonies which were established during this
triple league, such as Norba in the country of the Volsci,
Antium, and a few others, we cannot say that these colonies

were established in the name of the league. In the case of Antium, it is said by Dionysius that as there was not a sufficient number of Romans who were willing to give in their names, the Roman Senate permitted the Latins and Hernici to join the settlement. After B.C. 338 the Romans established in various parts of Italy colonies, which were named Latin colonies. As to the Roman colonies, which were established between B.C. 338 and the end of the Second Punic War B.C. 201, all but two, as far as we know, were settled on the east and west coasts of Italy for the protection of these parts. These were named the Maritime Colonies (coloniae maritimae), and it seems to be sufficiently proved that they were all colonies of Roman citizens. The settlers in the Latin colonies were the Italian people of all nations, who received grants of land in the new settlements, and they were dependencies of Rome. If a Roman citizen availed himself of permission to join a Latin colony, which permission was certainly sometimes given, he lost his citizenship, and his political condition was the same as that of the rest of the settlers in the colony.

These Latin colonies after B.C. 338 were established by virtue of a Lex under the superintendence of commissioners, named Triumviri; and some of these colonies consisted of several thousand persons, enough in fact to form a new community at once. If we may safely conclude from the example of the later foundation of Nemausus (Nimes) in the south of France, the condition of each colony was determined by a Formula or instrument which fixed the constitution of the colony, the extent of the territory and the duties of the colony to Rome. Cicero, it is true, in one passage, gives to the Latini the name of "foederati" or people who had a Foedus or treaty with Rome; and this passage is sometimes quoted to prove that the Latin colonies were enumerated among the Foederate towns of Italy; a conclusion which cannot be derived from this passage of Cicero, and is also absolutely inconsistent with the nature of a Latin colony. It is not easy to determine what kind of administration prevailed in a Latin colony, and much that is said by modern

writers on this matter rests on a very weak foundation.
Savigny supposes that the Latin colonies, like the Roman
colonies, were bound by the laws of Rome, and so we must
suppose that Roman law prevailed in them, whether these
colonies had magistrates of their own or were administered in
some other way.   These Latin colonies, as already observed,
formed, together with the old Latin towns, the Nomen
Latinum, a term which expressed no political unity; but
it did express, as we must conclude from the term, a uniform
relation of dependance on Rome, though it does not follow
that the internal condition of the Latin colonies was the
same as that of the Latin towns.   It is true that there is no
evidence of there having been any difference in the internal
condition of these Latin towns and the Latin colonies; but
our knowledge ends with this negative fact, and no conclusion
can be got from it.

It is certain that these Latin towns had not the Roman
citizenship with the suffrage; but it is uncertain whether
they had the other part of the Roman citizenship, Commercium and Connubium, or the Commercium only.   We learn
from Cicero that there were twelve Latin colonies, and among
them Volaterrae and Ariminum (Rimini), which had the
Commercium and consequently the legal faculties or capacities
which have already been mentioned (p. 176, and vol. i., p.
135). If we can trust this passage of Cicero, it seems to be a
safe conclusion that the other Latin colonies and towns had
not the Commercium.   But on this point modern critics are not
agreed.   Nor are they agreed on the question whether the
inhabitants had Connubium with Roman citizens, or in other
words, whether marriages contracted between them and
Roman citizens had for a Roman citizen all the consequences
of a Roman marriage, and for a Latin all the consequences
of such a marriage as he might contract with a Latin woman.
At a later time than this of which we are speaking, if a man
in a Latin colony filled an office of honour, a magistracy, he
might thereby claim the Roman citizenship.   It is sometimes
assumed, for there is no proof, that this was so in a Latin
town before the Social War and the Lex Julia which gave

the Roman citizenship to all Italy. This assumption being granted, it follows of course that every Latin colony had a town community and a constitution like that of a Roman colony; and if the assumption is not granted, every Latin colony may still have had such a constitution, and we may say further it must of necessity have had it. The Lex Servilia de Repetundis of Glaucia (p. 100) gave the Roman citizenship to any man who conducted a prosecution under this law to conviction, but this Lex was enacted after the claims of all the dependent states to the citizenship had been often urged, and the clause was probably put in the law merely as a conciliatory measure towards all the Italians.

There remains to be considered another method by which the Latins had sometimes irregularly got the Roman citizenship. In B.C. 187 there was an embassy from the Latin Socii to Rome, men sent from all Latium, to complain to the Senate that a great number of their citizens had migrated to Rome and had been registered in the Roman census (Livy, 39 c. 3). A praetor was instructed to inquire into the matter, and it was declared that if the Latini could prove that any Latin or his father had been registered among the Latin Socii in the censorship of C. Claudius and M. Livius (B.C. 204) or since, such Latin must be compelled to return to the place where he had been registered, that is, to his own Latin city. The consequence of the inquiry was that twelve thousand Latins returned home, for Rome was at that time crowded with aliens born who were passing as citizens. Ten years later (Livy 41, c. 12) the Latins renewed their complaint at Rome: they said that if their citizens were allowed to migrate to Rome and be entered on the Roman census, it would happen that after the census had been held a few times more, their towns would be depopulated, their lands would be deserted, and they would be unable to furnish a single soldier to the Romans. Livy also speaks in this chapter of a law which allowed Latins to become Roman citizens, if they had left children behind them at home. This is the only notice of such a law that exists. This law, he adds, was abused, for, to avoid leaving their children behind, the Latini

sold them to Roman citizens on the condition that they should
be manumitted and so become citizens of the class of Libertini or free men who had been slaves; and some who had no
children to leave at home still contrived to become Roman
citizens.   Thus without any regard to the law, without
leaving any children at home to supply their place, the Latins
insinuated themselves into the Roman citizenship by migrat-
ing to Rome and getting their names put on the census.   It
may be remarked that if so many Latini had settled in Rome,
it is hardly possible that the Latini had not the Commercium,
for though they would acquire it by being entered as citizens
on the Roman census, it would be very difficult for them
to take the first step of settling in Rome, if they did not
possess by virtue of their condition as Latini all the faculties
which a Roman citizen possessed for the acquisition and
disposition of property.   The prayer of the Latini was, that
the Romans would order the Latini to return to their homes,
and provide by law against the abuse of selling children for
the purpose of their becoming Roman citizens, and if any one
should thus become a Roman citizen, it might be declared
that he was not one.

Those difficult passages of Livy are explained by Savigny
thus.   After the enactment of the Lex Julia, a new status
named Latinitas was introduced, as we shall hereafter see.
But there was an important difference between the older
Latinitas, which existed before the Lex Julia and the new
Latinitas.   The new Latins were allowed to acquire the
Roman citizenship by having held the office of a magistratus
in their own town.   Some modern writers, Madvig for
instance, assume that the Latins had this mode of acquiring
the Roman citizenship before the Lex Julia, but the assumption, in Savigny's opinion, has nothing to rest on.   It is
certain that there is no evidence for it.   On the other hand,
observes Savigny, the old Latins could obtain the Roman
citizenship on easier terms, simply by removing to Rome,
provided they left children at home to fill their place.
Madvig supposes that this law about the Latini obtaining the
Roman citizenship, provided they left children at home, was

only a measure enacted for a particular occasion, and that by
virtue of it those Latini would not be driven from Rome, who
happened to have left children at home. Savigny objects to
this explanation also, and with good reason. There is no
sign in Livy that he understood the law as intended only
for a particular occasion, and the second application of the
Latini to Rome and the terms of their petition imply that
the law, whenever it was enacted, was existing in B.C. 177,
and the Latins only asked for a fresh enactment to prevent
the abuse of the first. Savigny has a further remark: he
says that it is improbable that this mode of a Latin acquiring
the citizenship by removing to Rome and getting his name
on the censors' books would have subsisted at the same time
as the privilege of obtaining the Roman citizenship by filling
the office of a magistratus in a Roman town. This also
must be admitted; and as the Latini certainly had for a time
at least the power of acquiring the citizenship by virtue of
this law, it is a fair conclusion that they had not also the
power of acquiring it by the exceptional method of filling the
office of a magistratus in their native towns. A passage of
Cicero (Pro. P. Sestio, c. 13) has been urged in support of
Madvig's interpretation of Livy, but it proves nothing. The
final conjecture is, that as the passage in Livy (41, c.
12) is defective, it contained something about the repeal of
this law, but this is a method of solving a difficulty
which cannot be accepted. The conjecture is also confuted
by the very next chapter of Livy (41, c. 13), in which
we read that measures were taken to satisfy the petition
of the Latini, by an addition to the law and not by repeal-
ing it.

It is certain that after the enactment of this law the
Romans did more than once drive aliens out of Rome, and
in B.C. 95, as we have seen, this was done by the Lex Licinia
Mucia (p. 128). If this law then mentioned by Livy (41,
c. 12) still existed, we must suppose that they drove out
all aliens who had no claim to citizenship in any way,
and also such Latini as had no claim to the citizenship even
under this law mentioned by Livy. The passage in Livy

(25, c. 3) which has been alleged as evidence of the Latini having the suffragium or power of voting, is supposed to be corrupt. If it is not corrupt, it is unintelligible, for it is certain, if any thing is certain, that the Latini as a rule had no vote in Rome.

All the rest of the dependants of Rome are comprehended under the name of Socii, for the words Socii et Nomen Latinum, as already observed, express all the Roman dependencies in Italy. These dependant states are sometimes comprised under the name of Federate states (civitates foederatae) for many of them, perhaps all, had a Foedus or treaty which regulated their duties to Rome. They were independent communities as to their internal administration, but they were bound to supply Rome with troops or ships and sailors for the wars. We know the names of many of these Federate towns, such as Praeneste, Neapolis (Naples), Nola, Rhegium, Tarentum, and others. We may conjecture that all the Greek towns of Italy had a treaty with Rome.

Such is a general view of the condition of the Roman state in B.C. 90. As far as I have attempted to describe it, this view is consistent with the antient authorities and with the opinions of those modern writers who have most carefully investigated this difficult subject. If it is not altogether satisfactory, it may be as near the truth as we can come in the present state of our knowledge.

CHAPTER XV.

THE Italian states appear to have been preparing for war before B.C. 90. The confederates selected the town of Corfinium for their head quarters and the capital of the league. Corfinium was in the mountainous country of the Peligni, on the river Aternus (Pescara) east of the Lake Fucinus (Celano). The confederates gave to their capital the new name Italica. They built a large forum or public place, and a senate house, and stored the place with all the necessary supplies for war. They formed a senate of five hundred men, who had the general administration of the new league. It is not said how the Senate was chosen, but we may assume that the members were in some way selected from the different states which formed the new confederation. As Corfinium was merely selected for the convenience of the situation, and the confederates could not consistently with the nature of their league acknowledge it as a sovereign city, it follows that there could be no body of citizens in Corfinium corresponding to the citizens in Rome. The league was of necessity feebly held together, and if such a body as this Senate had not been formed, it could not have existed at all. The Senate ordained that two consuls should be annually appointed, and twelve praetors. Strabo, in speaking of the election of the consuls and praetors, uses a word which implies popular election, but an election by the citizens of Corfinium alone would be an absurdity, and an election by all the members of the confederation would be an impossibility; and so in the

absence of evidence we know nothing at all of the way in
which these elections were managed. The confederate consuls
were Q. Pompaedius Silo and C. Aponius Motulus as he
is named by Diodorus; but if we follow the coin, his name
was C. Papius Mutilus [1] and this is also the name in Appian.
Silo belonged to the nation of the Marsi, a small but warlike
mountain people who occupied the basin of the Lake Fucinus, and had long been the trusty allies of Rome. This great
struggle was indeed frequently called the Marsic War by
the Roman writers, either because the Marsi were the most
dangerous enemy or because they set the example of resistance
to Rome after the outbreak at Asculum. Motulus or Mutilus
was a Samnite, and the most distinguished man of his nation.
The insurgents raised a confederate force of one hundred
thousand men, foot and horse. The several towns had also
their own troops for their defence.

Two signal instances of fidelity to Rome among the
Italians have been recorded. There was one Minatius
Magius of Asculum, as it stands in the common texts of
Velleius, but we should probably read " Magius of Aeclanum
or Aeculanum," a town of the Hirpini, for it was in their
country that Magius, who was an ancestor of the historian
Velleius Paterculus, raised some troops and did good service
with the Roman army at Herculaneum, Pompeii, and Cosa.
The little town of Pinna (Penne) in the country of the
Vestini also maintained its fidelity. The Italian insurgents
had in some way got possession of the children of the people
of Pinna, or probably only of some, though Diodorus says all;
but whether they had received them as hostages or how, the
story does not tell. These children were placed in front
of the walls of Pinna by the insurgents, who threatened

---

[1] In the Catalogue of Lord Northwick's coins (1859), there is a coin struck
by the Confederate Italians with the legend " C. Papius Mutilus," and the title
" Imperator " in Oscan characters.

In the Bibliothèque Impériale, Paris, there is a denarius struck during the
Social War, which has the legend " Italia " in Roman characters, and on the re-
verse the name of the Samnite commander Papius Mutilus in Oscan characters
(Histoire de Jules César, i. 332, note).

to kill them before the eyes of their parents, unless the town
would revolt from Rome. The people refused, and they saw
their children murdered. It is difficult to understand how a
small town remote from Rome on the east side of the Apennines refused to join in the general rising in those parts.
On the west of the Apennines the Etrusci and Umbri, though
wavering in their fidelity, were on the Roman side in the
beginning of the war. The Latins too kept to their allegiance; and part of Campania at least was either held in
subjection or made no active resistance to Rome, and the
rich lands of this garden of Italy contributed to the maintenance of the Roman armies. The great city of Capua was
occupied by the Romans during the Social War, and served
as a stronghold for the armies of the republic and a place for
military stores.

The Romans resolutely prepared for the contest, which
must have cost them an enormous sum of money. L. Piso
Caesoninus, the father of him whose daughter C. Caesar
afterwards married, was appointed to superintend the
fabrication of arms, and, as Cicero says, he made a large
sum of money; for war, which is a national loss, brings profit
to a few. The Romans raised a force equal to that of the
insurgents, and sent the two consuls L. Julius Caesar and
P. Rutilius Lupus into the field. The men who were left at
home guarded the city. Rutilius had for his Legati, Cn.
Pompeius, the father of Pompeius Magnus, Q. Caepio,
C. Perperna, C. Marius the conqueror of the Cimbri, and
Valerius Messala. Caesar had with him P. Lentulus, whom
Appian names Caesar's brother, T. Didius, P. Licinius
Crassus, L. Cornelius Sulla, who had been praetor the year
before, and M. Marcellus. The jealousy of Marius and Sulla
might have damaged the Romans, if both of them had served
under the same consul; and accordingly they were kept apart
either because they wished it, or perhaps the consuls prudently separated these two rival generals, who hated one
another sincerely.

The confederates divided Italy into two military depart-
ments. They gave to Pompaedius the country from a place

which Diodorus names Corcola as far as the Hadriatic,
comprising the parts turned to the north and the west.
Pompaedius had six generals under him. Mutilus had that
part of Italy which was towards the east and the south; and
he also had six generals under him. This is the statement of
Diodorus. Appian (D. C., i. 40) gives a list of the confederate
commanders, but the names are corrupted in the ancient
books, and it is very difficult in some cases to determine
the true forms [1]. The confederates imitated the Romans in
forming their constitution and in their preparation for war.
They had often asked to be incorporated in the Roman state
as citizens, but they now aimed at something more. They
were resolved to establish an independent confederacy, and
to succeed in this they must destroy the tyranny of Rome.
But it was impossible to combine by a single effort the
Italian nations in a league which should be a match for a
power that had grown slowly and steadily for centuries, and
though it seemed at first that the great City must fall beneath
her rebellious dependencies, she had still vigour enough
to sustain the contest and bring it to a successful issue. If
we cannot discover all the causes which secured victory to
the Romans, we may assign the result to the Fortune of
Rome, which we often read of, but fortune is only another
name for causes which are obscure or undiscoverable.

We only know the military events of this war from
the incomplete narrative of Appian and the fragmentary
notices of Diodorus and other writers. Appian may have
followed chiefly L. Cornelius Sisenna, who treated of the
Social War in the first five books of his history, and was
a contemporary writer. The history was also written by
L. Lucullus (Plutarch, Lucullus, c. 1). The war appears to
have begun with the attempt of the Romans to reduce
Asculum in Picenum, where the insurrection had broken out.
Cn. Pompeius was sent against this town, which could only
be taken by a siege, for it was in a strong position and well
defended by walls. When the Roman commander was close

---

[1] There is a note by Freinshelm on the names of the confederate generals
(Florus, Duker. iii. 18).

to Asculum, the people placed a few old and infirm men on
the ramparts in order to deceive the enemy, and then
suddenly sallying out, they defeated Pompeius and dispersed
his men.

The consul L. Caesar led his troops into Samnium, where
he was defeated with the loss of two thousand men by the
confederate leader Vettius Cato or Scato, or whatever his
true name may be, who then advanced to make the siege of
Aesernia (Isernia) a Latin colony high up the valley of the
river Volturnus. Two Romans, L. Scipio and L. Acilius, had
been put into the town to direct the defence, but they made
their escape in the dress of slaves. The confederate general
blockaded Aesernia and reduced the people to such extremities that to save their food they turned the slaves out of the
town, but these poor wretches were kindly treated by the
besiegers. Aesernia made a stout resistance and was not
surrendered till the townsmen had devoured the dogs and
every animal in the place. The siege lasted, it is said, some
time, and if this is so, we can hardly understand why no
attempt was made by the Romans to relieve the place.
Indeed Orosius says that Sulla was sent to Aesernia with
twenty-four cohorts, and that he saved the city after inflicting
great loss on the enemy. There is however better evidence
that this town, with M. Marcellus in it, fell into the hands of
the confederates during the war, and we may conclude that
it suffered much, for it was a deserted place when the geographer Strabo was writing. Venafrum (Venafro), which is
lower down the valley of the Volturnus than Aesernia, was
treacherously given up to the confederate general Marius
Egnatius, who massacred two Roman cohorts that he found
in the town. According to Livy's Epitome, the confederates
also began the siege of Alba about the same time that
Aesernia was invested. This Alba, named Fucentia or
Fucensis, was situated on a hill a few miles north of the lake
Fucinus and at the base of the great Monte Velino. It was
made a Latin colony in B.C. 303. The result of the siege
of Alba is not recorded.

Perperna, who served under Rutilius, and had ten thousand

men with him, was defeated by the confederate general
P. Pracsentaeus, but the place of the battle is not named.
Perperna lost four thousand men; and the greater part of
the survivors threw away their arms, which were picked up
by the enemy.   After this disgraceful defeat Rutilius
deprived Perperna of his command and joined what remained
of his army to the troops of C. Marius.

The Romans were unsuccessful on all points.   P. Licinius
Crassus, who had been sent into Lucania, was opposed by the
confederate general M. Lamponius.   The Roman camp was
placed near some forests and thick underwood, which was
probably very dry, for the enemy contrived to set fire to the
wood, and eight hundred men perished either by fire or by
the hands of the enemy who had put them into confusion by
this stratagem.   The remnant of the army of Crassus escaped
to Grumentum, a Lucanian town high up the valley of the
Aciris (Agri) and due south of Venusia (Venosa).   The
inference from an anecdote in Seneca (de Ben. iii. 23) and
in Macrobius (Sat. i. 11) appears to be, that the town was
besieged and taken by the confederates.   The anecdote is
told as an example of the fidelity of slaves.   During the
siege some slaves left their mistress in the town and went
over to the enemy.   When the place was taken, the slaves
hurried to the house of their mistress, and dragged her out
with threatening gestures.   They said to those whom they
met that at last they had an opportunity of being revenged
on the cruel woman, and so they took her off as if they were
going to kill her.   But this was only an ingenious trick
to save a mistress whom they loved.

The confederate consul Mutilus now came down from
the hill country into Campania, and the town of Nola,
which lies in the plain between Vesuvius and the Apennines,
was treacherously surrendered to him.   He also induced two
thousand Roman soldiers who were in the place to change
sides and join him.   The officers and the commander L.
Postumius, who refused to be traitors to their country, were
imprisoned till they died of hunger.   The fall of Nola was
followed by the capture of Stabiae on the bay of Naples, and

the Roman colony of Salernum. Mutilus compelled all his prisoners and all the slaves that he could lay hold of to join his army, from which it would appear that he was either short of soldiers, or foolishly added to his forces a body of men whom he could not rely on. To strike terror into the Campanians, he wasted the fertile country round Nuceria (Nocera), which lies between Naples and Salerno. Indeed it is probable that Nuceria was also taken and plundered, though we have only the authority of Florus for the fact. The neighbouring towns submitted to Mutilus, and on his demand supplied him with ten thousand foot soldiers and a thousand horse. He now commenced the siege of Acerrae (Acerra) which is on the Clanius, north of Naples. If this place was taken, the insurgents might march upon Capua, and the Romans would be in danger of losing all Campania.

The consul Caesar advanced to the relief of Acerrae with a force which he had increased by the addition of ten thousand Gauls, probably from north Italy, and some Numidians both horse and foot. Upon this Mutilus took Oxyntas, a son of Jugurtha, whom the Romans had kept prisoner at Venusia, and putting on him a royal dress showed him to Caesar's Numidian troops. Many of these Africans went over to Oxyntas, whom they considered to be their king, and Caesar, not trusting the rest, sent them back to Africa. Oxyntas served the purpose of Mutilus, and nothing more is said of him. The success of Mutilus made him despise the Roman consul, and he endeavoured to storm his camp. But while the Italians were tearing down the earthworks and palisade, Caesar sent out his cavalry at another part of the lines, who, falling on the flank and rear of the enemy, killed six thousand of them. The meagre narrative of Appian only tells us that Caesar retired from Acerrae, and we must suppose that Mutilus continued the siege. The news of Caesar's victory was joyfully received at Rome, and the "sagum," or dress of mourning, which had been assumed at the outbreak of the war, was laid aside for the usual garb.

In the south of Italy the confederates had the superiority. The towns of Canusium, Venusia, and many others went over

to the confederate commander Judacilius; and he stormed
those places which refused to surrender. The Romans of
rank who were found in those towns were massacred: the
common sort and the slaves were compelled to join the confederates.

The consul Rutilius and C. Marius were advancing towards
the mountain region about the Lake Fucinus in the country of
the Marsi. They had reached a river, which Appian names
the Liris, but other authorities the Tolenus, which is a branch
of the Velinus. As the highest part of the Liris and the
small river Tolenus are very near one another, the difference
in the name is not material; the country in which the
Roman army was moving is sufficiently indicated. The
Romans made two bridges over the stream, at no great
distance from one another, for the purpose of taking the
troops across the river. Vettius Cato was on the other side,
near the place where Marius was making his bridge. Marius
had advised Rutilius to avoid a battle with the enemy and to
prolong the war, for he said that the Romans would never
want supplies, and as the war was carried on in the enemy's
country, they could not hold out long. The advice of the
old soldier was good, but Rutilius suspected that Marius was
not sincere, and that he was looking out for his seventh consulship with the hope of putting an end to the war himself.
In the night Vettius placed an ambuscade in a ravine near the
bridge of Rutilius. The consul crossed the river at early dawn,
and was suddenly attacked. Many of his men were killed,
others were driven into the river, and the consul received a
wound in the head of which he died. Marius, who was at
the lower bridge, knew what had happened when he saw the
bodies of Roman soldiers floating down the stream. He
quickly crossed the river, drove back the enemy, and stormed
the camp of Vettius, which was protected by a small force.
The confederate general was obliged to pass the night on the
ground where he had gained his victory; and having lost his
camp and being in want of food he retreated the next morning. The bodies of Rutilius and of many other men of rank
were carried to Rome for interment. It was a sad sight for

the citizens to see the mangled body of the consul and so
many others who had fallen. There was mourning in Rome
for many days. In consequence of this consternation the
senate made an order that those who perished in battle should
be buried where they were killed, that the sight of the dead
might not deter others from joining the army. The enemy
hearing of this made the same order about their own dead.
The fight in which Rutilius fell is registered by Ovid in his
Calendar (Fasti vi. 557—560). The day was the third of the
Ides of June, the festival of Matuta (June 11), B.C. 90. No
successor was appointed to Rutilius, for the consul Caesar had
not time to go to Rome to hold the Comitia. The senate gave
the army of Rutilius to C. Marius and Q. Caepio.

About this time Servius Sulpicius gained a victory over the
Peligni. But the folly of Q. Caepio brought another disaster
on the Romans. He had been blockaded in his camp by the
enemy, and had the good luck by a timely sally to put them
to the rout. It was in consequence of this success, according to Livy's Epitome, that Q. Caepio received an independent
command, and he and Marius separated their forces. Caepio
was opposed to the confederate consul Pompaedius, who came
to him as a deserter bringing as hostages two slave children,
dressed in the fashion of children of free birth, and he passed
them off as his own. To convince Caepio of his sincerity he
also brought some ingots of gold and silver, as they appeared
to be, but it was only lead covered over with the precious
metals. He entreated Caepio to follow him quick with his
army that he might seize the camp of the confederates while
it was without a commander. Caepio did as he was told and
followed Pompaedius, who, when he was near an ambuscade,
which had been formed to receive the unwary Roman, ran up
a hill on the pretext of looking out for the enemy and gave a
signal. The men of Pompaedius rose from their place of concealment and falling on the Romans killed Caepio and destroyed a part of his army. The trick seems almost too
absurd to be credible, but every Roman was not a good general and a man of sense. The senate gave to Marius what
remained of Caepio's army.

The great contest of the war was for the possession of the
rich Campanian country. The consul Caesar was somewhere
in these parts with thirty thousand foot and five thousand
horse.   He was passing through a narrow defile when he was
suddenly attacked by the confederate general Marius Egnatius
and driven back.   The consul, who was sick, made his escape
in a litter to a river on which there was a single bridge,
insufficient for the whole army.   The greater part of his men
were overtaken and destroyed, and the rest threw away their
arms and fled.   Caesar with great difficulty reached Teanum
Sidicinum (Teano), a town on the Latin road due south of
Venafrum, and about half way between Venafrum and Capua.
The Roman consul armed again as well as he could the soldiers
who rallied at Teanum, and being joined by fresh troops he
advanced southward past Capua to Acerrae, which was still
blockaded by Mutilus.   The two armies were encamped opposite to one another, but both were afraid to attack.   The
fact that Mutilus had been allowed to continue the siege
of Acerrae shows that the Romans were sufficiently employed
by the enemy in other parts of Italy.

The narrative of Appian does not explain why Marius and
Sulla were now acting together, but as the Romans had been
driven out of southern Campania, they must have made
an effort to maintain themselves by concentrating their forces
in north Campania and in the parts adjoining.   The Marsi
fell upon the troops of Marius, but they were vigorously repelled and driven back to the inclosing walls of a vineyard,
which they got over with difficulty, and Marius did not think
it prudent to follow them.   Sulla, who was posted on the
opposite side of the vineyard and saw what had happened,
met the Marsi as they were flying, and killed many of them.
In this battle the Marsi lost six thousand men ; and Herius
Asinius fell, who commanded the Marrucini.   A great quantity of arms was taken by the Romans.   But this defeat only
exasperated these brave mountaineers.   They recruited their
ranks with the intention of attacking the Romans, who did
not venture to attack them.   Marius always acted on the
defensive during this campaign, nor could he be induced by

any insult or challenge to give his enemy battle. Plutarch, following some authorities, describes him as slow in his plans and rather too cautious, either through age, for he was now his sixty-seventh year, or through failing strength, as Marius himself alleged. But as to refusing to fight when the enemy wished, Marius only acted like a prudent general, and as he had done in the Cimbric war. Pompaedius Silo was opposed to Marius after the defeat of Asinius, and when Marius was intrenched, Silo sent him a message to this effect, " If you are a great general, Marius, come down and fight," to which Marius made the sensible reply, " Nay, do you, if you are a great general, compel me to fight against my will." There was however one occasion when the enemy presented an opportunity for the Romans to attack, but they lacked courage, and Marius scolded his soldiers well for their want of spirit.

Diodorus has preserved a story not improbable in itself, which may help to explain the subsequent policy of the Romans in this war. Marius, as the historian says, had led his forces to the level country of the Samnites, and was encamped near the Marsi, who were commanded by Pompaedius. The two armies being within sight, many of the Marsi and Roman soldiers recognized one another as old friends, or as comrades who had served together, or as kinsmen by virtue of the law of intermarriage (connubium). Old sympathies were revived; the men called out to one another by name; they exhorted each other to abstain from this cursed fratricidal war, and finally dropping their arms the soldiers on both sides shook hands and embraced. This brought Marius out from the ranks. Pompaedius also came forward, and the two generals talked together like friends and kinsmen. They said a good deal about peace and about the Roman citizenship, which the confederates desired. Both armies were delighted and full of hope about a peaceful termination of the contest. It seemed as if two hostile bodies had been changed into a great meeting on some festal occasion. The generals themselves invited the men to cease from mutual slaughter, and the soldiers were eager to follow the exhortation. It is impossible to say how far this part of

the historian's narrative is exact, but it is certainly a probable
story, and not like a fiction.   The Romans and the Italian
nations had long served together in the armies of Rome; the
Latin tongue must have become familiar to the allies; and
marriages between Romans and Italians would be common,
for we know that whenever two nations have any communion
the men of one nation will seek the women of the other.
The passage of Diodorus indeed affirms that intermarriage
existed legally between the Romans and the Italian nations,
and if this were so, the marriage of a Roman with an Italian
woman had the same legal consequences as if he had married
a Roman woman.   But if this capacity of marriage did not
exist between a Roman and Italian, still the marriage of
persons of those two nations would be a marriage, though it
would not be a Roman marriage.

While Rome was fighting for her supremacy in Italy,
there was a rising in the Transalpine province of Gallia.
The Salluvii or Salyes, who had been reduced to subjection
(Vol. i. p. 310), took up arms, but the rebellion was suppressed
by C. Caecilius.   Nothing is known of this affair beyond the
brief notice in Livy's Epitome.

The military operations on the east side of the Apennines
are very obscure.   Cn. Pompeius was the Roman commander
in those parts.   Judacilius, Titus Laphrenius, as Appian
names him, and P. Ventidius, for which name it has been
conjectured that we should read Vettius in Appian's text,
combined their forces in the neighbourhood of the hills
of Falernum, where they defeated Pompeius and drove him
to Firmum (Fermo), about six miles from the coast of the
Hadriatic.   Firmum was a Latin colony established about
the beginning of the first Punic war.   There is a mistake in
Appian's text in the name Falernum, which cannot be the
Falernus Ager of Campania, if Pompeius fled to Firmum.
Accordingly it is conjectured that the battle was fought
about Fulcria on the left bank of the river Tinna (Tenna) in
Picenum, and about twenty miles from the Hadriatic.
Laphrenius undertook the siege of Firmum, while the two
other generals went on some expedition.   Pompeius armed

the remainder of his men, but he still kept within the walls
of Firmum, while another Roman army was coming from the
south to his relief under the command of Servius Sulpicius,
who was instructed by Pompeius to place himself in the rear
of Laphrenius. While Pompeius sallied out and attacked the
enemy in front, Sulpicius set fire to the camp of the confederates, who being panic-struck fled in disorder to Asculum
without a commander, for Laphrenius fell in the battle.
Pompeius now commenced the siege of Asculum. This town
was the native place of Judacilius, who hurried to relieve it
with eight cohorts, having first sent a message to the people
to announce his approach. As soon as they should see him
advancing to Asculum, they were told to make a sally on the
enemy, while he attacked the Romans in the rear. The
people of Asculum were not bold enough to second the plan
of Judacilius, who however made his way through the
Romans into the city with as many of his men as he could.
He reproached the townsmen with their cowardice and disobedience of his orders. Despairing of saving the city he
massacred his political enemies, who had always opposed him
and now had prevented the people from obeying his commands. We see from this example that there were factions
in some of the Italian towns, and probably some of them
were driven unwillingly into the war with Rome. Judacilius
expecting no mercy from the Romans, if he fell into their
hands, made a great pile of wood in one of the temples, and
placing a table on it feasted with his friends. While the
drinking was going on he took poison and lying down on the
pile bade his friends set fire to it. They would not be sorry
to be rid of such a desperate madman.

The campaign of B.C. 90 had not been favourable to the
Romans. They had not reduced any part of Italy to obedience, and the Tyrrheni and Umbri with other peoples who
bordered on them were supposed to be ready for revolt.
There was danger that Rome would have enemies all round
her. Accordingly the Senate gave orders for occupying the
coast from Cumae in Campania to the mouth of the Tiber.
But there was a want of men, and now for the first time, as

it is said, the class of Libertini, or manumitted slaves, were
employed in military service.

Before the close of the year B.C. 90 we must assume that
the consul Caesar came to Rome to hold the Comitia. The
consuls of the next year were Cn. Pompeius Strabo and L.
Porcius Cato. Near the end of the year B.C. 90 Caesar also
proposed the law which bears his name, the famous Lex
Julia. The condition of the Roman state was very bad.
The republic was surrounded by enemies in Italy, and the
sign of revolt in Transalpine Gallia might be followed by
other risings in the provinces. But the greatest danger was
in the east, where Mithridates Eupator, the sixth king who
bore the name of Mithridates, was threatening the Roman
possessions in Asia. In these difficulties the Senate yielded
to necessity, and the Lex Julia de Civitate, as it was named,
was hastily enacted. The terms of this Lex have not been
preserved. Gellius says that by this law the Roman citizenship was given to all Latium, by which he probably means
all Latium and the Latin colonies. Cicero states that the
citizenship was offered to the Socii and the Latini, that is, to
all the people in Italy except the province of Gallia Cisalpina.
According to Appian, the Lex offered the citizenship to the
Italians who still remained faithful to Rome; and he adds
that the Etrurians readily accepted the offer. The Epitomator of Livy has not mentioned the Lex Julia, though there
can be no doubt that Livy had spoken of it in his seventy-
fourth book. This omission shows how imperfectly the
Epitomator did his work. The Epitome records a defeat of
the Umbri by Aulus Plotius, and a defeat of the Marsi by a
praetor L. Porcius, both of these nations, as the Epitome
states, having revolted from Rome. But there is a manifest
blunder of the Epitomator in the name of the Marsi, though
it is by no means certain that we should read Etrusci in place
of Marsi. If Plotius defeated the Umbri, this event may have
happened before the enactment of the Lex Julia. This concession on the part of Rome confirmed the friendship of those
states which were still well disposed or wavering, and it
tended to diminish the animosity of those who were still in

arms, for they had hopes of receiving the same offer of the Roman citizenship, which was the ostensible object of the war.

The Romans did not affect to legislate for the Latins or the Italians. Cicero remarks that if the Romans enacted a law, such as the Furia on testaments, the Voconia, and many others on matters relating to the ordinary affairs of life, the Latini accepted such of them as they chose. This Lex Julia de Civitate also was not a law imposed on the Socii and Latini, by which they were compelled to become members of the Roman state: it was an offer which they might accept or refuse. Those who did accept the offer were said according to the Roman phraseology to be "fundi facti." There was, says Cicero, a great dispute among the people of Heraclea, a Greek city on the Tarentine gulf, and also among the people of Neapolis (Naples) about accepting the offer of the Lex Julia, for a large number in both these cities preferred the freedom which they enjoyed under their treaties to the proffered citizenship. Cicero says that the register office (tabularium) of Heraclea was burnt during the Italic war, from which it is a possible, but not a necessary conclusion, that the ravages of this great struggle extended as far as Heraclea.

As to the Lex Julia, Appian remarks that the Romans did not enrol their new citizens among the five-and-thirty tribes which then existed, and this was done in order that the new citizens, who would be more numerous than the old, might not outvote them. They made some new tribes to receive them, in which they voted last. Such may be the meaning of Appian, but there is a difficulty about one word that he has used (δεκατεύοντες). If this arrangement was made, the votes of the new citizens might be useless, for the five-and-thirty old tribes, which were called to vote first, were more than half the number. The design of this contrivance was either not seen by the Italians, or they were content for the time, but they found out the purpose and effect of this arrangement afterwards, and so it was the cause of fresh trouble. Velleius says that the new citizens were distributed into eight tribes, and he gives the same reason for this measure that Appian does. It is conjectured from a fragment of the third book of the historian L. Cornelius Sisenna (Lib. iii.) who wrote the history of the Social War, that L. Calpurnius Piso added two tribes pursuant to a decree of the Senate. If these two tribes were added in or after B.C. 89, this confirms the statement of Velleius.

CHAPTER XVI.

THE SOCIAL WAR.

B.C. 89.

THE war still continued. The consuls Strabo and Cato took the field. L. Julius Caesar, the consul of B.C. 90, was appointed to command an army with the title of proconsul. He fell on the enemy somewhere, while they were moving from one place to another, killed eight thousand of them as the number is reported, and picked up the arms of many more who fled. The siege of Asculum was continued by Caesar, but he fell sick before the town, and being unable to stay any longer he appointed C. Baebius his successor.

The confederates on the Hadriatic coast, before they heard of the change of disposition in the inhabitants of Etruria, sent by a long circuitous path over the Apennines fifteen thousand men to help the Etrurians. The consul Cn. Pompaius Strabo fell on these men and killed five thousand of them. The rest attempted to find their way home through a country without roads and in bad weather. They had nothing to eat except the mast from the trees on the Apennines, and half of them died of hunger and fatigue.

It is impossible to make a satisfactory chronology of the events of this war. We have nothing to guide us except the meagre Epitome of Livy and Appian's compilation. The Epitome records a defeat of the Marsi by the consul Cn. Pompeius, and we have Cicero's evidence to the fact that Pompeius in his consulship was opposed to the Marsi. Cicero,

at this time a mere youth, was serving in the Roman army,
and he records a conference between Pompeius and P. Vettius
Cato or Scato, as the name is written in the manuscripts.
The meeting took place between the two camps, and there was
present, besides the Roman and the confederate generals, Sextus
Pompeius, the brother of the consul, a learned and wise man.
Cato saluted Sextus Pompeius, who said, "By what name
shall I address you?" Cato replied, "As one who wishes to
be your friend, and by necessity is your enemy." The conference was conducted fairly, without any fear or suspicion,
and no great signs of animosity. The Romans and the Italian
nations had become by long intercourse almost one people,
and so the folly of the Romans appears still greater in
refusing to admit the Italians to the citizenship.

In this year the services of Sulla were more conspicuous.
The Italian Minatius Magius, with the legion which he had
raised in the country of the Hirpini, took Herculaneum in
Campania in conjunction with the Roman commander T.
Didius, the man who had distinguished himself by the bloody
massacre in Spain (p. 138). Didius was killed in this campaign, and perhaps in the assault on Herculaneum. Stabiae,
which had fallen into the hands of Papius Mutilus in B.C. 90,
was recovered by Sulla on the last day of April B.C. 89, but
the town was destroyed, and when the elder Pliny wrote it
was only a village. While Sulla was encamped near the
hills about Pompeii, and as it seems was besieging the town,
the confederate commander, L. Cluentius or Juventius, as
Orosius names him, took a position within three miles of
Sulla's camp. The Roman commander was irritated at
seeing an enemy so near him, and without waiting for some
of his men, who were out foraging, he attacked Cluentius.
The Romans were driven back, but being joined by the
foragers, they put Cluentius to flight, and he removed his
camp to a greater distance. Cluentius was now joined by
some Gauls, who must have come along the east side of the
peninsula and have crossed the Apennines into Campania.
When the two armies again approached, a Gaul of huge
stature came forward and challenged any Roman to single

combat. This is a usual story in Roman history; but instead of a Roman on this occasion accepting the challenge, a Moor of short stature fought and killed the big man. The Gauls fled on seeing their countryman fall, and the rest of the troops of Cluentius being thrown into disorder, fled towards Nola. Sulla pursued the enemy and killed thirty thousand. The people of Nola opened only one gate to receive the fugitives for fear of the Romans entering with them, which gave Sulla another opportunity of attacking the enemy under the walls of Nola, and slaughtering twenty thousand more, among whom was the commander Cluentius. Thus according to this very improbable story fifty thousand of the confederates fell on one day. Orosius indeed reduces the twenty thousand to eighteen thousand, but that does not materially diminish the loss of the enemy. The confederates, it may be true, were completely beaten and no quarter would be given, but the soldiers of the enemy could run as fast as the Romans could pursue, and some of them would certainly escape. There is no notice of the capture of Pompeii by Sulla. If he did take the place, we must conclude that it did not suffer like Stabiae, for Pompeii continued to exist until it was covered with ashes by the eruption of Vesuvius A.D. 79.

An event happened about this time which shows that the Roman discipline was either not well maintained, or that one commander at least had made himself intolerable to his men. Aulus Postumius Albinus, whom Livy's Epitome names commander of the fleet, was murdered by his own soldiers. Orosius terms Albinus a man of consular rank and the legatus of the consul Sulla, but Sulla was not consul till the next year (B.C. 88). Both Orosius and the Epitome place the murder of Albinus before the defeat of Cluentius. Albinus appears to be the consul of B.C. 99, the colleague of M. Antonius. The soldiers of Albinus were placed under Sulla, but he did not punish them for their mutiny. He said that "the soldiers would bestir themselves the more in the war and make amends for their fault by their courage." Sulla was looking to the consulship and to the command against Mithridates, and as he wished to be popular with the army,

he would not punish the mutineers who had killed their
general. These men fought bravely in the battles with
Cluentius and thus made good the expectations of their
general.

Sulla now advanced south to the country of the Hirpini to
attack the town of Acculanum or Acclanum, which was on
the Via Appia about fifteen miles south-east of Beneventum
(Benevento). The people of Acculanum were expecting the
arrival of the Lucani on that very day to bring them help,
and they asked Sulla to allow them time to consider what
they would do. Sulla saw their purpose and he gave them
one hour, during which he surrounded the walls, which were
made of wood, with bundles of vine cuttings, and when the
time had expired, he made ready to burn the place. The
townsmen were terrified and surrendered. Sulla gave up
Acculanum to be sacked by his men. He spared the other
towns which voluntarily surrendered, and finally reduced to
submission all the country of the Hirpini.

After this success Sulla entered Samnium which was the
stronghold of the confederates. The Samnite general Papius
Mutilus held the passes which led into this mountain region,
but Sulla took his men by a circuitous way and fell suddenly
on the enemy. The confederates being surprised were completely defeated with great loss. Their army was dispersed,
and Mutilus who was wounded in the fight made his escape
with a few of his men to Aesernia, which was in the possession of the confederates. This is Appian's narrative. The
name of Mutilus does not occur again in the history of the
Social War. We might conjecture that he died of his wound,
but a man of the same name, Papius Mutilus, afterwards
perished in Sulla's proscription, which fact has led to the
conjecture that Mutilus survived the war. There is also a
passage in Appian's Civil War (iv. 25) which by a correction
of a name has been referred to this famous confederate
leader, who, if this correction is accepted, lived to the time
of the proscription of the triumviri. Frontinus records a
stratagem of Sulla, which seems to show that he entered the
country of the Samnites by the upper part of the valley of

the Volturnus, and that the enemy was not taken by surprise. According to Frontinus, Sulla was hemmed in by the enemy in the narrow valley near Aesernia; but he was a man who never failed to get out of a difficulty. He asked for a conference with Mutilus about terms of peace. The conference came to no result, but an armistice was made, during which Sulla observed that the enemy relaxed his vigilance. Accordingly one night he led all his men off, leaving a single trumpeter behind, who was ordered to sound the different watches just as if the Romans were in their camp, and as soon as the fourth and last watch was sounded, the trumpeter might follow. Thus Sulla got all his men safely away with his baggage and military engines. A dark night might render such a retreat possible, but unless the enemy was at a great distance, it is difficult to conceive how Sulla's retreat was not discovered by the noise which would be made by the removal of his heavy material; and the distance between the two camps was not sufficient to prevent the sound of the trumpet being heard, for that is the essential part of the stratagem. We may suppose that Mutilus followed Sulla when his retreat was discovered, and the battle which was fought may be that which Appian has described; but even this supposition does not entirely reconcile the two narratives.

Sulla left Aesernia behind him and crossed the ridge of the Apennines to Bovianum, where the confederate congress was then sitting. Bovianum (Bojano) is in the midst of the mountains near the source of the river Tifernus (Biferno), which flows down a long narrow valley into the Hadriatic. It may be conjectured that the confederates had been already driven from Corfinium and that their cause in the northern part of the confederation was in a bad condition. The old town of Bovianum was on an eminence, for Appian describes it as having three heights or citadels. While the townsmen in one of these places were directing all their attention to Sulla's movements, some of the Roman soldiers were sent round to seize either of the other two heights, and if they succeeded, they were ordered to give a signal by raising a smoke. When the smoke appeared, Sulla attacked that part of

Bovianum opposite to which he had placed himself, and after
three hours hard fighting he took the town. This ended the
campaign of Sulla. The winter was approaching and he
went to Rome to canvass for the consulship, the great object
of his ambition. He was elected Consul for the year B.C. 88
by the almost unanimous vote of the electors, with Q. Pompeius Rufus for his colleague.

Appian has recorded the success of Sulla in a continuous
narrative; but if we follow the Epitome of Livy we must
place the death of the consul Cato somewhere between the
early part and the close of Sulla's campaign. Cato commanded the troops which had served under Marius. He
defeated the Marsi several times, but he lost his life in an
attempt to storm the enemy's camp, and his army was repulsed.
Orosius has reported from some authority that Cato was
killed in the confusion of a battle by a son of C. Marius. He
was the second Roman consul who perished in this war. The
campaign in the south-east part of Italy was conducted by
the praetor O. Cosconius and Q. Lucceius, the father of the
Lucceius who afterwards wrote a history of the war. They
burnt Salapia (Salpi), one of the chief towns of Apulia on the
coast of the Hadriatic; and Cannae submitted. Cosconius
then undertook the siege of Canusium (Canosa), but he was
attacked by the Samnite army, and after great loss on both
sides, Cosconius was defeated and retired to Cannae. In
some of these battles, according to Livy's Epitome, the confederate leader Marius Egnatius lost his life. According to
Appian's narrative, the Samnite commander, after the retreat
of Cosconius to Cannae, was Trebatius, a name which some
critics have proposed to alter to Egnatius; but it is impossible
to reconcile Livy and Appian by this alteration, for the
Trebatius of Appian was not killed, and the Egnatius of
Livy was killed. A river separated the Samnite and the
Roman army, perhaps some small branch that entered the
Aufidus on the right bank, for Cannae the head-quarters of
Cosconius, and Canusium the head-quarters of Trebatius are
south of the main stream of the Aufidus. The confederate
general wished to have a fair fight in the open field, and he

proposed that either Cosconius should cross the river to his
side or retire and allow him to cross over. Cosconius thought
it better for him to let the enemy have the river in the rear,
and he allowed the confederates to cross. Probably the
Roman hardly gave his imprudent enemy time to put his
men in order. The Samnites were defeated and compelled
to recross the river with the loss of fifteen thousand men.
The remnant of the Samnites with Trebatius escaped to
Canusium.

Appian's brief notice of the rest of the campaign of
Cosconius is proved to be worthless by his own geography.
He says that Cosconius overran the territories of Larinum,
Venusia, and "of the Asclaci," which appears to be the
Asculum of Apulia. It is possible that Cosconius took
Venusia and Asculum; but we may ask why he did not take
Canusium. Perhaps he did take Canusium and the compiler
has forgotten to record this fact. But Larinum, which is
near the river Tifernus, is beyond the limits of Cosconius'
campaign. Cosconius also reduced the territory of the
Peucetii or Poediculi, which he might easily do, for they
were a small people on the Hadriatic, south of the Aufidus.
He also entered the peninsula of Iapygia, which lies between
the Tarentine gulf and the Hadriatic. The defeat of Trebatius
laid open all the south-east of Italy to the Romans. The
Iapygian peninsula once contained thirteen towns and was
very populous, but in Strabo's time the only large towns were
Tarentum and Brundisium. The rest were reduced to villages.
This country had suffered ever since the Romans began the
contest for the supremacy in Italy, and the Social War completed the ruin of a once flourishing country. The Romans
carried on the war in the enemy's territory, which they
wasted, and they burnt the towns with a savage ferocity, as
if they preferred the ruin of the Italian dependencies to a
friendly union which would strengthen the Roman republic.

The great southern peninsula, which lies between the
Tarentine gulf and the Tuscan or lower sea, was still scarcely
touched by the Roman arms. It contained two nations, the
Lucani and Bruttii. A. Gabinius entered Lucania, and it

appears that he defeated the enemy in the open field and
took several of the Lucanian towns. But the confederates
had still an army, and Gabinius foolishly attacked them in
their entrenched camp. He found by experience that the
capture of ill-fortified towns was a different thing from
storming a position which the enemy had chosen, and he lost
his life.

The defeat of the Marrucini by P. Sulpicius Rufus, the
legatus of Pompeius, is placed in the Epitome after the
death of Gabinius. Orosius, who observes the same order of
events, adds the Vestini to the peoples whom Sulpicius
reduced to obedience. The Marrucini and Vestini were on
the east side of the Apennines, and bordered on the Marsi.
Pompeius and his legatus were carrying on the war in the
same country; but according to the Epitome the Vestini,
with the Peligni who inhabited the high Apennines east of
the lake Fucinus, submitted to Pompeius, who is incorrectly
named proconsul by the Epitomator. The confederates were
exhausted and there was treachery among them. C. Vettius,
one of the Peligni, was seized by his own troops, who
intended to deliver him to Pompeius; but a faithful slave to
save his master from disgrace stabbed him, and then killed
himself. The Marsi about the same time were defeated by
L. Murena and Q. Caecilius Metellus Pius, as the name
should probably be written in the Epitome. The submission
of these warlike nations compelled the confederates to remove the seat of their government finally from Corfinium in
the country of the Peligni. They may indeed have changed
their head-quarters before the Marsi were completely defeated, if it is true that the supreme council was at Bovianum, when Sulla attacked that town. It is possible that the
congress had been moving about from one place to another.
At last they removed over the Apennines to the Samnite
town of Aesernia. They appointed five praetors or generals,
and they gave the chief command to Q. Pompaedius Silo,
who was one of the five. The confederates raised fresh
troops, and made up an army of thirty thousand men. They
also manumitted slaves and armed them as well as they

could, to the number of about twenty thousand infantry and
a thousand cavalry. This was the last desperate resource of
these brave people. It is hard to conceive how they could
maintain so many men in a country, which for two years had
been devastated by contending armies.

After the submission of the warlike nations east of the Lake
Fucinus, or about the same time, for it is impossible to determine, Pompeius returned to the siege of Asculum in Picenum,
the town where the resistance to Rome first showed itself.
Here was fought the great battle of the war, in which
seventy-five thousand Romans were opposed to sixty thousand Italians, a statement hardly credible, when we consider
that both sides had still other armies on foot in various parts
of Italy. The Italians were defeated with the loss of
eighteen thousand Marsi and their commander Francus, as
Orosius names him, and three thousand prisoners were taken.
It was after this great defeat, according to Orosius, that
Judacilius had his last feast and poisoned himself in Asculum;
but Orosius is untrustworthy in any matter where there is a
question of chronology. Four thousand of the confederates,
who escaped the slaughter of this dreadful day, fled to the
mountains, where they were surprised by the snow and cold,
for the winter had begun. They were found frozen to death,
some resting on stumps and rocks, others on their armour,
with staring eyes and grinning teeth. After the battle
Asculum was taken, or it surrendered. Pompeius whipped
and then beheaded all the commanders and centurions, with
all the principal people. The slaves and booty were sold by
auction. He allowed the free people to leave the town, first
stripping them of all that they had, and sent them off naked,
as we are told, but half naked may be nearer the truth. The
Roman senate expected that the plunder of Asculum would
help to replenish their exhausted stores, but the consul
brought nothing into the treasury. His son Cnaeus was
afterwards called to account for his father's peculation (B.C.
86). A single word of Florus of doubtful meaning has led
some modern writers to affirm that Pompeius destroyed
Asculum, but this is very improbable, for we find it men-

tioned as a town a few years later. The consul had a triumph
for the capture of Asculum and the reduction of Picenum a
few days before his term of office expired, on the twenty-
seventh of December, B.C. 89. Among the prisoners who
walked in the triumphal pomp was a woman of Asculum, who
carried a young male child in her arms. Fifty years later
this captive child entered Rome himself as a triumphant
conqueror. This is the romantic history of P. Ventidius
Bassus. Dion Cassius and others detract from the effect of
the story by informing us that Bassus fought against the
Romans in the Social War, and appeared in chains in the
triumph of Pompeius. However he did triumph in B.C. 38;
and he must have been very young in B.C. 89. Pompeius
had the honour of establishing colonies north of the Po, the
Transpadane colonies, as they were named. These were not
new colonies, as Asconius informs us, but old towns to which
was given what the Romans termed the Jus Latii or Latinitas,
by virtue of which every man who filled the office of a magistrate might have the Roman citizenship (p. 182). It is
reasonable to suppose that this privilege was given to the
Transpadane colonies by an enactment (lex) or a Senatusconsultum, and Pompeius himself may have proposed it after
his triumph, and before his term of office expired.

Money was scarce in Rome owing to the war, and there
was a great struggle between debtors and creditors. Appian
represents the trouble as arising solely from loans of money,
which the lenders demanded with interest, and the debtors
could not or would not pay. There was an old law, it is said,
which forbade the lending of money on interest, and punished
with a penalty the man who lent on these terms. But if such
a law ever existed, it fell into disuse, and if it had been observed, there would have been an end of lending and borrowing. The practice of lending on interest being now established
by custom, the creditors were calling for their interest and
principal, and the debtors, as it happens in time of war and
civil disturbance, deferred making payment, and some even
threatened that they would make their creditors pay the
penalty. Asellio, who was Praetor Urbanus in this year

(B.C. 89), after making a fruitless attempt to reconcile debtor and creditor, appointed, according to Roman practice, judices, that is, persons to sit as judges and to hear and determine the questions arising from this conflict of law and custom. The creditors, who were vexed at the attempt to enforce an old law, did themselves justice in this way. Asellio was offering a sacrifice in the Forum before the temple of Castor and Pollux, and the people were standing round. A stone was thrown at the praetor, on which he cast down the cup and ran towards the temple of Vesta, but some of the crowd put themselves before him and barred the way. He then made his escape into a shop, where he was murdered. Many of the pursuers, supposing that the praetor had made his escape to the Vestal virgins, broke into places where no man was allowed to enter. Thus a Roman praetor, while he was performing a religious ceremony, dressed in the splendid robes of his office, was murdered early in the morning, when the Forum was full of people. The senate gave notice that whoever would give information about the murderers should receive a reward; if he was a free man, a sum of money; if a slave, he should have his freedom; and if an accomplice, he should be pardoned. But no man could be found to inform, and the creditors, who were the guilty men, contrived to keep all quiet. If the conjecture is true that in this year was enacted the Lex Plautia de Vi, it is very probable that the immediate occasion of this enactment was the murder of the praetor Asellio. This law is mentioned by Cicero and his commentators several times, and also by Sallust. There is however no evidence for assigning it to the year B.C. 89 except the name Plautia, and that is not enough. We know that the law was enacted before B.C. 63, and that is all. The object of the law was to prevent acts of violence which disturbed the public peace. Such acts were rioting, violence to magistrates or the senate by armed men, the forcible occupying of public places, and carrying weapons. These provisions of the law are collected from several passages of Cicero, one of which shows that the law also contained a chapter or chapters on the appointment of the jury (judices),

who should try such offences. It is conjectured that the
penalty of the Lex Plautia was exile, but for what time we
cannot tell.

Some time in this year B.C. 89, but the time is uncertain,
there was also enacted the Lex Plautia Papiria, so called from
the tribunes M. Plautius Silvanus and C. Papirius Carbo who
proposed it. The object of the law appears to have been to
conciliate the states which were at war with Rome and to
secure the fidelity of the Federate or allied towns (foederatae
civitates).   One part of this law is quoted by Cicero in his
defence of the poet Archias (c. 4), who claimed the Roman
citizenship under the Lex Plautia Papiria. The words of
Cicero are these: "The Roman citizenship was offered under
the law of Silvanus and Carbo to any persons who had been
enrolled as citizens of the Federate states, if their domicile
was in Italy at the time when the law was enacted, and if
within sixty days they made a declaration before a praetor "
of their intention to become Roman citizens. Cicero merely
quotes this part of the law because it applied to the case of
his client Archias. But it is certain that this was only one
particular clause of the law of Silvanus and Carbo, and that
the purpose of this enactment, which would properly apply
to town communities and peoples, was to complete in some
way what the Lex Julia had not accomplished, or was not
adapted to accomplish. Appian remarks that the Social War
lasted until all Italy came over to the Roman polity, except
the Lucani and the Samnites, who did not come over at that
time; "but they also, as I suppose, afterwards obtained what
they wished : and they were severally enrolled in the (new ?)
tribes like those who had already obtained the citizenship,
that they might not by being mixed with the old citizens
prevail in the voting, for they were superior in numbers "
(B. C. i. 53). There is some error in Appian's text, for he
says simply "in the tribes," whereas the close of the sentence
shows that these tribes, as he understood the matter, were
not the old tribes, and accordingly Musgrave conjectured
that the word "new" is wanting.

Censors had been elected in B.C. 92, and censors were again

elected in B.C. 89, P. Licinius Crassus, consul B.C. 97, and
L. Julius Caesar, consul B.C. 90. It appears that these extraordinary censors were appointed for the purpose of enrolling the new citizens in the new tribes, but yet there was no
census, as Cicero says, perhaps because the times were
troubled. However the Lustrum was celebrated, but inaus-
piciously, for it was done without the authority of the augurs.
Crassus had proposed the sumptuary law named the Lex
Licinia, and the censors now made an edict for the suppression of luxury. They declared that no person should sell
"unguenta exotica," a term under which were comprehended
costly oils and perfumes of foreign growth used by women
and effeminate men. If the law was enforced, there must
have been informers, and we may assume that shops might be
visited by the magistrates to discover any violations of the
edict.

Cicero speaks of a Lex Plautia or Plotia Judiciaria, of
which he says, "I remember when for the first time the senators together with the Roman equites were acting as jurymen
(judices) under the Lex Plautia, Cn. Pompeius, a man hateful
to the gods and to the nobility, was tried under the Lex
Varia de Majestate." It is generally assumed that this trial
took place before Pompeius commanded in the Social War,
and that therefore the Lex Plautia must have existed then.
But Asconius states that this Lex Plautia was proposed by
the tribune M. Plautius Silvanus in the consulship of Cn.
Pompeius Strabo and L. Porcius Cato (B.C. 89) in the second
year of the Italic War, at a time when the equestrian order
was in possession of the office of juryman (judex). The law
was proposed with the support of the nobility, and it was to
the effect which Cicero's words indicate; for by virtue of
this law the people elected fifteen men out of their respective
tribes to discharge the office of jurymen for that year. The
result of this mode of election was that even senators were
elected and some also from the plebs—that is, from those who
were neither senators nor equites. This positive statement
of Cicero, supported and explained with great precision by
his commentator, must be accepted, and consequently Cn.

Pompeius, if he was ever tried for Majestas or treason, was
tried after he was consul.　This short notice of the Lex
Plautia on the constitution of the jury lists is another example
of the great difficulty in understanding the subject, for we
have no other evidence about the Lex Plautia, and we have
Cicero's statement elsewhere that the jury lists were made up
of Equites only during nearly the whole period from the time
of Gracchus to the legislation of Sulla.

CHAPTER XVII.

THE TRIBUNATE OF P. SULPICIUS RUFUS.

B.C. 88.

THE Romans had now as one of their consuls the best soldier of the Republic and a man of great and varied talents, L. Cornelius Sulla. He was fifty years of age when he was elected (B.C. 89), according to Plutarch, but in his forty-ninth year as Velleius says.

The war still continued. Q. Pompaedius Silo fought a great battle early in this year with the Roman commander Mamercus Aemilius, in which the confederates lost above six thousand men, and the Romans only a small number, as their historians reported. Silo had still an army, for he recovered Bovianum and entered the place in triumph, but this was a good omen for the Romans, because a triumphal procession ought to enter a victorious city, and not a city which had been captured like Bovianum. Q. Caecilius Metellus Pius, the successor of Cosconius, took by storm the town of Venusia, which contained a strong garrison, and he made above three thousand prisoners. Silo, the brave and skilful confederate commander, fell in some battle after he had recaptured Bovianum. According to Appian, he was defeated by Metellus in Iapygia, and his men who fled from the battle and were dispersed came in singly and submitted to Metellus. Orosius reports that P. Sulpicius had the honour of finally defeating this formidable enemy of the Romans. Orosius places the battle at a river Theanum,

which does not exist, but it is possible that he may mean the
town of Teanum in Apulia on the river Frento (Fortore).

After these defeats, according to the narrative of Diodorus,
and when the affairs of the Italian allies were desperate, they
sent to Mithridates VI. king of Pontus, who possessed a large
army and great resources. They invited the king to lead his
forces into Italy, and promised him an easy victory, if he
would join his army to the troops of the confederates.
Mithridates answered that he would bring his army into Italy,
when he had settled the affairs of Asia according to his
pleasure, and he was already engaged in the business.
Appian indeed states (Mithridat. c. 112) that Mithridates
did make a treaty with the Samnites, if we accept
Schweighaeuser's emendation of a corrupt word. But
the confederates had no hope of immediate help. A few of
the Samnites still held out, and the people who were
shut up in the town of Nola. There were also the confederate commanders Lamponius and Clepitius at the head of
the remnant of the Lucanian forces. The war was in fact
terminated, but the Romans had on hand another war in the
east. The Social War, according to the estimate of Velleius,
had carried off above three hundred thousand of the men of
Italy. Some of the fairest portions of the peninsula were
wasted, and flourishing towns were plundered or burnt.

Mithridates had begun the war with the Romans by
invading their province of Asia. The consul Sulla was appointed to the Asiatic war, but as Nola still held out and
was besieged by a Roman army, Sulla went to assist in
reducing the place. While he was before Nola, a Samnite
army came to relieve the town and encamped near it. Sulla,
who had great confidence in omens, was encouraged by
favourable signs to attack the fortified camp of the Samnites,
which he stormed and captured. The siege of Nola still
continued, and Sulla was recalled to Rome by more serious
matters.

In this year P. Sulpicius Rufus, who had served with distinction in the war, was one of the tribunes. He was ten
years older than the orator Hortensius, a fact which fixes his

birth in B.C. 124, for Hortensius was born in B.C. 114. We
know the place which Sulpicius occupied in public affairs
by the company which he kept. Cicero introduces him in
his dialogue on the Orator, in which Sulpicius and C. Cotta
accompanied L. Crassus to his Tusculan villa during the
Ludi Romani (p. 156), where they were joined by Q. Mucius
Scaevola, the augur, and by the orator M. Antonius. On the
day after the first day's conversation, Q. Lutatius Catulus,
now an old man, and C. Julius Caesar Strabo, his half-
brother, were added to the company. Sulpicius and Cotta
were very intimate with the tribune M. Livius Drusus, and
great expectations of their future career were entertained by
the older men of their party. Cicero says that Sulpicius and
Cotta were the best speakers of all the young men of their
age; and Cicero well knew the style of Sulpicius, for during
the year B.C. 88 he heard the tribune daily addressing the
people. Cicero has described the style of his oratory (Brutus, c. 55) in those precise terms which none but a master of
the art could use. "Sulpicius," says Cicero, "was of all the
orators that I have heard the most dignified, and I may say,
the most tragic: his voice was powerful, sweet, and clear;
his gesture and the movements of his body were full of grace,
and yet his action was that of a man trained for the forum
and not the stage: his language was rapid and flowing, and
yet not redundant or diffuse. He chose Crassus as his
model: Cotta preferred Antonius: but Cotta did not possess
the energy of Antonius, and Sulpicius did not possess the
suavity of Crassus." This accomplished orator did not leave
a single written speech behind him. Cicero had often heard
him say that he was not accustomed to writing, and that he
could not write. Antonius discovered the talents of Sulpicius when he was a young man, and gave him some advice,
which Sulpicius followed so well that in less than a year he
prosecuted Norbanus (B.C. 94), whom Antonius defended.
On this occasion, says Antonius, it is past all belief what a
difference there was between his oratory at the trial of Norbanus and what he had displayed at the time when I gave
him my advice.

In the tribunate of Sulpicius an attempt was made to
recall those men who had fled from Rome for fear of prosecution under the Lex Varia and had not had the opportunity
of defending themselves, but Sulpicius interposed as tribune and
prevented the return of the exiles.   C. Julius Caesar Strabo
was a candidate for the consulship, though he had not been
praetor, and he could not be legally elected.   Both Sulpicius
and his colleague P. Antistius opposed Caesar's claim, and
Antistius spoke better than Sulpicius.   On this occasion Sulpicius was on the side of constitutional law, and the attempt
of Caesar to seize the consulship was illegal.   The resistance
of Sulpicius made a breach between him and the party to
which Caesar belonged, and if it was not the beginning of
the troubles of this year, it contributed to embitter the rival
factions against one another.   Sulpicius had been on very
friendly terms with Q. Pompeius Rufus, the colleague of
Sulla in the consulship, but in this year they quarrelled and
became deadly enemies.   Plutarch, probably following Sulla's
Memoirs and the writers of that faction, represents Sulpicius
as a cruel, rapacious, and audacious villain : he says that " he
sold the Roman citizenship to libertini or men of the freedmen class and resident aliens, and publicly received the
money at a table in the Forum."   Though Plutarch may
have found this abuse in some of his authorities, it is a charge
which without further evidence ought not to be accepted.
Certainly many, probably most, of the libertini, were citizens
without paying for the privilege of a vote, and the aliens
who became citizens under the Julia Lex and the Plautia
Papiria would be numerous enough without increasing the
citizens by such a strange method as selling the franchise.
It is possible that Sulpicius did in some way contrive to bring
a great number of men to the ballot-box who were not
entitled to vote; and the transfer of the command against
Mithridates from Sulla to Marius is evidence of his unscrupulous character, for Marius was not fit to conduct such a war,
and Sulla, besides being entitled to the command as consul,
was the ablest general that Rome then had.   The early years
of Sulpicius gave promise of better things, as we know from

Cicero's testimony, and as we might infer from the character of the men with whom he had associated. But the possession of power showed the true temper of the man, and those who had formed great expectations of him did not know his real character, and we may add, that he did not know it himself, for who can say what he would do, if he were elevated to place and power? One of the measures of Sulpicius, as it is reported, is so absurd that we must suppose that Plutarch has misunderstood it. "He caused a law to be passed that no senator should contract debt to the amount of more than two thousand drachmae (Roman denarii), and yet at his death Sulpicius left behind him a debt of three millions." Here it is stated that this law was not only proposed, but carried; a law by which the popular assembly affected to regulate the Roman Senate. That would have been a revolution greater than any that Rome had seen. The absurdity of such a law, the absolute impossibility of executing it, will be apparent to any man who considers what the law is said to have forbidden, the evidence that would be necessary to procure a conviction, and what should be the constitution of the court that would give judgment in such a case. The very notion of conceiving such a law would prove Sulpicius to have been a fool; and we know he was not. He seems however to have been guilty of great inconsistency in his tribunate, for the same authority which states that he at first opposed the return of the exiles, affirms that he afterwards proposed a law for their restoration, and he attempted to justify his inconsistency by now saying that they were not exiles whom he proposed to recall, but persons who had been forcibly ejected from Rome: and yet the exiles whose return he had opposed and the men whom he afterwards proposed to recall were the same.

The ancient writers assign as the immediate cause of the civil war the rivalry of Marius and Sulla. Some modern writers are of a different opinion. The question is not very important to decide, for when a state is on the way to ruin, the end may come in various ways. Marius, now an old man, wished to have the command in the war against

Mithridates. He was mean and greedy, and though no
statesman, he was a clever intriguer. He is said to have
gained over Sulpicius by many promises, and he encouraged
the new Italian citizens to hope for a place in the old tribes,
instead of being registered in new tribes, where their votes
went for nothing. Marius did not let these people know
what his object was, for his intention was to use their votes
for his own ends. Plutarch's lively story in his life of
Marius says nothing of Sulla having obtained the command
in the Mithridatic war. He represents the contest for the
command as lying between Marius and Sulla; but this
cannot be true. The Senate, pursuant to a law of C. Gracchus, would name in B.C. 89 the consular provinces for the
year B.C. 88, and if they had determined on the war against
Mithridates at the time when the consular provinces were
named, we may safely affirm that the conduct of this war
would be one of the consular provinces. The consuls would
determine between themselves by lot or otherwise who should
lead the Romans against Mithridates, and Appian states that
Sulla got the command. It is possible however that early in
B.C. 88 it was not settled who should be sent out to oppose
Mithridates, and accordingly Plutarch represents Marius as
intriguing for the command, and the people as divided
between him and Sulla. The biographer's narrative is here
the more entertaining, and is a faithful picture of popular
canvassing. Some of the voters told Marius to go to the
warm baths of Baiae and look after his health, for Marius
had a sumptuous house at Misenum near Baiae furnished in
a style of luxury which was not creditable to an old soldier.
To show the electors of Rome that he was not past active
service, Marius went daily to the Campus Martius and took
his exercises on horseback with the young men, though he
was fat and heavy. The people came to look at the old
general, who was now near seventy years of age, and had
many infirmities: some admired his spirit, but the wiser
sort lamented his greediness and ambition, and they pitied
a man who having risen from poverty to enormous wealth
and to the highest station from a low degree, had not sense

enough to enjoy quietly what he had got, and wished now, at his advanced age, to set out to the east to oppose Mithridates and his skilful generals. Marius attempted to justify himself, but his excuse was ridiculous. He said that he only wished to serve in the campaign against Mithridates that he might teach his son the art of war.

With a view to securing the election of Marius to the command in the war against Mithridates, Sulpicius proposed a law for the distribution of the new citizens among the old tribes; for if this was done, Marius and Sulpicius expected that they could do what they liked, the new citizens being much more numerous than the old. The old voters were roused to hostility against the men, who, as they supposed, would overpower them at the ballot-box, and the two parties came to blows. They fought with sticks and stones, and the disturbance increased daily. In order to prevent the law of Sulpicius from being put to the vote the consuls proclaimed a "justitium," as the Romans termed it, a kind of holiday during which no public business could be done.

The new citizens, as Appian explains, had no power by their vote, because they were all classed in the new tribes, which voted after all the old tribes, and even did not vote at all, if the old tribes were unanimous, or if a sufficient number of them to constitute a majority of all the tribes had voted the same way. Sulpicius also proposed to allow the freedmen to vote in all the tribes, for as they had lately been allowed to serve in the army, they were well entitled to be placed on the same footing with the rest of the citizens. But the law of Sulpicius could not be enacted, if the old voters were against it, and the law could only be carried by fraud or force or intimidation, which the consuls feared. This fear implies that many of the Italians were in Rome, brought there by the promises and inducements of Marius and Sulpicius.

The suspension of public business deranged the plans of the tribune, but he was ready for the emergency. He had in his pay three thousand men armed with daggers; and he had formed for himself a kind of body-guard composed of six

hundred members of the Equestrian class, whom he named an
opposition senate. He summoned his partisans to come to the
Forum with their daggers concealed, which they were told to
use, if it should be necessary, even against the consuls. Sulpicius declared the "justitium" to be illegal, and he required
the consuls to put an end to it that the vote might be taken
on the law which he had proposed. There was a great
tumult, daggers were drawn and the consuls were threatened.
Pompeius escaped, but his son, who had married a daughter
of Sulla, was murdered. There was a story current that
Sulla fled to the house of Marius and thus avoided his pursuers who ran past, and that Marius let him out by another
door. Sulla in his own memoirs admitted that he did go to
the house of Marius, but not to seek protection : he went to
consult with Marius about the demand of Sulpicius, and
finally he returned to the forum and put an end to the "justitium." But he saw that he was no longer safe in Rome,
and he went to Capua, where the army was assembled which
he was going to take across the Hadriatic for the campaign
against Mithridates. Appian suggests that Sulla did not
suspect that the object of Sulpicius was to deprive him of the
command, but it is impossible that Sulla could be ignorant
of this design, if Plutarch's more circumstantial narrative is
true. He fled to Capua for his own safety and to secure the
fidelity of his soldiers. The law of Sulpicius about the tribes
was enacted, and then by another vote of the popular assembly the command against Mithridates was transferred to
Marius, or if we admit that it had not yet been conferred on
Sulla, it was now at least given to Sulla's intriguing rival,
which was the object of this coalition of Marius and Sulpicius.

Plutarch in his lives of Marius and Sulla has reported this
affair of Sulpicius with some variety. He says in his life of
Sulla that Sulpicius deprived Pompeius of the consulship,
which we know that he could not do legally, though it is
possible that he might affect to do it by a popular vote, as
Tiberius Gracchus had done in the case of his colleague
Octavius (vol. i., p. 185). But Sulla was not a man to sub-

mit to be cheated out of the great object of his ambition,
the command against Mithridates, which as consul he was
entitled to ; and he also knew that no man in Rome was so
fit for it as himself. He called together his soldiers who were
eager to go to the east, for they expected rich booty, and they
feared that if Marius had the command he would take other
troops. Sulla discoursed to his men of the treatment that he
had received from Marius and Sulpicius, for he did not venture to tell them his intentions, and bade them be ready to
obey orders. But the men knew what he intended, and they
called out for him to lead them to the city. A fact reported
by Plutarch, but omitted by Appian, is consistent with the
course of events. Two tribunes had been sent from Rome
to receive the army from Sulla, and both of them were murdered by the soldiers. This would be a lucky affair for Sulla,
and he could now trust his men.

Sulla marched on Rome with six legions, though he was
deserted by all his superior officers except one quaestor. The
rest either would not join in this act of military violence or
they were too timid. The Senate sent two of the praetors to
forbid Sulla to advance. These commissioners assumed a
bold countenance before Sulla, but they narrowly escaped
with their lives. The soldiers broke their fasces, stripped them
of their senatorian dress, and sent them back with insult.
They reported at Rome that the rising could not be checked
and was past all remedy. The commissioners had asked Sulla
why he was leading his army against Rome, to which question
he had a ready and a just answer: he was coming to release
Rome from her tyrants. This was the only answer that he
would give to a second and a third message. At last he said
that if the Senate would meet him and Marius and Sulpicius
in the Campus Martius, he would do whatever should be
determined after deliberation. But the proposal could hardly
be serious, for the Senate to meet in the open plain a man
who had six legions ready to do his bidding. As Sulla
approached the city, he was joined by his colleague Pompeius,
but Plutarch reports that Pompeius had gone to Sulla at
Nola. Appian's history is probably a faithful abridgment

of his authorities, but he omits those circumstances which give to Plutarch's narratives the lively colouring that has made him the most amusing of all biographical writers. There is no doubt that Plutarch made great use of Sulla's memoirs, and though Sulla may not have been always veracious, we may believe some things that he tells us. He had some hesitation about attacking Rome, for he feared the risk, which is just what we might expect in a man who combined great daring with great caution. But he was encouraged by a sacrifice and the declarations of the haruspex Postumius. Sulla had great faith in dreams, and he had a most favourable one. In his sleep he saw the goddess, whose worship had been brought to Rome from Cappadocia. "Sulla dreamed that the goddess stood by him and put a thunderbolt in his hand, and as she named each of his enemies, she bade him dart the bolt at them, which he did, and his enemies were struck to the ground and destroyed" (Plutarch). Sulla told the dream to his colleague, and at daybreak began his march to Rome. He left it recorded in his memoirs, that what he had resolved on without deliberation and on the spur of the moment turned out more successful than what he had well considered. But there was only one thing for him to do now; there was no choice—he must crush his enemies or be crushed by them.

Marius and Sulpicius were not prepared to resist, and they sent fresh commissioners in the name of the senate to request Sulla not to approach within five miles of Rome, until the senate had determined what they would do. This was a trick to gain time. The consuls promised that they would comply, but as soon as the commissioners were gone, they followed after. Sulla with one legion occupied the gate which Plutarch names the Caelian, perhaps the Caelimontana and the adjoining part of the wall. Pompeius with another legion seized the Colline gate on the north side of the city. A third legion occupied the wooden bridge over the Tiber, named Pons Sublicius. The site of this bridge is not certain, but the narrative of Appian might imply that it was not included within the walls, and the same conclusion has been derived from the story of the flight of C. Gracchus, as it is told by two Latin writers of no authority. A fourth legion was placed outside the walls as a reserve. With the two remaining legions Sulla entered Rome. The people pelted his soldiers with stones and tiles from the house-tops, and stopped the progress of the troops until Sulla threatened to burn the houses. Marius with Sulpicius and his partisans had hastily armed as many men as they could, and a fight was made about the market on the Esquilino. Sulla was at first repulsed, but he seized a standard, and advancing to the front rallied his troops. He then summoned his legion that was lying out of the city, and sent some of his men round by the quarter named Subura to attack the enemy in the rear. As the men of Marius were unable to resist these fresh assailants and were in danger of being surrounded, Marius attempted to collect together the citizens who were still pelting the invaders from the house-tops, and he summoned the slaves by a promise of freedom; but only three came, and finally Marius and his faction were driven out of the city. Sulla now advanced to the great street named the Via Sacra in the centre of Rome. Here some of the rabble or the soldiers were beginning to plunder, but Sulla promptly checked the pillage and punished the thieves. To secure the safety of the city he placed troops in different parts, and he and his colleague visited the posts during the night to prevent any disturbance either on the part of the citizens or their own men. At daybreak they called an assembly of the people, before which they spoke of the wretched condition of the commonwealth, which had long been in the hands of turbulent men, and protested that they had been compelled by necessity to do what they had done. This was the first time that a Roman army entered the city with a hostile purpose, and the first time that a consul commanded his troops within the walls. There were some men of the opposite faction whom it was necessary to get rid of, the tribune Sulpicius, Marius and his son, and a few more, about twelve in number. They had compelled the Senate to obey their orders, they had begun a civil war, they had been guilty of the unpardonable offence of attempting to

excite the slaves to rise, they were guilty of treason in its
worst form, and they deserved to die.   Whether, as Plutarch
says, the Senate was intimidated to become the instrument
of Sulla's vengeance, or he made use of the popular vote, as
Appian's words imply, is not material; but Sulla would be
too wise to do by his own authority what he could accomplish
under legal form.   If only a dozen ringleaders were declared outlaws, and so far as our evidence goes, no others
were punished, the moderation of Sulla or his prudence was
conspicuous.   If he acted without any direct authority from
the Senate, which in fact had lost its power, he did no more
than what as consul it was his duty to do, to protect the
State and crush an insurrection, as we do sometimes by pro-
claiming martial law, which means the will of him who for
the time wields the power of the sword.   The leaders of the
expelled faction were declared enemies to the State; any
man might kill them; and their property was confiscated.
Men can always be found to execute the will of those who are
in power.   His own slave betrayed Sulpicius to the pursuers,
who caught him in his country house near Laurentum and
put him to death.   Velleius alone affirms that the head of
Sulpicius was stuck up in front of the Rostra, "as an omen
of the coming proscription."   But this rhetorical phrase
gives us good reason for suspecting that the statement is
false.   The head of Sulpicius would be the best proof that
he was dead, but Sulla was not so foolish as to irritate
and disgust the Romans at a time when he wished to be
popular.   Sulla gave the slave his freedom, for this was
the promised reward of his treachery; but he gave more
than was promised, for he ordered the wretch to be pitched
down the Tarpeian rock.   The story that Sulla set a price
on the head of Marius is not credible, for under the general
terms of the declaration his life might be taken by any
man, and a reward would be given without being promised.
Marius fled to a farm which he had in the Solonium, a
district bordering on the road from Rome to Ostia.   He
sent his son to get some supplies from the estates of his
father-in-law, and himself went to Ostia where one of his

friends had provided a vessel in which he set sail with his
stepson Granius, as Plutarch names him, without waiting
for his son. The young man was surprised by the approach
of day while he was packing up what he wanted, and some
horsemen were in the neighbourhood suspecting that Marius
was there. The overseer of the farm, who had spied the approach of mounted men, put Marius in a waggon loaded with
beans, and yoking his oxen met them on his road to the city
with the waggon. He passed unmolested, and Marius was
thus conveyed to the house of his wife, where he got what he
wanted. By night he made his way to the coast, and embarking in a vessel bound for Africa he arrived there safe.

The consuls now set about restoring order. They proposed
the following changes, as Appian reports them : That for
the future no measure should be brought before the popular
assembly for their vote, unless it had received the approbation of the Senate. This was an old practice, but it had long
fallen into disuse. They also proposed that the votes should
not be taken in the Comitia Tributa, but in the Centuriata,
and according to the ordinance of King Servius Tullius.
They thought that by these two measures, by no law being
proposed to the popular assembly unless the Senate had
deliberated on it, and by the suffrages not being in the hands
of the poor and turbulent, but in the possession of the richer
and more prudent, all causes of revolutionary agitation would
be cut off. The theory of the Roman constitution allowed
the tribunes and the higher magistrates, consuls and praetors,
to propose any measure to the legislative assembly.   But
such a power was inconsistent with good legislation, for in
the popular assembly discussion and debate were impossible.
The Senate had practically long had the initiative in legislation, as we see by numerous instances in the history of Rome,
and if any attempt was made to carry a measure, which the
Senate had not approved, they had means at their command
for preventing it or declaring it null, as in the case of the
legislation of Drusus (p. 161). But since the commencement
of the revolutionary epoch, those who wished to effect constitutional changes, would attempt to destroy this power of

the Senate, of which we have an example in the Agrarian Law of Saturninus (p. 112), who compelled the Senate by oath to abide by his enactment. It was wise policy to declare that the Senate should deliberate upon an act of legislation before it was proposed to the people, who could only reject or accept it. Appian also reports that the tribunes were deprived of much of their power in other ways. He gives no explanation, but the tribunitian authority would be greatly limited by the necessity of obtaining the consent of the Senate before they could propose any measure to the people. By restoring the ordinance of King Servius Tullius, Sulla again gave the preponderance to those citizens, whose property entitled them to a place in the first class, which as it contained nearly half the votes would, according to the Roman system of voting, practically destroy the votes of the poorer sort. One advantage of this change would be a diminution in the number of votes, and a consequent improvement in the quality of them, for those who had some property would at least be the friends of order and the enemies of agitation and turbulence. Further, the Senate, which had been much diminished in numbers, and consequently in authority, was increased by the addition of three hundred men from the Optimates or aristocratical class. All that had been done on the motion of Sulpicius after the removal of the "justitium" was declared to be illegal and null. These measures were probably enacted in legal form, but the revolution of the following year undid the work of Sulla and his colleague.

A single imperfect notice in Festus is the only authority for a law respecting interest that was passed in this year (B.C. 88). It was entitled Unciaria Lex or a law on the uncial rate of interest, and we may suppose that it was enacted to settle the disputes which had terminated in the murder of the praetor Asellio. Nothing whatever is known of the provisions of this law. The Epitome of Livy also speaks of Sulla settling some colonies, but there is no notice of this fact in any other author. Sulla behaved with great moderation at this difficult crisis. He was going to leave Italy for the

war against Mithridates, and it was his interest to put the
power at Rome in the hands of his own party. He might
have named the consuls for the next year, for a man with
six legions under his command could have done what he
pleased. At this time Sulla had perhaps not conceived
the design of making himself master of the Roman State;
or, if we suppose that he had, he showed his good sense by
waiting for the better opportunity that he would have
when he returned from a successful campaign against the
great enemy of Rome. At the elections the voters rejected
Nonius, the son of Sulla's sister, and a man whom Plutarch
simply names Servius, probably Servius Cornelius, Sulla's
brother, who were candidates for offices, as Plutarch has
it; but the offices were evidently the consulship. He
further says that Sulla even aided L. Cornelius Cinna in
obtaining the consulship, though Cinna was of the other
faction, and that Sulla did this in order to recover some of
the popularity that he had lost since he entered the city with
his troops. However Cinna was bound by a solemn ceremony to be faithful to Sulla's policy. One man who cared
neither for promises nor oaths exacted them from another
whom no promise or oath could bind. In the presence of
many spectators Cinna ascended the Capitol with a stone in
his hand, he took the oath which Sulla required, and pray-
ing, that if he did not keep his promise he might be cast out
like the stone from his hand, he hurled it on the ground.

The colleague of Cinna was Cn. Octavius, who was of
Sulla's faction. The truth perhaps is that Sulla contrived
to secure the election of Octavius and could not prevent the
election of Cinna. Octavius was unknown as an orator
before his election, but during his office he made many good
speeches to the people. Cicero however does not enumerate
him among the great orators of Rome, and in his treatise
entitled Brutus he dismisses Octavius with a brief notice.
Octavius was feeble in body and in mind, weak and superstitious, but an honest man, and quite unable to maintain the
preponderance of his party.

The Social War was not ended with the defeat and death

of Pompaedius (p. 215). The Samnites and Lucani were still
in arms, and the siege of Nola continued. Sulla had sent his
soldiers back to Capua, and was exercising his functions as
consul in the regular way. The partisans of the exiles were
thus encouraged to agitate for their restoration, and they
were aided by many rich women. Neither money nor pains
were spared to further their intrigues, and designs were even
formed against the lives of the consuls. It was now near the
end of their year of office. Sulla, who was going against
Mithridates, would be safe with his army, but his colleague
Q. Pompeius Rufus could easily foresee what his fate would
be when Sulla was gone. Accordingly by a vote of the
people the command of the army in Italy was given to him
with proconsular authority for the year B.C. 87.

This army was with the proconsul Cn. Pompeius Strabo,
who was vexed at being deprived of the command, and he
was an ambitious and unscrupulous man. The consul Rufus
was received within the quarters of the army, and on the next
day when he was transacting some business Strabo retired,
being now a private person. The consul was addressing the
soldiers who were standing around, when some of the men
fell upon him and murdered him. Those who took no part
in the assassination fled from the spot, and Strabo immediately coming up made a display of great indignation at this
atrocious deed. But this was all that he did, and immediately he resumed the command. The general belief was
that he instigated his men to kill their new commander, and
this is the only conclusion that we can make from his
character and conduct. This was the first time that a Roman
consul fell by the hands of his own men. It was a sign that
the old Roman discipline no longer existed, and that anarchy
was approaching.

Sulla was still in Rome, when the news of the assassination
of his colleague came. He made no attempt to punish Strabo
or his men. He feared for his own life, and his friends kept
guard about him by day and by night. A tribune, named
Virginius, moved by Cinna, as it is said, was even threatening
him with a prosecution, for Sulla was now (B.C. 87) no longer

consul. He left Rome, joined his troops at Capua, got every
thing in readiness, and shipping his men at Brundisium took
them over to the opposite coast. He who in a few years returned victorious to Italy and trampled his enemies under
foot, fled for his life from his fellow-citizens. There is no
historian of this period who has attempted to explain the
motives of Sulla's conduct, when he had an army which was
devoted to him. Still we may see that he acted wisely and
like a patriotic citizen. The enemy was master of Greece,
and Italy might be attacked next. A civil war at home
would weaken the Romans, and Italy might again see a formidable foreign host wasting her lands. If Sulla could
defeat Mithridates and save Italy, he would be welcomed on
his return by his fellow-citizens. Of course he foresaw that
in his absence the opposite faction would prevail, and he knew
how they would use their victory; but their triumph would
only be for a time. He judged wisely both for the interests
of Rome and his own. He left the civil broils behind, and
deferred his vengeance to another day.

Sulla must have heard of the occupation of Asia by Mithridates before he sailed from Italy, and of his invasion of
Greece. If the king had not been opposed by the naval force
of the Rhodians, he might now have sent troops into the
south of Italy to join the few confederates who were still in
arms. Diodorus in his corrupted text states that the remaining confederate generals after Sulla had left Italy, and when
affairs were in a disturbed state at Rome, attempted to seize
Rhegium at the extremity of Italy, with the intention, if
they captured the town, of transporting their troops into
Sicily and securing this fertile island. If they had succeeded,
the Romans might have had another war on their hands in
a country from which they had derived great help in their
contest with the revolted Italians. But the praetor of Sicily
C. Norbanus got together a large force and made such
vigorous preparation that the invasion was not attempted, and
the last effort of the confederates ended in nothing.

CHAPTER XVIII.

C. MARIUS.

B.C. 88.

THE ship in which Marius embarked was carried southward along the coast of Italy. But tho wind changed and blew from the sea with a great swell, and tho storm became so violent that with difficulty the vessel was brought to shore at Circeii (Monte Circello). Marius had suffered from sickness, and the provisions were falling short. Accordingly he and his companions landed, and wandered about without any definite purpose. In this dreary country they met with a few herdsmen, who had nothing to give, but they knew Marius, and told him there were horsemen in those parts looking after him. He and his friends were suffering from want of food, but to save their lives they plunged into the forest, where they spent a wretched night. The next day hungry and desponding they continued their weary journey along the coast, encouraged by Marius whose hopes were sustained by an old prediction. When he was a boy he took an eagle's nest with seven young eagles in it; and the sooth-sayers predicted that he would attain the highest office seven times. Some people believed the story: others say that Marius told it to those who were with him, and that they believed what he said, though it was a fable, for an eagle has not more than two young ones at a time. However it was the universal belief that Marius in his greatest troubles clung to the hope that he should be consul the seventh time.

They were approaching Minturnae, a city of Campania on the Liris and near the coast, when they spied a troop of horse

riding towards them. Luckily two merchant vessels were
near the shore, and the fugitives swam to them. Granius got
into a vessel which carried him to the island of Aenaria
(Ischia). Marius was with difficulty kept above the water
by two slaves and placed in the other vessel, while the horsemen from the shore were calling out to the sailors to throw
him overboard. The men refused and set sail, but wishing
to get rid of their dangerous charge, they came to anchor at
the mouth of the Liris, where they advised Marius to land
and to take some rest till the wind should spring up. He was
carried to the shore and laid on the grass, not expecting what
happened, for the sailors immediately went back to their
ship and left him. In this low flat country there were no
paths, and Marius with difficulty made his way through the
swamp and ditches to the hut of an old man who lived in the
marshes. The lonely wanderer entreated this poor fellow to
save his life, and made great promises if he should escape
from his pressing dangers. The man, who either knew
Marius or suspected his rank, said that he could conceal him
from his enemies, and taking him into the marsh he hid him
in a hole near the river and covered him with reeds and
grass. The pursuers were soon on the spot, and began to
threaten the old man for concealing an enemy of the Romans.
As the noise reached Marius in his hiding-place, he stripped
off his clothes and threw himself into the water, but he was
seized by the pursuers and dragged naked and covered with
mud to the neighbouring town of Minturnae. Here he was
lodged in the house of a woman who treated him kindly,
while the magistrates were deliberating what they should
do, for instructions had been sent to the authorities of every
town to look for Marius and put him to death. Even in
this extremity a good omen was not wanting, and it came
from an ass. As Marius was approaching the woman's house,
an ass ran out to drink at a spring: he stood and looked the
Roman in the face boldly and briskly, and then with a loud
bray sprang past him frisking with joy. From this sign
Marius drew the conclusion that his safety would come from
the sea, for the ass turned from him to the water.

The magistrates after much deliberation determined that Marius must die, but as none of the citizens would do the deed, a Gaul or Cimbrian, probably a slave, was sent to kill him. The fellow with a sword entered the room where Marius was lying. The place was dark, and the eyes of Marius seemed to flash fire. Rising from his bed as the assassin approached he called out, "Man, do you dare to kill Caius Marius?" The terrified barbarian fled like a madman from the room crying out, "I cannot kill Caius Marius."

The magistrates now changed their mind. The terror of the Gaul caused general alarm, and there was compassion too for a man who had saved Italy from the barbarians. According-ing to one story they let him go, and sent him off to ramble where he pleased, and so he finally escaped. The other story, which seems more probable, is that they put him on board a vessel, which was supplied by one Belæus, who afterwards had a picture painted to represent the scene and dedicated it in the temple of Minturnae. However in some way Marius passed over to an island, which in Plutarch's narrative is Ischia, and there he found Granius and his friends. They all set sail for Africa, but on the voyage they put in at Eryx in the north-west angle of Sicily to get water. The Roman quaestor in that part was on the look-out, and he was near taking Marius when he landed. Marius continued his voyage to Africa, and reached the island Meninx, now Jerbah, which is in the smaller Syrtis and separated from the mainland by a narrow arm of the sea. In this fertile spot he would find supplies, and here he heard that his son and Cethegus another fugitive had escaped and were going to ask aid of Hiempsal, king of Numidia, who is supposed to have been a descendant of Massinissa. This news encouraged Marius to sail to the Roman province Africa, and he landed near Carthage. The governor, who is named Sextius or Sextilius, sent an officer to forbid Marius to set foot in the province, with a threat that he would be treated as an enemy, if he did not go away. Indignation choked the utterance of Marius, and he looked at the man steadily without saying a word, until he was asked what answer he made to the governor's order.

With a deep groan he replied, "Tell him you have seen Caius Marius a fugitive sitting on the ruins of Carthage." Here we probably detect the legendary element in those romantic adventures of the old Roman. His flight was a theme for declamation in the age of rhetoric under the Empire. Juvenal half satirist and half declaimer speaks of Marius'

> " Exile and prison, and Minturnæ's marsh,
> And bread at conquer'd Carthage meanly begg'd."

We may admit that Marius landed somewhere in the province Africa ; but to produce effect, it was necessary that the place should be Carthage, and the effect would be heightened if he sued for alms like a beggar on the ruins of a city once the rival of Rome.

The king of Numidia treated young Marius and his companions with respect, but he always found some pretext for not letting them go, which made them suspect his motives. At last they did escape and by the help of a woman, as we read of Christian captives in Algiers in former days owing their deliverance to some fair heathen. Young Marius was a handsome man. One of the king's concubines who had seen him felt pity for his wretched condition, and pity became love. At first Marius rejected the woman's proposals, but as he saw no other way of getting out of the king's power, he accepted her proffered favours, and by her assistance with his friends he escaped to his father. The story does not say whether young Marius carried off the woman. He certainly ought to have taken her with him. The father and son now embarked in a fishing-boat and passed over to the island Cercina, which was no great distance from the mainland. They had only just set sail, when some of the king's horsemen reached the place where they had embarked.

The island Cercina is one of the Kerkennah, two low islands, one much larger than the other, and opposite to Sfax on the east coast of Tunis. The soil is fertile and the surrounding sea abounds in fish.

There are two narratives of the adventures of Marius,

one by Appian and the other by Plutarch. Appian's story
agrees in the main with Plutarch's, but the narrative in
Plutarch is much more lively, and it is embellished with
circumstances, which in themselves are not improbable. The
fact of Plutarch mentioning the islands Jerbah and Kerkennah
appears to show that he found somewhere a long story of the
wanderings of Marius, which could only be derived from the
report of the general or his son and companions. Plutarch
in his life of Marius quotes an historian, C. Piso, who is
otherwise unknown, as authority for Marius conversing with
some of his friends a few days before his death, and talking
of all the incidents of his busy life from his boyhood, and
all the vicissitudes of his fortune. There would be no want
of stories about Marius both during his lifetime and after his
death ; and as it happens with all human events, truth and
falsehood would be mingled together. We may accept this
bit of history as true in the main, without troubling ourselves
about some inconsistencies in it.

As soon as Sulla had left Italy, the friends of the exiles
with the consul Cinna at their head began to agitate.
They encouraged the new citizens to claim what Marius had
promised them, a place in the old tribes. This led to a
quarrel between Cinna and Octavius, and was the immediate
cause of the restoration of Marius. It was said that Cinna
was gained over by a bribe of three hundred talents from the
Marian faction. Cinna's men assembled in the Forum with
daggers concealed, calling out for the enactment of the same
measure which the tribune Sulpicius had once carried. The
opposite faction, who were also armed, assembled about
Octavius, who was still in his house waiting to see what
would happen. When it was reported to Octavius that a
majority of the tribunes were opposing Cinna, and that the
new citizens with bare swords were climbing the rostra and
threatening the tribunes, he came down the Via Sacra with a
dense mass of his partisans, and falling furiously on his opponents dispersed them. The consul avoided Cinna, and made
his way to the temple of Castor and Pollux, either to secure
this strong position, or because the Senate may have been

there, for they often held their sittings in this place. Octavius was satisfied with dispersing the crowd, but his men were not. Without any command they fell on the opposite faction, killed many of them and pursued the rest to the gates of the city. Ten thousand men, according to Plutarch, perished on the side of Cinna, which is doubtless a great exaggeration.

Cinna seeing that his plans had failed summoned the slaves in the city to join him by promising them freedom, but as none came he left Rome, and visited the neighbouring cities, such as Tibur and Praeneste, to stir up his partisans and prepare for a fresh contest. Cinna was joined by some senators of his faction, among whom was Q. Sertorius, who had distinguished himself in the wars with the Cimbri and Teutones, and in Spain. Sertorius, who was a quaestor at the time when the Social War was breaking out, was appointed to raise troops and procure arms, a commission which he executed successfully, and he distinguished himself in the war, when he obtained a command, by his skill and courage. Sulla opposed Sertorius when he was a candidate for the tribuneship, and so Sertorius lost his election. He now joined Cinna : an honest man attached himself to the faction of a villain, for such things happen in civil wars. Cinna had begun a fresh revolution, he had attempted to rouse the slaves, and he had left the city after his designs had failed. The Senate responded to these illegal acts by another illegal act. They declared that Cinna was no longer consul, and L. Cornelius Merula, Flamen Dialis or priest of Jupiter, was elected in his stead. The Samnites or some of them were still in arms, and Appius Claudius was with a force at Capua. Cinna took the bold resolution of attempting to seduce the men of Claudius, having first gained over the officers and some of the senators who were on the spot. He came among the soldiers as a consul, but he laid down the fasces as if he were now a private man, and addressed the soldier citizens. He said that the senate had taken away what the people by their votes had given him, and they had done this without the consent of the people ; he grieved not for himself,

but for them; what would be the use of soliciting the votes
of the electors, and what would become of their power, if the
honours which they conferred should not be secure? Having
thus roused the angry passions of the men, he went on to
excite their sympathy, and finally he rent his clothes, and
leaping down from his elevated position, threw himself on the
ground, where he lay for some time. This piece of acting,
which among us would excite ridicule and contempt, had
effect among a people of a different temperament. The soldiers
raised him up, seated him again in his place, and elevating
the fasces bade him take heart, for he was still consul and
might lead them where he pleased. The tribunes followed the
example of the soldiers: they also took the usual military
oath to Cinna, and each officer tendered the oath to his men.
Cinna now felt himself secure, for the sanctity of an oath was
still respected by a Roman soldier. He visited many of the
cities of the Italian allies of Rome, where he could count on
support because he had suffered chiefly on their behalf. The
towns furnished men and supplies, and many of the powerful
Romans who were friends to the new revolution flocked to
Cinna. In the mean time Octavius and Merula fortified Rome.
They also sent for men to the cities which adhered to their
cause, and into Gallia Cisalpina. Cn. Pompeius, who had
the title of proconsul and the command of an army east of
the Apennines, was hastily summoned to protect the city.
His behaviour made it suspected that he was waiting to join
the successful side. If he had come to Rome earlier, his
services would have been more useful. When Pompeius did
bring his troops to Rome he encamped near the Colline gate,
being accompanied by his youthful son afterwards known as
Pompeius Magnus, who showed great presence of mind in
frustrating a conspiracy against his own life by a companion
and tent-mate, and in checking a mutiny of the soldiers who
hated his father. Cinna came up shortly after and made his
camp near the position of Pompeius.

The news of this revolution reached Marius in his exile,
and he determined to try his fortune in Italy. Probably he
was invited to return by Cinna, as Plutarch reports in his life

of Sertorius. Marius took with him some Moorish cavalry,
and a few Italians who had joined him in Africa. He landed
at Telamo (Telamone) on the coast of Etruria, between the
mouth of the river Umbro (Ombrone) and the Albinia (Al-
bogna), with about a thousand men. Here he was joined by
some of the exiles and by many slaves to whom by proclamation he offered their freedom, and also by freemen who were
employed as agriculturists and herdsmen in the maremme
or marsh lands of Tuscany; out of which materials he made
up a legion. The old general encouraged his adherents by
talking of his campaigns, his triumphs over the Cimbri and
his six consulships: he promised to make a settlement of this
long disputed question about enrolling the new citizens in the
old tribes. He sent to Cinna and proposed to join him, and
Cinna gladly accepted the offer, but not without opposition on
the part of Sertorius, who either thought that Cinna would
pay him less respect, if Marius were present, or because he
knew and feared the ferocious temper of Marius, and anticipated what would happen if he again entered Rome. It is
said indeed that Marius and Cinna with the chief men of
their faction consulted on the best way of securely establishing
themselves in power, and they came to the conclusion that
they must get rid of all the leaders of the opposite party, and
so they would be able to settle affairs just as they pleased,
when their opponents were destroyed.

When Marius had joined Cinna, they formed their plans.
Cinna with Cn. Papirius Carbo took up a position on the
Tiber opposite to Rome; Sertorius was on the river above the
city, and Marius below Rome towards the sea. Sertorius and
Marius barred the Tiber above and below Rome, and nothing
could be brought into the city by the river. With his ships
Marius attacked and plundered the corn vessels that were
coming to Rome, and thus furnished himself while he cut off
the supplies of the city. The port of Ostia at the mouth
of the Tiber was treacherously surrendered to him, and then
plundered. Marius now moved with his army to Rome and
seized the hill named Janiculus on the west side of the Tiber.
In the mean time Cinna sent a force to occupy Ariminum

(Rimini) on the Hadriatic that no help might come to the city from North Italy.

The consuls Octavius and Merula wanted more troops for the defence of the city. Q. Caecilius Metellus Pius had an army with which he was still continuing the war against the Samnites, and he received orders from the Senate to come to any honourable terms with the enemy, and then hasten to the relief of the city which was blockaded. The Samnites saw that their time was come to demand good terms, for they would know that Metellus was intending to withdraw his troops for the defence of Rome. They demanded that the Roman citizenship should be given to themselves and to all who had passed over to them; that they should keep all their booty, and that the Romans should surrender all the Samnite captives and all who had passed over to the Romans. In fact these were such terms as conquerors impose on the conquered. Metellus refused to grant the demands of the Samnites; but Marius or Cinna through the agency of Flavius Fimbria agreed to give them all that they asked. Thus through the quarrels of the Roman nobles the nation, which Rome had oppressed and humbled, became the instrument by which she was compelled to submit to a bloody tyrant.

At the beginning of the year three Roman armies under Claudius, Metellus, and A. Plotius were watching the Samnites. Cinna had carried off the troops of Claudius, and Metellus after the failure of his negotiation was recalled to defend the city. There now remained only the army of Plotius, who was attacked and defeated by the Samnites before they marched upon Rome. The siege of Nola appears to have been raised before Metellus left Campania, and the garrison advanced to the neighbouring town of Abella (Avella) and burnt it. Abella, we must assume, was in the Roman interest.

The treachery of a tribune named Appius Claudius let Marius into Rome. This man had the charge of the Janiculum, but being solicited by Marius, from whom he had once received favours, he opened the gate early in the morning

and let him in and Cinna also. This part of Appian's
narrative is not clear. Perhaps he means that the tribune
had the charge of the city gate nearest to the Janiculus, for
Marius and his partisans were in possession of all the country
on the west side of the Tiber. Octavius and Pompeius
hurried to meet their enemies, who after a fierce fight were
driven out of the city. Six thousand men fell on the side of
Octavius, and seven thousand of the opposite party. The
Janiculus might have been recovered at the same time, if
Pompeius had not persuaded Octavius to advance no further
and to recall Crassus from the pursuit. His object was to
prolong the war till the Comitia, when he expected to be
elected consul. Pompeius is charged with playing a double
part all through this civil contest. In this difficult crisis it
is reported that the Senate followed the policy of their
opponents and promised the Roman citizenship to all who
had submitted. The design of the Senate was to obtain aid.
They got plenty of promises, but only about sixteen cohorts.
The miseries of civil war were aggravated by famine and
pestilence. In the camp of Pompeius there died eleven
thousand men, and six thousand of those who were under
the command of Octavius. These numbers must be grossly
exaggerated, but we have the testimony of Velleius in addition to that of Licinianus and Orosius that there was
pestilence in the armies. A thunder-storm shortly after
broke out, and Pompeius, who was lying sick in bed, was
struck by the lightning. He lived only a few days. When
he was carried out for interment, the people who feared and
detested him while he was alive, pulled the body from the
bier and treated it with the utmost indignity. The soldiers
of Pompeius were transferred to the camp of Octavius.

Marius having cut off all supplies from Rome by sea and
also by the river above Rome, turned to the towns in the
neighbourhood where there were magazines of corn. He
surprised Antium, Lanuvium, and Aricia which was on the
Via Appia and the first stage out of the city. Other places
were treacherously surrendered to him. Marius now con-
fidently advanced against the city along the Via Appia, and

together with Cinna and the legati Carbo and Sertorius he took a position about twelve miles from Rome. Octavius, P. Licinius Crassus, and Q. Caecilius Metellus were at the foot of the Alban hills, looking out on the movements of the enemy. Octavius, it appears, had gone out of Rome and taken with him all the troops that were not necessary for the defence of the city. If there was pestilence in Rome, this alone would be a sufficient reason for withdrawing as many of the men as he could, and as no supplies could be brought into the city, it would be necessary to seek them outside. The Via Appia was in possession of the enemy, but the Via Latina would still be open, and some of the other roads between the Latina and the Tiber. So long as Rome held out and the Senate had an army outside the walls, there was still hope. The forces of Octavius were superior in numbers and discipline to those of Cinna and Marius, but Octavius would not trust the fortune of his party to a decisive battle, and herein he appears to have made a great mistake. Cinna sent criers about the city walls who promised freedom to all the slaves who would join him, and the slaves made their escape and came in great numbers. The Senate were alarmed, and there was danger also of a popular insurrection if the scarcity of provisions lasted much longer. Accordingly they sent to Cinna to see what terms he would grant. The commissioners were asked by Cinna a question which they might have anticipated: he wished to know whether they came to him as a consul or as a private person, and as they could not give him an answer, they returned to the city. Large numbers of the citizens now broke out of Rome and came to Cinna, some fearing starvation, and others, who had long been favourable to Cinna's faction, saw clearly what turn affairs were taking. Cinna was now emboldened to approach close to the walls, and encamp under them. Octavius still remained inactive, while Cinna was receiving additions to his force by deserters, and the Senate were negotiating. He would not follow the advice of his friends, who urged him to invite the slaves by a promise of freedom. Octavius was an honourable man, and wished to save his country without violating the law, but his conduct showed that he was not equal to the emergency. In fact he gave up the contest when he moved from his position and again entered the city by one of the gates that was not occupied by Cinna's troops. It is not certain whether it was after the return of Octavius to the city or while the army was still outside that many of the soldiers of Octavius came to Q. Caecilius Metellus Pius and urged him to take the command : they said that if they had a good general, they would fight with pleasure and win the victory. Metellus rebuked the men and told them to go back to the consul, upon which they passed over to the enemy. This defection appears to be the same event which Licinianus has described in a different way. Metellus had led his troops against Cinna, but when the armies were near one another, the men of Metellus saluted Cinna's men, who returned the greeting ; on which Metellus in alarm led his men back, and made a useless attempt to negotiate terms of peace with Cinna. Either then there was defection on the part of the Senate's troops, or their fidelity was suspected, and resistance was no longer possible. If these events happened before Octavius's return to the city, they will explain his conduct. All was lost, and Metellus in despair left Rome and went to Africa.

There were now three consuls, Octavius, Cinna, and Merula, who had been put in Cinna's place. The Senate would not deprive Merula of his office, for he had done nothing that could be blamed. Merula, who was an honest man, and had been made consul against his wish, addressed both the senate and the people, declaring that he would take the first step to reconciliation by laying down his office, and accordingly he abdicated. The Senate sent again to Cinna, and now they acknowledged him as consul. They expected little from him, and they only asked him to swear that he would shed no blood. Cinna would not swear, but he promised that he would not voluntarily be the cause of any man's death, and he advised that Octavius should get out of the way, for fear that he might suffer against Cinna's wish. Perhaps he really wished to save Octavius. Cinna returned this answer from his consular seat, while Marius stood by and said nothing ;

but his heavy brow and gloomy look showed that he was
bent on revenge. The Senate accepted Cinna's promise and
invited him and Marius to enter the city, for they knew that
Marius directed every thing and Cinna merely gave his assent.
Cinna entered, but Marius halted at the gates, saying with
an ironical smile that it was not lawful for exiles to come in.
The tribunes immediately removed this scruple by calling the
people together, who repealed the enactment by which Marius
and his partisans were banished in Sulla's consulship.

The narratives of Appian and Plutarch agree as to the
chief facts; but Appian had no other purpose than to tell a
story simply, while Plutarch as a biographer wished to
delineate character. It is therefore sometimes very difficult
to determine whether Plutarch added embellishment to the
plain facts or derived some of his more striking pictures from
memoirs, or finally retained some of those graphic touches
which Appian would purposely omit in his compilation.
However in this matter there is a material difference between
them, for Plutarch says that Marius himself summoned the
people to the Forum, which would be an irregular act, but
perfectly consistent with the man's arrogant temper. Only
three or four of the tribes had voted when Marius put an end
to the farce by entering Rome with a body-guard composed
of the slaves who had flocked to him, and the work of
plunder and murder began. Both Marius and Cinna had
sent to Octavius their promise confirmed by oath that he
should suffer no harm, and the soothsayers and diviners had
assured the superstitious consul that he was safe. His friends
judged better and advised him to fly, but Octavius said that
he was a consul and would not leave the city. However he
crossed the river to the Janiculus with some of the chief of
the nobility and some of the soldiers who still obeyed him.
Here he seated himself in his chair of office with all the
insignia of his rank upon and around him. Censorinus with
a body of horse was now approaching, and again his friends
and the soldiers urged him to fly and brought him a horse.
But the consul obstinately refused. He would not even rise
from his seat, and he resolutely waited for the assassins. He

died nobly like a Roman of the best times, an honourable man who did his duty faithfully at a time when men's tempers are tried in civil strife. If he had been less scrupulous, he might perhaps have saved Rome from the horrors that followed, and we learn from this example that the best men are not the fittest to command in troubled times. The head of Octavius was carried to Cinna, and placed in front of the Rostra in the Forum. This was the first time that a consul's bloody head was set up in public, but other heads were soon added to the ghastly spectacle, and the barbarous practice now begun was followed in the civil broils of Rome until the days of C. Caesar Octavianus.

Rome now suffered all the horrors of a city taken by storm. The armies of Marius and Cinna contained Samnites and Lucanians, men who remembered what their countrymen had endured from Rome in times past, and what they had suffered themselves in the Social War. There was also a large body of slaves, invited by the promise of freedom, and eager for plunder and blood. Cinna's appetite for slaughter was soon satisfied, but Marius thirsted for vengeance on all whom he hated or suspected. His rabble massacred those whom he pointed out: a nod was enough to determine their fate, and if Marius did not salute a man whom he met or return the salute, the man was cut down. The pursuers went forth into the roads and the towns near Rome, seeking for senators and men of the equestrian class. The Equites were murdered and left on the spot, but the heads of the senators were placed on the Rostra. Ties of hospitality and friendship proved no security to those who were hunted down, and fugitives were betrayed by those with whom they sought shelter. All regard for the gods, says the historian, all fear of retribution from men was gone. These savage murders were not done in secret. The assassins did their work mercilessly in the open light of day. If they found a man dead, they would sever the head from the body. Such sights would gratify the ferocious temper of some and strike terror into others. For five days and nights in succession the city was given up to robbers and murderers. Words make little

impression when we attempt to describe great calamities in
general terms. It is only the tale of individual suffering
that reaches our hearts and makes us feel for others. The
ancient writers have left on record some signal examples of
this kind.

The brothers C. Julius Caesar Strabo and L. Julius Caesar,
consul of the year B.C. 90, perished. Caius was betrayed by
a Tuscan friend. The heads of the two brothers were placed
side by side on the Rostra. P. Crassus, consul in B.C. 97,
the man who had visited the Cassiterides (p. 138), flying with
his oldest son was overtaken by the pursuers. The father
killed his son, and then, as Cicero says, died by his own
hand. Cornutus was saved by the fidelity and ready wit of
his slaves. He was hiding in a hut, when the men of blood
were looking for him. The slaves had got the body of some
obscure person, and laid it on a pile of wood, to which they
set fire when the pursuers approached. They said that it was
the body of their master who had strangled himself: the
men believed them and looked no farther.

Marcus Antonius fled to the house of a poor man, who
gave him shelter and protection. The man sent a slave to a
neighbouring wine-shop to buy wine for the use of Antonius;
and either because the slave was more careful than usual
about the quality of the wine, or as another version of the
story runs, came oftener than he used to do, the dealer was
curious to know the reason. The slave, who was a simple
sort of person and had long known the wine-dealer, whispered
in his ear that his master had Marcus Antonius concealed in
his house. The wine-dealer immediately hurried to Marius,
who happened to be at supper, and told him where Antonius
was. Marius was so pleased at the news that he sprung up
from table, and would have gone himself to the place, but his
friends stopped him, and he sent a tribune named Annius
with some soldiers to bring the head of Antonius. The
tribune waited at the door of the house while his men went
up-stairs, and entered the room where Antonius was concealed. When the soldiers saw Antonius, each man began
to urge his companions to the deed, which all of them were

unwilling to do. In this extremity so powerful was the eloquence of Antonius, when he pleaded for his life, that the soldiers could not look him in the face: they turned their eyes on the ground and wept. The tribune ran up-stairs to see what was the cause of the delay, when he found the men softened and awed by the eloquence of the great orator. He abused them for their faint-heartedness, and seizing Antonius, while he was still speaking, cut off his head and sent it to Marius.

Q. Ancharius, one of those who were marked for death, watched an opportunity when Marius was going to sacrifice on the Capitol. He thought that the sanctity of the place and the solemnity of the occasion might save his life. When the ceremony was beginning, Ancharius approached and saluted Marius, who replied by ordering those about him to kill the man. His head was fixed up in public with that of M. Antonius, and of others who had been consuls and generals. On the very Rostra, says Cicero, from which in his consulship Antonius had steadily defended the public interest, which in his censorship he had adorned with the spoils that he gained as commander of the Roman forces against the pirates, that head was placed which had saved the lives and fortunes of so many Romans. No man was allowed to inter the bodies of those who were murdered. Headless trunks were pitched into the streets, trampled under foot, and devoured by birds and dogs. The men of opposite factions murdered one another, and no one inquired or cared about it. Others were driven from their houses, stripped of their property, and deprived of their offices. All the laws that had been enacted in Sulla's consulship were repealed, and all his friends who could be caught were put to death. Sulla's house was pulled down, his property was confiscated, and he was declared an enemy to the state. His wife Metella only saved herself and her children by flight.

After so much blood had been shed, there was a show of things returning to the regular form of administration; but it was only a show. A charge was made against Merula the priest of Jupiter and once consul. His offence was that he

had allowed himself to be elected in the place of Cinna.
Appian also speaks of some charge being made against
Q. Lutatius Catulus, but he does not say what it was.
Catulus had been the colleague of Marius in the Cimbrian
war (B.C. 102), and owed his safety to him, and yet he was,
says Appian, ungrateful and had been very active in driving
Marius into exile. A notice of trial at this time was a farce.
Neither Merula nor Catulus was tried. Merula opened his
veins and letting the blood flow on the altars, where he had
often prayed to the gods for the safety of the State, he called
down curses on the heads of Cinna and his faction, and so he
bled to death. He left a small writing-tablet near his body,
in which he declared that when he was opening his veins he
had taken off the apex or official cap, for it was not lawful
for the flamen of Jupiter to die with it on his head: so
careful was this honest man to observe all the ceremonial,
absurd as it may seem to us, which his sacred office required.
No person was appointed to fill Merula's place, and the office
of Flamen Dialis remained vacant for more than seventy
years.   The friends of Catulus interceded for him with
Marius, but the only answer was " he must die;" and Catulus
did die by his own act instead of waiting for the assassin.
He shut himself up in a new plastered room, and lighting a
fire of charcoal he was suffocated by the vapours.

Cinna and Marius had put to death or driven out of Rome
all their enemies, but they found a fresh enemy of their own
making. The slaves who had flocked to them on the promise
of freedom were now free and armed; but they abused their
freedom by breaking into houses to plunder and kill. Some
of them directed their attacks against their old masters,
defiled their children and violated their wives. Plutarch
twice calls these men Bardiaei, which may be a form of
Ardiaei or Vardaei, the name of a people on the east coast of
the Hadriatic (vol. i., p. 111); and we may conjecture that
these men had been brought to Italy as slaves. Cinna made
frequent attempts to check the villains, but they would not
listen to him. At last he and Sertorius, or Sertorius alone,
for the story is told both ways, surrounded them with a body

of Gauls by night when they were asleep and destroyed them
to a man. The number was four thousand. Orosius found
a story rather different. The liberated slaves were insatiable
in their appetite for plunder, and they would not give the
consuls a share of it. Being invited into the Forum on
pretence of receiving their pay, they came unarmed and were
surrounded by the soldiers and massacred to the number of
eight thousand. The fact is certain that the revolutionary
faction after using the slaves for their own purpose got rid of
them by a general massacre.

After the murder of the consul Octavius B.C. 87 no consul
was elected in his place. Marius perhaps exercised consular
authority, about which he would have no scruples, especially
if it is true, as Livy's Epitome reports, that he and Cinna
declared themselves consuls for B.C. 86 without the form
of an election. On the first of January B.C. 86 Marius
entered on his seventh consulship, and thus the omen of the
seven young eagles, was accomplished. On this same day he
ordered Sextus Licinius, a senator, to be thrown down the
Tarpeian rock.

There were reports at this time, as Plutarch says, that
Sulla had finished the war against Mithridates and was
coming against Rome. He had indeed gained some advantages in Greece, and was besieging Athens and the Piraeus,
but his return was delayed for several years. Marius was
terrified at the prospect of a new contest with his mortal
enemy, and his spirit was broken by age and all the trouble
that he had endured. His mind was disturbed, sleep left
him, and as he dreaded wakeful nights he gave himself up to
intoxication. The traveller and philosopher Posidonius, who
was on a mission from the Rhodians to Rome, says that he
had an interview with Marius in his last illness, and talked
with him on the subject of his embassy. In his restless state
of mind Marius was seized with a kind of pleurisy, as Posidonius states, and this was the immediate cause of his death.
The historian C. Piso, already mentioned, reports that after
a conversation of Marius with his friends on the vicissitudes
of his life, he said that no man of sense ought to trust fortune

after such reverses, upon which he took leave of his friends, and keeping to his bed for seven days he died.   There is no inconsistency in the two narratives.   Both may be true. There was also a third report, that he died by his own hand. It was said that in his illness he became delirious: he thought that he was conducting the war against Mithridates, and he would then put his body into all kinds of movements and attitudes as in battle, and shout out loud as if he were cheering his men.   His ruling passion was strong even in death. He died on the seventeenth day of January B.C. 86, according to Plutarch, or, as Livy's Epitome has it, four days earlier. There was great rejoicing at Rome, and men hoped that the death of the tyrant would release them from tyranny, but they were disappointed.

CHAPTER XIX.

DOMESTIC EVENTS.

B.C. 80.

L. VALERIUS FLACCUS, a man hitherto unknown, was elected consul in the place of C. Marius. The only act of his consulship that is recorded is an enactment by which he relieved debtors at the cost of creditors. This Lex Valeria declared that a debtor might satisfy a creditor by a payment of one-fourth of his debt; a most disgraceful act, says Velloius, for which within two years Flaccus met with well-deserved punishment. But in these troubled times it could not be expected that accounts between debtor and creditor could be settled as in peaceful days. Property would be depreciated, money scarce, and provisions dear. Many persons had lost their slaves, and the ordinary course of industry was interrupted. The law of Flaccus was a general act for the relief of insolvents, and if the creditor got five shillings in the pound, that is a good deal more than our creditors sometimes got from bankrupt or insolvent debtors. The fault of the law of Flaccus was that it relieved a debtor whether he was solvent or not, if we are rightly informed about it, and in this respect it would resemble an enactment by which in our own days a borrower might pay his creditor in depreciated paper money instead of paying in money of the same value as that which he received.

To this year also probably belongs the restoration of the denarius, the principal Roman silver coin, to its standard weight, which was effected by M. Marius Gratidianus. This man's history is connected with that of Cicero's family.

M. Gratidius of Arpinum had a sister Gratidia, who married M. Tullius Cicero of Arpinum, the grandfather of the orator M. Tullius Cicero. Gratidius proposed a Lex tabellaria or a law for voting by ballot at Arpinum, which was opposed by his brother-in-law Cicero. Gratidius also prosecuted at Rome on a charge of malversation (Repetundae) C. Flavius Fimbria, who was consul with C. Marius in B.C. 104. It is uncertain at what time this prosecution took place, but it was before Fimbria was consul, for Gratidius was under M. Antonius in Cilicia in B.C. 103, where he was killed. This M. Marius Gratidianus was the son of M. Gratidius, and he was adopted by M. Marius, a member of the family of C. Marius, and as some suppose his brother. If this is so, M. Marius Gratidianus would be the nephew of C. Marius, who was seven times consul. Gratidianus is the man whose case M. Antonius defended (p. 93) against Orata. Asconius reports that he was a very popular man and twice praetor. It is supposed, but it does not appear quite certain, that Gratidianus was praetor in this year B.C. 86. Cicero tells us not very clearly that an Edictum or order was drawn up about the coinage (res nummaria) by the tribunes in conjunction with the praetors; but Gratidianus who hunted after popularity anticipated his colleagues and announced the measure himself from the Rostra, as if it was his own. Accordingly an enactment was made on the matter, and Gratidianus had the pleasure of seeing statues erected to him by the grateful people in all the quarters of the city. The pound of silver, says Pliny, ought to be coined into eighty-four denarii, but at this time there had been falsification at the mint, and the measure of Gratidianus appears to have consisted in restoring the true weight of the denarius, and introducing some test for proving it. The matter is imperfectly made out by the fragmentary notices which remain, but we may infer that the silver coinage had been depreciated during the troubles of the last few years.

Cnaeus Pompeius, the son of Strabo, succeeded a father who was universally detested, but he would probably have had no trouble on this account, if Strabo the father had not been an opponent of the Marian faction. The father was guilty of peculation when he captured Asculum (B.C. 89), and we must conclude from proceedings being instituted against the son, that the father's property was liable in the son's hands. Peculatus (peculation) was the misappropriation of public money, and there were special enactments about this offence at a later time, but there is no evidence that any existed in the year B.C. 86. However there was a form of trial for this offence, and in the present instance it was in fact a proceeding on the part of the State as creditor against the goods of Strabo. Pompeius was defended by L. Marcius Philippus, who said on the occasion that it was nothing strange if Philippus loved Alexander, by which words he alluded to the supposed resemblance of young Pompeius to Alexander the Great, for some of the Romans who liked him as much as they hated the father gave him this name. The orator Hortensius, and Cn. Papirius Carbo also spoke for Pompeius. It is reported that Pompeius in the preliminary proceedings showed such acuteness and firmness that the praetor Antistius, who presided at the trial, conceived a great affection for him and offered him his daughter Antistia to wife. Pompeius accepted the proposal and an agreement was made between them, the acquittal of Pompeius probably being the condition of his marriage. If Antistius was looking out for a husband for his daughter, he showed that he was a man of business by selecting a handsome young man, with a large fortune, who had already given promise of great talent and a distinguished career. However it is said that Pompeius had a good defence. He proved that most of the property which his father was charged with taking had been appropriated by one of his freedmen. Young Pompeius himself was charged with having in his possession some hunting-nets and books, which his father gave him out of the plunder of Asculum. The prosecutor must have been at loss for evidence to support his charge, if he relied on such small matters as these. However Pompeius denied that these things were in his possession, for Cinna's men had broken into his house in Rome and plundered it. The verdict was in favour of Pompeius, who was greatly indebted to Carbo on this occasion. We shall see afterwards what return Pompeius made.

The faction of Marius had the power at Rome, but they had two enemies abroad, Mithridates and Sulla, and they feared Sulla most. Sulla had now taken Athens and defeated Archelaus, the general of Mithridates in Greece; he had a veteran army which was attached to him, and he had the wrongs to avenge which the opposite faction had inflicted on himself and his family. It was necessary therefore to get rid of this formidable enemy, who might at any time return to Italy. Accordingly the faction at home sent the consul Flaccus over the sea from Brundisium with two legions to supersede Sulla and take the command in the war against Mithridates. They sent against Rome's best general a man of no talent, and no experience in war. He was accompanied however by C. Flavius Fimbria, who had some pretensions to military skill, but was one of the greatest villains in Rome. He was one of the most active and unrelenting among those who sought out the partisans of Sulla in the massacres which followed the return of Marius; and he is accused of having made an attempt on the life of Q. Mucius Scaevola at the funeral of Marius. This man was not the consul of B.C. 104.

In this year (B.C. 86) L. Marcius Philippus and M. Perperna were censors, and they held a lustrum. One authority gives the number of citizens who were registered as 463,000. Perperna attained the age of ninety-eight and died in B.C. 49. Thus the life of one man comprehended all the period from the destruction of Carthage to the invasion of Italy by C. Julius Caesar.

In the beginning of the eightieth epitome of Livy it is said that "the Roman citizenship was given to the Italians by the Senate;" and the next event recorded in the epitome is the union of the Samnite troops with those of Cinna and Marius, and the defeat of Plotius (p. 240). This passage about the citizenship is difficult to explain. We know that it had already been offered to the Italians and accepted by some, but that the new citizens were dissatisfied at not being

placed in the old tribes. If the effect of this senatus consultum was to give them what they wished, it is not easy to see
why the demand of the Samnites made to Metellus was refused, for though it contained other claims besides the
citizenship, there was reason enough in the circumstances for
granting the Samnites any thing that they asked, if they
would only aid the Senate against Marius and Cinna. If
this passage of the Epitome contains a truth, it may be that
the senate made a last appeal to the insurgents and promised
the citizenship to all who were still in arms. That something
was done this year (B.C. 87) about the Italians and the franchise appears probable from a census being held in the next
year by Philippus and Perperna.

CHAPTER XX.

MITHRIDATES VI. EUPATOR, KING OF PONTUS.

MITHRIDATES EUPATOR[1], says Strabo, possessed the country bounded (on the west) by the river Halys and extending eastward to the Tibareni and the Armenians; also the country west of the Halys as far as the town of Amastris, and some parts of Paphlagonia. He also acquired on the west side the coast as far as Heracleia, and on the east side as far as Colchis and the Less Armenia, which he united to the kingdom of Pontus. These were the limits of the kingdom of Pontus in Asia Minor when Cn. Pompeius took possession of it after the death of Mithridates. The kingdom may accordingly be described as occupying the south coast of the Black Sea nearly as far west as the river Sangarius. The boundaries on the south were formed by Galatia and Cappadocia. Within the limits fixed by Strabo were the towns of Trapezus (Trebisond), Amasia the birthplace of Strabo, Sinope, and Amastris. A large part of this country is mountainous, but it contained many fertile plains near the sea, which produced grain, oil, and various fruits. The mountains supplied ship timber. Iron was worked in the

---

[1] The name on coins is Mithradates, and this form sometimes occurs in the MSS. The more usual form in the ancient writers is Mithridates. It is supposed that the first part of the name contains Mithra or Mitra, the Persian word for the sun, and a termination "dates," which corresponds to the Greek termination dotes in such words as Diodotus and others of like form.

country of the Chalybes; and in the neighbourhood of Oenoe
(Unieh) on the coast there are still some people who make
iron from the ore which they find in the hills. Here we
have an example of a native industry that has existed for
centuries before the Christian era to the present day. This
name Pontus first occurs in a passage of Xenophon. Pontus
was in fact a part of Cappadocia. When the Macedonians
took Cappadocia from the Persians, they found it divided into
two satrapies, which partly with their consent, and partly
against it (the expression is Strabo's) were changed from
satrapies to kingdoms, one of which was simply named
Cappadocia, also Cappadocia bordering on the Taurus, and
sometimes Great Cappadocia; the other was called Pontus or
Cappadocia on the Pontus. The Pontus was the sea which
the Greeks called Pontus Euxinus, now the Black Sea. It
was a tradition that the remote ancestor of the dynasty of
the kings of Pontus was one of the seven Persians who over-
threw the power of the Magi B.C. 521. But though Pontus
was a satrapy under the Persian kings, we cannot admit
without evidence that it was an hereditary satrapy from the
time of Darius the First until it became a kingdom. Polybius,
the best authority that we have on this matter, states that
Mithridates, king of Pontus, the fourth of the name, professed
to be a descendant of one of the seven Persians who destroyed
the usurping Magus; and, he adds as his own remark, that
Mithridates had maintained the possession transmitted from
his ancestors, which was originally given to them by
Darius.

Clinton's list of the kings of Pontus begins with Ariobarzanes I., of whom we know nothing. The real founder of
the kingdom of Pontus was Mithridates II., as he stands in
Clinton's list. He was named Ctistes or the "founder" of
the dynasty, and is properly Mithridates the First. Appian
makes Mithridates VI. or Eupator the eighth in descent from .
Ctistes, and the sixteenth from Darius, the son of Hystaspes,
but he would have had some difficulty in tracing the pedigree
from Darius. This Mithridates Ctistes was at one time with
Antigonus, one of Alexander's successors, in what capacity

wo know not; but Antigonus having had a dream, which
portended the future power of Mithridates, attempted to
assassinate him. Mithridates escaped and fortified a strong
place in Cappadocia, where he was joined by many adventurers during the troublesome times when Alexander's successors were quarrelling among themselves. He got possession
of Cappadocia and the parts adjoining on the coast of the
Euxine, and founded a kingdom which he transmitted to his
descendants. Mithridates was assassinated in B.C. 302, and
succeeded by a son Mithridates III., who died in B.C. 266.
The successor of Mithridates III. was Ariobarzanes the Third,
as he is named, but he ought to be called Ariobarzanes I.,
for the two other kings named Ariobarzanes I. and II. preceded Mithridates Ctistes, and ought not to be enumerated
among the kings of Pontus. This Ariobarzanes got possession of the city of Amastris (Amasserah) on the coast of the
Black Sea and west of Sinope. He died about B.C. 240 as
some have conjectured, but the date of his death may be
earlier, and was succeeded by Mithridates IV., as he is
named. This Mithridates married a sister of Seleucus Calli-
nicus king of Syria, and he gave one of his daughters,
Laodice, in marriage to Antiochus III. the son of Seleucus.
Thus the kings of Pontus, who were said to be of Persian
stock, became by intermarriage mingled with princes of the
Greek race. Mithridates made an attempt to gain the important town of Sinope. The time of his death is uncertain,
but it is fixed by conjecture about B.C. 190. Pharnaces I.,
the successor of Mithridates IV., besieged and took Sinope
(Sinab) a Milesian colony, well situated on the coast of the
Euxine, and the most flourishing Greek settlement within
that sea. Mithridates V. Euergetes, the son of Pharnaces I.,
succeeded his father. The year of his accession is unknown,
but it was before B.C. 154, as appears from a passage of
Polybius. He formed some alliance with the Romans and
probably received the title of "friend," which the Republic
sometimes deigned to bestow on a prince whom they expected
to be useful to them. During the third Punic war (B.C.
149—146) Mithridates sent the Romans some ships and a

small force to aid them against the Carthaginians.   His services in the war of the Romans against Aristonicus (B.C.
131) have been already mentioned (vol. i., pp. 206, 212), and
he was rewarded with the province of Phrygia.   This king
was assassinated probably about B.C. 120 by his friends, as
they were named, but in fact by enemies at Sinope.   His wife
and several children survived him.

Mithridates VI., named Dionysus and Eupator, was eleven
years old when his father was murdered.   He was born and
passed his early years at Sinope, where he became acquainted
with the literature as well as the language of the Greeks, for
he was himself half Greek.   He was fond of music, and had
so great a capacity for learning languages that he mastered
the tongues of more than twenty nations whom in his long
reign he reduced under his dominion.   On his father's death
it is said that his guardians tried to get rid of him by compelling him to ride on a wild horse and to throw the javelin
from it, but as he managed the horse better than boys of his
age, his guardians tried to take him off by poison.   The
youth however was more than a match for his assassins: he
fortified his body by using antidotes, which had such an effect
that when he was an old man, no poison would kill him.
This is the romantic story of Justinus, which is unworthy of
credit; but still it may be true that the young king had
enemies, and that by the precocious vigour of his understanding and resolution he saved himself from their designs.
Justinus further says that in order to protect himself against
these domestic traitors, he gave himself up to hunting and
for seven years never came under the roof of a house: he
wandered about the forests and the mountains, where he
learned to avoid or pursue wild beasts, and to fight with
them.   It is possible that the young king was for some years
after his father's death a wanderer, and that he was formed in
adversity for the great part which he afterwards played.
Few men have equalled Mithridates in strength, activity, and
endurance.   He had talent too, but it was the talent of a
barbarian, not of a wise administrator.   He was cruel, sensual and vindictive, greedy and audacious; but events will

show that his abilities were not equal to his daring and his
ambition.

The historian Memnon reports that Mithridates was thirteen when he succeeded to the throne, and that not long
afterwards he imprisoned his mother, who had been appointed
by his father to share the royal power. Perhaps the mother
was only the guardian, and the youth was impatient of a
woman's authority. The queen died in prison, and her son,
a brother of Mithridates, was also put to death. The chronology of the early part of the reign of Mithridates is unknown, but he began his active career when he was very
young, and continued it as long as he lived. His chief city
was Sinope, the acquisition of which by the kings of Pontus
gave them a fleet, which enabled Mithridates to extend his
conquests to the north shores of the Black Sea. The narrative
of Appian fixes the acquisitions of Mithridates to the east
and to the north in the early part of his reign, before his
contest with the Romans. He conquered the Colchi and
even carried his victorious arms beyond the Caucasus, as
some authorities state. It is certain at least that he got a
footing in the Crimea and in the countries on the north shore
of the Euxine. Paerisades, the last king of Bosporus of his
dynasty, being hard pressed by his barbarian neighbours, applied for help to Mithridates, who sent a force to the Crimea
under two Greeks named Neoptolemus and Diophantus. The
Roxolani, a warlike people, occupied the steppes between
the Tanais (Don) and Borysthenes (Dnieper). They had
helmets and jackets of ox-hide, shields made of osiers; and
for offensive weapons, spears, swords, and arrows. They wore
a nomadic people. Waggons covered with skins were their
moveable homes. Their wealth was cattle, which supplied
them with milk, cheese, and flesh. They went from place to
place in search of pasture for their beasts: they passed the
winter in the marshy parts along the Maeotis or sea of Azof,
and the summer in the wide, treeless plains of the interior.
These were the men who threatened the feeble settlements of
the Greeks on the north side of the Euxine, and were met by
the troops of the king of Pontus. The result showed the

weakness of brave men when opposed to disciplined soldiers with superior arms. Six thousand men under Diophantus defeated nearly fifty thousand Roxolani, the greater part of whom were slaughtered. The generals of Mithridates either now or some time after led their troops beyond the Borysthenes, westward to the Hypanis (Boug) and the Tyras (Dniester). Near the mouth of the Hypanis was the Greek settlement of Olbia, which probably became dependent on the kingdom of Pontus. A tower near the mouth of the Tyras, named the tower of Neoptolemus, may be evidence that the general came so far, and that this tower was built as a fort to protect the entrance of the river or for a look-out. At the mouth of the Tyras there was a village Hermonax, and fourteen or fifteen miles higher up the river two towns, Niconia and Ophiusa, both of which, as the names show, were Greek settlements. It seems that there was a third town lower down named Tyras, if we admit that the Milesian colony Tyras is different from Ophiusa. The Greeks originally planted themselves here for the fisheries in the river and for trade with the barbarians. Mithridates finally obtained possession of the little kingdom of Bosporus in the Crimea or Tauric Chersonesus by the cession of Pacrisades, and he formed some kind of alliance or connexion with the native tribes that lived north of the Euxine. His acquisitions in these parts would furnish him with useful supplies in his wars with the Romans, for the kingdom of Bosporus exported corn, skins, and salt fish in abundance.

Ariarathes VI. king of Cappadocia had married a sister of Mithridates VI. king of Pontus. The death of Ariarathes VI., the murder of his son Ariarathes VII. by Mithridates, and the revolutions which ended in the final establishment of Ariobarzanes I. as king of Cappadocia by Sulla B.C. 92, have been already told (p. 141). Mithridates submitted to the imperious commands of Sulla, but he waited for his opportunity. It may have been after the return of Sulla to Rome, though it is impossible to fix the time, that he left home with a few friends and in disguise visited the Roman province of Asia, and made himself acquainted with the

position of all the cities. He visited also the neighbouring
kingdom of Bithynia, which he coveted. It was supposed at
home that Mithridates had perished in his daring enterprise,
but he came back at last and found that in his absence his
sister Laodice, who was also his wife, had borne him a son.
Amidst the rejoicings on his return Mithridates narrowly
escaped assassination. Laodice believing that her husband
was dead sought for lovers among her friends, and to prevent
her infidelity from being discovered, she designed to poison
her husband. A female slave informed the king of his wife's
treachery, and she received the punishment that she deserved.
We have only the authority of Justinus for this romantic incident in the life of Mithridates, and though it may be easy
to raise objections to the story, we cannot judge the acts of
the king of Pontus by the rules applicable to common men.

Nicomedes II. king of Bithynia died probably in B.C. 91
at a great age. About ten years before, upon the death of
Pylaemenes, king of Paphlagonia, a country on the Pontus
between Bithynia and Pontus, Mithridates VI. and Nicomedes
seized Paphlagonia and divided it between them. The
Roman senate however commanded the two kings to give up
their conquest and restore Paphlagonia to its former condition.
Mithridates refused. He said that the kingdom of Paphlagonia belonged to him in right of his father, to whom the last
king had bequeathed it. Nicomedes promised to restore his
own part to the rightful king. However he gave it to his
own son after changing his name to Pylaemenes, which was
the name of the kings of Paphlagonia. Nicomedes II. was
succeeded by his son Nicomedes III. Philopator, against
whom Mithridates sent an army under the command of
Socrates, surnamed Chrestus or the good, a younger brother
of Nicomedes. Socrates expelled Nicomedes, and took possession of the kingdom of Bithynia (B.C. 90). At the same
time Mithridates drove out of Cappadocia Ariobarzanes I.,
whom the Romans had restored in B.C. 92. Both the kings
applied to the Romans, who were at this time engaged in the
Social War, and could spare no troops for a campaign in Asia.
However, the Senate declared that the kings must be restored,

and they sent to Asia for this purpose certain commissioners, at the head of whom was Manius Aquillius, the man who had put an end to the slave war in Sicily.   L. Cassius, the governor of the province Asia, who had only a small force, was ordered to assist in restoring the kings, and Appian states that Mithridates himself was commanded to co-operate with the Roman troops. The king did not comply, but he made no opposition. Perhaps he did not yet think the opportunity favourable for beginning that contest with Rome, for which he had long been making preparation. Cassius and Aquillius taking the forces which were in the province Asia, and adding to them a large number of Galatæ or Gauls of Galatia, and Phrygians, set the two kings again on their thrones. Socrates was put to death by Mithridates himself, to please the Romans, as he said. But those greedy Romans went beyond their commission. They urged Nicomedes and Ariobarzanes to invade the territory of Mithridates and promised them help from Rome, though they knew that it would not come. The kings were unwilling to attack so formidable an enemy, but the commissioners insisted, and Nicomedes at last unwillingly consented.   He had promised large sums of money to the commissioners and the Roman commanders for his restoration, and the money was still unpaid.   He had also borrowed largely from the Roman capitalists who followed the army to make profit out of the king's necessities. Dunned by his creditors and driven by the commissioners, he plundered the possessions of Mithridates as far as the city Amastris without meeting any resistance. The king of Pontus had an army ready, but he retired before the invader. Appian suggests that he wished to have fair grounds for making war on the Romans, and so he allowed Nicomedes to plunder his country; but justice was not a thing that a man like Mithridates would care for. He either could not check the invasion, or he thought it better to wait till he could strike a decisive blow.

When Nicomedes had retired with his booty, Mithridates sent his general Pelopidas to the Roman commissioners. He knew that the invasion was their work, but he dissembled.

Pelopidas reminded the Romans of the friendship between
them and the king, and even the king's father; and what had
the Romans done in return for the services of the kings of
Pontus? They had taken from Mithridates both Phrygia
and Cappadocia, though Cappadocia had always belonged to
his ancestors, and had been recovered by his father. Phrygia
had been given as a reward for the help of Mithridates V.
in the war against Aristonicus (vol. i., p. 212); and the
same general Aquillius who gave Phrygia had been well
paid for it by the king of Pontus. Pelopidas concluded with
reminding the commissioners that Mithridates had the title
of friend and ally of the Romans, and he called on his
friends and allies to aid him, or to stop the aggression of
Nicomedes.

Ambassadors from Nicomedes were present at this interview between Pelopidas and the Romans. The answer which
they made to the complaints of Pelopidas has no historical
value, but it is of some use as serving to explain the position
and means of Mithridates. They said that Mithridates had
stirred up Socrates to expel his brother the king of Bithynia,
who was under the protection of Rome, and that this was in
fact an attack on the Romans; that contrary to the order of
the Romans that the Asiatic kings should not set foot in
Europe, Mithridates had seized a large part of the (Cimmerian)
Chersonesus; that he had a great force and had made preparations, as if he had already determined on war; besides his
own troops he had Thracian and Scythian mercenaries, and
men from all the neighbouring nations; he was connected by
marriage with the king of Armenia, and seeking an alliance
with the kings of Syria and Egypt; he had three hundred
decked ships, was building more, and sending to Phoenice and
Egypt for helmsmen and captains: all this preparation could
only be intended against the Romans, who, if they were wise,
would look to the acts of Mithridates and not to his specious
words.

Pelopidas prudently replied, that Mithridates was willing
to submit to the Romans his old disputes with Nicomedes, but
the present matter required no discussion, for the Romans

had seen the country of Mithridates plundered, and they
know that he was excluded from the Euxine. He demanded
that the Romans should either stop Nicomedes from further
hostilities, or should help their ally Mithridates, or finally,
that they should stand aside and allow him to protect himself.
All this the commissioners listened to, though they had made
up their minds to support Nicomedes. Still they did not know
what to say to the last demand of Pelopidas, for Mithridates
was an ally of Rome, and they had no direct quarrel with him.
At last they hit on a reply worthy of a modern diplomatist,
when he intends to lie and yet wishes to seem fair. They said:
We should neither wish to see Mithridates molested by Nicomedes, nor will we allow war to be made on Nicomedes, for
we think that it is against the interest of the Romans for
Nicomedes to be injured. Pelopidas attempted to show that
this answer was no answer, but he was ordered to go away.

Mithridates found no difficulty in understanding what was
meant, and he immediately sent his son Ariarathes with a
large force into Cappadocia. King Ariobarzanes was ejected,
and Ariarathes took his place. Pelopidas again visited the
Roman commissioners and proposed that they should do one
of three things: that they should keep Nicomedes from
wronging Mithridates, who was an ally of Rome, and if they
would do this, Mithridates would aid them against the revolted
Italians; or they should formally renounce their show of an
alliance; or that they and the king of Pontus should go to
Rome and appeal to the Senate. The commissioners thought
that Pelopidas made an insolent demand: they replied that
Mithridates must not attack Nicomedes and that they would
restore Ariobarzanes. Pelopidas was sent away and told not
to come again unless his master would obey their orders.

Without waiting for instructions from Rome the commissioners prepared for war. Their forces were collected from
Bithynia, Cappadocia, Paphlagonia, and Galatia. L. Cassius
took his position on the confines of Bithynia and Galatia;
Aquillius at the point where Mithridates might enter Bithynia; and Q. Oppius on the mountains of Cappadocia. Each
of these three commanders had about forty thousand men and

some cavalry. The Romans also were in possession of the
entrance to the Black Sea near Byzantium with a fleet under
the command of Minucius Rufus and C. Popillius. Mithridates had, as the Romans reported, two hundred and fifty
thousand foot, forty thousand cavalry, and three hundred
docked ships on the sea, besides a hundred other vessels
named "dicrota," with two banks of oars. His commanders
were the two brothers Neoptolemus and Archelaus, but the
king himself looked carefully after the conduct of the war.
Arcathias, also a son of Mithridates, commanded ten thousand horsemen from the Less Armenia; Dorylaus commanded
the troops which were drawn up in phalanx; and Craterus
was the captain of one hundred and thirty war chariots armed
with scythes.

A battle was fought (B.C. 88) between Nicomedes and the
generals of Mithridates in a broad plain on the banks of the
Amnias or Amnius, a river which Hamilton identifies with a
western affluent of the Halys. The Amnias has various
modern names, one of which, Giaour Irmak, indicates its connexion with the Halys or Kizil Irmak. Nicomedes was in
this plain with all his forces. Neoptolemus and Archelaus
had only their light-armed troops with the cavalry of Arcathias and some of the chariots, for the phalanx had not yet
come up. The generals of Mithridates had seized a rocky
eminence in the plain that they might not be outflanked by the
more numerous army of the enemy; but when they saw that
their men were being dislodged from the height, Neoptolemus
and Arcathias came to their help, and there was a fierce
struggle. The men of Nicomedes put their opponents to
flight, but at this critical moment Archelaus moving from
the right fell on the pursuers, who again turned round to
face the fresh assailants. Archelaus now retired slowly to
allow the division of Neoptolemus time to rally, and then
again he attacked the enemy. The scythe chariots were
driven against the mass of the Bithynians, and cut their way
through, splitting the enemy's army into two parts, and by
fresh assaults breaking them again. The horrid spectacle of
mangled men still breathing, or cut to pieces, and quivering

limbs hanging from the chariots terrified the Bithynians and
threw them into confusion. They were now attacked both in
front and in rear, and after great slaughter Nicomedes with
the remnant of his army fled to Paphlagonia. His camp and
all that was in it fell into the hands of Mithridates. A large
number of prisoners were taken, whom the king treated
kindly, and supplying them with provisions sent them off to
their homes. By this prudent conduct, which he repeated on
subsequent occasions, he no doubt expected to secure their
services at some future time.

Nicomedes joined Manius Aquillius, and Mithridates advanced to the mountain Scorobas on the borders of Bithynia
and the Pontic kingdom. Manius retreated before the enemy,
but he was overtaken by Archelaus and compelled to fight.
Nicomedes had gone off to join L. Cassius, but Aquillius had
still above forty thousand men. However he was defeated
with great loss, his camp was taken, and he escaped to the
river Sangarius (Sakaria), which he crossed by night and
fled to Pergamum in the province Asia. Cassius with king
Nicomedes and such of the Roman commissioners as were
present removed their camp into Phrygia to a strong place
named the Lions' Head, where they attempted to train their
men to military discipline. But they had only a rabble of
artisans, agriculturists, and idle fellows lately brought together, with some Phrygians whom they added to the number.
At last the Roman commanders seeing that they could not
fight with such men, broke up their army and went away.
Cassius went to Apameia with his troops, probably Apameia
Cibotus near the source of the Macander; Nicomedes retired
to Pergamum; and Manius Aquillius endeavoured to reach
Rhodes. Those who were guarding the outlet of the Black
Sea gave up the ships to Mithridates. Being now master of
all Bithynia he attempted to restore order in the country.
He next entered Phrygia, and thence advanced into Mysia, and
the Roman province Asia. The fame of the king's generosity
had preceded him. The cities sent commissioners to invite
him to visit them: in the extravagance of their joy they
called him god and saviour; and when he approached, all the

population poured out to meet him in their best clothes and
with great rejoicings. No Roman governor had ever such a
reception. By his emissaries also in Lycia and Pamphylia
Mithridates attempted to draw those countries into friendly
relations with him. The town of Laodiceia (Eski Hissar) on
the Lycus, a branch of the Maeander, held out against Mithridates under Q. Oppius, named proconsul in Livy's Epitome, who had a few horse and some mercenaries. Mithridates
sent a herald to Laodiceia with a promise that the people
should not be injured, if they would surrender Oppius. The
townsmen accepted the offer, sent off the mercenaries, and
brought Oppius to the king preceded by his lictors by way
of mockery. Mithridates took Oppius about with him to
show every body that he had captured a Roman general.
Manius Aquillius did not reach Rhodes; he was lying sick
at Mitylene in the island of Lesbos, when he was seized by
the islanders with some other Romans and given up to Mithridates with the view of conciliating his favour. The king
set him on an ass in chains, and took him about the country,
compelling the wretched man to call out that he was Manius
Aquillius. Posidonius says that a huge barbarian was mounted
on a horse and fastened by a long chain to Aquillius, who
was dragged after him on foot. On arriving at Pergamum
Mithridates ordered melted gold to be poured down his throat,
a fit punishment, as the king alleged, for his greediness.

Mithridates appointed governors over the provinces which
he had captured. He was gladly received by the towns of
Magnesia on the Maeander, Ephesus and Mitylene. The
people of Ephesus were so delighted at being freed from their
oppressors, that they threw down the statues of the Romans
which they had doubtless set up themselves to please their
former governors. Stratoniceia in Caria made some resistance,
but it was captured, the people were fined, and a garrison was
placed in the town. The king found a prize here which he
valued more than money. He saw a beautiful young woman
whom he added to his collection; "and if any man," says
Appian, "cares to know her name, it was Monime, and her
father was Philopoemen." Plutarch says that Monime was

a Milesian, and that the king tempted her with the offer of
fifteen thousand gold pieces, but she refused till an agreement for marriage was made and she received a diadem and
the title of queen.

These events took place in B.C. 88, when Sulla was consul.
The Romans had lost their province Asia and they determined
to recover it.   Sulla, as we have seen, was appointed to take
the command against Mithridates, but he was still detained
by the civil dissensions and the war in Italy. Money also
was wanted for this foreign expedition. It was accordingly
resolved to sell, as Appian has it, what Numa Pompilius had
set apart for the ceremonials of religion, certain pieces of
land about the Capitol ; and the sale produced nine thousand
litrae of gold or nine thousand Roman librae, as it is stated.

Mithridates was occupied with attempting to reduce the
Asiatic town of Magnesia near Mount Sipylus which had
not submitted to him, and in building more ships for the
purpose of assaulting the island of Rhodes, which remained
faithful to the Romans. In the mean time he gave secret
orders to his commanders and the magistrates of the Asiatic
cities to massacre on the same day every Roman and Italian
among them, men, women, and children, to leave the bodies
unburied and to share the property of the strangers with the
king. If any man buried a corpse or concealed a Roman or
Italian, he must be punished ; rewards were offered to those
who discovered or killed any of the foreigners who tried to
hide themselves ; slaves who murdered or denounced their
masters were to have their freedom ; and debtors who killed
their creditors were to be relieved of half their obligations.
The day fixed for this general massacre was the thirtieth
day from the time of the notice.   The province of Asia
swarmed with the officers of the Publicani, who farmed the
taxes, and with Roman and Italian money-lenders and speculators who had resorted to this rich country to make gain.
The way in which the Greeks of Asia assisted in executing
the savage orders of Mithridates shows how odious was
Roman dominion and Roman greediness.

At Ephesus the foreigners fled to the great temple of

Artemis (Diana) and clung to the sacred statues, but they
were dragged out and killed. At Pergamum the Romans
fled to the temple of Aesculapius and were pierced with
arrows while they were still holding to the statues. At
Adramyttium some tried to escape by swimming out to sea,
but they were followed and killed, and their children were
drowned. The people of Caunus, who lived on the mainland
nearly opposite to Rhodes, had been made tributary to the
Rhodians after the war with Antiochus (B.C. 190), but they had
been set free from this dependence by the Romans not long
before this event. This act of favour however did not save
the wretched Italians who were among them and had fled for
refuge with their wives and children to the hearth of Vesta
in the town hall. They were dragged from the sacred hearth,
the children were murdered before the face of the mothers,
and then the wives and husbands. The people of Tralles
having some scruple about staining their own hands with
blood, hired a savage Paphlagonian, named Theophilus, to do
the work for them. This fellow having brought his victims
into the temple of Concord despatched them without mercy.
Some had their hands cut off as they were clinging to the
statues. P. Rutilius Rufus, who was living in exile at
Mitylene, escaped from the general massacre by disguising
himself. Theophanes, a flatterer of Cn. Pompeius Magnus,
reported that when the private writings of Mithridates were
afterwards seized in the fort of Caenum, there was among
them a letter from Rutilius to the King in which he urged
the massacre of the Romans in Asia. But this was no doubt
a lying invention of Theophanes, made perhaps with the
view of pleasing Cn. Pompeius, whose father's bad character
had been exposed by Rutilius in his historical works. No
man knew the number of those who perished in this fearful
massacre, and accordingly it was magnified to an incredible
amount, which is better omitted than repeated. This event
showed, says Appian, that the inhabitants of Asia were not
moved by fear of Mithridates so much as by hatred to the
Romans; but it is probable that both motives were combined.
They suffered for their cruelty afterwards; for Mithridates

treated them like a tyrant, and Sulla like a Roman. Mithridates now received the submission of the island Cos, the only
place where the Romans were saved during the massacre. They
took refuge in the temple of Aesculapius, and the sanctity of
the asylum was respected. Mithridates found here the son
of Alexander I. of Egypt, who had been left in Cos by his
grandmother Cleopatra. He brought up the young man in
regal state, but he possessed himself of a large part of the
treasure of Cleopatra, consisting of fine works of art, valuable
stones, women's ornaments, and a great quantity of money
which he sent off to Pontus.

The town of Rhodus was built at the northern extremity
of the island. It was founded during the Peloponnesian war
and planned by Hippodamus of Miletus, the same architect
who built the Athenian Piraeus. This is the remark of
Strabo, who also compares Rhodus with the Athenian
Munychia. Aristotle says more clearly that Hippodamus
laid out the streets of the Piraeus, and so before he made the
plan of Rhodus he had experience in building towns. Rhodus
rose from the sea like the seats of a theatre, a circumstance
which gave it a picturesque appearance, but caused on one
occasion great loss, when a violent storm of rain and hail
descended from the hills and flooded the lower parts. In
the first century before the Christian era no city of Asia
could be compared with Rhodus in respect of harbours,
streets, walls, and other great works. It was famed for
wise laws, the excellence of the administration, and for
superiority on the sea. The Rhodians excelled in ship-
building; they had excellent naval architects, and abundance
of workmen for the dockyards, whom they took care to provide always with sufficient means of subsistence. No man in
the town was allowed to want. The rich voluntarily contributed to the support of the poor. There were also officers
whose business it was to look after the supply of provisions.
The object was to maintain a navy for which they would
never want men; and they kept up stores of machinery,
armour, and every thing necessary for the equipment of a fleet.
The Rhodians were a great maritime people long before the

foundation of the town of Rhodus, and, according to tradition, even before the institution of the Olympic games. They founded Rhode (Rosas) in Spain on the coast of Catalonia, a town which the Massaliots afterwards possessed (vol. i., p. 305). In Italy they founded Parthenope, as Strabo affirms, which was either the original site of Naples or near it; and they had a settlement, probably Salapia, in the part of Italy named Daunia. The town of Gela in Sicily was also a Rhodian settlement. The fame of the island and its wealth are recorded in the list of the Hellenic peoples who went against Troy, whatever may be the date of this portion of the Iliad. The long commercial experience of the Rhodians led them to form a maritime code, some of the provisions of which were accepted by the Romans and thus have been incorporated in the maritime law of European states. The Lex Rhodia de Jactu (Dig. 14, 2. 1) provided that when goods were thrown overboard to lighten a ship and save the rest of the cargo, the loss to the owner of the goods must be made up by a general contribution of all who had an interest in the ship and the remainder of the cargo. This is the foundation of the modern doctrine of general average.

The Rhodians prepared to receive Mithridates by strengthening their walls and harbours, and placing military engines on them. Some men came over from the mainland to help them, from Telmessus in Caria and from Lycia. The Italians who escaped from the massacre also fled to Rhodes, and L. Cassius with them. While the fleet of Mithridates was approaching, the Rhodians demolished the suburbs of the town that they might not shelter the enemy. They closed the harbours with chains and prepared to resist Mithridates from the walls. The king encamped near the city and frequently assaulted the harbours, but failing in all his attempts he waited for the arrival of his army. In the skirmishes which took place the Rhodians had the advantage and gained confidence. They kept their ships in readiness to attack the enemy, if an opportunity should offer.

A royal transport was sailing near the coast when a

Rhodian dicrotos or bireme went out against it, and this brought on a general battle. Mithridates had the advantage in number of vessels, but the Rhodians having superior skill sailed round his ships and pierced them. They took one trireme and towed it off with all the crew. A Rhodian quinquereme was taken by the enemy, and the Rhodians not knowing what had become of it sent six of their best sailing ships with their admiral Damagoras to look after the lost vessel. Twenty-five of the enemy's ships came against them, but Damagoras kept out of their reach till it was dark, when seeing that the enemy's vessels were drawing off, he suddenly fell on them, sank two, and driving the rest to the coast of Lycia returned safe to Rhodes in the night. During the action while Mithridates was sailing from ship to ship and encouraging his men, a vessel of Chios, which was in his service, fell foul of the king's ship in the confusion. The king took no notice of it at the time, but he afterwards punished the helmsman and the man stationed at the head, and was in ill humour with all the Chians. Perhaps he suspected treachery.

At this time the army of Mithridates was coming from Asia in transports and ships of war, carried towards Rhodes by a wind blowing from the Asiatic coast. There was a great swell in the sea, and the Rhodian vessels attacked the ships of Mithridates while they were tossed by the waves and dispersed. They carried off some, and pierced others or set them on fire. Mithridates now tried a stratagem, the success of which depended on certain combinations, and it had the usual luck of such schemes. Some deserters from the Rhodians pointed out to him an eminence near the city which might be easily taken, and was crowned by a temple of Zeus Atabyrius. This place cannot be what was called Mount Atabyris, for that was in a different part of the island. Mithridates embarked his men by night, some of them furnished with scaling-ladders, and gave them orders to assault both the harbours and the walls, when a beacon signal blazed from the top of Atabyrius. The men of Mithridates silently approached the town, but the Rhodian watches discovered them and raised a fire signal.

The assailants took this to be their own signal, and the deep silence was broken by a loud shout from the men with the scaling-ladders and from the fleet. The Rhodians answered by a cheer from the walls, which were manned with all their force. The enemy were afraid to attack in the dark, and when they made the assault at daybreak, they were repulsed.

The king had prepared one of those great military engines, which the Greeks named Sambuca. A ladder four feet wide was made, the sides of which were protected by wood-work, and it was also covered over. It was high enough when it was brought up on ships against a sea wall to enable men to step off upon the battlements. Two ships were laid side to side, all the oars on the right side of one and on the left side of the other having first been cleared away, so that the ships might be fastened close together. The ladder, which was in fact a moveable covered gallery, was laid over the sides of the ships along the line of junction, with the head projecting far beyond the beaks. At the top of the ships' masts pulleys were fixed with ropes. When the ships approached the wall, the ropes were attached to the upper end of the ladder, which was elevated by men at the stern of the ships who hauled the ropes through the pulleys. Other men at the same time at the head of the vessel supported the ladder with props to secure its elevation. By the use of the oars on the two outer sides the vessels were brought close up to the land, and the top of the ladder to the level of the enemy's sea wall. A kind of stage was fixed at the top of the ladder and protected on three sides by a breastwork. It was wide enough to hold four men, who fought against those on the wall who attempted to prevent the ladder from being fixed. When the top was securely placed, the men on the stage let down the breastwork on each side and stepped on the walls or towers, while the rest followed them by the ladder, which was planted securely on the two ships. This is Polybius's description of the Sambuca (viii. 6) which Marcellus used at the siege of Syracuse, and he adds that it was aptly called a Sambuca or harp, for when the ladder was raised, the outline of the two ships and of the ladder which was planted on them was like a harp.

The Sambuca of Mithridates was brought up to that part of the wall of Rhodus which was near the temple of Isis, and it alarmed the townsmen "by sending out at the same time many missiles and rams' heads and javelins;" from which it appears to have been a larger piece of machinery than the Sambuca of Marcellus. It was surrounded by numerous boats containing men with scaling-ladders, who were to ascend through the Sambuca upon the walls. It seems that this machine had a large stage at the upper end, and it was not high enough, otherwise small ladders would not have been required. The Rhodians made a brave resistance, until the huge engine broke down by its own weight, and the phantom of Isis opportunely appeared and showered fire upon it. The king seeing that he could not take the place withdrew all his troops from the island. But perhaps he intended to return, for he crossed over to Patara on the south-west coast of Lycia, a country in which he would find abundance of timber; and he began to cut down the trees which were about the temple of Latona for the purpose of constructing military engines. But he was alarmed by a dream and spared the sacred trees. He now left Pelopidas to carry on the war against the Lycians and sent Archelaus into Greece. From this time he committed most military matters to his generals, and employed himself at Pergamum in raising recruits and preparing arms for them. He also sat in judgment on such as were charged with designs against his life, or with attempting revolution or favouring the Roman interest. His leisure time was spent in the company of his new wife Monime.

CHAPTER XXI.

SULLA IN GREECE.

B.C. 87.

It was in B.C. 87 that Mithridates sent Archelaus with a
large armament to Greece with the view of expelling the
Romans from that country also. Archelaus, or a commander
under him, named Menophanes by Pausanias, surprised the
island of Delos, which had revolted from the Athenians, and
took some other places, the names of which are not mentioned;
but Appian's narrative implies that they were places dependent on Athens, to which city we must suppose that the
Romans had attached them, in conformity with a common
practice of "attributing," as the Romans styled it, various
smaller towns or districts to some larger political community
which they favoured. A great number of men were killed in
these revolted places, most of whom were Italians, and they
were again made dependencies of Athens, the object of
Archelaus being to gain the aid of the Athenians. In Delos,
which was a great entrepôt of commerce, the merchants
were massacred, and all the men of the island : the property
of the merchants was seized and all the sacred offerings : the
women and children were made slaves, and the town was
laid in ruins. Some of the merchants who escaped from
Delos in their vessels waited for Menophanes until he set
sail from the island, and attacking him on the open sea sent
him to the bottom. The sacred treasures of Delos, it is said,
were conveyed to Athens by Aristion an Athenian, and two

thousand soldiers were sent with him to protect the money. Aristion employed the men, probably according to the intention of Archelaus, for his own ends, and made himself master of Athens. He was a cruel master, though he professed to be an Epicurean philosopher, as Appian names him, and at the same time takes the opportunity of making a remark on the tyrannical conduct of many Greek philosophers, who had acquired political power and turned out more cruel than common tyrants. Hence he is led to doubt about philosophers generally, whether they pursue philosophy because they love virtue, or merely employ it as a consolation in their poverty and exclusion from political life. The philosophy that Appian alludes to is political and moral philosophy; and his remark has this practical value, that men who devote themselves to speculation and have not been always engaged in public affairs, are very dangerous men, if they should ever attain political power, for they may be, as Appian suggests, philosophers from necessity and dishonest; and even if they are honest, they will reduce their speculations to practice at any cost, for such men care not for the sufferings of mankind, if they can only try their theories on them.

Posidonius, the philosopher, wrote a very particular account of Aristion, which is preserved in a long extract of Athenaeus (Lib. v.), where he is named Athenion. However this discrepancy of name may be explained, the man is the same. He was the son of an Athenian also named Athenion, who had him by an Egyptian slave woman, or somebody else begat the boy, and Athenion brought him up. The mother and her child used to lead the old fellow about when he was far advanced in years, and when he died they got his money. The young Athenion or Aristion, as we shall call him now, contrived to be registered as an Athenian citizen, and married a comely young woman. He and his wife devoted themselves to the sophistic business, or the teaching of rhetoric and philosophy, took youths as pupils at Messene and also at Larissa in Thessaly, and at last came back to Athens with a good sum of money. When Mithridates was beginning his victorious career, Aristion was elected ambassador by the

Athenians and sent to the king, whose favour he gained. In his letters to Athens Aristion encouraged the people to hope for the re-establishment of the democracy and for great things from Mithridates. All Roman Asia was now in the hands of the king, and Aristion set sail to return to Athens. A storm carried him to Carystus in Euboea, from which place the Athenians sent some ships of war to convey him to Athens and a litter or chair with silver feet. The whole city turned out to welcome the ambassador and admire the caprice of fortune, who had exalted a schoolmaster to such high dignity. Aristion entered Athens in the silver-footed litter, which was covered with purple cloth, and he was splendidly lodged in the house of a rich man. When he next made his appearance in public, he wore a fine cloak which trailed on the ground, and a gold ring with the likeness of Mithridates engraved on the stone, and he was followed by a great train. There was a religious ceremony in honour of his advent. On the next day a crowd assembled about his residence to wait for the appearance of the great man, and the citizens without being summoned ran to the place of public meeting. Aristion at last came out of the house surrounded by a body-guard composed of all who wished to be popular. Every man was anxious to be near him, and to touch, if possible, the garment of the illustrious friend of king Mithridates. Aristion ascended the Bema or pulpit, which stood in front of the colonnade of Attalus and had been built for the use of the Roman commanders when they made a public speech. After looking round at the immense crowd and then turning his eyes upwards, he said that the state of affairs and the interests of his country compelled him to tell what he knew, but the great importance of what he had to say and the strangeness of the late revolutions made him hesitate. The crowd bid him take heart and speak out. He did speak, and told them of the glorious victories of Mithridates, of the disgrace of the Romans, of the armies of the king that were entering Thrace and Macedonia, and of the combination of the east and the west under Mithridates for the ruin of the Roman power. Here the orator paused to let his hearers talk a little with one another and admire the great news. He then rubbed his forehead and said, Well, what must I advise you to do? He answered his own question by advising them to put an end to the present state of affairs in which the Roman Senate kept them, and to resume their independence. The result was that he was elected general of the Athenians, and all the munitions of war were put into his hands. The new general thanked the electors and said, Since you are now your own masters, and I am the head, if you will give me your help, I shall be able to do whatever you can do by your united strength. He now appointed all his own officers, men who were his tools, and in a few days he declared himself master or tyrannus, as the Greeks named a usurper. Thus an ignorant buffoon by the popular vote was invested with supreme power, and men soon found out that they had made a fool and a knave their master and could not get rid of him. Some, who were wiser than the rest and saw how the farce would end, attempted to leave the city, but the gates were watched, and if the fugitives made their escape by letting themselves down from the walls, they were followed by mounted men and killed or brought back in chains. Aristion put to death all whom he suspected, and got together all the money that he could. Every man was ordered to keep within doors after sunset, and no one was allowed to go out even with a light. Posidonius has a story about the sacred treasure of Delos, which is different from Appian's. After Aristion was elected president of Athens, he sent Apellicon to Delos to seize the money. Apellicon landed on the island with some troops, and finding it undefended, as it appears, took no precautions against a surprise. Orobius, as Athenaeus names the Roman commander, who had to look after Delos, though the name Orobius is not Roman, one dark night disembarked some soldiers on the island and fell on Apellicon's men who were drunk and asleep. He massacred the Athenians and those who were with them to the number of six hundred, and took four hundred prisoners. Apellicon escaped from the slaughter. We can only make a consistent narrative by supposing that this affair of Apellicon happened before Archelaus took the island of Delos on his voyage to Greece, when it was so completely plundered that it remained a waste when Strabo wrote.

The movements of Archelaus in Greece before the arrival of Sulla are very obscurely told by Appian. He says that Archelaus was joined by the Lacedaemonians, and the Achaei, but it is impossible to say exactly what he means by Achaei. Boeotia too declared for him, except the small town of Thespia to which he laid siege. Metrophanes, another general of Mithridates, about this time seized the island of Euboea and the town of Demetrias (Volo), which is well situated on the mainland at the head of the gulf of Pagasae. C. Sentius, the Roman governor of Macedonia, sent his legatus Bruttius Sura against Metrophanes, who was defeated in a naval fight and escaped with the help of a fair wind. Sura took the island of Sciathos, where the enemy had deposited his plunder. He hung some of the slaves whom he found there and cut off the hands of the freemen. Sura then advanced into Boeotia, having received a small reinforcement from Macedonia, and fought on three successive days with Archelaus and Aristion without any decisive result, as Appian says; but Plutarch reports that he compelled Archelaus to retire to the coast, and Pausanias agrees with him. Appian reports that Archelaus was joined by more Greeks, and Sura seeing that he was not a match for them all "retired towards the Piraeus," till Archelaus came with his fleet and occupied it. Here there is evidently some blunder. Sura would never have advanced upon the Piraeus with his small force and then waited till Archelaus came with his fleet, which we must suppose had first taken him to the Boeotian coast. Plutarch's story is more consistent. After the success of Sura in Boeotia, L. Licinius Lucullus a legatus of Sulla arrived, and gave Sura notice to make room for Sulla, who was coming and had a commission to carry on the war in these parts; on which Sura returned to Sentius in Macedonia. He had done good service to the Roman cause, but he knew that Sulla would not allow a rival to rob him of his expected glory, and

Sulla had a force large enough to compel Sura to withdraw.

Sulla left Italy in B.C. 87 with five legions and some auxiliary cohorts and cavalry. He would sail from Brundisium and land somewhere on the opposite coast of the continent. It was a long and difficult march to Athens. He got some money, men, and supplies from Aetolia and Thessaly. In passing through Boeotia he received the submission of nearly all that country; and Thebes which had hastily taken the side of Mithridates, still more hastily and more wisely now declared for the Romans. When Sulla had entered Attica, he employed part of his force in blockading Aristion in Athens, and with the other he commenced the siege of the Piraeus or port town in which Archelaus had shut himself up. The Piraeus was surrounded by a strong wall, forty Greek pecheis, about sixty feet, in height, says Appian, and built in the time of Pericles, when he led the Athenian democracy, and induced them to strengthen the fortifications of the seaport town. But the wall round the Piraeus was built in the time of Themistocles, as Thucydides states, for the purpose of protecting the three natural harbours, and it was demolished by the Lacedaemonians in B.C. 404, with the Long Walls which united Athens with the ports. Conon rebuilt both the walls of the Piraeus and the Long Walls (B.C. 393) after the battle of Cnidus, or he restored them, if the Lacedaemonians did not completely destroy these massive constructions, as our authorities say that they did. The Lacedaemonians destroyed three long walls, the wall to the Phalerum and the two Long Walls to the Piraeus. Thucydides when he speaks of the Long Walls simply, means the wall to the Phalerum and the wall to the Piraeus; but he indirectly informs us that the wall to the Piraeus was a double parallel wall, the northern having been built when the Phaleric long wall was built, and the southern having been built after. Conon's restored walls were only two, and they are the walls of which some remains still exist.

Appian then has made a mistake in naming the wall round the Piraeus a work of Pericles, unless we accept Leake's sug-

gestion that the fortification of the Piraeus was not completed
till B.C. 449, when Pericles was in power.   Leake founds this
hypothesis partly on a passage in Andocides, and confirms
it by this passage of Appian; but Appian instead of being
a confirmation requires confirmation himself.   The words of
Thucydides (i. 93) appear to mean that the fortifications of the
Piraeus were finished soon after the close of the Persian wars.

Sulla attempted to scale the wall of the Piraeus, but he
was driven back, and retired with part of his troops to
Eleusis and the other part to Megara, where he constructed
military engines, for his intention was to raise an agger, as
the Romans termed it, or bank of earth against the wall and
place his engines on it.   By means of Megara Sulla kept
open his communication with the Peloponnesus, and from
Eleusis he had a road open to Thebes, as appears from what
follows.   He got workmen with all necessary tools, iron,
catapultae, and every thing else of this kind from Thebes.   He
cut down the trees in the Academia, one of the suburbs of
Athens, and also the trees of the Lyceium, another of the
suburbs, for the construction of his engines.   Sulla also used
the materials of the Long Walls for his embankment.   Appian (Mithrid. c. 30) says that "he began to demolish the
Long Walls, converting stones and wood and earth to the
purposes of his embankment."   The structure of the sentence
might signify that he took stones, wood, and earth from the
Long Walls; but if the passage does mean this, it is hardly
possible that this can be the author's meaning, and the fault
is in his way of writing.   We cannot conceive that there
should be any wood in the Long Walls, and Sulla might find
earth any where.   It appears from a passage of Livy (31,
c. 26) that Philippus IV. in B.C. 200 nearly surprised Athens
by breaking "into the narrow part of the half-ruined wall,
which by two branches unites Piraeus to Athens."   Livy
seems to mean that the wall was in a ruinous state then.
We do not know whether it was repaired between that time
and the siege of Athens by Sulla.   If it was repaired, it is
very probable that the breach was filled up with any material
that was at hand.

It happened that two Athenian slaves in the Piraeus, either because they favoured the Roman side or wished to secure their safety, if the place should be taken, communicated with the Romans by inscriptions on balls of lead, which they threw with slings. This was done for some time before the intention of the slaves was known to the Romans, but the value of the leaden balls was opportunely discovered before it was too late. One day the leaden balls announced that on the following day the besieged would sally out against the men who were employed on the siege works, and that the cavalry would attack the Romans in flank. Sulla was thus prepared and the attempt of the enemy failed. The Roman earthworks were daily rising higher, and Archelaus constructed towers on the walls opposite to them and placed his engines for discharging missiles. He sent to Chalcis in Euboea and to the islands in the Aegean for reinforcements. He also armed the rowers in the fleet, for he was hard pressed, though he had more men than Sulla. Archelaus made a sally at midnight and burnt one of Sulla's two " testudines " or covered sheds under which the men worked at mining the walls, and he burnt also the engines which were stationed near the testudo. Within ten days Sulla repaired his loss, and placed his new testudo where the former had been. Archelaus built opposite to it a tower on the walls.

Mithridates was enjoying himself in Pergamum, but he did not neglect the war. He sent to Archelaus some fresh troops under a general named Dromichaetes. There had been however an unlucky omen, which greatly troubled the king. He was in the theatre of Pergamum one day, when a figure of Victory bearing a crown was let down by some machinery, but unluckily the Victory was broken in pieces just as it was touching the king's head, and the crown fell down and was destroyed.

Archelaus having received this reinforcement hazarded a battle under the wall of the Piraeus, the result of which was doubtful, until a Roman legion that had been looking out for wood came up in time, and Archelaus was defeated with the loss of two thousand men. The rest were driven

back within the walls. Archelaus himself, who had shown
great courage in this fight, delayed his retreat too long. The
gates were closed and he was hauled up by a rope from the
walls. On this occasion some of the Roman soldiers, who had
formerly disgraced themselves, did good service and recovered
their character. Sulla released these men from the "igno-
minia," the Roman term for the disgrace of cowardly
soldiers, and he rewarded the rest well. In fact he was
fighting not only for victory against Mithridates, but for the
mastery of Rome, and he secured the fidelity of his men by
profuse liberality. He required large sums for the expenses
of the war, and as he could not have money from Rome, he
helped himself. The Greek temples still contained great
wealth in the precious metals. Sulla took some of the most
costly offerings from Epidaurus and Olympia, and he sent
Caphis a Phocian to Delphi with a message to the Amphic-
tyons, by which he demanded the treasures of the god on the
ground that they would be safer in his keeping; or, if he
used them, he would replace them. Caphis did not like the
business on which he was sent, and lamented to the Amphic-
tyons that it was imposed on him. Upon this some of them
said that they heard the sound of the lute in the temple, and
Caphis either believing it or wishing to divert Sulla from his
sacrilege sent him information of what had happened. Sulla
replied by a jest: he wondered that Caphis did not understand the music; it was a sign that the god was pleased, and
he ordered him to take the treasure, for the deity offered it.
The Roman general believed in dreams and signs, or he pretended that he did, but like many men in all ages, who accept the religion of their country, he never allowed it to
deter him from any thing that he had set his heart on.
Most of the things were sent from Delphi secretly, perhaps
for fear of some popular disturbance, but one of the silver
jars, the gift of king Croesus, was too large to be taken off
slily. Croesus had sent four jars, but the other three, we
must suppose, had been carried away before, probably when
the Phocians plundered Delphi in the Sacred War (B.C. 357).
This valuable jar was cut in pieces. The precious metal

taken from the temples was coined into money in the Peloponnesus under the superintendence of Lucullus, whence it
was named Lucullean and came into circulation during the
war in Greece. The conduct of Sulla was contrasted by the
Greeks with the behaviour of the Roman commanders who
drove Antiochus out of Greece and defeated the kings of
Macedonia. These men did not touch the temples: they
even sent presents to them. But things were changed now.
Roman generals employed their arms against one another as
much as against the enemies of Rome, and they purchased
the services of their soldiers and thus "made the Roman
state a thing for bargain and sale, and themselves the slaves
of the vilest wretches that they might domineer over honest
men." Sulla was the man who did most to establish this
system by his profuse expenditure on his own men, and he
afterwards employed money in corrupting the soldiers of
other Roman commanders. The remarks are Plutarch's, and
they are just and pertinent. Sulla did more than any
Roman towards the ruin of Rome by corrupting the soldiery,
and all his subsequent attempts at reform were idle efforts to
restore stability to a system of government in which the
soldier was ready to obey the man who paid him best. It
is a true remark of Livy that any kind of government may
last, so long as military discipline is maintained.

The winter was now coming on, and Sulla made a camp at
Eleusis, a town which stood on the eastern end of a low
rocky hill, parallel and near to the shore of the magnificent
bay of Eleusis. He dug a deep ditch extending from the
interior down to the sea to prevent the enemy's cavalry from
annoying his position. He had to skirmish with the enemy
daily at the ditch while his work was going on, and the men
of Archelaus made frequent sallies from the Piraeus. Appian's abridgment gives no reason why Sulla made a camp
at Eleusis on the approach of winter. But he had no ships,
and as the siege of the Piraeus was protracted, he must have
found it difficult to get supplies for his army before Athens
and before the Piraeus. He would find some supplies in the
fertile plain of Eleusis, and he might keep open from this

place his communication with Bœotia and his friends in
Thebes by the pass of Phyle. Eleusis also was connected
with Athens by the Sacred Way, and a road led from Eleusis
between Mount Korata and the sea to Megara and the Isth-
mus. Sulla sent to the Rhodians for ships, but Mithridates
commanded the sea, and the Rhodians could not comply with
the demand. Accordingly Sulla despatched Lucullus to the
east to get ships from the kings of Syria and Egypt, and
from the maritime cities in the east part of the Mediterranean.
Lucullus embarked on a small vessel, and changing from ship
to ship to escape detection at last reached Alexandria. We
shall see afterwards what he did.

The siege of the Piraeus was continued. The traitors
within the walls informed Sulla by their leaden missiles, that
on a certain night Archelaus would send some corn to Athens,
which was in great want of provisions. Sulla laid an ambuscade and took all the corn with the men who were
carrying it. About this time, a Roman commander, whom
Appian names Munatius, defeated Neoptolemus in the neighbourhood of Chalcis in Euboea, and took many prisoners.
Shortly afterwards, the Romans before the Piraeus, while the
enemy's watches were asleep at night, availed themselves of
their engines to fix the scaling-ladders and mount the walls.
The men on guard at this spot were surprised and killed;
others fled in alarm, but some of the enemy made a brave
resistance, killed the captain of the scaling party and pitched
the rest from the walls. The enemy then sallying from the
gates attempted to burn one of Sulla's towers, which was
only saved by the great exertions of the general all through
the night and the next day. Archelaus had now completed
his great tower on the walls, which stood face to face with
Sulla's tower, and missiles were constantly discharged from
one against the other. Sulla sent from his catapults twenty
very heavy leaden balls at once, which destroyed many of the
enemy, and shook the tower so much that it was near falling,
and Archelaus drew it back. Athens was still suffering from
famine, and the traitors announced to Sulla that another
attempt would be made to send corn by night. But Arche-

laus now suspecting some treachery set men at the gates with
torches to sally out, if Sulla should attack those who were
carrying the corn. Both plans succeeded. Sulla took the
corn, and Archelaus fired some of Sulla's engines.

Mithridates saw that the struggle between himself and the
Romans must be decided on the west side of the Aegean,
and he sent one of his sons, Arcathias, with an army into
Macedonia, from which the small force of the Romans was
easily expelled, and all the country was brought under the
king's dominion. Arcathias appointed governors of Macedonia and began his march southward to Athens. The
design was to relieve Archelaus, who was shut up in the
Piraeus. On the way Arcathias fell ill and died. His army
subsequently joined Archelaus in Boeotia.

Sulla was conducting two sieges at once, and it is not easy
to conceive how he found men enough to shut in Athens and
to attack the Piraeus at the same time. He must have had some
Greeks in his army. In Athens indeed there was probably
no great force, but the extent of the walls made the blockade
difficult. If it was not relieved, famine would compel a
surrender, and with this view Sulla constructed numerous
castella, or forts round the city, to prevent any of the inhabitants from making their escape and so to increase the
sufferings of all.

When Sulla had completed his embankment against the
Piraeus, he placed his engines on it. Archelaus in the mean
time was undermining the work of Sulla and carrying off the
earth. At last the embankment suddenly sank in, on which
the Romans withdrew their engines and set about repairing
the embankment. They also began to undermine the enemy's
wall, and as their excavations and those of the besieged
met underground, the men fought in these subterraneous
galleries. The battering-rams of Sulla at last throw down
a part of the wall, which was near to one of the enemy's
wooden towers, and the tower itself was fired. Sulla seized
the part where the wall had fallen, and at the same time
filled with sulphur, tow, and pitch the mine which he had
carried under the walls. The upper part of his mine was

sustained by the timber, which had been placed there to
protect the excavators from the earth falling in. When the
combustibles had destroyed the wood-work, the wall gave
way, first in one place, and then in another, burying in the
ruins the men who were upon it. The consternation of the
enemy encouraged the Romans, and Sulla urged them on
to the assault. He continually relieved his men, when they
were exhausted, by sending fresh men in their place to scale
the walls. Archelaus also brought up fresh troops to resist
the assault. Many men fell on both sides, but at last Sulla
finding the defence more easy for the enemy than the attack
for himself drew off his soldiers. In the night Archelaus
worked at a new wall, which was constructed in the form
of a crescent with the convex side turned inwards, for
the purpose of closing the breach. Sulla attempted to
destroy this wall which was fresh constructed and weak, but
his men were assailed both in front and on the flank when
they advanced within the hollow of the crescent. Failing in
this attempt, Sulla gave up all hope of taking the Piraeus by
assault, and blockaded it with the view of reducing it by
famine. But if this was his purpose, as Appian says, he
must have known that Archelaus, who had the command of
the sea, could supply himself with provisions better than
Sulla could furnish his own army ; and though Archelaus
might have taken off his men by the ships when he pleased,
he had no intention yet of giving up the stronghold which
he possessed.

The provisions in Athens were now exhausted. A modim-
nus of wheat, something less than twelve gallons, was selling
for a thousand drachmae (above 40*l.*). All the animals had
been eaten, and skins, shoes, and leather bottles were cooked
for food ; even the dead were devoured. Men ate the wild
chamomile that grew about the Acropolis. Aristion all the
time was enjoying himself, for he had laid in a store of good
things for himself and his own crew. The members of the
Senate and the priests entreated him to come to terms with
Sulla, and at last being persuaded he sent some of his boon
companions to treat of peace. When they came to the

Roman general, they had no proposals to make, but they
began a pompous speech about Theseus and Eumolpus, and
the Persian wars, which Sulla cut short by telling them to be
gone with their fine talk: he had not been sent to Athens to
learn a lesson, but to compel rebels to submit. He completed
his line of contravallation round the city, and it was now
impossible for a single person to escape. It happened that
the Roman soldiers who were stationed at the outer Ceramicus,
a suburb on the west side of Athens, overheard some old men
in the city abusing the tyrant for not guarding the approach
to the wall about the Heptachalcum, the only part, as they
said, where it was easy to get in. The story of the over-
hearing is improbable, and we must assume that the Romans
could see where the wall was weakest. However, this was
the part where the Romans entered. Sulla levelled the wall
between the Piraic and the Sacred Gates, as Plutarch reports,
or we may rather suppose that he levelled enough to make a
wide entrance. Any further labour at this time would have
been useless. The resistance was feeble. About midnight
the infuriated besiegers broke into the city, striking terror
into the inhabitants with the sound of trumpets and horns
and loud cries. The men were so weakened by want of food
that they could not fly, and the women and children were
massacred without mercy. Sulla's orders were to kill all
before them. Many of the Athenians seeing no hope presented themselves to the soldiers, and some killed themselves.
A large number fell about the Agora, and the blood streamed
down the inner Ceramicus, and, as many say, even flowed
through the gates into the suburbs. A few escaped to the
Acropolis with Aristion, who first set fire to the Odeium
of Pericles or music hall, that Sulla might not use the timber
for an attack on the Acropolis. Sulla would not allow the
city to be burnt, but his men had permission to plunder as
much as they liked. They found in many houses human
flesh prepared for food. According to Plutarch's statement,
two Athenian exiles, who were with Sulla, and some Roman
senators also who were in his army, at last prevailed on him
to stay the slaughter. The city was taken, as Sulla says in

his Memoirs, on the Calends or first of March (B.C. 86) after
a siege of several months.

Sulla left an officer C. Scribonius Curio to besiege Aristion
in the Acropolis. The tyrant and those with him were compelled by famine to surrender. Aristion was put to death,
and all those with him who had been his guards or had held
any office since the rebellion, or who in any way had acted
contrary to the rules established by the Romans at the conquest of Greece. Sulla raised some money by selling all the
slaves that he took in the city. It is not reported that he
sold any free persons, an act of grace which is more than the
Athenians could have expected. He took out of the Acropolis
forty pounds of gold and six hundred of silver. Sulla is not
charged with carrying off any of the works of art from
Athens. All that he is said to have taken were some columns
from the Olympicium, which were used in the Capitoline
temple at Rome. But these columns must have been sent off
some time after the capture of Athens, for Sulla had no ships
now, and he had more weighty business on hand than the
collecting of works of art to adorn Rome. If he did not
carry off plunder of this kind, it was not from any scruples.
He could do nothing with it, so long as Rome was in the
possession of his enemies, and he would not send it home,
even after he had cleared Greece of the armies of Mithridates,
to fall into the hands of the opposite faction. We must conclude that it was the circumstances of the times that saved
Athens from being plundered of her statues, or possibly
Sulla's indifference to such things, though that is less likely,
for he was a man of education and well acquainted with the
value of Greek art. The only statue that he is said to have
carried away from Greece was an ivory statue of Athena
from Alalcomenae in Boeotia.

After the capture of Athens Sulla made another attempt
to storm the Piraeus. He broke down a part of the new
wall which Archelaus had constructed, but he found that the
enemy had built other similar walls behind this. However
Sulla pushed the assault so vigorously that Archelaus gave up
the defence of the circuit of the Piraeus and retired to the

strongest part of the Piraic fortifications, or the Munychia, which was surrounded by the sea except where the neck of the peninsula was joined to the mainland, and here he was safe. When the Romans broke into the Piraeus, they burned the greater part of it with the sheds of the dry docks and the noble arsenal constructed by the architect Philo.

Another army from Asia was now coming against Sulla under Taxiles a general of Mithridates. He was moving from Thrace and Macedonia with one hundred thousand men, ten thousand horse, and ninety scythe chariots. He summoned Archelaus to join him, an important fact, which Appian has omitted, and Plutarch has recorded. Probably Mithridates, who was in Asia, directed the operations of the war, as military movements have been directed in modern times by men who sit at home and know not what they are doing. Archelaus could stay in the Munychia as long as he pleased, for he had the command of the sea. His plan, says Plutarch, was to protract the war and to cut off Sulla's supplies. When Archelaus took off his men in the ships and landed them in Boeotia, Sulla also left Attica and crossed the mountains. Pausanias says that Sulla hearing of the advance of Taxiles from Elateia in Phocis left the siege of Athens and met Taxiles in Boeotia, and that the news of the capture of Athens reached him three days after, and on the very day that he won his victory at Chaeroneia. He also states that Sulla returned to Athens after his victory, and shutting up his prisoners in the Ceramicus put to death every tenth man on whom the lot fell. A fragment of Licinianus seems also to agree with Pausanias, but the passage is so defective that we cannot safely rely on it. This discrepancy has perhaps been caused by a confusion between the capture of Athens, and the capture of the Acropolis, which, as Appian remarks, took place a little after the entrance of the Romans into the city. Sulla may have visited Athens after the capture of the Acropolis, and in the interval between the battle of Chaeroneia and the battle of Orchomenus. However this may be, it is safer to follow the continuous narrative of Appian.

u 2

Some people blamed Sulla for leaving the rough country of
Attica and leading his men into Boeotia, which was open and
well suited for the war chariots and cavalry of the enemy.
But Sulla was compelled to leave Attica for want of provisions, and he was under that necessity which sometimes
befalls the most prudent commander; he must hazard a
battle or lose all the advantages that he had gained. His
force was small and his first object was to form a junction
with L. Hortensius, supposed to be a brother of the famous
orator, who was leading some troops from Thessaly. The
enemy had occupied the pass of Thermopylae, but Caphis,
apparently Sulla's old friend, though Plutarch here names
him a Chaeroneian, led Hortensius by a circuitous route over
the rugged mountain mass of Parnassus "close by Tithora
(Tithorea), which was not at that time so large a city as it is
now, but only a steep rock scarped all round, to which place
in time of old the Phocians who fled from Xerxes escaped
with their property and were there in safety " (Plutarch).
The city Tithorea of Plutarch's time was situated at Velitza,
which is at the north-east base of the great mass of Parnassus, near the small river Cachales, which flows into the
Cephissus. There Hortensius rested during the day and repelled an attack of the enemy. At night he descended to
Patronis by a difficult path and joined Sulla.

Plutarch took great pains in describing this Boeotian campaign. His narrative, which is founded on Sulla's Memoirs,
is much clearer, and more circumstantial than Appian's.

Sulla and Hortensius occupied an elevation in the midst of
the rich plain of Elateia. This elevation, named Philoboeo-
tus, was fertile and extensive, and had water at the base.
Sulla in his Memoirs highly commended the natural qualities
and position of this place, which Leake identifies "with the
remarkable insulated conical height between Bissikéni and
the Cephissus." If this conjecture is true, Sulla was encamped on the right side of the Cephissus, in the country
which lies between the Cephissus and the stream named
Platania, which joins the Cephissus on the right bank just
below the narrows by which a man passes from Phocis into

Boeotia. Here the Romans would find some supplies, and
they had water. Archelaus, according to Appian, reached
Thermopylae and united his forces with those of Dromichaetes,
and the army of Arcathius, which had entered Macedonia.
He was also joined by those whom Mithridates had just sent,
the army of Taxiles as it seems, but Appian does not name
Taxiles. The combined troops marched from Thermopylae
into Phocis, passing down the valley of the Cephissus by the
town of Elatcia (Lefta), which they attempted to take, but
they were beaten off by the citizens, for which service the
Romans afterwards declared Elateia to be a free city. The
barbarian army was composed of Thracians, men from Pontus,
Scythians, Cappadocians, Bithynians, Gauls from Galatia,
Phrygians, and others who were included in the new acquisitions of Mithridates, in all one hundred and twenty thousand
men, as Appian reports. Sulla had his Italian troops with
those Greeks and Macedonians who had lately come over to
him from Archelaus, and the few that had joined him from
the adjacent parts. But all his force was not a third of
the enemy's. Plutarch, no doubt following Sulla's statement,
says that he had not fifteen thousand infantry, and the
cavalry was not more than fifteen hundred. The other
generals of Mithridates were impatient for battle, against the
advice of Archelaus, who knew his own men and the Romans
too. But the numbers of the enemy who filled the plain,
their horses and chariots, the barbaric splendour of their arms,
and the shouts and cries of many tongues, struck terror into
the small body of the Romans. Sulla being unable to remove
their fears, and not choosing to fight a battle with his men in
this mood, kept quiet. The contempt of the enemy for the
Romans led to the neglect of their own discipline, and the men
of Archelaus straggled from their camp to plunder. They
destroyed the town of Panopeus, plundered Lebadeia, and
robbed the oracular shrine of Trophonius. In order to keep
his soldiers from idleness, Sulla led them down to the banks
of the Cephissus, and compelled them to divert the river
from its course and to dig ditches, with no other view, as
Plutarch supposed, than to tire his men and make them

prefer the hazard of a fight. Frontinus (Strat. i. 11, 20)
says that Sulla at the siege of the Piraeus, finding his men
slack, imposed hard work on them that they might be the
readier to battle with the enemy. But the text of Frontinus
is incorrect as to the place.

On the third day the soldiers were weary of this labour,
and prayed Sulla to lead them against the enemy. There
was an elevated place near the Cephissus, once the Acropolis
of the Parapotamii, a city which had been destroyed. This
elevated place was a rocky precipitous hill on the north side
of the Cephissus, and separated from Mount Hedylium by
the river Assus, which there flows into the Cephissus, as
Plutarch says[1]. The enemy was moving towards this spot
with the view of seizing it, but Sulla's men anticipated them.

The river Cephissus enters the west side of Lake Copais, a
basin which receives the drainage of the Cephissus and of
Northern Boeotia. In the level country west of the lake and
south of the lower course of the Cephissus is the plain of
Chaeroneia, which is the entrance to the wide plains of Boeotia. Archelaus, after failing in his attempt on the acropolis
of the Parapotamii, advanced towards Chaeroneia. Some of
the men of this town were in Sulla's army, and they entreated
him not to let the place fall into the enemy's hands. Sulla
accordingly allowed them to go, and he sent a legion under
Gabinius with them to Chaeroneia. "Thus," says Plutarch,
"our city had a narrow escape;" for Chaeroneia was Plutarch's
birth-place, and he retired there after his residence at Rome.

Appian represents Archelaus as seeking a fight, and Sulla
as declining a battle, but keeping a sharp look out for convenient times and places. The object of Archelaus seems to

---

[1] " In this passage there is a difficulty :—The testimony of Theopompus, of
Strabo, and of Plutarch himself, shows that Paleókastro is the ancient Parapotamii, and the rocky summit above it Edylium; in which case there is no
stream which can correspond with the Assus but that named Kinéta, which
flows from the marsh of Sfaka, and is joined by the torrent of the vale of
Khúbavo. The river however does not divide the hill of Paleókastro from
Mount Edylium, as Plutarch leads us to expect, but leaves it on the left and
joins the Cephissus a little below the hill of Paleókastro, which is in fact a low
extremity of the mountain itself."—Leake, Travels in Northern Greece, ii. 106.

have been to exclude Sulla from the more fertile parts of
Bocotia, and to confine him to the valley of the Cephissus,
for Archelaus had thrown up a strong intrenchment at a
place named the Assia on the north side of the lower Cephissus between Mount Hedylium and Mount Acontium which
is nearer the lake than Hedylium ; and Sulla quitting his
position at the Acropolis of the Parapotamii and crossing the
Assus, had encamped at the foot of Mount Hedylium, near
the intrenchment of Archelaus. Leake conjectures that
Assia may be in that recess of the plain between Hedylium
and Acontium, through which a small branch of the Cephissus
runs, and where the modern village Karamusá stands. Plutarch adds that the spot where Archelaus was encamped
was " called Archelaus from his name up to the present
day ;" and so we may conclude that there is no doubt about
the site of the camp. Leaving L. Licinius Murena at the
camp with one legion and two cohorts to watch the enemy,
Sulla crossed the Cephissus and advanced south with the
object of effecting a junction with his own troops in Chaeroneia, and examining a place named Thurium or Orthopagus
which was occupied by a detachment of the enemy. Thurium
is a conical-shaped hill south of Chaeroneia, and part of a
small range which separates the plain of Chaeroneia from
the plain of Lebadeia. A stream named Morius flows under
Thurium and enters the Cephissus on the right bank opposite to Assia. Sulla joined his troops in Chaeroneia, where
he found two men of the town, who undertook to dislodge
the enemy from Thurium, if he would give them a few
soldiers. Sulla allowed the two Chaeronoians to make the
attempt, and in the mean time he formed his troops in the
plain, with his cavalry on each flank, himself commanding
the right and Murena the left. We must conclude from this
that, when Sulla crossed the river to Chaeroneia, Archelaus
followed him, and Murena, who would then have nothing to
do on the north side of the river, crossed it also and joined
the general with his legion and two cohorts in the plain
between Chaeroneia and the Cephissus. Sulla's legati Galba
and Hortensius with some reserved cohorts in the rear occu-

pied the neighbouring heights to prevent the enemy from
attacking Sulla's flank, for Archelaus had placed a large body
of cavalry and light infantry on his wings with the manifest
design of extending his line and surrounding the Romans.
The two Chaeroneians under the command of Ericius (probably a corrupted name which should be Hirtius) started on
their enterprise from a precipitous rock which rises above the
town of Chaeroneia, and is named Petrachus. They made
their way unseen round Thurium to the highest point of the hills
behind Chaeroneia, and suddenly appeared above the enemy.
The barbarians fled in disorder, but they suffered most from
themselves, for as they ran down the hill and were entangled
among their own spears they shoved one another over the
rocks. Three thousand of the enemy perished in the confusion. Part of those who got safe to the foot of the hill fell
in with Murena and were destroyed, and the rest forcing their
way to the main body of Archelaus caused alarm. Sulla
seized the critical moment, and by quickly leading his men
up to the enemy, deprived them of the use of their formidable
scythe chariots. The efficacy of these chariots depended on
traversing a space sufficient to enable them to acquire velocity
and momentum. They were now driven feebly against the
Romans, who easily pushed them aside, or opened their lines
and let them pass to the rear, where before they could turn
round, the horses and drivers were pierced with the Roman
javelina. It was now a fight between long pikes and swords.
The barbarians pushed forward with their spears and locked
their shields in order to maintain their line: the Romans
threw their pila against the enemy, and then with their
swords attempted to beat aside the spears. Archelaus had
placed in his front fifteen thousand slaves, who had been
invited from the Greek cities by a promise of freedom and
armed. These men fought better than could have been
expected, but the slingers and light javelin men assailed
them in the rear, and at last they turned and fell into
complete confusion.

Archelaus was now extending his right wing to surround
the Romans, and Hortensius with his cohorts advanced at

a run with the view of taking Archelaus on the flank. But
Archelaus with two thousand horsemen suddenly wheeled
round, and Hortensius overpowered by numbers retreated to
the hills, and thus becoming separated from the body of the
army was in danger of being hemmed in by the barbarians.
Sulla on the right wing, which was not yet engaged, hastened
to relieve Hortensius; but Archelaus conjecturing from the
dust raised by Sulla's troops what he was going to do, quitted
Hortensius, and wheeling round moved to the place which
Sulla had left on the right, expecting to find the soldiers
there without their general and to defeat them. At the same
time the Chalcaspides under Taxiles attacked Murena on the
left. This dextrous movement of Archelaus would have been
successful against a bad general. The shouts of the two
armies were re-echoed from the hills, and Sulla hesitated
which way he should move. But he was not disconcerted by
an unexpected movement. He sent Hortensius with four
cohorts to support Murena, and ordering the fifth to follow
him he turned to the right wing, which was bravely resisting
Archelaus. As soon as Sulla appeared, the Romans broke
the line of Archelaus, and pursued the barbarians in their
disorderly flight to the river and Mount Acontium. The
river must be the Cephissus, on the north side of which and
near Acontium Archelaus, as we have seen, had his camp.
When Archelaus fled, Sulla hastened to aid Murena, but
finding that Murena had defeated Taxiles, he joined in the
pursuit. Many of the barbarians were cut down in the plain,
but the greatest part perished in the attempt to regain their
intrenchments, and only ten thousand made their escape to
Chalcis (Egripo) in Euboea. It appears that the main camp
of the barbarians was near Acontium, and if they fled from
Chaeronia to their camp, the survivors must have retired to
the coast along the north side of the lake Copais. Appian's
account of the battle, which differs from Plutarch's, states
that the Romans completed their victory by breaking into
the camp of Archelaus. He also makes the survivors of
Archelaus' troops ten thousand, and the loss of the Romans
only fifteen men, and even two of these afterwards came

back alive. Plutarch quotes Sulla's Memoirs for the statement that he missed only fourteen of his own soldiers, and
ten of the fourteen showed themselves in the evening. Sulla
made many prisoners, and got a great quantity of arms and
booty. That which was of little use was piled up in a great
heap, and, according to Roman custom, fired by the general
as an offering to the deities of war. Sulla erected two
trophies, one in the plain where the men of Archelaus first
gave way, and the other on the summit of Thurium. Both
those trophies existed when Pausanias travelled through
Greece in the second century of our era. Sulla followed
Archelaus with some light troops to the Euripus or the channel which separates Euboea from the mainland, but he was
still without vessels, while Archelaus in his ships sailed about
in security and pillaged the sea coasts like a pirate. Returning from the pursuit Sulla celebrated at Thebes a festival for
his victory and had a dramatic representation. The judges
were Greeks invited from the other cities of Greece, for
Sulla did not pardon the Thebans for having once joined
Archelaus. He took from them half of their lands, which he
dedicated to Apollo of Delphi and Zeus of Olympia, ordering
the revenues from these lands to be paid to the two deities
in place of the money of which he had robbed Delphi and
Olympia. Thus Sulla made other people pay his debts. He
also showed his piety at the cost of others. He placed a
statue of Dionysus on Mount Helicon, but it was a statue
which he took from the town of Orchomenus, and one of
Myron's best works. This was, according to a Greek saying,
a way of worshipping the gods with other people's incense.

CHAPTER XXII.

SULLA AND MITHRIDATES.

B.C. 86—84.

When Mithridates heard of the defeat of Archelaus, he was greatly alarmed, but he immediately set about raising another army. Fearing that this misfortune would bring fresh enemies on him, either now or when some other opportunity offered, he seized all those whom he suspected. He first laid hold of the tetrarchs of the Galatians, both those who were living with him on friendly terms, and those who had not submitted, and put them to death with their wives and children, all except three tetrarchs who escaped. Some of those chiefs were treacherously surprised, and others were murdered one night at a banquet. The king also seized all the property of the Galatian chiefs, and putting garrisons in their towns sent Eumachus to govern the country as a satrap. But the three surviving chiefs collected a force and expelled Eumachus and his men from Galatia.

The vindictive king had not forgotten the ship of Chios which accidentally fell foul of the royal vessel in the sea-fight with the Rhodians. He began with confiscating the property of the Chians who had fled to Sulla, and seizing what belonged to the Romans in Chios. Zenobius, his commander, being sent with a force to the island got possession of the town of Chios and all the other strong places. He then summoned the natives to a public meeting, and told them that the king suspected the city on account of the Roman party in it, but he would be satisfied, if they would give up their arms and put in his hands as hostages the

children of the first people of the island. The Chians seeing
that their city was occupied by Zenobius gave what he asked
for, and both arms and hostages were sent to Erythrae on the
mainland. A letter now came to the Chians from Mithridates in which he charged them with favouring the Romans,
and being hostile to himself, but, though his friends advised
him to put them to death, he was content with imposing on
them a fine of two thousand talents. The Chians wished
to send commissioners to the king to remonstrate, but Zenobius would not allow them, and with sorrow they were
reduced to the necessity of making up the sum demanded
of them by taking the ornaments from the temples and
all the women's decorations. But Zenobius alleging that
the full weight was not made up summoned all the inhabitants to the theatre, which he surrounded with armed
men, and he also lined with troops the ways from the
theatre to the sea. The people were then taken out of the
theatre, and put in ships, the men by themselves, and the
women and children by themselves, and being carried to
Mithridates they were sent off to some of the parts bordering
on the Black Sea.

Zenobius with some troops was now sent to Ephesus, but
the people would not admit him till he had laid down his
arms at the gates. He entered this great city with a few of
his followers, and lodged with Philopoemen, the father of
Monime, and now by the king's favour governor of Ephesus.
Zenobius invited the Ephesians to a public meeting, but they
knew the man and put off the meeting to the next day. In
the night the citizens having assembled seized Zenobius and
put him to death in prison. They then took possession
of the town, formed themselves into military companies,
brought in supplies from the country, and managed their own
affairs as they pleased. This revolt encouraged the citizens
of Tralles, Hypaepa, Metropolis, and other places to do the
same. Mithridates attempted to reduce the insurgents, and
he severely handled those who fell into his power, but he
relied more on other measures. To prevent further defection
he declared the Greek cities to be free, proclaimed a general

remission of debts, which would please debtors better than creditors, gave the citizenship to the resident aliens in the Greek towns, and freedom to the slaves, hoping, as it turned out, that debtors, aliens, and slaves would be faithful in the expectation of keeping what he had given to them. The king was still in danger from conspiracies. Two men of Smyrna and two of Lesbos combined to kill him, but things turned out as they often do when several men are engaged in a conspiracy. Asclepiodotus one of the conspirators betrayed his accomplices, and he convinced the king of the truth of his information by placing him where he could hear one of the conspirators talk without being seen. The conspirators were put to a painful death, and the king's suspicious temper led him to greater cruelty. Eighty persons were seized in Pergamum on a charge of conspiracy, and the same thing happened in other cities. A reign of terror began. Agents of the king were sent about the country who laid hold of those who were denounced out of private enmity, and put them to death. Sixteen hundred persons are said to have lost their lives by this cruel inquisition. Not long after, when Sulla entered Asia, some of the informers were caught and executed, some did justice on themselves, and others fled with Mithridates to Pontus. The inhabitants of Asia had exchanged Roman tyranny for the worse tyranny of an Asiatic despot.

In the course of this summer Mithridates sent another army into Greece, eighty thousand men under Dorylaus to join the ten thousand that Archelaus still had. Sulla had left Bocotia, and advanced as far as Melitaea in Phthiotis with the view of meeting the consul L. Valerius Flaccus, who was crossing the Hadriatic with a force to oppose Mithridates, as it was said, but in fact to oppose Sulla also. The news of Dorylaus landing at Chalcis brought Sulla back to Bocotia, which was again occupied by the king's troops. Dorylaus paid no attention to the advice of Archelaus, and was eager to draw Sulla to a fight. Indeed he said that so many thousands could not have been destroyed by the Romans, if there had not been some treachery. However a slight skirmish

with the Romans near Tilphossium about fifty stadia from
Haliartus on the south side of Lake Copais, made Dorylaus
wiser, and he formed the opinion that it was not prudent to
hazard a decisive battle, and that it would be better to
prolong the war until the Romans should be exhausted by
want of supplies.   The king's generals had taken a position
near Orchomenus at the west end of the lake of Copais.   The
town of Orchomenus stood on an elevation round the southern
base of which the Cephissus flows into the lake.   The north
end of the hill of Orchomenus is opposite to Mount Acontium.
The little river Melas rose on the east side of the hill of
Orchomenus, and was a copious stream even at its source; but
the greater part of the water was lost in obscure marshes
overgrown with shrubs, and only a small part flowed into the
Cephissus near the point where this river entered the lake.
The ground near Orchomenus was favourable for the enemy
who had a superiority in cavalry, "for of all the plains in
Bœotia noted for their beauty and extent, this, which commences at the city of Orchomenus, is the only one which
spreads without interruption and without any trees, and it
reaches the marshes in which the river Melas is lost" (Plutarch).   The Romans, who were encamped near the enemy,
began to dig trenches "on both sides with the view, if
possible, of cutting off the enemy from the hard ground and
those parts which were favourable to cavalry and driving
them into the marshes."   But the barbarians making a
vigorous attack drove the Romans from their trenches, and
dispersed most of the men who were placed to protect the
workers.   At this critical moment Sulla leapt from his horse
and seizing a standard made his way through the fugitives,
calling out to his men that when they should be asked where
they deserted their commander, they must remember to say
that it was at Orchomenus.   This reproach rallied the Romans,
and they repulsed the enemy.   Sulla then withdrawing his
men for a time and allowing them to take some food, began
again to work at the trenches with which he designed to
shut in the enemy.   The barbarians again assaulted the
Romans, but they were driven back to their camp, where

they spent a wretched night. In this battle Diogenes, the son of the wife of Archelaus, fell while he was fighting bravely. At daybreak Sulla again led his men up to the enemy's camp, and again began working at his trenches for the purpose of shutting him in. The camp was at last assailed. The Romans protected by their shields tore down one angle, but the barbarians leaping from their rampart were ready to receive them with their swords, and they checked the Romans until Basillus a tribune jumped into the breach and killed the first man that he met. Basillus was followed by his soldiers, and the camp was stormed. The barbarians attempted to escape, but some were killed, and many were driven into the lake and drowned. Archelaus hid himself in a marsh till he got a boat in which he crossed the lake and escaped to Chalcis in Euboea, whither he summoned all the troops of the king that were in Greece. Even in the time of Plutarch, two hundred years later, many barbarian bows, helmets, pieces of iron cuirasses, and swords were found buried in the marshes of Orchomenus. The descriptions of this battle by Plutarch and Appian agree in some respects, but neither description is clear. There is a much better description by Frontinus. It is true that Frontinus does not name Orchomenus, but as his narrative cannot refer to the first battle between Sulla and Archelaus, it must refer to the second. Frontinus says: Archelaus in the battle with Sulla placed his scythe chariots in front: behind them he placed his Macedonian phalanx; in the third line he placed his auxiliaries who were armed in Roman fashion, and among them were deserters of Italian stock, on whom Archelaus greatly relied, for these men could expect no mercy from the enemy. His light-armed troops were in the rear. On both flanks he placed his numerous cavalry with the view of surrounding the Romans. Sulla, who had his camp in his rear, dug on each side of the ground which he intended to occupy with his troops two broad ditches which extended from his camp into the plain, and he placed two forts at the extremity of these ditches. He thus prevented the enemy from falling on his flanks. Sulla arranged his infantry in three lines behind one another, with intervals in the lines through which the light troops and the cavalry, which was in the rear, could pass when the opportunity came. Those who were in the second line were ordered to fix firmly in the ground numerous stakes close set; and the ante-signani or men in the first line were ordered to retire within the stakes, when the scythe chariots approached. The battle cry was then raised, and as the chariots advanced, they came upon the stakes and were received with a shower of missiles from the light troops which were sent forward. The chariots attempted to turn round to retreat, but this movement threw the phalanx of spearmen into disorder and they fell back. Archelaus then brought up his cavalry to the front, but Sulla's cavalry coming up quick from the rear fell on them and completed the rout. All this is intelligible and explains how Sulla with his small army defeated the superior force of Archelaus. He showed his military talent by arranging his troops in an unusual order, but an order which secured him a victory (Frontinus, Strat. ii. 3, 17; Machiavelli, Dell' arte della guerra, Lib. iv.). Caesar made a similar disposition for the protection of his camp when he was in presence of the great army of the Belgian confederation (B. G. ii. 8).

The day after the battle Sulla rewarded the brave tribune with a military crown and gave prizes to others. Bocotia had been very unstable in fidelity to the Romans, and Sulla allowed his men to plunder the country. One authority reports that above twenty-five thousand prisoners were made and sold by auction. This would bring a large sum of money to Sulla and enable him to pay his men. Sulla wintered in Thessaly, where he waited for Lucullus and the ships that he was expecting, but as he heard nothing of Lucullus, he set about building ships himself.

Plutarch places the interview between Sulla and Archelaus before Sulla left Boeotia for Thessaly. He also says that many who had fled from the tyranny of Cinna and Carbo at Rome resorted to the camp of Sulla and formed a sort of senate about him. But Plutarch may not be quite accu-rate here, for Cinna and Carbo were not consuls until the next year B.C. 85. Plutarch also represents Metella with her children as not coming to Sulla until after the battle of Orchomenus, and entreating him to go to the aid of his friends in Italy. But Sulla could not leave the war with Mithridates unfinished, and a man of his sagacity must have seen that he would more easily put down his enemies at home after he had humbled the great enemy of Rome. He had an interview with Archelaus at Delium on the sea-coast of Boeotia, or at Aulis, which was near Delium. Archelaus urged Sulla to give up the war against Mithridates and to return to prosecute the war against his enemies at Rome: he offered Sulla money, ships, and troops on behalf of the king. Sulla in reply advised Archelaus to assume the kingly title, to become an ally of Rome, and give up the ships of Mithridates. But Archelaus was a more faithful servant than his master deserved, and he refused to become a traitor. Sulla then asked Archelaus how he could venture to propose to him to be a traitor to Rome, to him a Roman who had inflicted on Archelaus two severe defeats at Chaeroneia and Orchomenus. Finally they came to the following terms as Plutarch has reported them: Mithridates was to give up the province Asia, and Paphlagonia, and to surrender Bithynia to Nicomedes, and Cappadocia to Ariobarzanes, to pay down to the Romans two thousand talents, and to give them seventy ships fitted with brass and completely equipped. Sulla agreed to confirm Mithridates in the rest of his possessions and to recognize him as an ally of the Romans. The form of the agreement, as reported by Appian, expresses the surrender of territory in general terms, but it contains some other things which it is reasonable to suppose that Sulla would insist on, such as the surrender of Roman generals, commanders, captives, deserters, and fugitive slaves, with the Chians and others whom the king had sent to Pontus. Appian may have had other authorities besides Sulla's Memoirs for the history of this campaign, and it is certain that in his description of the battle of Chaeroneia at least he must have followed a different authority. The veracity of Sulla's Memoirs cannot be estimated by a comparison with

other contemporary historians, for we have none. Granius
Licinianus, supposed to be a contemporary of Sallust, is the
nearest writer in time to Sulla's period, and a fragment of
his Annals contains the terms of this treaty, which agree in
the main with Plutarch and Appian, though there are some
variations. The fragments of Dion (ed. Reimarus, p. 73)
relating to this treaty are nearly a verbal copy of Plutarch.
According to Licinianus, Archelaus agreed to surrender his
fleet to Sulla, and the king was to retire from all the islands,
also from the province Asia, from Bithynia, Paphlagonia, and
Galatia ; to give up Q. Oppius and M'Aquillius, and set free
all the captives, the number of whom was not small. It was
also agreed, as Licinianus says, that the king should give
seventy ships decked and equipped to the Socii or allies, and
furnish them with corn and pay. But who are meant by the
Socii ? That is not easy to say, nor perhaps did the man who
wrote these words know what they meant. Though we do
not possess the exact terms on which Sulla agreed with
Mithridates, perhaps we know the chief conditions; but it
seems as if none of our extant authorities took the pains
to report the terms of the treaty completely.

After the agreement was made Sulla began his march
towards Asia in company with Archelaus. At Larissa in
Thessaly Archelaus fell ill, and Sulla stopped his march and
treated him with as much attention as if he had been one of
his own generals. Sulla's behaviour to Archelaus gave rise
to suspicion that the battle of Chaeroneia had been won
through treachery on the part of Archelaus, and this suspicion was confirmed by Sulla giving up all the friends of
Mithridates whom he had taken prisoners, except Aristion
whom he had put to death, and Aristion was an enemy of
Archelaus. Sulla also gave Archelaus ten thousand plethra
of land in the island of Euboea, and the title of friend and
ally of the Roman people. Sulla, says Plutarch, makes his
apology or defence about these matters in his Memoirs, but
whether he admitted or denied them, Plutarch does not say.
He thought it necessary however to explain his behaviour
towards Archelaus. If he told the truth, his explanation

might be that it was his policy to come to terms with Mithridates and to end the war with some credit to himself, and
so to be at liberty to turn against his enemies at home. He
had also a Roman army to contend against which was now in
Asia under Fimbria an audacious villain, whose success
against Mithridates threatened to rob Sulla of the honour of
humbling the king of Pontus. Sulla was in great straits.
He had no help from Rome: indeed he was declared an
enemy by his political opponents. It was necessary to employ all the resources of his fertile genius to accomplish his
purpose, and as success is the test by which we generally
measure the ability of a politician and a general, we must
admit that Sulla conducted his affairs in this difficult crisis
with rare ability and courage.

When Sulla was in Thessaly, or it is possible that it was
after he had advanced into Macedonia, ambassadors came
from Mithridates about the terms of peace made by Archelaus. Appian and Plutarch agree that Mithridates objected
to the surrender of Paphlagonia, but Plutarch adds that he
positively refused to confirm the agreement about the ships.
Upon this Sulla fell into a great passion, and said that Mithridates would speak a different language when he should see
Sulla in Asia. The ambassadors had nothing to say in reply,
but Archelaus attempted to pacify Sulla, and at last he
obtained permission to go to Mithridates on a promise to
conclude peace on Sulla's own terms: if he should not succeed, he said he would kill himself. Appian reports that the
ambassadors of Mithridates told Sulla that Mithridates could
have obtained better terms from Fimbria. But Sulla replied
that he would punish Fimbria too, and as soon as he arrived
in Asia, he would know whether Mithridates was for peace or
war.

The consul L. Valerius Flaccus had crossed the sea from
Brundisium in B.C. 86 and perhaps late in the year. On the
voyage the greater part of his ships were dispersed or
damaged by bad weather; and some vessels which were
despatched before the rest were burnt by a force sent for
that purpose by Mithridates. This is Appian's brief narra-

tive, which continually perplexes us, as abridgments and
summaries always do, by reporting facts without the necessary explanation, and by bringing facts into juxtaposition,
which were in no ways connected. If any of Flaccus' ships
wore burned by Mithridates, it must have been some vessels
that had been sent forward to the northern parts of the
Aegean, to meet the troops which would march from the
coast of the Hadriatic along the Via Egnatia through Macedonia and Thrace.   Flaccus, who was a poor commander and
a cruel disciplinarian, disgusted his army, and part of his
troops which had been sent forward into Thessaly passed over
to Sulla; but there is no evidence whether this defection took
place when Sulla had advanced into Phthiotis before the
battle of Orchomenus or after. Fimbria, who served under
Flaccus and was a man of some ability, contrived to keep the
rest of the soldiers together. It happened that on one occasion there was a dispute between Fimbria and the quaestor
of the army about quarters, and Flaccus decided the dispute
against Fimbria, who was much vexed, and threatened to
return to Rome. Flaccus took him at his word and put
another in his place. Fimbria watching his opportunity,
when Flaccus had crossed over from Byzantium to Chalcedon, deprived of the fasces Minucius Thermus, who had been
left in charge of the forces by Flaccus, and usurped the command of the army. Flaccus recrossed the Bosporus in great
passion to recover his authority, but the army had mutinied and
he was glad to make his escape to Chalcedon by night, and
from thence he fled to Nicomedia and closed the gates of the
town. Fimbria followed the fugitive general, discovered him
hid in a well, cut off his head and ordered it to be thrown into
the sea. The body was left unburied. This is the most audacious act of villainy recorded in Roman history. A man who
had followed the army on the invitation of Flaccus and was
employed by him, murdered his own general, a Roman consul, who had been appointed to conduct the war against
Mithridates in Asia. Fimbria now assumed the command
and conducted the campaign with great vigour. He fought
several battles with a son of Mithridates and defeated him at

the river Rhyndacus, by a stratagem like that which Sulla used
at the battle of Orchomenus (Frontinus, iii. 17. 5). From
the Rhyndacus Fimbria pursued the king to Pergamum.
Mithridates however did not venture to stay there, and he
continued his flight to Pitane on the coast, still followed by
his active enemy, who began to make a line of trenches
round the town, and would have caught the king, if he had
not crossed over to Mitylene on the opposite coast of Lesbos.
We must suppose that Mithridates had exhausted his men in
the wars in Greece, or he might have made head against the
small force of Fimbria.

Asia was now cleared of the king's troops and was at the
mercy of Fimbria, who punished those who had sided with
Mithridates and plundered the lands of such towns as would
not open their gates to him. The people of Ilium being
besieged by Fimbria sent messengers to Sulla in Europe to
ask him to come to their help. Sulla promised that he would
come, and in the mean time advised them to tell Fimbria that
they were under his protection. Fimbria replied that he was
glad to hear that they were friends of the Romans, and he
invited them, as he was a Roman, to let him into their town.
He reminded them also with a sneer of their kinship with the
Romans, alluding to the old legend of Aeneas and his Trojans
settling in Italy. When Fimbria was let into the town, he
massacred all whom he could seize, and he burnt the place to
the ground. He put to a cruel death the men who had been sent
on a mission to Sulla. He did not spare even the temples.
Those who fled to the temple of Athena were burnt alive
together with the building. Appian fixes the date of this
event at the close of the 173rd Olympiad, which was the
middle of B.C. 85. He remarks that Ilium was now treated
worse by a kinsman than it had been by Agamemnon, for he
supposed in accordance with the common opinion of antiquity
that this Ilium was on the site of the Ilium of the Iliad.
Fimbria, it is said, even dug down the walls or threw them
down by undermining them, but Ilium still existed as a town
after Fimbria's savage treatment of it.

We know little of the affairs at Rome during this time.

310 DECLINE OF THE ROMAN REPUBLIC.

It is stated by Livy (Epit. 83) that L. Cornelius Cinna and Cn. Papirius Carbo appointed themselves consuls for two years or rather during two successive years B.C. 85 and 84.

Sulla spent the winter of B.C. 85 and the early part at least of B.C. 84 in Macedonia. This province had been completely disorganized by the occupation of Mithridates' troops and the incursions of the barbarians on the frontiers. Sulla with his legatus Hortensius reduced these marauders to submission, and thus at the same time gave employment to his men and enriched them with plunder. It was prudent policy for Sulla to settle the affairs of Macedonia before he advanced into Asia.

The adventures of Lucullus after he was sent off by Sulla near the end of B.C. 87 are briefly told by Plutarch. Lucullus sailed to Egypt and Africa to get ships. He set out with three Greek piratical vessels and three Rhodian biremes, as Plutarch says in his life of Lucullus, but this statement does not agree with what Plutarch has said in his life of Sulla. The sea was filled with the cruisers of Mithridates, but Lucullus safely reached Crete, and made the people friendly to his cause. From Crete he passed over to Cyrene, and settled affairs there, which were in great confusion. In his voyage from Cyrene to Egypt Lucullus was attacked by pirates and lost most of his ships, but he escaped himself and was well received at Alexandria by King Ptolemaeus VIII. Plutarch calls the king a young man, but that is a mistake. Ptolemaeus declined the alliance which Lucullus proposed, for the king was afraid of taking any part in the war, but he gave Lucullus ships to convey him as far as the island Cyprus. In his voyage along the coast of Syria Lucullus got some vessels from the maritime towns, and probably some also from the south coast of Asia Minor, but Plutarch observes that he did not take any vessels from "such as participated in piratical iniquities," and these piratical towns, as we know, were on the coast of Cilicia. When Lucullus was in Cyprus, he heard that the enemy was lying in wait for him "at the headlands;" but it is uncertain whether this was some place on the coast of Cyprus, or these "headlands" were some of the bold projections of the opposite coast of Asia Minor. Lucullus hauled up his ships and wrote to the cities about winter-quarters and supplies, as if he intended to stay in Cyprus till the fine season began. But this was only a feint. As soon as he had an opportunity, he put to sea and reached Rhodes, where he got more ships from the Rhodians. This was the successful issue of the adventure of the young Roman commander. Lucullus persuaded the people of Cos and of Cnidus to desert the king and to join him in an attack on the Samians. He also drove the king's party out of Chios and released the people of Colophon from their tyrant, who was probably a creature of Mithridates. These events must have occupied some time. When Mithridates had left Pergamum and was shut up in Pitane by Fimbria, the king summoned all his ships in order to secure his escape by sea, for he had no chance of getting away by land. Fimbria, who had no naval force or very little, sent to Lucullus and prayed him to come to Pitane with his fleet, and thus Mithridates would either be caught, if he put out to sea, or he would be compelled to surrender to the army which was investing Pitane. Fimbria said that the capture of Mithridates would be glorious both to himself and Lucullus, and the Romans would think nothing of the vaunted victories of Chaeroneia and Orchomenus in comparison with the capture of Mithridates. But Lucullus would not listen to Fimbria's proposal, though if he had blockaded Pitane, Mithridates would have been taken and the war ended. It is difficult to say whether Lucullus acted like a good citizen or not on this occasion, for Mithridates was an enemy of Rome, and every Roman was bound to do him all the harm that he could. But if Lucullus blockaded Pitane with his fleet and prevented the escape of Mithridates by sea, the king must surrender to Fimbria, who would have had the credit of taking him. Lucullus would see this, and he could not consent to aid a man, who had murdered his own general and seized the command of the army. Besides, Lucullus was serving under Sulla, and he could not co-operate with a man who was Sulla's enemy as much as Mithridates was. Whatever may have been his reasons, Lucullus refused to

assist Fimbria, and so Mithridates escaped to Mitylene, as
already has been said. But Lucullus attacked and defeated
some of the king's ships off Lectum in the Troad ; and he
had a second naval fight near Tenedos with Neoptolemus,
who had a larger naval force, but was compelled to fly before
Lucullus.

When Archelaus returned from Mithridates, he found Sulla
at Philippi, which town he had taken. Archelaus brought
back a favourable answer, and reported that Mithridates
wished to have an interview with Sulla. Plutarch has stated
that it was fear of Fimbria that inclined Mithridates to make
a friend of Sulla; and this is very probable. Mithridates
could expect no terms from Fimbria, and indeed he might
fear that any agreement with him would not be ratified at
Rome, but that in dealing with Sulla, he would be dealing
with a man who could impose terms on Rome as well as on
himself. Sulla had his own reasons for coming to an agreement with the king. He wished to return to Rome and
to strengthen himself against his enemies in Italy by the
ships and money of Mithridates. Lucullus met Sulla in the
Thracian Chersonesus and took him over the Hellespont to
Dardanus in the Troad, which had been declared a free city
by the Romans after the peace with King Antiochus B.C.
190. Dardanus is about midway between the promontory of
Sigeium and Abydus. Mithridates had still two hundred
rowing-ships, twenty thousand heavy armed soldiers, six
thousand horsemen, and many of his scythe chariots. If he
had all this force, when he fled before Fimbria, he was either
a coward or he knew that he could not trust his men.
Fimbria must have retired from Pitane after the escape of
Mithridates to Mitylene, and the king then returned to the
mainland, for Appian states that he advanced from Pergamum
to meet Sulla at the place appointed for the conference. Sulla
had with him only four cohorts and two hundred horsemen,
as Plutarch reports. Sulla and the king met in a plain, each
attended by a small number of men, and in the presence of
the two armies. When they met, Mithridates advanced and
held out his hand, and Sulla asked him if he agreed to the

terms made by Archelaus. As the king made no reply, Sulla
said, "Those who sue must speak first : conquerors may remain silent." Appian has reported the conference which
followed, and the speeches of the king and Sulla, which are
the rhetorical embellishments of the historian. Mithridates
threw the blame of the war on the greediness of the Roman
commissioners and commanders, and, whatever his own
ambitious designs may have been, he had certainly good
cause of complaint. Sulla replied by recapitulating all the
crimes of Mithridates, and the many proofs of his hostility to
the Romans, especially in taking advantage of the time when
Rome was engaged in war with the revolted Italians. It is
possible that all the talk was mere show, and that both Sulla
and the king were desirous to end the war. Mithridates at
last agreed to the terms made by Archelaus, and Sulla embraced and kissed him. He then produced kings Ariobarzanes and Nicomedes and reconciled them to Mithridates.
The king gave up to Sulla seventy ships, and sailed off to
the Pontus. This was the termination of the first Mithridatic
war (B.C. 84). Sulla's men were dissatisfied with this settlement. They thought it a shame that the greatest enemy of
the Romans, who had massacred so many thousands in the province of Asia, should be allowed to sail off with the spoils of the
country, which he had been plundering for four years. Sulla's
apology to his soldiers was that he could not oppose both
Fimbria and Mithridates, if they should unite against him.
Such a union would not have been impossible, and Sulla
acted like a wise man with reference to his own interests.

Sulla now advanced against Fimbria, who was encamped
near Thyateira, an inland town of Lydia on a branch of the
river Hermus. When Sulla was within two stadia of Fimbria,
he summoned him to give up his army, and when this was
refused, he began to make his trenches for the purpose of
shutting up Fimbria. Many of Fimbria's men passed over
to Sulla, and the rest declared that they would not fight
against their fellow-citizens. Fimbria tried to induce his men
to take the oath of obedience to him, and he first called on
one Nonius, who had been his adviser in all things. Nonius

refused to take the oath, and Fimbria drawing his sword
threatened to kill him. This only made matters worse, and
Fimbria found it prudent to desist. He then engaged a slave
by bribes and the promise of liberty to pass over to Sulla as
a deserter and kill him. The man's trepidation, as he was preparing to do the work, betrayed him, and being seized he
confessed. Sulla's men were infuriated at this attempt on the
life of their general, and standing round Fimbria's intrenchments they abused him and called him Athenion, the name of
the slave king in Sicily, who had a short reign. Fimbria, who
had now no chance of escape, appeared on the rampart and
asked for a conference with Sulla, who would not go himself,
but sent Rutilius. Fimbria asked for pardon if he had done
any thing wrong, and urged his youth as an apology. Rutilius
promised that Sulla would allow him a safe conduct to the
sea, if he would leave Asia of which Sulla was proconsul.
Fimbria might have been well satisfied with such terms, but
perhaps he did not trust Sulla. His answer was that he had
a better way than that, and thereupon he retired to Pergamum, and going into the temple of Aesculapius stabbed
himself. The wound was not mortal, and Fimbria ordered
his slave to despatch him, which the man did, and then
killed himself on the body of his master. Plutarch says that
Fimbria feared Sulla's unforgiving temper and committed
suicide in the camp; and this seems a more probable story,
for it is not easy to conceive how Fimbria could make
his escape to Pergamum, more than forty miles distant from
Thyatira, nor why he should go there merely to die. Sulla
allowed Fimbria's freedmen to bury the body : he said that
he would not imitate Cinna and Marius, who had deprived
many persons in Rome of life and their bodies of interment. Sulla's conduct was prudent, whatever was his
motive. He immediately received the submission of Fimbria's
army, which he joined to his own. He commissioned C.
Scribonius Curio to restore Nicomedes III. named Philopator,
to his kingdom of Bithynia, and Ariobarzanes to Cappadocia.
He sent a despatch to the Senate, as any other Roman
general would have done under the circumstances, but he

took no notice of the fact that he had been declared an enemy.

Sulla had now leisure for the affairs of the province Asia. The people of Ilium, of Chios, the Lycians, Rhodians, the town of Magnesia which had resisted Mithridates, and some other places, in consideration of the help which they had given, or as a compensation for what they had suffered in the cause of Sulla, were declared free states and friends of the Roman people. Sulla sent soldiers round to the other towns, and made proclamation that all the slaves, who had been declared free by Mithridates, should return to their masters. Many of the slaves took no notice of the order, and some of the towns resisted. The consequence was a great massacre both of free men and slaves. The walls of many cities were destroyed, and in various parts the people were reduced to slavery and their lands wasted. Those Ephesians, who had been the chief leaders in the rebellion, were beheaded. Sulla issued an order that the chief persons in the several towns should meet him at Ephesus on a certain day. When they came, he addressed them from his tribunal. He told them that the Romans first entered Asia when Antiochus king of Syria was wasting the country. When the Romans had driven Antiochus out, they made the river Halys and the range of Taurus the western limits of the possessions of Antiochus, but they allowed the people of Asia to enjoy their independence, except such as they placed under the protection of King Eumenes of Pergamum, or under the Rhodians, both of whom had been allies of the Romans. When King Attalus bequeathed his kingdom of Pergamum to the Romans, the people of Asia joined the usurper Aristonicus and aided him for four years against the Romans. When Aristonicus was taken, the greater part of his adherents submitted through fear. After this they had peace for four and twenty years[1], during which time individuals grew rich and communities flourished, till again the people of Asia broke out against the Romans. Taking advantage of the

---

[1] There is an error in "four and twenty."

Social War in Italy, some of them invited Mithridates to enter
Asia, and others joined him when he came. They obeyed
the cruel order to massacre all the Italians in Asia in one
day with the women and children, nor did they spare even
those who fled for refuge to the temples. They had paid some
penalty for their crimes even to Mithridates, who broke his
promises to them, put them to death, seized their money and
lands, abolished debts, made slaves free, set tyrants over some
of the towns, and allowed pirates to scour the seas and
robbers to overrun the country; from all which they might
learn what kind of a master they had taken in place of the
Romans. Some of the ringleaders had been already punished,
but it was right that all the people should pay the penalty
of their offences, and it was just that the penalty should
be of the same kind as their own deeds. The Romans
however would never make cruel massacres, nor indiscriminate
confiscation of property, nor encourage the rising of slaves
and such other acts as were only the work of barbarians.
After this terrible denunciation Sulla concluded thus : " But
still as I wish to show some regard to the Greek race and
name, and the fame of the people of Asia, and out of consideration too for the reputation of the Roman people, I
impose on you only a penalty of five years' taxes to be paid
immediately, and further all the expenses of the war, and
whatever other expenses I shall have in settling the country.
I shall distribute this sum among the several cities, and
appoint a time for the payment; and those who do not
observe the terms will be punished as enemies." It was
simply an act of prudence in Sulla not to ruin totally a
people from whom he might draw so much money, and
though he cared not for human life and spared no man who
stood in his way, he was far above such ferocious tyrants as
Mithridates, who loved cruelty and gratified his revenge even
with his own loss. Sulla, who was a man of great ability
and foresight, was not guilty of this folly.

The contribution which Sulla levied on the province Asia
was the large sum of twenty thousand talents, which, though
a heavy charge on a people who had already suffered so

much, might yet have been borne. But this was not all.
The inhabitants of the province were reduced to beggary by
the violence and exactions of the soldiers who were quartered
on them. "Sulla issued an order that the master of a house
should daily supply the soldier who was quartered on him
with four tetradrachma and with dinner for himself and as
many of his friends as he chose to invite; a centurion was to
receive fifty drachmae daily, and to be supplied with two
garments, one to wear in the house and the other when he
went abroad" (Plutarch). It is said that there is nothing
new under the sun, nothing new at least in knavery and
oppression. We have heard in recent days of soldiers being
quartered on the peaceable inhabitants of an invaded country,
who had to feed them well and even furnish them with
luxuries. Lucullus was appointed by Sulla to collect the
precious metal and to coin money. Fortunately for the
people of Asia, Lucullus was a man of mild temper. He
behaved honestly and justly in the discharge of his odious
duty. But the sufferings of the people were great. The
cities were compelled to borrow money at heavy interest.
The lenders would be the Italians who followed the Roman
armies, and the Italian "negotiatores" who would come down
on the province like a shower of locusts, as soon as it was
safe to venture there with their capital. The cities gave as
security their theatres, gymnasia, harbours, and whatever
public property they had. The wealth of the temples was
probably used also in satisfying the demands of Sulla. Some
of the towns had productive property, which they could
mortgage, as we may see from the case of Ephesus. The
great temple of Diana possessed the revenue arising from the
fish that were taken in two salt lakes near the city. Sulla
received the whole of the contribution before he left Asia.
The province was now in a wretched condition. After being
plundered by Mithridates and drained by Sulla, it was left to
the mercy of pirates, who infested the seas with numerous
ships like regular fleets. Mithridates turned these villains
loose to do all the mischief that they could, when he saw that
he could not hold the country long. The pirates not only

took the traders whom they found on the sea, but they
attacked the seaport towns. Iassus or Iasus a town of Caria
on a small island, Samos, Clazomenae, and Samothrace were
captured, while Sulla was still in Asia. It was reckoned
that these marauders carried off from the temple of Samothrace valuable things to the amount of a thousand talents,
as it was supposed. Appian does not determine whether
Sulla allowed these people to be plundered for their defection
from Rome or whether he had no time to put down the
pirates, for he was in a hurry to return to Italy. The second
is doubtless the true reason. Sulla was not so foolish as to
wish that pirates should plunder towns, which might furnish
valuable contributions to himself, and he had weighty business on hand at home. Lucullus remained in Asia, as we
shall afterwards see.

Sulla distributed the province into districts for the purpose
of raising this extraordinary contribution; and it is assumed
by some writers that the arrangement, which he then made,
was the foundation of the division of the province into
districts for the purpose of letting the taxes (vectigalia). It
is some confirmation of this opinion that Cassiodorus speaks
of Sulla dividing Asia into forty regions or districts (or forty-
four, as Clinton quotes Cassiodorus) in the fourth consulship
of L. Cornelius Cinna and in the second consulship of Cn.
Papirius Carbo, or B.C. 84. Cicero also speaks of Sulla's
arrangements for the raising of the taxes of Asia, which he
calls Sulla's "descriptio," if the word is right, but it should
probably be "discriptio." He observes that Cn. Pompeius
and Flaccus followed Sulla's arrangement in levying money
in Asia. The inhabitants of Magnesia also even in the time
of the Emperor Tiberius relied on the arrangements (con-
stituta) of Sulla, which declared that the temple of Diana
Leucophryna in Magnesia should be an inviolable asylum.
This however was granted or confirmed by Sulla as a reward
for the services of the town in resisting Mithridates, and is
only evidence that Sulla did affect to settle some things in
the province Asia. It is observed by Becker that these forty
districts of Sulla were not the same as the Conventus Juridici,

or the larger divisions of Asia made for the administration of justice. These Conventus or divisions we must assume to have been made when the province was settled by M'Aquillius and the ten Roman commissioners (vol. i., p. 211). The names of ten of these Conventus may be collected from the ancient writers: they are Ephesus, Tralles, Alabanda, Laodicoia or the Jurisdictio Cibyratica consisting of twenty-five towns with Laodiceia at the head of them, Apamea Cibotus near the site of Celaenae with fifteen towns, Synnada with twenty-one dependent places, Sardes, Smyrna, Adramyttium, and Pergamum. Decker observes that this list is probably incomplete, and there is little doubt that it is. The Conventus or diocese (διοίκησις), as it was named in Greek, took its name from the chief town, which the governor or his deputy visited on circuit for the administration of justice and for doing other acts necessary for the administration of each Conventus.

As these Conventus or administrative divisions existed when Sulla was in Asia, it does not appear why he did not make use of them for the purpose of levying his extraordinary demand for twenty thousand talents. It may be however that these districts were too large, and that, as the money was wanted soon, it would be more easily raised by dividing the country for that purpose into more numerous and smaller divisions, and employing more men in collecting it. But then it would seem likely that Sulla's division was only made for the particular occasion. In the war between Caesar and Pompeius, when a requisition for money was made upon Asia, a definite amount was imposed "on the several Conventus and the several towns," as Caesar expresses it.

CHAPTER XXIII.

SULLA IN ITALY.

B.C. 84—83.

Sulla left L. Licinius Murena in Asia with the two legions of Fimbria. He sailed from Ephesus with all his ships and on the third day entered the Piraeus. During his stay in Attica he was initiated in the Eleusinian mysteries, and he got possession of the valuable library collected by Apellicon, who was now dead. This library contained, as Plutarch says, most of the writings of Aristotle and Theophrastus, which were not then well known to people in general. Strabo has a curious story about Aristotle's writings. Neleus, a native of Scepsis in the province Asia, was a pupil both of Aristotle and Theophrastus. Aristotle gave his library to Theophrastus, his successor in his school, and Theophrastus left his own library and Aristotle's to Neleus who brought the books to Scepsis. Neleus left the books to his descendants, who were ignorant persons and took no care of them. When the kings of Pergamum, in whose dominions Scepsis was, were looking for books to form their great library at Pergamum, these people hid the books of Aristotle and Theophrastus in a cellar underground, where they were damaged by damp and worms. At last they were sold to Apellicon for a large sum. Apellicon had the books copied, and published them with the damaged passages incorrectly restored, and many errors. The old Peripatetics after the time of Theophrastus possessed few of Aristotle's works, and those chiefly of the kind called Exoteric, such as could be understood by those who were not of the school, or in other words, such as were generally intelligible. Consequently the older Peripatetics could not learn the philosophy thoroughly, but only furbished up common-places in a rhetorical manner. The later Peripatetics, after these books were published, could teach the philosophy better and follow Aristotle's principles, but yet owing to the many errors in the text they were often compelled to guess at the meaning of the philosopher. When Apellicon's library was brought to Rome, it was carefully preserved. Some time after, Tyrannion a Greek grammarian, who had been taken prisoner by Lucullus (B.C. 72) and carried to Rome, became acquainted with the keeper of the Aristotelian library, and through his permission occupied himself with the books. Strabo's words do not clearly express what Tyrannion did. Plutarch says that he arranged most of the books, whatever he may mean. The booksellers also, Strabo says, made bad copies of the writings, and did not carefully compare the copies with the originals, which, he observes, is the case with other books which are copied for sale both at Rome and in Alexandria.

It might be inferred from Strabo's story that Aristotle only published a few of his writings of the class already mentioned, and that after the death of Theophrastus the Peripatetics were ignorant of at least a large part of Aristotle's works until they were published by Apellicon. There is great improbability in such a conclusion, and some direct evidence that Aristotle's works were well known and indeed published by himself. Accordingly Strabo's story has been rejected by several critics; but it is possible that there may be some truth in it, and the original manuscripts of Aristotle may have passed into Neleus' hands, and finally have been sold by some of his descendants to Apellicon. Andronicus of Rhodes, who was living in Rome about B.C. 50, got copies from Tyrannion, published them and made the tables which are now in use (Plutarch). Andronicus, it is said, critically revised the writings of Aristotle and published them arranged according to the subjects in divisions named pragmateiae (πραγματεῖαι). It is not probable that Sulla cared much for such matters as Aristotle laboured on; but as Sulla knew Greek well and was a man of education, we may suppose that he was well pleased to secure the valuable library of Apellicon. We may conclude from the use which Andronicus made of it at Rome that Sulla by carrying off the books to a safe place contributed to the preservation of the text of Aristotle.

The news of Sulla's great exploits and of the large force that he was bringing caused alarm among his enemies at Rome. The consuls Carbo and Cinna sent agents all through Italy to collect money, men, and supplies of provisions. They tried to secure the support of all the Romans of note, and stirred up the new enfranchised Italian cities by telling them that it was through them that the Roman State was threatened with such danger. They also set about refitting their ships; and sending for those which were in Sicily they kept a look-out on the coasts. It was probably after Sulla had arrived in Greece, when he was elated with his success in bringing the war to an end and confident in the powerful armament under his command, that he wrote to the Senate.

This is the conclusion which we may derive from Appian. The Epitome of Livy (Ep. 83) might lead to a different conclusion as to the time, but such conclusion would by no means be safe. The Epitomator states that when Cinna and Carbo, who had made themselves consuls for two years, were preparing to make war against Sulla, L. Valerius Flaccus induced the Senate to send to him a mission about peace. Accordingly the mission might be placed in B.C. 85 before Sulla had crossed over to Asia, and while Fimbria was still there at the head of a victorious army. But it is safer to follow Appian. Sulla's letter was to the following effect: He enumerated his services against Jugurtha, and then in the war with the Cimbri, and what he had done when he was praetor of Cilicia, and in the Social War, and in his consulship. Finally he spoke of his success against Mithridates, which he exaggerated greatly. He also dwelt particularly on the fact that he had received those who had been expelled from Rome by Cinna, and that he had protected and relieved them in their troubles. "In return

for all this," he said, "his adversaries had declared him an
enemy to the Roman State, they had demolished his house,
murdered his friends, and his wife and children had with
difficulty made their escape. But he would soon come and
punish both his adversaries and all those who had done him
wrong. To the rest of the citizens and those who had
been lately made citizens he declared that he should have
no charge to make against any man among them." Such a
letter from such a man caused general alarm. L. Valerius
Flaccus, the Princeps Senatus, made a speech on the state of
affairs, and he and others, who were desirous of peace, prevailed on the Senate to send commissioners to Sulla, who should
attempt to bring him to terms with his opponents, and
should tell him that if he required any assurance for his own
safety, he must let the Senate know what his demands were.
Cinna and Carbo were also instructed to stop their military
preparations until Sulla's answer came; and they promised
that they would. But as soon as the commissioners were
gone, Cinna and Carbo proclaimed themselves consuls for the
next year, that after leaving Rome they might have no occasion to return soon for the sake of holding the Comitia. From
this we must collect that Cinna and Carbo left Rome
in B.C. 84 not long before the usual time of the consular
elections.

The consuls intended to send their troops over the
Hadriatic to Liburnia, as Appian names it, for the purpose of
meeting Sulla, who was expected to come into those parts on
his way to Italy. The first division of the troops which were
embarked landed safely on the opposite coast. A second
division was overtaken by a storm, and all those who got
back safe to the Italian shore immediately went off to their
homes, being unwilling to fight against their own countrymen. The rest of the men hearing of this refused to embark
for the voyage across the sea, and there was a mutiny. The
place of embarkation is only mentioned by one authority, who
says that it was Ancona. Cinna summoned the soldiers,
whom he intended to scold well for their disobedience. The
men assembled to hear what the consul had to say, but they

were in no humour to submit   One of the lictors who was
clearing the road for Cinna struck a soldier who stood in the
way, on which another soldier struck the lictor.   Cinna
ordered the man to be seized, but this was only the signal for
a general uproar and the consul was pelted with stones.   The
soldiers who happened to be near Cinna drew their swords
and stabbed him; and so he died, the second consul who was
murdered in these troublesome times.   Plutarch gives a
different account of the immediate cause of Cinna's murder,
though the hatred of his men was the real motive.   He says
that young Cn. Pompeius was in Cinna's camp, and that
being alarmed in consequence of some false charge and accusa-
tion he stole away.   A rumour spread that Cinna had put
the youth to death, and the soldiers made an assault on the
general, who attempted to escape, but he was overtaken by a
centurion, and died a coward's death, if the story is true that
Cinna fell down at the centurion's knees and offered him his
seal ring, which was very valuable.   The centurion contemptuously refused the bribe and said, "I am not going to
seal a contract, but to punish an abominable and unjust
tyrant," and so he killed him.   Carbo recalled the men who
had been sent over the sea.   He would not return to Rome,
though he was summoned there by the tribunes for the election of a consul in the place of Cinna, but when the tribunes
threatened that they would depose him, he came and gave
notice for an election.   The omens however were not favourable,
and Carbo named another day, which turned out still worse,
for the lightning fell on the temples of Luna and Ceres.   The
voting was accordingly deferred by the advice of the augurs
until the summer solstice should be passed; from which we
learn that Cinna was murdered in the first half of the year
B.C. 84, unless the calendar was much out of order at that
time.   Carbo was now sole consul.   He was even a more
violent and tyrannical man than Cinna, and Sulla's arrival in
Italy was eagerly expected, for it was thought that any
change of masters would be an improvement.   The Roman
State was a prey to anarchy and to brutal soldiers: freedom
was gone, and the only hope was that men might live under a

moderate slavery, and a more reasonable despot. It is difficult
to conceive how order could have been restored at Rome without Sulla ; and the restoration of order required the destruction of his political enemies.

As soon as the commissioners from the Senate had found
Sulla, they got their answer. He said that he would never
be reconciled to the men who had committed such crimes ;
that the Romans might pardon them, if they chose ; as to
assuring his own safety, which they spoke of, he said that he
would rather secure the safety of the Senate and the people
and that of those who had fled to him, for he had an army
that loved him. This answer showed that he did not intend to
disband his troops, and that he intended to be master. As
to his demands, Sulla said that his rank must be restored,
and his property, and that a certain priestly office which he
had held, and all honours that he had enjoyed, must be given
back to him. He sent some of his own friends with the
commissioners to support his demands before the Senate.
They all landed at Brundisium, where they heard of Cinna's
death and that the Republic was in a state of anarchy, upon
which without going any farther Sulla's friends returned to
him. Appian's narrative shows that he supposed Sulla to be
in Greece when he sent this answer ; and it was probably
now about the close of B.C. 84. He had five Italian legions,
six thousand horse, and some troops that he had raised in the
Peloponnesus and Macedonia, in all forty thousand men. He
had sixteen hundred, or as Plutarch says, twelve hundred
ships, probably a large part of them stored with supplies, for
he could not expect to find much in Italy on his arrival.
His armament sailed from the Piraeus round the Peloponnesus to Patrae (Patras) in Achaea, from which place it
would follow the coast to the parts of the mainland opposite
to Brundisium.

Sulla did not accompany the fleet from the Piraeus. While
he was staying at Athens, he was seized with a numbness in his
feet and a feeling of heaviness. Strabo, whom Plutarch quotes,
called it a " stammering of gout." Sulla went to Euboea to
try the effect of the hot springs of Aedepsus (Lipso) on the

west coast of the island. The springs, which still exist, were
much resorted to by the Greeks in Plutarch's time (Sympos.
iv. Probl. 4). They are more copious than the springs of
Thermopylae on the opposite mainland, but of the same
kind. The water rushes into the sea in a copious stream, the
vapour of which is seen at some distance. Sulla used the
waters, and enjoyed himself in the company of actors, of
whom he was very fond. One day when he was walking on
the shore, some fishermen gave him some very fine fish,
which Sulla was much pleased with, but hearing that the
fishermen were from Halae in Boeotia, he said, "What, is
there a man of Halae still alive?" After the victory of
Orchomenus Sulla pursued his enemies, and destroyed Halae,
Larymna, and Anthedon, all on the coast. Probably the
fugitives sought to protect themselves in these places, and the
towns were taken by storm. Sulla's remark frightened the
poor fishermen, who seem to have crossed over from the
opposite mainland to make their offering to the great Roman
general. However Sulla smiled, and told the men to go
away in good heart, for their fish were powerful intercessors.
On this it is said that the people of Halae took courage and
again occupied their little town.

From Euboea Sulla went through Thessalia and Macedonia to meet his fleet on the coast of the Hadriatic. He
was going to lead his men against their own countrymen, and
he had some fears that when they landed they might disperse to their several homes. But his men voluntarily took
an oath that they would stay with him and not do any
mischief in Italy. They knew that his enterprise would
require much money, and they all contributed to raise a fund,
each according to his means. Sulla refused to accept their
money, and commending their zeal he set sail from Dyr-
rhachium to "oppose," as he said in his Memoirs, "fifteen
hostile commanders at the head of four hundred and fifty
cohorts." If there is no error in the numbers in Plutarch's
text, and the cohorts contained at that time five hundred
men, as Appian states, the Senate had 225,000 men in arms
when Sulla landed. Appian reduces the force of the Ro-

public to two hundred cohorts or twenty legions, but he adds, that there were more afterwards. It was a bold undertaking to invade Italy, when such a force was on foot, but the invader was a man who trusted in his good fortune, had proved himself a skilful commander and negotiator, and possessed courage and cunning in a degree that is rare. The town of Brundisium received Sulla without making any resistance, for which the townsmen were afterwards rewarded with certain privileges, which, says Appian, they still retain. Plutarch's statement that Sulla landed near Tarentum is difficult to explain, for he had just before said that Sulla made preparation to cross from Dyrrachium to Brundisium, which was the usual landing-place of the Romans when they passed from Greece to Italy, and the most convenient place. It is true that Brundisium is near Tarentum, the two towns being on opposite sides of the narrow peninsula, which forms the south-eastern part of Italy, but if Plutarch meant to refer to Brundisium in these words, it is singular carelessness. Freinsheim suggests that Sulla's fleet was so large that one port would not hold all the ships. But the harbour of Brundisium was at that time in good condition, and large enough for all such ships as Sulla had; and therefore he would have no occasion to send part of them to Tarentum. Sulla in his Memoirs would certainly say where he landed, and we have evidence that Plutarch constantly used them. It is plain also that he referred to them on this occasion, for he says that the deity gave Sulla sure prognostics of success. He sacrificed immediately on landing "near Tarentum," when it was found that the liver of the animal had on it the figure of a crown of bay with two ribands attached to it. This was the triumphal crown, which is represented on some Roman medals in the hand of a winged Victory. Such a fact was one that Sulla would not fail to record in his Memoirs, for he believed in signs and omens, and that he was favoured by the gods. But Plutarch has through carelessness or ignorance confused all the narrative by speaking of Sulla landing near Tarentum. There has been some difference of opinion about the time of Sulla's landing in

Italy, but Clinton's conclusion that it was early in the year
B.C. 83 is most consistent with the evidence [1].

The eighty-fourth book of Livy, as we learn from the
Epitome, contained an account of the measures which were
taken in B.C. 84 to resist Sulla's invasion. Some time after
his colleague's murder Carbo was compelled by the tribunes
to hold the consular Comitia for B.C. 83, in which L. Cornelius
Scipio Asiaticus and C. Norbanus were elected consuls. Sextus
Lucilius, as Paterculus names him, was one of the tribunes
of B.C. 84, and he was punished for his opposition to Carbo
by being thrown down the Tarpeian rock by P. Popillius
Laenas one of the tribunes of the next year. The colleagues
of Lucilius received notice that they would be brought to
trial, on which they fled to Sulla, and the interdict of fire
and water was passed against them. The Epitome of Livy
records a Senatus consultum by which the suffrage or right of
voting was given to the new citizens. This is all that the
Epitomator tells us, and it is very obscure. In the eightieth
book (Epitome) we have read that the citizenship (civitas)
had been given to all the Italians, at a time when the Social
War was not entirely ended (p. 254). This Senatus consultum
of B.C. 84 may have been designed to conciliate the Italians
by putting them on the same footing as the old citizens with

---

[1] There is a description and a plan of the port of Brindisi in Swinburne's
Travels in the Two Sicilies. There is an outer port, and an inner port. The inner
port has two arms which embrace the site of the town of Brindisi. Caesar
damaged the port of Brundisium by attempting to stop up the channel between
the inner and the outer port, when he was blockading Pompeius. I have
received some valuable information about the present state of Brindisi from Mr.
F. R. Conder. He says that he has seen a vessel of 500 tons lying in the inner
harbour of Brindisi. There is a bar at the entrance of the inner port, which is
the result of Caesar's operations; and before this damage was done, Mr. Conder
observes that the port of Brindisi must have been equal to Cork, not in size, but
in safety and convenience. He adds that there is a chain of rocks outside,
which could be converted into a breakwater, and thus a noble outer port would
be made. This the finest Italian port in the Hadriatic was neglected by the
Government of Naples, and consequently the harbour has been damaged and the
salubrity of the place destroyed. The new kingdom of Italy could not employ
itself better than in restoring this valuable harbour and making the railroad to
Brindisi the highway to the East.

respect to voting. It was the policy of Sulla's opponents to secure the help of those warlike nations, which had wrested from Rome the concession of political equality, and to show them that their only chance of keeping what they had got was to resist the invader, who belonged to the party which had so steadily opposed the claims of the Italians. The Epitome also records that the libertini or emancipated slaves were distributed among the five-and-thirty tribes. Many slaves had received their freedom in the time of Marius, and the design of this measure seems to have been to secure their fidelity by placing them on the same footing as other citizens.

Though Sulla had so formidable a force opposed to him, his enterprise was not so desperate as it might seem. His enemies were only united by fear of him, and many of them hated one another. Sulla was the sole director of his own plans, and he pursued them consistently to the end. He had friends too, on whom he could rely. M. Licinius Crassus, the son of Publius Crassus, who perished in B.C. 87, escaped to Spain, a country which he had become acquainted with during his father's proconsular command. His adventures, as told by Plutarch, are like a romance, but there was authority for the story. Crassus with three friends and ten slaves sought refuge on some land belonging to Vibius Pacianus, and they hid themselves in a large cave near the sea. Crassus being in want of provisions sent a slave to Vibius to sound his disposition. Vibius was pleased to hear of the escape of Crassus, and he took a slave to a spot near the cave, and ordered him to carry food daily to the place and then under pain of death to go away without making any inquiry. The slave brought the provisions daily, but he never saw those who were concealed, though they saw him, for they knew the time of his coming and kept watch. The fugitives were well fed by their liberal host. But Vibius did not think this was enough, and considering that Crassus "was a very young man and that provision should be made in some degree also for the pleasures suitable to his age," he took two handsome female slaves and went down to the coast with them. Vibius pointed out to the girls a small path along the precipices, and told them to enter the cave. Crassus seeing them approach was afraid that his retreat had been discovered, and he asked them what they wanted and who they were. The girls answered, as they had been told, that they were looking for their master, who was concealed there. Crassus understood what was meant and received the girls, who stayed with him the rest of the time and carried messages from Crassus to Vibius. Plutarch found this story in the historian Fenestella, who says that he saw one of these slaves when she was an old woman, and that he had often heard her speak of this adventure and tell the story with pleasure. Fenestella was born about B.C. 51, and it is therefore possible that he might have seen this old woman. Crassus lived eight months in this way, but as soon as the news of Cinna's death (B.C. 81) reached Spain he came out of his concealment, and got together above two thousand men, with whom he went round to different towns, to get money and supplies, as we must suppose. Many writers, says Plutarch, affirm that he plundered Malaca (Malaga), an old Phoenician settlement on the south coast of Spain, but Crassus denied it. He got some vessels, probably he seized them at Malaca, and crossed over to Africa to Q. Metellus Pius, who had collected there a considerable force. But Crassus and Metellus soon quarrelled, and Crassus went to Sulla, whom he seems to have joined somewhere in Greece after Sulla's return from Asia. When Sulla landed in Italy he sent Crassus into the country of the Marsi to raise a force. The road lay through a territory which was in the possession of the enemy, and Crassus asked for a guard to protect him. Sulla vehemently replied, "I give thee as guards thy father, thy brother, thy friends, thy kinsmen, who were cut off illegally and wrongfully, and whose murderers I am now pursuing." Stung by this reproach, Crassus set out, and making his way through the enemy he collected a strong force, and actively assisted Sulla in the prosecution of the war. We may conjecture that Crassus had friends and clients among the Marsi.

Q. Metellus Pius, the son of Metellus Numidicus, first served under his father in Numidia against Jugurtha (vol. i.,

p. 441). He commanded, as we have seen, in the Social
War, and defeated the Marsian general Q. Pompaedius
(B.C. 88). When Marius returned to Italy (B.C. 87), Metellus
left Rome (p. 243) and went to Africa, where his father's
memory still lived, and he got together a force. It was probably after Crassus left him that Metellus was expelled from
Africa by the praetor C. Fabius, who was of the faction of
Marius. Metellus returned to Italy, and remained in the
mountain fastnesses of Liguria until he heard of Sulla's landing, when he joined him somewhere in South Italy with such
forces as he had. Sulla and Metellus were of the same
party, and Sulla's wife Caecilia Metella was the cousin of
Metellus.

But Sulla's chief support came from a youth twenty-two
years of age, Cn. Pompeius, the son of Strabo. Whatever
other motives he may have had for declaring in favour of
Sulla, he had the sagacity to see to which side victory would
incline; and if Sulla should lose his life in the coming contest, he had audacity and self-confidence enough to aspire to
be the head of a party. After Sulla's arrival in Italy and
probably after Sulla had gained some advantages, Pompeius
attempted to rouse the people of Picenum, in which country
he had estates. He did not deign to steal to Sulla as a
fugitive: he intended to join him with a force sufficient to
command respect. He assumed the command in Auximum
(Osimo) a large inland town south of Ancona, placed a tribunal in the forum, and ordered out of the place two brothers
Ventidii, who were among the chief inhabitants and in the
interest of Carbo. He enlisted soldiers, and appointed centurions, and then visited other towns of Picenum, where he
did the same. The men of Carbo's party fled from the towns,
and the young self-made general met with no opposition in
those parts. There was, as events showed, a large body of
people in Italy who were tired of the tyranny of the last
few years and glad of any change. Pompeius raised three
legions, and supplied himself with provisions, beasts, waggons, and every thing necessary for war. If he raised this
large force, he must have had credit, and he would require

some ready money. Our extant authorities give no information on such matters, and we must conjecture that Pompeius used his own means, which would not go far, even if he was rich, and that he made up the rest that was wanted by borrowing and levying contributions.

CHAPTER XXIV.

THE CIVIL WAR.

(B.C. 83—82.)

APPIAN has given a brief narrative of the civil war which followed Sulla's landing in Italy, and we learn something from Plutarch's Life of Sulla, and a few passages of Roman writers. But the events are very imperfectly related. Appian computes that the war lasted three years until Sulla obtained the mastery, but it was not three complete years.

Sulla led his troops from Calabria into Apulia without doing any damage to the lands or any injury to the people. This politic conduct gained him friends. According to Velleius he made fair proposals of peace to his opponents before there was a fight; and the Epitome of Livy also records the sending of commissioners about peace to Norbanus and the consul's rough treatment of them. Appian has omitted this fact. It is his fashion to make a brief and dry narrative of events, and he often omits minute particulars. Sulla's proposals for peace are only worth notice as evidence of the man's character, for we cannot believe that he wished to make peace, or that he would have trusted any promises made by men of the Marian party.

Sulla and Metellus found the consul Norbanus about Canusium (Canosa) in Apulia, where a battle was fought, in which Norbanus was defeated with the loss of six thousand men, while Sulla lost only seventy, but he had a large number wounded. Norbanus made his retreat across the mountains to Capua. Velleius has quite a different story.

He says that Sulla overpowered the consuls Scipio and Norbanus near Capua; that Norbanus was defeated in the field, and Scipio was betrayed by his army. But Velleius is not an historian. If the several facts which he relates are true, they are not always placed in chronological order nor in any connexion which explains them. Both the brevity of his work and the plan of it make Velleius a very difficult writer to use. Appian simply abridged his authorities, and certainly attempted, though he may not always have done it, to place his facts in chronological order. Though it is improbable that Sulla met with no resistance before he crossed the Apennines, the circumstance of Norbanus taking shelter in Capua after his defeat seems to imply that he was defeated not very far from that city, and Drumann has suggested that Canusium in Appian is a mistake for Casilinum, which is on the Vulturnus and near Capua. There is, indeed, decisive evidence that Norbanus, if he was defeated in Apulia, had also a defeat near Capua. The plain of Capua is bounded on the east by Tifata, a ridge which belongs to the Apennines, and in the plain between Capua and the hills Norbanus, according to Velleius, was beaten. Sulla to show his gratitude to Diana, the patron of all that region, gave to the goddess, that is, to her temple, certain springs famed for healing properties, and all the lands of the district. An inscription on the door-post of the temple, still extant in the time of Velleius, and a bronze tablet within the temple testified to Sulla's victory and his piety.

Plutarch reports that when Sulla was at Silvium (Garagnone) in Apulia, a slave met him and declared that he brought from Bellona assurance of victory, but he added that the Roman Capitol would be burnt, if Sulla did not make haste. The temple on the Capitol was in fact burnt this year, and the fire is said to have happened on the very day which the slave foretold, the day before the Nones of Quintilis, which month, says Plutarch, we now call Julius. This building had stood, it is said, four hundred years. Nobody knew how the fire happened, but various conjectures were made. The Sibylline books perished in the conflagration. Obsequens, who records the wonders of this year, places the burning of this temple among them, from which we may perhaps conclude that the cause was unknown.

When Sulla and Metellus had crossed the Apennines into Campania, they were met by the consul Scipio about Teanum between the rivers Liris and Vulturnus. Scipio's army was not in high spirits at the prospect of a fight, and the men wished for peace. Sulla having ascertained their disposition sent to Scipio to propose terms of agreement, not because he either expected or wished for a quiet settlement of affairs, but because he had hopes of corrupting Scipio's men. Scipio received hostages and was persuaded to have an interview with Sulla or Sulla's agents, though Sertorius warned Scipio of the danger. There were only three persons from each side present, and nobody else knew what was said. It was supposed that Scipio determined to consult his colleague Norbanus before finally coming to terms, for he sent Sertorius to him. In the mean time the two armies kept quiet. Sertorius in going to Norbanus passed by Sucssa, which lies between Teanum and Minturnae on the river Liris. This town had declared for Sulla, but Sertorius seized the place. Sulla sent to Scipio to complain, and Scipio, either because he was privy to the act or did not know what answer to make, sent back Sulla's hostages. The army was much displeased with the seizure of Sucssa during the truce and with Scipio sending back the hostages, when they had not been demanded: in fact the men had no heart nor inclination to fight against Sulla, and only wanted an excuse for going over to him. Sulla was now informed that Scipio's men would desert their general, if he would approach the camp. As soon as he came, the whole army went over to him, and Sulla seized the consul and his son Lucius in their tent; on which Appian observes that it was an imputation on Scipio's generalship to have been so ignorant of the treachery of his own men. But Scipio may have known that he could not trust his men ; and as he could not run away from his army, he must wait for the event. Sulla thus carried off from the enemy forty cohorts, having entrapped them, as Plutarch says, like so many tame birds. It was on this occasion that Carbo remarked, that in Sulla he had both a lion and a fox to contend against, but the fox gave him most trouble. Sulla attempted to persuade Scipio and his son to join him, but they refused, and were allowed to go away.

It might be concluded from the statement about Sertorius seizing Suessa on his way to Norbanus that Norbanus had left Capua, for Suessa is not on the road from Teanum to Capua, and Appian has apparently made some mistake, which it is impossible to explain. Norbanus, he says, was still in Capua, and we must conjecture that Sulla had left a force there to watch him, or otherwise he might have joined Scipio. Plutarch indeed, whose narrative we may occasionally use as a supplement to Appian, says that Sulla was surrounded by many hostile camps and large forces, when he invited Scipio to a conference. It is therefore possible that when Sulla crossed the Apennines and came down from Tifata into the plain, he defeated Norbanus, who fled to Capua, and then advanced against Scipio, who was on his way to join Norbanus. However this may be, Appian states that, after the capture of Scipio, Sulla sent persons to Capua to Norbanus to propose terms to him also, but as he got no answer, he moved on probably northwards, wasting the lands of all those who were not of his party. Norbanus also left Capua and advanced northward, as we must assume, but by a different road.

Carbo, who was probably in the north of Italy, hurried to Rome, and induced the Senate to declare Metellus and all the senators who had joined Sulla to be enemies to the State, for many men of rank had gone over to his side. Among them was P. Cethegus, a friend of Caius Marius, and once one of the most violent enemies of Sulla. He now came as a suppliant and offered his services. He was ready to do any thing, and Sulla had no objections to use any man as his tool. C. Verres also, afterwards known as the most notorious scoundrel that Rome ever produced, came over to Sulla. In B.C. 84 he was the quaestor of Carbo, and he embezzled a large sum of public money with which he was entrusted.

Cicero is our authority for this fact. Verres said that he left in Ariminum (Rimini) all the money that he had not disbursed as quaestor, but the money was never seen again, and Verres, as we shall find, had a good reason for mentioning Ariminum as the alleged place of deposit. If Verres deserted the consul Carbo and robbed the state in B.C. 84, as Cicero says, he must have taken an early opportunity of joining Sulla, for he would be in great danger. The conduct of M. Pupius Piso, the quaestor of the consul L. Scipio, is contrasted by Cicero with the behaviour of Verres. Piso did not touch any of the public money, nor did he join Scipio's army. The conclusion seems to be that he joined Sulla, for he could hardly remain neutral. Yet this man was then the husband of Annia, the widow of the consul Cinna, who was murdered in B.C. 84. He afterwards divorced Annia to please Sulla.

Appian places the burning of the Capitol after Carbo's return to Rome, which gave some people the opportunity of saying that he fired the temple, though it would be difficult to discover any reason why either Carbo or any body else should have done it. However as the fire happened in July, it is probable that Plutarch has made a mistake in supposing that Sulla was still in Apulia in the month of July B.C. 83 (p. 334). After the affair of Suessa, Sertorius, who was a praetor, fled to Spain, of which country one of the two divisions had been assigned as his province some time before. This is Appian's statement, but another authority says that he withdrew to Etruria, and did not go to Spain until B.C. 82. Something will be said on this matter in a subsequent chapter. It appears certain that Sertorius was not actively engaged in the campaign against Sulla.

There is no clear account of the operations of Pompeius before he joined Sulla. All that we know of them is in Plutarch's Life of Pompeius. Three commanders were advancing against Pompeius in Picenum. Plutarch names them Carinna, Cloelius, and Brutus. Carinna is C. Carrinas; Cloelius may be C. Caelius Caldus; and Brutus was either M. Junius Brutus, the father of him who was afterwards one

of the assassins of Caius Caesar, or he was L. Junius Brutus
Damasippus. If these three men had united their armies,
Pompeius could hardly have resisted them; but from jealousy
or some other cause they did not co-operate. Pompeius met
the force of Brutus, who had a body of Gallic horsemen
probably raised in North Italy, and there was a fight between
the cavalry on each side. A horseman one of the strongest
men among them was brought down by the spear of Pompeius, upon which the rest of the Gallic cavalry fled, and
putting the infantry in confusion caused a general rout.
After this defeat the three commanders quarrelled, and retreated as well as they could. The consequence of this panic
was that all the towns in those parts declared for Pompeius.
Plutarch also speaks of Scipio the consul advancing against
Pompeius, and of the soldiers of Scipio deserting their general, who made his escape. But this appears to be only
another version of the story of Scipio's army going over to
Sulla, as Plutarch himself reports in the Life of Sulla.
Again Plutarch speaks of Pompeius defeating Carbo on the
river Aesis (Esino), which flows into the Hadriatic between
Sinigaglia and Ancona, but Appian places the defeat of
Carbo in the next year B.C. 82.

When Sulla heard of Pompeius being surrounded by three
armies, he was alarmed for his safety and advanced to relieve
him. Of course Sulla must have marched northward, but the
biographer does not inform us where the two commanders
met. Pompeius, on hearing of Sulla's approach, ordered his
men to be under arms and to receive Sulla with gallant show.
As Sulla came near, he admired the fine appearance of the
men, and he was met by Pompeius, who according to custom
saluted him by the title of Imperator. Sulla got down from
his horse, and saluted Pompeius by the same title of Imperator, which was an extraordinary distinction for a youth
of two-and-twenty. Pompeius was sent by Sulla into North
Italy, where Metellus now was. Pompeius was willing to
serve under Metellus, and Metellus was glad to have assistance, for by reason of his age, says Plutarch, his warlike and
courageous temper was becoming extinct. But Metellus was

not fifty years old, and he was younger than Sulla, who was
about fifty-five. So the biographer's remark about the age
of Metellus is one of his blunders.

Nothing more is reported of the military operations of this
year. The consuls Scipio and Carbo were raising more men.
They had still the greater part of Italy on their side, and
strong partisans in the parts about the Po. Sulla was equally
active. A large part of Southern Italy was either favourable
to him or unable to oppose him; and by threats and coaxing,
by a liberal use of money and promises, he increased his army.
The latter part of the year was thus spent by both sides in
preparing for the next year's campaign. The Senate took
from the temples gold and silver vessels and coined them
into money.

The consuls of B.C. 82 were Cn. Papirius Carbo for the
third time, and C. Marius, whom Appian here names a
nephew of C. Marius, the conqueror of the Cimbri, though
he had before called him the son. It has been conjectured
that the consul of B.C. 82 was an adopted son of C. Marius;
but all the authorities except Appian name him a son. He
was a young man, not twenty years of age, as Livy's Epitome
states, with the further remark that his election was secured
by violent means. Perhaps the youth's name did something
for him, for a son or a nephew may rise to place and power
upon the reputation of an uncle or a father. Marius however may have been older than the Epitomator states. Appian
says that he was seven-and-twenty. The beginning of this
year was very cold, and the hostile armies kept in their
quarters.

The Epitome places early in B.C. 82 the tragical story of
C. Fabius Hadrianus, the governor of the Roman province
of Africa, who had expelled Metellus. The government of
Fabius was oppressive to the Roman citizens of the province,
and he was also vaguely charged with stirring up the slaves
to rise, with the view of making himself master of the province. Whatever was his guilt, there is no doubt about his
end. He was blockaded in his own residence at Utica, and
burnt alive. No inquiry was made into the matter, and it

was generally agreed that he deserved his fate. Haverkamp in his edition of Orosius has given a denarius, which he attributes to this Hadrianus. The reverse represents a Victory in a biga with an ostrich running in front.

The affairs of Sulla gained by the prolongation of the contest. In the island of Sardinia the praetor Q. Antonius was defeated and killed by L. Philippus, a legatus of Sulla. There is no other L. Philippus whom we know than L. Marcius Philippus, who had been consul in B.C. 91. We have no reason to suppose that he was a violent partisan of the Marian faction, though he had passed safely through the late revolution. He now prudently came to the winning side. The acquisition of Sardinia, a corn-producing island, would furnish Sulla with supplies, for we may assume that he had ships sufficient to command the sea. Sulla also entered into negotiations with the Italian states, or with some of them at least, who were nearest to him. These people were afraid that, if Sulla were victorious, they should lose the Roman citizenship, and the suffrage "which had been lately given them;" such are the words of Livy's Epitomator. Sulla promised to secure to these people what they had got, and he confirmed his promise by a formal treaty.

Early in the spring Metellus, who was near the river Aesis in Picenum, fought a battle with Carrinas, one of the legati of Carbo. It was a well-contested day, but Carrinas at last was routed with great loss, and all the adjacent parts submitted to Metellus. Carbo now came up and held Metellus in check, until he heard of the defeat of his colleague Marius, when he retreated north to Ariminum, followed by Pompeius, who harassed his rear. The retreat of Carbo to Ariminum shows that the party of Marius was still strong in those parts.

It is not said where Sulla passed the winter. In the spring (B.C. 82) he got possession of Setia (Sezze), which stands on a height at the western margin of the Volscian mountains and looks over the wide level of the Pomptine marshes. Marius, who was encamped near Setia, retreated slowly to a place named Sacriportus. Plutarch says that

Marius made a stand near Signia (Segni), which is on the borders of the valley of the Sacco. He does not mention Sacriportus, but as this was the battle-field, and Marius retreated from Setia towards Praeneste, he would march through the valley which separates the Volscian from the Alban hills, and we may therefore place Sacriportus in the upper valley of the Sacco between Signia and Praeneste. Marius had eighty-four cohorts, and he offered Sulla battle. Sulla was ready, for he had dreamed in the night that the elder Marius was advising his son to beware of the following day. The two armies fought with great obstinacy, but when the left wing of Marius began to give way, five of his cohorts and two companies of cavalry throwing down their standards passed over to Sulla. This defection decided the battle. The soldiers of Marius fled to Praeneste followed by Sulla, who slaughtered them in great numbers. Those who first reached the town got in, but as Sulla was pressing close on the fugitives, the gates were closed, and a great many of Marius's soldiers were killed about the town. Marius himself escaped by being hoisted up the walls by a rope. Some historians, and among them Fenestella, say that Marius saw nothing of the battle. Being exhausted by fatigue he was lying on the ground, and fell asleep as soon as the signal for battle was given, and was roused with difficulty when the flight began. Sulla in his Memoirs says that he lost only twenty-three men and killed twenty thousand of the enemy, a statement which is incredible, though we have the general's own words for it. He took eight thousand prisoners, some of whom were Samnites, a nation that had always been the most stubborn of the Italian enemies of Rome, and the most dangerous opponents of the Romans in the Social War. Sulla massacred all his Samnite prisoners. About the same time Metellus defeated another army of Carbo, five of whose cohorts passed over to Metellus in the battle. Pompeius also routed C. Marcius Censorinus near Sena (Sinigaglia) on the Hadriatic, and took the town, which he allowed his soldiers to plunder. According to a passage of Frontinus, Pompeius crossed the Po and captured Mediolanum (Milano).

There is no other time, as it seems, to which this event can be referred. Some of his men massacred the senate of Milan, and Pompeius had resort to a stratagem to punish them. He was afraid of a mutiny, if he summoned only the guilty, and he therefore called together all the army. The murderers came with little fear, because they were confounded with the rest, and did not think that they were summoned to be punished; but the men, who had no share in the massacre, aided in picking out the guilty, that they might not participate in their crime by letting them escape.

The signal defeat of Marius in the open field was the ruin of his party. It was the greatest folly to oppose an inexperienced youth to a veteran soldier, who had always been victorious and was the best general of the age. The stronghold of Praeneste, which was the base of Marius's operations, had been held by Cinna in B.C. 87, when he was driven from Rome. The modern town, named Palestrina, is at the termination of an abrupt offset of the Apennines, a part of the same range on which Tivoli stands. The ground rises in terraces up to the highest point of the hill, where is the village of Castel San Pietro, formerly the strong citadel of the ancient city of Praeneste. The road from Palestrina up to San Pietro is steep. The huge Cyclopean walls of limestone are traced on both sides from the lower town up to the citadel. In the Cyclopean walls there are portions which are of Roman construction, and others of a later period. The hill on which the citadel stood is connected at the back by a lower neck of land with the mountain range. Castel San Pietro is 2400 feet above the sea, and commands an extensive and beautiful prospect. On the south are seen through the opening between the Alban and the Volscian hills, Astura and Porto d'Anzo, with the islands of Ponza and Palmaruola. On the south-east is the valley of the Sacco, and the towns of Segni and Anagni. The Campagna of Rome, out of which rise the Alban mountains, and Rome itself at the distance of twenty-three miles by the road through Gabii, are before the spectator, who may see to the north of the Tiber the solitary height of Soracte, and the distant mountains of the Umbri and the Sabines. This strong place could only bo taken by siege. Sulla inclosed the town with his works, and left Q. Lucretius Ofella to reduce Praeneste by famine.

Marius was shut up in Praeneste with no hope of escape, but before he perished, he determined to be revenged on his enemies. He found an instrument in L. Junius Damasippus, one of the praetors, who was in Rome. It is said that Marius sent a message to him, but as that would be difficult, Marius may have given his orders before he was blockaded; or the bloody deeds committed in Rome may have been the work of Damasippus only. The Senate was summoned to the Curia Hostilia on the pretence of business. Among those who came were P. Antistius, the father-in-law of Pompeius, and C. Papirius Carbo, a cousin of the consul Cn. Carbo. Both of them were murdered in the senate house by some assassins who were brought in for the purpose. Calpurnia, the wife of Antistius, stabbed herself when she heard of her husband's death. C. Carbo was the man who with his colleague M. Plautius Silvanus proposed the law (B.C. 89) for giving the citizenship to the Italians, but he was of the party of the Optimates, and the only Carbo, as Cicero says, who was a good citizen. L. Domitius, another senator, was killed at the entrance of the senate house as he was attempting to escape; and Q. Mucius Scaevola, the Pontifex Maximus, the head of religion, in front of the building, as Appian reports. But Cicero, who knew the facts well, says that Scaevola fled to the temple of Vesta and the ever-burning fires, where he was massacred before the goddess, whose statue was sprinkled with his blood. Q. Mucius Scaevola was the son of the consul of B.C. 133. He was the most eloquent of jurists, and the most learned jurist among orators, and a man of great moderation, but his political opinions attached him to the party of the Optimates. After the death of the Augur, Q. Mucius Scaevola, to whom Cicero was taken by his father to profit by the wise old man's instruction, Cicero attended at the house of the Pontifex Scaevola, after the manner of the young Romans of that day, and he has affectionately recorded the virtues and the talents of one, who as an administrator,

an orator, and a lawyer is among the most illustrious men of
any age or country. Scaevola, the Pontifex Maximus, is the
first Roman, so far as we know, to whom we can attribute
a scientific and systematic handling of the Jus Civile, or the
Roman Law, a work which was divided into eighteen books.
Nothing remains of his writings except a few fragments in
the Digest; but Scaevola's name lives in the imperishable
monument of Roman law which he laboured to build, and in
the eloquent words of his grateful pupil, who has well said
on another occasion, "The life of the dead rests in the remembrance of the living." The bodies of the murdered men
were thrown into the Tiber. It was now the fashion to
refuse even the rites of burial to an enemy. The news of
this massacre brought Sulla to Rome, and Damasippus ran
off to the consul Carbo in Etruria. It is probable indeed
that the approach of Sulla alarmed his enemies, who could
not defend the city against him. Sulla's army advanced
upon Rome in several divisions. As they marched along,
all the towns through terror made their submission, and the
citizens of Rome, who were suffering from famine, opened the
gates. Sulla stationed his army in the Campus Martius and
entered Rome. All his enemies were gone. Their property
was immediately seized and sold on the public account. Sulla
then called a meeting of the citizens in which he deplored the
necessity of taking harsh measures, but he bade them be of
good cheer, for the troubles would now soon be over and
order would be restored to the Commonwealth. Having
settled such affairs as were urgent, Sulla set out for Clusium
(Chiusi) in Etruria, where Carbo was with the main body of
the army. Carbo had some Spanish horsemen, who had been
sent to him from the Roman governors in Spain. There
was a cavalry skirmish on the banks of the Clanis (Chiana),
one of the branches of the Tiber. About fifty of the Spanish
horsemen fell, and two hundred and seventy of them passed
over to Sulla. Carbo, either enraged at the treachery of the
Spaniards or fearing that he should lose the rest of them,
butchered every man that remained. The abridgment of
Appian is often very unsatisfactory. He says no more of

Carbo, who, as we must conjecture, retreated before Sulla, or shut himself up in Clusium. Sulla gained another victory near Saturnia, an Etrurian town, south-west of Clusium and on the river Albegna. Etruria was the stronghold of Sulla's enemies in the north, and the Etrurians afterwards paid dear for their resistance.

Metellus with a fleet sailing along the east coast to Ravenna occupied the level country in those parts which was rich in grain. Sulla appears to have secured the command of the sea by the ships which he brought with him to Italy; and the occupation of Sardinia and of the country about Ravenna show that he was compelled to look after supplies of corn in distant places. Italy had been devastated in the Social War, and this civil contest must have impeded agriculture and caused great suffering all over the country. The important city of Naples was still in the hands of Sulla's enemies, but some of his men were treacherously let into the city by night, and massacred all except the few that escaped. Some galleys which belonged to the town were also seized. The operations of Sulla after the skirmish on the Clanis are omitted by Appian, but the armies of Sulla and Carbo must have kept near one another, for there was at last a general battle near Clusium with no decisive result. The fight lasted all day and was only ended by darkness.

While Sulla and Carbo were about Clusium, Pompeius and Crassus defeated Carrinas in the plain of Spoletium (Spoleto), an Umbrian town a few miles west of the Nar, a branch of the Tiber. Carrinas lost three thousand men and retired to Spoletium. Carbo sent a force to relieve Carrinas, but Sulla laid an ambuscade on the way and destroyed two thousand of Carbo's men.

One night when there was a heavy shower of rain Carrinas left Spoletium and made his escape. The enemy who were blockading him knew what was going on, but they did not care to stir in the darkness and the rain. Carbo hearing that Marius was suffering from famine in Praeneste, sent C. Marcius Censorinus with eight legions to his relief. This force came unexpectedly upon Pompeius, who was waiting for them

in a narrow pass, and was completely routed. Marcius lost
a great number of men, but he made his escape with the rest
to a hill, where Pompeius blockaded him. In the night
Marcius leaving his watch-fires burning to deceive Pompeius
stole off quietly, but his men mutinied, for they charged their
general with negligence in allowing himself to be surprised.
A whole legion with their standards left the general and
crossed the Apennines to Ariminum; others went off to their
several homes, and Marcius, who had only seven cohorts left,
returned with them to Carbo.

Another attempt was made to relieve Praeneste by Marcus
Lamponius from Lucania, Pontius Telesinus from Samnium
and Gutta of Capua. Lamponius had led the Italians
against the armies of Rome in the Social War, which
in a manner was continued in this contest between Sulla
and the Marian faction, for Sulla was the representative
of that party which had resisted the claims of the Italians.
The amount of the force brought to relieve Praeneste is
stated by Appian at seventy thousand. His narrative implies that this large army advanced in a body, for he says that
Sulla occupied a narrow gorge through which they had to
pass, and stopped them. This is all that he tells us, and we
cannot explain what he has left imperfect. Marius seeing
that there was no hope of relief constructed a kind of fort in
the wide interval between the city and the lines of the
blockading army, and here he brought his military engines
and all his men. His object was to force a way through
the enemy, but after making the attempt for many days
and in various ways he retired again within the walls of
Praeneste.

The chronology of the events of this year is not certain,
but the safest guides are Appian and the Epitome of Livy
(88). Sulla, it appears, had left Carbo behind in order to
oppose his enemies who were advancing in great force from
the south. Carbo and Norbanus took advantage of the
opportunity to cross the Apennines with the hope of crushing
Metellus. It was near evening, and their army had been
marching all day, when they found Metellus at Faventia

(Faenza), a town on the Via Aemilia, about half way between Rimini and Bologna. Though there was not more than an hour of daylight remaining, and the ground was close planted with vines, Carbo and Norbanus determined to attack Metellus, expecting that he would be alarmed at the surprise. But they were repulsed and driven among the vineyards, where they were cut down in large numbers. Near ten thousand men were killed ; six thousand surrendered or passed over to Metellus, and the rest were dispersed. A thousand men only kept together and made good their retreat over the Apennines to Arretium (Arezzo). A legion of Lucanians, which was advancing under the command of P. Tullius Albinovanus, deserted to Metellus on hearing of this great rout. Albinovanus who had in vain tried to prevent this defection joined Norbanus. But he saw that the affairs of his party were desperate, and he secretly negotiated with Sulla, who promised him pardon, if he would do some great service. Albinovanus was one of those who had fled to Africa when C. Marius was driven out of Rome, but Sulla was willing to pardon and employ any man whom he could make useful, and Albinovanus was ready to show that he deserved Sulla's favour. He invited to a banquet Norbanus and his officers C. Antipater, and Flavius Fimbria, the brother of the Fimbria who lost his life in Asia, and also all the other commanders of Carbo who were there. All came except Norbanus, and they were all massacred by order of Albinovanus. This bloody and traitorous murderer, in crime but not in talent a Cesare Borgia, made his escape to Sulla. Ariminum and other places now fell into the hands of Sulla's party, and may have been plundered. Ariminum was certainly sacked. Norbanus seeing that he could now trust nobody got on board of a merchant vessel and sailed to Rhodes. Sulla afterwards demanded his surrender, and while the Rhodians were deliberating about the matter, Norbanus killed himself in the public place.

Carbo seems to have had no ability as a general. Instead of directing all his efforts against Sulla, he wasted his strength on fruitless attempts to relieve Marius. He sent for this

purpose Damasippus with two legions, a force too small
to be of any use, even if it had reached Praeneste, but it was
stopped on the road, for the passes were occupied by Sulla. All
Cisalpine Gallia from Ravenna to the Alps now submitted to
Metellus. A victory gained by M. Lucullus, the brother of
Lucius, over one of Carbo's commanders at Fidentia between
Parma and Piacenza, completed the subjection of Northern
Italy. Probably about the same time M. Crassus took the
strong Umbrian town of Tudor (Todi) near the upper Tiber
and between Spoletium and Clusium, the head-quarters of the
consul Carbo. Tudor is only about thirty miles from Clusium,
direct distance. The town was pillaged, and Crassus was
suspected of appropriating most of the plunder to his own use,
which was afterwards made the ground of a charge against
him before Sulla. Carbo had still thirty thousand men at
Clusium, besides the two legions of Damasippus, and other
troops with Carrinas and Marcius Censorinus. The forces of
the Samnites also were vigorously struggling with Sulla for
the pass, wherever it was, by which they were attempting to
reach Praeneste. Yet Carbo like a coward left his army and
fled with a few friends to Africa, on the pretext, for it was
only an excuse for betraying his men, that as Italy was
lost he would secure the province Africa. After Carbo's
flight a battle was fought between Cn. Pompeius and the
army near Clusium, in which Pompeius gained a decisive
victory, and those of Carbo's men who survived the battle
dispersed and went to their homes. According to Velleius
it was the two Servilii who defeated Carbo's army at Clusium
after the consul's flight; and Urnini possessed a denarius
which, as he supposed, commemorates this victory of the
Servilii.

Carrinas, Marcius Censorinus, and Damasippus uniting
their forces marched to the pass, where the Samnites were still
held in check by Sulla. This place, to which Appian gives
no name, must have been an important position, for Sulla
had left his generals in the north to look after Carbo. Sulla's
object was to prevent a junction between this formidable
enemy from the south and the forces of Carbo. Carrinas and

the other Roman commanders finding that they could not
force the pass, suddenly turned off to Rome, expecting to find
the city unprotected, and they knew that the people were
suffering from famine. They took a position in the Alban
territory about twelve miles from Rome and made a camp.
We must conjecture, for Appian's scanty abridgment leaves
the story very imperfect, that this advance upon Rome may
have been designed to draw Sulla from his strong position.
Part of the Samnite forces may have moved off unseen by
Sulla to aid in the capture of Rome. At all events when
Sulla moved towards the capital, the whole force of the
enemy was already there, and the decisive battle was fought
under the walls of Rome. Sulla had sent forward his cavalry
to annoy the rear of the enemy on their march, and himself
advancing with great speed with all his army encamped
about noon at the Colline gate near the temple of Venus.

Plutarch's narrative of the last struggle for the supremacy is founded, as we may assume, on Sulla's Memoirs;
and his story is this. Telesinus and Lamponius had advanced
with forty thousand men, as Velleius has it, the bravest of
the Samnites and southern Italians, to the relief of Praeneste.
The Samnites, says the Epitome, were the only Italians who
had not yet laid down their arms. The enemy however
found that Sulla was in the way, and Pompeius was coming
on their rear. They could not advance: they could not
safely retreat; and there remained only one thing to do.
They broke up their camp by night, took the road to Rome,
and were very near surprising the city. They passed the
night about ten miles from Rome. At daybreak some of the
most distinguished young men came out of the city on horseback to oppose the enemy, but they were defeated with great
loss. Rome was in alarm, women were shrieking, and men
hurrying in all directions, expecting that the city would be
stormed by the most inveterate and bravest of their Italian
enemies. The Samnites under their gallant leader saw the
unexpected opportunity of destroying a city, which sheltered
the wolves that preyed on Italian liberty. The forest, said
Telesinus, must be rooted up, which is the lair and refuge of

these wild beasts [1]. Sulla had sent forward Balbus with a
body of cavalry to oppose the enemy; Plutarch says, seven
hundred men : but this was too feeble a force to engage the
Samnites, though it is said that it did attack them. Sulla
soon came up with his men, and ordering them to take some
refreshment he prepared for the battle under the walls of
Rome near the Colline gate, though his soldiers were exhausted by a long march. His friends urged Sulla to let the
men have rest, though as the enemy was before him, it
cannot be certain that Sulla could have followed their advice,
even if he had been willing. It was about the tenth hour of
the day, two or three hours before sunset of the first of
November B.C. 82. The signal was given and the battle
began. It was the fiercest fight of all the campaign. Crassus,
who commanded the Roman right, defeated the enemy, but
the left was hard pressed, when Sulla came to the relief,
mounted on a spirited white horse. Two of the enemy's men
recognizing the Roman commander made ready to discharge
their javelins at him. Sulla did not see them, but his groom
did, and he whipped Sulla's horse, which made a bound and
just carried him so far beyond the range of the spears that
they stuck in the ground. Sulla had in his bosom a small
golden figure of Apollo, part of the spoil of Delphi. He
kissed the image and prayed to the god not to desert him in
this final struggle. By threats and persuasion he tried to
stop his men, who were giving way, but the left wing was
completely broken, and Sulla mingling with the fugitives
made his escape. This was the only battle in which this
successful commander had ever turned his back on an enemy.
Appian says that the left wing fled to the gates of the city
followed by the enemy, and that the older citizens who manned
the walls, let down the gates, and so killed many of their own
men and some of the senators among them. The Romans
finding the gates closed, turned again on the enemy, and the

---

[1] A Samnite medal represents a bull, the symbol of Italy, throwing down a
wolf. The medal has the name C. Papius Mutilus with the title of Embratur,
an Oscan word which corresponds to the Latin Imperator (Histoire de Jules
César, L. 241, note).

battle continued through the night. This is hardly consistent with Plutarch's statement, and indeed Plutarch's narrative, though we assume it to be founded on Sulla's Memoirs, is hardly consistent with itself. But after all the victory remained with Sulla. Crassus had pursued the routed enemy as far as Antemnae, and there he rested. In the confusion of a battle it is sometimes not easy to discover which side is victorious. In the night Crassus sent to Sulla for something to eat for his wearied soldiers, and Sulla then learned that the left wing of the enemy was nearly destroyed. Lamponius, Marcius Censorinus, Carrinas, and the other generals of Carbo's party escaped for the present. Some fugitives quickly carried the news of the fight to Praeneste, and urged Ofella to raise the siege immediately, for Sulla was killed and the enemy was in Rome. But Ofella had soon evidence that Sulla was victorious. Marcius Censorinus and Carrinas were overtaken in their flight and brought to Sulla, who ordered their heads to be cut off and sent to Ofella, who fixed them on poles round the walls of Praeneste. The head of Damasippus was sent in company with the rest, but it is uncertain whether he fell in battle or was taken alive. Telesinus was found the next day on the battle-field, not yet dead, and his head too was cut off and sent to Praeneste. On both sides it is said that fifty thousand men fell, a number which may be much above the truth, but in such battles no quarter was given, and when men fight obstinately hand to hand, the numbers that fall must not be estimated by the result of modern battles.

Sulla came up with Crassus at Antemnae by daybreak. The enemy were still there in force. Three thousand of them proposed to surrender, and Sulla promised to spare them, if they would punish the rest of his enemies before joining him. The men trusted to his promise, and attacked their comrades. When a great number had fallen on both sides, Sulla took the survivors to Rome, who were six thousand, or eight thousand, as Appian says, the greater part of them Samnites. He pretended, as one authority informs us, that he was going to enroll them among his troops. Probably the men were deceived, or they would not have gone quietly to the shambles. They were placed in the Circus Flaminius, or in the Villa Publica, as the Epitome and Dion say, and the Senate was summoned in the neighbouring temple of Bellona. As soon as Sulla began to address the Senate, the men who were appointed for the work began to cut the prisoners down. The shrieks startled the Senate, but Sulla told them to attend to what he was saying and not to trouble themselves about what was going on outside: it was only some villains who were punished by his orders. The bodies were thrown into the Tiber. The victory of Sulla at the Colline gate was celebrated by the institution of the Games of Victory, which took place on the twenty-seventh of October, from which we might infer that this was the day on which Sulla gained his decisive victory under the walls of Rome; but it was, as above observed, the first of November.

The people of Praeneste seeing that further resistance was hopeless surrendered to Ofella. Marius attempted to get out of the place by one of the subterranean passages, which supplied the town with water and were also intended for the purpose of escape; but finding that the outlet was blocked up by the enemy he killed himself. Another version is that he and Telesinus, a younger brother of Pontius Telesinus, were together in the subterranean passage, and that, when they found it impossible to get out, they drew their daggers to kill one another. Telesinus was killed by Marius, who not being mortally wounded prevailed on a slave to despatch him. Whether he perished thus, or, as Velleius says, was caught, as he was just putting his head out of the hole, is uncertain. The same event is generally told several ways. Ofella sent the head of Marius to Sulla, who set it up in the Forum in front of the Rostra, and repeated with a sneer at the youth of Marius the line of Aristophanes,

" You should first have worked at the oar before you ventured to handle the helm."

When Ofella was in possession of Praeneste, he put to death some of the senators whom he found in the place, and kept others prisoners till Sulla came, who soon despatched them. Sulla ordered all the men in Praeneste to lay down their arms and to come into the plain. He picked out a few, who had been of service to him, and the rest he formed into three divisions, Romans, Samnites, and Praenestines. He told the Romans that they deserved punishment, but he would pardon them. All the rest were massacred, but the women and children were spared. The number that perished is variously reported: Plutarch says twelve thousand, of whom five thousand are said to have been Praenestines. The city was plundered. It was one of the richest of the Italian towns.

Norba still held out. Norba, a Latin colony, was near the modern Norma, between Cora and Setia, on the margin of the Volscian mountains, which here rise abrupt above the plain. From the heights of Norba there is a wide prospect over the Pomptine marshes and the coast as far as the mouth of the Tiber. The circuit of the ancient walls is about two miles. They are of the style named Cyclopean and constructed of the mountain limestone, in some parts of large polygonal blocks, in others of smaller stones more neatly put together, and in other parts again of stones nearly squared; from which it is inferred that the walls were constructed at different times. In some parts there is a double wall, one within the other. On the highest point was the citadel which also had its wall. This strong fortress was betrayed to M. Aemilius Lepidus, who entered it by night. The townsmen indignant at the treachery resolved to avoid the fate of their neighbours of Praeneste. Some stabbed themselves, others perished by mutual slaughter, and some died by hanging. In desperate extremities men still prefer one kind of death to another. Some of the citizens barricaded their doors and set fire to the houses. A strong wind happened to be blowing, and the flames spread so fast that the whole town and all that was in it were destroyed. There was no booty here for Sulla's men. Norba remained uninhabited when the elder Pliny wrote. If any of the inhabitants survived the ruin of their city, they sought a home elsewhere.

There was no longer any serious resistance to the conqueror.
Fire and sword had done their work. Sulla sent his officers
round to put garrisons in the suspected towns. He rewarded
all those who had served him well: he gave them wealth,
places, any thing that they asked for. He saw the talents of
Cn. Pompeius, and thought it prudent to attach him more
closely to his cause. Sulla's wife Caecilia Metella had a
daughter Aemilia by her former husband M. Aemilius
Scaurus the consor. Aemilia was the wife of M'Acilius Glabrio,
who was persuaded or compelled by Sulla to divorce her,
though she was then with child. Pompeius also consented
to put away his wife Antistia, who had lately lost both her
father and mother. It was an ungenerous act to desert a
woman, whose father Antistius had been murdered, because
his son-in-law Pompeius had joined Sulla. Aemilia was
taken to the house of Pompeius where she died in childbirth.

Pompeius was now sent by Sulla in pursuit of the consul
Carbo, and to clear Sicily of the Marian party. M. Perperna,
who had once been praetor, had escaped from Italy to Sicily
about the same time that Carbo and Domitius had gone to
Africa. On the arrival of Pompeius, Perperna left Sicily.
Carbo with some of his friends had passed over from Africa
to the island of Cossura (Pantellaria) in order to hear what
was going on in Italy; and he sent M. Junius Brutus, who
had been praetor B.C. 88, in a fishing-boat to Lilybaeum on
the west coast of Sicily to find out if Pompeius was there.
Brutus being surrounded by the enemy's vessels killed himself to avoid being taken. Carbo was seized in Cossura and
brought in chains before Pompeius, who sat on his tribunal
while he passed sentence on a Roman consul. It was just
that Carbo should die, and necessary too, but it was unfortunate for Pompeius to be the executioner of a man who
had once done him a great service by speaking in his defence
(p. 253). If it is true that Pompeius ordered those who
seized Carbo and his companions to put the rest immediately
to death, but to bring Carbo before him, it is a proof that
he was not an unwilling instrument of Sulla's vengeance.
Carbo's enemies may have invented the story of his cowardly

behaviour, but we can easily believe it of a man who ran away from Italy before the means of defence were exhausted. When he was dragged away for execution and saw the sword bared, his heart failed and he begged in vain for a little delay. Carbo's head was sent to Sulla as the best evidence that his orders were obeyed. Pompeius put to death all the enemies of Sulla who were of chief note, and were brought to him. Indeed he could not do otherwise without displeasing his master at Rome; but he allowed others to escape and even aided them in getting away. Sicily was restored to tranquillity without the calamities which befell Italy.

CHAPTER XXV.

SULLA, DICTATOR.

B.C. 82—81.

MARIUS, observes Plutarch, was always cruel, and the possession of power did not change his disposition. He was a rough, uneducated, brutal soldier. But Sulla from his youth was fond of pleasure and jollity. He loved a joke and was witty. He loved wine and women and theatrical shows, and delighted in the company of actors, singers, and dancers. Active and energetic when he had business on hand, he laid aside all serious thoughts at table and was a jovial companion. He was a man of letters too, well versed in the learning of the Greeks, a good administrator, a courageous soldier, and a bold and able commander, sometimes cautious, sometimes even rash, quick to seize opportunities, with a resolute will, and a presence of mind that never deserted him in danger. From his early years he was tender-hearted and easily moved to tears; and yet he became the most cruel tyrant that ever scourged a conquered nation. It has been said of Marat, who resembled Sulla in nothing except this, that he had great "sensibilité," a French word for which our English word "sensibility" is perhaps hardly a complete equivalent, but it is near enough. Marat was driven half mad by revolutionary frenzy, but he had some method in his madness. This man, who thirsted after human blood, said that he could not bear to see an insect suffer. Michelet has explained this apparent contradiction. People, he says, confound sensibility with goodness of disposition; they do not know that exalted sensibility may become fury. Women have moments of cruel sensibility; and Marat in temperament was a woman and more than woman, nervous and sanguine. Sulla was, as Carbo said, both lion and fox. He was both man and woman too: he felt like a woman, but he had the energy of a man. His character was not fully shown till opportunity came. His behaviour when he was absolute master led some to think that power changes men's tempers and makes them violent, proud, and inhuman. Plutarch raises the question without settling it, whether change of fortune really changes a man's temper, or whether power merely discovers the bad qualities which have hitherto been concealed. The answer to the question is not difficult; most men, nearly all, are capable of crime under certain circumstances. Fortunately for the world opportunity does not come to all; but no man who has lived half a century and observed human nature can doubt that we always are what we were born, somewhat improved or made worse according to the circumstances by which we have been surrounded. Experience shows that power, place, opportunity, adversity, prosperity, and temptation discover in a man qualities unknown to others, and not suspected even by himself. Sometimes the man becomes great and noble; sometimes mean, cruel, and contemptible. It is power which gives the greatest opportunity for the display of bad qualities. We see it daily in men who rise to high station, and even in those who are invested with the smallest authority over others. A Greek said truly that power shows the man.

Sulla only thought of securing the fidelity of his friends. He never thought of conciliating enemies. He had only one way of dealing with them: he exterminated them. He had wrongs of his own to revenge, and greedy adventurers to satisfy. A Roman cared little for human life, and Sulla less than any Roman. When a man has once begun to rule by terror and bloodshed, it is not easy for him to stop in his career, for all violent passions grow stronger by use. Such a man's name and memory would be execrated after his death, and we cannot say how far we can trust all that is reported of Sulla and of his cruel partisans. But we know that the horrors of these times left an impression among the Romans that was never effaced from their remembrance, and the great Revolution of France is an example of what man can do when fear and hate, revenge and cupidity are let loose in the midst of civil discord. Sulla had also a victorious army, who expected to be paid for their services, and both his inclination and his interest bade him satisfy their demands. In an address to the people of Rome Sulla spoke proudly of his own exploits, and let his enemies know what they might expect. He concluded by saying that he would alter things for the advantage of the people, if they would obey him, but he would not spare any of his enemies, and would punish with all his power every man who had aided his adversaries since the day when the consul Scipio violated the terms of his agreement.

Blood now began to flow freely, and many persons were put to death. Some, who had taken no part against Sulla, were murdered through private enmity, and Sulla consented to their death to please his partisans. At last a young man boldly asked him in the Senate house, when these things would end; he did not ask for mercy to those whom it was determined to destroy, but he intreated Sulla to release from uncertainty those whom he intended to spare. Sulla replied that he had not yet determined whom he would spare. Then tell us, said the senator, whom you intend to punish. Sulla said that he would; and the proscription list appeared. But even this monstrous act was done in legal form, for Cicero affirms that there was an enactment (lex) for the sale of the property of the proscribed and of those who fell in arms against Sulla (Pro Q. Roscio Amerino, c. 43).

A proscription was a list of persons set up in public, and every man whose name was in the list might be killed by any one who chose to do it. The first list contained the names of forty senators and about sixteen hundred equites. Rewards were offered to those who committed the murders, and to those who discovered the hiding-places of the proscribed; and severe penalties were imposed on those who concealed them. Another list soon appeared, which contained the names of other sena-

tors. Some of these unhappy people were killed on the spot
where they were caught, in houses, in streets, and in temples.
Others were dragged before Sulla and their carcases pitched
down in front of him, or hauled along the roads and trampled
under foot. Cicero, if we take his words literally, saw, or if
he did not see himself, others saw and told him of senators
being killed and their heads fixed up near the reservoir of
Servilius, in one of the most public parts of Rome, and of
crowds of assassins scouring the streets. The spectators
looked on in silence, for terror tied their tongues. Those
who fled from Rome were followed by the pursuers, and
killed wherever they were found. The property of the
proscribed was sold, their children lost all title to it, and contrary to the old Roman principle of not punishing children
for the crimes of their parents, they were excluded from the
honours, that is, the offices of the State. This penalty bore
some resemblance to the English old barbarous doctrine of
attainder and corruption of blood. In the same way after
one of the revolutions of Florence, the Ghibellini were excluded by their political opponents from the offices of the
republic. It is not certain whether those penalties were
fixed now or by a subsequent Lex Cornelia de Proscriptis.
Valerius Maximus is the only authority that has recorded the
whole number of the proscribed and murdered, whose names
were entered on the public records. He says that it was four
thousand seven hundred; but the number was much increased
by those who were secretly assassinated from motives of
revenge or lucre. Many names were inserted also in the
proscription lists merely because the men were rich. One,
whom Plutarch names Q. Aurelius, who never meddled in
public affairs, happened to be reading the list of the proscribed
in the forum, and found his own name there. He said, "Alas,
it is my farm at Alba that is my persecutor;" and he had
not gone far from the spot before he was murdered by a man
who was in search of him.

A horrible act of vengeance and cruelty is recorded; and
the chief guilt is fixed on Sulla. M. Marius, a senator as
Livy names him, a man of Prætorian rank, was a relation of

C. Marius. Florus names him the brother of Marius, meaning probably the younger Marius, but it appears that he was the cousin, for the man was M. Marius Gratidianus (p. 252). He was given up by Sulla to be tortured at the prayer of Q. Catulus, the son of Q. Catulus who had killed himself to escape from the cruelty of C. Marius after his return from exile. Marius Gratidianus was taken from a goat-pen in which he was hid and dragged across the Tiber to the tomb of Catulus. He was whipped, his limbs were broken and mangled, his nose and hands were cut off, and his eyes torn out. Lucan has elaborated in his Pharsalia (ii. 175) a painful description of this abominable torture. Plutarch simply reports of the death of M. Marius, who is no doubt Gratidianus, that L. Catilina cut off his head and brought it to Sulla in the Forum, and then went to the temple of Apollo, which was close by, and washed his hands in the sacred font. The only contemporary writer known to us who speaks of the death of Gratidianus, is Cicero's brother Quintus, in the letter to his brother Marcus when Marcus was a candidate for the consulship. He affirms that Catilina flogged Gratidianus through the streets of Rome, drove him to the tomb of Catulus, tortured him cruelly, and after cutting off his head carried it in his hands streaming with blood. We learn from the notes of Asconius on M. Cicero's oration, delivered when he was a candidate for the consulship, and when L. Catilina was a competitor, that Marcus Cicero also charged his opponent with the murder of Gratidianus. But Gratidianus, according to the story, was made an offering at the tomb of Catulus, and if the son prayed for the victim, we may conclude that he was also guilty of the torture. The charge against Catilina by the two brothers after such a lapse of time and in the excitement of an election requires further evidence, but we have none except the fact that Catilina was tried and acquitted in B.C. 64 for murders committed during Sulla's proscription. Perhaps the bad character of Catilina and his subsequent fate may have been the cause of his being charged with this crime as well as with others. Plutarch reports twice that Catilina murdered his own brother before

the termination of the war, and asked Sulla to proscribe him
as if he were alive; and the request was granted. Q. Cicero
does not mention Catilina's murder of his brother, but he
charges him with putting to death his brother-in-law, Q.
Caecilius, a Roman Eques, and his sister's husband. Indeed
Quintus affirms that Sulla placed Catilina over the assassins
who looked after the Roman Equites, and the murder of this
class of men was the act by which Catilina began his political
career. The vengeance of the triumphant party was not
satisfied with the blood of the living. The remains of C.
Marius, which rested on the banks of the Anio, were taken
from the tomb by Sulla's order and thrown into the river.
Lucan alludes to this contemptible act of vengeance, when he
describes among the omens of the civil war between Caesar
and Pompeius the frighted rustic on the banks of the Anio
flying from the spectre of Marius

" Raising his head above the shattered tomb."

The Italians suffered as well as the Romans. Death, exile,
and confiscation were the punishment of those who had aided
with Sulla's enemies. Commissions sat all through Italy to
try those who had served the vanquished party as officers
or soldiers, or had furnished money, or aided in any way the
faction of Marius. It was made a matter of charge to have
been a host, a friend, a lender or a borrower, when one of
the parties was not of Sulla's faction. Any thing indeed was
enough, when the object was to get rid of men for the sake
of their money. Whole communities were punished: the
citadels were destroyed, the walls taken down, and heavy
contributions and fines imposed on the people. Sulla's
soldiers were planted in most of these towns, and held them
as garrisons. These men received land and houses, which
had been taken from those who were put to death or had
fled and abandoned their estates. Some of Sulla's men
were made so rich that they lived in regal state. L. Luscius
a centurion acquired a property which was estimated at
ten millions of sesterces, or 88,540 pounds sterling. This
liberality secured the fidelity of the soldiers even after Sulla's

death, for they knew that they could not keep what they had
got, unless all Sulla's acts were confirmed.

An event, which happened during this civil war, gives us
a lively picture of these dreadful times. A man named M.
Aurius, a citizen of Larinum (Larino in the Neapolitan province Capitanata), was made prisoner at Asculum. He fell
into the hands of Q. Sergius a senator, who made him a
slave and kept him in chains. The mother of Aurius,
who had long believed her son to be dead, at last received
evidence that he was still alive, and a slave on an estate
in North Italy, and she urged her kinsfolk to find and
restore to her this her only surviving child. But before this
could be done, the mother died, having bequeathed to this
lost son a large legacy, and having made a grandson named
Oppianicus her heir. This fellow instead of restoring his
uncle to freedom contrived his death, and thus secured the
legacy for himself. When the murder was known at Larinum, A. Aurius a kinsman of M. Aurius declared that he
would prosecute Oppianicus, and the clamour against him
became so loud that he left the town and sought refuge in
the camp of Q. Metellus. When Sulla's arms were victorious,
Oppianicus hurried to Larinum with an armed force, got rid
of the Quatuorviri or four magistrates, who had been elected
by the municipality, and put himself and three others in
their place, alleging that he was following Sulla's order.
He also declared that he had Sulla's authority for putting to
death the kinsman of M. Aurius who had threatened him
with a prosecution. By the massacre of this enemy and
some others he established a reign of terror and ruled in this
country town like some of the petty lords that we read of in
later times when Italy was cursed with a host of tyrants.
One example like this tells us more of the sufferings of Italy
during the civil war than all the vague descriptions of
battles.

Spoletium, Interamna (Terni), Praeneste and Florentia
(Firenze) on the Arnus, are enumerated by Florus as towns
which were sold by auction, one of this foolish writer's
vague expressions, to which we must give what meaning we

can. The mention of their names is perhaps evidence that all these towns were severely punished by heavy contributions and loss of their land. Florentia at that time was an insignificant place, and we can only interpret Florus by supposing that the lands in this part of the valley of the Arno were given to Sulla's soldiers. The destruction of the Latin town Sulmo is also attributed to Sulla.

The final reduction of Nola in Campania was also Sulla's work. This place had made an obstinate resistance to the party of Sulla, and it was severely punished. The lands were distributed among Sulla's soldiers. We may guess what became of the people. The confederate leader Papius Mutilus, who was in Nola, made his escape to Teanum, where his wife Bassia lived (p. 204). The fugitive general came by night to his wife's door and prayed for admission, but the woman refused to receive him, because, as she said, his name was on the list of the proscribed. Upon this the unfortunate man stabbed himself, and the doors of the house were stained with his blood.

Volaterrae (Volterra) in Etruria was the last Italian town that submitted. Volterra stands on the flat summit of a hill which rises precipitously above the valley of the river Caecina (Cecina). The steep and difficult ascent to the top from the surrounding country is reckoned by Strabo to be fifteen stadia, or nearly two Roman miles. Some of the Etrurians and those who were proscribed by Sulla took refuge here with a considerable force and held out for two years. Populonium (Populonia) which stands on a high peninsular promontory, which rises above the sea opposite to the island Ilva (Elba), also sustained a siege at the same time as Volaterrae. It was probably ruined, for Strabo describes the town in his time as deserted, and containing only the temples and a few dwelling-houses. The haven at the foot of the hill was better inhabited. The territory of Volaterrae, which extended to the sea, was declared by Sulla to be the property of the Roman people, and consequently was forfeited. The territory of Arretium also was forfeited, but neither the territory of Arretium nor of Volaterrae was ever distributed in allotments. Probably Sulla died before he could finish his work. It was urged on the occasion of a certain trial about the freedom of a woman of Arretium that this town was deprived of the Roman citizenship, but Cicero, who defended the freedom of the woman, maintained that this could not be done, and Sulla was still living when Cicero made his speech, probably in B.C. 79. We are not told directly to what condition Sulla reduced the citizens of Arretium and Volaterrae, but the passage in Cicero's oration Pro Caecina (c. 35) shows that he left the people of these towns only the Commercium (p. 180), a term which has been explained.

Sulla settled matters in Rome just as he pleased, for no man ventured to oppose him. Appian speaks of some legislative act or resolution of the Senate, by which every thing was confirmed that Sulla had done as consul or proconsul. A gilded equestrian statue was also set up in front of the Rostra with the inscription Cornelius Sulla Imperator Felix, which means the Fortunate; for so his flatterers named him, or he assumed the title himself, and it appears on some of his medals. Though he had kingly power, Sulla wished to give his usurpation the show of being regularly constituted, for even a tyrant is compelled to acknowledge ancient forms. As there were no consuls, no election could be made without the creation of an Interrex or temporary king, which was an old Roman institution. Accordingly for form's sake Sulla left Rome for a time and directed the Senate to appoint an Interrex. The Senate elected L. Valerius Flaccus in the expectation that there would be an election of consuls; but Sulla wrote to Flaccus and told him that he thought that the interests of the State required the appointment of a Dictator, and he recommended that the man who should be elected should not hold the office for a fixed time as of old, but until he should have completely restored tranquillity all through the dominions of Rome. It was easy to collect from the letter whom Sulla would recommend as a fit person for this office, but that there might be no mistake, he added that he thought himself the best man for the purpose. It was impossible to resist such a candidate, and accordingly the votes of the popular assembly, as Appian states, made Sulla perpetual Dictator. In fact he was elected king and more than king for life, and he might have had the name too, if he chose; but he was too wise to take an odious title. The election was invested with a little decency by the declaration that Sulla was made Dictator for the purpose of framing such laws as he might think useful, and for the settlement of the State. The old office of Dictator, which was limited both in time and power, had not been filled for one hundred and twenty years, but in cases of great emergency the consuls had been invested with extraordinary powers by virtue of the commission which was expressed by the terms, That the consuls should see that the commonwealth sustained no damage. The dictatorship of Sulla was in fact an imperial power conferred in the form of a popular election, which was directed by the man who proposed himself as the sole candidate, and asked for votes which could not be refused.

Still further to maintain the appearance of ancient forms Sulla allowed two consuls to be elected, M. Tullius Decula and Cn. Cornelius Dolabella, for the year B.C. 81. But his supreme authority was shown by the twenty-four lictors who preceded him, a thing never seen before in Rome, and by a strong guard. He settled public matters according to his pleasure, but all these changes require a separate consideration. The Senate was greatly reduced in numbers; and Sulla added to the body about three hundred selected from the best of the Equites, as Appian says, but Sallust affirms that some of them had been common soldiers, which is not credible. The people voted for each new senator, but we must assume that Sulla nominated or proposed the candidates. However, if he used the popular vote on this occasion, Sulla set an example which usurpers may follow. It is prudent to found power and revolutionary measures on the apparent consent of the people, when it can be done. Sulla also gave freedom and the Roman citizenship to above ten thousand of the youngest and most vigorous slaves, whose masters had been killed. These men were all named Cornelii, after the Gentile

name, Cornelius, of their great patron Sulla, and thus he had
ten thousand strong fellows in Rome always ready to do his
bidding.   In order to secure a body of partisans all through
Italy he distributed among his soldiers a large part of the
public land which had not yet been given in allotments, and
other land of which the Italians had been deprived as a
penalty for their resistance.   The men of three-and-twenty
legions were thus provided for, or forty-seven legions, as the
Epitome states.   But even twenty-three legions were a much
larger force than Sulla brought with him to Italy, and this
number must include the soldiers of Pompeius, Metellus, and
of other commanders, and the men who joined him in Italy
during the civil war.   Those who fell in the contest with
Sulla or were murdered afterwards would lose all that they
had, and there would be a great quantity of vacant land.
Many owners fled or were turned out of their estates to make
way for the soldier.   The misery that women, children, and
old people would suffer may be easily conceived, and when
we add to this, the neglect of agriculture during the war, and
the loss of slave labourers, it is certain that the population
and products of Italy must have been greatly diminished.
But our scanty historical records say nothing of these
matters.   The new settlers of Sulla would not be the kind
of men who were adapted to restore the prosperity of the
country, many of them old soldiers accustomed to a camp
life, to plunder, and the licence which Sulla allowed his men
in order to secure their attachment.   Thus Sulla laid the
foundation of fresh revolutions, and he who affected to be the
restorer of the State was in fact the man who hastened
its ruin.   But he only did what was unavoidable.   His men
fought not for their country, but for a faction, and they
expected to be paid for it.

   The land which was seized was the prize of the victorious
party, but it was not all given.   It was the policy of Sulla
that Roman citizens should be purchasers of confiscated
property, for they would thus have an interest in maintaining
the new state of affairs.   In revolutionary times fortunes are
rapidly lost and won.   M. Crassus, who had served Sulla

well, enriched himself by buying large properties at low
prices, for at such a time when ready money was wanted,
there would be few purchasers. C. Verres had passed over
to Sulla (p. 330), who however would not trust the man, but
he allowed him to enrich himself with the property of some
of the proscribed in the territory of Beneventum. P. Cornelius Sulla, a kinsman of the dictator, was one of the men
who got good bargains; and Sulla's wife Metella also bought
confiscated estates. Though property must have been greatly
depreciated through so much being brought into the market
at once and the want of purchasers with ready money, still
it is stated (Livy, Ep. 89) that the sale of the confiscated
estates amounted to three hundred and fifty millions of sesterces, or nearly three millions sterling. A fact like this
tells us more of the suffering and misery caused by this
revolution than the most eloquent words. A large part of
the land of Italy must have changed hands in consequence
of the grants to the soldiers and the sales. Those who were
robbed, if they did not perish by the hands of the assassin or
fly to other countries, must have died of starvation.

These sales were openly made in Rome by Sulla himself,
and he disposed of the money which was produced just as he
pleased. Handsome women, musicians, actors, and freedmen
received largely of the tyrant's bounty, which he distributed
with a profuse hand. He got rid of enemies in order to
secure himself, and he got rid of friends too when they stood
in his way. Ofella presuming on his services canvassed for
the consulship, though he was only an Eques, and had not
filled any office. Sulla attempted to persuade Ofella to desist
from his pretensions, but Ofella refused and lost his life. It
is possible that Sulla feared there might be some disturbance,
for Ofella entered the Forum with a large body of his sup-
porters, while Sulla was seated on his tribunal in the temple
of Castor. Sulla sent a centurion to kill Ofella, and the man
promptly obeyed his orders. The people seized the centurion
and brought him before Sulla, who silenced their clamours by
declaring that the centurion had done what he was bid. At
the same time he told them a story. "The lice," he said,

"were very troublesome to a clown as he was ploughing. Twice he stopped his ploughing and purged his jacket. But he was still bitten, and in order that he might not be hindered in his work, he burnt the jacket; and I advise those who have been twice humbled not to make fire necessary the third time."

Sulla celebrated a triumph for his victories in the war with Mithridates on the 29th of January B.C. 81. It lasted two days. On the first day there were exhibited fifteen thousand pounds weight of gold and one hundred and fifteen thousand pounds of silver, the produce of Sulla's victories and pillage: on the second day, thirteen thousand pounds of gold and six thousand pounds of silver, which Marius had carried to Praeneste from the ruins of the capitol and from the other temples in Rome. The men, who had been driven into exile by the Marian faction, and were now restored by the victory of Sulla, walked in the procession with chaplets on their heads. After the triumph the Dictator made a speech before the people in which he recounted all the events of his life, his good fortune as well as his great deeds, and in conclusion he bade them salute him by the name of Felix or the Fortunate, the nearest Greek for which, says Plutarch, is Eutyches. Whenever he wrote to Greeks, he signed himself Epaphroditus; and the name Lucius Cornelius Sulla Epaphroditus appeared also on his trophies in Boeotia, but this inscription may have been added by Sulla's orders after he left Greece. Some time after his return Metella bore him twins, a boy and a girl. He named the boy Faustus and the girl Fausta. This word Faustus also means happy and fortunate, and may represent Epaphroditus, though this Greek word strictly denotes one who enjoys the favour of Aphrodite or Venus.

Appian found somewhere an oracular answer which had been given to Sulla in the usual form of Greek hexameters. The answer assured him that Cypris (Aphrodite) gave great power to the progeny of Aeneas, and exhorted him to make annual offerings to all the gods, and to send presents to Delphi. There is, says the Oracle, as you ascend the heights below snow-clad Taurus a Carian city, which takes its name from Aphrodite: if you give the goddess an axe, you will acquire great power. The city is Aphrodisias in Caria, where there are the remains of an Ionic temple of Aphrodite. Sulla sent to the goddess a present of a golden crown and axe, probably when he was in Asia, with an inscription on one or both, which we may assume to be his own composition:

> "Sulla to thee this offering, Aphrodite,
> He to whose might the conquer'd nations yield,
> He saw thee in a dream amidst the ranks,
> Clad in Mars' armour, battling in the field."

Though Sulla could rob a temple when he wanted money, he believed in the religion of his time. He was a religious man after the fashion of his age. We should call him superstitious; and a man who is superstitious is capable of any crime, for he believes that his gods can be conciliated by prayers and presents. The greatest crimes have not been committed by men who have no religious belief.

L. Licinius Murena, who had been left in Asia by Sulla (B.C. 84), was eager to gain a triumph and to get plunder. He had the two legions of Fimbria, and he raised other troops. The Milesians were required to furnish ten ships, and the other cities of Asia in proportion to their ability. Mithridates, who had gone off to Pontus after his agreement with Sulla, was at war with the people on the Cimmerian Bosporus and with the Colchi, who had revolted. The Colchi asked the King to give them his son Mithridates for their ruler, and when he was sent they submitted. But the father suspecting that his son had encouraged the Colchi invited him to come and see him. The young man came and was put in golden fetters, and soon after executed, though he had done his father good service in the war with Fimbria. The King was now building a fleet and collecting a great force to reduce his rebellious subjects on the Bosporus. The magnitude of his preparations made it generally supposed that he intended to attack the Romans, and this was confirmed by the fact that he still kept some part of Cappadocia, which he had promised to give up to Ariobarzanes. Archelaus also had fled to Murena for fear of the king, who charged him

with yielding too much to Sulla in the negotiations for peace.
Murena seeing the great preparations for war and being
instigated by Archelaus entered Cappadocia and advanced to
Comana. There were two places of this name, Comana in
Pontus, and Comana on the river Sarus in that part of Cappadocia named Cataonia. As Murena afterwards crossed the
Halys, it appears that it was the Comana of Cappadocia
which he took. It is supposed that Comana was at or near
the modern town Al-Bostan, which stands in a large well-
cultivated plain. Comana contained a temple which had
many priests devoted to the service of the goddess and possessed numerous slaves. The chief priest was next in rank
to the King and generally a member of the royal family.
When Strabo visited the place, it had six thousand men and
women slaves, who cultivated the estates of the temple.
Murena surprised some of the cavalry of Mithridates at
Comana, and when commissioners came to him from the
King and appealed to the treaty, he said that he could see no
treaty, and in fact Sulla had no written agreement with
Mithridates. Murena set about collecting booty, and he
even took the money from the temple, the plunder of which
was doubtless the object of his march across the mountains
to this remote spot. He spent the winter in Cappadocia.
Mithridates sent to Rome to complain of Murena. He addressed himself to the Senate and Sulla, as Appian states, but
if Mithridates appealed to Rome at the end of B.C. 84 or in
B.C. 83, he would hardly apply to Sulla, who in B.C. 83 had
not possession of Rome. In the spring of B.C. 83 Murena
crossed the great river Halys when it was swollen by the
rain, and ravaged numerous small places. The King, who
was waiting for the return of his ambassadors from Rome,
did not oppose Murena, who retired into Phrygia and Galatia
loaded with booty. There he found a man named Calidius,
who had been sent from Rome in consequence of the complaints of Mithridates. Calidius brought no formal instructions, but he declared publicly that the Senate ordered
Murena to abstain from disturbing the King, who had a
treaty with Rome. It was observed however that Calidius

had a private interview with Murena, who immediately
renewed hostilities. In the state of affairs then in Italy
Murena would not feel afraid of disobeying the order of the
Senate, if an order really was sent to the effect which
Calidius stated. Mithridates was now compelled to fight,
and he sent Gordius to waste the country in which Murena
was. Gordius seized many beasts and waggons, and made
some prisoners. He found Murena encamped on a river and
took his position on the opposite side. Neither general was
willing to hazard a battle, but Gordius gained by the delay,
for Mithridates came to his support with the larger part of
his army, forced a passage across the river and inflicted on
Murena a signal defeat. The Roman general retreated to a
strong position on an eminence, where he was again attacked
by Mithridates, and after losing many of his men he retreated
through the mountains to Phrygia, harassed in his rear by
the enemy.

When this victory was noised abroad, many changed sides
and joined Mithridates, who now expelled the garrisons
which Murena had left in Cappadocia. He celebrated his
victory after the manner of the Persians by a sacrifice to the
god of battles. On a lofty mountain he built up a huge pile
of wood. It was the fashion for the Persian kings to carry
the first logs on such an occasion. When the great central
pile was constructed, it was surrounded by a lower range of
wood. On the upper pile were placed milk and honey and
wine and oil and all kinds of aromatics : on the lower there
was laid out a feast for those who were present. This was
done in imitation of the royal sacrifices at Pasargadae in
Persia. When the pile was fired, the blaze was seen by the
mariners on the Black Sea at the distance of more than a
hundred miles.

Sulla was now in power, and he sent Aulus Gabinius to
inform Murena that he must not carry on war against Mithridates. When this final order came, Murena was not
in a condition to continue the war. Gabinius was also
instructed to reconcile Ariobarzanes and Mithridates.
When the kings met, Mithridates betrothed to Ariobarzanes

a daughter who was only four years old, in return for which
he was allowed to keep those parts of Cappadocia which were
in his possession and to take others. He also feasted all who
were present, and proposed prizes for drinking, eating, joking,
singing, and other things usual among his people in such
festivities. Gabinius was the only man who took no part in
these amusements. Murena left his province, in which he
was succeeded by M. Minucius Thermus. He had a triumph
in Rome probably in B.C. 81, though instead of a triumph he
deserved a severe punishment. But Sulla could not forget
the services of Murena at the battle of Chaeronea, nor could
he refuse any favour to those who had stood by him in the
contest for power. The second Mithridatic war, as it was
called, ended in the third year, as Appian observes; by which
he means that it was carried on during one year and part of
two other years.

While Pompeius was settling the affairs of Sicily (B.C. 81),
he received orders to pass over into Africa, where Cn. Domitius Ahenobarbus had got together a large force. Pompeius
left C. Memmius, whom Plutarch names the husband of
Pompeius' sister, to command in Sicily, and crossed the sea
with a hundred and twenty large vessels and eight hundred
transports loaded with corn, arms, money, and military engines. This large fleet was doubtless partly composed of the
vessels which Sulla had brought with him from Greece; and
Sicily would be required to make contributions for the war.
Part of the troops were landed at Utica and the rest at
Carthage. Seven thousand of the men of Domitius came
over to Pompeius, who had six complete legions of his own.
It happened that some of the soldiers found a hidden treasure in the ruins of Carthage, and when this was known in
the army, the rest of the men thought that there must be
more, for it seemed probable that money had been buried
when Carthage was attacked by Scipio. For many days the
soldiers were busy with looking after these supposed treasures, and Pompeius could do nothing with them. He
prudently let them have their way and went about laughing
and looking on while they were turning up the ground. At

last the men grew tired of the useless search and told the commander to lead them against the enemy.

Domitius had placed himself in a position where there was a deep ravine in front of his camp. During a violent storm of wind and rain he gave the order for retreat, and Pompeius taking advantage of the opportunity crossed the ravine. The men of Domitius were in disorder, and made a feeble resistance. The wind also veered round and blew right in their face. The men of Pompeius also were put in confusion by the storm, and the general narrowly escaped being killed by one of his own soldiers who did not easily recognize him. At last the enemy were repulsed with great loss, and the army of Pompeius saluted him with the title of Imperator, but he said that he could not accept the title until the enemy's camp was taken. Upon this it was vigorously assaulted and Domitius was killed. The cities which had sided with Domitius surrendered or were taken by storm. Hiempsal the Numidian king had been ejected by the Numidians, and a man named Hiarbas had assumed the title of King and was on the side of Domitius. He was taken prisoner, and Hiempsal was restored to the throne of Numidia. Orosius reports that Hiarbas made his escape from the battle, but was afterwards taken in the town of Bulla Regia and put to death.

After this victory Pompeius entered Numidia. We must therefore conclude that the battle was fought in the Roman province Africa, which was in the possession of Domitius. Pompeius advanced into the interior of Numidia and completely subdued the country. A few days were spent in hunting lions and elephants. The lion is common in North Africa, but it is doubtful if the elephant was ever native in that part of the continent. Plutarch indeed must have supposed the elephant to have lived in a wild state in Africa, or he could not have spoken of Pompeius hunting it. Herodotus (iv. 191) enumerates elephants among the beasts of North Africa, west of the lake Tritonis, but his information was derived from hearsay. When Pliny (H. N., viii. 1) speaks of elephants in the forests of Mauretania, he probably only copied

Herodotus or some other writer, just as he tells us that there are lions in Europe between the rivers Nestus and Achelous, a statement which he found in Herodotus. A little farther on Plutarch speaks of the elephants which Pompeius brought from Africa as "the king's elephants that he had taken," as if the elephants belonged to Hiarbas or Hiempsal and had been captured after breaking loose. The elephant had long been tamed and used by the Carthaginians and the African kings, and if the animal was not found in North Africa, it must have been brought from the country south of the Great Desert. The elephant is represented on some Roman medals, and it is the African elephant, as we see from the largeness of the ears, which is one of the differences between the Asiatic and the African species.

When Pompeius returned to Utica, he found orders from Sulla to disband the army except one legion, and to wait there with it until the arrival of his successor. Pompeius was annoyed, though he did not show his dissatisfaction, but the army did, and refused to obey Sulla's commands. It seems strange that Sulla should have ordered the soldiers to be disbanded in Africa, for if they had been left there, they would be like so many hungry lions let loose on the people of the province. Besides, all these men were entitled to their reward for serving Sulla, and their commander expected a triumph. It seems probable that Plutarch has misreported or misconceived Sulla's orders. However this may be, there was a mutiny, which Pompeius with great difficulty appeased and set sail for Italy. A report had reached Rome that Pompeius had revolted, on which Sulla remarked that it was his fate in his old age to fight with boys. However the truth was soon known, and Sulla seeing that the Romans were eager to welcome Pompeius on his return, prudently went to meet the conqueror of Africa as he approached the city. Sulla received him with all possible expressions of goodwill, and saluted him by the name of Magnus or Great. The services of the young general indeed deserved all praise, for in about forty days he had cleared Africa of the enemy and restored order. Pompeius did not adopt the name Magnus until he was in Spain, where he was afterwards sent to oppose Sertorius. It was nothing strange that a Roman should receive such an honourable title, for the name Maximus or Greatest had been conferred on others before. The young general was not very modest, and he asked for a triumph. Sulla at first opposed the demand, for triumphs were only granted to dictators, consuls, or praetors, and the victory of Pompeius had been obtained over a Roman and not over a foreign general. Pompeius also was only an Eques, not even a member of the Senate: indeed he was not entitled to be admitted into that body in a regular way, as he had not yet filled a magistracy, and was far short of the necessary age. We cannot wonder then if Sulla was jealous of this forward youth, who went so far as to say that more men worship the rising than the setting sun. His meaning was plain enough, and when the words were reported to Sulla, the dictator who was surprised at his boldness, said twice, Let him triumph. This concession is a proof that Sulla did not think it prudent to oppose the claims of Pompeius, and he was always wise enough to yield to circumstances when he could not have his own way. Pompeius was in his twenty-fifth year, according to the Epitome, when he triumphed; but Licinianus says that he was twenty-five and that his triumph was on the twelfth of March, which would be in B.C. 80. He made preparations to enter the city in a car drawn by four elephants, but as the gate was not wide enough, his chariot was drawn by horses. The soldiers who returned with him had not got as much as they expected, and showed that they intended to make some disturbance at the triumph ; but Pompeius declared that he would rather give up the triumph than humour them, and so they were content to be quiet for the present.

In the year B.C. 81 another young man was rising to distinction in a different way. M. Tullius Cicero, a native of Arpinum, who was nearly nine months older than Pompeius, delivered his speech for P. Quintius before C. Aquillius Gallus, who was afterwards a colleague of Cicero in the praetorship. This was not Cicero's first speech in court, as we learn from the oration itself, but it is the earliest of his extant

orations.   The subject of the speech was a claim of Sextus
Naevius against P. Quintius, which originated in a partner-
ship between Naevius and C. Quintius who at his death left
his brother P. Quintius his testamentary heir.   Cicero was
opposed to Q. Hortensius, the advocate of Naevius.   Hortensius, who was eight years older than Cicero, had already
attained great reputation as an orator.   The whole matter of
this speech is very difficult to understand.   It has given
employment to several learned critics, but the only commentary worth reading is by a modern German jurist[1].

[1] "Semestrium ad M. Tullium Ciceronem Libri Sex" by F. L. Keller, Zürich,
1842. A young student should not read this oration. He will certainly not
understand it. The legal question, which is before the Judex Gallus, is not
easily apprehended; and neither Cicero's statements nor arguments are clear.
Keller thinks that Cicero had a bad case to defend, and there are good reasons
for this opinion.

CHAPTER XXVI.

C. JULIUS CAESAR AND M. TULLIUS CICERO.

B.C. 80—79.

PLUTARCH reports that when Sulla got the power, he confiscated the marriage portion of Cornelia the daughter of Cinna, because he could not by promises or threats induce Caesar to part with her. C. Julius Caesar, the son of C. Julius Caesar and Aurelia, was first betrothed to Cossutia, who was very rich, but only of an equestrian family. It is uncertain whether he was married to Cossutia, but perhaps he was not, for Cossutia was dismissed, as Suetonius expresses it; and after Cinna's death Caesar married his daughter Cornelia in B.C. 83, the year in which Sulla invaded Italy. If Caesar was born on the twelfth of July B.C. 100[1], in the

---

[1] "Mommsen proposes the date 652 for Caesar's birth, because from the time of Sulla, the age required for the aedileship was thirty-seven, forty for the praetorship, forty-three for the consulship, and as Caesar was curule aedile in 689 (B.C. 65), praetor in 692 (B.C. 62), consul in 695 (B.C. 59), if he had been born in 654, he would have held each office two years before the legal age." (Histoire de Jules César, i. p. 251.) But the author of the "Histoire" remarks that the law was not strictly observed in the case of eminent men, and he takes the instances of L. Licinius Lucullus, and Cn. Pompeius Magnus. Lucullus was consul B.C. 74, but we do not know when he was born. Pompeius was born B.C. 106, and he was consul B.C. 70. But his election was irregular, and there is no evidence that Caesar was elected to a magistracy before the legal age. The author further observes: "If we admit Mommsen's opinion, we must fix Caesar's birth not in 652, but in 651 (B.C. 103); for if he was born in July 652, he would not be forty-three before July 695, and as the election of the consuls took place six months before they entered on office, he would attain the legal age in July 694, and this would throw his birth back to 651." This also is no answer to Mommsen's opinion, for it appears that a man might enter on his consulship in his forty-third year, as Cicero did. If we accept the evidence of

year of the city 654, he was in his seventeenth year in the
beginning of B.C. 89. His father died suddenly at Pisae
when the son was in his sixteenth year. There is no mention
of Caesar during the contest in Italy between Sulla and his
enemies, but as he was old enough to bear arms, and was so
closely connected with Cinna and the Marian faction, for he
was the cousin of the younger Marius, it is probable that he
served against Sulla. It is strange that Sulla spared his life,
if Caesar was ever in his power, and it appears that he was.
Plutarch says that Caesar was not content to be let alone by
Sulla, who after his final victory was occupied with the proscriptions and other matters, and that he even presented
himself to the people as a candidate for a priestly office,
though he had hardly arrived at man's estate. Sulla, he
adds, contrived to prevent Caesar's election, and even thought
of putting him to death, and when it was observed to him by
those who interceded for his life, that there was no reason for
getting rid of such a youth, Sulla replied that they had no
sense if they did not see how many Marii in such a boy.

But Plutarch has made a mistake here. Caesar was created
Flamen Dialis after the death of Merula, through the favour
of his uncle C. Marius and Cinna (B.C. 87). There was
nothing to prevent a youth thirteen years old from being
made Flamen of Jupiter. A like instance of early ecclesiastical promotion once occurred in modern Rome. Gio-
vanni de' Medici, the son of Lorenzo, and afterwards Pope
Leo X., was made a cardinal in his thirteenth year. Marius
died early in B.C. 86, and though his party was in power till
Sulla's return in B.C. 83, Caesar was never inaugurated, and
the office was not filled up until the time of Augustus
(p. 248). Sulla of course would not allow Caesar to have the
priesthood; and if Caesar was not in the proscription lists,
he was certainly followed by the inquisitors of blood and
only escaped out of the city by night in disguise. Plutarch
relates that the words which Sulla uttered, when it was urged

Appian and Suetonius as to Caesar's age when he was murdered, he was born in
B.C. 100; but the difficulty above stated still remains. See a note in Barker's
" Handbuch," etc., ii. 2. 21 (1810).

to him that there was no reason for putting such a youth to
death, came to Caesar's ears and gave him the alarm. He
wandered about the Sabine mountains sick with fever, and
changed his hiding-place nearly every night.   Once he fell
in with Sulla's men, who were scouring those parts, and he
only got off by bribing Cornelius Phagita, the commander of
the band whom he had at a future time the opportunity of
punishing, but he did not do it.   Being released by Phagita
Caesar made his way to the coast, and taking shipping sailed
to Bithynia to King Nicomedes.   As Suetonius tells the
story, it was after his wanderings and buying his life from
the men of blood that Caesar was pardoned by Sulla through
the intercession of the Vestal virgins and others, and it was
on this occasion that Sulla made the remark that there were
many Marii in Caesar.

But if Caesar was hunted and saved himself by bribing
his captors, there is an inconsistency in saying that his
friends asked for his pardon after he had made his escape.
It seems then that the true order of events is this: that
Caesar was at one time in Sulla's power, that the tyrant
deprived him of his wife's portion, and perhaps of his property, but for the time he proceeded no farther, either
because Caesar had powerful friends to speak for him, or for
other reasons; but the murderers would let him have no rest,
and he escaped from Rome and made his way to Asia.   We
cannot conceive Caesar being sent to Asia by Sulla after
he was pardoned at Rome, or even being allowed to go abroad.
The history of this early part of Caesar's life is interesting
on account of the future fortune of the man.

The town of Mytilene in Lesbos had joined Mithridates,
and refused to submit to Lucullus, whom Sulla left in Asia
B.C. 84.   Lucullus brought his fleet to Lesbos, defeated the
islanders, and after establishing the blockade of Mytilene, he
sailed off with his ships to the town of Elaea on the opposite
coast of the mainland.   But this was only a feint.   He returned by stealth and laid an ambuscade near the city.   The
Mytilenaeans came in a disorderly way, expecting to plunder
a deserted camp; but Lucullus falling on them took a great

number of prisoners and killed five hundred of the enemy.
He also carried off six thousand slaves and made a large
booty. Lucullus did not get possession of Mytilene, and he
must have left Asia shortly after the attack on the town. At
least his name is not mentioned in the campaign of Murena
against Mithridates.

When Caesar reached Asia, M. Minucius Thermus was
in command there, and Caesar served under him. Though
Plutarch says that Caesar went direct to Nicomedes III.,
king of Bithynia, the true story may be that he joined
Thermus, who sent him to Nicomedes to procure ships for
the siege of Mytilene. The town was again assaulted, and
this time it was captured. Caesar saved the life of a soldier
in the attack, for which gallant act Thermus rewarded him
with a civic crown. There are Roman denarii of the Minucii
which contain on the reverse a representation of two men
fighting and a third between them on the ground, who is
defended by one of the combatants, but there is no reason for
supposing that this denarius was struck in honour of Caesar,
as one of the commentators on Suetonius assumes. The capture of Mytilene may most probably be placed in B.C. 80,
being noticed at the end of Livy's 89th Epitome, but without
any mention of the name of a praetor Minucius Thermus, for
which Suetonius is the only authority. Caesar again visited
Nicomedes either during the siege of Mytilene or soon after.
It was an unfortunate visit, for his intimacy with the Bithy-
nian king was the foundation of a foul charge against Caesar,
which his enemies invented, as we suppose, and maintained
and propagated as long as he lived. His biographer has
minutely recorded all this scandal without expressing any
opinion of the truth or falsehood of the imputation (Sueton.
Caesar, 2. 49). In this year Sulla was consul a second
time with Q. Caecilius Metellus Pius for his colleague.

The misery which Italy suffered from the civil wars extended to the provinces. Some of them had been ravaged in
the contest between Sulla and Mithridates, and all places
which were accessible from the sea were exposed to the
pirates who swarmed in the Mediterranean. The Roman

treasury was exhausted, and contributions were levied on the provincials to fill it again. Nations and kings under the protection of Rome, towns which in consideration of past services had hitherto been exempted from making any payments, and even those whose relation to Rome was fixed by treaty, all were called on for contributions. Some cities were deprived of the income which they derived from their ports, and even of their lands, though both were secured to them by treaty. Sulla even tried to make a little profit out of Egypt. Alexander, the son of Ptolemaeus IX. of Egypt, sometimes named Alexander I., had been given up to Mithridates by the people of Cos (p. 271), but the young prince after a time made his escape to Sulla, with whom he lived on terms of intimacy. Alexander's father had been driven out of Egypt in B.C. 89, and his father's brother Lathyrus, Ptolemaeus VIII., was restored to the throne, which he kept until he died in B.C. 81. As Alexander I. was dead and Lathyrus left no legitimate sons, the crown of Egypt came to his daughter Berenice, named also Cleopatra. Sulla thought that there should be a man on the throne, and if Alexander was made king, the Romans might get some money out of so rich a country. Alexander accordingly was sent to Egypt and received as king. Cleopatra was already seated on the throne, and it was a condition of the agreement with the people of Alexandria, that the claims of Alexander and Cleopatra should be united by a marriage. Alexander performed his promise and took his cousin to wife. But he must have been both stupid and cruel, for in a few days he put her to death. He had been educated in a school of murder under two of the greatest teachers of the day, a brutal king and a savage aristocrat. In other ways too he conducted himself so outrageously, relying on Sulla's support, that on the nineteenth day of his reign, as Appian states, the people of Alexandria dragged him from the palace to the gymnasium and killed him. But there seems to be some reason for supposing that his reign was not quite so short. He was succeeded by Ptolemaeus XI., commonly called Auletes, an illegitimate son of Ptolemaeus Lathyrus.

In B.C. 80 Cicero, now twenty-six years of age, made his speech in defence of Sextus Roscius of Ameria. This oration, delivered when Sulla was in the possession of power, is a valuable historical document. It was a bold act to undertake the defence of a man, who had been wronged by one of Sulla's favourites. Circumstances compelled the advocate to be cautious in what he said, but he has spoken more freely than we could expect of the murder and pillage, which, if not always done with Sulla's consent, were at least not checked and punished by him. There is no evidence which brings before us so clearly the sufferings of Italy after Sulla's victories as this speech of Cicero, who was living in the midst of a dreadful revolution and was a witness of the atrocities committed. He could hardly venture to exaggerate them, and fear of Sulla, as we plainly see, made him say no more than would serve the interest of his client. To read this speech is the next thing to having seen what is described in it. We almost touch the tyrant with our finger.

Cicero had not yet filled any public office, for he was too young to be eligible. He could therefore, as he says, speak more freely than those whose superior age and position in the State made their acts and words more observed. He tells the court and the audience the reason why many men older than himself and men of distinction could not venture to defend Roscius, who was accused of the monstrous crime of killing his own father. The property of the father had come into the possession of L. Cornelius Chrysogonus, a Greek as his name shows, and a freedman of Sulla, perhaps one of the ten thousand Cornelii. This fellow, now one of the most powerful men in Rome, affirmed that he had bought of Sulla for two thousand sesterces the property of Sextus Roscius' father, which was valued at six millions of sesterces. But Chrysogonus was afraid that he could not keep what he had got, unless the son was put out of the way. It was not easy to find an advocate bold enough to expose the villainy of Chrysogonus, though, as Cicero says, Sulla did not know it. The courts were now open again after a long interval, and Sulla had taken the office of Judices or jurymen from the

Equites and restored it to the senators. Consequently the jury in this case was composed of senators, many of whom had been lately brought into the senate by Sulla to fill up the places of those who had perished or were in exile. Cicero's client was probably tried under Sulla's Lex De Sicariis et Veneficiis, a law for the trial of assassins and poisoners. The history of Sextus Roscius the father is this.

Sextus Roscius belonged to the Umbrian town of Ameria (Amelia), which lay between the Tiber and the river Nar (Nera). He was one of the first men in the town both for rank and wealth, and on intimate terms with some of the great families of Rome, the Metelli, Servilii, and Scipios. He was also a partisan of the nobility, and during the contest between Sulla and his enemies he had exerted himself in opposition to the Marian faction. Such a man might well think that after the victory of his party he had nothing to fear. During the proscriptions he was often at Rome, in the Forum and other public places, where he might rejoice with his friends and exult over the unhappy men whom Sulla's triumph devoted to destruction. But he had enemies in his native town, who coveted his great possessions, two men of the same name, each a Titus Roscius, one of whom had the cognomen of Capito and the other of Magnus. Both of these men, as Cicero affirms, were practised villains. While Sextus Roscius the son was living at Ameria and looking after his father's estates, Titus Roscius Magnus was in Rome. One evening as the father was coming home from supper accompanied by some of his slaves, he was assassinated near the Palatine Baths. There was no evidence as to the assassin, but a presumption was raised from what happened after. On the very evening of the murder a man named Glaucia Mallius, a freedman and client of T. Roscius Magnus, set out to carry the news to Ameria, where he arrived at daybreak the following morning, having travelled fifty-six miles in about ten hours. Glaucia did not carry the news to the murdered man's son, but to his enemy T. Roscius Capito. Within four days the intelligence of the death of Sextus Roscius reached Chryso-

gonus, who was with Sulla in the camp before Volaterrae.
Chrysogonus was informed of the great wealth of Roscius,
who had thirteen farms, most of them near the Tiber: the
father had been easily despatched, and the son, who was
unknown at Rome and altogether engaged in agricultural
occupations, might be got rid of without any trouble. Capito
and those who carried the news to Chrysogonus promised
him their aid in disposing of the son also; and a bargain
was made about the division of the spoil. So Cicero represents the matter, but probably without any direct evidence.
The bargain was an inference from the subsequent conduct
of the Roscii and Chrysogonus. The proscription was now
over, and those who had fled for fear were beginning to
return to Rome; and yet the name of the deceased Roscius
was entered on the proscription lists, though he had been a
strong partisan of Sulla. Three of the man's best farms
were given to Roscius Capito, and he was in possession of
them when Cicero made this speech. Titus Roscius Magnus
took possession of all the rest of the property in the name of
Chrysogonus. Sextus Roscius was ejected from his paternal
estates; and though he had not yet discharged all the funeral
rites of his father, he was even turned out of his home.
Roscius Magnus openly carried off many valuables to his
own house, and he removed others secretly. He liberally paid
those who helped him in stripping the unfortunate son of all
his father's lands, which were sold on account of the State,
for they were confiscated under the proscription law by the
fact of the owner's name being in the lists, and Chrysogonus
was the purchaser for two thousand sestertii, as already said,
and so the State was defrauded. Here Cicero remarks that
he is well aware that all this was done without Sulla's
knowledge, which may either have been the fact, or Cicero
said so to avoid offending Sulla, while he was attacking one
of his favourites. He excuses Sulla by reason of his occupations: in his hands alone was the power of making peace and
war, all eyes were turned to him, he was sole ruler, and there
were always men ready to take advantage of any opportunity
to commit crime when Sulla was too busy to look about him.

This may be so far true that the villains who were about the Dictator murdered and plundered without asking his consent, but we cannot believe that Sulla took much pains to punish or to check them. A single word from him would have been enough.

The people of Ameria were roused by this cruel spoliation of a respected fellow-citizen; and the Decuriones or Senate of the town made a resolution to send ten of the chief men of their body to Sulla to remonstrate and ask for restitution of the property of Roscius. Cicero produced the resolution (decretum) as evidence of the truth of his statement. When the commissioners came to Volaterrae, Chrysogonus was afraid that he was ruined, if Sulla should see them. He went to the commissioners himself, and also induced certain " noble " men to treat with them. These friends of Chrysogonus persuaded the commissioners not to approach Sulla, and they promised that Chrysogonus should do what they wished. These simple-minded men, as Cicero names them, were quite satisfied with the promise of Chrysogonus to erase the name of Sextus Roscius the father from the proscription lists, and to give up the estates to his son. Titus Roscius Capito, who was one of the ten commissioners, added his promise to that of Chrysogonus, and so the commissioners returned without seeing Sulla. But nothing was done, and the matter was put off from time to time, till at last Sextus Roscius fearing that he might have his father's fate fled to Rome where he was kindly received and protected by a lady named Caecilia, a daughter of Metellus Balearicus, as it is said in one passage of this oration. His persecutors finding that they could not assassinate the man, and fearing that they could not keep their ill-gotten property so long as he was alive, resorted to the desperate expedient of bringing him to trial on the charge of murdering his own father, or rather procuring his murder; for the fact of the son being at Ameria, as Cicero affirms, when the father was killed, would be easily proved and a sufficient answer to the charge of being the murderer himself. Indeed, as Cicero says, Erucius the prosecutor did not affirm that Roscius committed the murder (c. 29), nor could he say whom Roscius employed to do it, nor could he say any thing more than this, that the father was murdered at a time when assassinations were common and passed unpunished. Erucius then might have been the murderer himself; and his argument would throw suspicion on those who paid him for his services in this case, for they had the property of the murdered man and used it for the ruin of the son. It is almost impossible to imagine how a man was brought to trial for murder without some distinct allegations to which he might answer. Yet Cicero represents it so; and if it was as he says, he could truly affirm that the vague charge of Erucius required no defence. The evidence for the prosecution had not been given when Cicero made his answer to the speech of Erucius, but if Cicero has truly represented the case, there was no evidence against Roscius, and there could not be any. Accordingly Cicero shows that as a matter of probability all the circumstances point to T. Roscius Magnus as the guilty man, and not to the son; to him who had been enriched by the father's death, not to the son who had thereby lost all; to him who was at Rome and had the opportunity of doing the deed, not to him who was not at Rome and had no opportunity or motive for committing the crime. But it is certain, notwithstanding the vague character of the charges against Roscius and the want of evidence, that he was in danger, or Cicero would not have thought it necessary to make such a defence as he has.

All the father's slaves were seized by the knaves who charged the son with the murder, and when he asked for two of them to be questioned by the torture as to his father's death, his opponents refused to give the slaves up. The demand of Roscius was at least evidence of his innocence, and the refusal of his enemies was evidence of their guilt, as Cicero argues.

After disposing of the vague charge of Erucius, and showing the probable guilt of the two Titi Roscii, Cicero comes to that "famous golden name of Chrysogonus," as he terms it in allusion to the meaning of this Greek's name. He charges Chrysogonus with ordering the sale of Roscius' property, and

being himself the purchaser for a nominal sum.   He affirms
that the property could not be sold under the proscription
law (p. 358), Valeria or Cornelia, whichever it was, for he did
not know nor did he care what the name of this law was.   He
affects even not to know the provisions of the law except from
report.   However, as he was informed, the proscription law
declared that the property of those only should be sold, whose
names were in the proscription list, or of those who had lost
their lives while they were fighting on the side of Sulla's
enemies.   But the name of Roscius was not in the list when
he was murdered, and so long as any men were under arms,
he was on Sulla's side.   The law also fixed a time after
which no confiscated property should be sold, and Roscius
was murdered and his property sold some months after the
time fixed by the law.   Therefore there could be no legal
sale of the property, and indeed Cicero seems to say
that there was no sale at all, but it was only said that
there was a sale in order to colour the knavery.   He
charges Chrysogonus with putting the name of Roscius the
father in the proscription list.   Here again Cicero takes
great pains to clear Sulla from all imputation in this
affair.   If Chrysogonus like other vile freedmen should
attempt to shelter himself under the name of his great
patron, nobody would listen to him.   Here the orator
has a passage, which like some others in this speech, his
maturer judgment must have condemned, and good taste
turns from with disgust.   He says, "If Jupiter, who rules
all things, sometimes plagues men with tempests, excessive
heat or excessive cold, destroys cities and ruins the harvest:
not that he does it purposely, for mischief's sake, but this
happens 'through the very force and magnitude of things,'
while we see that the good which we enjoy is his gift: how
can we wonder that when L. Sulla was sole governor of the
Roman State and of all the world, and was securing by his
legislation the grandeur of the republic, he failed to observe
some things; unless we wonder if human wisdom could not
do what divine power cannot accomplish ?"

Cicero declares that he was never an enemy to the "cause

of the nobility," that is, to the cause of Sulla. He appeals to all who knew him to witness the truth of what he says; that as far as his poor means would go, when all possibility of peace between the contending parties was at an end, he did all that he could to aid the party which was ultimately victorious; though he admits that he did not bear arms in the war between Sulla and the Marian faction. He was safe somewhere during this troublesome time, and it is a certain conclusion that he declared for Sulla early in the contest, and put himself under the protection of that party. Nor can we blame him. He chose the better, and it turned out to be the successful side. How could he have joined the men who murdered his venerable teacher the Pontifex Scaevola, or how could he foresee that Sulla's victory would be so much abused? After all he declares his satisfaction with the result, which had been brought about with the full consent of the gods, by the efforts of the Roman people, and by the wisdom, authority, and good fortune of L. Sulla. He cannot find fault with the punishment of those who obstinately resisted, nor with those being rewarded who had done good service to the victorious cause. But if the war was carried on in order that the meanest wretches might be enriched out of the spoil of others, and if so far from preventing this, a man must not even blame it, then indeed the war had not restored liberty to Rome, but had crushed and enslaved the State. However this was not so. If such villains should be resisted, the better cause so far from being injured, would be strengthened and confirmed. The conclusion was that the judices should acquit Roscius, by which verdict they would satisfy honest men and give security to all. Not a word is said by Cicero about Roscius recovering his father's property. He says that if Roscius can only escape all suspicion of being his father's murderer, he will be content to lose his property. Cicero acted wisely here. The first thing that he had to do was to secure his client's acquittal. If that could be accomplished, then it might be considered whether it was safe to claim restitution of his property; but as far as we can judge from this speech, such restitution was not expected by Cicero.

Plutarch says that Roscius was acquitted, and Cicero himself says so also. But it is very probable that Roscius owed his safety as much to the interest of Caecilia and other great friends of his father as to the eloquence of the young advocate. In his Orator (c. 30) Cicero has passed judgment on this juvenile production, which has some faults and great merits. It was his fashion to write out and improve his speeches, and we cannot be certain that the written speech which we have was exactly that which was delivered. Indeed we may accept the suggestion which has been made, that a few passages which might have offended Sulla were either not spoken just as they now stand or were added afterwards. I have dwelt at some length on this oration, tho first speech of the great orator in what the Romans called a public trial. The study of it is a good introduction to the life of a man who for the next eight-and-thirty years is the most prominent person in Roman history as a politician and a writer. It is also a kind of commentary on the times which immediately followed the acquisition of power by Sulla; and though we must read it with caution, considering the circumstances under which it was delivered, it is the only piece of direct contemporary evidence that we possess for this part of Sulla's history.

Cicero had been studying oratory for some years when this speech was delivered. In B.C. 88, in the consulship of Sulla and Q. Pompeius, he was a pupil of Philo, the chief of the Academy, who with others had fled from Athens during the war with Mithridates. He also attended the Rhodian Molo, a great forensic orator and teacher, who was at that time in Rome (B.C. 87). Cicero has himself told us in his treatise entitled Brutus (c. 89, &c.) how hard he was working during the three years from the death of Marius to the return of Sulla. He learned Dialectic from the Stoic Diodotus, who subsequently lived in Cicero's house and died there. It was his habit daily to practise speaking with M. Piso and Q. Pompeius surnamed Bithynicus, or some other teacher. Sometimes he declaimed in Latin, but more frequently in Greek, either because the Greek language supplied more rhetorical ornament, and the practice of speaking in Greek improved his Latin style; or because he could not have the advantage of being corrected or taught by Greeks, who were the best instructors in oratory, unless he spoke in Greek, for these men did not know Latin well enough to listen to their pupil in his native language. The practice of translating from the Greek orators into Latin, which L. Crassus used (p. 89), was Cicero's own practice also. The return of Sulla (B.C. 83) was followed by the Civil War, but when order was restored, the courts were again opened, and Cicero began his career as an advocate, not, as he says, to learn his art in the courts, as most persons did, but he appeared in the courts to practise what he had learned out of them. Molo was again at Rome in B.C. 81, having been sent by the Rhodians to ask for some compensation from the Senate for their fidelity in the Mithridatic war and the aid that they had given to Sulla. Cicero placed himself under Molo also during this second visit of the Rhodian to Rome. His success in the case of Sextus Roscius established his reputation, and he was employed in other cases. He defended before a court of decemviri against C. Aurelius Cotta the rights of a woman of Arretium (p. 363). The real state of this case can hardly be extracted from Cicero's words, but he finally succeeded in maintaining the woman's rights, though he was opposed to an eloquent advocate, and Sulla was still living. Cicero's conduct in the case of Sextus Roscius and the woman of Arretium seems to show that after the proscription was over, the regular course of administration was restored, and that an advocate at least might venture to defend a client before the courts.

In the year B.C. 79 Cicero went abroad. Plutarch found somewhere that fear of Sulla was the cause of his leaving Rome, and it is likely enough that he was glad to be out of the way for a time; but he says himself that he travelled for the sake of his health. He was very slender and weak; his neck was long and thin, and this bodily conformation seemed to threaten danger to his life, if he continued his laborious studies and exerted himself much in speaking. His friends were uneasy about him, because he spoke without pause or variation, with his voice at the highest pitch and with violent action of the whole body. In fact he did not yet know how to speak, and he had need of a good teacher. Both his friends and physicians advised him for the present to give up speaking, but he could not be prevailed on to abandon a profession for which he felt that he had great natural powers. However he thought that by adopting a different style he might avoid danger and manage himself better, and accordingly he set out on his travels, after he had been practising two years in the courts and had already acquired a great reputation. He first visited Athens, where he renewed his philosophical studies under Antiochus, a very distinguished professor of the Academy. In company with his friend Atticus, who was then at Athens, Cicero often attended the lectures of Zeno the Epicurean, who was the chief of that sect and now an old man. From Athens Cicero crossed over to Asia, and he visited all the province for the purpose of seeing all the great masters of the oratorical art and practising himself with them. The chief teachers were Menippus of Stratoniceia, in Cicero's judgment the most eloquent of the Asiatic orators, Dionysius of Magnesia with whom Cicero spent most time, Aeschylus of Cnidus, and Xenocles of Adramyttium. These were at that time the principal rhetoricians, as Cicero terms them, or teachers in Asia. Not satisfied with these instructors in the art of oratory, Cicero went to Rhodes and placed himself once more under his old master Molo, who was not a mere rhetorician, but a man used to speaking in the courts and an excellent writer. He was also most expert in observing faults and teaching the principles of his art. He took pains in pruning the redundancies and superfluities of the youthful orator's style. After all this discipline Cicero returned home almost a different man. His former bad habit of excessive straining of the voice was cured: his style of speaking, as he expresses it, had cooled down: his lungs were strengthened, and his health was improved. He came back to Rome in B.C. 77. Sulla was then dead.

CHAPTER XXVII.

SULLA'S DEATH.

B.C. 80—78.

SULLA was consul in B.C. 80, and the electors of Rome wished to appoint him again for the year B.C. 79, supposing that it would please him. But he refused the honour and named or allowed to be elected P. Servilius Vatia and Appius Claudius Pulcher. It was probably early in this year that Sulla formed the resolution of giving up his power, the first example, it is said, of a man resigning supreme authority not to his children, but to those whom he had governed. He seized the power by violence and crime, and when he had enjoyed it, he voluntarily abdicated. He who had caused the death of so many citizens, who had destroyed his enemies without mercy; senators, men of consular rank, and equites; who had driven so many into exile, confiscated their property, and cruelly treated the cities of Italy which had resisted, now returned to the condition of a private citizen. There is a savage grandeur in his contempt of danger and his way of dealing with mankind from the time when he went on his hazardous expedition to seize Jugurtha up to the day of his death. In courage, self-confidence, ability, and success in daring enterprise, he is unequalled by any man in the records of history.

In the public address in which he declared his intention to retire, he said that he was willing to give an account of all that he had done, if any person chose to ask for it. He then sent away his lictors, dismissed his guard, and walked about for some time with his friends, the people looking on the while with wonder and fear. It is said that a young man at last found courage to address Sulla when he was going home, and followed him to his door with abuse. Sulla submitted to the insult, and only observed when he had entered his house, that this young man's behaviour would prevent any one in future from resigning such power as he had held. The story is one of those which people will accept or reject according to their notion of probabilities. If the remark of Sulla were omitted, the rest of the story might be believed. It was a trivial observation, and not in fact true, for he had not parted with his real power. He had above a hundred thousand soldiers settled in different parts of Italy, who had served under him, and been enriched by his bounty. In the city he had his ten thousand Cornelii ready to obey his orders, besides a large body of other partisans. These men who were devoted to him and formidable to his enemies, rested their hopes of immunity for all that they had done on the continuance of Sulla's life. The reasons for Sulla's abdication are not difficult to discover. He had seized the supreme authority more from necessity than ambition, and he loved pleasure more than power with all its troubles. If he had lived a little longer, the state of Italy and the war of Spain would have called him again to active life, unless he had chosen to make way for other and younger men who were aspiring to be leaders in the State. He wisely gave up what he could not have maintained; and he was not guilty of the low and foolish ambition of attempting to secure to his son an impossible imperial power, or raising his family above the condition of Roman citizens. Appian says that he was still in vigorous health, but that may be doubted. He was weary of war and the toils of business and a city life: he wanted quiet, and he sought it on his estates near Cumae on the pleasant coast of Campania, where he amused himself with hunting and fishing, and writing his Memoirs.

Plutarch as a biographer tells us many things about Sulla's private life, which an historian might omit. He also records those facts which belong properly to political history, but he often makes a confused jumble and neglects the order of events. The last public act of which Sulla, as far as we know, expressed an opinion, was the election of consuls for B.C. 78: both Appian and Plutarch place this event after his abdication. The consuls elected were Q. Lutatius Catulus of the party of Sulla, and M. Aemilius Lepidus of the opposite faction. These two men hated one another and began to quarrel as soon as they were in office. Pompeius had canvassed for Lepidus and secured his election contrary to Sulla's wish, who seeing that Pompeius was pleased at the result told him that he was only strengthening a rival. Sulla's foresight was just, as events soon showed.

Before Sulla retired from the city and after he had abdicated, if we follow the order of his biographer, he performed a solemn act of piety. He made an offering of the tenth part of his substance to Hercules, and feasted the people. So great was the preparation for this entertainment that a large amount of provisions was daily thrown into the river, as we are told, and wine forty years old was drunk. In the midst of this feasting, which lasted several days, Metella Sulla's wife fell sick, and her illness was mortal. As Sulla was a Pontifex, he could not allow a person to die in his house, and accordingly in pursuance of the advice of the priests who were learned in ecclesiastical law, Sulla sent his wife a writing of divorce, and ordered her, while she was still alive, to be removed to another house. So far he complied with the custom; but he spared no expense in the funeral of Metella, though he was violating one of his own sumptuary laws. A few months later Sulla was at a show of gladiators, where his attention was attracted by a very beautiful woman named Valeria. She was a daughter of Valerius Messala, and had lately separated from her husband. The mode in which the woman attracted Sulla's notice, and the passion that he immediately conceived for her, and the marriage that followed make an amusing chapter in Plutarch. It seems probable that this marriage took place no long time before his death, as he left Valeria with child. Valeria was Sulla's fifth wife, for he had been married three times before he took Metella.

Plutarch who has got together all the scandal about Sulla says that he still continued his dissolute course of life, and spent his time with women and actors, and in drinking. Among his companions was the famous actor Q. Roscius, who was a man of talent and great taste. Sulla's way of living soon brought on disease. Some authorities say that his flesh became so corrupt that his body swarmed with lice, and it was impossible by any care to keep him free from vermin. The want of contemporary evidence throws some doubt on the manner of his death, and it has been urged that a man in such a state of health could not have left a wife pregnant. It is also argued that Sulla in his Memoirs said nothing of this loathsome disease, as Pliny observes, and this negative evidence is supposed to counterbalance such evidence on the other side as we have. But Sulla, who prided himself on his good fortune, could hardly be expected to report such a calamity.

Sulla was still busy with his Memoirs; he finished the twenty-second book only two days before his death. In this part of his work he said that the Chaldaeans once foretold him that he should have a happy life and die at the height of his prosperity, which passage may be some evidence against the report of his having the lousy disease. He was warned, as he wrote in his Memoirs, that his end was near. One of his sons, who died a short time before his mother, appeared in a dream, and entreated his father to rest from his troubles and join Metella with whom he would live in tranquillity. Sulla had no remorse for what he had done: he gloried in his acts and his good fortune, and he was ready to die when his time came. He had enjoyed the favour of his gods during life, and he expected a happy existence after death. He went on working to the last. Ten days before his death he settled some disputes among the people of the neighbouring town of Puteoli and gave them a constitution. The very day before he died Sulla sent for Granius, one of the chief men of Puteoli, who had in his hands the money raised by the town council (decuriones) of Puteoli as a contribution towards the restoration of the Roman Capitol, or if Granius had not the

money, he had at least not taken pains to collect it. The
dedication of the Capitol was the only thing wanting to complete Sulla's good fortune, as he said in his Memoirs, and he
wished to have the honour of performing this solemn ceremony. He was in a violent passion when Granius came, and
owing to his excitement and shouting he vomited a quantity
of blood and died (B.C. 78). But as Plutarch tells the story,
Sulla's slaves by his order strangled Granius first. Sulla
was in his sixtieth year. Appian's story of his death is this:
Sulla had a dream, in which the deity summoned him. At
daybreak he told the dream to his friends, and immediately
began to make his will, which he completed on that day.
He appointed his friend L. Lucullus the guardian of his
children, and entrusted him with the final arrangement and
correction of his Memoirs which were also dedicated to
Lucullus. In the evening he was seized with fever and he
died in the night. Both in his death and in his life he was
considered the most fortunate of mankind, "if indeed," adds
the historian, "a man should consider it good fortune to
obtain all that he desires."

When the news came to Rome, there was great commotion.
The friends of Sulla wished to bring the body to the city and
to give it a public funeral. Lepidus and his faction resisted
this proposal, but it was carried by Catulus and his partisans.
Even Pompeius was on the side of Catulus, though he was
the only friend whom Sulla had not mentioned in his will,
and such an omission was in Roman opinion a mark of want
of respect. It was the fashion of the Cornelii to bury their
dead, but L. Philippus, who anticipated future disturbances,
advised that Sulla's body should be burnt, lest he should have
the same fate as Marius, whose body the soldiers had dragged
from the tomb and torn in pieces. The corpse of Sulla was
carried to Rome on a gilded couch with regal decorations,
attended by trumpeters and horsemen. Others followed on
foot, and armed. The soldiers who had served under Sulla
flocked from all parts of Italy to do honour to their great commander, and as they came took their place in the procession.
A mighty crowd, such as had seldom been seen, came to

gaze on the spectacle. The insignia of office and the axes, which used to accompany Sulla when he was dictator, were carried in the funeral pomp.

When the body reached the city, it was brought in with still greater solemnity. More than two thousand golden crowns made hastily for the occasion were carried in the procession, the gifts of cities, of the legions which had served under Sulla, and of his friends. There were other costly things also sent to decorate the ceremonial, and more than words can tell. All the sacred colleges were there, not through affection, but through fear of the great military force that was assembled: even the Vestals were present. All the Senate joined in the procession, and the magistrates, in their several costumes. The Roman Equites followed in their proper dress, and all the legions which had fought under Sulla, each in its place, carrying gilded standards, and wearing armour plated with silver. The number of those who blew wind instruments was almost past counting. The notes were by turns soft and plaintive. The immense multitude responded to the music, first the Senate, then the Equites, then the army, and the people last. Some really regretted Sulla; others feared his soldiers, and looked with terror even on the corpse. They had before their eyes a strange spectacle, and they could not forget what Sulla had done. The body was placed before the Rostra, and the funeral oration was pronounced by the best orator of the day, whose name however is not recorded. Faustus, Sulla's son, was too young to discharge this pious duty. Some of the senators, robust men, then took up the bier and carried it to the Campus Martius, where the ancient kings of Rome were interred. The day was cloudy and threatened rain; but a strong wind came down on the funeral pile and raised a great flame. Around the burning body the Equites and soldiers moved in solemn pomp. When the pile was sinking and the fire going out, there was just time to collect the ashes before the rain descended in torrents. "So Sulla's good fortune seemed to follow him to his funeral and to stay with him to the last. His monument is in the

Campus Martius. The inscription, which they say that he
wrote and left behind him, is in substance that none of his
friends ever did him a kindness, and none of his enemies ever
did him a wrong, without being fully repaid" (Plutarch).
When the consuls were returning from the funeral, they fell
to quarrelling and abusing one another.

CHAPTER XXVIII.

SULLA'S REFORMS.

WE find frequent mention of Leges Corneliae. These were laws enacted in the usual form during Sulla's consulship and dictatorship, but proposed and prepared by Sulla or his advisers. There are indeed some Leges named Corneliae, which were not the work of L. Cornelius Sulla; but in general when Leges Corneliae are mentioned, they are the Leges enacted under Sulla's administration. Not one of those laws is extant in the original form, and we only know them from the writings of Cicero and other authors, and from the Pandects or Digest of Justinian. Some of Sulla's laws related to constitutional forms, and others to the repression of Crimes or to Criminal Law.

If Sulla had any clear object in his legislation about Constitutional forms, it was to strengthen the aristocratical element, so far as he could, not by any positive enactments, but by weakening the power of the Tribunes of the people and of the Comitia Tributa. Accordingly the Lex Cornelia de Tribunicia Potestate was designed to put a muzzle on the demagogues. The tribunes at this time possessed a double power, the power of preventing the action of other magistrates, and the power of acting themselves without being checked. This Cornelian law deprived the tribunes of the power of proposing any measure (rogatio) to the assembly named the Comitia Tributa, which consequently lost all legislative functions. The tribunes would also as a matter

of course lose the power of prosecuting any man before this
popular body. It seems a safe inference that they were also
deprived of the power of holding meetings for the purpose of
addressing the people, and this conclusion is fully confirmed
by a passage of Cicero (Pro Cluentio, c. 40). In fact Sulla
thus suppressed liberty of speech. He did the same kind of
thing that is done now by checking the liberty of the press
in those countries where freedom is in fetters. It is generally
said that this Cornelian law left the tribunes their Intercessio
or Veto (jus intercedendi). Zachariae, who adopts this
opinion with some qualification, considers it evidence that
Sulla was not in favour of despotism, and that he was a far-
seeing statesman. Sulla, he says, thought that a republican
government, especially where the form is aristocratical, cannot exist without some securities for stability, and some
means of preventing hasty measures. This end is effected in
modern States, both constitutional monarchies, as they are
called, and democracies, by establishing two deliberative
bodies, whose consent is necessary for any enactment. But
it is very unlikely that Sulla's law reserved to the tribunes
that extravagant power which they formerly possessed of
stopping every act of the administrative body, and throwing
all things into confusion. Cicero says that he greatly approved of Sulla's law, which deprived the tribunes of the
power of doing mischief, but left them the power of giving
their aid and protection (auxilii ferendi). This passage will
not decide whether the tribunes retained the full power of
the Veto, though it proves that they retained some power of
interposing in certain cases. The passages in the commencement of Caesar's history of the Civil War (i. 5. 7), if
they are taken literally, would prove that under Sulla's law
the tribunes retained the full power of their Veto; but it
would be a very unsafe conclusion from the words of a man
who wished to put the best colour on his own case. Sulla's
law on the tribunate also declared that a man who had been
tribune could not enjoy any other office; and consequently
those who expected to attain the highest honours of the State
would not consent to take the tribunate. Sulla thus left the

office a mere form without a reality, as Velleius says. Perhaps he thought it more politic to make the office contemptible than to abolish it. As he did not abolish it, the Comitia Tributa must have been still held after the enactment of this law for the election of Tribunes annually, and the lower magistrates. Appian observes, " I cannot say whether Sulla transferred the tribunate, as is now the case (when Appian was writing), from the people (δῆμου) to the senate;" which has been interpreted to mean that Sulla made none except senators eligible to the tribunate. Suetonius in the life of Augustus (c. 40, and c. 10) says that if there were no senatorian candidates at the Comitia for electing the tribunes, the people might elect them from the Equites. It appears then that some rule had been established about the eligibility of Senators to the office of Tribune. But it is not easy to reconcile this statement of Appian, as it is explained, with the rule that a man who had been tribune should not be capable of holding any other office.

From this time the legislative power would be exercised solely by the Comitia Centuriata. A passage in Appian states that in Sulla's consulship after he had entered Rome as a conqueror it was established that the voting should be not by Tribus, but by Centuriae, according to the ordinance of King Servius Tullius. This matter has been already explained (p. 227). In other ways too, Appian says, Sulla abridged the tribunitian power, which had become very tyrannical. These great changes were made, as Appian states, during Sulla's consulship, and they seem to be the same changes which are mentioned by other writers as part of Sulla's constitutional reforms. It is possible that Appian has placed them in the wrong order of time, in Sulla's consulship instead of his dictatorship. If he has placed them right, we must suppose that those reforms were re-enacted when Sulla became dictator, for it is certain that after he left Rome for the war in Greece, his enemies would undo the work of his consulship.

It may be useful to explain how the Romans had two kinds of public assemblies for legislation and some other purposes,

the Comitia Centuriata and the Comitia Tributa. The nature
of the constitution of the Comitia Centuriata has been briefly
explained (vol. i., p. 136). The origin and foundation of the
Comitia Centuriata was a census or valuation of property,
according to which the people were distributed into classes,
which distribution determined the services that each individual owed to the State and his place in the popular
assembly. The institution of a census is one of the evidences
of the capacity of the Romans for civil administration. Tradition ascribes it to the reforming king, Servius Tullius. For
the purpose of government territorial divisions are also necessary, and the territorial divisions of the early Roman State
are also attributed to Servius Tullius. He divided the whole
Roman land into Regiones, and the population of the several
regions were called a Tribus. The city with the exception
of the Capitolium and Aventinus was distributed into four
Regiones, occupied by as many Tribus, named Tribus Urbanae or City Tribus. These Tribus were the Suburana,
Esquilina, Collina, Palatina. The rest of the territory was
distributed into six-and-twenty Tribus, named Rusticae, so
that the whole number was thirty. It appears that some
great political change had caused an alteration in the number of the Tribus, and possibly in the territorial boundaries ;
for it is stated by Livy that in B.C. 495 there were only
twenty-one Tribus, and this remained the number for above
a century. Other Tribus were added at different times until
the number was five-and-thirty. The two last were added in
B.C. 241, from which time the number thirty-five remained
unchanged. Each Tribus added to the number of twenty-one
existing in B.C. 495 must be supposed to imply an addition
of territory ; and among the names of those fourteen now
Tribus we find Pomptina, Aniensis, and others, which seem to
derive their names from some natural feature in the localities.
When the Italians received the Roman citizenship by virtue
of the Leges Julia and Plautia (B.C. 90 and 89), it was proposed, as we have seen, to make eight or ten new Tribus,
among which the new citizens should be distributed, the
object being to nullify their votes by not allowing these new

tribes to vote until the five-and-thirty old tribes had voted
(p. 199). In B.C. 88 the tribune P. Sulpicius Rufus proposed
a law for the distribution of the new voters among the five-
and-thirty old tribes (p. 221). Appian says that the law of
Sulpicius was enacted, but he appears to contradict himself
in another passage farther on, where he states that in the
following year when Cinna was consul, the friends of the
exiles urged the new citizens to claim a place in the thirty-
five tribes, and Velleius says that Cinna promised to do what
they demanded. It may be that the measure of Sulpicius
had been carried, for Appian informs us that Sulla in the
same year undid all the work of Sulpicius, and so we can
understand that after Sulla left Rome for Greece, Cinna and
his faction attempted to re-enact the measure of Sulpicius
which Sulla had repealed, and it is consistent with Appian's
narrative to suppose that the measure of Sulpicius was again
enacted. But there may have been some doubt about the
legality of what was done in these turbulent times, for the
matter was only settled, according to Livy (Ep. 84), during
Sulla's campaign in Asia by a Senatusconsultum; and the
same Epitome also records the distribution of the Libertini
among the thirty-five Tribus (p. 328). Consistently with this
fact we are told that when Sulla returned to Italy he made an
agreement with the Italian populations, or perhaps only with
those who were willing to treat with him, that he would not
deprive them of the citizenship and the suffrage, which had
lately been given to them; which can only mean that suffrage
for which there had been such a violent struggle, the distribution of the new citizens among the old tribes. This was
the end of the great dispute.

These territorial divisions, named Tribus, had some kind
of organization for civil purposes. The Rustic Tribus were
subdivided, as we are told, into Pagi, hamlets, or small
communities. The Urban Tribus were subdivided into
Vici, or quarters. Originally, we must suppose, every
man lived within the territorial limits of his Tribus.
But if this was so, such a rule could not be maintained. Afterwards a man might live where he liked, in his

Tribus or out of it. When the Italian nations received the citizenship of Rome and were enrolled in the Tribus, the possession of the franchise and the enrolment in a Tribus must have been quite independent of a citizen's residence or domicile.

A question has been raised whether the original division into Tribus had reference only to the Plebs, or whether it comprehended also the Patricians and their clients. It is difficult to understand how a territorial division should not comprehend every person, for every man lived in some Tribus, and had his property necessarily within some one or more of the Tribus. We may safely affirm that the territorial divisions comprehended all the Roman population, for if the Patricians and their clients were not within them, in what part of space within the Roman territory can we fix them ? The reason of this strange notion having been suggested seems to be that the Patricians did not originally vote in the Comitia Tributa; but there is no inconsistency in this, for the establishment of the Comitia Tributa was a work of a later time, in no way connected with the original division of the State into Tribus, though this division was the foundation of that particular popular assembly which afterwards had the name of Comitia Tributa, as we shall presently see [1].

The condition of the Libertini or manumitted slaves with respect to their tribes varied at different times. It was a tradition that King Servius Tullius placed them in the four Urbanae Tribus, which would contain a larger number of the poor than the Rusticae. It appears that the Libertini were afterwards (B.C. 311) permitted to be enrolled in all the Tribus; then again they were placed in the Urbanae Tribus.

---

[1] If the Tribus comprehended all the Roman population, who were the Aerarii, of whom mention is occasionally made ? It is said that they were persons who were not included in the Tribus. They must then have been persons, originally at least, who had no landed property. In some way certainly they formed a kind of inferior class, for we read of the Censors degrading a man for moral offences, and this degradation was expressed by the terms of removing him from his Tribus (tribu movere), and also making him an "aerarius" or classing him among the "aerarii" (aerarium facere, in aerarios referre). Those who would examine into this matter must read what has been written on it, but perhaps they may as well save themselves the trouble.

But the rule was not observed, and these men still contrived
to introduce themselves into the other Tribus, for in B.C. 220,
according to Livy (Epit. 20), the Libertini were again confined to the four city Tribus, having up to this time been
dispersed among all the Tribus. Again we find this despised
class enrolled in the Tribus Rusticae, from which they were
finally expelled in B.C. 169, and the whole body was placed
in one Tribus Urbana selected by lot, the Exquilina, by the
censor T. Gracchus, the father.   When this class of electors
was dispersed among all the Tribus, their vote would have
some effect, if they were numerous, as we may suppose that
they were.   The object of placing all the Libertini in one
Tribus was to destroy the effect of their vote, for the majority
of each Tribus determined the vote of the Tribus, and the
vote of each Tribus counted one.   It is said that still another
change was made, by which the Libertini were not confined
to this one city Tribus, but were again allowed to be enrolled
in any of the four city Tribus.   It has been conjectured
from a passage of Aurelius Victor that this last change was
made by M. Aemilius Scaurus (B.C. 115; vol. i., p. 336).
All this proves that in the later Republic the class of
Libertini was looked on as a dangerous body by the party of
the Optimates.   Cicero (de Or. i. 9), who speaks of Ti-
Gracchus the father in his censorship confining the Libertini
to the four Urbanae Tribus, instead of placing all of them in
one Tribus, as Livy has it, says that if this had not been
done, the constitution which even after this change was
hardly maintained would have ceased to exist altogether.
As complete Roman citizenship meant not only the enjoyment of all the civil capacities of a citizen, but also the possession of a vote in the elections, the Romans were a little
perplexed about dealing with a large class, whom the aristocratical party at least believed to be dangerous citizens.   It
was not possible to exclude them from voting : all that could
be attempted was to render their vote of no effect.   When Sulla
was expected in Italy, the Libertini were distributed among
the five-and-thirty tribes (pp. 329. 403).   But this arrangement
may not have continued after Sulla had defeated his enemies.

In some modern states the difficulty is of a different kind. The electoral franchise is not co-extensive with citizenship; or, in other words, there are modern political communities, in which a man may have all the rights and capacities that belong to any member of such communities, except the right to vote. In such states the question may arise how far the electoral franchise shall be extended; whether it shall be confined to those who possess it by virtue of paying certain rates or taxes, or whether a larger number shall be admitted to the franchise either by lowering the amount of such rating, or in some other way. In modern states where the electoral franchise is limited, there is no admission of the principle that citizenship carries with it the electoral franchise, as was the case at Rome. In fact it does not, and accordingly the extension of the franchise is discussed simply as a question of policy. The difficulty in this discussion appears to be this. There can be no sufficient reason why any particular amount of rating should be preferred to another amount in determining an elector's qualification, and so we come to the conclusion that there should be none at all. But, if there were no particular qualification, we might find that we had got a large class of electors too ignorant to know how to use their power, or who blinded by false opinions might give their votes to men who would flatter their prejudices in order to secure their own election, and then use their opportunities as representatives of the people to further their own instead of the general interests. There is also in countries where great wealth is in the hands of a few the danger that, if suffrage is made universal, the votes of a very large number of poor electors will be either sold, or given at the bidding of the rich on whom the electors depend. However, those modern states, where the functions of electors are simply limited to the choice of representatives in a national assembly, can never suffer from universal suffrage as Rome did, where there were annual elections of nearly all the functionaries in the state from the highest to the lowest. At Rome the Libertini or freedmen had the franchise, but not the capacity of attaining to the high offices (honours) in the state. In modern states we may find examples of citizens who are eligible to a representative assembly, and have the capacity of rising to the highest places in the state, and yet have not the electoral franchise. This seems to be an inconsistency; but in political matters theoretical inconsistencies may have little or no practical effect on the liberty and happiness of a nation.

Not only were the Libertini or Freedmen at Rome excluded from the high offices of the state, but their children also were excluded. But it appears from what we read of the Senate, that the grandson of a freedman was admissible into that body, and consequently he could attain those offices which qualified a man for admission into the Senate. Libertini were also deprived of the privilege of bearing arms in the service of the state, at least in the legions, and they were only conscribed on extraordinary occasions. During the war with the Italian allies the Libertini were for the first time enrolled in the legions. Men were scarce then, and necessity compelled the Romans to fill their ranks in any way that they could. It is sometimes said that an Ingenuus, that is a citizen born free, could not marry a Libertina or woman who had been emancipated; but before the close of the Republic we certainly find examples of such marriages.

We know nothing of the origin of the Comitia Tributa, or the meetings of the Plebs according to their Tribus. Livy (ii. 58) records the first election of the Tribuni Plebis at the Comitia Tributa; but we may assume that such meetings of the Plebs existed before they elected their own magistrates. The Tribuni Plebis were originally appointed only to protect the Plebeians against the abuse of power by the Patrician magistrates; but they soon obtained or exercised the power of holding public meetings and addressing the Plebs; and this was a sufficient foundation for all the subsequent usurpations. The law of Publilius Volero (B.C. 471) gave the Plebs the election of their own Magistratus by declaring that they should be appointed at the Comitia of the Tribus, and Livy records this first election of Tribunes at these Comitia. Nobody can tell, for no authority has told us, how the Comitia Tributa obtained legislative power. It may be assumed that

they first legislated in matters that concerned only the
interests of their own body. But we are told how the enactments of the Comitia Tributa were made binding on the
whole Roman people. A law was passed in the Comitia
Centuriata (B.C. 449), after the overthrow of the Decemviral
authority, by which law it was declared that Plebiscita, or
enactments made in the Comitia Tributa, should be binding
on the Populus, where the Populus must mean the Patres or
Patricians. As such enactments were made binding both on
the Plebs and the Patres, we see the origin of a natural
extension of the old meaning of Populus, which now might
signify the whole Roman people. It may be assumed that
after this enactment the Patricians would not be excluded
from a vote in the Comitia Tributa; and this assumption
appears to be the foundation of the common assertion in
modern books that after the overthrow of the Decemviral
power the Patricians voted in the Comitia Tributa. A law of
the Dictator, Q. Publilius Philo (B.C. 339), to the same effect
as the law of B.C. 449 is recorded (ut plebiscita omnes Quiri-
tes tenerent), but we are not informed why the same thing
was enacted twice. It may be that it was thought necessary
to reaffirm a principle which was not established without
opposition from the Patricians. The Lex Hortensia, B.C. 287,
again declared that Plebiscita should be binding on the
whole people, and from this time there was certainly no
difference between a Plebiscitum or a statute enacted at the
Comitia Tributa, and a Lex or a statute enacted at the
Comitia Centuriata. Both were laws or statutes. Thus the
Romans had two legislative assemblies.

After the Lex Valeria of B.C. 449 had constituted the
Comitia Tributa as a legislative body, we find that the
Senate used to propose measures to the assembly through
the Tribunes; and if the Tribunes proposed a measure themselves, it was the practice for them first to lay it before the
Senate, and then with the authorization of the Senate (ex
auctoritate Senatus) to propose it to the assembly. Thus the
initiative or the first step in legislation belonged to the
Senate in the case of laws enacted both in the Comitia Cen-

turiata and Tributa. Cases are mentioned in which enactments were made at the Comitia Tributa without the previous consent of the Senate, and it seems as if there was often
an effort made to get rid of this restraint. The Senate however had means of resisting the encroachments of the tribunes, and they had means of impeding the execution of a
law, as we have seen in the case of the Gracchi. In B.C. 100
the turbulent tribune L. Appulcius Saturninus compelled the
Senate to swear to the observance of his Agrarian law within
five days (p. 112), and other examples of like compulsion
occur afterwards. This measure of Saturninus made the
Comitia Tributa independent of the Senate, whose only
remaining means of resistance consisted in the power of
annulling a Plebiscitum on the ground of informality in the
enactment, or in gaining over one or more tribunes to inter-
pose a veto on the acts of the others.

The powers of the Comitia Tributa were of gradual growth.
In their complete form these powers comprised the election
of certain magistrates, the enactment of laws which concerned
both internal and foreign administration, and the exercise of
judicial authority. As to the magistrates, the Comitia Tributa
elected those magistrates who were originally Plebeian, the
Tribuni Plebis and the Aediles. These two offices differed
in this from the magistracies which were originally Patrician,
that a man was not bound to fill the office of Tribune and
Aedile, whereas he must have been Quaestor and Praetor
before he could be elected Consul. The Comitia Tributa
also elected the Magistratus Minores, as they were named,
and commissioners for various purposes. The further inquiry
into this subject belongs to works which treat of Roman
antiquities.

The power of directing the foreign administration, and of
making peace and war, was originally the prerogative of the
Senate. But the principle became established in the course
of time that the Roman State was not bound by any agreement with another State without the consent of the people
(jussu populi). Accordingly Polybius (vi. 14) says of his time
that the popular assembly (δῆμος), by which he means the

Comitia Tributa, "decides upon peace and war; and with
respect to alliances and the putting an end to them, and
with respect to treaties, it is the popular assembly which
confirms and ratifies them, or the contrary; so that for this
reason again a man might fairly say that the people have
the greatest share of power, and that the constitution is
democratical." As to the legislative functions of the Comitia
Tributa, it appears that the oldest laws passed by these
Comitia were framed with the view of extending the influence
of the Plebeians; but these laws, it is said, in the early periods
of the Republic required the confirmation of the Senate and
of the Comitia Curiata or the assembly of the Patrician body.
After the end of the struggle between the Plebeians and the
Patricians, we find that the laws proposed by the consuls in
the Comitia Centuriata were generally such as the nobility
and the rich would approve, while the measures proposed by
the tribunes were of a popular nature. But we read of cases
in which the Senate seem to have sought popularity by encouraging the consuls to propose measures to the Comitia
Centuriata, which the tribunes might have proposed at their
Comitia. It was however the nature of the Roman constitution that its development was always in the popular direction,
and so we find that legislation in the latter part of the
Republic was chiefly exercised by the people in the Comitia
Tributa, and the functions of the Centuriata were limited to
such matters as either positive law or usage had appropriated
to them.

The judicial authority of the Comitia Tributa was a pure
usurpation, so far as we can judge; but it hardly seems a sufficient explanation of this usurpation to say that it was founded
on the "auxilium tribunicium," or the authority by virtue of
which the tribunes could protect a plebeian against arbitrary
treatment by the Roman magistrates. The usurpation was
probably gradual, but it was sure. The tribunes could ar-
raign magistrates before the Comitia Tributa after the expiration of their office, as we see from many examples (vol. i.,
p. 80). But the judicial activity of the popular assembly
was limited by Sulla and even before his time by the es-

tablishment of regular courts for the trial of offences. The
first of these was the court established for the trial of
governors charged with the offence of Repetundas (vol. i.,
p. 26). The tribunes carried their usurpation so far that
we find an instance in which some vestals, who had been
tried and acquitted by the court of the Pontifices, were again
brought to trial through the agitation of the tribunes (vol. i.,
p. 342).

The Comitia Centuriata was then the proper assembly of
the sovereign people of Rome from the time of Servius
Tullius, and when the word Comitia alone is used, it means
the Comitia Centuriata. The functions of these Comitia were
legislation, which required the confirmation of the Comitia
Curiata, the election of the higher magistrates, the declaration of war, and the exercise of jurisdiction in capital cases,
that is, such as affected the status or condition of a Roman
citizen. The Senate originally had the power of concluding
peace, which power, as we have seen, was afterwards obtained
by the Comitia Tributa. It is maintained by some modern
writers that the Comitia Centuriata never had this power.
The criminal jurisdiction of the Comitia Centuriata was
originally founded on the right of appeal (provocatio) of
every Roman citizen within the limit of one mile from the
city against any sentence of a magistrate which imposed
corporal penalties. This right of appeal, which was given
by the Lex Valeria (B.C. 509), and confirmed by other laws
(vol. i., p. 255), was a limitation of the power of the magistrates; and it was expressly declared in the Twelve Tables
that neither a Privilegium, which here means a proceeding
in the nature of a bill of pains and penalties, nor any penalty
that affected the Caput (condition) of a Roman citizen could be
inflicted except by the Maximus Comitiatus or sovereign assembly. In extraordinary cases the assembly transferred the
judicial authority to the Senate, who appointed a commission
(quaestio) under a presidence of a Praetor or Consul, and in this
case there was no appeal, as there was none also in later times
from the sentence of the regularly constituted courts for
criminal matters (quaestiones perpetuae). During military

service there was no appeal from the sentence of the commander. In the field he was supreme. Nor was there any
appeal against the decisions of the Pontifex Maximus which
were made in the exercise of his ecclesiastical authority.

It is distinctly stated by Cicero that after the decemviral
legislation appeals and capital prosecutions were brought
before the Comitia Centuriata, and this continued to be the
practice in Cicero's time in all cases, where offences were not
prosecuted in some particular court established by a special
law or statute. Cicero himself was banished by a legislative
act of the Comitia Tributa; but he maintains that the proceeding was irregular.

The Comitia Centuriata became by the reformation of
Servius Tullius the great assembly of the State; and on the
expulsion of the kings it may be said to have become the
sovereign assembly. It comprehended both Patricians and
Plebeians. The voting in the Comitia Centuriata was by
divisions named Centuriae, and a majority in each Centuria
determined the vote of the Centuria. Consequently each
Centuria had one vote. Now as the classes into which King
Servius distributed the Roman citizens were determined by a
property qualification, it would follow that the first Class and
the higher Classes would contain fewer voters than the lower
Classes; and yet the higher Classes contained a larger number
of Centuriae than the lower and could outvote them (vol. i.,
p. 136).

Thus by the system of Centuriae the votes of a small number of the wealthier citizens could overpower the vote of a
large majority of the electors. But this result was further
secured by the order in which the Centuriae voted. It is the
best opinion that according to the old constitution the
eighteen Centuriae of Equites were first called to vote, and
they were accordingly named "praerogativae," for the "rogatio" or question was first proposed to them. This first vote
would naturally have some effect in determining the votes
which were given afterwards, if the result was made known
before any other votes were given; and it is assumed that it
was made known. Next to the eighteen Centuriae of Equites,

the 80 Centuriae of the first class were called to vote, and these 98 Centuriae are named by Livy the " primo vocatae," or " first called." If these 98 Centuriae were unanimous, no further voting was necessary, and the votes of the other Centuriae were not given. Thus though the plebeians had a vote, and those plebeians, who had the necessary property qualification, would be in the first Class, yet the votes of the patricians might still be sufficient to carry any election or any legislative measure, for the patricians in the early Republic also possessed the wealth. But the constitution of Servius, or at least that which we suppose to be his constitution, as we read of its operation in the early ages of the Republic, gave the initiative in legislation to the Senate, as already observed, for without the consent of the Senate given in regular form no measure could be proposed to the Comitia Centuriata. So we find the formula " ex Senatusconsulto ferre ad populum," " to propose a measure to the sovereign assembly pursuant to a resolution of the Senate." This initiative of the Senate is named by the Latin writers " auctoritas Senatus," and by the Greek writers on Roman affairs a προβούλευμα. It is also maintained by some modern writers that every vote of the Comitia Centuriata required the confirmation of the Comitia Curiata or the original assembly of Roman citizens, which consisted only of Patricians and existed before the reform of Servius Tullius created the new assembly called the Comitia Centuriata. If this was so, the power of the Roman electors in the Comitia Centuriata was at first small. It is further said that the confirmation of the Curiae in matters of legislation was virtually dispensed with by a law (Lex Publilia) enacted in B.C. 339; and in the matter of elections a law of B.C. 287 reduced the confirmation by the Curiae to a mere form.

It would seem probable that the organization of the Comitia Centuriata would undergo some changes in the course of time, and that the Classes and Centuriae, as supposed to have been established by Servius Tullius, could not remain what they originally were. The fact of the increase of wealth in the Roman State would make the

original rating for the first Class a small sum, and would
greatly increase the numbers of those who were included in
it. A change was made in the constitution of the Comitia
Centuriata, but we do not know when it was made, and it
is impossible to say what it exactly was. An unsatisfactory
passage of Dionysius (Roman Antiqu. iv. 21) informs us that
the constitution of Servius Tullius lasted many generations,
but "about his time" (the time of Dionysius) it was changed
to a more democratic character, not by the destruction of
the Centuriae, but by not observing the ancient strict form of
calling the Centuriae (to vote), "as I have observed," he
says, "by often being present at the elections." This passage, which we might understand, if we knew what the
change was, does not help us much towards discovering in
what the change consisted. It shows however that the
Centuriae still existed, that some change was made in the
order of calling them to vote, and that the change was in a
democratical direction.

A passage of Livy (i. 43) states that at some time after
the thirty-five Tribus were constituted, the number was
doubled by making Centuriae of Seniores and Juniores in
each Tribus; consequently there would be seventy half Tribus,
and it appears that each of these half Tribus was designated
by the name of the original Tribus in which it was contained. Livy does not say how many of these Centuriae of
Seniores and Juniores were contained in each original Tribus,
and the critics are divided in opinion on this matter. But
we know that in the Comitia Centuriata the voting was still
by Classes, and we may conclude that instead of these Classes
being formed out of the whole body of the citizens, as in the
constitution of Servius Tullius, and consisting of unequal
numbers of Centuriae, the division into Classes was applied
to each Tribus, and the old Servian distribution into Seniores
and Juniores was maintained, as Livy describes it (i. 43).
If the new Classes in each Tribus had still contained unequal
numbers of Centuriae, as in the old constitution, no real
change would have been made, and the division of Classes
would only have become more complicated by making it with

reference to each Tribus, instead of forming them out of the
whole body of citizens without reference to the division into
Tribus. It has accordingly been conjectured that under the
reformed system each half Tribus was distributed into five
Centuriae, five of Seniores and five of Juniores, making ten
Centuriae in each Tribus. Under this arrangement then
the first Class would contain thirty-five Centuriae of Seniores,
one from each half Tribus, and thirty-five Centuriae of Juniores, one from each half Tribus; and so on through all the
five classes. Accordingly under this new constitution there
would still be five Classes, determined, as we assume, by a
property qualification, but there would be the same number
of Centuriae in each Class, 350 in all, and so far the first
Class would lose the preponderance which it had under the
Servian constitution. Some critics have supposed that thirty-
five Centuriae of Equites were also included in the first
Class, which would consequently contain 105 Centuriae, and
increase the whole number to 385, and to 386 if we add a
sixth class of the Capite censi and Proletarii, containing a
single Centuria. Others add eighteen Centuriae of Equites
to the first Class, which would thus contain eighty-eight,
and the whole number of Centuriae would be 368.

This hypothesis of the new constitution of the Comitia
Centuriata is due to Octavius Pantagathus. Savigny explained
it in an essay in 1805, which is printed in his Vermischte
Schriften (vol. i.), with some additional remarks. Many
critics have attempted to explain this new constitution of the
Classes, and some have introduced conjectures for which there
is no foundation. It is a most perplexing and difficult subject, which unfortunately cannot be settled by the evidence
which we possess.

In remains to speak of the order in which the Centuriae
were called to vote. Under the reformed system we read of
one Centuria Praerogativa, or Praerogativa, as it was often
simply called, and it was determined by lot. This Centuria
voted first, and we must presume, for we have no reason to
suppose any departure from the old usage, that the Centuriae
of the Equites and of the first class voted next; and then the

Centuriae of the second class, and so on until a majority was obtained. It is still doubtful, and must remain so, whether the Centuria Praerogativa was chosen by lot from all the Centuriae or only from those of the first Class.

The attempt of C. Gracchus to change the order of voting by Classes, and to determine by lot the order of voting for all the Centuriae, is founded on very poor evidence (vol. i., p. 264). The passage in Appian about Sulla's reform (Civil Wars, i. 59), which passage has been already referred to (p. 227), is ambiguous. If we assume it to mean that Sulla abolished the Comitia Tributa, the fact is not true. If we take it literally, we must admit that he restored the Centuriae as they were in the time of Servius Tullius, or as they existed according to the constitution which is attributed to him. But it is impossible to believe that he either accomplished or attempted such a change; and it seems more probable that Appian means to say that Sulla gave all the legislative power to the Comitia Centuriata.

CHAPTER XXIX.

SULLA'S REFORMS.

As to the Senate, Sulla, as we have seen, restored to this body the initiative in legislation. No legislative measure could be proposed to the popular assembly, unless the Senate had given their consent. He also restored to the Senators the office of Judices or jurymen in criminal trials, of which this body had been deprived by the legislation of C. Gracchus. Other changes that were made after the time of Gracchus have been already mentioned (pp. 3. 98). We have seen (p. 365) how Sulla filled up the vacant places in the Senate by the election of three hundred from the body of the Equites; but we do not know what was the whole number of the Senate as thus reconstituted. If we can trust a passage in one of Cicero's letters to Atticus, the whole number of the Senate about twenty years after Sulla's time was above four hundred.

A Scholiast on Cicero's oration against Caecilius (c. 3) affirms that Sulla abolished the office of tribune and censor. We know that the first part of the affirmation is false, for the tribunate still existed. It may not be true, nor is it probable, that the office of censor was abolished, though there was no Lustrum after Sulla's Dictatorship until B.C. 70. The words of Cicero, on which the Scholiast has made his remark, do not prove that the censorship was abolished, but they prove that at the time when Cicero delivered this oration (B.C. 70) the office was not exercised. It is not material to determine what Sulla did as to the censorship, for the office certainly existed after his time, but he may have deprived

VOL. II.

the censors of their power of making and revising the lists
of the Senate. If this was done, then a man must have
obtained admission to the Senate according to the new arrangement solely by virtue of having been elected to an
office. The lowest office which qualified a man for the Senate
was the Quaestorship. Sulla took an unusual way of filling
the vacant ranks of the Senate, and it is quite consistent that
he should not consent to the Censors revising his work.

Sulla increased the number of Praetors to eight by adding
two to the number that already existed. Pomponius (De
Origine Juris, § 32) says that Sulla added four Praetors,
which must be a mistake. Pomponius mentions the addition
of the four praetors together with the fact of Sulla establishing certain Quaestiones Publicae or Criminal Courts, from
which we conclude that the number of Praetors was increased
with the view of supplying six judges to preside in the new
criminal courts. The Praetor Urbanus and Peregrinus would
administer law within the city, as in former times. After
the expiration of their annual office, all the eight praetors
might be governors of provinces, with authority as Proprae-
tors or Proconsuls. The number of Quaestors was also increased from eight to twenty, in order to keep the Senate
supplied with members, as Tacitus observes; a remark which
helps us to conjecture how Sulla proposed for the future to
settle the admission into the Senate without the sanction of
the Censors.

It was also established that no man could be elected
Praetor unless he had held the office of Quaestor, nor elected
Consul unless he had filled a praetorship; and further that
no man should hold a magistracy (probably a curule office) a
second time, unless at an interval of ten years. Thus the
older practice was revived, and the more recent rule as to a
man not being twice eligible to the consulship was repealed
(vol. i., p. 85).

Sulla restored to the Colleges of Pontifices, of Augurs, and
of the Decemviri sacris faciundis, who had the care of the
Sibylline books, the power of filling up the vacancies in their
own body (p. 40). He also raised the number of members

in the Colleges of Pontifices and Augurs to fifteen; and it is probable, though there is no direct evidence for it, that he raised the number of Decemviri to fifteen, for that is the number which Cicero and other writers assign to this body.

Sulla, as we shall presently see, made great changes in the constitution of the courts for criminal matters. It is not certain whether he made any changes in civil procedure. In Rome the jurisdiction in civil matters was in the hands of the Praetor Urbanus and the Praetor Peregrinus. If both the parties to a suit were Roman citizens, they appeared before the court of the Praetor Urbanus. If one of the parties was not a Roman citizen, or, in other words, if he was an alien (peregrinus), or if both were aliens, the matter belonged to the jurisdiction of the Praetor Peregrinus. The course of proceeding before the Praetor Urbanus, when he did not decide summarily, was this. He decided whether there was a ground of action, and if there was, he named a Judex or judge for the occasion, whose business was to investigate the facts by evidence produced before him, and to pronounce judgment in conformity with the facts and the directions contained in the Praetor's instructions (formula). If, for instance, it was a simple action of debt, the instructions would be to ascertain if a debt was proved or not, and to pronounce judgment accordingly. The procedure before the Praetor Peregrinus was similar.

Now the question is from what class of persons was a Judex in civil cases taken in Sulla's time. The expression used by the Roman writers is this, that Sulla restored the "Judicia," that is the office of Judex, to the Senators, who had it before the legislation of Caius Gracchus. It has been the general opinion that these long disputes at Rome about the "Judicia" referred only to the determination of the class from which Judices should be taken in criminal trials or certain kinds of criminal trials. No evidence has been alleged to prove that the term "Judicia" as applied to these disputes comprehended trials for civil matters; nor is there any evidence, so far as I know, that at this time the Praetor Urbanus appointed a Judex out of any particular class. The office would be troublesome, the matter in dispute often of a trifling nature, and we can conceive no reason why the Senators should care for exercising such a function, though it is true that it might be one way to popularity, or to unpopularity, just as it might happen. The functions of the Praetor Peregrinus must have become more limited after the Italian nations became Roman citizens, and they could only extend to cases in which a Peregrinus, that is a provincial, was a party to a suit, or two provincials were the parties.

A Lex Cornelia, and as it is assumed, a Lex of L. Cornelius Sulla about the provinces is mentioned by Cicero. It determined that the retiring governor of a province could not stay in it more than thirty days after the arrival of his successor. It also limited the expenditure which a province should make in sending a deputation to Rome to thank the Senate for the governor who had last retired. Such an abuse had grown up in course of time, that a governor was not satisfied with having done his duty in a province; he must have a public declaration of it at Rome, and by persons sent at the expense of the province. We might almost conjecture that such a practice originated in the attempt of some knavish governor to save himself from prosecution by the testimony of those whom he had misgoverned.

It has been remarked (vol. i., p. 26) that a new period in Roman criminal legislation began with the Lex Calpurnia Repetundarum (B.C. 149). We do not know what more was done in this kind between B.C. 149 the date of this law and Sulla's time. Three of the laws of Sulla relating to criminal matters are well known. The Lex Cornelia Majestatis was apparently the model on which the later Lex Julia Majestatis was formed. Though the name of Majestas was not known in early Roman legislation, yet the crime was, for the legislation of the Twelve Tables declared that if a Roman stirred up an enemy against his country, or delivered up a citizen to an enemy, he must be put to death (Dig. 48. 4. 3). The meaning of the term "Majestas minuta, or imminuta," has been explained (p. 115). Among the later Roman writers it is named "Majestas laesa," which term is still preserved in the French lèse-majesté. The notion of "Majestas minuta," when it was fully established, may have comprehended all that the old term Perduellio comprised, and even more, and so the offence, which Perduellio denoted, and the term itself would drop into disuse. There is however one example of a trial for Perduellio after Sulla's time, and that was the peculiar case of C. Rabirius, whom Cicero defended in a speech which we have. We know very little of the provisions of Sulla's law on Majestas. Cicero informs us that it was a violation of the Lex Cornelia Majestatis for a "governor to quit his province, to lead his army out of it, to make war without instructions, to enter any kingdom without the authority of the Roman people and Senate;" and "to let the enemies of the Roman people escape for a bribe." We may conclude that Sulla's law contained an enumeration of all the cases which it was considered useful to comprise under the term of Majestas, and so this act of legislation gave the word an exact signification. The penalties of the Lex are unknown.

We know more of the Lex Cornelia de Sicariis et Veneficiis, the law on assassination and poisoning. Many of the provisions of this law are contained in the Digest (48. 8. Ad Legem Corneliam de Sicariis et Veneficiis). The crimes which this law was directed against were murder, arson, going about armed for the purpose of committing murder or stealing; and in a magistrate or a presiding judge, the offence of inducing a person to give false evidence for the purpose of securing the condemnation of an innocent person. A man who made poison for the purpose of destroying another, or sold it, or had it in his possession, was subject to the penalties of this law. It contained, as was usual with Roman laws, several chapters. The fifth chapter is quoted in the Digest (48. 8. 3). The penalty of the law was transportation or, as the Romans termed it, deportation to an island in the Mediterranean, and forfeiture of all a man's property. It is true that the term "deportatio" is not used in this sense even by Cicero, and therefore it is not probable that the word was in

Sulla's law; but still this penalty may have been fixed by the law, as it is expressly so stated in the Digest, though the name of the penalty may have been different. The "deportatio," as Ulpian says, took the place of the "aquae et ignis interdictio," or the interdict of water and fire. By this law of Sulla the intention or evil design (dolus malus) was equivalent to the commission of the act, a principle of criminal law which is indisputable, for we do not punish a man simply because he has done a certain act, but because he has done it intentionally and maliciously. A rescript of the Emperor Hadrian, which is quoted under the title of this Cornelian law on assassinations and poisonings, merely expresses this rule of law in another form when it states that "in crimes the intention is considered, not the result." The Romans knew how to distinguish between the facts which were evidence of intention and those which left the intention doubtful or disproved it; and so they could distinguish between what we call murder and manslaughter. But they inferred the murderous intention in some cases, where we less consistently often refuse to admit it (Dig. 48. 8. 1. § 3).

Sex. Roscius Amerinus, whom Cicero defended against the charge of killing his father (p. 381), was probably tried under this law of Sulla. In the Digest (48. tit. 0) there is a title "on the Pompeia Lex on parricides" (B.C. 55), in which the definition of parricide is extended to killing father, mother, grandfather, grandmother, brother, sister, and a great number of other relations, and it is added that the punishment was the same as that in the Lex Cornelia de Sicariis; and in another excerpt under this title (0) it is said that the punishment of parricide derived from ancient usage was the "culleus" or sack. We may infer then that there was a chapter in the Lex Cornelia de Sicariis on parricide, and that it was punished according to the ancient usage; further, that the Lex Pompeia merely extended the definition of parricide and retained the same penalty.

Sulla had himself been an assassin and the leader of the assassins of Rome, but he did his work in regular form. In the proscription the heads of the murdered were brought in,

registered, and paid for out of the treasury. It was a piece
of business conducted with as much order as any other part
of the public administration. Sulla, however, took care to
protect his agents, for he introduced a clause into one of his
enactments, and most probably into this very law on assassination, by which those, who had brought in the heads of
Roman citizens and received the money for them, were
exempted from the penalties of the law.

The Lex Cornelia de falsis or on forgery and frauds comprehended a great number of cases (Dig. 48, tit. 10; Paulli
Recept. Sent. V. tit. 25). It comprehended the cases of a
man giving false evidence or not giving the true evidence for
a bribe, or bribing another to give false evidence or not to
give the true evidence ; and the case of a man conspiring
with others to deceive a judge by false evidence, and bribing
a judge or causing him to be bribed. It also applied to the
case of a man who knowingly and wilfully wrote a false will
or any other false instrument, or used it as evidence, or who
produced a forged will; or suppressed or hid or unsealed or
destroyed a will, or who opened the will of a man in his lifetime without the testator's consent; or who made or used a
false seal, or took off a seal from an instrument or broke it.
The law also comprehended the offences of debasing the gold
and silver coinage, or melting it, or buying or selling coins
of tin or lead with a fraudulent purpose. The penalties of
this law are not mentioned in any of the extant authorities.

There was also a Lex Cornelia de injuriis, which provided
for cases in which a man was assaulted with blows or his
house was forcibly entered. It is disputed whether this law
treated such acts of violence as criminal offences, that is
imposed some penalty on the offender, or merely gave an
action to the injured person, or whether it contained both
penalties and provision for damages to the plaintiff. So far
as the law might contain penalties, they would be enforced
and enlarged by the subsequent Leges Juliae de Vi Publica
and de Vi Privata, and this part of the Lex Cornelia de injuriis might become obsolete.

In order to understand the changes introduced or estab-

lished by Sulla in the constitution of the criminal courts we
must go back to the principle of the Twelve Tables, which
declared that a judgment which affected the Caput (condition)
of a Roman citizen could only be passed in the Maximus
Comitiatus or Comitia Centuriata (Dirksen, Uebersicht, &c.,
p. 645). This term Caput, as already explained, comprehended all that are usually called the personal rights of a
Roman citizen—life, freedom, citizenship. Such a procedure
must have originated in a small community, and even in
such a society it could not be long maintained as the only
way of bringing offenders to punishment. Accordingly we
read of commissions of inquiry (quaestiones) being established
on particular occasions by the popular vote, which thus constituted the consuls or a praetor an extraordinary court.
Such commissions were also appointed by the Senate with or
perhaps sometimes without a popular vote. The establishment (B.C. 149) of a court for the trial of the offence briefly
named Repetundae was an improvement on the old system.
This was named a Quaestio Perpetua, a permanent court, as
contrasted with those which had hitherto been formed for a
temporary purpose. It is assumed by some writers that in
the interval between the establishment of this first Quaestio
Perpetua and the commencement of the Social War other
permanent courts (Quaestiones Perpetuae) for the trial of
criminals were established by particular laws. Such a supposition seems probable, but the direct evidence for it is
wanting. Some support to this opinion is supposed to be
derived from a passage of Asconius (in Cornel. p. 73, ed.
Orelli) which states that during the Social War the Senate
resolved that the courts ("judicia" in the original, rather a
vague word) should not be held. We can easily understand
that during this conflict between Rome and her subjects, the
regular administration of law was suspended; and that is all
that we can conclude from the passage.

There were two kinds of Magistratus of ancient date, which
require a brief mention, the Duumviri Perduellionis, and the
Quaestores Parricidii. It is singular that only three cases
are mentioned in our extant authorities of the Duumviri

Perduellionis passing a sentence, and the first two belong to the early periods of Roman history. The first is the case of the Horntius who killed his sister (Livy i. 26). The second is the case of M. Manlius, who lost his life through being charged with aspiring to royal power (Livy vi. 20). The third is the case of C. Rabirius, which was after Sulla's time, and will require particular consideration. It is sufficient for the present to state that the Duumviri Perduellionis did not form a permanent court, but were named by the people for the occasion.

The office of the two Quaestores Parricidii seems to have been, as we may infer from the name, for Quaestores is a shorter form of Quaesitores, to inquire into cases of murder and other crimes also (res capitales). It was their duty to collect the evidence, to seize the suspected person, and to bring him before the Comitia for trial. If these officers were appointed during the kingly period, as we must admit if we accept such evidence as there is, the Comitia by which they were named and before which a man was tried on their charge would originally be the Curiata, and afterwards, we must suppose, the Centuriata. But we know little about these Quaestores Parricidii, though instances are recorded in which they acted, as in the case of Spurius Cassius. It is possible that these Quaestores may have executed the sentence of the people; or, as it has been suggested, the Triumviri Capitales did it for them. No mention, it is said, occurs of the Quaestores Parricidii after B.C. 366; and some of their functions, perhaps all, were transferred to the Triumviri Capitales, for Varro says that the office of the Quaestores Parricidii, the inquiry into crimes, was exercised in his time by the Triumviri Capitales. It is observed that in the fragments of the Lex Servilia (p. 102) the Triumviri Capitales are mentioned, though we should rather have expected to find the Quaestores Parricidii mentioned, if that office still existed. This then is one piece of negative evidence from which Zachariae would infer that the office of the Quaestores Parricidii had ceased to exist at the date of the Lex Servilia.

The chief authority for the history of Roman law is Pomponius (Dig. 1, tit. 2 de origine juris et omnium magistratuum, &c.). He says that Cornelius Sulla settled (constituit) the Quaestiones Publicae or Courts. He did not originate or found them, which fact would be expressed by a different word (instituit), as Zachariae correctly observes. Sulla therefore confirmed and enlarged what he found subsisting, for the purpose of withdrawing criminal jurisdiction from the popular assemblies and giving it to permanent courts, and also for the purpose of rendering the appointment of extraordinary commissions unnecessary; though instances occur even after Sulla's time of persons being tried otherwise than by these courts. It is however certain that from Sulla's time criminal jurisdiction was as a rule exercised by these courts. They were named Quaestiones Perpetuae (permanent) and the titles of the following nine courts are certain: the Quaestio Majestatis; de vi; de sicariis &c.; de veneficiis; de parricidio; de falso; de repetundis; peculatus (peculation); and ambitus (bribery at elections). Zachariae, who names these nine courts, asks if there were not also two others, one de adulterio (on adultery) and one de plagiis (the offence of making a freeman into a slave); but he does not answer his own question by producing any evidence.

The constitution of these courts was this. A Praetor or Judex quaestionis presided; and a jury, who were named Judices, by the verdict of a majority determined the guilt or innocence of the accused. The Lex Cassia (vol. i., p. 109) introduced the use of the ballot in the Judicia Populi. We see by the Lex Servilia (p. 104) that the ballot was used at least in some criminal trials, when there was a jury; and it is generally supposed that the ballot was used in all the Quaestiones or Criminal Courts. But Cicero (Pro Cluentio, c. 20) in one particular case speaks of the presiding judge asking whether the accused wished to have the votes of the jury taken openly or secretly. Cicero says that the question was put by the judge conformably to the Lex Cornelia, "which then was," from which we may infer that some change was afterwards made in this matter. The Praetors

had their several courts assigned by lot for their year of
office, unless the law which constituted the particular court
had named a Praetor, in which case it would be, we must
suppose, either the Praetor Urbanus or the Praetor Peregrinus. The jury was chosen for every particular case.
The procedure was the same in all the courts, as far as we
know. The courts were open, the proceedings were oral;
every thing was done in the presence of the accused and the
public. The publicity of criminal trials is a valuable principle, which the Romans established, and maintained until
the declining days of the Empire.

Zachariae supposes the existence of a Lex Cornelia Judiciaria, or a law which regulated the constitution and procedure
of all the criminal courts. This is likely enough. There
was a subsequent Lex Julia judiciorum publicorum, and it
may have been founded on a Lex of Sulla. We have seen
that Sulla raised the number of praetors to eight, but nine
courts of criminal judicature have been mentioned, and there
may have been more. This difficulty is supposed to be solved
by the hypothesis that when the different courts for each
year were assigned by lot, certain Senators (as Zachariae
supposes) were added to the praetors, and if the lot fell on
them, they would exercise the office of presiding judge (judex
quaestionis) in the court to which the lot assigned them.
This "judex quaestionis" is only mentioned by Cicero, in an
excerpt in the Digest (48. 8. 1), and in a late legal compilation (Collatio Legum Mosaicarum et Romanarum, i. 3). We
may conclude then that a "judex quaestionis" was sometimes
appointed to preside in a criminal court, and though he was
not a regular magistratus, he acted for the occasion as such
(Dig. 48. 8. 1, "quive quum magistratus esset publicove
judicio praeesset;" and further on "quive magistratus judexve
quaestionis "). But there is no evidence how these "judices
quaestionis" were appointed.

The legislation of C. Gracchus made the juries (judices)
eligible from the Equites only, though, as we have seen, the
question of determining the class from which juries should
be taken was still agitated after the time of Gracchus. Sulla,

as already observed, made the "judices" eligible only from the
Senators. The number that was employed in any case is not
known. As to the mode of selecting the jury for each trial,
all that we know with certainty is that the whole body of
judices were divided into Decuriae, three Decuriae, as some
modern writers say, of one hundred members each. When
a trial was coming on, the Praetor wrote down the names of
the members of the Decuria, which was to furnish the jury
for that occasion, threw the names into an urn, and then
drew out as many as the law required in the particular case.
Both the prosecutor and the accused had the right to challenge (rejicere) a certain number of the jury; and the place
of those jurymen, who were struck off the list, was supplied
by the Praetor drawing the same number of fresh names from
the urn. The number of jurymen that the prosecutor and
the accused respectively could challenge was three. If the
accused was a senator, he could challenge a larger number,
but we do not know what that larger number was. The jury
when finally constituted were sworn to the discharge of their
duty.

The court of Centumviri, as far as we know, remained
after Sulla's time what it was before. This court really consisted of one hundred and five members, three elected by
each of the thirty-five tribes, and thus in fact they were
magistrates directly elected by the people. The matters which
came before this court were not such as to lead Sulla to interfere with it. Among other things we know that it decided
on questions of succession to the property of persons deceased (p. 133). It continued to exist under the Empire, for
the younger Pliny practised in this court in the time of
Trajan. The Romans had long had this court, and there were
no political reasons for meddling with it, but it does not seem
to us a well-constituted court for the decision of difficult
questions of property.

Zachariae raises the question how far did the criminal
legislation of Sulla extend, that is, did it extend to other
parts of Italy than Rome; and what were the limits of the
jurisdiction of those who presided in the criminal courts

at Rome. So far as these laws applied to any abuse of power by a magistrate, the offender would be tried at Rome, wherever the offence was committed. As to other offences, it seems that they would be tried by local courts. All Italy with the exception of the north part, or Gallia Cisalpina, was now Roman, and even the Latin colonies of Gallia Cisalpina were Roman. Consequently all the people within the limits of Italy who had become Roman citizens would be subject to Roman law. But we know that by the Lex de Sicariis, for instance, the jurisdiction of the magistrate to whom this Quaestio had been assigned by lot, was limited to crimes committed in Rome and within a mile from the city walls. Indeed the civil jurisdiction of the Praetor Urbanus was originally confined within these narrow limits (Gaius iv. 104), though it was afterwards extended by virtue of the authority contained in the Imperium, as the Romans termed it. It seems then that we must conclude that those citizens who committed crimes out of the jurisdiction of the city of Rome, must have been tried by some of the courts established in various parts of Italy, for they could only be tried at Rome when the offence was committed within the limits mentioned above.

In Polybius' description of the powers of the Roman Senate (vi. 13) he includes the inquiry into criminal acts committed in Italy, such as treason, conspiracy, poisoning, and assassination. The term Italy here must mean so much of the Italian peninsula as in the time of Polybius was dependent on Rome. It would therefore be no novelty if under the legislation of Sulla, or after his death, provision was made for the administration of criminal justice all through Italy, as the Senate had in former times inquired into crimes by the appointment of extraordinary commissions, of which we find examples recorded. There is however no evidence of any thing having been done by Sulla to regulate the administration of justice in those Italian towns which had obtained the Roman citizenship in consequence of the changes which followed the outbreak of the Social War.

The final settlement of the administration of the Italian

towns belongs to a later time, but it may be useful to indicate it here in a general way, and also to show by what steps
the unity of Italy was established. The Lex Julia gave the
Roman citizenship to the Latini (p. 198), which some able
critics suppose to mean the few towns of the old Latin nation
which had not received it before, and the numerous Latin
colonies. The law would therefore apply to the Latin colonies even in Gallia Cisalpina, and they would become Municipia by receiving the Roman citizenship. There were
founded in Gallia Cisalpina before the Social War the Latin
colonies of Placentia (Piacenza) and Bononia (Bologna).
Mutina and Parma founded in B.C. 183 were Roman
colonies. North of the Po there was the colony of Cremona,
founded at the same time as Placentia, and also Aquileia, and
Eporedia (p. 119). The Lex Plautia Papiria enacted in B.C.
89 is supposed to have completed what the Lex Julia had not
accomplished (p. 212). In this same year Cn. Pompeius
Strabo gave to the towns north of the Po the Latinitas or
Jus Latii, which placed them in a condition with respect to
Rome, which was above that of Peregrini or aliens, but below
that of citizens (p. 210). There remains a difficult question
to decide, What was the political condition of the people in
Gallia Cisalpina south of the Po, when the Transpadani or
people north of the Po received the Latinitas in B.C. 89?
Savigny has come to the conclusion that at the time when
the people north of the Po were raised to the condition of
Latini, the people south of the Po received the Roman citizenship.

After Caesar had crossed the Rubicon in B.C. 49, the
people north of the Po also received the Roman citizenship.
At this time Gallia Cisalpina was still a province, for it had
been under Caesar's administration up to B.C. 49. Probably
about B.C. 45 a Lex Julia made a general provision for
the administration of all communities of Roman citizens.
In B.C. 41 Gallia Cisalpina ceased to be a province, and all
the country on each side of the Po was incorporated with
Italy. The towns of Gallia Cisalpina, which had hitherto
been under the government of a proconsul, now received a

new organization. But these changes will be more particularly considered hereafter.

As to the laws attributed to Sulla for the improvement of morality, if we may use such a term, little is known. Plutarch certainly speaks of Sulla legislating about marriage and expense. If he legislated about marriage, he may have legislated about adultery, but there does not appear to be any direct evidence that he did. The great legislative act for adultery was the work of Caesar Augustus. Sulla certainly legislated, as the Romans had done before, with the view of checking lavish expenditure, though he was not a pattern of good living himself. Gellius (ii. 24) in his chapter on the Sumptuary laws of Rome says that Sulla proposed a law to the popular assembly for limiting the expense which a man might make at a dinner or supper, as he calls it. The reason for this legislation was, as he says, that the former Sumptuary laws were neglected; which we might readily suppose to have been the case, even if Gellius had not told us so. Macrobius (Sat. ii. 13) describes the law as not prohibiting magnificent entertainments, nor putting restraint on the luxury of the table, but as fixing the prices of rare articles, such as choice fish and other things, as if the object of the law was to enable those who were fond of good eating to indulge their appetites at less cost. The law contained an enumeration of many delicacies, which in his time, Macrobius observes, no man had even heard of. This law then among other things attempted to fix the price of certain articles of consumption, and is a proof that Sulla and his advisers were not wise in some things. By the same law or by another the expense of funerals was limited.

It is supposed on some small evidence that Sulla stopped the distributions of corn to the poor Roman electors. These distributions of corn at a low price had begun in the time of C. Gracchus (pp. 114. 151); and after the death of Gracchus other attempts were made to provide cheap corn for the poor at the public cost. It was not Sulla's policy to seek popularity or votes; and if by any public act he declared that the poor must not expect relief from the State, he did this less from wise economical views than from dislike or contempt of the populace. He had bought the fidelity of his soldiers, who were his support. He could gain nothing by buying the votes of the poor citizens. All we can really affirm is that such people got nothing from him while he lived. The enactment of a law for giving aid to the poor (Lex Frumentaria) was one of the proposed measures of the consul Lepidus after Sulla's death.

Sulla, as already observed, settled his soldiers all over Italy and gave them lands. In fact such was the state of the peninsula after the civil wars, so great was the loss of life, and so many were turned out of their homes, that Sulla had more land to give than he required. He settled Aleria in Corsica for some reason, the only settlement that he made out of Italy, for he had no occasion to seek abroad for the means of rewarding his legions. It seems likely that Sulla's settlements were made pursuant to a Lex Cornelia, which indeed Cicero mentions, for he informs us that the law declared that the allotments made by Sulla (sortes assignatae) to his men should not be alienated. But this absurd prohibition, which had been also made before (vol. i., p. 178), had no effect. The allotments soon passed by death of the holders or by sale into other hands.

The acts of Sulla during the short period that he was in power show his activity. The mischief that he did by his proscriptions and by turning so large a number of people out of their property was enormous. He made Italy a desert, and put idle soldiers in the place of industrious farmers. He made indeed an attempt to cure some of the evils, which were hurrying Rome to ruin, but he did not and could not prolong the existence of such a state. His services in giving form and consistency to the criminal law of Rome cannot be disputed. His laws on criminal matters were the foundation on which Caesar Augustus afterwards built. If he did not himself frame these enactments, he had at least the merit of finding able men to do it.

Sulla might have had a conspicuous place among the writers of Rome, if his Memoirs had not perished; for only a few lines have been preserved by Gellius and others. Plutarch, as we have already seen, used them for his biography of Sulla. The Memoirs were written in Latin. Sulla's freedman L. Cornelius Epicadus completed the twenty-second book, which, as Suetonius says, had been left unfinished. We have no means of knowing what was the historical value of these Memoirs, and we must form a guess from the character of the man. We may safely assume that self-glorification was not wanting, and that Sulla's good fortune and success were continually proclaimed. As he was a good general and a man of ability, we may believe that he formed his military plans well and explained them clearly, but our confidence in his veracity is weakened when he speaks of the number of his enemies who fell, and of his own losses being in fact nothing. The Memoirs of the Dictator Sulla would have formed a curious contrast with the Commentaries of the Dictator Caesar.

CHAPTER XXX.

M. AEMILIUS LEPIDUS.

B.C. 78—74.

THE work of Sallust, which he entitled Historiae, began with the consulship of M. Aemilius Lepidus and Q. Lutatius Catulus. This history has perished except a few fragments, which have been diligently collected from various writers. One of the longer fragments of the first book is a speech of Lepidus to the people against Sulla, and it is undoubtedly one of Sallust's fictitious orations. But though the speech is the work of Sallust, the facts which it contains ought to be true, if Sallust had any regard to the duties of an historian. Lepidus addresses the people as consul, and urges them to recover their liberty of which they had been deprived by the usurpation of Sulla, whom he speaks of as still living and in the possession of power.

We might suppose that Lepidus commenced his attack on Sulla and his policy in the interval between his election and entering on his office on the first of January B.C. 78. But in this oration Lepidus does not speak as consul elect (designatus); he speaks as consul in office, and therefore Sallust makes Lepidus attack Sulla in B.C. 78, and he represents Sulla as not having yet abdicated. Now Sulla, as we have seen, abdicated in B.C. 79 and died in B.C. 78, but we do not know at what time of the year he died, nor how long the interval was between his abdication and his death. But if the facts, on which this fictitious oration is founded, are truly represented, Lepidus in his consulship declared his intention to undo the work of Sulla; and Sulla had not abdicated at

the time of this declaration of hostility. The date of Sulla's
abdication then, if we follow Sallust's authority, is incorrectly
placed in B.C. 79, in the consulship of P. Servilius and Appius
Claudius, and we must suppose that Sulla abdicated after
Lepidus entered on his consulship in B.C. 78, and that he died
shortly after.

Lepidus had been praetor in Sicily (B.C. 81), and he got a
bad name for his administration of the island. Two Metelli,
Celer and Nepos, began a prosecution against him, but gave
it up because they found that he was a popular favourite.
His policy in his consulship appears to have been to make
another revolution in the popular interest, or rather in his
own interest under the popular name. Though he belonged
to a noble family, he affected the side of the people, and his
marriage with Appuleia the daughter of the turbulent tribune L. Appuleius Saturninus might seem to give him
additional credit with the faction which Sulla had crushed.
The historians speak of the revolutionary measures which
Lepidus proposed in his consulship, and though we might
easily guess what his designs were, we have no particular
evidence about them beyond a few words in Appian, his
speech in Sallust, and the speech of L. Marcius Philippus
which was delivered in the following year.

Lepidus in his harangue to the people recapitulated the
violent measures by which Sulla had deprived Roman citizens
of their life and property, driven into exile those who were
fortunate enough to escape from his bloody emissaries, and
made himself the master and the tyrant of Rome. He
says that Sulla charged him with having got the property
of some of those who had been proscribed. His answer
was that this charge was one of Sulla's greatest crimes,
for that neither himself nor any one else was safe in the
terrible days of the proscription, when to act honestly
would have been a man's ruin. He says that he bought
the property of the proscribed through fear, and he was
ready to restore it to the owners on repayment of the
purchase-money. He concluded by calling on the people
to follow him as their leader in the recovery of liberty, a

kind of language which any man may use when his design
is to make a revolution.

The purpose of Lepidus was to recall the proscribed, and
to put them in possession of their property which had passed
into other hands, and a great part of it into the hands of
Sulla's old soldiers. He proposed to restore civic rights to
those towns which had been deprived of them by Sulla. The
restoration of the tribunitian authority was also in the designs of Lepidus, according to the speech of Philippus made
in B.C. 77, but Licinianus states that the proposal to restore
the tribunitian authority was made by the tribunes themselves to the consuls, and that Lepidus was the first to reject
the proposal. He declared in an address to the people, which
is referred to by the annalist Licinianus, that it was not for
the interest of the state that the authority of the tribunes
should be restored, and a large part of the audience signified
their assent. If then Lepidus did design to restore the
antient authority of the tribunes, it was at some time later
than that assigned by the annalist to his refusal, and when
his affairs were in such a state that he was ready to strengthen
himself by any means in his power. A fragment of an
ancient writer might appear to refer to Lepidus, but it refers
to C. Aurelius Cotta, consul B.C. 75. The writer says: I do not
find either in Sallust, or in Livy, or in Fenestella mention of
any other law proposed by him except that which he proposed
before the popular assembly, against the will of the nobility,
but greatly to the satisfaction of the people, and it was to
this effect, that those who had been tribunes should be allowed
to hold other offices (magistratus), which was forbidden by a
law of the Dictator Sulla enacted a few years before. But
some measures of Lepidus showed that he relied on the favour
of the people for support : he carried or proposed a Lex
Frumentaria, or law for the gratuitous distribution of grain,
one of the usual baits with which unprincipled men in those
times fished for popularity.

The Senate had declared in B.C. 79 that the provinces of
the consuls should be Italy and the Provincia or south of
Gallia, and Lepidus had the Provincia. But instead of

going into the south of France, he remained in Etruria and
received all the discontented who flocked to him.   The
Senate had attempted to secure the peace by binding Lepidus
and Catulus by an oath to abstain from mutual hostilities,
but Lepidus interpreted the oath as only valid during the
year of his consulship, and it was his intention on the
expiration of his office to declare war against the partisans
of Sulla. Accordingly though Lepidus was so near Rome,
he would not come to the Comitia, and when the Senate,
who were aware of his designs, invited him to come, he
advanced with all his force, intending to enter the city.
Catulus had no talent for military affairs, and the hopes
of the Senate rested on Cn. Pompeius, who attached himself
to the party of the Optimates and received the command of
a force to oppose Lepidus. According to Appian, Catulus met
Lepidus not far from the Campus Martius and drove him back.

The year B.C. 77 began with an interregnum.   Lepidus
was now proconsul and at the head of a large force.   All
Etruria was in arms, there was disturbance in Spain, and in
the east the attitude of Mithridates was threatening.   The
encouragement which Lepidus had given to those who had
been deprived of their lands by Sulla led to a violent reaction.
The people of Faesulae (Fiesole) near Florence attacked the
strong forts of Sulla's veterans, killed many of them and re-
entered into the possession of their property which had been
given to Sulla's soldiers.   The Senate attempted to negotiate
with Lepidus, but his demands were too extravagant to be
granted: he asked for a general restoration of the property
which had been confiscated in Sulla's time, a restoration of
their civil rights to those who had been deprived of them, the
complete re-establishment of the tribunitian authority, and a
second consulship; as we learn from the speech of L. Philippus,
who concluded his address to the Senate with this motion, that
Appius Claudius the Interrex with Q. Catulus Proconsul, and
all the rest who had the Imperium, should look after the
defence of the city, and provide that the Commonwealth
should sustain no damage.   This declaration of war was
followed by prompt action.

M. Junius Brutus, a partisan of Lepidus, held Cisalpine Gallia
or North Italy with an army, but he was too far off to join
Lepidus, who appears to have been still in Etruria when he
made a second advance on Rome. He had few friends in the
city, and no man of note joined him. C. Julius Caesar was in
Asia at the beginning of B.C. 78, and he joined the expedition of P. Servilius against the Cilician pirates, but he left
Servilius as soon as he heard of Sulla's death and the attempt
of Lepidus to make another revolution. He found however
on his arrival at Rome that the prospect was not so good as
he expected; and he would not place himself on the side of
Lepidus, though he was invited by great promises. He had
no confidence in the ability of the man, nor did he think the
opportunity favourable for attempting a change. Caesar's
brother-in-law L. Cinna was less cautious. He followed the
fortunes of Lepidus and after his defeat fled to Sertorius in
Spain.

We collect from the speech of L. Philippus in Sallust that
Lepidus had advanced already once upon Rome, for he asks
the Senate if they were waiting till he came again. Appian's
narrative, which is very brief, implies that the attack of
Lepidus was made in his consulship, and he appears to be
speaking of the same attack, which Florus describes, when
he says that on the approach of Lepidus, Catulus and Pompeius occupied the Pons Milvius and the Janiculus with an
armed force, that Lepidus was easily repulsed, and was
declared an enemy by the Senate. Some modern writers
place this repulse of Lepidus in B.C. 77; but it is absolutely
impossible to construct any clear narrative of the events from
the miserable fragments that remain. Lepidus retreated into
Etruria.

Pompeius advanced into North Italy to put down the
partisans of Lepidus, which he accomplished with little difficulty. Brutus, who had shut himself up in Mutina (Modena),
surrendered to Pompeius, who allowed him to retire with a
small escort of horse. But the next day Pompeius sent
P. Geminius after Brutus, who was taken near Regium
(Reggio) between Modena and Parma, and put to death.

Pompeius was much blamed for his conduct on this occasion.
He first wrote to the Senate to say that Brutus had voluntarily surrendered, and then he sent a letter containing
various charges against the man after he was dead. This
Brutus was the father of the Brutus who was afterwards one
of Caesar's assassins. The town of Alba on the river Tanarus
in Cisalpine Gallia was taken at this time, and a son of
Lepidus who was found in the place was also put to death by
the order of the cruel Roman commander. The fate of
Lepidus was soon decided. He had gained some advantage
on the coast of Etruria, probably over Catulus, but Pompeius
crossing the mountains from North Italy defeated him near
Cosa, and Lepidus placing the remnant of his troops on
shipboard made his escape to Sardinia. His object was to
get possession of this fertile island, to stop the supplies of
corn from going to Rome, and perhaps to join Sertorius in
Spain. But the Roman governor of Sardinia made such
good preparations that Lepidus was foiled in all his attempts
on the strong places of the island. He soon fell sick, and
"died of vexation, not at the state of affairs, as they say, but
from finding some writing by which he discovered that his
wife had committed adultery" (Plutarch). The story may
be taken for what it is worth, which is probably nothing at
all. Lepidus attempted a revolution, and as he failed, he
has had the usual fate of all who are unsuccessful in great
enterprises, and he is numbered among the ambitious and
the incapable. His army was broken up, but Perperna led
the greater part of the men to Sertorius in Spain. The defeat
of Lepidus was not followed by any severe measures against
his partisans. Nobody wished to see the times of Sulla revived, and the ruling party had work enough on their hands
in foreign parts without making more enemies at home.

In the year B.C. 77 the Romans made an attempt to clear
the Eastern parts of the Mediterranean of the Cilician pirates.
P. Servilius Vatia, the consul of B.C. 79, was sent against
them with a fleet and an army. He was engaged for three
years on this hazardous service, for he did not complete his
work till B.C. 75.

The great inland sea, round which lie nearly all the
countries which formed the ancient world, has been from
time immemorial infested by pirates. The eastern shores of
the Hadriatic, the Grecian peninsula, the numerous islands
of the Aegean, and the west and southern coasts of Asia contain innumerable bays and inlets, which are convenient for
receiving such small vessels as the ancients used. Commerce
by sea must be older than piracy, but it is probable that as
soon as ships traversed the waters of the Mediterranean,
robbers followed in their track. The long unsettled state of
the countries, which border the north shores of the great sea,
is proved by the continual migrations of the people from one
place to another in early ages, and the general insecurity of
life and property. Necessity would drive many men to live
by plunder; and others, who loved a roaming and unsettled
life, would prefer the excitement, the dangers, and the great
though uncertain gains of piracy to the hard labour and the
dull existence of common life. The occupation of sea robber
became glorious: it was only another kind of warfare. It
was an old Thracian notion, as Herodotus reports it, that to
do nothing was most honourable; to till the earth was a great
disgrace; and to live by war and plunder was the mark of
a gentleman. These ideas have not yet been completely
eradicated from men's minds. A successful brigand is still
a great personage. Thucydides reports an old tradition that
a king named Minos cleared the Aegean of the pirates as
well as he could, in order that his revenues might come in
the better, for this maritime potentate had reduced to his
obedience the group of islands named the Cyclades, and
piracy would have disturbed the profits which he derived
from the commerce of his subjects. It has been necessary to
repeat the work of King Minos at intervals to the present
day. Within the memory of many of us who are still living
the south coast of Asia Minor, from which Servilius drove
the Cilician pirates, has been infested by villains who plundered the flags of all nations, and often massacred their unfortunate prisoners.

The southern coast of Asia Minor extends from a point

opposite to the island of Rhodes to the entrance of the bay of Iskendroon or Scanderoon. The outline of the coast is formed by two huge rounded peninsulas separated by the Gulf of Adalia. The western peninsula is the ancient Lycia, a country of mountains, forests, and valleys. Along the rough irregular shore of Lycia the mountains press close upon the sea. A little north of the town of Olympus, one of the haunts of the pirates, rises the huge mass of Takhtalu, the ancient Solyma, which is 7800 feet high. The eastern peninsula is Cilicia the rough (Trachea) or the mountainous, a name by which it was distinguished from the level or Plain Cilicia. Strabo says that the mountainous Cilicia extends from Coracesium (Alaya) eastward to the river Lamus (Lamas). The coast of Cilicia Trachea presents a rough outline, backed by mountains from Coracesium to the promontory Sarpedon, a distance of one hundred and fifty miles. A high bluff named Anemurium (Cape Anamour) is the most southern point of the Cilician peninsula and also the most southern point of Asia Minor. From the plain of Selinus (Selinty) eastward to Anemurium, " a distance of thirty miles, the ridge of bare rocky hills that forms the coast is interrupted but twice by narrow valleys, which conduct the mountain torrents to the sea " (Beaufort). At the river Lamus the rocky coast terminates, and the wide plains of the Level Cilicia commence, which extend inland to the base of the range of Taurus and eastward to the bay of Scanderoon. The high mountains which back the plain of Cilicia are visible from the sea, and the peaks are covered with snow as late as the month of June.

After the death of Alexander Balas in B.C. 146, Demetrius II. named Nicator reigned in Syria; but Diodotus, surnamed Tryphon, set up Antiochus the infant son of Balas as a rival to Demetrius. Tryphon soon put the child to death and usurped the Syrian throne. His career was short. He was defeated and put to death in B.C. 139. Coracesium was the stronghold which Tryphon used as his head-quarters in his attack on Demetrius. After Tryphon's death, the Cilicians whom he had employed continued the

piratical practices which their leader had begun, and the
kings of Syria were too weak to keep them in check. The
most profitable employment of the Cilicians was the capture
and sale of prisoners in the market of Delos, from which the
Romans were supplied. After the destruction of Carthage
and Corinth the demand for slaves among the Roman capitalists increased greatly, and the Cilicians finding so good a
market for their wares prosecuted vigorously the business of
catching slaves. They found along the south coast of Asia
Minor safe places from which they could sally forth to plunder, and where they could retire with their booty or take
shelter in bad weather. One of those places was Phaselis
(Tekrova), on the east coast of Lycia, north of Olympus.
The people of Phaselis made profit by the visits of the
pirates to their port, and they became partners in their in-
famous gains. The Egyptian kings, who were at enmity
with the Syrian kingdom, did not interfere with the pirates
either when they visited Egypt or the dependent island of
Cyprus. The Cilicians pretended that they only dealt in
slaves, and those who received them into their ports professed to believe them. The Rhodians also, who had a good
navy, did not attempt to check the piracy in the eastern
Mediterranean. Perhaps the Cilicians took care to give the
Rhodians no pretext for attacking them. The Romans were
for some time too busy to look after the distant coast of Asia,
and when they were compelled to attack the pirates in order
to secure their own ships and commerce, they found that
they had a formidable enemy to contend with.

In B.C. 103 the orator M. Antonius, as we have seen above
(p. 60), was sent against the pirates, and had a triumph for
some victory over them. During the first Mithridatic war
the pirates again made their appearance on the coast of Asia
and in the waters of the Aegean, being encouraged by Mithridates, when he found that he could no longer retain his
hold on the Roman province of Asia. Sulla had no time to
punish the marauders, for he was in a hurry to return to
Italy to crush his enemies at home.

Servilius set about the war against the pirates with an

honest intention to put an end to their plundering. With a well-equipped fleet he drove from the sea the vessels of the Cilicians, which were small craft, and quick sailers, but no match in a fight for the more powerful Roman vessels. He then attacked the strongholds of the pirates, which were well fortified and contained the rich produce of many years' robbery. The town of Olympus, situated on a mountain of the same name, was in the possession of Zenicetas, who also held Phaselis, Corycus in Cilicia, and many places in Pamphylia. Servilius stormed and set fire to the robber's strong place, and Zenicetas with all his family perished in the flames. Phaselis was also taken by the Roman commander, Attalia in Pamphylia, Corycus, and other places on the coast. Servilius even penetrated into the interior of this rugged country, and was the first Roman who led an army over the range of Taurus into Isauria, which was reckoned a part of Lycaonia. The chief city of this country, which was named Isaura, was situated on the north side of the Taurus, but the site of the place is not quite certain. The Isaurians were robbers, and probably leagued with the Cilician pirates. Servilius rooted them out of their nests, and took possession of their strong place Isaura by diverting a stream which supplied the town with water. For this exploit he obtained the title of Isauricus. Strabo's remark that he had seen this P. Servilius Isauricus has caused the critics some difficulty. Though Strabo was not born when Servilius conquered the pirates, the Roman commander lived to be a very old man, and Strabo must have seen him somewhere, even though he does not tell us where he saw the man. It is not likely that he confounded so distinguished a soldier with any other person.

The conquests of Servilius were in Lycia, Pamphylia, and Isauria. The only place that he took in Cilicia Trachea is Corycus, and he did not advance into the Level Cilicia. If a province of Cilicia was formed after the victories of Servilius, it certainly comprised very little even of western Cilicia; and the name Cilician was applied to the new province with as little accuracy as the war against the pirates was named the Cilician war. This province which the Romans named Cilicia consisted of Isauria, Pamphylia, and Pisidia. It has been observed (p. 143) that the Romans used the term province of Cilicia even before the conquests of Servilius. Both Sulla in B.C. 92 and Cn. Cornelius Dolabella in B.C. 80 and 79 had held the province named Cilicia; and we know from Cicero that Dolabella's offences during his praetorship, with which he was charged, were limited to Lycia, Pamphylia, Pisidia, and Phrygia.

Servilius had a triumph in B.C. 75. In the procession were displayed the statues and other valuable things which were taken from the captured cities. All that had been acquired in the war was carefully registered by the general in his accounts, which were deposited in the Roman treasury. He did not enrich himself. Many of the piratical captains, and among them a noted one named Nico, appeared in the triumphal pomp. It was a day of great rejoicing at Rome. The prisoners were kept to gladden the eyes of the Roman people, and as the living proof of the defeat of these formidable enemies. When the car of Servilius reached the Forum and began to turn towards the Capitol, the captives, according to Roman usage, would be led off to prison and to death.

C. Julius Caesar had returned to Rome, but he was still too young to come forward as the leader of a party. The attempt of Lepidus had ended ignominiously, and the friends of Marius were powerless. Caesar made an effort to gain popularity by the prosecution (B.C. 77) of Cn. Cornelius Dolabella for malversation (Repetundae) in the government of his province Macedonia. Dolabella was a friend of Sulla: he had been consul in B.C. 81, and when he had the government of Macedonia he gained some victory over the Thracians for which he had a triumph. C. Aurelius Cotta, probably a brother of Caesar's mother Aurelia, and Hortensius defended Dolabella, and he was acquitted by the jury, which was formed according to Sulla's constitution. But though Caesar failed in his prosecution, he laid the foundation of his great reputation as an orator. In the next year (B.C. 76) he attempted to bring to justice another of Sulla's friends, C.

Antonius, the younger son of the great orator M. Antonius.
Caius Antonius was with Sulla in his Greek campaign, and
on some occasion when he had the command of several
troops of cavalry he plundered the Greeks. The men now
came to Rome to complain, and Caesar undertook their case.
Antonius was brought before M. Lucullus, who was then
Praetor Peregrinus, in order that the necessary preliminaries
to the trial might be gone through. Lucullus granted what
the Greeks asked, but we are not told what it was for which
they applied to the Praetor. We may however conclude
that it related to the manner of conducting the trial.
Antonius however appealed to the college of tribunes against
the decision of Lucullus, having declared on oath that he
could not have a fair trial. So he escaped for the present,
but six years later the censors L. Gellius and Cn. Cornelius
Lentulus expelled him from the Senate on this very ground
of having plundered the allies of Rome, evaded his trial, and
being greatly in debt.

Having failed in these two prosecutions, Caesar left Rome
again in order, as Suetonius says, to be out of the way of his
enemies and to improve his oratorical powers under the
instruction of the great rhetorician Molo of Rhodes. A
modern writer affirms that fear of the men, whom he had
attacked, was no part of Caesar's motives for leaving Rome,
but we can easily believe that he did not find his residence
in the city very pleasant. It was in the winter of B.C. 76
that he crossed the sea, and fell into the hands of pirates near
Pharmacusa (Farmaco), a small island off the coast of Asia
Minor and south-west of Miletus. Servilius was still engaged
in the war with the pirates, and we might suppose that Caesar
would have rejoined his old commander, but there is no
evidence that he intended to do so, and the island Pharmacusa did not lie on the road to the Cilician coast, nor
indeed on the direct course to Rhodes. Plutarch has a
wonderful story of Caesar's behaviour while he was with
the pirates. The men demanded twenty talents as his
ransom, but Caesar only laughed at them for not knowing
the value of their prize, and he promised to give them

fifty talents.   While he sent off some of his companions
to the neighbouring cities of Asia to raise the ransom money,
he was left alone with one friend who was his physician, and
two attendants.   During his stay of near forty days among
the pirates, he was more like a prince surrounded by his
guards than a prisoner among cruel robbers.   It is a
characteristic feature in this story, the truthfulness of which
we cannot estimate, that Caesar employed himself in writing
poems and speeches.   All through his active life, as we know
from undoubted evidence, Caesar was always busy with
literary occupations, even in the midst of his marches and
campaigns.   That he read his compositions to these pirates,
as we are told, each man may believe or reject as he pleases.
He joined them in their sports and exercises, and made himself a pleasant companion.   The fellows were pleased with
their prisoner, and of course did not believe him when he
used to tell them with a laugh that he would hang them
all.   When the ransom was brought, Caesar was released
and set off straight for Miletus, where he manned some vessels
which he found in the port.   With this force he returned to
the island, surprised the pirates, dispersed part of their fleet,
sunk some ships, and took others with the men in them.
Caesar lodged the pirates in prison at Pergamum, and then
went to the proconsul Junius Silanus, who being the governor
of Asia had the power of punishing the pirates.   The proconsul, who, according to one story, was in Bithynia, whither
he had gone on some business, said that he would sell the
prisoners, or he gave some other answer not satisfactory to
Caesar, who immediately returned to Pergamum and crucified
them.   It is said however that the men were put to death
before they were fastened to the cross.   Fenestella's report
that they were beheaded is only worthy of notice as an
example of the perversions to which all historical narratives
are subject.

   The date of this event in Caesar's life appears to be fixed
by a passage in Pliny (N. H. ii. 35), who names Junius
Silanus proconsul, and fixes his proconsulship in the consulship of Cn. Octavius and C. Scribonius Curio B.C. 76.

Plutarch places the event immediately after Caesar's visit to King Nicomedes in Bithynia about four years earlier, but he is mistaken. This Junius Silanus must be D. Junius Silanus, who was afterwards consul in B.C. 62. The events of Caesar's early life are very imperfectly known, and many tales were in circulation about him, which were false or perverted from the truth. Polyaenus in his book of Stratagems tells the adventure with the pirates in a way, which in some respects agrees with the authorities already mentioned, and in others differs entirely from them.

It is not said how long Caesar continued his lessons under Molo. Suetonius alone has recorded the fact that at the commencement of the third war with Mithridates Caesar crossed over from Rhodes into Asia, "and having got together some auxiliary troops and expelled the king's governor from the country, he kept to their allegiance the states which were doubtful and wavering." The third war with Mithridates began in B.C. 74. Caesar's uncle C. Aurelius Cotta, who had been consul in B.C. 75, had the province of Gallia in the following year. The Senate granted Cotta a triumph for some victory, of which we know nothing; but an old wound, which Cotta had once received in battle, broke out before the day of the triumph, and he died suddenly. Cotta was a very distinguished orator. He is one of the speakers in Cicero's dialogue on the Orator, and in the third book of the treatise "De Natura Deorum." Cotta was a Pontifex, and Caesar's friends in his absence secured his election to the vacant place. It has been already observed that Caesar at an early age was appointed Flamen Dialis by the influence of Cinna and his uncle Marius, but owing to the civil disturbances he was never instituted in this high office. He now hurried back to Italy to take possession of his ecclesiastical dignity. The seas still swarmed with pirates, and Caesar was compelled to cross the Hadriatic in a small boat with two friends and ten slaves. He knew what he might expect from the pirates, if he was caught, but he was prepared for the worst, and had resolved not to fall into their hands alive. Fortunately he saw nothing of them.

Plutarch's chronology of the early part of Caesar's life is all in confusion. Both he and Velleius place the prosecution of Dolabella after the adventure with the pirates. Plutarch could not do otherwise, because he supposed that Caesar was taken by the pirates shortly after his visit to King Nicomedes in Bithynia; but Velleius has made an unpardonable blunder in doing so, for he tells us that Caesar was elected a Pontifex in the place of C. Cotta, and he ought to have known that Cotta was one of the two orators who defended Dolabella against Caesar's prosecution.

It was after his return to Rome that Caesar was elected a military tribune, but there is no evidence of his serving in the army either in the war against Sertorius or in the third war against Mithridates.

CHAPTER XXXI.

SERTORIUS IN SPAIN.

B.C. 82—76.

It is hardly possible to determine whether Sertorius retired to Spain in B.C. 83 or in B.C. 82. Appian fixes the event after the capture of Suessa B.C. 83 (p. 335), but that does not determine the time. The narrative of Plutarch (Sertorius, c. 6) perhaps implies that the younger Marius and Carbo had entered on the consulship, and that Sertorius was still in Italy in the beginning of B.C. 82. Drumann collects the same conclusion from the passage of Julius Exsuperantius (c. 8), who may have correctly copied his authority, probably the History of Sallust. Julius states that the consuls, and other heads of the party wished to get rid of Sertorius, either because he found fault with their conduct of the war against Sulla, or because they thought it necessary to secure Spain. Accordingly Sertorius was despatched to Nearer Spain, as Julius says, with instructions to settle affairs in Transalpine Gallia by the way.

Quintus Sertorius was a native of Nursia (Norcia) a Sabine town in the lofty Apennines near the source of the Nar. He lost his father when he was young, but he was carefully brought up by his mother, whom he loved most tenderly. He got some practical knowledge of law by attending the courts, and some reputation in Rome as a speaker, even in Cicero's judgment.

This man was fitted for the part which he played in

Spain. He possessed courage, strength, endurance, presence of mind in the midst of danger, and all the qualities that are necessary for a commander. His military career commenced in B.C. 105, when he was present at the great battle on the Rhone (p. 8). The other events of his life have been already mentioned. In some of his campaigns he had lost an eye, and accordingly Plutarch enumerates him among those one-eyed commanders "who have accomplished most by a union of daring and cunning," Philippus of Macedonia, Antigonus, and Hannibal. Sertorius found in Spain a country well suited for carrying on an irregular warfare against his enemies; and he had the example of the Lusitanian Viriathus, who had long defied the armies of Rome and was only conquered by treachery.

Sertorius passed through the south of France to the Eastern Pyrenees, where he paid the barbarians money to allow him quietly to cross the mountains. He found the people of Spain dissatisfied with the Romans owing to the tyranny and greediness of their governors, but he gained their goodwill by the remission of taxes, and most of all by not quartering his soldiers on them. He was the first who set the example of placing his men under winter tents in the suburbs of the towns. Prudence however may have led him to make this change, for he would remember what had happened at Castulo (p. 106); and he could keep his men in better order under tents than if they were dispersed through a town. He also armed the Roman settlers in Spain, and employed his time in building vessels and making other preparations for war. It was not before the end of B.C. 82 or the beginning of B.C. 81 that Sulla had leisure to attend to foreign affairs. He sent C. Annius Lusous, who had served under Metellus Numidicus in the Jugurthine war, with the title of proconsul to Spain. Annius had with him two Quaestors, C. Fabius and Q. Tarquitius. When he reached the Pyrenees, he found the pass occupied by Julius Salinator the legatus of Sertorius with six thousand men. Seeing that the position of Sertorius' lieutenant could not be attacked Annius waited at the base of the mountains. He was extri-

cated from his difficulty by treachery, for one Calpurnius
Lanarius murdered Salinator, upon which the men of Sertorius left the strong places which they occupied and Annius
crossing the mountains advanced southward without any
opposition. Sertorius was so ill prepared to meet the enemy
that he fled with three thousand men to New Carthage (Car-
tagena), where he either had ships of his own, or he found
in the noble port of this great town merchant vessels enough
to receive his troops. He then crossed over to Africa to the
Mauritanian coast, but his men were attacked by the barbarians while they were getting water, and Sertorius again
embarking sailed towards Spain. On the sea he met with
some pirates, who are named Cilicians, for this was now a
common term for any pirate. Being joined by these robbers
Sertorius attacked the island Pityussa (Iviza), where there
was a Roman garrison and drove it out. But Annius soon
came up with a well-equipped fleet, which Sertorius ventured
to attack with his light ships. The biographer does not
distinctly say that Sertorius was defeated, though we may
perhaps infer that he was; but if he was not defeated, some
of his ships were driven ashore by the bad weather, and the
rest were roughly handled by the storm. When the wind
abated, Sertorius with the remnant of his shattered fleet
steered to the south-west and passing through the Straits of
Gibraltar entered the Atlantic Ocean. He brought his vessels to land near the mouth of the river Baetis (Guadalquivir), and we may assume in the bay of the great
commercial town Gadeira or Gades (Cadiz).

In this market of nations Sertorius fell in with some
sailors who had returned from the Atlantic islands, which
they reported to be two, separated by a very narrow channel
and ten thousand stadia from the African coast. They were
called the islands of the Happy, but it is not said that they
were inhabited. The soil of the islands was rich, and they
produced fruit spontaneously and in abundance. The climate
was pleasant, owing to the mild temperature and the slight
changes. The barbarians, as the people in the south of Spain
are termed, believed that these islands were "the Elysian

Plains and the abode of the Happy which Homer has celebrated." It has been conjectured that the sailors whom Sertorius saw had been to the Canary islands, but the description suits better the Madeira islands, which are two, though neither the distance of these islands from one another nor their distance from the African coast is truly stated. Sertorius, who was now probably near fifty years old, was seized with a strong desire to live in these happy islands far from tyranny and the turmoil of war. His Cilician associates wanted neither peace nor quiet. They were bent on fresh adventure and set out to Africa to restore to his throne a Mauritanian prince whom Plutarch names Ascalis. In order to employ his men and keep them together Sertorius took them over to Africa to support the king's enemies, and so he would have to fight against his Cilician allies. Sertorius defeated the king and besieged him in Tingis (Tangier) to which Ascalis and his brother fled. Sulla sent help to Ascalis from Rome under a commander named Paccianus, but he was defeated by Sertorius and lost his life. After the death of this general his troops passed over to Sertorius, who now took Tingis, and, we may assume, made the king his prisoner. We are not told how Sertorius settled affairs in Mauritania, but he treated liberally those whom he had vanquished, and got from them, as we may infer from the narrative, such supplies as he wanted.

It was a lucky accident for Sertorius which brought Roman troops into Africa. He who had fled from Spain without knowing where to seek a refuge was now at the head of the Roman soldiers who had been sent against him, and the fame of his success brought him new allies. The Lusitani, the old enemies of Rome, were preparing to rise against their tyrants, and they sent to Sertorius, whose character was well known, to invite him to be their leader. Sertorius again crossed the Mediterranean. It was probably when he was passing the straits on his return that he gained a naval victory over Cotta, who was apparently attempting to prevent him from landing in Spain with his small force of two thousand six hundred Romans and seven hundred Africans who followed his fortunes. A fragment of Sallust indeed says that Sertorius after leaving a small garrison in Mauritania, took advantage of a dark night and a favourable sea, and thus by a stealthy movement he endeavoured to avoid a fight in his transit. The fragment goes no further, but it confirms a probable conjecture that the Roman fleet was on the watch to stop his passage from Africa to Spain, and as Sertorius never had the means of opposing the Romans successfully on the water, and after his return to Spain had occupation enough in defending himself by land, we cannot fix any other time for his naval victory than that of his passage from Mauritania to put himself at the head of the Lusitani. This victory then over Cotta, as Plutarch names it, in the Straits, may be no more than a passage successfully accomplished in spite of the Roman cruisers. The Lusitani had seized a mountain position named Ballers, where they waited for Sertorius and his men, who all crossed the Straits in safety.

Sertorius immediately set about bringing the Lusitani into discipline, and he gained allies among the neighbouring Spaniards by his mild behaviour and his activity. He had a rude people to deal with, but his sagacity taught him how to manage them. A native made him a present of a white fawn, which became so tame that it would come when it was called, and accompany him when he was going about among his men. Sertorius conceived the idea of making this fawn a useful instrument in governing the superstitious barbarians. He said it was a gift from Diana, and as a proof of this assertion he declared that the fawn showed him many hidden things. When he got secret information of the movements of the enemy, he pretended that the fawn had spoken to him in his sleep; and when he heard of any of his officers having been successful he would conceal the news, and produce the fawn crowned with chaplets, which was usual on the occasion of a victory, and tell his men to rejoice for they would hear of some good luck.

His whole force at first was small, but by his prudence and success it rapidly increased. Probably we may place in B.C. 80 the defeat of Fufidius, the governor of Further Spain, who was sent from Rome against Sertorius. The battle was fought on the banks of the Guadalquivir. The governor of Nearer Spain was L. Domitius Ahenobarbus, but we know nothing of what was done in that part of the peninsula during his government.

In B.C. 80 Q. Caecilius Metellus Pius, the son of Numidicus, was consul with Sulla. It was in the next year perhaps and not in his consulship that Metellus was sent to Spain to oppose Sertorius. Plutarch repeats what he had said on another occasion (p. 339) that Metellus was growing old, though he was now only about fifty, and Sertorius must have been very little younger than Metellus, and perhaps no younger. But Metellus was fond of his ease, and he commanded men who had only been used to regular war. With such troops he was no match for Sertorius, whose strength, activity, and endurance were unsurpassed, and his men like himself could make long marches and subsist on the scantiest food. It seems a correct conclusion from a fragment of Sallust's history that Metellus summoned L. Domitius from Nearer Spain to aid him against Sertorius. Domitius advanced as far as the Guadiana, where he was defeated by Hirtuleius, one of Sertorius' commanders and lost his life. Another commander of Metellus, named Thorius, had the same bad luck, and perished probably in the same battle. Metellus also, it is said, sustained several defeats, but this vague statement is all that we are told. If we follow Caesar's authority, Sertorius had stirred up the Aquitani of Gallia against the Romans. L. Valerius Praeconinus was defeated in Aquitania and lost his life; and L. Manilius or Mallius Nepos, the Roman Proconsul of the Provincia, only escaped by flight, and left all his baggage behind. The defeat of two Roman generals north of the Pyrenees by the people of Aquitania, while Sertorius was opposing Metellus in Spain, leads to a probable conclusion that this war in Aquitania was instigated by Sertorius and that his object was to close the passes of the Eastern Pyrenees against the Roman armies. Orosius indeed reports that Manilius entered Spain with three legions and fifteen hundred horse; that he fought a battle with Hirtuleius, lost his camp and all his stores, and escaped with only a few of his men to Ilerda (Lerida) in Catalonia on the river Segre. This statement is clear and precise, but it does not agree with Caesar.

A narrative, which pays no regard to chronology, written by a man who knew nothing of the geography of Spain, and only intended to show the character of Sertorius by selecting a few striking facts and events, cannot be converted into a history. Such is Plutarch's life of Sertorius. All we can learn as to this part of the war is the fact that Metellus gained no advantages over the famous guerrillero, and was often defeated. The story of the siege of Langobriga in Lusitania may serve as an example of the daring and success of Sertorius. The only place of this name that we know was near the mouth of the Douro, but it is very improbable that this remote spot was the town mentioned in Plutarch's narrative. Metellus attempted to take Langobriga, because the townsmen gave great help to Sertorius. He expected to reduce the place in a short time by blockade, for it had only one well of water, and it was easy to cut the people off from getting any supply outside of the walls. But Sertorius came to the aid of the townsmen, and soon got ready two thousand skins of water. The Spaniards and Moors volunteered to convey the skins into the town, which they succeeded in doing, and they brought back with them all the useless hands, that the water might last longer for those who were able to defend the place. Metellus, who had sat down before Langobriga with only five days' supplies for his men, was obliged to send out some troops to forage, but the men fell into an ambuscade laid by Sertorius and sustained great loss. Metellus finally gave up the siege and made a disgraceful retreat.

Sertorius by his success gained the love and admiration of his barbarian allies, and by introducing the Roman discipline he converted them into an efficient regular army. He also employed gold and silver in the decoration of their helmets and for the ornament of their shields, and accustomed them to the use of flowered cloaks and tunics. He knew that a handsome dress and fine armour please soldiers and would be a means of attaching his allies more strongly to him, and bringing fresh recruits. Sertorius was fighting for his life and his party; but the men of Spain for the independence of their country. The Spanish mothers sent their boys to the war, and encouraged them by the tale of what their fathers had done. Sertorius devised another plan for pleasing the chiefs and securing their fidelity. He got together the boys of noblest birth and placed them at Osca (Huesca), where he established a college. Huesca is in Aragon, in the country of the ancient Ilergetes, about half way between the Ebro and the Pyrenees. The fact of Sertorius establishing his college here shows that he was master of part of the country north of the Ebro. The boys had teachers of Greek and Roman learning, and while they were brought up in a way to qualify them to assist in the administration, they were in fact hostages in the hands of Sertorius. The fathers however were well pleased that their sons should be dressed like young Romans and go to the college of Sertorius free of cost. The boys were frequently examined and received rewards, and the golden ornament for the neck which the Romans named a "bulla." Sertorius also availed himself of the Iberian custom of having about him a number of men who were designated by a term which may be expressed by the word "devoted." It was an Iberian usage that those who were placed about a commander should never desert him, and if their commander died, they died with him. Caesar in his Commentaries on the Gallic war describes a similar usage among the Aquitani and the Galli. The officers in the army of Sertorius could only secure a few of these faithful followers, but those who were devoted to die with Sertorius were thousands. On one occasion when the army of Sertorius was routed near a city and the enemy was close upon them, the Iberians saved Sertorius by raising him on their shoulders to the top of the wall, and when their general was safe, they took to flight, each man looking after himself.

We gain a settled chronological point in the perplexed narrative of Plutarch by the fact of M. Perperna joining Sertorius with the remnant of the troops of Lepidus and such other forces as he had raised. This M. Perperna was the grandson of M. Perperna who was consul B.C. 130 (vol. i. pp. 208, 238), and the son of M. Perperna, who was consul in B.C. 92, and served in the Social War. When Perperna entered Spain in B.C. 77 with money and a large force, he intended to act independently of Sertorius and to carry on the war against Metellus. He was proud of his noble family and his wealth, and if he brought above five legions with him, as Plutarch reports, he had an army sufficient to support his arrogant pretensions. However it is certain that he could not have brought five legions from Sardinia which he had lately left, nor can we conjecture where he got fresh men, though it is likely enough that there were plenty of old soldiers ready to take service under any man who would promise them pay and booty. It is not clear how long Perperna kept apart, but we are told that he did not join Sertorius till he was compelled by the clamour of his own soldiers, when they heard that Cn. Pompeius was crossing the Pyrenees to support Metellus. Pompeius came the next year B.C. 76.

Sertorius established a senate composed of those Roman senators who had fled from Rome. If the arrival of Perperna did not lead to the formation of this rival senate, we may assume that this body would be increased in numbers by the addition of refugees with Perperna. It consisted of three hundred men, and was named by Sertorius the Roman senate, by way of insulting the true Senate, as Appian says, which remark is probably only his opinion. We cannot literally accept Plutarch's statement that this senate was composed of senators who fled from Rome, if Appian is to be trusted for three hundred being the number. Sertorius appointed his quaestors and generals from this body, and arranged every thing according to Roman usage. He made use of the men and resources of Spain not to establish the independence of the country, but, as he said, to recover freedom for the Romans who had been oppressed by the tyranny of Sulla and his party. It was consistent with this design that he appointed only Romans to command under him.

Appian has omitted all mention of what Metellus did against Sertorius before the arrival of Cn. Pompeius in Spain, and Plutarch's biography is useless for the purpose of an historical narrative. The junction of Perperna and his forces with Sertorius roused the Roman Senate to a sense of their danger, for though Sertorius may not have conceived the bold design of invading Italy, yet if he succeeded in driving the Roman forces out of Spain, he might follow Sulla's example and enter Rome as a conqueror. It was better policy to fight the battle in Spain than in Italy, and the Senate looked about for a general whom they could send, not to supersede Metellus but to put some life into the Spanish campaign. There was a young man ready to go, but the Senate would rather have taken somebody else. However, there was no choice, for the aristocracy of Rome was in a pitiable condition, and there was not a single man of mature age able and willing to command in Spain. Cn. Pompeius, it is said, retained an army under him after the defeat of Lepidus, as if he expected to be soon employed; "and though Catulus ordered him to disband his force, he would not obey, but kept under arms in the neighbourhood of the city continually inventing excuses, until the command was given to him on the proposal of Lucius Philippus" (Plutarch). We are compelled to take such statements as these for want of others, but we can hardly believe that a young man, who held no public office could keep a force together without the consent of the Senate and without money from the treasury, unless we make the very improbable assumption that his troops were regularly paid by the state at the time when he was keeping them together against the wish of the governing body. However it was determined to give Pompeius a command in Spain with the title of proconsul. Some senator asked Philippus if he thought that Pompeius should be sent as Proconsul (proconsule), to which Philippus, who was a witty man, replied "Not as Proconsul, but in place of the consuls," a joke which is better in the original than in the translation ("Non pro consule sed pro consulibus.") Cicero has told the story twice. In one of the passages he says that the command against Sertorius was given to a private person, because the consuls refused it. The consuls of the year B.C. 76 were Cn. Octavius and C. Scribonius Curio, whom Cicero names " most energetic and illustrious," though he said so merely for the purpose that he then had in hand (De Imp. Cn. Pomp. c. 21). If the consuls' had been energetic and illustrious, the Senate would certainly have sent one of them to Spain; for at this time, before the restoration of the tribunician authority, the Senate had the whole administration in their hands, and gave commissions in cases where according to the old practice a vote of the people would have been necessary.

CHAPTER XXXII.

CN. POMPEIUS IN SPAIN.

B.C. 76—75.

In forty days Pompeius was ready to march to Spain. It is uncertain whether he set out at the close of B.C. 77 or in the beginning of B.C. 76. He crossed the Alps, not indeed with so much difficulty as Hannibal, but he cut a new road at a part which Appian describes as situated about the sources of the Rhone and the Po, which rivers, he adds with his usual ignorance of geography, rise in the Alps not far from one another. Pompeius probably made his road by the pass of Mont Genèvre, which seems to be the route that Caesar took in the first year of his Gallic campaigns. In his letter to the Senate Pompeius says that the enemy was threatening Italy by the Alpine passes, and he drove them back to Spain. He crossed the Pyrenees and received the submission of the Laletani and the Indigetes, two nations on the coast between the Pyrenees and the Ebro. Meeting with no enemy here Pompeius advanced southwards through the plain of Valencia to relieve the town Lauron which Sertorius was besieging. Lauron was probably situated near the mouth of the Sucro (Xucar). Orosius reports on the authority of a writer named Galba (Sueton. Galba, c. 3) that Pompeius had thirty thousand infantry, and a thousand horsemen; and Sertorius double the number of infantry and eight thousand horsemen. The hostile camps about Lauron were near to one another, and both Sertorius and Pompeius were compelled to forage for supplies. There were only two places which could furnish the armies, one near the camps, and the other at a distance. Sertorius ordered his light troops to scour the part that was near, but he would not allow them to visit the remoter spot, his design being to make the enemy believe that they might safely forage there. The men of Pompeius having been thus led to seek supplies in the more distant place, Sertorius sent forward Octavius Graecinus with ten cohorts armed in Roman fashion, ten cohorts of light armed Spaniards, and Tarquitius Priscus, with two thousand horsemen, to lay an ambuscade for the enemy. This man seems to be the Q. Tarquitius who accompanied C. Annius into Spain (p. 450), and if so, he must have changed sides. After carefully examining the ground the officers of Sertorius by night placed their troops in a wood near the foraging ground of the enemy. In the front they put the Spaniards, who were well fitted for operations which required speed and stealth; a little distance behind them were posted the heavy armed troops, and furthest in the rear the cavalry, in order that the ambuscade might not be betrayed by the neighing of the horses. All were ordered to keep quiet till the third hour after sunrise, for the foragers would of course come in the early morning. The men of Pompeius after well loading themselves were making ready to return, with no apprehensions about their safety, and even the picquets, seeing that all was quiet, were dispersed to look after supplies, when on a sudden the nimble Spaniards fell on the enemy who being scattered in all directions were surprised by this unexpected attack. Before they could make any resistance, the heavy armed troops rushed out of the wood and put to flight the foragers while they were attempting to form their ranks. The cavalry then coming up pursued and cut down the fugitives all along the road by which they were making their escape to the camp of Pompeius, who seeing the confusion sent a legion under D. Laelius to protect the foragers. Upon this the enemy's cavalry turned off to the right as if they were taking to flight, but as the soldiers of Pompeius advanced, the cavalry fell on their rear, and at the same time those who were pursuing the fugitives attacked them in front. The legion thus placed between two bodies of the enemy was destroyed together with the commander. Pompeius indeed began to put his whole army in motion to save the legion, but Sertorius had placed his men on the hills ready for action, and thus he deterred Pompeius from leaving his position. Sertorius thus inflicted a double loss on the Roman general, and compelled him to be a passive spectator of the destruction of his own men. This was the first contest between Sertorius and Pompeius. Livy wrote that Pompeius lost ten thousand men and all his baggage, but this statement has been disputed, because according to the narrative there was no general battle and it is not said that Pompeius was compelled to leave his camp. But if a whole legion perished, and also all the men who were sent out to forage, and the beasts with them, the loss would correspond pretty exactly to Livy's statement and to the narrative of Appian.

There was a height near the city well situated for enabling an enemy to attack Lauron, and both Pompeius and Sertorius had attempted to secure this valuable position. Sertorius succeeded in getting it; and Pompeius was well pleased with the result, or affected to be, thinking that Sertorius would be hemmed in between the town and his own army. He encouraged the townsmen to hold out, and to look on while Sertorius was blockaded. But Sertorius smiled when he heard of this, or more probably he would see without being told what the design of his adversary was. He encouraged his men by reminding them that he had still six thousand regular soldiers on the ground which he held before he seized the hill, and that if Pompeius should attack them, he would be himself attacked in the rear. Thus Sertorius made good his words when he said that he would teach Sulla's pupil, for so he contemptuously named Pompeius, that a general should look behind him rather than before. We cannot tell at what time of the siege of Lauron the affair of the foragers happened, but we learn from Frontinus' narrative of the successful stratagem of Sertorius that

he was then in the possession of the heights. Pompeius saw
when it was too late that the enemy, whom he was expecting
to blockade, had so disposed his force that it was not safe to
attack him. Want of supplies and the heavy loss that he
had sustained may have led Pompeius to retire before Lauron
surrendered, for as Sertorius was superior in numbers, he
could not have stayed safely. Lauron was burnt, and the
inhabitants who survived the slaughter were sent as slaves to
Lusitania. Plutarch says that Sertorius spared the people
and let them all go; but after he had burnt their houses and
taken all their property, there would be less mercy in turning
them loose to starve than in selling them for slaves. Sertorius boasted that Pompeius saw the city perish and was
near enough to warm himself by the flames. Pompeius in
his letter to the Senate simply says that he sustained the
attack of Sertorius though his forces were very inferior in
numbers; but he indirectly admits that he was forced to
retire. The young general made his hasty retreat northward from a burning town which he had come to save, and
from a wasted country, where he had left thousands of his
men to rot. He had learned something of the art of war by
sad experience, and he had at least the merit of escaping
from his terrible enemy.

An event happened at the capture of Lauron which gives
us some notion of the difficulty that Sertorius had in keeping
his men under discipline and of his prompt punishment.
When Lauron was surrendered or taken, for the fact is
doubtful, a soldier attempted unnatural violence upon a
Spanish woman, who tore out the villain's eyes. Sertorius
heard of what happened, and as the whole cohort had a bad
name for such vices, he destroyed every man, though they
were all Roman soldiers.

The winter was coming on, but Sertorius did not rest. He
began the siege of Contrebia, a town which has been mentioned already in the history of the Spanish wars (Vol. i.
p. 65). The site of this place is unknown, but it must have
been somewhere near the Ebro. As Contrebia held out
against Sertorius, we must assume that it was in the Roman

interest; and it is said that it was defended by deserters from
Sertorius and by runaway slaves. After a siege of four-and-
forty days and great loss to Sertorius the town surrendered.
He took hostages from the people, demanded a small sum of
money, and deprived them of all their arms. The freemen,
who had deserted were given up; the runaway slaves, who were
much more numerous, were massacred by the townsmen at
the command of Sertorius, and their carcases were thrown
over the walls. Sertorius left in the town an officer named
L. Insteius with some men, and led his forces to the Ebro to
the neighbourhood of a place named Aclia Castra, where he
built huts and put his army in winter quarters.

Here he held a meeting of the Spanish states, which were
on his side. He had given orders all through the Nearer
province, in which he now was, that the several peoples
should furnish arms according to their ability. When the
arms thus furnished were approved, the soldiers were ordered
to bring in their old arms, and they received a new supply.
The cavalry received fresh equipment, and pay. Arti-
zans were collected and employed in a public workshop. A
calculation also was made of the amount of work that could
be turned out every day. Thus all kinds of weapons and
military material were prepared, for the states in alliance
with Sertorius eagerly seconded his designs. The general
thanked the deputies of the several states and towns for what
they had done, laid before them an account of his own operations, and exhorted them to prosecute the war.

In the spring of B.C. 75 Sertorius sent Perperna with twenty
thousand foot and fifteen hundred horse to the territory of the
Ilercaones, who were on the coast near the mouth of the
Ebro, to protect the maritime parts of that country and to
watch Pompeius. At the same time he wrote to Herennius
or Herennuleius, as he is named in Livy, who was in the
same parts to which Perperna was sent. We know nothing
of the operations of Metellus in the preceding year (B.C. 76).
One of Sertorius' commanders, named L. Hirtuleius, was now
somewhere in the neighbourhood of Metellus, and Sertorius
sent him instructions for the conduct of the war: he was

directed to protect the states, which were friendly to Sertorius, but to avoid a battle with Metellus, whose reputation as
a commander was superior to that of Hirtuleius, and he had
also a larger force. Sertorius said that he did not himself
intend to fight Pompeius, and he did not think that Pompeius would seek a battle, if the war was prolonged. Pompeius, he said, had the sea in his rear and all the provinces
under his orders and so he could get supplies by his vessels;
but that he himself had consumed in the previous summer
all his stores and would be in want of every thing. Perperna
had been sent to the sea coast to protect those parts which
had not yet been wasted by the enemy, and, if any opportunity should offer, to harass and surprise him. This passage
from a fragment of the 91st book of Livy, when it is properly understood, gives a clear insight into the state of affairs
in Spain. Metellus occupied the Farther province with a
force superior to any thing which Sertorius could send against
him. Pompeius, who had been compelled to leave the kingdom of Valencia, had retired into Catalonia on the coast
where the Roman ships could send him supplies, while the
cruisers would prevent any thing from reaching Sertorius by
sea. A war, which had now lasted several years, had undoubtedly wasted the resources of Spain. Sertorius admits
that he was short of supplies, and perhaps neither the
army of Metellus nor Pompeius could have subsisted, if the
Roman fleet had not commanded the sea. In these difficulties the policy of Sertorius was the only hope of safety in a
country like Spain. He could not fight regular battles, at
least he could not trust his lieutenants with such a hazardous
authority. He advised them to carry on the guerilla warfare,
for which the people and the country, particularly in the
mountainous parts of Spain, are peculiarly adapted. The
advice was the same that the Duke of Wellington gave to the
Spanish Government during the Peninsular war, to wage a
defensive war with their bands of hardy, daring, enduring
men, and not to fight regular battles for which the Spaniards
were not trained, nor to let Spanish generals pretend to command armies, a thing which they did not understand.

Sertorius led his troops along the south side of the Ebro through a friendly people without committing any devastation. When he came into the lands of the Bursaones, Casuantini and Graccurritani, he wasted all the country and his men trampled down the crops that were on the ground. His course was up the river. When he reached Calagurris (Calahorra) a friendly city near the Ebro, he made a bridge over a river, which was near the city, and pitched his camp. Calahorra stands on rising ground on the borders of Aragon and Navarro near a river, which flows into the Ebro. From this encampment M. Masius was sent into the neighbouring country of the Arevaci to enlist men and to get corn for the provisioning of Contrebia. C. Insteius, the commander of the cavalry, was sent to Segovia in Old Castile and into the territory of the Vaccaei to get together more horsemen. He was also ordered to repair to Contrebia, when he had discharged his commission. Sertorius now advanced through the country of the Vascones into the territory of the Berones, a tribe on the upper Ebro, and one of the Celtic peoples, which at some unknown time had settled in Spain. Their chief town Varcia (Varea) stood on the Ebro, where there was a ford over the river, which from this point was navigable. Varcia was the strongest city of the Berones, and Sertorius probably tried to take it; but here the fragment of Livy's 91st book ends abruptly.

Sertorius had made Contrebia his head-quarters because it was the most convenient position for him to pass by on his return from the territory of the Berones, to whatever part of Spain he might intend to lead his army. The Berones and their neighbours the Autricones had often applied to Pompeius for assistance during the past winter while Sertorius was engaged in reducing some of the Celtiberian towns, and they had sent men to point out the roads to the Roman army. The cavalry of these two nations had also harassed his men while they were foraging during the siege of Contrebia, and had attempted to draw off the Arevaci who were friendly to Sertorius. The object of the operations of Sertorius on the upper Ebro and the parts west of it is plain. He wished to

secure all the countries along the higher part of this great
river, and to recruit himself both with men and supplies.
Pompeius was on the coast in the parts on the lower Ebro,
which were favourable to Sertorius. Metellus was a long way
off in Lusitania or at least in the south-west part of Spain.
Sertorius could choose whether he should advance against
Pompeius or Metellus.

But his plans were spoiled by the defeat of Hirtuleius who
found Metellus or was found by him in the neighbourhood of
Sevilla. Hirtuleius was the assailant, for at daybreak he led
his men up to the entrenchments of Metellus. It was the
hottest season of the year. Metellus kept his men within his
lines to the sixth hour of the day, and so gained an easy victory
when he attacked an exhausted enemy with troops which were
quite fresh. Such a commander as Hirtuleius was enough to
ruin any cause. He lost, it is said, twenty thousand men,
but we may doubt if he had so many in his army, and escaped
with a few followers into Lusitania. However Hirtuleius
must have recruited his forces, for he engaged in a second
battle with Metellus at Segovia, where he was again defeated
and lost his life. If the place where Metellus gained this
second victory over Hirtuleius is rightly fixed, we must conclude that Metellus was advancing to the north of Spain after
the battle near Sevilla.

In B.C. 75 Pompeius left Catalonia and again marched
southwards into the kingdom of Valencia. He had probably
been half starved in his northern winter quarters, and changed
them with the view of feeding his army and defeating the
lieutenants of Sertorius. Herennius and Perperna, who had
united their forces, were on the river Turia (Guadalaviar)
in that vast and fertile plain which is called the Huerta or
Garden of Valencia, the Paradise of Europe. A battle was
fought near Valentia (Valencia) in which Herennius and
Perperna were defeated by Pompeius with great slaughter,
and Herennius lost his life. The town of Valentia fell into
the hands of Pompeius, who says that he destroyed it. This
was the place where D. Brutus had settled some of the rest-

less Lusitani (vol. i., p. 73), and it is very probable that they now turned against the Romans.

Sertorius may have intended to join Herennius and Perperna, when Pompeius turned to the south, but he was too late. He determined however to risk a battle with him before he was joined by Metellus, and Pompeius himself was eager to try the fortune of war in the hope of gaining all the honour of a victory over his formidable antagonist. The two commanders met near the town of Sucro which was on the river of the same name (Sucro). Sertorius contrived that the fight should not begin before the approach of evening, for he thought that as the enemy did not know the country, the darkness would be a disadvantage to Pompeius whether he gained the victory or was defeated. The battle was fought in a thunderstorm, which burst out of a clear sky, but the hardy veterans on both sides were too well inured to war to care for such an unusual occurrence. Sertorius was on the right of his own army and opposed to L. Afranius who commanded the enemy's left; but he quitted the right on hearing that those on the other wing were giving way before Pompeius. Rallying the men on the left who were broken, and bringing them up to those who still kept their ground, he made a fresh charge on Pompeius, who was pursuing the fugitives. In this encounter Pompeius nearly lost his life. A tall man, an infantry soldier, attacked him on his horse, and in the struggle Pompeius was wounded, though he cut off the man's hand with his sword. The Roman general only escaped by leaving behind him his horse with its trappings of gold and costly ornaments, for the Libyans of Sertorius in their eagerness to secure the tempting prize delayed the pursuit, and were too busy with plundering and quarrelling to make the most of the victory. During this battle on the Sucro a barbarian brought the news to Sertorius of the final defeat and death of Hirtuleius, but as soon as he had delivered his message, Sertorius stabbed the man with his dagger, that he might not spread the report and dishearten his army. The victory of Sertorius was only partial. The right wing, which he had quitted, was completely defeated by Afranius, who put the Spaniards to flight, drove them back to their camp and entered it with the fugitives. His men knew nothing of the defeat of Pompeius and began to plunder, but Sertorius returning from the pursuit of the enemy fell on the men of Afranius who were all in disorder and slaughtered a large number of them. The loss on each side was estimated at ten thousand. In the morning Sertorius was ready to renew the contest, but learning that Metellus was near he said "If that old woman had not come up, I would have given this boy a good drubbing by way of lesson and have sent him back to Rome." Appian (Civil Wars, i., 110) speaks of Pompeius and Metellus coming down from the Pyrenean mountains where they had wintered, and fighting the battle at Sucro against Sertorius and Perperna, who had marched thither from Lusitania; but he appears to have confounded this battle with a subsequent engagement at Saguntum.

At daybreak Sertorius and Pompeius were again preparing for battle, each of them having rallied his men, but when Metellus came up, Sertorius retired, and his men dispersed, which was their mode of retreat, and a safe one with such soldiers in such a country, for the enemy could not pursue a scattered army. Pompeius and Metellus now met for the first time since Pompeius had entered Spain. When Pompeius went to meet Metellus, after the battle, he ordered his lictors to lower the fasces out of respect to a general who was of higher rank, but Metellus would not allow this, and did not assume any superiority in respect of his age and consular dignity, except that when the two armies encamped together, the watchword for both was given by Metellus. However the two armies generally encamped apart.

In this campaign in Valencia Sertorius had lost his favourite fawn, and was much dispirited, for he was deprived of one of his means of cheering the barbarian troops. However it happened that some men who were rambling about at night fell in with the animal and caught it. Sertorius hearing this good news gave the men money to keep the secret, and after concealing the fawn several days he told the barbarian chiefs

that the Deity had shown him in his sleep signs of great good
fortune. He then ascended his tribunal to transact business,
and the fawn being let loose by those who had charge of it
bounded up to Sertorius on his seat, placed its head on his
knees and kissed his right hand, as it had been used to do.
The two friends embraced, and Sertorius even shed tears, or
pretended to do so. This incident restored the hopes of the
barbarians, and they were ready to meet the enemy again. It
was the design of Sertorius to drive the Romans from the
rich garden of Valencia. He cut off the communications
between the armies of Metellus and Pompeius, intercepted
their supplies, wasted the country, and even got the command
of the sea in those parts so as to shut out all relief on that
side. Metellus and Pompeius were reduced to act on the defensive, as appears from the fact that they had retired
northwards to the stronghold of Murviedro on the Palancia,
the site of the famous Saguntum which Hannibal ruined, an
almost impregnable position which commands the approach
to the city of Valencia from the north. The Romans came
down from the heights of Murviedro to forage in the plain,
where Sertorius was ready to meet them. It was a well-
fought battle, which lasted from midday till the stars were
lit. Sertorius defeated the division of Pompeius who lost six
thousand men and his quaestor Memmius, who was his brother-
in-law. Sertorius lost only half that number. Metellus,
though he was wounded in the battle, defeated Perperna,
whose loss was five thousand. On the following day about
dusk Sertorius made a sudden attack on the camp of Metellus,
who was saved by the prompt arrival of Pompeius, and Sertorius prudently retired. He had not succeeded in destroying
his enemies, and he had hardly escaped defeat. His design now
was to gain time, to recruit his own army, and to tire out the
enemy by luring him to a fruitless pursuit. He ordered his
men to disperse after he had fixed the place where they should
meet again. The rallying point was Clunia, a town of the
Arevaci on a branch of the upper Douro. It was a long and
weary road from the coast of Valencia over the high plateaus
of central Spain; but Pompeius followed Sertorius, and

blockaded him in Clunia. After suffering a good deal before the place from the sallies of the besieged, the severity of the season and want of food Pompeius retired to winter in the country of the Vaccaei, the kingdom of Leon. His more prudent colleague Metellus probably sought winter quarters between the Ebro and the Pyrenees, though Plutarch says that he retired into Gallia; but as we know that Pompeius wintered in Gallia in the following year, it has been assumed that Plutarch has made a mistake and confounded the operations of two different years. From his winter quarters Pompeius sent to the Roman Senate a letter of grievous complaint, which Sallust has reported in his Histories, or after his fashion he has composed a letter in the name of Pompeius. The historian makes him say that he was weary of writing and sending messengers, that his resources both public and private were exhausted, and that for the space of three years the Senate had hardly sent him sufficient supplies for a single year. But the historian has here made a mistake. Even if Pompeius left Italy at the end of B.C. 77, he had not been more than two years in Spain, for this letter was written in B.C. 75 and reached Rome before the end of the year, as we learn from Sallust himself. Pompeius further said that he and his enemy were just in the same condition: neither army received pay. He warned them not to compel him to look after his own interests. All Nearer Spain, he said, which was not held by the enemy, was utterly wasted either by Sertorius or the Roman armies, except the maritime states, and they were only a cause of cost and a burden. In the year before (B.C. 76). Gallia had supplied Metellus with money and corn, but it was now itself suffering from a deficient harvest. He ended by telling the Senate that he had not only spent all that he had, but that even his credit was gone; and if they did not help him, the armies must quit Spain and the war would be transferred to Italy.

CHAPTER XXXIII.

THE DEATH OF SERTORIUS.

B.C. 74—72.

THE events of these years are very imperfectly recorded. A fragment of Sallust speaks of Metellus returning into Further Spain after a year's absence, and Drumann has perhaps correctly referred this passage to the year B.C. 74. The campaign of the previous year had on the whole been favourable to the Romans, and Metellus was received with great demonstrations of joy by the people of Southern Spain many of whom were Romans and many were in the Roman interest. The quaestor C. Urbinus and others made great preparations to honour the advent of the proconsul. He was treated with splendid entertainments, stage performances, and the most extravagant adulation. He appeared in a triumphal robe at banquets; and while he was seated, a figure of Victory descended accompanied by a noise in imitation of thunder and placed a crown on his head. When he went abroad, incense was burnt and he was worshipped as a god. He indulged freely in the pleasures of the table, to supply which not only the province was ransacked, but the purveyors even crossed the sea into Mauritania to look for birds and animals hitherto unknown. The more sober part of the people looked with disgust on all this pomp and luxury.

The consuls of B.C. 74 were L. Licinius Lucullus and M. Aurelius Cotta. There was again war with Mithridates, and Lucullus was intriguing for the command of the Roman

army in the east. But he was afraid that Pompeius might
leave Spain and get the conduct of the war, for though
Pompeius was still a young man and had filled no public
office, there was no Roman who had so high a military
reputation. Accordingly Lucullus bestirred himself to get
men and supplies sent to Spain that he might not have a
rival to dispute with him the honour of again humbling the
Asiatic king. The letter of Pompeius was answered by the
despatch of two legions to Spain.

In this year probably we may place the negotiations
between Mithridates and Sertorius, and the king's embassy to
Spain. Two Romans named L. Fannius and Magius, who had
escaped from Fimbria's army, when it went over to Sulla,
happened to be at Myndus in Caria, when C. Verres, then
the proquaestor of Cn. Cornelius Dolabella (B.C. 80, 79) came
there in an armed vessel of Miletus, which the citizens had
lent him to ensure his safe passage. Verres sold the vessel
to Magius and Fannius and put the money in his pocket.
These men had probably fled to Mithridates as early as
B.C. 84, and we cannot conjecture what they were doing at
Myndus in B.C. 80 or 79, unless they were there as agents
of Mithridates. However this may be, they now advised
the king to negotiate with Sertorius, and it seems that
they were in the embassy to Spain. The design of Mithridates was to keep the Romans employed in the west,
while he again attacked their province Asia. He offered
Sertorius money and ships, both of which Sertorius wanted,
and in return he demanded a confirmation of his title
to the province Asia, which he had been compelled to
surrender to Sulla. The king believed or he had been
persuaded by his flatterers that Sertorius would be finally
victorious and would make himself master of Rome, as Sulla
had done. The senate of Sertorius recommended him to
accept the king's terms, but he would not consent to separate
Asia from the Roman dominion. A treaty was made between Sertorius and Mithridates on these terms: Mithridates
should keep Cappadocia and Bithynia, though the last king
of Bithynia had by testament in this very year bequeathed

his kingdom to the Romans: Sertorius should receive three thousand talents from Mithridates and forty ships, and send him a general and soldiers. But Appian states that Sertorius consented to give up to the king the province Asia, with Bithynia, Paphlagonia, Cappadocia, and Galatia. Sertorius sent a general, a Roman Senator, who is named M. Marius or Varius; but it is not said that he sent soldiers, and for a good reason. He had none to send. The ambassadors with the new general sailed from Dianium (Denia) on the east coast of Spain (vol i., p. 306). Sertorius used this place as a station for his ships, and we may assume that the negotiation with the ambassadors of Sertorius was conducted at Dianium on some occasion when Sertorius was in the plain of Valentia and in the adjoining parts on the river Sucro. The ambassadors from Mithridates, says Cicero, sailed from Dianium in the very vessel which the knave Verres had sold to them, and they visited all the peoples who were hostile to Rome on their voyage to Sinope (Sinab) in the Black Sea, where they arrived in safety. The treaty, as far as we know, had no result.

Such a treaty may have been considered as treason to Rome by the enemies of Sertorius, and may have been the immediate cause, though it is merely a conjecture, of Metellus setting a price on the head of his enemy. The father of Metellus in the Jugurthine war had attempted to take off Jugurtha by bribing those about him (vol. i., p. 420), and the son now followed the example of his father: to such a degraded condition had even the best of the nobles of Rome descended. Proclamation was made that if any Roman killed Sertorius, he should have a hundred talents of silver and twenty thousand jugera of land: if the assassin were an exile, he should have permission to return to Rome.

Whether it was owing to the proclamation or to other causes, many of the men of Sertorius went over to Metellus, and those who remained with him were discontented. Sertorius is charged with having cruelly treated many of those about him and made himself odious. He also got rid of his Roman guard and put Celtiberians in their place. It is not strange if Sertorius did use severity when a price was set on

his head, and his men were deserting. But he might have
maintained his ground still longer in spite of all his difficulties, if treachery had not come from a quarter where it
was least expected.

Metellus, to whom Perperna was opposed, had easy work
this year. He got possession of many towns which were on
the side of Sertorius and carried off the men to other parts. In
the north Pompeius undertook the siege of Pallantia (Paloncia)
on the river Carrion in the wide plains of the kingdom of
Leon. He undermined part of the walls of Pallantia, but he
was interrupted in his operations by the sudden arrival of Sertorius and led his troops away, having first fired the timbers
which supported his subterranean galleries and thus brought
down the wall. Pompeius made a junction with Metellus,
and it seems that both of them advanced to attack Calagurris
(Calahorra) on the river Ebro, but Sertorius again disturbed
the operations of the two generals, and destroyed three
thousand of their men. The winter was coming on, supplies
were wanted, and Pompeius and Metellus were obliged to
seek better winter quarters. Metellus retired into Further
Spain, and Pompeius crossed the Pyrenees into the south of
France. This was the end of the campaign of B.C. 74.

The events of the year B.C. 73 are unknown, for the extant
authorities supply no information. All that we are told is
that Metellus and Pompeius took many towns which were on
the side of Sertorius, but there was no great battle. The two
Roman generals continued to prosecute the war successfully,
and they now despised an enemy whom they had once feared.
The inactivity of Sertorius is explained by the fact, if it is
true, that his character was entirely changed. According to
the old doctrine, the deity, who was leading him to ruin,
devised the surest means of accomplishing the end; for
Sertorius became indolent, indulged in luxurious living, and
spent his time in drinking and in the company of women.
The natural consequence was that he was defeated in every
conflict with the enemy. In his waning fortune his temper
became irritable and suspicious; he trusted no man, and he
punished with cruel severity. But Sertorius was surrounded

by enemies, and all that is reported of him has come down to us through corrupted sources. Metellus had set a price on his head, and his own officers were traitors. Perperna was the man who plotted against his commander's life, foolishly thinking that he could retrieve the fortunes of his party. The misconduct of the officers of Sertorius, and the heavy demands which they made on the barbarians in the name of the commander-in-chief caused revolt and disturbance in the Spanish cities. These outbreaks led to acts of severe repression by Sertorius or by others in his name, for it was easy to lay all the blame on Sertorius, when he was dead. The last act, the worst of all, was the execution of some of the youths who were brought up at Osca, and the sale of others into servitude. As these boys were held as hostages for the fidelity of the Spaniards, the alleged justification for this cruelty must have been the treachery of their fathers and kinsmen.

At last a conspiracy was formed against Sertorius. The conspirators were Perperna and nine other Romans. Some of these men however were detected and punished: others saved themselves by flight. Perperna, who had escaped detection contrary to his expectation, and was now in fear for his life, hurried the execution of his plot. The story in Appian is told in his shortest and driest way. As Sertorius was always surrounded by his guard, and it was not easy to reach him, he was invited by Perperna to a banquet, where he and his men were made drunk, and murdered.

But Plutarch has preserved a more particular and a more probable account of the death of the famous guerillero, who had so long defied the arms of Rome. It appears also from a fragment of Sallust's histories that there was extant a very minute record of the assassination of Sertorius; for the fragment describes the places occupied by Sertorius and others at the fatal banquet. The story is this. Perperna was waiting for an opportunity, when he was urged to the immediate execution of his plot by the imminent fear of discovery. One of the conspirators Manius Antonius a bragging fellow had talked about the plot to a youth, who was thus made acquainted with the whole design. There was no safety now except in prompt action. The conspirators engaged a man to carry a forged letter to Sertorius, which announced a victory gained by one of his generals. Sertorius offered a sacrifice for the good news, and Perperna, who was giving a great banquet on the occasion, after much entreaty prevailed on Sertorius to come. He came with a scriba or secretary to an entertainment in the town of Osca at which the conspirators were present. At other times when Sertorius was at a banquet, great propriety was observed, for he would not allow any indecency or excess, but on this occasion, as the conspirators were seeking to begin a quarrel, they used obscene talk and pretended to be drunk for the purpose of irritating him. Being vexed at their behaviour or perhaps half-suspecting their designs in consequence of their insulting manner, Sertorius changed his posture on the couch, and threw himself on his back as if he were paying no attention to what was said. Perperna seized the opportunity, and taking a cup of wine drank part, and then dashed the cup down. This was the signal. Antonius who was next to Sertorius struck him with his sword. The general turned round and attempted to rise, but Antonius throwing himself on his chest held his hands, while the other conspirators murdered him. This event took place some time in B.C. 72.

When the death of Sertorius was known, his soldiers were ready to mutiny. However unpopular their commander had been during the latter part of his career, this shameful murder committed by men whom he trusted, awoke their old affection and revived the memory of his great exploits. The natives were as indignant against Perperna as the Romans; and the Lusitani most of all lamented the death of the brave leader whom they had so long and faithfully followed through all his varying fortunes. The hatred against Perperna increased when it was known that Sertorius by his testament had given part of his property to the very man who was now the murderer of his commander, his friend, and his benefactor. Perperna had great difficulty in preventing the soldiers from rising against him. He bribed some, made promises to others,

and terrified the rest by his savage threats and the execution
of some of the most active of the mutineers. The natives of
Spain were pacified by the release of some of their countrymen, whom Sertorius had put in prison, and by the surrender
of others who were hostages.   By such means Perperna
secured the unwilling obedience of those who had served
under Sertorius, and took the command ; but he soon showed
his cruel and jealous disposition by putting to death three
Romans of rank, who had fled with him to Spain, and also
the son of his own brother.

Metellus had retired to another part of Spain and left Pompeius to deal with Perperna, whose forces were probably much
weakened, for many of the Spaniards submitted to Pompeius
and Metellus after the death of Sertorius.   There were slight
skirmishes for some days between Pompeius and Perperna,
but at last both the commanders resolved on a general engagement.   Pompeius despised his opponent who had no
military talent, and Perperna knew that he could not long
secure the fidelity of his troops.   Pompeius sent forward a
legion to meet Perperna's army with instructions to disperse
in flight when they were attacked by the enemy.   While
Perperna was engaged in the pursuit, Pompeius appeared
with all his force and inflicted on his opponent a complete
defeat. Perperna, who feared his own men more than the
enemy, did not attempt to escape. He hid himself in some
bushes from which he was dragged by the horsemen of Pompeius amidst the curses and execrations of his own soldiers.
To save his life he offered to give information about the designs of some of his own faction in Rome.   When his capture
was announced, Pompeius refused to see the contemptible
villain and ordered him to be executed. This politic behaviour was much approved, and increased the reputation of
Pompeius. Perperna had got possession of the papers of
Sertorius, among which were autograph letters from consular
men and persons of influence in Rome, who invited Sertorius
to come to Italy, and assured him that there were many persons who wished for a change in the present state of affairs.
Pompeius took possession of all these letters together with the

papers of Sertorius and burnt them without reading them himself or letting any one else read them. He thus took the most effectual means of relieving those who were implicated in treasonable designs from the fears and suspicions which might drive them to desperation and fresh revolutionary attempts. All the conspirators against Sertorius came to a bad end. Some were put to death, and others who escaped to Africa perished there. Only one of them named Aufidius survived, and he lived to old age in some obscure Spanish village, poor and despised.

The war against Sertorius was ended, but some of the Spanish towns still held out. The natives had not fought for Sertorius only: they wished to throw off the Roman yoke. Pompeius destroyed Uxama (Osma) a town on the upper Douro in the country of the Arevaci. The town of Calagurris (Calahorra) on the river Ebro made a desperate resistance to L. Afranius, one of the generals of Pompeius. The place was reduced to such extremities that the men killed their wives and children for food, and salted for future use what was not immediately consumed. The city was at last stormed and burnt. This was the last memorable event in a war which had lasted ten years, if we reckon from the time when Sertorius went to Spain. If the peninsula was not entirely reduced to its former condition of subjection, at least all active resistance to Roman authority ceased, and Pompeius had leisure to settle the affairs of Spain before returning to Italy. The great commercial town of Gades had taken the Roman side during the late struggle, and Pompeius with the advice of his council gave the Roman citizenship to some of the Gaditani. Among the men who were thus honoured was L. Cornelius Balbus. Balbus was the family name of this Gaditanian citizen, and he took the Roman praenomen and gentile name Lucius Cornelius. This Balbus had fought on the Roman side to the end of the war, and had been in the great battles of the Sucro and the Turia. In B.C. 72 the consuls L. Gellius and Cn. Cornelius Lentulus at Rome proposed an enactment which confirmed the Roman citizenship to all those to whom Pompeius had given it severally. This was the beginning of the fortune of the Gaditanian, who worked his way dexterously to wealth and influence, and finally became a Roman consul.

Before Pompeius left Spain he erected a memorial of his victories in the eastern pass of the Pyrenees, through which ran the road from Narbo (Narbonne) in Gallia to Juncaria (Junquera) on the Spanish side of the mountains. This pass is now the Col de Pertus; and here Pompeius built his trophy at the Summus Pyrenaeus, as the place is named in the Roman Itineraries. It was the natural boundary between Gallia and Spain. The inscription recorded in exaggerated language that from the Alps to the limits of Further Spain eight hundred and seventy-six towns had been reduced to subjection. Pompeius had however the modesty and the good sense not to place the name of Sertorius in the inscription. After the death of Sertorius some of his men took to brigandage and infested the passes of the Pyrenees. Pompeius prudently stopped the mischief by settling them in Aquitania at a place named originally Lugdunum, but afterwards Convenae or Lugdunum Convenarum, apparently so called from the inhabitants being brought together here. The place is now St. Bertrand de Cominge which is seated on a hill in the upper valley of the Garonne, in the French department of Haute Garonne.

END OF VOL. II.

GILBERT AND RIVINGTON, PRINTERS, ST. JOHN'S SQUARE, LONDON.